# Police Special

## Also by William P. McGivern

THE ROAD TO THE SNAIL

SEVEN LIES SOUTH

SAVAGE STREETS

ODDS AGAINST TOMORROW

NIGHT EXTRA

MARGIN OF TERROR

THE BIG HEAT

THE CROOKED FRAME

SHIELD FOR MURDER

VERY COLD FOR MAY

HEAVEN RAN LAST

BUT DEATH RUNS FASTER

# POLICE SPECIAL

*including*

## *ROGUE COP*
## *THE SEVEN FILE*
## *THE DARKEST HOUR*

By William P. McGivern

DODD, MEAD & COMPANY

New York   1962

# Contents

*Rogue Cop*

# 1

THEY HAD BEEN PLAYING POKER FOR SEVERAL HOURS NOW, NOT WITH ANY particular enthusiasm but simply to kill this quiet stretch of Saturday evening. Later, as the night wore on, the city's tempo would rise to a harder, sharper beat; then murders, knifings and shootings would bring the game to an end. But now the police speaker was silent and the detectives played cards on a cigarette-scarred table in a smoky, unventilated office. Outside, in the large, brightly lighted file room, a clerk was typing up reports, working with severe concentration, stopping only to sip cold black coffee from a cardboard container at his elbow. The glazed-glass door that led to Lieutenant Wilson's office was dark; the lieutenant was out in the districts now, but would be back at Headquarters by ten or eleven. There would be work then for him and his men.

Standing at the brown wooden counter that ran the length of the room was a reporter named Murphy, a bulky, untidily dressed man with a round florid face and thoughtful gray eyes. He was applying himself to the evening paper's crossword puzzle, frowning intently, apparently immune to everything but this immediate preoccupation.

At the card table Sergeant Mike Carmody was dealing now, his big clean hands spraying the cards about with expert speed. He was an arrestingly handsome man in his middle thirties, with a silvering of gray in his thick blond hair. Everything about him looked hard and expensive; his gray flannel suit had cost two hundred dollars and was superbly fitted to his tall, wide-shouldered frame; the planes of his lean tanned face were flat and sharply defined, and his eyes were the cold gray color of winter seas. Even when he smiled there was no softness in it; his smile was a small, direct challenge, a projection of his sure confidence in his own strength and brains.

"Okay, make up your mind," he said to the man on his right. "The spots won't change, Myers."

Myers, a small man with thinning brown hair and a cautious mouth, studied his cards and shook his head slowly. "It's by me, Mike," he said.

The other two players—Abrams, a solemn grandfather and Dirksen, a bean-pole with a thin freckled face—both passed.

Carmody held two queens. He flipped in a half-a-dollar and said, "It's off then." He was bored with the game and made no attempt to conceal it.

Myers and Abrams called the half-dollar bet, but Dirksen threw his cards in. "I haven't seen anything higher than a ten for the last hour," he said, yawning. Then he glanced at Mike Carmody and said conversationally, "Say, Mike, that was a nice pinch your kid brother made the other day. How about that, eh?"

There was a sudden small silence around the table.

Carmody studied his cards, ignoring it. "He didn't make the pinch," he said, glancing at Abrams. "How many, Abe?"

"Sure, but he made the identification," Dirksen said. "He caught Delaney with the gun in his hand, but Delaney got away." Dirksen's voice was patient and explicit, as if this were a difficult matter to explain. "Then Delaney got picked up later and your brother made the identification. That's what I meant by saying—"

"I read the story in the paper," Carmody said, catching Dirksen directly with his hard cold eyes. He smiled then, the bright quick smile in which there was no warmth or humor. "But we're playing cards now, remember?"

"Well, I'm not stopping you," Dirksen said, shrugging and looking away from Carmody's eyes.

"That's fine," Carmody said, still smiling. He wondered fleetingly if Dirksen had been needling him; Dirksen was dumb enough to try it, after all.

Myers took one card, Abrams three. Carmody drew three to his pair of queens and without looking at them pushed in a dollar. He wasn't interested in Myers' one-card draw. If Myers caught a flush or straight he'd raise, but the amount involved wasn't enough to buy a decent steak. Myers caught. Carmody guessed that from the way his eyes flicked from his cards to his little heap of money.

"I'll bump it five," Myers said.

"You can't," Abrams said. "The limit is two."

"Who said anything about a limit?" Myers demanded.

"Well, it's always been a limit," Abrams said, shrugging his big shoulders. "But it don't make any difference to me. I'm out."

"We didn't establish a limit tonight," Myers said, wetting his lips and glancing at Carmody.

"Make it five if you want," Carmody said, only slightly irritated. Myers had hooked and now he wanted to get rich on one hand. Let him, he thought. Glancing at his cards he found that he had drawn another queen to go with his openers, and a pair of tens. He grinned at the fantastic luck and tossed in ten dollars. "Once again, my friend," he said.

"You're bluffing," Myers said. He stared into Carmody's hard quick smile, trying to keep a weary premonition of defeat from showing in his face.

"Raise then," Carmody said.

"I'll just call," Myers said, pushing in his last five dollars. He had to use silver to make up the amount, and then he put down a king-high straight and looked hopefully at Carmody.

Carmody stared at his cinch hand. He knew all about Myers, as he knew about all the detectives on his shift. The damn fool had two young daughters, and a wife in a sanitarium, but here he was throwing away fifteen dollars in one hand of poker.

Carmody hesitated, annoyed with himself, and Myers watched him with mounting confidence.

"Come on," Myers said. "What've you got?"

"It's your money," Carmody said shortly, and tossed his cards in, face down. The gesture would be wasted, he thought, as he leaned back and lit a cigarette. Myers, pulling in his money triumphantly now, was like most cops, brave, honest and dumb. Carmody felt no sympathy for him, only a blend of exasperation and anger. He'd never have a cent more than his salary and not even that unless he learned to stop drawing to inside straights. That's what bothered him, Carmody thought, his face expressionless. Myers was a fool and he didn't like fools.

"Caught you bluffing, didn't I?" Myers said, arranging his money happily. "Thought you could run me out with a five-dollar bet, eh? Well, my luck's changing. I'm starting back now, remember that."

"You'd better start by remembering the limit," Carmody said, his irritation sharpened by Myers' yapping. "You won't get rich by changing the rules in the middle of a deal."

"Is that how you got rich?" Myers said, stung by Carmody's tone. "By following the rules?"

There was tense silence then, as if everyone at the table had suddenly held his breath. Myers had skated onto thin ice; he was on an area that had mile-high danger signs posted on it. The unnatural silence lasted until Carmody said very quietly, "Let's play cards, Myers. It's your deal, I think."

"Sure, that's right," Myers said, and began quickly to shuffle the cards. There was a white line showing around his small cautious mouth.

Murphy, the reporter, drifted and leaned against the doorway, hat pushed back on his head, a little smile on his big florid face. "I should have been a cop," he said sighing. "Nothing to worry about but filling straights."

No one answered him.

"Say, when's Delaney's trial?" he asked of no one in particular.

Dirksen looked up at him, his freckled face blank and innocent. "Next month sometime, I guess. That right, Mike?"

Carmody nodded slowly, studying his cards. "That's right. The thirteenth."

"The unlucky thirteenth for Delaney," Murphy said, watching Carmody's sharp handsome profile. "That should be a big day for your

brother, Mike. Any cop would be happy to finger a hoodlum like Delaney."

"I'd be glad of the chance," Myers said, risking a quick glance at
Carmody.

They were needling him cautiously, a dangerous pastime, cautiously
or any other way. He knew they were watching him over their cards,
ready to drop their eyes swiftly if he raised his head.

Without looking up he said quietly, "Murph, we just got through talking
about my brother's case. We kind of exhausted the subject, too. So why
don't you run off and find a good exciting accident to cover? Let us play
our little game in peace."

Murphy smiled and raised his hat to Carmody. "I depart, O Sergeant,"
he said, his thoughtful eyes contradicting the smile on his lips. "The city
calls me. Full of heartbreak and tragedy, but laced with dark laughter
withall, it beckons and whispers that its secrets are mine."

Carmody smiled slightly. "Why don't you try that to music?"

"Good idea. Music is getting popular in town," Murphy said in a
changed voice. "Singing particularly. Maybe even Delaney will take it
up. Well, adios, chums."

He strolled out and Dirksen shook his head. "Odd ball," he murmured.

Carmody swallowed a dryness in his throat and said, "Okay, let's play
cards."

Ten minutes later the phone in the file room rang. The clerk answered
it, listened for a few seconds, then said, "Yes, sir. Right away." Covering
the receiver with the palm of his hand, he called out, "Sarge, a call for
you."

"Who is it?" Carmody said.

"Dan Beaumonte."

There was another little silence at the card table. Carmody stared at his
cards for a few seconds, then tossed them in. "Deal me out," he said,
and walked into the file room, moving with an easy controlled grace that
was somehow menacing in a man of his size.

Abrams began to whistle softly through his teeth. The three detectives
avoided one another's eyes, but their ears were turned to the open door
of the file room.

Carmody lifted the phone and said, "Hello, Dan. How're things?"

"It was a bad day," Beaumonte said. His voice was deep and rich,
stirred gently by an undercurrent of humor. "I had three tips at Jamaica
but they all ran out. Do you know of any glue factory that's looking for
three good specimens?"

"It's a good thing to get a day like that behind you," Carmody said.
He knew what Beaumonte wanted and he wished he'd get to it; but you
didn't hurry Beaumonte.

Then it came. "I want to see you tonight, Mike. You're working four-to-twelve?"

"That's right."

"Twelve is too late. How about making it now? I'm at my apartment."

Carmody knew the clerk and the detectives at the card table were listening. "Well, I'll see you around," he said.

"Right away, Mike. He's your brother."

"Sure."

He put the phone down and walked back to the smoke-filled card room. Dirksen began talking loudly. "The thing is, you can't figure the odds in Hi-Lo poker. You never know, for instance, whether—"

"I'm going out," Carmody said to Abrams. "Take over till I get back."

"Okay, Sarge."

"Tell the lieutenant when he comes in that I'll be about an hour."

Dirksen smiled as Carmody buttoned his shirt collar and pulled up his tie. "I wish I got calls from big men like Beaumonte," he said. "That'd make me feel like a real operator."

Carmody guessed that Dirksen was trying to be funny but he was in no mood for it. He put his big fists on the table and leaned forward, fixing Dirksen with his hard, bright smile. "Now listen to me," he said gently. "If you want to talk about telephone calls talk about your own. Get your wife to call you and talk about that. But stop talking about mine. Okay?"

Dirksen's freckled face got red. "Hell, there's nothing to be touchy about," he said. "I just passed a remark. It's still a free country, ain't it?"

Carmody smiled and let the tension dissolve. "Free country? Try that on your landlord and grocer and see what happens."

A relieved laugh went around the table. Carmody straightened up and said, "Take it easy, I'll see you later."

He went downstairs, walked past the House Sergeant's office and through the silent roll call room, where the Magistrate's bench loomed up like an altar in the darkness.

Outside on the sidewalk he paused, savoring the welcome freshness of the spring air against his face. From here, at the north entrance of City Hall, he looked down the glittering length of Market Street, blazing with light against the black sky. The Saturday night crowd jammed the sidewalks, and the traffic was flowing in thick, noisy streams. Somewhere off to his right a police siren was screaming faintly. West, he thought, the Tenth district. He nodded to three patrolmen who went by him on the way to work, and then lit a cigarette and walked down the block to his long gray convertible.

The traffic made his trip across town slow and difficult; but he was grateful for the time it gave him to think. He had done a lot of thinking in the past week, but now he was meeting Beaumonte and the chips would be down. Thinking wouldn't be enough; there had to be a solution. He stared through the windshield, turning the problem around slowly in his clear, alert mind. Waiting at a stop light, he suddenly pounded his big fist on the rim of the steering wheel. If only his brother hadn't identified Delaney. Anyone but Eddie. And if only Delaney weren't threatening to sing. If only a hundred things.

The trouble stemmed from the fact that Delaney worked for a gambler and racketeer named Dan Beaumonte.

And so did Mike Carmody.

There was a girl standing at the terrace window when Carmody walked into Beaumonte's long, elegantly appointed living room. She turned slowly, smiling at him, her figure slim and graceful against the backdrop of the lighted city.

"Hello, Mike. Come over and look at our little village. It's like being high up in a castle."

Carmody joined her and they inspected the view for a few seconds in silence. The city was beautiful now, the lights spreading over it like an immense sparkling carpet. Beaumonte's apartment was on the twenty-fifth floor of a massive building which overlooked the park and a long curving stretch of the river. Like a castle, Carmody thought. With a safe view of the slaves.

"Where's Beaumonte?" he asked her.

"Changing. Would you like a drink?"

"No, thanks."

She patted his arm and he saw that she was a little tight. "I hate to drink alone. Dan says that's my trouble. But what's a girl to do when she's alone?"

"Have a drink, I guess," Carmody said.

"Absolutely right," she said, and poked him in the chest with her finger. "You don't mind if I go ahead?"

"Not a bit." Carmody felt vaguely irritated as he watched her stroll to the bar. Not with her or Beaumonte, but with himself for some curious reason. The girl's name was Nancy Drake, and she had been Beaumonte's mistress for years. She was a slender blonde with piquant, good-natured features and fine gray eyes. Everything about her blended neatly with the perfection of the room; the oil paintings, the balanced groups of furniture, the nice integration of form and color, were all an appropriate backdrop for her pale, well-cared-for beauty. It made a pretty picture, Carmody thought. Well-organized luxury without time payments or mortgages. The room and the girl had been bought and paid for by Beaumonte with good hard cash.

This was what irritated him, Carmody decided. The room looked like an art gallery and Nancy looked like the daughter of a duke. It was the big lie that disgusted him; they should do their business in the back of a saloon, and if women were present they should be the kind who hung around saloons. But it was Beaumonte's lie so that made it all right.

Carmody realized his thoughts were running in illogical circles. Why should he object to Beaumonte's pretenses? Weren't his own just as bad? But he was a little sick of Beaumonte at the moment and he didn't bother applying logic to his judgments. When I'm fed up I'll walk out, he told himself, frowning slightly, disturbed by his thoughts. I'm not in so deep that I can't take a walk.

A door opened and Beaumonte came into the room. He held a slim cigar in one hand and wore a dinner jacket cut of black raw silk.

"Sorry to keep you waiting, Mike," he said, in his deep rich voice. "I'm glad you could get right over."

Carmody said something appropriate and watched Beaumonte as he put an arm around Nancy's waist and kissed her bare shoulder. Sometimes Beaumonte's expression gave him away; but there was nothing to learn from it now. He seemed in good spirits but his mood could change drastically and without warning, Carmody knew.

Physically, Beaumonte was impressive, with a big well-padded body, thick gray hair and a complexion like that of a well-cared-for baby. His lips were full and red, his brown eyes clear and untroubled. He spent about a third of each day taking steam baths, sun-lamp treatments and suffering the ministrations of his barber, masseur and trainer. His manner was sensuous and complacent; he could bear nothing but silk against his skin, and fussed pretentiously with his chef on the subjects of sauces and wines. There were times when Carmody half expected him to start stroking himself or purring.

"Mike won't drink," Nancy said.

"Not a bad habit," Beaumonte said, glancing at her appraisingly.

"I'm okay," she said.

"Yeah, so far. Won't change your mind, Mike?"

"All right, make it a mild Scotch," Carmody said.

"I'll have sherry, the Spanish with the crowns on the label," Beaumonte told Nancy. He glanced at Carmody. "It's a fine one. I have it imported especially. You have to watch sherry, Mike. It's splendid when it's right. But when it isn't, I mean if it's off even a shade, well it's not worth drinking."

"Sure," Carmody said, managing to keep his annoyance from showing in his face. Beaumonte had grown up on bootleg whiskey; he had been a small-time hoodlum in the Thirties, a skinny punk in pin-striped suits and a gray fedora, which he wore pulled down all around in the style favored by Capone's bums in Chicago. Money, carloads of it, had brought out the art lover and wine bibber.

Nancy brought their drinks on a round silver tray, and Beaumonte's expression changed as he noticed that she had made herself another highball. "You've had enough," he said. "Leave that here and go lie down."

"Dan, don't be dull," she said, trying to soften his face with an impudent, gamin smile. "You'll spoil the party."

"You've had your ration for today," he said, and now he meant business. His face and manner were unpleasant. "It's sloshing in the scuppers. Beat it. Sleep it off."

"All right, Dan," she said quickly, her little pose melting under the hard anger in his eyes. "So long, Mike."

Here was the art patron and wine sipper, Carmody thought, and the irony of it was enough to check his irritation. For some reason Beaumonte enjoyed humiliating her; and by a freak of timing the scenes always seemed to occur when he was playing the grand gentleman to the hilt. Maybe she planned it that way, Carmody thought. Beaumonte had picked her out of a chorus line six years ago, and since that time had transformed her into a lady. She had been trained to walk and talk, to manage a dinner party for thirty and to dress herself with quiet taste. Beaumonte had hired trainers and coaches for her, he had schooled her like an intelligent dog until she could perform any social trick with ease. And somewhere on the way she had started hitting the bottle. She would probably be dead in five years, Carmody knew, and he wondered if that was why Beaumonte was so rough on her. Because the investment wasn't paying off; the bought-and-paid-for little lady had crossed him by turning into a lush. But there was something else, Carmody guessed. Beaumonte would have enjoyed humiliating a real lady, but no genuine article would take it; so he had created Nancy as a stand-in for the real thing. By hurting her he took a small revenge against a class which had always intimidated him; people whose English was correct and whose manners were casual and right.

Beaumonte sat down in a deep chair, the glass of sherry in one hand, the slim cigar in the other. He looked up at Carmody, a small frown gathering on his pampered features. "Let's get right to it, Mike. Sit down and get comfortable." He sipped some of the sherry and wet his full lips. Then he turned his clear brown eyes directly to Carmody. "It's this, Mike. If your brother fingers Delaney it can cause us trouble. Because Delaney has told our lawyer that he's going to talk, unless we take him off the hook. So your brother's got to be sensible. You understand?"

Carmody shrugged his wide shoulders and said nothing. The silence stretched out awkwardly until Beaumonte, still frowning, said, "Well, do you see it?"

"Part of it," Carmody said. "What's the rest of it?"

"All right, let's start at the start," Beaumonte said, settling in the chair and crossing his fat legs. "Delaney, who's worked for us off and on for years, shot and killed a man named Ettonberg. That was last month. It was a stupid murder, and not tied up with us in any way. Ettonberg and

Delaney had a fight about a woman and Delaney killed him after he'd been drinking so much that he couldn't hit the ground with his hat. As you know, this happened in a boardinghouse on your brother's beat. He went in and found Delaney standing over Ettonberg with a gun in his hand. If he'd killed the bastard right then, he'd have done us a favor. But Delaney slugged your brother and got away without being seen by anyone else. So he went to Martin's joint where there was a poker game and fixed himself up an alibi."

"I guess we both know the story pretty well," Carmody said. "The cops picked up Delaney on my brother's description. Eddie testified at the Grand Jury hearing and the D.A. got a true bill."

"Okay, now we're up to the present," Beaumonte said. "When Delaney goes to trial your brother can finger him right into the chair. And that can't happen. If it does, Delaney talks."

What did Delaney know? Carmody wondered. "Can he hurt you by talking?" he asked.

Beaumonte looked annoyed. "Don't talk about me being hurt. I don't like that kind of talk."

Carmody shrugged. "No point in not being realistic. I talk pretty damn much."

"We're going to save Delaney," Beaumonte said. Carmody's remark had brought spots of color into his cheeks, but he didn't let his anger get him away from the subject. "So you talk to your brother, Mike?"

"What do I tell him?"

"You tell him he don't identify Delaney at the trial."

"Will that do any good?" Carmody said. "My brother has already testified against Delaney at the Grand Jury hearing."

"Don't you worry about the legal end of it," Beaumonte said. "That's what we pay lawyers for. And here's the way they've figured it. Delaney's attorney waived a hearing before the Magistrate the night of the murder. So your brother didn't have to identify him then. Naturally, Delaney was held for the Grand Jury without bail. In this state defendants don't appear at the Grand Jury hearings, so your brother didn't confront Delaney and make an identification. He just testified that to the best of his knowledge a man named Delaney was standing over Ettonberg's dead body when he came on the scene. That gave the D.A. his true bill. Your brother won't confront Delaney until the trial. And that's when he blows the case up by refusing to finger him."

"It will look raw as hell," Carmody said.

"To hell with how it looks," Beaumonte said angrily. "They'll know he's lying but they won't be able to prove it. The jury is what counts. And our attorneys will make them believe that your brother's an honest cop who won't send an innocent man to the chair just to fatten up some D.A.'s score of convictions. Delaney will beat the rap. And, by God, Mike, he's got to beat this rap. You understand?"

"They'll boot my brother off the force."

"So is that bad? We'll take care of him. Offer him ten thousand to start with, and see what he thinks of it. And we can go higher. A lot higher."

Carmody hesitated a moment. Then he said, "Why do you want me to handle it, Dan?" A phrase came into his mind from his forgotten religion and forgotten values: *"Let this chalice pass from me!"* He didn't want this job, and in some intuitive manner he was afraid of it. But there was no one he could ask for help. Not Beaumonte, that was certain. And there was no one else. *Let this chalice* . . . Why had those words occurred to him?

Beaumonte was rolling the cigar between his full red lips, watching him carefully. "I want you to handle it because it's a big job," he said at last. "I'll tell you this: Ackerman is watching it personally."

Carmody nodded slowly. It was important then, no doubt of it. Ackerman was number one. He controlled the city's gambling and numbers racket. Beaumonte ran the west side personally, and acted as a link between Ackerman and the other districts; he supervised the operations of Fanzo in Central, Nick Boyle in Meadowstrip, and Lockwood in the Northeast. But all of it was under Ackerman's thumb. He juggled the judges and magistrates and cops, he put the collar on the politicians he needed and he fought the reform movement on the high inside levels. Thinking about it, Carmody felt a brush of anxiety; there was a lot of muscle stacked up against his brother.

"Why is Ackerman so interested?" Carmody asked.

Beaumonte was silent a moment. Then he said quietly, "Don't start guessing about him. You know that's stupid. Just remember he's interested. That's enough. Now there's one other point. I don't want any hard feelings between you and me."

"I don't get that," Carmody said.

Beaumonte got to his feet and glanced at his gold wrist watch. "Hell, it's later than I thought," he said. Carmody had risen also and Beaumonte put a hand on his arm, turning him toward the door. "This thing has got to be handled, one way or the other," he said. "I want it peaceful. I hope your brother is smart and winds up with a nice little bundle in his pocket." They stopped at the door, facing each other, and something had changed in Beaumonte's smooth plump face. He was still smiling but the smile meant nothing now. "We're not kids, Mike," he said. "I'm putting it on the line. If your brother don't play ball we'll have to handle it our way. That's why you're making the first pitch. If you don't sell him the deal, you can't blame us for doing what we got to do. Is that clear enough?"

"I'll talk to my brother," Carmody said evenly.

"How do you get along with him?"

"So-so."

"What's the matter? He's your kid brother, he should do what you tell him."

"We don't see much of each other," Carmody said.

"That's too bad." Beaumonte looked at him, his head tilted slightly. "Don't he like your friends?"

"Lots of people don't," Carmody said, holding his irritation in check.

"Not smart people," Beaumonte said, smiling. "When'll you see him?"

"As soon as I can."

"Make it tonight. He doesn't go to work until twelve."

"How do you know?"

Beaumonte shrugged. "I told you this was important. We're keeping tabs on him. You see him now, then come back. I'll be here all night. Got that?"

Carmody hesitated. "Okay, Dan," he said finally.

Beaumonte smiled. "We want this peaceful. Good luck."

# 2

CARMODY DROVE FROM BEAUMONTE'S APARTMENT TO A DRUG STORE ON Market Street and called his brother's home. There was no answer. He replaced the receiver and remained seated in the booth, thinking coolly and without emotion of Beaumonte's words: *We want this peaceful . . . but if your brother won't play ball we'll have to do it our way.*

Beaumonte meant that. There was no phoniness about him when it came to business. He squandered his bluff on paintings and horse shows and the Mayor's council on human relations, catering generously then to his itch for approval and respectability. But this was business. His and Ackerman's. And they'd order Eddie killed with no more emotion than they'd order a steak.

Carmody wasn't worried yet. The confidence in his own strength and brains was the hard core of his being, impervious to strain or pressure. Somehow, he would save Eddie. He accepted Beaumonte's deadly injunction as a factor in the equation. They—Beaumonte and Ackerman—meant business. Therefore, something else would have to give. That was Eddie.

After a ten-minute wait he dialed Eddie's number again and let it ring. Eddie might be outside watering the lawn, or at the workbench in the basement, repairing a lock or mending a screen. Something important, Carmody thought.

The phone clicked in his ear. Eddie's voice said, "Yes? Hello."

"This is Mike. How's the boy?"

"Mike? How are you?" Eddie's tone was neutral, neither friendly nor unfriendly. "I was splicing a hose out in the back yard. You been ringing long?"

Splicing a hose, Carmody thought, shaking his head. "Eddie, I want to see you tonight."

"I'm going out pretty soon," his brother said.

"Well, I can meet you anywhere you say. This is important. Where will you be?"

"Vespers at Saint Pat's."

"Vespers?"

"Sure. You might remember if you put your mind to it."

Eddie's tone, hard and sarcastic, warned Carmody off the subject. "How about afterward then?" he said.

There was a short silence. Then Eddie said, "I've got a date later, Mike."

"Well, something you've been keeping from me, eh?" Carmody said, trying for a lighter touch.

"I know what's on your mind," Eddie said shortly. "And the answer is no, Mike."

"Don't jump to conclusions," Carmody said. This was no time for anger; that would tear it for good. "I've got something to tell you in person. So how about it?"

"Okay," Eddie said, after a pause. "There's a club at Edgely and Broad called the Fanfair. I can meet you there at eleven."

"Fine." He tried once more for a lighter mood. "You're moving in swanky circles, kid."

"It's just a neighborhood joint," Eddie said, keeping it cold and distant. "I'll see you, Mike."

Carmody left the booth and glanced at his watch. It was almost eight-thirty and there was no point in going back to Headquarters. He ordered a lemon Coke at the fountain and looked over the magazine rack while he drank it. Then he phoned in and left a message with the clerk for Lieutenant Wilson, saying he was on something important and would be in later. The clerk told him everything was still quiet, and added that the card game could go on all night if things stayed this way.

"Yes, we've got snap jobs," Carmody said, and replaced the receiver.

With almost two hours to kill, he left the drug store and strolled down Market, trying to dismiss the memory of Eddie's coldness. It hadn't always been that way. Carmody was eight years older than his brother and as a boy Eddie had idolized him, which was inevitable, considering the difference in their ages. He had taught Eddie to swim, to play ball, to fight and had bought him clothes and lent him money for his first dates. Eddie had been a nice little guy, Carmody thought, walking along the bright crowded street. A serious kid, not bright or shrewd but straight-forward and dependable. Almost too pretty in the soft, dark-pale Irish manner; flawless fair skin, long-lashed blue eyes, thick, curly black hair. In his cassock and surplice with the round white collar under his chin he had always stolen the show at St. Pat's Christmas and Easter proces-sions. But he'd never been spoiled, Carmody remembered. He was just a likable little boy, shyly earnest and direct, with a thousand little-boy questions always buzzing in his head. Carmody smiled slightly. *Why don't footballs float like balloons? Could the old man lick Jack Dempsey? How come you have to leave home when you marry an old girl?* Carmody had always felt like smiling at him when he asked questions like that, his face serious, his long-lashed eyes staring at Mike as if he knew everything in the world. They'd got along fine then and maybe that was the only way two people ever got along—when one of them was so trusting that he accepted the other's every word without doubt or resentment. But it couldn't stay that way. Eventually, the dumb one got smart and saw that his idol was just another poor fool.

Time was standing still, Carmody thought, looking at his watch. The crowds went by him, charged with night time excitement and a traffic cop waved and gave him a soft, smiling salute. He crossed the street and stopped to look at the bright posters in front of a movie house. Buying a ticket, he went inside and took a back seat. The audience sloped down from him to the screen, a dark, intense unit. There was an irritating smell of stale smoke and popcorn in the heavy air.

After twenty minutes he lost interest in the picture and left. It was the kind of junk that annoyed him thoroughly, a sticky, phony story about a man and woman who ran into trouble because they ignored the standards of their society. Who in hell made those standards? A group of frightened ninnies who clung for protection to the symbols of reversed collars and nightsticks, and wanted only a kind boss, an insurance policy and a two-room apartment with babies.

There was no penalty for smashing the rules made by these timid people; Carmody had proved that to his satisfaction. The truth they gave lip-service to didn't exist; there was no mystery about life, no hidden value, no far-away beauty and happiness. The true life spread around every human being, a dog-eat-dog slaughter for money and power. Those who didn't see it were blinded by fear; they closed their eyes to the truth because they were afraid to fight. They wanted a handout, a pension, a break, from some other world. They can't take this world, and that's why we take it away from them, Carmody thought.

Finally, he turned into a night club on Fifteenth Street, a big splashy place with a name band and a Hollywood star doing an M.C. turn between pictures. Carmody had a drink with the owner, a worried little man named Ventura, who was going into court the following month to explain some tax irregularities. They talked about the case and Ventura wanted to know if Carmody had heard anything about it, or did he know the judge, and how the hell did things look anyway?

"That's all Federal," Carmody said, relieved that there was no way he could help. That was odd; normally he didn't mind doing a favor. Maybe I want a favor, he thought. But what? And who can help me? While Ventura was off greeting a chattering bunch of expensive-looking college kids, Carmody paid the check and left.

Now it was time to see his brother.

Eddie was sitting at the bar, his broad back to the entrance, and Carmody came up behind him and slapped him on the shoulder. His brother turned, smiling awkwardly, and they exchanged hellos and shook hands.

"What'll you have?" Eddie asked him.

"It doesn't matter. Scotch, I guess."

"I'll coast on this," Eddie said, nodding at his half-filled glass of beer.

The Fanfair was a pleasant spot, several notches above a neighborhood tavern. There was a piano on a dais at the end of the long bar and beyond that double doors led to the dining room. The lighting was soft and the decorations were attractive; it was the sort of place a young man would take his girl after the movies, or where a married couple would bring their in-laws for Sunday dinner. There was no bouncer, no drunks or cigarette girls, no unescorted women.

"Let's take a booth," Carmody suggested.

"Sure." Eddie picked up his beer and crossed to a row of dark-wood booths, moving with solid strides that were in sharp contrast to Carmody's easy but powerful grace. Eddie was several inches shorter than his brother, but his shoulders were heavier. At twenty-eight he was in good shape, but he would have trouble with his weight in a few years. There was still the suggestion of the choir boy in his square pale face and in the shyly earnest expression around his eyes. Despite his bulk, there was a vulnerable look about him; he had never learned to camouflage his emotions. His hopes and hurts and disappointments were nakedly apparent, mirrored for everyone to see in his embarrassingly clear and honest eyes.

"What's on your mind, Mike?" Eddie said, after a quick glance over his shoulder at the piano.

"Does your girl work here?"

"Yes, she's a singer and plays her own accompaniments." Eddie smiled. "She's pretty good, I guess."

He was very proud of her, Carmody saw. "Well, let's get this over with," he said, moving his glass aside, fixing Eddie with his hard eyes. "You got yourself into a mess on this Delaney business."

"That's your version of it, not mine."

"Damn it, let me finish," Carmody said. "Delaney's in a position to embarrass the men who run the city. He's threatening to talk unless they take the heat off. You're the heat, Eddie. Do you understand?"

Eddie put his elbows on the table and leaned closer to Carmody. "You want me to say it wasn't Delaney I saw standing over Ettonberg with a gun in his hand? Is that what you want?"

"I want to keep you out of trouble," Carmody said.

"Thanks all to hell," Eddie said shortly. "I don't need your help."

"Kid, be sensible. Why be a hero for a bum like Delaney?"

"If he's such a bum, why are the big boys worried?"

"He can embarrass them; put it that way."

"They embarrass real easy, don't they?" Eddie said.

"Be a humorist," Carmody said dryly. "But see if this strikes you as comical. Unless you testify sensibly, you won't testify at all."

Eddie stared at him for a few seconds, his big chest rising and falling rapidly. "I'll get killed for doing my job," he said at last. "Is that what you're telling me?"

"I'm just a carrier pigeon, a Western Union boy," Carmody said. "I'm delivering a message. But you wouldn't be getting this treatment if it weren't for me. They'd step on you like a bug if you weren't my brother."

"I owe you a lot," Eddie said bitterly. "I get a reprieve because my brother works with the big boys."

"Don't talk like a fool." They were both becoming angry and Carmody knew that would ruin everything. He lit a cigarette and drew a long breath. This always happened with him and Eddie; he could handle other men without his emotions interfering, but this kid brother of his always got under his skin. Eddie was too stubborn to see the truth, and that made Carmody furious. "Now look," he said, keeping his temper in check. "You're not just getting a reprieve. You'll get ten thousand bucks to go with it, which is more dough than you can save in twenty years pulling police boxes. You get that for just saying, 'I'm not sure' when you look at Delaney in court."

"I'll tell the truth so to hell with you," Eddie said, his big hands tightening into fists. He was bitterly angry but beneath that was a deeper feeling; his soft clear eyes were like those of a child who has been hurt by a trusted adult.

A chord sounded from the piano and he turned his head quickly.

The big baby, Carmody thought helplessly. He doesn't understand how the world is run, he doesn't know anything except the nonsense the old man pounded into him. Carmody wondered how he would handle this as he glanced past Eddie to the girl at the piano. She was older than Eddie, thirty or thirty-two maybe, a slender girl with brown hair and a small serious face. She began to sing a sentimental ballad in a voice that was low and pleasant, but not much else. Carmody wondered what her appeal was to Eddie. What would his brother want in a woman? Carmody didn't know. They had stopped communicating on all but superficial levels long before he got to know Eddie's needs and taste in women. This one didn't seem to be the party type. She looked brave and thoughtful, but that might be part of the act. She wasn't voluptuous or sexy, in fact she didn't even look very strong; her arms were white and thin against her black evening gown, and he could see the deep shadowed hollow at the base of her throat. A demure clinging vine maybe. Would Eddie like that? Someone he could baby and protect? Carmody sipped his drink and shook his head. That would be a great union. Two babies hugging each other in the big windy world.

Something about her touched a faint responsive chord in his memory. There was a teasing familiarity in the way she sat at the piano, her back perfectly straight, thin shoulders squared and her small head raised as if watching for something on the horizon. Carmody ran her face and body through his mind as if it were a fingerprint card in a selector machine. He tried to match her up with friends and enemies, with places and crimes, but the effort produced no answer to the little query in his mind.

"She's good," he said to Eddie, making it warm and friendly. "What's her name?"

"Karen Stephanson."

That meant nothing to Carmody. "Is she a local product?"

"No, she was born in New York. But she's worked all over the country, I guess."

"How did you get to know her?"

"Well, this place used to be on my beat. I came by one night when it was raining and she was waiting for a cab. She lives near here, at the Empire Hotel. I called the district from the pull box and got one of the squads to drive her home."

Carmody smiled. "Very neat!"

"Well, I stopped in to hear her sing a few times, and then asked her for a date. That's all there was to it."

"Is this a serious deal?"

"With me it is. I don't know about her."

Carmody patted his brother's shoulder, still smiling. "Look, if any ninety-eight-pound female thinks she is too good for you just tell her about the Kings of Ireland. Hell man, we're direct descendants."

"Don't forget the family castles and hunting lodges," Eddie said, responding to the lighter mood. "There must be castles every square yard over there. I never met a Mick whose family didn't own one or two at least."

Smiling at him, Carmody thought, he's serious, all right. And with Eddie that wouldn't mean one-night stands. He'd want it all the way, with an apartment, babies, diapers on the radiators, the works. "You want to marry her?" he asked.

"I guess I would," Eddie said, coloring slightly.

"Good, keep that in mind," Carmody said. "Now without getting sore, let's go back to Delaney."

"We've settled that," Eddie said shortly, his mood changing.

"Listen to me, Goddamnit. You won't marry anybody unless you play ball. Get that through your thick head. You'll be dead." I've got to sell him this, Carmody thought, but for the first time he felt a tug of anxiety. Supposing he couldn't? What then?

"Let's drop it," Eddie said angrily. Then his face softened, and his eyes became helpless and vulnerable. "I'm not judging you, Mike. Maybe you're the smart one. And maybe I'm a dope, like you say. But I like it the way I am. Can't you see that? I don't like fighting you. It gives me a charge to see you, and to kid around about the Kings of Ireland. That's fine, for some reason. But let's drop this other thing."

"If I do you get killed."

Eddie smiled crookedly. "Well, I haven't anything too big on my conscience."

"Damn it, stop talking like the old man," Carmody said, snapping out the words. "What about this girl? Will you do her any good lying on a morgue slab?"

"Leave the old man out of this," Eddie said.

"Okay, forget him. But stop talking like a child."

"I'm no child. I can handle myself."

"Dear God," Carmody said, raising his eyes to the ceiling. "Now you're going to be a hero. Stand right up to a crowd that just about holds the whole state in its hands."

"Maybe I'm not so alone as you think," Eddie said. "Supposing I go to Superintendent Shortall with your deal. What about that?"

Carmody smiled gently. "Shortall's no knight in armor. He works for the same boss as I do."

"That's not straight."

"Wouldn't I be likely to know?"

Eddie stared at him, swallowing hard. Then he said bitterly, "Yeah, you'd know about that, I guess. So Shortall is on the take too." He suddenly pounded a fist on the table. "The big phony. Him and his speeches about our responsibility to the community, about being good citizens first and good cops second."

"Fine, get mad," Carmody said, nodding approvingly. "That's a healthy reaction. It's the first step toward getting smart. Now listen to me," he said, fixing Eddie with his cold hard eyes. "I've been through all this. Do you think they'll let you be a good cop? Sure, if you don't bother them.

You can be as efficient as you like on school crossings, but they'll break you in two if you stick your nose into their business."

Watching Eddie's troubled face, Carmody realized that it was time to ease off, to let the seed he had planted grow. "What happened to our drinks?" he said. "Let's have another round; okay?"

"Does that include me?"

It was the girl, Karen, who spoke. She was standing beside their booth, smiling pleasantly at Eddie.

"Good gosh, I didn't even notice you'd stopped singing," Eddie said, and started to get to his feet. But she put a hand lightly on his shoulder and said, "Never mind, I'll slide in beside you."

"This is my brother, Mike, Karen. Mike, this is Karen."

They smiled at each other, and Carmody said, "What would you like to drink?"

"Scotch, please. On the rocks."

Carmody gave the waiter their order, then looked at Karen. "We were just talking about you in connection with Kings of Ireland," he said.

"Cut it out, Mike," Eddie said, grinning uncomfortably.

"I don't understand. Should I?" Karen said, smiling at Eddie.

"No, it was just a gag," he said.

She's a cool little cookie, Carmody thought, studying her with interest. She realized that he was taking her measure but it didn't disturb her; she sipped her drink slowly and gave him time to draw his conclusions. There were girls who would have resented his deliberate appraisal, but her manner remained poised and friendly. She was better-looking up close, he thought. Her eyes were very lovely, deeply blue and steady, and there was a hint of intelligence and humor in the turn of her soft, gently curving lips. She wore her brown hair parted in the middle and clipped behind with a small silver barrette. Against the dark wood of the booth her bare shoulders were white and square. She held herself very handsomely, chin raised, back straight and her hands resting in her lap.

They talked casually until Eddie glanced at his watch.

"I'm taking Karen out for a sandwich, Mike," he said. "This is her only break before she gets through at two."

"Perhaps Mike would like to come with us." She spoke to Eddie but she was watching Carmody, taking his measure as he had taken hers.

"No, I've got to get back downtown," he said, knowing Eddie didn't want him along. Karen understood that, he saw. She finished her drink and put out her cigarette, changing the mood with these little gestures. "We'd better go then, I think," she said.

Carmody paid the check. Karen excused herself to get a wrap and Eddie went off to make a phone call. Carmody stood alone, flipping a coin in one hand, and staring at his tall, wide-shouldered figure in the bar mirrow. He'd made a good start. Eddie had something to think about now, and when a man started thinking he was usually getting on the right track.

He turned, still flipping the coin, and saw Karen coming toward him with light quick steps. She carried a stole over one arm and he could hear the click of her high-heeled sandals above the murmur of laughter and conversation. And then he noticed that she was limping. It was a very small limp, just a slight favoring of her left leg, but the sight of it touched the responsive chord in his mind. Where had he seen her before? Then, when she stopped and smiled briefly at him, the cogs in his sharp brain meshed together smoothly. And he had the answer to his query.

It was in Miami, two seasons ago, when he'd been down with Beaumonte for an unscheduled winter vacation. He had seen her in the expensive lobby of an expensive hotel, making her way on crutches. That was why he had remembered her, because she had been on crutches. That had stuck in his mind.

Smiling down at her he said suddenly, "Where were you on the night of December 15th two years ago? Don't huddle with your attorney. Let's have it without rehearsal."

"What do you mean?"

"Miami, wasn't it?"

"That's right." She watched him gravely. "How did you know?"

"I was there. I remembered you."

"Yes, I expect you would," she said.

His mind was working smoothly and sharply. Could she help him with Eddie? She looked smart; maybe she could pound sense into his head. The chance was well worth taking.

"I want to talk to you," he said. He smiled into her steady blue eyes and put his hands lightly over her bare shoulders. "I've got a proposition to make. Concerning Eddie, so don't haul off and slug me yet. How about having a drink with me when he's out safeguarding the ash cans in the neighborhood?"

"Let me go," she said quietly; but her voice was tight with anger. "Take your hands off me."

Carmody put his hands on his hips and studied her closely, bewildered by her reaction. "Take it easy," he said gently. "You're jumping to conclusions, I think."

"The Miami phase is over and done with," she said. "You'd better get that straight."

He didn't understand this. "I'm sorry you got the wrong idea," he said.

She was pale and defiant, but he saw that her lower lip was trembling. "Don't take it so hard," he said, still puzzled. "What can I say after I say I'm sorry?"

"You don't believe me, of course," she said.

"Why shouldn't I?"

"Stop grinning like an adolescent at a burlesque show," she said angrily.

"They whistled in my day," Carmody said. "But that was quite a spell back. You know you're awfully touchy. Does it worry your psychiatrist?"

"You're very funny. I'll bet you do imitations, too."

"Don't try to creep into my heart with flattery," Carmody said, smiling at her. "I know you just want to borrow my badge to give to some police dog."

She started to say something but Eddie came swinging down the room, grinning cheerfully, and she turned her back to Carmody and let Eddie take her arm.

"We've got to rush it up a little," he said, patting her hand. "You two have a chance to get acquainted?"

"We sure did," Carmody said, looking at Karen. He half expected her to tell Eddie about their little flare-up, but she avoided his eyes, said nothing. It would come later, he guessed. When she could flavor her version to Eddie's taste.

Outside they said their good-bys and Eddie and Karen walked away together in the soft clean darkness. Carmody stared after them, frowning slightly and flipping the coin in his hand.

He would save Eddie all right. With or without help from this cool, poised little character. But probably with her help, he thought, smiling slightly.

She knew the score. She could count; all the way up to ten thousand.

He drove into the city on Broad Street and parked in a restricted zone on Fifteenth Street under the eye of a friendly traffic cop. Beaumonte was waiting for him but first he would have to check in with Lieutenant Wilson. There was always the need to preserve the illusion that he was a responsible member of the department.

Carmody called from a drug store. Wilson, a sharp and businesslike cop, sounded annoyed when he got through to him. "I can't run a shift without a sergeant, Mike," he said. "Where've you been?"

"Something developed on that Fairmount Park murder," Carmody said. "I'm meeting a character who wants to make a deal."

"Another Carmody exclusive," Wilson said dryly.

"Don't be sensitive. You can give it to the papers," Carmody said.

"I don't give a damn about that," Wilson said. "We've had two jobs tonight, a knifing in South with no leads and a murder in the Wagner Hotel. Everybody's out but me and I'm holding down your desk."

"I'll stop at the Wagner and take a look," Carmody said, checking his watch. The delay wouldn't improve Beaumonte's disposition, he knew. "Who'd you send on that one?"

"Dirksen and Myers."

"I'll take a look. And stop worrying."

"Gee, thanks," Wilson said. "It's real friendly of you to pitch in this way."

Carmody laughed and dropped the receiver back in place. He went out to his car and drove through center-city to the Wagner, a well-run commercial hotel near the railroad station. There he found Myers browbeating an hysterical little man in whose room the girl had been shot, and Dirksen talking baseball with a lab technician. The girl lay on the floor beside the rumpled bed, a heavily built blonde in her middle thirties. She wore only a slip and her make-up stood out like clown markings against the white emptiness of her face. Dirksen digressed reluctantly from the baseball to give him the story. The elevator operator had heard the shot and summoned the night manager, who had opened the room with his passkey. The girl was on the floor, a bullet hole under her heart, and the man, a furniture salesman from Michigan, was sprawled on the bed out cold.

"It was his gun fired the shot," Dirksen said in conclusion. "It's open and shut. He's playing dumb but he's our boy."

Carmody glanced around the room, frowning slightly. He noticed a tray of smeared highball glasses on the bureau with two whiskey bottles beside it. One was empty, the other full, and they were of different brands.

"What's our boy's name?" Carmody asked.

"Samuel T. Degget."

"Did you check his wallet? Was anything missing?"

"No, he's got all his money."

Carmody stared at Degget for a moment or so, trying to get an impression of the man. He was married and had grown daughters (Degget was telling Myers now in a high squealing voice). You couldn't be sure, Carmody thought, but he didn't seem to fit this kind of trouble. The girl, yes; the shooting, no. Degget looked like a cautious methodical person, and was probably a pillar of rectitude in his own community. When he cut loose it would be far from home and with all risks reduced to the absolute minimum. Everything bought and paid for, anonymous and artificial, and no unpleasant after effects except a big head in the morning. Why would he louse himself up with murder?

"What do you have on the girl?" he asked Dirksen.

"She works as a waitress in the coffee shop in the lobby. No folks in town. She lives in a boardinghouse on Elm Street with another girl. One of the waiters in the coffee shop remembers that Degget and she were pretty friendly. You know, he kidded around with her a lot."

Carmody frowned and looked once more at the whiskey bottles. Two different brands, one bottle empty, the other full. He checked his watch. The State liquor stores had closed two hours ago; he was wondering where Degget had got the second bottle. It wasn't likely that he had bought them both at the same time; if so, they would have been the same brand.

He glanced at Dirksen, who wet his lips. "Something wrong?" Dirksen asked, worried by Carmody's expression.

"Call the bell captain and ask him if there was any service to this room tonight," Carmody said.

Dirksen was on the phone a moment, and then looked over the receiver at Carmody. "No service, but somebody from here asked to see a bellhop."

"They may have run out of booze and wanted another bottle," Carmody said sharply. "Bellhops can find one for a price. Get the name of the boy who came up here, and find out if he's still on duty."

"Sure, sure." Dirksen looked up from the phone a moment later. "It was a fellow named Ernie, but he's not around. Do you think—"

"Get his address and send a car out there. And put him on the air. He can't be far away. Take Degget in as a material witness but get this guy Ernie."

"Right, Sarge." With routine to absorb him, Dirksen was crisp and confident. Myers drifted over, looking puzzled. "What's all this, Mike?"

"It was Jack the Ripper, really," Carmody said, smiling coldly at him. "I spotted it right away."

"What's funny about it?" Myers said, irritation tightening his cautious mouth.

"Nothing at all," Carmody said. "Actually, it's pretty sad."

"We got the man who—"

"No you haven't," Carmody said. "Not if my hunch is right. But Dirk can fill you in. I've got to be going."

It was nearly midnight when he got to Beaumonte's, and by then the night had turned clear and cool. Beaumonte opened the door and said, "Well, you and your brother must have had quite a talk." He wore a crimson silk dressing gown and held a pumpkin-sized brandy snifter in one hand.

"Sorry to keep you waiting," Carmody said. He strolled into the room and saw with a slight shock that Bill Ackerman was sitting in a deep chair beside the fireplace. The Delaney business was very big, he knew then. Nothing but high-priority operations could get Ackerman in from the country.

"Hello, Mike," Ackerman said, smiling briefly at him.

Carmody smiled and said hello. There was another man sitting in a chair with his back to the window, a powerfully built young man with wide pale features and dull observant eyes. Carmody said hello to him, too. His name was Johnny Stark and he had been a highly touted heavyweight contender until something went wrong with his ears. He was slightly deaf, and worrying about it had stamped a solemn, surprised look on his face. Ackerman owned his contract when he was fighting, and had taken him on as bodyguard when the medical examiners barred him from the ring. Stark sat with his huge hands hanging between his legs, his fairly good ear cocked toward Ackerman and his dull eyes flicking around the room like those of an inquisitive dog. He mumbled his answer to Carmody's greeting; this had become a habit since his hearing had gone bad. He was never sure what people said to him and he covered up with grunts and mumbles which could mean anything.

"Well, how'd it go?" Beaumonte said, easing himself into the sofa.

"The kid was sensible; he'll cooperate," Carmody said. This wasn't a lie, he thought; he'd bring Eddie around some way.

"That's just fine," Beaumonte said, smiling at him. "I told you I didn't want trouble."

"There won't be any."

Ackerman stood and stretched leisurely, his hands stuck deep into his trouser pockets. Carmody didn't know whether he had been listening or not; it was impossible to guess accurately about anything connected with Bill Ackerman. He was a tall man in his middle fifties, with the lean, disciplined body of a professional soldier.

There was nothing to be learned from his features, which were tanned and hard, nor from his eyes which were merely sharp black globes beneath bushy gray eyebrows. His hair was the color of well-used and well-kept silver, and he dressed like a banker in town and a rancher in the country. He was a cold, controlled man who emanated a quality of blunt, explosive power; there was none of Beaumonte's phoniness in him. He lived in the country because he liked it there. The fact that it was pleasant for his wife and two daughters was simply coincidence. Had he wanted to live in the city, that's where he would live. Ackerman was driven by cool, dispassionate greed; he wanted to expand and expand, consolidate his gains and expand again. There was no definite goal on the horizon; it was the struggle as well as the victory that pleased him. Greed dominated his life. His farms and stock paid for themselves and his foreman and hands admired his shrewd tough efficiency. Everything in Ackerman's operations paid its way or was dropped. His world was money, and rivers of it flowed to him from handbooks and policy wheels throughout the state. More of it rolled in from his trucking and contracting firms, from fleets of cabs and packing houses. The money mounted faster and faster, and with a fraction of it he bought immunity from the law. Every cop he hired, every politician he subsidized, every judge he elevated became a prop to his empire, chained into place forever by guilt. No one got away from him; men were chattels, and he was as greedy for them as he was for money.

Carmody wasn't afraid of Ackerman; but he wondered why he bothered to tell himself this so often. If there was anyone to fear in this deal, it was Ackerman. He had fought his way up in the rackets with cold and awful efficiency; he had begun in Chicago with Dion O'Bannion's hoodlums, had run his own mob after repeal and had moved East to crash into the unions and the black market during the war. His past was marked with terror and violence but somehow he had come through it without being killed or jailed for life.

Now he stared at Carmody, his eyes narrowed under the bushy gray brows. "Your brother is a smart man, Mike. Runs in the family, I guess."

Carmody felt a sharp surge of anger at that. But he said quietly, "He's smart enough."

"Specifically, he won't identify Delaney at the trial. Is that right?"

"That's the agreement."

"What is it costing us?"

"Ten thousand. That's what Beaumonte said."

"It's a fair price," Ackerman said, rubbing his jaw. He didn't like paying off; it wasn't natural for money to flow the other way. "Probably more dough than he's ever seen in one piece, eh?"

"Sure," Carmody said.

Ackerman said casually, "I want to talk to him, Mike. Fix it up for tomorrow night."

"Will that look good?" Carmody asked. He knew Ackerman had tried to jolt him, and that was ominous. It meant that Ackerman hadn't believed him completely. He smiled coldly, his tough strength and brains responding to the challenge. "If you're seen huddling with him before the trial it won't look good when he double-crosses the D.A."

"I said I want to talk to him," Ackerman said, watching Carmody curiously. He looked more surprised than angry. There was never any discussion about his orders; he insisted on automatic compliance. "You bring him here tomorrow night. Let's say ten o'clock. Got that?"

Beaumonte was watching them over the rim of his brandy snifter, and Johnny Stark had cocked his good ear anxiously toward the edge in Ackerman's voice. The tension held in the long graceful room until Carmody dismissed it with a little shrug. "Sure, I've got it. Ten o'clock."

"That's about all then, I guess," Ackerman said. "I'll see you, Mike."

"So long."

After he had gone Ackerman sat down and lit a cigar. When it was drawing well he glanced at Beaumonte through the ropey layers of smoke. "I don't know too much about Carmody," he said. "What kind of a guy is he?"

"He's tough," Beaumonte said, nodding. "But he's all right."

Ackerman said nothing more and Beaumonte became uneasy. He waved the heavy smoke away from his eyes, and said, "What's the matter? Don't you trust him?"

Ackerman used one of his rare smiles. "I'm like a guy in the banking business. I don't do business on trust. What's Carmody's job?"

"Just a job," Beaumonte said. "He keeps an eye on the bookies in West, does some collecting, checks the records of a guy who wants to open a horse room or run a policy game. That kind of thing. And he settles beefs. He's good at that."

Ackerman rubbed his smooth hard jaw and was silent again for several minutes. Then he said, "Well, we've got a beef. Think he's the man to settle it?"

"Well, that's up to you," Beaumonte said. Ackerman's manner was making him nervous. He liked straight, direct orders; but Ackerman wasn't giving orders. He was giving him an unwelcome responsibility in the deal. Beaumonte frowned, watching Ackerman hopefully for a crisp, final decision. In his heart he was a little bit afraid of Carmody; there was a look on the detective's face at times that made him uneasy.

"We'll give him a chance to settle it," Ackerman said tapping his cigar on the side of an ashtray. "But just one. I don't like the brother angle."

"Blood is thicker than water, eh?"

"That's it," Ackerman said, using another rare smile. "But it's not thicker than money. Anyway, I'm going to hedge the bet just in case. You call Dominic Costello in Chicago and ask him to line us up someone who can do a fast job."

Beaumonte liked this much better. The decision was made, the orders given and he was in the clear. "I'll take care of it," he said. "How about a nightcap?"

"Okay. Make it light though, we're driving to the country tonight."

# 3

CARMODY DROVE DIRECTLY ACROSS TOWN TO HIS HOTEL WHICH WAS NEAR the center of the city and about a block from the river. He parked a car length from the canopied entrance and told the doorman that he would be going out again shortly.

Carmody had lived here for six years, in a three-room suite on a premium floor high above the city's noise and dust. Letting himself in, he snapped on the lights and checked the time. Twelve-thirty. He had missed his shift completely, which would give Wilson something to complain about tomorrow. Let him, he thought. There was more at stake now than eight hours of routine duty.

First he had to get fixed on Karen Stephanson. She might be the lever to pry Eddie off the spot. Carmody paced the floor slowly, thinking over each word of their conversation, trying to recall every expression that had shifted across her small pale face. Finally, he sat down at the phone and

called a man named Tony Anelli, a gambler who spent six months of
each year in Miami.

Anelli sounded a little tight. "Howsa boy, howsa boy?" he said cheerfully. Carmody heard a woman's high laughter in the background.

"I'm looking for some information," Carmody said.

"Came to the right party," Anelli said. "We got a party going, as a
matter of fact." This struck him as comical and he began to laugh. Carmody let him run down and then said, "Do you know anything about a
girl named Karen Stephanson?"

"Karen Stephanson? Sounds Swedish," Anelli said. He was silent a few
seconds. "It's familiar, Mike. I wish I wasn't loaded. The old head is turning around like a merry-go-round. Wait a second. I met her a couple of
times, if she's the same dish. Thin girl, brown hair, kind of serious. Does
that fit?"

"Yeah, that fits," Carmody said. "What do you know about her?"

"Well, nothing much. She was Danny Nimo's girl."

"Danny Nimo?"

"He ran a string of handbooks in New Orleans. Pretty rough character."

"She was his girl, eh?"

"Yeah, that's right. He's dead though. Died a year or so ago of pneumonia," Anelli said. "That's what always gets those big chesty guys. Let's
see now. I met her in Miami in '50 or '51. She'd been in a hell of an
accident. Nimo took me up to the hospital to see her, and that's why I
remember her, I guess."

"What kind of an accident?" Carmody asked. He was thinking of her
coldly and savagely. The pale little face, the poised and regal manner,
and twisting his brother around in her slim hands like a piece of helpless
clay. A bitter smile appeared at the corners of his mouth. He'd put an
end to that act.

"It was an automobile accident," Anelli said. "Nimo was driving, and
the story was that he was drunk. They hit a truck head-on; he told me
her legs were broken in a dozen places."

In spite of his anger, Carmody winced. He hated the idea of physical
suffering, not for himself but for others. It was about the only crack in his
hard, iconoclastic shell. But her suffering was over, he thought, and now
she was staging a cheap, phony act for Eddie. He understood her flare-up
at his offer of a drink; she had thought he knew about her relationship
with Nimo and was attempting to blackmail her into two-timing Eddie.
A nice sweet kid. *The Miami phase is all over.* That's what she'd said.
Sure, he thought, sure. Miami and Danny Nimo were a little trip along
the primrose path, but now she was back on the strait and narrow, re-
deemed in the nick of time, saved by the bell, cheating the devil with a
shoestring catch of her virtue. That would be her story, Carmody knew;
told with a tactful tear or two and Eddie would buy it at any price.

"Thanks, Tony," he said into the phone. "See you around."

"Sure, keed. Take it easy. Wish I could do the same, but the night's going to be bumpy, I think."

Carmody hung up and walked into the bedroom, stripping off his suit coat. He showered and shaved, then opened the closet doors to choose his clothes. A dozen suits faced him in a neat row, and there was a line of glossy shoes with wooden blocks inside them in a rack on the floor. On either side of the suits were cedar-lined drawers filled with shirts, socks and underwear, and smaller trays containing cuff-links, tie-clips, handkerchiefs, a wallet and cigarette cases. Carmody took out a blue gabardine suit, a white shirt and a pair of cordovan shoes which had been shined and rubbed until they were nearly black. After dressing he glanced at himself in the full-length mirror. His thick blond hair was damp from the shower and there was an unpleasant little smile on his hard handsome face. All set for fun with Danny Nimo's ex-passion-flower, he thought. It should be good. He wondered what would happen to her when he dropped Danny Nimo's name into her lap. Fall apart in nice delicate pieces probably.

Carmody walked into the living room, made himself a light drink and put on an album of show tunes. She wound up her turn at two o'clock and Eddie had told him she lived at the Empire Hotel. Two-thirty should find her home, unless she was out with someone else. Staring at the gleaming sweep of the river, he realized he was letting himself get emotional about her. And that was no good. Anger could upset his judgment as drastically as any other passion. What he thought of her didn't matter; it wasn't his job to strip away her defenses. His only job was to make her help him with Eddie. So to hell with what he thought of her, to hell with everything but his dumb kid brother.

Still staring at the river, he lit a cigarette and sipped his drink. The music wrapped itself around him, filtering into his mind with stories of love—love lost, love found, love dying, love growing. Every kind of love there is, he thought irritably. The songs were as bad as the movie he had walked out of tonight. All promise, hope, and sickly enchantment. Did anyone know love as it was defined by these groaning singers? Where was this nostalgia, this grandeur, this thing that could enrich a man even as he lost or destroyed it?

Well, where was it? he asked himself. Not in this world, that was certain. It was like Santa Claus, and the big kind man with whiskers who looked down from the clouds with a sad smile on his face. Fairy tales for dopes who would fall on their faces if it weren't for these crutches.

To get his mind off it, he emptied an ashtray and straightened the pile of magazines on the coffee table. The room pleased him with its look of expensive comfort. It needed pictures, but he hadn't enough confidence in his own judgment to buy the modern paintings he thought he liked, and he balked at the hunting prints which a dealer had told him would go with just about anything. Glancing about, Carmody remembered the way his father had hung holy pictures around the house with a bland disregard for anything but his own taste. St. Michael with his foot on Lucifer's neck, the good and bad angels, St. Peter dressed like a Roman senator and St. Anthony looking like a tragic young poet. All over the place, staring at you solemnly when you snapped on the lights. Carmody hadn't minded the pictures as much as his father's stubborn insistence on sticking them in the most conspicuous spot in every room. It was like living in a church. Carmody hardly remembered his mother; she had died two months after having Eddie, when he himself was just eight years old. The old man had raised his sons alone; getting married again had never crossed his mind.

The stubborn old fool, Carmody was thinking, as he got ready to leave. He'd been sure he had a strangle hold on happiness and eternal bliss. Everything was settled, all problems were solved in advance by his trust in God.

I'd like to see him handle this problem, he thought bitterly. The old man would tell Eddie not to worry, to make a novena and do what he thought was right. That would be great except for the fact that Ackerman and Beaumonte didn't believe in novenas. Prayers were a waste of breath in their league. The old man couldn't save Eddie with a lifetime on his knees. But I'll save him, Carmody thought. Without prayers. That's my kind of work.

The Empire was a quiet, respectable apartment hotel in the Northeast section of the city. Carmody got there at two-thirty, parked on the dark, tree-lined street and walked into the tiled lobby. He found her name printed in ink on a white card and rang the bell. There was a speaking tube beside the row of cards. She answered the third ring.

"Yes? Who is it?"

"This is Mike Carmody. I want to see you."

She hesitated a moment, then said coldly, "It's a bit late, don't you think?"

"Wait a minute. What's wrong with a friendly chat?"

"You don't see anything wrong with coming up here at two-thirty in the morning?"

"People will talk, eh?" he said dryly. "Well, that's okay. I don't mind."

"Please, Mike, you're dead wrong about me," she said, her voice changing.

"Save all that," he said. "This concerns Eddie. Now press the buzzer before I get mad."

"Is this how you get what you want?" she said. "By kicking people around?"

"Press that buzzer," Carmody said. "I'm not kidding, bright eyes. Your virtue, such as it is, won't get a workout. Open up, damn it."

There was a short pause. Then the lock clicked sharply. Smiling slightly, he opened the door and walked down a short carpeted hallway to the elevator.

She was waiting for him at the doorway of her apartment, her small head lifted defiantly. She wore a blue silk robe and a ribbon held her hair back from the slim line of her throat. Without make-up her face was pale, but her steady blue eyes were bright and unafraid.

Carmody walked toward her, still smiling slightly. She would play this on a very high level, he guessed. All poise and dignity. She created an illusion of strength and dignity, but Carmody wasn't impressed. He had worked too long as a cop to be impressed by externals. Underneath that thin crust of confidence he knew there was nothing but guilt. What else could there be?

Smiling down at her, he said, "Thanks for letting me come up."

"I had no choice," she said shortly.

"That's a dull way to look at it."

She turned into her apartment and he followed her and tossed his hat into a chair. The living room was impersonal but comfortable; a TV set stood in one corner and a studio couch, made up now with sheets and blankets, was pulled out a few inches from the opposite wall. There were chairs, lamps, a coffee table with copies of *Variety* and *Billboard* on it, and a tall breakfront in which he saw shelves of dishes.

"Cosy," he said, nodding.

"You said you wanted to talk about Eddie."

"We'll get to him in a minute."

She shrugged lightly. "We'll do it your way, of course."

"That's right," he said.

"It's been a long day," she said. Her expression changed then, relieved by a tentative little smile. "Don't you have any soft spots? I'd be grateful if you'd make this brief and let me go to bed." She tilted her small head to one side. "How about it, Mike?"

"I'm covered with soft spots," Carmody said. "Sit down and be comfortable. This won't take long."

She moved to a chair and sat down slowly. The limp wasn't obvious; it was only suggested by the careful way she held her body—as if she were crossing a floor on which she had once taken a bad fall.

"What do you want?" she asked him.

Carmody sat down on a footstool in front of her, his big hands only a few inches from the folds of her robe. "Don't you want to guess?" he said.

"I expected you to be subtle about it," she said evenly, but a touch of color had come into her cheeks. "Flowers maybe, and a few kind words. But you've made this pretty cheap. Was that what you wanted?" Then she shook her head quickly and tried to soften his eyes with a smile. "You're wrong about me, Mike. What do I have to do to prove it?"

"Relax," Carmody said. "I'm here about Eddie. Listen now: he had the bad luck to identify a murderer last month, and the guy is important. Has he told you anything about this?"

"No."

"Well, Eddie stumbled on a shooting. The murderer got away, but was picked up on his description. At the trial next month Eddie can send him to the chair. But that can't happen. Eddie's got to refuse to make the identification. Unless he agrees to that he's in bad trouble. Do you understand this?"

"Yes, I think so," she said slowly. The color had receded from her cheeks. "It's always the same, isn't it? Important people can't be bothered going to jail." She studied him with a fresh awareness. "And you're a friend of the important people?"

"One of their best friends," Carmody said. "But Eddie's my brother and I don't want him hurt. That's why I need your help."

"What can I do?"

"To start with, answer my questions. I know he's crazy about you. But how do you feel about him?"

"I like him a lot. He's good-natured, gentle, he's straight and dependable, and—"

"Okay, okay," Carmody said, cutting across her words impatiently. "I don't want a litany. Do you love the guy?"

"Not yet."

Carmody looked at her in silence, trying to keep a check on his temper. Who in hell was she to dilly-dally with his brother? To play the shy maiden with an honest guy like Eddie?

"What're you waiting for?" he asked her coldly. "Butterflies in your stomach and stars in your eyes?"

"What right have you got to be sarcastic about it?" she said, leaning forward tensely. "It's none of your business. You don't have any authority to barge in here and grill me about Eddie. I'm not a suspect in one of your cases."

"Now listen to me, bright eyes," Carmody said, standing suddenly, and forcing her back into the chair with the threat of his size and power. "I know who you are and what league you played in. As Eddie's brother that gives me plenty of rights." Staring down at her he saw the fear in her eyes, the guilt that lay beneath her crust of angry innocence.

"You were Danny Nimo's girl, right?" he said coldly.

"That's right."

"That's right. Is that all you've got to say?"

"What else is there to say?"

"Where's the rest of it? Didn't he hold the mortgage on the family estate? Wasn't he trying to lure your sister into the white slave racket? Where's the cute story of how you got mixed up with him?"

"There's no cute story," she said in a low voice. "No estate, no lily-pure sister. I liked him, that's all."

"That's all?" Carmody felt a thrust of anger snap his control. He caught her thin arms and jerked her to a standing position. "You had to have a reason," he said, his voice rising dangerously. "What was it?"

"Let me go. Take your hands off me," she cried, struggling impotently against the iron strength in his hands.

"Did you tell that to Danny Nimo? Did you tell him to take his hands off you?"

She was beginning to cry, her breath coming in rapid gasps. "Damn you, damn you," she sobbed. "Why are you doing this to me?"

Carmody shifted his grip and held her effortlessly against him with one arm. "Cut it out, bright eyes," he said. "There's no need for a big act. I know you, baby, we're the same kind of people, the same kind of dirt." With his free hand he forced her head back until their eyes met and held in a straining silence. "Now look," he said softly, "I'm going to use you to save Eddie. You'll do what I say, understand?"

"Let me go," she whispered.

"When you understand me, bright eyes." He studied her pale, frightened face, hating her pretence of maidenly fear and virtue. She acted as if his touch would contaminate her innocence. What gave her the right to that pose? He kissed her then deliberately and cruelly, forcing his mouth over hers and pulling her slim struggling body against his chest. For a moment he held her that way, locked tight against his big hard frame, knowing nothing but violence and anger and bitterness. And then, slowly, reluctantly, there was something else; her lips parted under his and the anger in him was replaced by a wild urgency. Carmody fought against its overwhelming demand and pushed her roughly away from him. They stared at each other, their breathing loud and rapid in the silence. "Does that prove it, bright eyes?" he said thickly. "Does that prove we're the same kind of people?"

She twisted her arms free and began to pound her small fists against his chest. "You can't say that, you can't say that," she cried at him.

Carmody took her arms and put her down in the chair. "Take it easy," he said, still breathing hard. "It's a little late to start fighting for your honor."

She turned away, avoiding his eyes, and struck the arm of the chair with the flat of her hand. "You pig, you animal," she said in a trembling voice. Tears started in her eyes and ran down her pale cheeks. "Why did you do this? Have I ever hurt you? Am I so dirty you think you can wipe your feet on me?"

"Take it easy," he said again, running both hands through his hair.

Her tears made him angry and uncomfortable. He hadn't meant to hurt her; in spite of his deep cynicism about people, he had held on to an old-fashioned idea that women should be treated gently. He waited until she got herself under control. Then he said, "You think I'm a heel. Well, okay. But if I'm rough it's because this is no Maypole dance we're in." He realized that he was apologizing obliquely to her and this puzzled him. "Look, I don't care if you and Eddie get married," he said. "That's none of my business. Maybe it will work out great. But you can't marry a body in a morgue."

"Will they kill him? Are they that important?"

"Yes, they're that important," he said. "So let's get serious. Supposing you told Eddie you needed money, a lot of it. Would he try to get it for you?"

"I don't know," she said, shaking her head slowly.

"We may have to find out," he said. Glancing down at her slim legs, Carmody lit a cigarette and frowned thoughtfully. Then he said, "Supposing you told him you needed eight or ten thousand dollars for an operation? A spinal operation, or a series of them, to keep you out of a wheel chair. It ties in with your accident logically enough. How about it? Would he try to raise the dough for you?"

"I don't know. I don't know," she said. "But I couldn't tell him that. I couldn't ask him to turn himself into a liar and a thief."

Carmody took a long drag on his cigarette, and watched her with narrowed eyes. "We can all do things we think we can't," he said quietly. "Does he know about Nimo?" When she refused to meet his eyes, he said, "I didn't think so. Would you like him to find out about that? And what happened here tonight?"

She shook her head wearily. "Don't tell him about that. He thinks everything of you. And of me. No, don't tell him, Mike."

"We've made a deal then," Carmody said. "I'll see him tomorrow and make one more pitch at him. If I can't wake him up, then it's your turn. You'll have to put the pressure on him for money. And the only way he can get it is by co-operating with me."

"He won't do it," she said. "He's too straight to do it."

Carmody looked at her appraisingly. "Don't worry about that. He can bend a little to keep you out of a wheel chair. Will you be here tomorrow afternoon?"

"I can be."

"I'll call you." Carmody paused to light a cigarette. "You've got everything straight now?"

"Yes. Won't you go?" she said in a low voice. "Won't you please leave me alone?"

"Okay, okay, I'm going," Carmody said. He pulled the door shut behind him and strode along the corridor to the elevator. A noise stopped him; he turned, listening again for the sound. It had been a small helpless cry, distinct and lonely, like that of someone in pain. But the silence of the building settled around him and he heard nothing but his own even breathing and the beat of his heart.

# 4

THE PHONE WOKE CARMODY THE NEXT MORNING AT NINE-THIRTY. IT was Lieutenant Wilson. "What happened to you last night?" he demanded.

Carmody raised himself on one elbow, completely alert; Wilson's tone warned him of trouble. "I told you, I was working on that Fairmount Park murder."

"Did you make any progress?"

"I've got a lead." Carmody frowned slightly; he didn't like lying to Wilson. They had gone through the police academy together and had been good friends for several years. Wilson was a straight, efficient cop, a family man with kids in school and a home in the new development at Spring Hill. He was everything that citizens expected their police officers to be, intelligent, fair and honest. Carmody wondered occasionally why Wilson still liked him; they were on opposite sides of the fence, and Wilson normally had no use for cops who drifted toward the easy buck.

"You got a lead, eh?" Wilson said. "Well, supposing you get in here and tell me about it. I'll give it to someone to run down."

"What's the big hurry?"

"Damn it, Mike, do I have to send you an engraved invitation when I want to talk to you? Get in here."

"Okay," Carmody said, glancing at the alarm clock. He intended to see Eddie as soon as possible, and then, if necessary, Karen. "I'll be in at four o'clock," he said. "That's when my shift goes on."

"I want to see you now, right away," Wilson said.

"Okay, okay," Carmody said. He wasn't going in so there was no point in arguing about it. "How did that Wagner Hotel job turn out?"

"You struck gold, you lucky ape," Wilson said in an easier voice. "It was the bellhop, Ernie. Seems he brought a bottle up and found both Degget and the girl out cold. He was going through Degget's wallet when the girl woke and began to yell copper. He tried to talk her into a split, but she was too drunk to be sensible. Anyway, he got scared and shot her. He's put it all down on paper, so that winds that one up."

"The poor damn fool," Carmody said. "Why did he shoot her? You'd think a bellhop, of all people, would be smart enough to keep away from the big rap."

"He's not smart," Wilson said. "He's been in and out of trouble since he was a kid."

"This will be his last then," Carmody said. "How about the girl?"

"We got in touch with her mother. She's flying in to claim the body."

"It's a senseless mess all around," Carmody said. He glanced at his watch. "Well, get my name right for the papers."

"You're all right when you work at it," Wilson said. "I'll see you pretty soon, eh?"

"Sure." Carmody ordered his breakfast sent up, then showered, shaved and dressed. Eddie had worked twelve to eight and would still be asleep. Carmody decided to give him a few hours; he might be in a better mood if he had some rest. After coffee and orange juice he left his suite and drove across the city to the Midtown Club where he played three furious games of handball with a trainer. It was a punishing workout; the trainer had once been a semifinalist in the Nationals and he gave nothing away. Carmody was satisfied to win one of the three games and make a close fight of the other two. He baked out in the steam room afterwards and took an alcohol rub. Sitting in the dressing room later, a towel across his wide shoulders, he looked critically at himself in the mirror, noting the flat tight muscles of his stomach and the deep powerful arch of his chest. In good shape, he thought. The handball hadn't even winded him. Carmody's own strength and stamina had always surprised him slightly; his body simply ran on and on, meeting any demand he put on it, always more than equal to the occasion.

That's one thing I owe the old man, he thought; the indestructible constitution.

It was twelve-thirty when he left the club. He stopped at the Bervoort for cold roast beef with salad, then drank a bottle of cold beer and lit his first cigarette of the day. Relaxed and at ease, he sat for a few minutes at the table, savoring the fragrant smoke and the clean, toned-up feeling of his body.

Now he was ready for Eddie. This time he was sure of himself, charged with hard confidence.

The day was superb, clear and bright with sun. Carmody put the top of the convertible down before starting for the Northeast. He took the Parkway Drive, following the shining bend of the river, and enjoying the clean feel of the wind and sun against his face. Turning off at Summit Road, he wound into the Northeast, driving through quiet residential streets where children played on the lawns, with their mothers coming to the porches occasionally to see that they weren't in trouble. This was Carmody's background; he had lived in this neighborhood until he was twenty-seven, increasingly bored by the middle-class monotony of the people, increasingly annoyed by the sharp but worried eye the old man kept on him. Our break was inevitable, he thought, turning into Eddie's block. We just split on the big things. But why couldn't people be reasonable about these disagreements? The old man was a fool, not because of what he believed but because he was so blindly insistent that he was right. You could argue with him up to a point; but beyond that there was no sympathy or compromise. Well, it's all over and done with now, Carmody thought, as he went up the wooden stairs of the old frame house and banged the old-fashioned brass knocker.

He waited, rapped again, then tried the door. It was open as usual. Carmody walked into the hallway, hung his hat automatically on the halltree and turned into the familiar shabby living room. Nothing much had changed in the seven years that he had been gone; the old man's outsized leather chair stood with its back to the windows, his piano was still stacked with Irish songs and church music and the dark, shadowy copy of Rafael's *Madonna* hung over the mantel, slightly crooked as always. The room was clean and he wondered if Eddie did the work himself. Very probably, he thought.

"Eddie?" he called. "You up yet?"

Eddie's voice sounded from the basement. "Hey, who's that?"

"Mike. Come on up."

"I've got to wash my hands. Sit down and make yourself at home."

Make yourself at home! Carmody glanced around with a wry little smile. There was no place in the world where that would be less possible. He couldn't be comfortable here; he felt smaller and less certain of himself in the old man's home. The memories of his father crowded around him, evoking all the past pain and friction. That was why he hadn't come back even after the old man died; he hated the uncertainty and guilt this shabby, middle-class room could produce in him. But it wasn't just the room, it was his father, Carmody knew. His feeling about the old man had started long before he had gone to work for Beaumonte, before he had learned that his job could be made to pay off like a rigged slot machine. It had begun with those arguments about right and wrong. To his father those words defined immutable categories of conduct, but to Carmody they were just words applied by men to suit their convenience. It was an emotional clash between a man of faith and a man of reason, in Carmody's mind. His father was a big, gentle, good-natured person, who believed like a trusting baby in the fables of his childhood. Like Eddie, for that matter. But you couldn't tell them different. It only hurt and angered them. Maybe that's why I feel guilty, he thought. It's the reaction to destroying anyone's dream, even if you're only showing up Santa Claus as the neighbor across the street with a pillow under his shirt and a dime-store beard on his chin.

Turning to the mantel, he picked up a dried-out baseball from a wooden saucer. He was remembering the game in which it had been used, as he tossed it up and down in his hand. The police department against the Phillies' bench. A big charity blowout. Carmody had tripled home the winning run in the bottom of the tenth inning. This was the ball he hit off a pitcher who was good enough to win thirteen games in the majors that season. Eight years ago! He was working for Beaumonte then, taking the easy money casually and without much reflection; it seemed like just another tribute to his superior brains and strength. But he couldn't fool his father about the source of the money. The old man saw the new convertible, the good clothes, the expensive vacations, and that was when the sharp, worried look had come into his eyes. The blowup came the night after the game in which Carmody had tripled home the winning run.

He had picked up a set of silverware by way of celebration, the kind they'd never been able to own, and when he walked in with it trouble had started. Carmody tossed the baseball up and down in his hand, frowning at his father's piano. The old man had been singing something from the Mass the choir was doing the coming Sunday. It had got on Carmody's nerves. He had said something about it as he unwrapped the silver, and that touched off their last row.

Somewhere in the middle of the argument the old man had picked up the crate of silverware, walked to the door and had thrown it out into the street.

"And you can follow it, laddy me boy," he'd yelled in his big formidable voice. "No thief is going to sleep in my house."

That had done it. Carmody walked out and didn't see the old man until his funeral, a year later.

He heard Eddie on the basement stairs and quickly put the baseball back in the little wooden saucer. Eddie came in wearing a white T shirt and faded army suntan slacks. A lock of his hair was plastered damply against his forehead and his big forearms were streaked with sweat and dust. "Well, this is a surprise," he said, smiling slowly.

"You're up early."

"I had some work to do in the basement. How about a beer or something?"

"Sounds good."

"Sure, one won't hurt us," Eddie said. He went to the kitchen and returned in a few moments with two uncapped, frosted bottles of beer. Handing one to Carmody he tilted the other to his mouth and took a long swallow.

"That hits the spot," he said, shaking his head. "You working out this way today?"

"No, I'm here to see you," Carmody said, and watched the little frown that came on Eddie's face. "I told Ackerman and Beaumonte that you'd be sensible. They want to see you tonight at ten o'clock."

"You had no right to do that," Eddie said.

"Would you rather I sat back and let them blow your brains out?"

"Let me worry about that." Eddie looked badgered and harassed; a mixture of sadness and anger was nakedly apparent in his eyes. "I hate having you mixed up with those creeps," he said, almost shouting at Carmody. "I always have. You know that. But I don't want any part of them. Can you get that?"

"You should be grateful I work for them," Carmody said, holding onto his temper. "Do you think you'd get this break if you were some ordinary beat-tramping clown?"

"Grateful you work for them?" Eddie said slowly. "That's almost funny, Mike. Listen to me now. I always thought you were a great guy. Next to the old man, I suppose, you were the biggest thing in my life. I carried your bat home from games, I hung around Fourteenth Street when you were on traffic, watching you blow the whistle and wave your arms as if it was the most important thing anyone in the world could do."

"All kid brothers are that way," Carmody said.

"Then you had the blowup with the old man," Eddie went on, ignoring him. "I didn't understand it, he never talked about it, but it damn near tore me in two. Then I found out about it a little later when I was a rookie in the old Twenty-seventh. The cop whose locker was next to mine was talking about a guy who'd got into trouble for clipping a drunken driver for ten bucks. And he wound up by saying, 'Your brother's got the right idea, kid. Take it big, or don't take it at all.' " Eddie turned away and pounded a fist into his palm. "They had to pull me off him. I damn near killed him. Then I did some checking and you know where that led. I had to apologize to that cop, I had to say, 'You were dead right, my brother's a thief.' "

"You take things too seriously," Carmody said. "You sound like a recording of the old man."

"Is that bad?"

"No, hell no," Carmody said angrily. "It's great if you want to live in a dump like this and go through life being grateful to the gas company for a fifty-dollar-a-week job."

"That's all you saw, eh?" Eddie said in a soft, puzzled voice. "And you're supposed to be smart. The old man enjoyed his food, he slept a solid eight hours every night and when he died grown men and women cried for him. None of them had memories of him that weren't pretty good, one way or the other. They still miss him in the neighborhood. Those things are part of the picture, too, Mike, along with this dump as you call it, and the fifty-dollar-a-week job. But you never saw any of that, I suppose."

"Let's get off the old man," Carmody said shortly.

"You brought him up. You always do. You're still fighting him, if you want my guess."

"Well, I don't want your guesses," Carmody said. He knew he was making no progress, and this baffled and angered him. Why couldn't he sell this deal? Eddie stood up to facts as if they were knives Carmody was throwing at his father. That was why they came to the boiling point so quickly in any argument; in anything important the old man came between them. He was the symbol of their opposed values and Eddie was always fighting to defend him, fighting to prove the worth of what his brother had rejected. Carmody understood that now and he wondered bitterly how he could save him against those odds.

"Just listen to me calmly for a second," he said, drawing a deep breath. "Go along with Ackerman and Beaumonte. Tell them you won't identify Delaney. At the trial you can cross them and put the finger on him. They won't dare touch you then, the heat will be too big. Is there anything wrong with that?"

"You don't think so, obviously," Eddie said. He looked mad and disgusted. "You don't care about double-crossing them, eh?"

"I'm thinking about you," Carmody said, angered by Eddie's contempt. "Maybe I don't look very noble, but that's how the world is run." He had the disturbing thought that their roles had somehow become reversed; Eddie was calm and sure of himself, while he was getting more worried by the minute.

"Let's drop it," Eddie said flatly. "You couldn't change my mind in a million years. Now I've got to wash up. I'm meeting Father Ahearn at St. Pat's in fifteen minutes."

"More vespers?" Carmody asked sarcastically. He couldn't quite believe he had failed.

"No, it's a personal matter," Eddie said. He hesitated, then said in an even, impersonal voice: "I want to talk to him about Karen. She's not a Catholic and I'm going to find out where I stand."

"You'll marry her?"

"If she says the word."

"You're dumber than I thought," Carmody said, in a hard, clipped voice. He knew he had taken a step that could never be retraced but he was too angry to care. "Look that merchandise over carefully before you buy it, kid."

Eddie stared at him, swallowing hard. Then he said, "Get out, Mike. While you're in one piece."

"Ask her about Danny Nimo," Carmody said coldly. "See what happens when you do, kid."

"She told me about Nimo," Eddie said quietly.

"I'll bet she made a sweet bedtime story out of it," Carmody said.

But he was jarred; he'd been certain she wouldn't tell him about Nimo.

"She simply told me about it," Eddie said. "That's all. What you make of it depends on how you look at things. Everything in the world is twisted and dirty to you because you're always looking in a mirror."

"She's playing you for a fool," Carmody snapped. His anger had stripped away all his judgment; nothing mattered to him but blasting Eddie's ignorant trusting dream. "Ask her about me, about the scene we played last night. Maybe that will wake you up."

Eddie walked toward him slowly, his big fists swinging at his sides. There were tears in his eyes and his square face had twisted with anguish. "Get out, get out of here!" he cried in a trembling voice. He stopped two feet from Carmody and threw a sweeping roundhouse blow at his head.

He can't even fight, Carmody thought despairingly, as he stepped back and let the punch sail past him. Pushing Eddie away from him, he saw that he was crying, terribly and silently. Goddamn, he thought, as a savage anger ran through him, why doesn't he pick up a chair and bust me wide open? Doesn't he even know that much?

Stepping in quickly, he snapped a right into his brother's stomach, knowing he had to end this fast. Eddie went down, doubling up with pain and working hard for each mouthful of air. He stared up at Carmody in helpless agony. "Don't go, let me fight you," he whispered.

Carmody looked away from him and wet his lips. "I didn't mean to hit you, kid," he said. "I was lying about Karen. Remember that."

"Don't leave, let me get up," Eddie said, working himself painfully to his knees.

Carmody couldn't look at him; but he couldn't look at anything else in the room either. The piano, the *Madonna,* his father's chair, they were all as mercilessly accusing as his brother's eyes. He strode out the front door and went quickly down the steps to his car. It was torn open now, he thought bitterly. Karen was his last chance. Eddie's last chance. He pulled up at the first drug store he came to, went in and rang her apartment. When she answered he said, "This is Mike Carmody. I've got to see you. Can I come up?"

"I'll meet you downstairs," she said after a short pause.

"Okay, ten minutes," he said. She didn't want him in her apartment again; he knew that from the tone of her voice. "Don't keep me waiting," he said, and hung up.

She was standing at the curb when he got to her hotel, looking slim and cool in a chocolate-colored dress and brown-and-white spectator pumps. Her hair was brushed back cleanly and the sun touched it here and there with tiny lights. She had style, he thought irrelevantly, as she crossed in front of the car. It showed in her well-cared-for shoes and immaculate white gloves, in the way she held her head and shoulders. Phony or not, she looked like good people.

She slid in beside him, moving with the suggestion of tentativeness that was peculiar to her; that was the accident, he thought, glancing instinctively at her legs. What had Anelli said? A dozen breaks?

"We'll drive around," he said. "I just talked to Eddie and we wound up in a brawl."

"How did that happen?"

"It was about you." He headed for the river, frowning as he hunted for words. "You told him about Nimo, didn't you?"

"Yes, I told him," she said.

Carmody glanced angrily at her, then back to the road. "Why didn't you tell me that last night?"

"Would you have believed me?"

"I guess not," he said. What was he supposed to conclude from this? That she was playing it straight with Eddie? Or was she shrewd enough to know that he would be disarmed by a clean-breast approach?

When they reached the river he parked in a grassy, picnicking area. The water sparkled with sunlight and in the distance he could see the tall buildings of center-city, shrouded with mists of fog and smoke. It was a pleasant summer scene; a few boys were playing at the river bank and sparrows hopped along through the thick fragrant grass. Carmody twisted around in the seat and got out his cigarettes. "I made no impression on Eddie," he said. "So now it's your turn. But first I've got to tell you something. I told him about us." He went on hurriedly as she turned sharply on him, a touch of angry color appearing in her pale face. "Now listen to me; I told him to ask you about the scene we played last night. He took a swing at me and I had to hit him. Then I told him I'd been lying about you and me. Whether he believed me or not I don't know."

"You told him about us, and then you hit him?" She shook her head incredulously. "In God's name, why?"

"I had to," he said stubbornly.

"You had to! Who made you? Who forced you to?" She stared at him, her eyes blazing.

Carmody looked through the windshield at the city in the distance. Then he sighed heavily. "I don't know, it just happened," he said. "But I'm trying to save his life. I struck out, so it's up to you."

"What kind of threats will you use now?" she asked him bitterly. "He knows about Danny Nimo, and you told him about us. You don't have anything on me now. So what comes next? A session of arm-twisting? A gentle slapping around?"

"Unless you want him killed, you've got to help," Carmody said. Her words had stung him but he felt no anger at her, only a heavy dissatisfaction with himself. "Tell him you need ten thousand for an operation and you may save his life."

"Supposing it doesn't work," she said, watching him. "Then what will you do?"

"What can I do?"

"You're a detective, aren't you? Why don't you arrest them?"

"That's a pretty picture," he said, smiling ironically. "A pretty picture right out of a fairy tale. Will you see Eddie tonight?"

"Yes, at eight."

"Okay," Carmody said, switching on the ignition. "He leaves for the station around eleven-thirty, I guess. So I'll call you at twelve."

"All right," she said quietly.

"I'll drop you home. I've got to get to work."

"The nearest cab stand will do," she said. "Thanks, anyway."

"Okay," Carmody said, and rubbed his forehead tiredly. He wished this were over, with Eddie alive and Ackerman and Beaumonte satisfied with the way he'd handled it. He'd had no idea it would be so tough.

It was three o'clock when Carmody checked into Headquarters. He nodded to Dirksen and Abrams, who had come in early, and walked into Lieutenant Wilson's office.

Wilson glanced at him briefly. "Sit down, Mike," he said.

"Sorry I'm late," Carmody said, taking a chair and loosening his tie.

"What kept you? The Fairmount Park murder?"

"No, a personal matter." Carmody was becoming annoyed. Wilson was a short, powerfully built man with curly black hair and a set of belligerent, no-nonsense features. He seldom hounded Carmody because he knew there was no point in it. But now he was acting like a truant officer with a boy who'd been playing hooky.

"I said I wanted to see you this morning," he said, pushing aside a report. "Didn't that mean anything to you?"

"Frankly, not a hell of a lot," Carmody said. "I was off duty and I had some personal matters to take care of."

Wilson's face hardened as he left his desk and closed the door of his office. "You didn't see a paper this morning, I guess," he said looking down at Carmody.

"No. What's up?"

"Superintendent Shortall resigned. Because of his health."

Carmody started to smile and then he saw that Wilson was serious. He whistled softly. "Well, well," he said. There was nothing wrong with Shortall's health; he was sound as a hickory nut. The significant thing was that Shortall had been Ackerman's man. "Who'll get his job?" he asked Wilson.

"Somebody honest, I hope."

"You think that's likely?"

"Listen to me, Mike," Wilson said, sitting on the edge of his desk and studying Carmody with serious eyes. "I've known and liked you a long

time. I don't understand why. Maybe it's because you were the best cop
in the city for a half-a-dozen years. But, anyway, I'm giving you a tip;
don't be a smart guy too long. There comes a time when a city values a
bit of dumb, old-fashioned honesty."

Carmody lit a cigarette and flipped the match at the ashtray on Wilson's
desk. "What's on your mind, Jim?"

"Just this; I'm tired of the fix, I'm tired of guys like you and Shortall.
And if they put an honest man on top of this department I'm going to turn
in an unfitness report on you."

"Why the advance warning?" Carmody said, smiling slightly.

Wilson's face was troubled. "I told you, damn it. I like you, Mike.
And here's the rest of my deal. If you start right now being a full-time
cop again, I'll forget that report."

Carmody was silent a moment, staring at the curl of smoke from his
cigarette. It would be a relief, he thought, to have nothing on his mind
but being a full-time cop. He knew that this edgy feeling had grown from
his concern over Eddie, but that didn't help him to shake it; how could
he relax while his brother was stubbornly asking for a ticket to the
morgue?

"Think it over," Wilson said, watching Carmody's troubled face closely.
"And remember this; the city's changing. Big defense plants have come
into this town in the last few years, and the men running them pay a
houseful of taxes. And they want value from them. Parks, schools, things
like that. They don't want bookies and brothels and bars clipping their
workers every week. Neither do the unions. And when you get the unions
working with the men who run the companies you got a clout that can
stand right up to Ackerman and Beaumonte. Look at Shortall. They
made the Mayor can him. And they've got others on their list. You're a
tough guy, but don't get in their way, Mike."

Carmody had heard rumors of this before, but he hadn't been too
concerned. He still wasn't, as a matter of fact. He had too abiding a faith
in man's lack of goodness to believe in reform and regeneration. These
things were cynical, expedient measures that people forgot all about when
the baseball race got tight or the job of being good citizens became a
bore.

"Just think it over," Wilson said. "But don't take too long about it."

"Okay, Jim, thanks."

Carmody went out to his desk and checked the day's work with Sergeant
Klipperman who was going off duty. Everything was quiet; two man-
slaughters were pending and he sent Abrams and Dirksen out to wrap
them up. Myers came in fifteen minutes late, walking fast and trying to
look as if he'd been delayed by something important. Carmody glanced at
the big clock beside the police speaker but said nothing. He settled in his
chair and studied the reports on cases being handled by his shift.

Myers drifted over in his shirt sleeves and made some comment on the weather. Then he said, "That was pretty sharp guesswork on those whiskey bottles last night." He smiled cautiously, trying to analyze the brooding expression on Carmody's hard handsome face. "Dirk and I would have caught it, but you beat us to it, I got to admit that."

Yes, you've got to admit it, Carmody thought wearily. A frank generous admission that you're a dope makes everything just dandy. He started to say something sarcastic but changed his mind. Why jump on Myers? Why jump on anybody? "I came after you'd handled the routine," he said. "I had a better chance to look around."

"That's right, with the routine out of the way you can look around," Myers said, nodding. He sauntered away, looking relieved.

Carmody worked listlessly, almost hoping for a flurry of something to take his mind off Eddie. Finally, he left his desk and walked across the street to the drug store. He had to call Beaumonte and tell him Eddie couldn't keep the appointment with Ackerman. Putting it off any longer would only make matters worse.

Nancy Drake answered the phone and it took him a moment to get through her to Beaumonte. She was in a giggling, half-tight mood and insisted on telling him of some hilarious impropriety her dog had committed. Carmody listened impatiently, feeling the heat of the booth settling around him and aware that his temper was dangerously short.

"Great, hilarious," he said. "Funniest thing I've heard in the last two minutes. Now put Beaumonte on."

"We are in a most pleasant mood, I must say," she said with drunken dignity. Then she let out a little scream and giggled again. "Dan just whacked me on the tail. Would you do that to a girl, Mike? Come on, tell me."

Carmody swore softly and rubbed the back of his hand over his damp forehead. Then Beaumonte's soft rich voice was in his ear. "Mike, she had six brandy punches before breakfast, if you can believe it." He didn't sound angry, just tolerantly amused. "When she pickles herself for good I think I'll put her in a bottle over the mantel. Like a four-masted schooner, only she's missing a couple of masts."

Beaumonte had been drinking, too, Carmody guessed. "What's the deal on Shortall's resignation?"

"Where you phoning from?" Beaumonte said, after a short pause.

"A drug store."

"Oh. There's nothing to worry about, Mike. Ackerman will put a man in tomorrow probably. Is everything set for tonight, by the way? With your brother, I mean?"

"That's why I called," Carmody said. "He can't make it."

Beaumonte paused, and Carmody heard his long intake of breath. "This isn't good," Beaumonte said quietly.

"The kid had a date and wouldn't break it," Carmody said. "Should I put a gun in his back and march him up to your place?"

"Maybe that wouldn't have been a bad idea," Beaumonte said. "When can he make it?"

"Tomorrow night."

"Okay, I'll tell Ackerman. But he don't like being stood up."

"Don't worry, he'll be there tomorrow."

"I'm not worrying," Beaumonte said. "That's your job. Remember that, Mike."

When Carmody returned to the City Hall he saw Degget, the little man who'd been mixed up in the Wagner Hotel homicide, standing at the house sergeant's window, collecting his personal effects. Degget recognized him and smiled awkwardly. "Sarge, I know what you did for me," he said. "They had me down as a murderer until you came in."

"Well, it's all over now," Carmody said.

"No, it won't ever be over for me," Degget said, his small mouth twisting with embarrassment and pain. "You know how a small town is. They'll hold this over me and my family till we're in our graves. And I don't even know if my family will want me around any more. It was in the papers, you see. I wired my wife but she hasn't answered yet."

"These things blow over," Carmody said. He squeezed Degget's thin shoulder with his hand. "It won't last." Why should I give a good damn, he thought, watching Degget's worried hopeless eyes.

"Well, it's my goose that got cooked," Degget said. "And I asked for it." Then he said quickly, "Look, I want to show my appreciation for what you've done." He reached for his wallet but Carmody caught his arm. "Never mind," he said. "I don't want—" He paused, remembering Myers' invalid wife and young daughters. "I'll tell you what," he said. "If you want to buy someone a drink, buy one for Detective Myers. Leave something in an envelope with the house sergeant. He'll see that he gets it. And Myers can use it."

"I'll do that, I sure will," Degget said.

Carmody started for the stairs but stopped and looked back at Degget's doleful little figure. He winked at him and said, "Cheer up. The boys at home will think you're a hero."

"Well, they'll want all the details anyway," Degget said, smiling sheepishly.

The afternoon and evening wore on slowly. It was one of those nights when the city seemed to be inhabited by saints. But the inactivity irritated him because it gave him too much time to think. When his shift was finally over he was in a touchy, explosive mood. At his hotel he called the Fanfair and asked for Karen.

When she answered he said, "This is Mike. Did you talk to Eddie?"

"Yes—he's just gone." Against the background noise of the bar her voice was high and light.

"What happened?"

"I couldn't do it," she said. "I couldn't tell him I needed ten thousand dollars for an operation."

Carmody stared at the phone in his hand, his face hardening into cold bitter lines. "This is pretty," he said. "Did lying to him go against your principles?"

"No one has the right to put that kind of pressure on him. To force him to make that kind of decision."

"You sweet little fake," he said savagely. "You didn't have the right, eh? Well, do you have the right to let him get killed?"

"I begged him to take care of himself," she said, and he heard her voice break suddenly. "He said there was nothing to worry about. He said—"

"You missed your chance, baby."

"Then don't miss yours," she cried at him.

"What do you mean? Listen—"

The phone clicked in his ear. Carmody stared at the receiver a moment, then slammed it down in the cradle. She was checking out. The act was over; Danny Nimo's girl knew when it was time to switch roles. But with his anger there was a cynical respect for her; she was looking after Number One, and that was playing it smart.

Carmody crossed the room to the windows and stared out at the scene spreading below him; the river was shining palely and the high buildings loomed massively against the sky, their lighted windows forming irregular designs in the darkness. Eddie is my job, he thought, I was a fool to think anyone else cared a damn whether he lived or died.

# 5

CARMODY SLEPT UNEASILY THAT NIGHT AND WAS UP EARLY IN THE MORNing. One thing had occurred to him by then: Why were Ackerman and Beaumonte worried about Delaney? This was something he should have checked immediately, and he realized that his emotional concern over Eddie was ruining his cop-wise judgment. What had Beaumonte said? That if Delaney talked it would cause trouble. But for whom? Ackerman or Beaumonte?

Carmody sat down at the phone, a cigarette between his lips, and began a cautious check on Delaney. He talked with two Magistrates, a Judge and half-a-dozen bookies, trying to learn something from casual gossip. The word was around, he soon realized; they knew Delaney was threatening to sing and that the big boys were worried. But no one cared to speculate on the nature of Delaney's information. Carmody gave it up after a while, but he wasn't discouraged. The clue might be in Delaney's past; Delaney had been a muscle boy in the organization when Ackerman and Beaumonte were on-the-make hoodlums instead of semirespectable public figures. That would be the angle to check.

Delaney's evidence must be something tangible and conclusive; otherwise, his threats to sing wouldn't bother Beaumonte and Ackerman. The job was to find that evidence and destroy it; that would pull Delaney's stinger, take the pressure off the big boys and leave Eddie in the clear. It wasn't a simple job and it had to be done quickly, but Carmody wasn't worried; he knew how to handle this kind of work. The city couldn't keep any secrets from him; he had studied it too long for that. A map of the city blazed in his mind; he knew the look of a thousand intersections and could reel off the houses and shops on each corner as easily as he could the alphabet. He knew politicians from the Mayor down to precinct drifters, and he understood the intricate balancings and give-and-take of the city's administration. The brothels and bars, the clubs and cliques, the little blondes and brunettes tucked away in handsome apartments in center-city, guys on the make, on the skids, on the way up—Carmody had them all indexed and cross-indexed in his formidable memory.

No, finding Delaney's source of pressure wouldn't be impossible, he thought.

Carmody went into the bathroom to shower and when he came out the phone was ringing. He picked it up and said, "Yes?"

"This is Beaumonte, Mike. Can you get over here around four? Ackerman wants to see you."

"Four? Sure, that's okay," Carmody said easily. He stood with his feet wide apart, a towel around his middle feeling the drops of water drying on his big hard shoulders. "What's on his mind?" he asked. "My brother?" It was a stupid, dangerous question, but he had to know.

"Some friend of his wants to open a handbook in West," Beaumonte said. "Ackerman wants you to take good care of him."

"Sure, sure," Carmody said, releasing his breath slowly. "Four o'clock then."

"Right, Mike."

Carmody went out to lunch and got back to his hotel at three o'clock. He washed his hands and face, changed into a dark-gray flannel suit and was on his way to the door when the phone stopped him. A high-pitched irritable voice blasted into his ear when he raised the receiver. "Mike Carmody? Is that you, boy?"

"That's right. Who's this?"

"Father Ahearn. I want to see you."

"I'm just on my way out, Father," he said.

"I'm down in the lobby. This won't take long."

Carmody checked his watch and frowned. "Okay, I'll be down. But I'm in a hurry."

"I'll be waiting at the elevator so don't try sneaking past me."

Carmody hung up, finding a grim humor in the situation. The old priest acted as if he were talking to one of his altar boys.

When the elevator doors opened Carmody saw that the last eight years had been hard on the old priest. At his father's funeral, which was the last time Carmody had seen him, Father Ahearn had been lively and vigorous, a tall man with gray hair and alert flashing eyes. But now he was slightly stooped and the tremors of age were noticeable in his heavily-knuckled hands. His hair had turned almost white but his eyes hadn't changed at all; they still flashed fiercely above the bold strong nose. He looked incongruous in the smart glitter of the lobby, a tired, bent old man in a black suit which had turned a grayish-green with age.

Carmody shook hands with him and suggested they take a seat at the side of the lobby.

"You want to go off and hide, eh?" Father Ahearn said.

You never manage him, Carmody remembered. "What's on your mind?" he said, edging him tactfully out of the traffic flowing toward the elevators.

"What's the trouble with you and Eddie?"

"That's a personal matter, Father."

"None of my business, eh? Well, when one brother strikes another in my parish I make it my business."

"Eddie told you I hit him?"

"Yes. I could see he'd been hurt. But that's all he would tell me." The old priest tilted his head and studied Carmody with his fierce eyes. "What was it? The girl?"

"I suppose you could say that."

"And what makes it any of your business?"

"I'm his brother."

"Ah," the old priest said softly. "His brother, is it? His keeper, you are. Isn't that a new role for you, Mike?"

Carmody felt embarrassed and irritated. "Look, there's no point talking about it," he said. "What's between me and Eddie doesn't concern you or the church."

"Now you listen to me, boy. I don't—"

But Carmody cut him off. "It's no use, I've got to be going, Father." He didn't like doing this to the old man and he hated the hurt look his words brought into his eyes; Father Ahearn had been a family friend for years, and had done them a thousand favors. He had got him summer jobs, had sent him to college on an athletic scholarship and had seen that Eddie stuck out his last year of school after the old man died. But that was long, long ago, in time and in values; it belonged to another world.

"All right, I'll not keep you," Father Ahearn said.

"I'll get you a cab."

"Never mind, you go on about your important affairs. But don't interfere with Eddie and his girl."

"You've met her, I guess?"

"What have you got against her?"

She's fooled him, Carmody thought. Probably had a cup of tea with him and smiled at his Irish stories. "There's no point going into it," he said.

"Very well. Good-by, Mike." The old man walked away, threading through the group of expensively dressed men and women. Carmody watched him until he disappeared, and there was a small, unhappy frown on his hard face . . .

He got to Beaumonte's at ten of four and found Nancy alone in the long elegant drawing-room. She wore a black dress with a full flaring skirt and junk bracelets on her wrists.

"Where's everybody?" Carmody asked her.

"Everybody? Don't I count?"

"I mean Ackerman and Beaumonte."

"Are they everybody?" she asked, smiling at him, her eyes wide and thoughtful.

"No, you count, too," he said.

"Sometimes it seems like they're everybody," she said, sighing sadly. There was a comic quality to her gravity; with her swept-up blonde hair, jingling bracelets, she was hard to take seriously.

"Don't get deep now," he said.

"You're like them, in a way."

"That's a compliment, I hope."

"You wouldn't care whether it was or not." A frown gathered on her smooth childishly round forehead. "That's what frightens me about all of you. You just don't care. Not like other people do. Everything in the world is just to use. A girl, a car, a drink, they're all the same."

"What got you into this mood?" he asked her.

"Too many drinks, I guess. That's Dan's analysis for all my problems." She put an expression of mock sternness on her face and pointed a finger accusingly at Carmody. " 'You're a lush, you lush.' " Relaxing and sighing, she said, "That's his daily sermon. It's supposed to fix everything up dandy."

Carmody was touched by the unhappiness in her face. "You shouldn't worry so much," he said. He wondered why she stuck with Beaumonte. The same reason I do, he thought. The money, the excitement of being on intimate terms with power and privilege. Weren't those good reasons?

"The trouble is I don't feel like a girl any more," she said, making a studied pirouette on one small foot.

"Well, what do you feel like?"

"Like a faucet," she said, making a faster turn on her other foot. Her skirt flared out from her beautifully shaped, silken legs. "Look, I can dance. I'm a faucet," she said again, continuing the pirouettes. "Something Dan turns on and off, on and off. Whenever he wants to. Don't I dance gorgeously?"

"Just great."

She stopped spinning and looked at him, her eyes bright and excited. "I love to dance. Even when it was my work I loved it. Mike, how about taking me on a picnic some day?"

Carmody laughed. "Sure. We could stage it on the roof and have it catered by the Park Club. What gave you that idea?"

"No, the Park Club won't do," she said, sighing. "They'd send over ants in little tiny cellophane packages to give it a realistic touch. Excuse me. We need ice. Then I'll make us a couple of unwise drinks."

"Never mind me."

She looked at him thoughtfully. "How come you don't drink. I mean, get blind and drunk like the rest of us."

"I guess I don't want to be anyone else," Carmody said. "That's why people get drunk, I imagine. To forget what they are."

"That's a gloomy idea," she said. "It kind of hurts, too. Well, to hell with it. I'll get the ice and be somebody else. Maybe an ant at a picnic, who knows?"

A moment after she'd gone a key sounded in the front door and Beaumonte walked in, followed by Bill Ackerman and his huge watchdog, Johnny Stark, the ex-heavyweight. Something in their manner warned Carmody; Beaumonte, massive and immaculate in a white silk suit, looked sullen, and even Ackerman, who normally gave nothing away, was frowning slightly. Johnny Stark walked past Carmody and sat down in a straight chair with his back to the terrace windows. He flicked his eyes around the room but kept his good ear cocked toward Ackerman like a wary dog.

"More bum tips?" Carmody asked Beaumonte.

"We weren't at the track." Beaumonte stared bluntly at him, his eyes narrowed and unfriendly. "I've got more to do than sit on my tail in the clubhouse."

"I know you've got it rough," Carmody grinned.

"Don't be a comic. I'm in no mood for jokes."

"I worry a lot about your moods," Carmody said easily. "Sometimes they keep me awake all of five or ten minutes."

The silence stretched out as Beaumonte walked to the coffee table, picked up a cigar and faced him from the fireplace. This put Carmody in the middle of a triangle, with Ackerman standing before him, Beaumonte at his side, and Johnny Stark at his back. A faint warning stirred in him. Trouble was coming; he could sense it in their deliberate manner and hard watchful eyes.

"I expected to see your brother last night," Ackerman said. He was in a businesslike mood, his eyes frowning and black, his even features set in a closed, unrevealing expression. "What happened?"

"I explained that to Beaumonte."

"Explain it to me," Ackerman said coldly.

"My brother had a date and wouldn't break it."

"You're sure he hasn't changed his mind?"

"Of course not," Carmody said.

Ackerman smiled faintly but it didn't relieve the expression about his eyes. "I wanted to hear you say that, Mike." He glanced at Beaumonte. "There it is," he said.

"Yeah, there it is," Beaumonte said.

Ackerman opened his mouth but before he could speak Nancy came bouncing into the room, carrying a drink in one hand and humming a song under her breath. "Hello, Danny boy," she said, and skipped toward him with a series of intricate little steps. "I was dancing for Mike. He thinks I've got talent. Don't you Mike?"

Beaumonte swore violently at her and pulled the glass from her hand. Liquor splashed on the front of her skirt and over the tips of her black velvet pumps. She backed away, staring at him guiltily. Her face was white and her hands came together nervously over her breasts. "Why did you do that, Dan?" she asked in a small voice.

"Dancing! You've also been swilling my liquor like a pig."

"You said it was all right today."

"And now I'm telling you different," Beaumonte said, and hurled the glass across the room. It struck the wall beside one of his oils and shattered noisily. "I'll kick you back to the gutter if you can't stop acting like a rumhead." He caught her arm and shoved her toward the wide doors of the dining room. "Get out of here and sleep it off, you hear?"

"Don't shout at me, please, Dan," she said, regaining her balance. "I'll go, please."

Carmody said softly, "Your manners stink, Beaumonte. Why don't you try to match them up with your paintings and imported wines?"

"Keep out of this, Mike," Beaumonte said, staring at him with hot furious eyes.

"Everybody relax," Ackerman said, and the words fell ominously across the silence. Johnny Stark came quickly to his feet and moved in on the group, responding like a dog to Ackerman's tone. Nancy backed slowly to the bar as Beaumonte mopped his red face with a handkerchief. "Okay, we're relaxed," he said, breathing deeply and staring at Ackerman. "Let's get this over with."

"Okay," Ackerman said, in the same dangerous voice. He swung around on Carmody. "You've lied to us. You made no deal with your brother. We talked to him this afternoon and he threatened to arrest us if we didn't clear out of his house. Got anything to say to this, you smart bastard?"

"I was working on him," Carmody said slowly. Talking would help nothing; they had him cold. But he went on, anyway, stalling for time. "He didn't like the idea, but I was softening him up. I could have brought him around."

"You lied to us," Ackerman said. "You were crossing me up, Mike. There's a lot at stake in this deal but you couldn't take orders. Well, I got no room around me for guys like you. You beat it now, and beat it fast."

"You aren't talking to a bellhop," Carmody said. He didn't know where this was heading and he didn't care. "I don't come and go when you press a button."

"You'd better listen when I press a button," Ackerman said. "We've got a file on you a foot high. When it goes to the Superintendent you go to jail. Keep that in mind, bellhop."

It's a bluff, Carmody thought, watching Ackerman. But he knew he was kidding himself. Ackerman never bluffed; he had a leash on every man who worked for him. It was the fundamental rule of his operations.

"I don't trust anybody," Ackerman said, as if reading his thoughts. "And least of all the cops who work for me. You've already sold yourself once when you start using your badges as collection plates. And you'll sell me out if I give you the chance."

"Let's go, Mike," Johnny Stark said, moving toward him with his slow, flat-footed walk. "You heard Mr. Ackerman."

"Okay," Carmody said, looking about the room, letting his eyes touch Ackerman and Beaumonte. "I'll run along." He picked up his hat from the chair and walked to the door, feeling the silence behind him and aware of their looks on his back. With his hand on the knob he paused a second. He was alone now, cut off from everyone. There would be no help from any quarter; Karen, Ackerman, Father Ahearn, even Eddie himself, they were all ranged against him, watching his futile efforts with contempt. But I've always been alone, he thought, as a gentle, pleasurable anger began to stir in him; he had thrown away the hollow props of faith and family because he had to stand alone. Turning his head slightly he caught Ackerman with his cold gray eyes. "What about my brother?" he said.

"We'll take care of that," Ackerman said.

Carmody let his hand fall from the knob. For an instant he stood perfectly still, his big body relaxed and at ease. Then he turned and walked slowly back into the room. "What does that mean, Ackerman?" he said quietly.

"Don't make a big mistake now," Ackerman said. "Just beat it. I'm tired of talk."

They can't push me this last step, Carmody thought. I'm a crooked cop with thieves' money in my pocket, but I won't look the other way while they murder Eddie. Drawing a deep breath, he felt nothing but relief at reaching a line he wouldn't cross.

"There'll be just a little more talk," he said coldly to Ackerman. "And you'd better listen good. Nothing happens to my brother. Get that straight."

Ackerman looked at Johnny Stark and said irritably, "Take him out of here."

"What?" Johnny asked him anxiously.

"Get him out, you deaf ape," Ackerman yelled. "You think I want lip from a stupid flatfoot."

"I told you to listen good," Carmody said, and the hard bright anger in his face brought a nervous slack to Beaumonte's lips. Johnny was moving in on him, his massive chin pulled down into his neck, but Carmody kept his eyes on Ackerman. "Nothing happens to my brother. Figure out some other way to get off the hook."

"I heard you," Ackerman said. "I've listened to loud mouths like you before."

"Not like me, you haven't," Carmody said gently. "Remember that." Then he laughed and swung around to face Johnny Stark, his eyes alive with fury. "Now throw me out, sonny boy," he said. "Earn your dough."

"Mike, you and me don't want to fight," Johnny said.

"Why not? That's what you're paid for."

Johnny hesitated, a sheepish smile touching his wide pale face. Without taking his eyes from Carmody, he said, "Mr. Ackerman, Mike carries a gun."

"Don't let that worry you," Carmody said. He took the gun from his shoulder holster and flipped it suddenly to Johnny. "Now you've got one." While Johnny was turning it around gingerly in his massive hands, Carmody stepped in and hit him with a right that knocked him sprawling across the coffee table and into the fireplace.

Ackerman and Beaumonte scrambled aside, and at the bar Nancy screamed softly and put her hands to her mouth.

Johnny wiped his bleeding lips with the coat sleeve as he got slowly and purposefully to his feet. His little eyes were mean and hot. "You shouldn't have done that, Mike," he said, mumbling the words through split lips. "Now I'm going to hurt you."

"Come on, sonny," Carmody said, waiting for him with his hands on his hips. "You're no street fighter. I'll give you a lesson for free."

Johnny didn't answer. He came in fast, hooked a left into Carmody's side and tried for his jaw with an explosive right. It missed by half an inch but he recovered instantly and crowded Carmody back toward the wall with a flurry of punches that came out like pistons from his heavy shoulders. Carmody took a blow in the stomach and another that loosened a front tooth and sent a spurt of blood down his chin. Then he erupted; he could have handled it from a distance, cutting Johnny to pieces with his left, but that wouldn't have appeased his wild, destructive rage. He battered his way back to the middle of the room, trading punches with savage joy; he didn't want to do this the smart way, he wanted to be hurt, he wanted to be punished.

They stood toe-to-toe for half a minute, slugging desperately, and then Johnny broke it off and backed away, his breath coming in sharp whistles through his flat nose. He was cut badly around the mouth and there was a look of cautious respect in his narrowed eyes.

"Ackerman fixed your fights," Carmody said, grinning. "Didn't they ever tell you that."

Johnny leaped at him, swearing, and Carmody stepped back and let a punch sail past his head. Moving in fast he speared Johnny with a left and caught him off balance with a tremendous right that drove him across the room. Johnny bore back recklessly, but the right had weakened him; his breath was coming hard and he was down flat on his feet. Carmody hit him with another right and when it landed he knew the fight was over; the blow smashed into Johnny's throat and spun him around and down to the floor. Johnny screamed once in a desperate choking voice and his legs threshed as he fought to squeeze air into his lungs. He got enough down to quell his panic and then lay perfectly still, concentrating his strength on the painful work of breathing.

Carmody picked up his revolver, put it away in his holster and looked at Ackerman, his big chest rising and falling rapidly. "Remember what I told you," he said. "Nothing happens to my brother."

Ackerman smiled very carefully. The ingredients of death were in the room, he knew, and another jar might explode them in his face. "Maybe we can figure out something else," he said.

Beaumonte cried suddenly, "We don't want to hurt him, but the crazy sonofabitch hasn't got the brains of a two-year-old."

He had used the wrong word and he knew it instantly. Carmody walked toward him and Beaumonte said, "Now look," but that was all he got out; Carmody snapped a left up into his big padded stomach and Beaumonte's mouth closed on a sharp, disbelieving cry of pain. He sank to the floor slowly, settling like a punctured balloon, his face flushed with anguish and fear.

"It was just a manner of speaking," Ackerman said, still smiling carefully.

"It's a manner I don't like," Carmody said.

Nancy laughed suddenly, like a happy, delighted child, and skipped over to sit beside Beaumonte. She crossed her legs, spread her skirt out prettily then leaned forward and smiled into his crimson face. "Daddy got a tummy ache?" she asked him merrily. "Or is Daddy over his ration?" Beaumonte stared furiously at her, his face squeezed with pain, his mouth opening and closing soundlessly. "Look, it's sloshing in the scuppers," she cried, and raised her glass ceremoniously and poured the contents over his head. "See it slosh, Daddy? And what the hell are scuppers, anyway? I've always meant to ask."

The liquor darkened the shoulders and lapels of his white silk suit and dripped down onto his lap, but he paid no attention to it. He sat awkwardly, hunched over like a Buddha, staring at her with murderous eyes.

Ackerman smiled at Carmody. "There's still time to settle our problem smartly."

"The time ran out," Carmody said, moving toward the door but keeping his eyes on everyone in the room. "Remember what I told you, Ackerman. The guy you send after my brother has got to come through me first. He won't like that, I promise."

Ackerman shrugged slightly, and Carmody knew the break was clean and final. When he stepped from this room he wouldn't have a friend in the city. Okay, I don't need friends, he thought. I'm enough by myself, I'm Mike Carmody.

With a cold smile on his lips he turned and walked out the door.

Ackerman stood quietly for several seconds, frowning thoughtfully at the wall. Then, without looking around, he said, "Dan, did you get everything set with Dominic Costello?"

"He sent us a guy," Beaumonte said, his voice small and hoarse. "He's already on young Carmody's tail."

"Tell him to go to work," Ackerman said. "And you'd better figure out something to keep Carmody out of the way. Nobody will have a chance to get at his brother while he's around." His voice was flat and disgusted.

"Okay." Beaumonte still sat on the floor, watching Nancy. She smiled unsteadily at him as a slow fear began to work through her drunkenness. "I didn't mean it," she said in a sad, little girl's voice. "Honest, Dan."

Ackerman looked around then, his eyes dark and furious. "Maybe you can handle my business better than you handle your women," he said to Beaumonte. "You'd better, that's all I can tell you."

Johnny Stark climbed slowly to his feet, massaging his neck with both hands. "He caught me in the windpipe, Mr. Ackerman," he said in a squeaking voice. "I'd of got him if he hadn't caught my windpipe."

"You couldn't take him with an armored tank," Ackerman said, glaring at him. "What do I pay you for? To listen to birds singing?" Turning abruptly he walked to the door. Over his shoulder he said, "Don't bother coming along, Stark. I'm safer alone." He walked out and slammed the door shut behind him with a crash.

"Give me a hand, Johnny," Beaumonte said.

"Sure, sure," Johnny said quickly, glad to be useful to someone. He got behind Beaumonte, put both hands under his armpits and hauled him to his feet. Beaumonte swayed and put his hand for support against the mantel. "He could have killed me," he muttered. "He could have broke something inside me."

"Yeah, he can hit," Johnny said, nodding earnestly.

Nancy put a hand timidly on Beaumonte's forearm. "Look at me, Dan." She was pale and trembling, sobered by her fear. "It was just a joke. You do things like that to me sometimes, don't you? I was drinking too much, like you said. But I'm going on the wagon, I promise, Dan."

Beaumonte turned away from her, pulling his hand free from her arm. "You're going back where I found you," he said slowly.

"Dan, please!" She tried to turn him around but he shook her off with a twist of his big round shoulders. "Please, Dan! It was just a crazy joke," she said, beginning to weep.

"Johnny, you know where Fanzo's place is?" Beaumonte said to Stark.

"Yeah, sure, Mr. Beaumonte."

Beaumonte drew a deep breath. "Take Nancy there, take her if you have to break her legs and carry her," he said, in a slow empty voice. "You got that? I'll phone him so he'll have the welcome mat out."

"Dan, what are you going to do to me?" Nancy cried, backing away from the two men. She brought her hands to her mouth and the bracelets on her wrists jangled noisily in the silent room.

Beaumonte looked at her then for the first time since he'd got to his feet. "Why did you do a thing like that with Ackerman watching," he said thickly.

"I told you it was just a crazy gag."

"I'm going to pay you off good," he said. "You got no more loyalty in you than a stick of wood."

"Dan!" she cried softly, as Johnny Stark put a massive hand on her wrist. Her eyes were wild and unbelieving. "You aren't going to do this to me. It's a joke, I know. Tell me it's a joke, Dan."

"Get her out," Beaumonte cried. "Get her out of here."

When they were gone, Beaumonte drew a deep ragged breath and began to walk about in small aimless circles. Finally, he stopped and went quickly to the bar. He made himself a brandy and soda, slopping the ingredients into the glass, and then sat down in a deep chair and stared at the long silent room. For several minutes he remained motionless, his body slumping forward slightly, and then he moaned deep in his throat and began to pound his fist slowly against his forehead. But the sound of her weeping stayed loud in his mind.

# 6

CARMODY DROVE DIRECTLY TO HIS HOTEL, RECKLESSLY IGNORING LIGHTS
and traffic. It wasn't quite six yet, but he knew that Ackerman would plan
and act swiftly. The order might already be out, and that meant he had to
find Eddie fast. But a dozen phone calls to his home, his district and his
favorite bars, failed to turn up a lead.

Carmody rang Karen's apartment and drummed his fingers on the
table as the phone buzzed in his ear. Then the connection was made,
and she said, "Hello?"

"Karen, this is Mike. Have you seen Eddie today?"

"No. . . . What's the matter?"

"If you see him, tell him to call me at my hotel. Will you do that? I
couldn't stall the big boys any longer. Tell him that, too."

"Does that mean trouble?"

"Not for you, bright eyes. But it does for Eddie. If he calls you—"

The phone clicked dead. For a moment Carmody sat perfectly still and
then he swept the receiver off the table. She was staying in the clear. There
was trouble coming and Danny Nimo's girl would take a warm bath, do
her nails and keep nicely out of it. Well, what had he expected?

But underneath his anger there was a growing fear. He shouldn't have
tipped his hand to Ackerman; that spotted them a big advantage. Where
in hell were his brains?

He needed help in finding his brother but he didn't know where to
turn. Anyone who knew this was Ackerman's business would want no
part of it. The men on his shift were his only bet, but it wouldn't be easy
to find them; his shift had started its three-day relief that morning and
they might be out of town or visiting relatives. Some damn thing. Carmody
tried Dirksen first, because he was the dumbest, but got no answer.
Abrams' daughter talked to him and said that her daddy had gone to the
shore to do some fishing. Carmody thanked her and hung up. That left
Myers. He put through the call.

Myers sounded as if he had been sleeping. "Hi, Mike. What's up?" he
said.

"I need some help. My brother's in a little trouble and I've got to locate
him. But I need a hand. How about it?"

"In a little trouble, eh?" Myers said cautiously.

"That's right. Look, he lives on Sycamore in the Northeast. Number
two-eighty. Would you stake yourself out there and grab him if he shows
up? Tell him to call me right away at my hotel?"

Myers hesitated. "I was just going to take the girls to a movie. It'd be a shame to disappoint them."

"Sure, I know," Carmody said, rubbing his forehead. "But how about this? Make it tomorrow night and I'll get all three of you tickets to the new musical. And dinner at the Park Club first. My treat."

"A night on the town, eh? Sounds pretty fancy," Myers said dryly. "Well?"

"By the way, I got an envelope from Degget. Thanks."

"Degget?"

"Yeah, the little character we had in that Wagner Hotel murder. He sent me fifty bucks. And a note. Did you read the note?"

"No," Carmody said impatiently.

"Well, he said the smart detective told him I could use the fifty bucks." Myers laughed shortly. "That's you he meant. The smart detective."

"What're you getting at?"

"Yeah, you're the smart detective," Myers said, the words tumbling angrily from him. "And your brother's in trouble with Ackerman's bums and you want me to help you pull him out. Why don't you go to the hoodlums? They're your buddies, aren't they?"

"Forget it," Carmody said slowly. "I didn't know you felt this way."

"You wouldn't know how I feel," Myers said. "That would mean noticing me, asking me. But you're too much a big shot for that. What the hell was that address?"

"I said forget it."

"Give me that address. I'll get it from the book if you don't. I'm doing this for your brother. Because he's a cop, a dumb honest slob like me. Not for you, Mike."

"It's two-eighty." Carmody wet his lips. "Thanks, Myers."

"Go to hell."

The phone clicked. Carmody got to his feet, rubbing his forehead. What the devil had got into Myers? Had he been keeping this bottled up all these years? And what about the other men on his shift, and in the department? Did they feel the same way?

So what if they do, he thought, frowning and disturbed. It's there to take. If they had the brains they'd take it, too.

There was nothing to do but wait. He tried all the bars, and Eddie's home and district half-an-hour later but drew blanks. He left messages for Eddie everywhere to call him but that was all he could do.

The night deepened beyond his windows, moving slowly in wide black columns to the pink-gray streaks on the horizon. Lights came on in the tall buildings in the business district and the city spread out before him, a powerful exciting mass, cut through and through with white lines of traffic. Eddie was out there somewhere. Standing on a dark corner lighting a cigarette, swinging down a black alley on a short-cut to the district, stopping before a movie to look at the posters. And somewhere out there

Ackerman's killer might be starting slowly and carefully to work, asking questions, making calls, closing in on his brother's trail. And all I can do is wait, Carmody thought.

When the phone rang the sound of it went through him like an electric shock. He crossed the room in three strides and jerked the receiver to his ear. "Yes? Hello?"

"Hello, slugger," Beaumonte said with a laugh. "You pack quite a punch, or didn't anyone ever tell you?"

Carmody was caught off balance by Beaumonte's obvious good-humor. "Is that what you called to tell me?"

"No, this is business, Mike. I don't like being knocked around but I'm going to forget it. There's more at stake just now than a row between friends."

"Tell me about it," Carmody said.

"Ackerman and I had a talk after you left. He wants you to keep working on your brother. You said you could make him listen to reason. Does that still go?"

"Sure I can," Carmody said. The tension dissolved in him and he let out his breath slowly. With time he could work something out. "I'll need a few days," he said.

"Two days is the limit. That's Ackerman's final word."

"Okay, two days then," Carmody said. He was trembling with relief; Eddie wouldn't die tonight. "I can handle it in two days, I think."

"Good. And if you want to pound somebody, well, pound some sense into your brother."

"I'm sorry about tonight, Dan," Carmody said slowly.

"Don't worry about that. Let me know when you've made progress."

"Okay, Dan."

Carmody put the phone down and saw that his hands were trembling. Relief did that to you, just like fear. Eddie was safe for two days. Would it narrow down to hours? And then minutes?

Carmody turned on the record player and walked deliberately to the liquor cabinet. He took out a fresh bottle and put it on the table beside his chair. What had he told Nancy? That he didn't drink because he didn't want to be anyone else. Did that still hold? He sat down slowly, heavily, and let his big hands fall limply on either side of the chair. Not any more. I'd love to be someone else right now, he thought.

Carmody reached for the bottle the way a desperate man would turn on the gas . . .

He was awakened by a sound that seemed to be pounding at the inside of his head. Pushing himself to a sitting position, he stared blankly around the dark room. He checked his watch; the illuminated hands stood at one-forty-five. He had been out for hours. His coat lay beside him on the floor and his collar was open. There was a dull pain stretching across his forehead, and his stomach was cold and hollow.

The knocking sounded again, more insistently this time. Carmody snapped on a lamp, pushed the hair back from his forehead and went to the door.

Nancy stood in the corridor, swaying slightly; the night elevator man held her arms to keep her from falling. "She insisted I bring her up, Mr. Carmody," the man said. "I rang you but didn't get no answer."

"It's alright," Carmody said. "Come in, Nancy. What's the matter?"

She swayed toward him and he caught her shoulders. "Take it easy," he said.

"Beaumonte kicked me out," she said, grinning brightly at him; the smile was all wrong, it was as meaningless as an idiot's. "Got a drink for a cast-off basket case?"

"We can find one." Carmody led her to the sofa, put a pillow behind her head and stretched out her legs. Turning on the lights, he made a drink and pulled a footstool over beside the couch.

"Take this," he said. She looked ghastly in the overhead light; her face was like a crushed flower, lipstick smeared, make-up streaked with tears. "What happened?"

"He kicked me out, Mike. He gave me to some friends of his first. People he owed a favor to. Or maybe I'm flattering myself. Maybe they're people he doesn't like. They took me to a private house near Shoreline." She shook her head quickly. "They were real gents, Mike. They gave me cab fare home."

Carmody squeezed her hand tightly. "Take the drink," he said.

"I don't know why I came here. I shouldn't have. I guess it was seeing you in the fight. You're the only thing they're afraid of."

"Did you hear any talk about me after I left? From Ackerman, I mean? About me or my brother?"

She stared at him, her mouth opening, and then she shook her head from side to side. "Oh God, oh God," she whispered. "You don't know?"

"What?" Carmody said, as the shock that anticipates fear went through him coldly.

Clinging to his hands, she began to weep hysterically. "It's all over town. I heard it from Fanzo's men, and on the radio in the cab. Your brother was shot and killed a couple of hours ago."

# 7

SHE WAS CRYING SO HARD THAT IT TOOK CARMODY SEVERAL MINUTES
to get any details. When he learned where it had happened he stood up,
his breathing loud and harsh in the silence. "You stay here," he said in a
soft, thick voice. He picked up his coat and left the room.

The shooting had occurred a block from Karen's hotel. Carmody got
there in twenty minutes by pushing his car at seventy through the quiet
streets. The scene was one he knew by heart; squad cars with red beacon
lights swinging in the darkness, groups of excited people on the sidewalks
whispering to each other and women and children peering out from
lighted windows on either side of the street. He parked and walked toward
the place his brother had died, a cold frozen expression on his face. A cop
in the police line recognized him and stepped quickly out of his way, giving
him a small jerky salute.

Lieutenant Wilson was standing in a group of lab men and detectives
from Klipperman's shift. One of them saw Carmody coming and tapped
his arm. Wilson turned, his tough, belligerent features shadowed by the
flashing red lights. He said quietly, "We've been trying to get you for a
couple of hours, Mike. I'm sorry about this, sorry as hell."

Carmody stopped and nodded slowly. "Where's Eddie?" he said.

"They've taken him away."

"He's dead then," Carmody said. Nothing showed on his face. "I was
hoping I'd got a bum tip. What happened?"

"He was shot twice in the back. Right here."

Carmody stared at the sidewalk beyond the group of detectives and
saw bloodstains shining blackly in the uncertain light. In the back, he
thought.

"We'll break this one fast, don't worry," Wilson said. "We've got a
witness who saw the shooting. She was a friend of Eddie's. Karen Stephanson. You know her?"

"She saw it, heh? Where is she now?"

"At Headquarters, looking at pictures."

Carmody turned and walked away, his heels making a sharp, ringing
sound. Wilson called after him but Carmody kept going, shouldering
people aside as he headed for his car.

It took him twenty minutes to get back to center-city. He parked at
Oak and Sixteenth, a few doors from the morgue, and walked into the
rubber-tiled foyer. The elderly cop on duty got to his feet, a solemn,

awkward expression on his face. "He's down the hall. In B," he said. "You know the way, I guess, Sarge."

Carmody pushed through swinging doors and turned into the second room off the wide, brick-walled corridor. Three men were present, a pathologist from Memorial Hospital, a uniformed cop and an attendant in blue denim overalls. The square clean room was powerfully illuminated by overhead lights and water trickled in a trough around the edge of the concrete floor. The air smelled suspiciously clean, as if soap and brushes had been used with tireless efficiency to smother something else in the room.

Eddie lay on a metal table with a sheet covering the lower half of his body. The brilliant white light struck his bare chest and glinted sharply on the smears and streaks of blood. His shirt, which had been cut away from him, lay beside the table on the floor.

Carmody stared at his brother's body for a few moments, his features cold and expressionless. A lock of hair was curled down on Eddie's ivory-pale forehead and his face was white and empty and still. The choirboy who stole the show at St. Pat's, Carmody thought. Who wanted to play it straight, get married and have kids. That was all over, as dead as any other dream. One of the men said something to him hesitantly and awkwardly. "Damn shame, sorry . . ." Carmody couldn't speak; a pain was pressing against his throat like a knife blade. He nodded slowly, avoiding their eyes.

Someone came into the room behind him, and Carmody turned and saw old Father Ahearn standing in the doorway.

"I came as quickly as I could, Mike," he said.

Carmody turned and looked down at his brother. "We were all too late," he said, holding his voice even and cold. "Too late, Father." He put out a big hand and pushed the lock of hair back from Eddie's forehead. For another moment he stood there, staring at the pale quiet face, and then, moving deliberately and powerfully, he walked past the priest and out to the sidewalk. The night was cool and soft; a faint wind moved over the city and a diffused light was spreading thinly along the horizon.

The door behind him opened and Father Ahearn came to his side. "Why can't you face me, Mike?" he cried softly. "Who did this thing to your brother?"

"I warned him," Carmody said, swallowing hard against the pain in his throat. "I warned him, but he wouldn't listen to me."

"You warned him!" Father Ahearn took Carmody's big hard arm and tried to pull him around; but the detective's body was like a post set in stone. "What do you mean by that, Mike?"

"He wouldn't listen to me," Carmody said again. "They meant business but he wouldn't believe it."

"You knew this was going to happen?" the old priest said in a soft, horrified voice. "Is that what you are saying?"

"Sure, I knew it would happen . . ." Carmody said.

The old priest took a step backward, quickly and involuntarily, as if the face of evil had appeared before him without warning. "God have mercy on your soul," he said, breathing the words softly.

"Save the mercy for the men who killed him, Father." Without looking at the old priest, Carmody turned quickly and strode toward his car.

Half an hour later he pulled up before Karen's hotel. The street was quiet now, the squad cars had gone back to their regular duty. Only a few groups of people remained on the sidewalk, smoking a last cigarette and exchanging their final words on the shooting. Everyone prefaced his recapitulation with an "I was just—" "Just getting into bed." "Just locking up." "Just opening the ice-box—when it happened." For some reason, Carmody thought, listening to the eddies of talk in the silent street, they all felt these commonplace activities had assumed a shape and significance through their temporal relationship to tragedy. And maybe they did. I was just getting drunk, he remembered. Just passing out after accepting Beaumonte's word that Eddie would be spared for two more days.

A middle-aged patrolman was posted in the small foyer of Karen's hotel.

"Is the witness back yet?" Carmody asked him.

"Got in about fifteen minutes ago, Sarge."

"You'll be here all night?"

"That's right. And there's a man in back and one just outside her room. You going up?"

"Yes." The cop unlocked the inner door and Carmody walked by him and took the elevator up to her floor. He nodded to the alert-looking young cop who was on guard there and then rapped on her door.

"You'd better start asking everybody for identification," he said.

The young man flushed slightly. "I've seen your pictures in the paper lots of times, Sarge."

"Okay. But be on your toes when anyone gets off that elevator. If the guy she spotted comes up here he won't give you a chance. Remember that."

"I'm ready for him," the cop said, putting a hand on the butt of his revolver.

Carmody glanced at his youthful, clean-cut face, and swallowed hard against a sudden constriction in his throat. Another Eddie, confident and hard, willing to take on all the trouble in the city. How did they get guys like this for sixty bucks a week? Where did they find these brave dumb kids?

The door opened and Karen looked up at him. She had been crying but her face was now pale and composed. For a moment they stared at each other in silence. Then she said, "What do you want here?"

"The whole story, everything," he said, moving into the room and closing the door. She sat down slowly and locked her hands together in her lap. "Eddie was killed, that's what happened," she said, struggling to control her voice. "Just the way you said it would."

"You saw the killer. I want to know what he looked like. I want every detail you can remember."

"I've told the police everything."

"Tell me now."

"Why should I? You're a friend of the men who killed him. You stood by and let them murder him." She rose suddenly and turned away from him, her small face beginning to break and crumble with emotion. "You said we were the same kind of dirt, didn't you? But you let them kill your brother. I'm not in that class."

Carmody took her frail shoulders in his hands, twisted her around and sat her in the chair. When she attempted to get up, weeping helplessly now, he caught her wrist and forced her back with a turn of his hand. "I don't want any speeches," he said coldly. "There'll be plenty of speeches from everybody else. The Mayor, the newspapers, priests and ministers, they'll all make speeches. But they won't do any good. When they're all through talking, Eddie will be just as dead. So don't waste my time with a speech." His voice went low and hard, "Start with the beginning. Eddie was here tonight, wasn't he? When I called?"

"Give me just a minute," she whispered.

"Okay, take your time," Carmody said, releasing her wrist. He lit a cigarette and drew the smoke deeply into his lungs. Then he sat down and stared at a picture on the wall. Finally, he glanced at her. "Okay?"

"Yes. Eddie was here when you called. But he told me he didn't want to speak to you. He listened to the conversation and broke the connection when you began to yell at me. I begged him to be careful but he said you were more frightened of Ackerman than he was." She stopped, breathing slowly, and put the palm of her hand against her forehead.

"We watched television until eleven-thirty. When he left I tidied up the room and found his wallet in the chair he'd been sitting in. His badge was clipped inside it and I knew he'd need that on duty. So I went downstairs to see if I could catch him. The street was dark but I saw him walking toward the corner, about fifty yards away. I ran after him. I didn't call because it was late. Eddie didn't hear me until I was eight or ten feet from him. I'd changed into slippers and I didn't make any noise, I suppose. Then he turned around quickly and reached for his gun. When he saw me he laughed and started to say something. But he didn't get the words out." She shuddered and rubbed her arms with her hands. "That's when it happened. A man stepped from behind a tree and into the light of the street lamp. He had a gun and he shot Eddie twice in the back. Then he ran to the corner. I began to scream and he looked around and stopped. He started toward me but a woman came out on the balcony across the street and began to shout for the police. The man stopped again, under the light at the corner, and then he turned and ran into the next block."

"Okay. You've been looking at pictures at Headquarters. Did you find this man in any of them?"

She shook her head slowly.

"Tell me what he looked like. Everything you can remember."

"He was big. Not fat, but tall and wide. His hair was blond and long. I couldn't see his eyes, they just looked black, but his face was heavy and brutal."

"How old?"

"Young, not more than thirty."

"How about his clothes?"

"He was wearing a sports jacket and a sports shirt. The shirt was open at his neck and the jacket was a light color. Gray tweed or camel's hair, something like that."

Carmody frowned. He knew the local hoodlums who might have done this night's work: Sheen in West, Morgan or Schmidt in Northeast, Youngdahl who ran a bowling alley in Meadowstrip. But Karen's description fitted none of them. That meant an imported killer. And you couldn't get a man like that in ten minutes. It required arrangements, discussions, planning. So the double-cross hadn't been a spur-of-the-moment decision. It had been in the works all the time.

He began to smile slowly. "I'll get that man, Karen. Don't worry about it."

"What good will that do? Eddie's dead. You can't bring him back."

"I'm not doing this for Eddie," he said, still smiling coldly. "This is for me. They promised me time to work on him, and I believed them. They lied to get me out of the way. And it worked. Then they shot him down like a dog. Do you think I'll let them get away with that?"

"I might have guessed this," she said, staring at him with something like wonder in her eyes. "It's not for Eddie. It's not because the men who killed him are savage and cruel and evil. It's because your pride is hurt. Their great crime was to make a fool of Mike Carmody. Even your own brother's death can't penetrate your thick-headed arrogance."

"I told you to skip the sermons," he said, getting to his feet.

"I know you don't want to hear sermons," she said bitterly. "You don't want to hear a word about right and wrong or good and evil. Those things hurt you. You can't stand them, Mike."

"Shut up!" he said thickly. "Damn it, will you shut up?"

"No, you don't want anyone to tell you what kind of a man you are.

You sneer and laugh at the whole world but you're too damn sensitive to listen to its judgment on you. Well, some day you'll have to listen, Mike. You helped fire the bullet that killed Eddie, and you'll never be able to run away from that fact."

"I did what I could," Carmody said, catching her thin shoulders in his big powerful hands and lifting her to her feet. "Don't ever say I killed him. Don't ever say that to me again."

"You did nothing but advise him to become a thief like you," she said, staring into the pain and fury in his eyes. "When that didn't work you walked away from him. That's what you did, Mike."

The words framed the dark thoughts which he had been fighting to drive into the safe hidden depths of his mind. I didn't kill him, I didn't kill him, he thought, hurling the words like weapons at his growing sense of guilt. Then he released her arms so abruptly that she staggered to keep her balance. "You don't know anything about it," he said hoarsely.

"You're feeling it now," she said, watching his face. "It's something you'll never get away from. If I've done that, I'm glad."

"I'm tougher than you think," he said, forcing a smile onto his lips. "Listen to me; Eddie didn't die because of me. Eddie died because he was a fool."

She sat down slowly, watching him with a frown, and then shook her head sadly. "If you can say that, you're tough all right. You're not a man, you're just a slab of concrete. But some day you'll crack up anyway. And the crash will be that much louder."

"Don't bet on it," he said.

It was four in the morning when Carmody entered his own living room. The lights were on and Nancy Drake lay on the sofa, an empty whiskey bottle within inches of her trailing hand. Strands of her fine blonde hair fell across her damp cheek and there was a little smile on her lips. But it was a stiff, unnatural smile, the kind Carmody had seen on the lips of women who needed to scream. The line of her body was rigid and the smooth muscles in the backs of her calves were drawn up into small knots.

He shook her gently. "How do you feel, Nancy?"

"Feel?" The grin grew wider. "Hotsy-totsy." A spasm shook her body and she pounded her feet up and down on the cushions of the sofa. "Say something nice to me, Mike. Don't let me start crying."

"Let's have a drink. That's something nice, isn't it?"

"Real peachy," she said. "Let's just do that, Mike."

The phone rang suddenly, shrill and ominous in the silence. Nancy cried out softly and Carmody patted her shoulder. "Keep quiet while I'm talking," he said. "Okay?"

"Sure, Mike."

Carmody crossed the room and picked up the phone. "Hello."

"Mike, this is Bill Ackerman."

Carmody stared at the receiver. Then he said softly, "You made a mistake tonight, Bill. I'm going to prove it to you."

"Now get this!" Ackerman's voice was sharp and controlled. "We didn't kill your brother. I promised you forty-eight hours and I meant it. Whoever shot him was working on his own. We'll find the killer and when we do he's all yours. Do you understand me, Mike?"

Carmody smiled coldly. Was this the opening lead in another double-cross? Was he next on the list? "I thought you'd killed him, Bill. I thought you'd crossed me," he said.

"I don't work that way. I don't need to. I gave you forty-eight hours and I stuck to my word. My guess is that some hophead learned that your brother was causing us trouble, and decided to get in good with us by doing the job on him. He'll be in for a handout one of these days and you can take over from here. Is that clear?"

"That's your guess, eh?"

"I can't think of anything else."

The unpleasant little smile was still on Carmody's lips. Ackerman's confidence was almost funny, he thought. But where was this leading? Ackerman hadn't called to explain himself or apologize. There was no reason for that.

"I'm glad you weren't involved in it," Carmody said. "I'm going after the guy who did the job."

"We'll help you, Mike. Is there anything you need right now?"

"I'm okay. I don't need help."

"If you need it, it's here. Now here's why I called. Did you see Nancy Drake last night or this morning?"

Carmody frowned. What was Ackerman's interest in Nancy? "No, I haven't," he said, glancing at the slim figure on the sofa.

"That's funny. She was out with some of Beaumonte's friends last night. The last thing she told them was that she was going to your place."

"My place? She must have been drunker than usual."

"I imagine so. Anyway, Beaumonte wants to find her."

Now it's Beaumonte, Carmody thought. Why should Ackerman give a damn about Beaumonte's troubles? There had to be an answer to that one. Ackerman operated solely in the light of self-interest; nothing mattered to him unless it directly concerned his safety and money. "Did Beaumonte and Nancy have a row?" he asked casually.

"Yeah. He didn't like that baptismal job she did on him."

"Well, I'll check the elevator men here at the hotel," Carmody said. "You want me to go any farther?"

"Sure. Find her if she's still in town."

"Okay." Carmody hesitated, then: "I'll give Beaumonte a call if I get a line on her."

"No, let me know first," Ackerman said. Normally he never explained or discussed his orders, but now he said, "I'll hand her over to Dan as a little surprise."

"Sure."

"And, Mike, I'm sorry about your brother."

Carmody couldn't say thanks to that, the words would have stuck in his throat. "It was a rough deal," he said slowly.

When he put the phone down he walked over and sat down beside Nancy on the sofa. There was a pale morning light coming in the windows now and it glinted on her tumbled blonde hair and the backs of her slim silken legs.

"Can you talk to me a minute?" he asked her quietly.

She twisted around until she was lying on her back. "I'll get out," she said. "I shouldn't have bothered you."

"Don't worry about that," he said, taking one of her hands and rubbing it slowly.

"Why did Beaumonte do it to me?" she asked him in a small, weary voice. Then her eyes began to fill with tears. "I was as good to him as I knew how. I tried my best to do everything he wanted. Really, I did. And he must have liked me a little, Mike. In all the time he never had another girl. He used to laugh about that. Said he was growing old. But that wasn't it. He must have liked me. But he must have hated me, too. That's what I can't understand. Unless he hated me he wouldn't have done this, would he, Mike?"

"He doesn't hate you. He wants you back."

"I don't want to go back," she said, and her hand tightened in his like a frightened child's. "Can he make me?"

"No, of course not."

She sighed. "This is my chance, Mike. I don't want to wind up in some alcoholic ward. I'll lay off the booze, and try to get back into show business. I can do that, I know it."

"That was Ackerman who just called," Carmody said. "He wants you back, too. Does that make any sense to you?"

She shivered and rubbed her bare arms. "It just scares me."

"Is there any reason for him to be afraid of you? Have you got anything on him?"

She shook her head quickly, her eyes bright with fear. "I haven't got anything on anybody, Mike. Tell them that, please, Mike. Even if I could, I wouldn't bother them."

"I'm after them," he said gently. "Because they killed my brother. If you help me they'll never find out about it."

"I was sorry about your brother," she said, beginning to cry. "That was terrible, Mike." She was slipping away from him, he saw, retreating into irrational, nonspecific grief. "They shouldn't have done that."

"You're sure they did it?" He tightened his grip on her hand. "You know they did it?"

"They talked about it after your fight with Johnny Stark. After you'd gone." She stared pitifully at him, transfixed by his cold eyes. "Dan said there was a man tailing your brother, and Ackerman said to tell him to get to work."

Was this what Ackerman was worried about? Carmody wondered. Possibly. But there had to be something else. What Nancy had overheard wasn't evidence. And Ackerman would know that.

"They'll be looking for you," he said. "You told someone you were coming here."

"Don't make me go," she whispered.

"This isn't safe," he said. "Let me think." He had to hide her somewhere. Hotels and boardinghouses were out. If Ackerman were serious he could put a hundred men on her trail. Finally, Karen occurred to him; she was guarded by a detail of police and Nancy would be safe in her apartment. "Come on, let's go," he said. "Fix your hair and get into your coat."

"All right," she said. She seemed to have lost the power to act or think independently; she moved like a small battered puppet at the touch of his voice.

There was the problem of getting her past the police guard and Carmody put his mind to it on the trip across the dark city. Karen was an important witness, the only lead to Eddie's killer, and the police wouldn't stand for any casual boarders in her apartment. When he parked the car, a half-block from the Empire, he said to Nancy, "Now listen closely. We're going to the Empire Hotel. You can see the entrance from here. You go into the foyer alone and tell the cop that you live in the hotel but don't have your key. That's all, understand? I'll be right behind you and take it from there. Okay?"

Carmody walked into the foyer ten seconds after her and listened as she told her story to the patrolman. Then he said, "It's okay, officer. I've seen her around before. She lives here."

It worked smoothly, not because the cop was careless but because Carmody's endorsement had the stamp of rank and authority on it. In the elevator he punched a button that took them to the floor above Karen's. He led her along the warm silent corridor to the stairway and down one flight to the landing. "Wait right here," he whispered. Then he opened the door and stepped out into the hallway. The young cop stationed at Karen's apartment straightened alertly, but smiled as he recognized him.

"Everything quiet?" Carmody asked him.

"No one's been here since you left."

"Good. I'm going to be here half an hour going through some pictures with her. Why don't you go down and get some coffee?"

"Well, I'm supposed to stick right here."

"I'll take over. And coffee will keep you sharp the rest of the night."

It was that argument that sold the young cop. "I'll make it on the double," he said.

When the elevator doors closed on him Carmody went down the corridor to the stairway landing and brought Nancy back to Karen's apartment. He rapped sharply on the door and checked his watch. Five o'clock. He wanted to settle this and get to work.

There would be a restless ferment in the city today, precipitated by Eddie's death, and by fear of the cops' reactions to this defiant challenge from the big boys. This was the time to strike, Carmody knew, when people were ready to flinch.

The latch clicked and Karen opened the door. She wore a robe and slippers but he saw that she hadn't been asleep.

"I've got to ask you a favor," Carmody said.

"All right," she said, looking at Nancy.

"She's in trouble with the same guys who killed Eddie," he said. "She needs a safe place to stay."

Karen hesitated, still watching Nancy. Then she put a hand on her arm, and said, "Come on in. There's plenty of room."

"That's mighty hospitable of you," Nancy said, with a pitiful attempt at humor.

"She's had a rough time and is pretty loaded right now," Carmody said. "The cops won't let her stay if they find out she's here, so do your talking with the radio on. And if any detectives come up, put her in the bathroom or kitchen."

"I can manage it," Karen said.

The elevator cables hummed warningly and Carmody closed the door. He was standing with his back to it when the young cop came out of the elevator, carrying two cardboard containers of coffee.

"I brought one for you," he said.

"Fine," Carmody sipped the black coffee slowly, his thoughts ranging restlessly toward the city. The cop was silent until Carmody was ready to leave, then he wet his lips and told him awkwardly and hesitantly how sorry he was about his brother being killed.

"I worked with him and he was all cop," he said.

"I think you're right," Carmody said soberly. Then he left.

# 8

CARMODY WALKED THROUGH THE DOUBLE DOORS LEADING TO HEAD-quarters at five-thirty that morning. Abrams and Dirksen were there, along with a couple of men from Klipperman's shift. It was their day-off but they had come in when they'd heard the news. The same thing would happen in every station and district in the city, Carmody knew. Off-duty detectives and patrolmen would check in with their sergeants, grimly eager to join the hunt for a cop's killer.

The men stood when Carmody walked in and Abrams made an awkward little speech. "Rotten shame . . . we'll get the son, don't worry . . ." He was clumsy about it because the situation was marred by a make-believe quality; everyone in the room knew who had ordered Eddie Carmody's execution. And why. And they knew Carmody's relationship with Ackerman. But their sympathy was genuine, untouched by these considerations.

"Thanks," Carmody said, his hard face revealing nothing of what he was feeling.

Myers came out of the card room, a solemn expression about his small cautious mouth. "I'm sorry about it, Mike," he said simply. "I staked out at his home last night like you asked me to. But he never showed."

Carmody saw that the detectives were taking in every word. Well, so what? he thought. Should I be ashamed because I tried to save Eddie's life?

"Thanks, Myers," he said, "you did all you could." Then he turned into Lieutenant Wilson's office. Wilson was sitting at his desk with two empty containers of coffee at his elbow. His square pugnacious face was irritable from lack of sleep. He stood and patted Carmody on the shoulder. For a moment the two men looked at each other in silence, and then Wilson turned away and sat on the edge of his desk. The bright overhead light slanted through the smoky air and drew shadows along the lines of fatigue in his face. "Well, they killed a good boy, Mike," he said at last. "Just like they'd step on a bug."

"You made a proposition to me yesterday," Carmody said. "I'm taking it."

"Turning over a new leaf, eh?"

"I don't know. I can't make any pious speech. I'm a grown man, and I know the world isn't run the way some nun told me it was. But I'm going to get the guys that killed Eddie. That's what counts, isn't it?"

Wilson was silent, studying Carmody with a little frown. "You didn't hear the news, I guess?"

"What news?"

"We've got a new Superintendent of Police. They moved Captain Myerdahl up. Every paper in town is raising hell about your brother's murder. So the Mayor couldn't put a hack for the top job. Myerdahl's first order came in an hour ago. It was one sentence to every captain and lieutenant in the department: get rid of your rotten apples."

That was pure Myerdahl, Carmody thought. The old German was notorious for his shrewdness, his toughness and his defiant, uncompromising honesty. He knew the city as he knew the lines in leathery old hands, and he hated the men who were squeezing the heart out of it for their own profit. Until he retired, or was eased out, Ackerman's gambling operations would be shot to hell. Carmody saw a sharp significance in this; Ackerman must have known what would happen after Eddie's murder. And that meant he was more concerned about taking the heat off Delaney, than he was for the health of his rackets. What Delaney had on him was big!

"You see what that means?" Wilson asked him.

Carmody brought his thoughts back to the point. "I'm your rotten apple, eh?"

"It's a tough time for it to happen," Wilson said, rubbing his tired face. "I know you want to work on your brother's murder. But you're not going to, Mike." He picked up a sheaf of papers from his desk and held them limply in one hand. "This is an unfitness report on you."

"Now wait a minute," Carmody said sharply. "You can't boot me out now."

"If you are going straight for good I might put in a word for you," Wilson said. "But I don't want men who pick and choose their spots to be honest."

"Damn it, are you worried about my soul, or do you want Eddie's killer?" Carmody said.

"I've got an interest in both those deals," Wilson said quietly.

Carmody was silent for a moment or so, staring down at his big hands. "Okay," he said at last. "You aren't stopping me, Jim, you're just making it tougher. I want to work with you, but not at the expense of putting on sackcloth and ashes for Myerdahl's benefit. I'm a crooked cop. Those are dirty words but they fit. They're stuck to me with glue. I can't get rid of them by crossing myself and saying three Hail Marys."

"So you're going to free lance on this case?"

"He was my brother," Carmody said.

"That doesn't give you any exclusive rights. Eddie had five thousand brothers in this city."

"Brother cops, eh?"

"Don't sneer about it, Goddamnit. That's your trouble, Mike. Too much sneering."

"I wasn't sneering," Carmody said impatiently. He got to his feet. "Five thousand or fifty thousand cops won't break this case," he said, staring evenly at Wilson. "If you think so, I'll give you the killer's names as a head start. Ackerman, Beaumonte, Fanzo in Central, Shiller in Meadowstrip. There your murderers are, Jim. Along with assorted goons, bagmen, killers, judges and politicians. They killed Eddie, but you and your five thousand brother cops try to prove it. You won't in a million years. But I will. I know that crowd from the inside and I know the spots to hit." He gave Wilson a short, sardonic salute. "Take it easy, chief," he said, and started for the door.

"Hold on," Wilson said sharply. He got to his feet, his blunt face troubled and undecided. "Working together we can do it, Mike. With the department outside and you inside we could smash them for good."

"Make up your mind," Carmody said. "Am I on the team or off?"

Wilson tossed the unfitness report back on his desk. "I'll hold Myerdahl off somehow," he muttered. Then he looked at Carmody, his eyes sharp and unfriendly. "You get your way always, don't you? Do just what you want and to hell with everybody else."

"Why the analysis?" Carmody asked him. "Let's forget my personality and go to work. What's been going on?"

"We've got a detail of twenty men working out where your brother was shot," Wilson told him. "And when the shops and bars open we're putting out fifty more. Every section is throwing us men. The Vice Squad, Accident Investigation, even the Park guards. They'll fan out from the spot he was killed, making a street by street check of everybody who might have seen the killer. That girl's description will go on the air every fifteen minutes, night and day, to every squad in the city; an eight-state alarm has been out for hours." Wilson rubbed his face. "We'll get him if he's in the city. But that's what I'm worried about. That he may already be gone."

"He's still here," Carmody said. "Don't worry about that."

"How do you know?"

"Listen," Carmody said. The police speaker in the outer room had broken the silence. "To all cars," the announcer said in a flat, unemotional voice. "Be on the alert for murder suspect. Description following. Male, white, age twenty-five to thirty, tall muscular build, blond hair, wide face. Last seen in vicinity of Bering Street and Wilmer Avenue. Last seen wearing sports jacket, gray or tan, and sports shirt open at collar. This man is armed. Approach with caution."

The speaker clicked twice and was silent.

"That's going out every fifteen minutes," Carmody said. "The killer knows it. Would you move around if you were in his spot?"

"He might have caught a plane twenty minutes after the shooting."

"That might have been the original plan, but I doubt like hell that he followed it," Carmody said. "He flubbed the job. He shot Eddie in front of a witness."

"All the more reason for him to clear out fast."

"Reason for him perhaps, but not for Ackerman. The killer put Ackerman on the spot. And Ackerman won't let him go until it's safe. And it won't be safe until the witness is dead. Or the killer is dead. One or the other. That's why he's still in town. I'll bet on that."

"Then we'll find him," Wilson said sharply.

"Sure you will," Carmody said. "I'm going to work now."

"You've got another lead?"

"I don't know. When I find out I'll check in." Carmody hesitated at the door and looked back at Wilson with a small frown. "Thanks for the break, Jim," he said.

"Never mind that. I wouldn't use you if I didn't have to."

"You're honest at least," Carmody said, smiling crookedly.

He was walking through the bright early morning light to his car when Myers caught up with him and put a hand on his arm.

"Hold it just a second," he said. "I got something to tell you."

"What is it?" Carmody faced the small detective and tried to keep the impatience out of his voice. The city was coming awake; trolleys jangled on Market Street and the sidewalks were filling up with people. He wanted to be on the move.

"Well, look," Myers said. "Out at the sanitarium where my old lady stays, there's an attendant named Joe Venuti. A long time ago he worked for Capone in Chicago, and he knows the racket crowd pretty well."

"I've heard of him," Carmody said. "He's still wanted on some old charges, I think."

"Yeah, I guess he is," Myers said shrugging. "But he's been going straight for years and he's always been a big help with the old lady. You know how Italians are. They're the best people in the world with sick people and babies."

"What's the rest of it?" Carmody said.

"Sure. That's why I never bothered him I mean. Well, this morning I drove out there and woke him up. I gave him the girl's description of the killer. And he's going to call Las Vegas and Chicago tonight and gossip with some of his old friends."

"How come he's willing to help?"

"He's got to," Myers said, a grim little line going around his mouth. "I put it that way."

Carmody looked at him, slightly surprised. "He might turn something up, at that. But you watch yourself, Myers. Don't get hurt."

"You don't think I'm much of a cop, do you?" Myers said, smiling slowly at him. "Well, never mind that. Maybe I'm just a little dummy. But I can come up a notch or two for cop killers. I don't like them, Mike."

Brother cops, Carmody thought, studying the little man with a puzzled frown. Sighing he said, "You're okay, Myers. Don't worry about it."

"I'll find you when I hear from Venuti," Myers said, and Carmody saw that his tribute meant nothing to the little detective.

"Do that," he said slightly puzzled and angry. "And thanks."

Forty-five minutes later Carmody walked into the small lobby of the Milford Hotel, a quiet commercial establishment off Market Street. He had stopped at his hotel to shower and change. The loss of a night's sleep hadn't marked him; his eyes were clear and cold, and the muscles of his body were poised like powerful springs.

Showing the clerk his badge, he asked if Johnny Stark was in his room.

"Yes, sir. Shall I ring him?"

"No, I'll go up."

"Yes, sir. Of course."

Carmody rode up in the elevator and rapped twice on Stark's door, shaking the panels with his big knuckles.

Bedsprings creaked after a moment, and Stark said, "Who's that?"

"This is Mike Carmody. Open up."

There was a short silence. Then: "Sure, Mike. Right away."

The door opened and Stark blinked at Carmody, an uneasy smile touching his bruised lips. He wore a bathrobe and his face was thickened and dazed with sleep. "Come in," he said, still smiling uneasily. "I was asleep, out for the count."

"Where did you take Nancy Drake last night?" Carmody asked, walking into the small stuffy room. Stark cocked his good ear at him, frowning with the effort to hear. "Nancy Drake? What about her?"

"Where did you take her?"

Stark rubbed his big hands together, frightened and uncertain. "How'd you know that?"

"If they needed a delivery boy, you'd do. So where did you take her?"

"To Fanzo's bar in Central. I left her there and came home. That's all I did."

"Did you talk to her about anything on the way?"

"No." Stark wet his battered lips and looked away from Carmody's eyes. "She just did a lot of crying."

"What happened when you got there?"

"A guy I never saw before took her away. They were expecting us, I guess. Then I came home."

Carmody turned toward the door but Stark grabbed his arm. "Don't go, Mike. I want to tell you something."

"Take your Goddamn hand off me."

"All right, all right," Stark said quickly. "But listen to me. Ackerman fired me, Mike."

"That figures, doesn't it?"

"Sure; I'm supposed to be a fighter, not a clown. But that's not what's worrying me." Stark took a deep breath and rubbed a hand over his lumpy, unintelligent face. "I shouldn't have taken her to Fanzo's. That's what I'm trying to say. She was crying like hell and she begged me not to. It was a lousy thing to do."

"Well, why tell me about it? If you've got troubles go find a bartender or a priest."

"I just wanted to say it," Stark said. "I shouldn't have done it. Can I square it some way? Could I go out to Fanzo's and knock some heads together?"

"Stay away from there. They'd use you for a pin cushion."

"I'm a bum, I guess," Stark said, a little flush of anger coming up under his eyes. "Say it a thousand times. Go ahead. But are you any better? You work for 'em, too, don't you?"

"We aren't in a moral beauty contest," Carmody said, walking out of the room.

Stark followed him to the elevator in his bare feet, twisting his hands together anxiously. The anger was gone from his face; he looked scared and nervous. "One thing, Mike. Just one thing," he said. "You said Ackerman fixed all my fights? Was that straight?"

"No, the fix wasn't in," Carmody said, jabbing the elevator button impatiently. "What difference does it make?"

"It makes a difference to me," Stark said. "Don't you understand that?"

"Okay, I understand," Carmody said. "Go back to sleep."

"You don't believe I'm sorry about taking her out there, do you?" Stark said. "People can be sorry about things, can't they?"

"Sure they can," Carmody said shortly. "And they always are. But it doesn't do one damn bit of good."

"It makes you feel like less of a heel," Stark said. "It does that much."

Carmody didn't bother answering. The elevator door opened and he stepped in, glad to be leaving Stark and his big soggy burden of guilt.

Fanzo's bar had the name REALE lettered in gilt across a wide plateglass window. This was his home and headquarters; he lived above the taproom in a large gaudy apartment. Carmody parked his car and locked the doors. Central was that kind of neighborhood. Pool rooms, bars, pizza joints, littered streets, dismal alleys. The city's cesspool. Carmody walked into the tavern and nodded to the bartender, a tall, solemn Negro who wore a white apron pulled tightly across his big stomach. There were a dozen odd men lounging at the bar and in the wooden booths along the wall, bookies, minor hoodlums, all conspicuous and identifiable by their sharp clothes and casually insolent manner. They lived off the honest sweat of fools, and the knowledge of their cleverness had stamped arrogant little sneers on their faces.

"Is Fanzo around?" Carmody asked the bartender.

"Yes, sir, Mr. Carmody. He's upstairs. Want me to tell him you're here?"

"Never mind."

The bartender smiled, his teeth flashing in his solemn face. "You know he don't like being disturbed, Mr. Carmody."

"I'll remember to knock," Carmody said.

He walked through the bar, followed by a dozen pairs of alert eyes, and went up two flights of wooden stairs. The air was close and smelled of heavily spiced foods. Carmody knocked and the door was opened by a slim, dark-haired girl in a red silk robe and pink mules. She was eighteen or twenty, and very beautiful. Her skin was flawlessly smooth, the color of thickly creamed coffee, and her eyes were wide and clear.

"What is it?" she asked him sullenly.

"I want to see Fanzo."

"He expects you?"

From the front of the apartment, Fanzo called out in a high irritable voice: "Who the hell is that? Bring him in here, Marie."

The girl studied Carmody, her lips twisting into a smile. "Go in," she said, moving aside a few inches. Carmody brushed past her and walked through a short hallway to the living room, which was crowded with expensive inappropriate furniture and hung with heavy red draperies.

Fanzo was sitting at a wide table, eating breakfast. When he saw Carmody he got to his feet, a smile replacing the frown on his thin, handsome face. "Well, well, long time no see, keed," he said. "How's the boy? Tough about your brother, hey? I just been reading about it. A cop leads a hell of a life, don't he? No dough, nothing. And always the chance of that big boom sounding behind him." Fanzo shook his head and picked something from a front tooth. "Real tough. You had breakfast?"

"I'm not hungry."

"I'll go ahead. Funny thing, but when I read about people getting killed it makes me hungry as hell. Can't seem to get enough food." He sat down and gestured impatiently at the girl who was leaning in the doorway, one foot crossed over the other, a small smile twisting her full red lips. "Go find something to do," Fanzo said, waving her away with a thin nervous hand. "Go play with the television. Beat it."

She shrugged and sauntered from the room. Fanzo stared after her, smiling at her small round hips and the backs of her bare brown legs. "Screwball," he said, winking at Carmody. He picked up a peach from the bowl of fruit on the table and bit into it strongly, tearing a chunk free with big white teeth. "She's a Mexican. Slipped into Texas under a load of avocados. No entrance papers, nothing. She's crazier than hell. But she's

all right. And she does what she is told because if she don't she knows I'll
turn her over to the immigration people." Fanzo laughed and picked up
his knife and fork and began to eat. There was a staggering assortment of
food on the table; eggs, bacon, ham steaks, sausages, enchiladas, cold
melon and a variety of breads and rolls. "What's on your mind, Mike?"
he said. "You go ahead and talk. I'll eat."

"We're both going to talk," Carmody said.

"Sure, we both talk," Fanzo said, chewing away vigorously. He was a
tall lanky man in his early forties, with thin, cold features and glossy
black hair. Fanzo's conception of luxury was fundamental and primitive;
women, flashy cars, quantity rather than quality in food and liquor. He
was a shrewd and powerful factor in the racially mixed jungle that made
up Central. Unlike Beaumonte, he had no pretensions about himself; he
was a slum-bred hoodlum who lusted for power and cash. Respectability
wasn't his goal; he couldn't buy it so he didn't want it. He put no stock
in anything that didn't have a price tag on it. But in his district he held
more power than Beaumonte did in West. The district made the difference.
In Central, crime stalked the gutters and alleys like a bold cat. The city
didn't care about murders in this area. They weren't news. And this
indifference gave Fanzo a green light. He could enforce his orders by
gun or knife, without fear of reprisal. Everyone in Central knew this
and so they tried earnestly and fearfully to stay in line.

"What happened to Beaumonte's girl last night?" Carmody said.

Fanzo smiled briefly as he loaded his knife with food. "She's his girl,
keed. You better ask him."

"She was brought out here by Johnny Stark. What happened after
that?"

Fanzo lowered his knife and looked up at Carmody, still smiling slightly.
But his flat brown eyes were irritable. "Mike, I don't like this hard
talk," he said. "You come in here like a cop, for Christ's sake. Put that
away, keed."

"Start talking," Carmody said. "I'm in a hurry."

"You know, keed, you're making me mad," Fanzo said, looking at
Carmody with a puzzled frown. "I like you, but you're making me mad."
He gestured with both hands, a flush of anger staining his thin face.
"What's the deal, keed? You break up my breakfast, like you're grilling
some punk." He stood up abruptly, throwing his napkin aside furiously.
The short leash on his temper had snapped. "Goddamn you," he said
angrily. "Spoil a man's morning food on him. You beat it, Mike. You
beat it, you son of—"

Carmody hit him before the word was completed on his tongue. He
struck him across the face with the flat of his hand and the impact of the
blow knocked Fanzo sprawling over the table. Carmody picked him up
from the floor and dropped him into a chair. "Now talk," he said.

There was blood on Fanzo's lips and a smear of egg yolk on the white silk scarf he wore about his neck. He was breathing rapidly, his eyes flaming in his white face. In a high, whinnying voice he began to curse Carmody, spitting out the words as if they were dirt he was trying to get off his tongue.

"That's all," Carmody said softly. "Don't say anything else."

Fanzo paused as a strange fear claimed him completely; looking up at Carmody, he knew that he would die if he said another word.

They were silent for a moment, motionless in the gaudy room. Then Carmody said, "Tell me about the girl. Fast."

"Beaumonte sent her out with the fighter," Fanzo said, watching the detective carefully. "Before that, he called me and told me she needed a lesson. I didn't want to mix into this thing." Fanzo spoke slowly, never taking his eyes from Carmody's face. "Mixing with other guys' broads is no good. He takes her back tomorrow, next week and then he's mad at me for mixing in it. Mad at me because I know he's afraid to take care of her himself. But I do what Beaumonte says. I give her to three, four of the boys and they take her to a place of ours near Shoreline. Nothing real bad happens to her. You know what the boys would do with a little pink-and-white dish like that, they'd just—"

"Never mind the details." Carmody was having trouble controlling his voice. "What happened afterward?"

"They put her in a cab. She said she wanted to go to your hotel. She was kind of wild, still pretty drunk, too, I guess. She did some crazy talking."

"What kind of crazy talking?"

"She said she was going to put Ackerman and Beaumonte in jail." Fanzo smiled cautiously. "That kind of crazy talking."

"Anything else?"

"That's all the boys told me."

"Where are the boys now?"

"I could get them here. But it would take a few hours."

Carmody didn't want to wait that long. Later, if this lever wasn't strong enough, he could come back. Turning he started for the door, but Fanzo said, "Just a minute, Mike."

Carmody looked around. Fanzo was on his feet, holding one hand against the angry red mark on his cheek. "You shouldn't have hit me, Mike," he said slowly. "We were friends, but you put an end to it. I'll come after you some day. Sleep with that from now on, keed."

Friends? Carmody thought. Yes, he had given Fanzo the right to call him friend. They advanced the same interests, took their crumbs from the same table. They were closer than most brothers. Closer than he had been with Eddie. Why had he let this happen? he wondered. Why had he tossed away the privilege of having Fanzo as an enemy?

Walking back across the room, Carmody slipped the revolver from his holster and hefted it in his big hand. "You won't come after me, Fanzo," he said. His voice was soft and the strange cold smile was on his lips. "Because if you do, I'll feed you six inches of this barrel and then I'll put a bullet through your head. So you aren't coming after me, because you're smart, Fanzo."

Fanzo sat down slowly, his eyes dilating as he stared at the cold blue barrel of the revolver. Suddenly he felt cold and weak, as if he had just discovered that this grip on life was tentative and slippery. "No, I won't come after you, keed," he said, and wet his dry lips.

"That's very smart," Carmody said.

He left the room and went quickly down the stairs. A dozen heads turned as he stopped at the door of the smoky bar, a dozen pairs of eyes watched him alertly but cautiously. Everyone knew what had happened; the word had already come downstairs. A crooked cop had gone haywire and slugged Fanzo. But no one moved. The bartender discovered a spot on the bar that needed wiping, and someone whistled aimlessly into the silence. They all knew the legend of this particular cop and none of them was eager to add to its luster. For a moment Carmody let his cold eyes touch every face in the room, and then he walked through the bar and out to the sidewalk.

When the door swung shut a heavily built young man looked anxiously up toward Fanzo's apartment. "We should have stopped him," he said. "Fanzo won't like it that we just let him walk out."

The man beside him grinned. "Why didn't you stop him, boy? You lived a pretty full life, I guess."

# 9

ACKERMAN REPLACED THE PHONE, CHECKED HIS WATCH, AND THEN walked slowly down the sunlit length of Beaumonte's living room. There was an angry glint in his glassy black eyes, but his hard tanned face was expressionless. He glanced at a man who stood at the windows, and said, "Hymie, leave us alone for a few minutes. Go wash your hands or something."

"Sure, boss," Hymie Schmidt said. He was a slender, neatly dressed man with a pale narrow face and thinning brown hair. There was a nervous, charged quality about him, although his body was poised and deliberate in all its movements. The tension was in his dark eyes, which flicked nervously and restlessly from side to side as if constantly on the alert for trouble. "I'll go wash my hands," he said.

"And don't call me boss," Ackerman said shortly. "I'm Mr. Ackerman. Remember that."

"Sure, Mr. Ackerman," Hymie said. His dark eyes flicked angrily from side to side, but avoided Ackerman's. He didn't like this, but he kept his mouth shut. There was no percentage in being mad at Bill Ackerman.

"Come back if you hear the doorbell ring," Ackerman said.

"Right, Mr. Ackerman."

When he had gone Ackerman's mouth tightened slowly into a flat ugly line. He looked down at Beaumonte, who was slumped on the sofa in a blue silk dressing gown, and said very quietly, "That was Fanzo on the wire. Carmody just left after slapping him around like a two-bit punk. He's looking for Nancy."

Beaumonte rubbed a hand wearily over his forehead. The lack of sleep showed in his face; his eyes were bloodshot and tired, and his flabby cheeks and jowls needed the attentions of his barber and masseur. "I'm sorry," he said heavily. "I'm sorry, Bill."

"That doesn't do one damn bit of good," Ackerman said coldly. "I thought you had more brains than to spout off to a dame. Can't you impress them any other way?"

"I don't ever remember telling her," Beaumonte said, still rubbing his face wearily. "I must have been drunk."

Ackerman swore in disgust. "We've got enough trouble in town without worrying about where she is and who she's talking to," he said.

"We'll find her," Beaumonte said. "We got a dozen guys on her trail."

"And how about Carmody? Anybody watching him?"

Beaumonte nodded. "Sammy Ingersoll. But he hasn't got on him yet. Right now he's downstairs in the lobby. There's a chance Mike will turn up here."

"She's our number one job," Ackerman said. "I know she's been to Carmody's hotel. A cleaning woman remembered her. But the elevator men played dumb. Carmody's trained them not to talk about his business. It's an example you could damn well follow."

A touch of color appeared in Beaumonte's cheeks. He looked at Ackerman and said, "Let's don't get so mad that we forget business. You think Carmody believed you? About his brother, I mean."

"I don't know," Ackerman said slowly. "He's hard and he's smart. I'll never underestimate him again. That's why I told him to look for Nancy. I figured he'd reason it this way: if Ackerman wants me to find her, he isn't worried about her. So to hell with it." Ackerman shrugged. "I thought he'd think it was just another job and ignore it. But he didn't. He put aside looking for his brother's killer to look for Nancy."

"We'll find her first," Beaumonte said.

"We'd better. Remember that, Dan, we'd better."

Beaumonte got slowly to his feet and smoothed the wrinkled front of his dressing gown. "Just one thing I want clear," he said, meeting Ackerman's eyes directly. "She's not going to be hurt."

Ackerman grinned contemptuously at him. "You threw her out, remember," he said. "You gave her to Fanzo."

"All right, I did it," Beaumonte said, in a thick angry voice. "But I'm getting her back, understand? And in one piece."

"All right," Ackerman said easily. "That's the last thing in the world I want to do, as a matter of fact; you and I are friends, Dan. When we find her I'll send her on a vacation to Paris or Rio or Miami. Anywhere, as long as it is far away and she keeps her mouth shut."

"We understand each other then," Beaumonte said. "She'll be sensible, I'll guarantee that."

Five minutes later the doorbell rang. Beaumonte started to answer it but Ackerman stopped him with a gesture. "Hold it," he said quietly.

Hymie Schmidt appeared from the study, one hand in the pocket of his coat, his dark excited eyes switching from one side of the room to the other. Ackerman nodded toward the front door and Hymie moved to a position where he could cover anyone who entered. "All right now," Ackerman said to Beaumonte. "Go ahead."

Beaumonte walked across the room and opened the door. Mike Carmody stood in the corridor, his big hands at his sides, a faint cold smile twisting his lips.

"Hello, Dan," he said gently.

Beaumonte took an involuntary step backward. "We were hoping you'd show up," he said, breathing heavily.

"Sure," Carmody said. He walked into the room, and nodded to Ackerman and Hymie Schmidt, whom he knew to be fast and dangerous with a gun.

"You can relax, Hymie," he said, and smiled unpleasantly at him. "We're all friends here."

"I never relax," Hymie said, returning his smile. "The doc says it's bad for my nerves."

Beaumonte moved to Carmody's side, keeping carefully out of the line between the detective and Hymie Schmidt. "I'm sorry as hell about your brother, Mike," he said. "Ackerman told you that it wasn't our job, I know. But I want you to know I'm sorry."

"Sure," Carmody said, nodding. Nothing showed in his face. He had come here because it was essential to convince them that he was back on the team. Only by re-establishing that relationship could he set himself free to rip them apart from the inside. But it would take a hard, careful control to play this out, he realized. More than he had maybe. A dozen hours ago he had stood here fighting for Eddie's life. He had sworn that his brother wouldn't die and Eddie was now laid out in some undertaker's back room. But nothing else had changed; Beaumonte and Ackerman were still healthy and alive, making plans to perpetuate and enjoy their power and rackets. Only the poor grown-up choirboy was gone from the scene.

This went through Carmody's mind as he stared into Beaumonte's anxious eyes. "Well, it's all over," he said. "Talking won't bring the kid back."

"I told you we'll find the killer," Ackerman said. "When we do he's all yours. That's settled." He lit a cigarette and glanced through the smoke at Carmody. "Now, we'll get on to something that isn't settled. I had a call from Fanzo. He tells me you beat hell out of him. What's the story there?"

Carmody smiled slightly. "He called me a name I didn't like. Also, he wasn't being helpful. I traced Nancy to his place, and asked him about her. He got lippy so I had to calm him down."

Beaumonte put a hand on his arm. "What did you find out about her, Mike?"

Carmody turned to him and shrugged. "Nothing at all," he said. He was slightly surprised at the pain in Beaumonte's face. He must have loved her, he thought. The imitation lady, the little bottle girl, Beaumonte's true love. It was almost comical.

"Fanzo had no lead on her?" Beaumonte asked him anxiously.

"He was no help."

"She shouldn't have run off, damn it," Beaumonte said, rubbing his forehead.

"She was at your hotel, Mike," Ackerman said. His eyes were on Beaumonte, warning him to keep quiet.

"Was she?" Carmody said, turning to Ackerman. "I'm sorry I missed her."

Ackerman studied him for a few seconds. "One of the cleaning women saw her. But the elevator boys didn't know anything. Probably she just went through the lobby."

"That's odd," Carmody said, making a mental note to take good care of the elevator boys. Then he shrugged. "What's all the fuss about? She's raddled from too much booze, and scared to death after the job Fanzo's boys did on her. She'll turn up when she's had a night's sleep. Can't you wait a day or so until she comes to her senses?"

"No, we can't," Ackerman said. "Beaumonte wants her back right away because he thinks she's a cute kid. I want her back for another reason. She walked out of here with a bundle of bills, Mike, sixty-two thousand bucks to be exact. I want it back, and fast."

"Now that makes sense," Carmody said. He tried to keep the excitement from showing in his face. When they started lying they were scared. "How'd she get her hands on that kind of money?"

"Dan left the numbers pay-off for Northeast laying around," Ackerman said, shaking his head disgustedly. "So we've got to find her."

"Sure," Carmody said. "I'll let you know if I hear anything. By the way, Myerdahl's set to clamp down hard. I guess you know that."

"Let me worry about it, Mike," Ackerman said. "This is the seasonal slump in our racket. There'll be raids, arrests, public displays by all the reform groups. Our boys will have it rough for a while. But these things blow over."

"I wouldn't mind a fight," Beaumonte said. "We've made some of the biggest men in this town. If they try to unload us I'd like the chance to ruin the bastards."

"There isn't going to be any fight," Ackerman told him coldly. "I'm not tossing this city up for grabs. Remember that."

Carmody couldn't help marveling at their cool arrogance. The city was their private hunting ground, created and maintained for their express pleasure. They fed on it. Like protected vultures. How did they do it? he wondered. Just how in God's name did they do it? He remembered a phrase of his father's; in weakness there is strength. The old man had used it to spur them on in school. If you were weak at something, but worked like the devil on it, you would become strong through the weakness. Ackerman used a variation of the principle; the city's weakness was his strength. The average citizen's indifference, cynicism and willingness to compromise, was the weakness that Ackerman used as the foundation of his power.

"You'll keep in touch?" Ackerman asked him as he picked up his hat. "Remember, nothing's changed."

"Sure, nothing's changed," Carmody said. Just Eddie, he thought, forcing a small smile to his lips. Yesterday he'd been alive, today he was dead. That was the only change. "I'll keep in touch," he said to Ackerman. "Don't worry."

Downstairs in the lobby Carmody put through a call to Lieutenant Wilson. "I'm just checking," he said, when Wilson answered. "Any progress yet?"

"No. We've got seventy men in the street and they haven't turned up a lead. But I'm glad you called. A guy has phoned here three times wanting to talk to you. He says he's got some information you can use. He wouldn't tell me anything else, except that he was phoning from a drug store and not to bother tracing the call. I gave him your hotel number, and the number of your brother's home. He said he'd try both places till he got you."

"Okay," Carmody said. "He's probably a gravestone salesman. Now look; I suggest you start digging into Ackerman's background immediately. There's a loose end in his past that can trip him up, I think."

"The D.A. has covered that ground before, Mike. Ackerman always kept in the clear. You know that."

"I don't run the department, it's just a suggestion," Carmody said. "But take it to heart, Jim. I know what I'm talking about."

Wilson hesitated. Then he said, "I'll pass that upstairs. You got anything specific in mind?"

"No, that's the trouble. It could be anything, any time."

"I'll pass it on. Keep in touch."

"Of course, Jim," he said.

Half an hour later Carmody parked his car before Eddie's home in the Northeast. It was almost noon then. Sunlight filtered through the chestnut trees along the block, and faded to a softer tone as it struck the pavements and lawns. The kids playing ball in the street stopped their game to watch Carmody with round solemn eyes. They all know Eddie's dead, I guess, Carmody thought. He was probably a big favorite with them.

The front door was unlocked and he went inside. For a moment he stared about at the familiar furniture and pictures, frowning slightly. Then he walked upstairs to Eddie's room, which was at the rear of the house, overlooking the back yard. He had come here for two reasons: to look through Eddie's things and to wait for a call from the man who had been trying to reach him at Headquarters. Carmody went through Eddie's closet, drawers, desk, looking for nothing and anything. Eddie might have made notes of his identification of Delaney, or he might have noticed that he was being tailed and kept a record of that. Working with trained speed, Carmody opened insurance policies, police department circulars and a bunch of old letters, most of them yellowing notes he had scribbled to Eddie when he was away at school. In the bottom drawer of the bureau were athletic programs, news clippings, class pictures, English compositions with inevitable titles: My First Vacation, When I Grow Up, The Pleasures of Daily Mass. And there were pictures of Mike Carmody, dozens of them; running with a football, getting set to pitch, smiling in his rookie's uniform. There's nothing here, he thought bitterly, unless someone wanted details of the great Mike Carmody's career.

Downstairs again, he stopped with his hands on his hips and looked around the cool dim living room. He frowned at his father's big upright piano, and wondered why Eddie had never got rid of it. It was a space waster and dust trap. But the room played its usual trick on him; the gentle eyes of the *Madonna* stared at him reproachfully; the silent piano and empty chairs made him guiltily aware of the old rupture between him and his father. Exasperated with himself, he picked up a stack of music from the piano and looked at some of the titles. It was the old Irish stuff. *Kevin Barry; Let Erin Remember the Days of Old; O, Blame Not the Bard; Molly Brannigan.* Carmody had heard his father sing them all a hundred times. What had he got out of these songs? Each one told the same poignant story of betrayal and death, of vanished glories, of forsaken people dying grandly in fruitless battles for betrayed causes. Why did he cherish these bitter memories? They belonged a thousand years in the past; why were they important to him in America?

Footsteps sounded on the porch and Carmody put the music back in place hastily. The front door opened and Father Ahearn came into the living room, fanning himself with a limp Panama hat. He stopped in surprise when he saw Carmody standing in the shadows by the piano. "Well, this would make the devil himself believe in miracles," he said. "Coming up the street, I said a little prayer I'd find you here. I wanted to talk to you about Eddie." He sat down slowly and rubbed his eyes with a trembling hand. "The arrangements, you know. I can't get it through my head that the boy is gone."

"About the arrangements, you do what you think is right," Carmody said.

"As a matter of fact, I've done just that," the priest said. "But I thought you'd like to know. The wake will be at Kelly's, starting tonight at eight. Thursday morning at ten there'll be a Requiem High Mass at St. Patrick's. Eddie's district is supplying fifty honorary pallbearers, and the Superintendent is coming. And the Mayor, too, if he can possibly make it."

"That's great," Carmody said.

"It's good of them," Father Ahearn said, nodding slightly, and ignoring Carmody's sarcasm. "Now about the actual pallbearers. I've got five of his good friends from the neighborhood. I've left a place open for you, Mike."

Carmody turned away from him. "You'd better get someone else, Father. I'll be busy."

"Too busy to go to your brother's funeral?" the old priest said softly.

"That's right." He was staring at the music on his father's piano, a bitter look in his eyes. Maybe the old songs had a point. Betrayal and death. They were themes to haunt a man. "I'll be busy looking for his killer, Father," he said. "Let the Superintendent and the Mayor make a show at the funeral. They've got time, I haven't."

"So you're going to avenge Eddie," Father Ahearn said thoughtfully. "In that case, you're a bigger fool than I imagined. You can't avenge him, Mike. Don't you understand that much about yourself?"

"What are you talking about?"

"You don't believe in right and wrong," Father Ahearn said, shaking his head angrily. "In your heart you believe Eddie was killed because he was stupid. Because he wasn't like you. According to the rules you've made, there's no such a thing as sin. So how can you hate something that doesn't exist? By your standards, the men who killed him did no wrong. So how can you hold them to an accounting?" The old priest stood slowly, staring at Carmody with angry, impatient eyes. "Have the guts to be logical at least," he said. "You made the rules to suit yourself, so stick to them, man. Don't think you can flop from one side to the other like some sort of moral acrobat. It won't work, I tell you. You've lost the privilege of hating sin. That belongs to us poor fools who believe in right and wrong."

"All right," Carmody said slowly. "By my rules, I've got to get the men who killed Eddie. Right or wrong, you watch."

"It will do you no good," the priest said.

"I'm not trying to save myself. I'm after a killer."

Father Ahearn looked at him in silence for a few seconds, all the bright anger fading slowly from his face. "Well, I'll be going on," he said.

"Look, wait a minute. Won't you try to understand this?"

"No, I must be going on," he glanced around the room and shook his head slowly. "There was a lot of goodness and decency here, Mike. Stay a bit. Maybe some of it will soak back into you. Good-by, son."

Twenty minutes after the priest had gone the telephone rang. Carmody answered it and a man's voice said, "Is this Mike Carmody, the brother of that cop who got shot?"

Carmody had waited for the call because he knew the value of tipsters; the man with a grudge, the citizen who wanted to assist the law anonymously, even the busybodies—they had helped to break dozens of his cases.

About one in a hundred tips turned out to be helpful. But there was no short cut to find the occasionally reliable informant. The chronic alarmists and crackpots who flooded the police switchboard with calls every day could only be sifted out by patient investigation.

"Yes, this is Mike Carmody," he said. "Who's this?"

"The name wouldn't mean nothing to you. But I'm sorry about your brother."

"So am I," Carmody said. Would Father Ahearn take exception to that? he thought bitterly. Could he at least be sorry? "Well, what's on your mind?"

"Do you remember Longie Tucker?"

"Sure," Carmody said. The man's voice told him nothing; it was high and thin, with a tremor of nerves or fear in it. "What about Longie Tucker?" he asked. Tucker was a local hoodlum who'd drifted out to California six or eight years ago, a big and brutal man with black hair and blunt dark features.

"He's back in town, that's all. I saw him a couple of months ago. And his hair is gray now. The description of your brother's killer said blond hair. But at night under a street light gray hair might look blond."

Carmody nodded slowly. "Where did you see Tucker?"

"In a taproom on Archer Street, right at the corner of Twelfth. I thought of him when I read about your brother."

"I'll run this down," Carmody said. "Thanks."

"I hope it's him, Mr. Carmody."

"What's your interest in this? Paying off an old score?"

"You might say that," the man said in an unsteady voice. "Longie Tucker killed my son. I couldn't prove it, but he did it all right. And my boy never did any harm to anybody. He just got in the way. Well, I won't bother you with it. But I hope he's the man you want."

The phone clicked in Carmody's ear. He frowned at it a moment, then broke the connection and dialed Police. The record room would know where Tucker was hanging out. He wasn't wanted for anything here, as far as Carmody could recall, but some stoolie would have tipped off the police that he was back in town. The clerk at Records answered and Carmody asked for the chief, Sergeant Hogan. After a short wait Hogan came on, and Carmody asked him about Longie Tucker.

"We had a tip when he drifted back to the city," Hogan said. "The detectives in his district watched him for a few weeks, but he seems to be behaving himself. Wouldn't swear he'll keep it up though. He's a stormy one."

"Where is he living?"

"Just a minute . . . here it is . . . 211 Eighteenth Street. A rotten neighborhood, and just where he belongs. Anything else, Mike?"

"No, that's all."

Hogan hesitated, then said, "Tough about the kid brother, Mike."

"Yes, it was," Carmody said. "But we'll get the guy who did it."

"You're damn right."

Carmody hesitated a moment after replacing the phone, debating whether to run this down himself, or to pass it on to Wilson. It was now one-thirty. He wanted to see Nancy as soon as possible; now he knew she'd been lying when she said she had nothing on Ackerman. But Longie Tucker was an even stronger lure. When he got into his car he headed for 211 Eighteenth Street.

# 10

IT WAS AN UNPAINTED WOODEN BUILDING SET IN THE MIDDLE OF A block of municipal decay. Carmody got hold of the owner, a sullen little Spaniard, and asked him about Longie Tucker.

"There is one man on the third floor," the Spaniard said, shrugging carelessly. "I don't care about his name. Maybe you want that one, eh? I go to tell him."

"You go finish your lunch," Carmody said.

"You copper?"

"You just finish lunch, understand, *amigo?*" Carmody said quietly.

"Sure, I don't care," the man said and closed his door.

Carmody went up the stairs quietly. The wallpaper was torn and filthy, and he breathed through his mouth to avoid the greasy, stale smell of the building. Two doors stood open on the third floor, revealing the interiors of small, messy rooms. The third and last door was closed. Carmody eased his gun from the holster and tried the knob. It turned under his hand. He pushed the door inward and stepped into the room, his finger curved and hard against the trigger of his gun.

Longie Tucker lay fully dressed on a sagging bed, one hand trailing on the dusty floor. The room was oppressively hot; the single window was closed and the air was heavy and foul. Tucker breathed slowly and deeply, his body shuddering with the effort. There was an empty whiskey bottle near his hand, and two boxes of pills.

Carmody shook his shoulder until his eyelids fluttered, and then pulled him to a sitting position.

Tucker blinked at him, confused and frightened. "What's the beef?" he muttered.

Carmody's hopes died as he stared at Tucker's drawn face, at the gray skin shot here and there with tiny networks of ruptured blood vessels. The man was half his former size, a sick, decaying husk.

Tucker grinned at him suddenly, disclosing rows of bad teeth. "I get you now, friend. Mike Carmody. Is that right?"

"That's it," Carmody said, putting his gun away.

"I didn't do the job on your brother," Tucker said. "I couldn't do a job on a fly. I ain't left the room in two weeks. I got the bug in my lungs. Ain't that a riot? I go west and get the con."

"Who killed my brother? Do you know?"

"God's truth, I don't. I heard the job was open but I wouldn't have touched it if I could."

"You heard about it? Did they advertise in the papers?"

"Word gets around."

Carmody rubbed the back of his hand across his forehead and turned toward the door.

"Mike, can you spare a buck? I need something to drink."

"No."

"Coppers," Tucker said, making an ugly word of it.

Carmody looked down at him coldly. "Why didn't you save the money you got for shooting people in the back?" Then, disgusted and angry with himself, he took out a roll of bills and threw a twenty on Tucker's bed. "Don't die thinking all coppers are no good," he said.

"Thanks, Mike," Tucker said, grinning weakly as he reached for the money.

Carmody drove across the city to the Empire Hotel and went up past the police detail to Karen's apartment. She opened the door for him and he walked into the cool, dim room. The shades had been drawn against the afternoon sun and Nancy was lying on the studio couch, asleep, an arm thrown over her eyes.

"Must you wake her?" Karen asked him. "She just got to sleep."

"Yes."

"You have to, I suppose," she said dryly.

"Look, I didn't invent this game," Carmody said. Then he felt his temper slipping; the pressure inside him had reached the danger point. Wilson, Father Ahearn and now Karen. They couldn't wait to give him a gratuitous kick in the teeth. "Stop yapping at me," he said abruptly. "If you think I'm a heel write your congressman about it. But lay off me; understand?"

"I understand," she said. "I'm sorry."

The reply confused him; it was simple and straightforward, with no sarcasm running under it. He sat down on the sofa facing the studio couch and lit a cigarette. "I'll give her a few minutes," he said. "How has she been?"

"Not too good. She cried a lot and tried to leave several times. I gave her a few drinks and that seemed to help."

"She had a rough time."

"Yes, she told me about it," Karen said. She sat down beside him on the sofa and shook her head slowly. "What kind of men are they, Mike?"

"Big men, tough men," he said. "With the world in their pockets. They don't believe in anything but the fix. They never heard of Judgment Day."

She didn't answer him. He glanced at her and saw that she was rubbing her forehead with the tips of her fingers. She was wearing a white linen dress and her hair was brushed back above her ears and held with a black ribbon. The faint light in the room ran along her slim legs as she moved one foot in a restless circle. She looked used up; pale and very tired.

"She told me about your break with Ackerman," she said quietly. "And the fight. She thinks you're the greatest guy in the world." Again her voice was simple and straightforward, with no bitterness or sarcasm in it. "That's why I told you I was sorry. You tried to save him. I didn't know that this morning."

"I was a big help," he said bitterly.

"I can't believe he's dead," she said, moving her head slowly from side to side. "Just last night he sat here full of health and hope and big plans. And now he's gone."

"Well, he lived in a straight line," Carmody said, "no detours, no short cuts." He spoke without reflection or deliberation, but the words sounded with a truth he hadn't understood before; it was something to say of a man that the shape and purpose of his life had remained constant against all pressure and temptation.

"It's been a ghastly day," she whispered.

"You ought to get some rest." Without thinking of what he was doing, he put a hand on her back and began to massage the taut muscles of her shoulders and neck. He felt the malleable quality of her body under his fingers, and the small thin points of her shoulder blades, and he wondered irrelevantly what held her together, what supported all of her poise and strength. There was something inside her that was impervious to attack. She had countered his contempt with a confident anger, as if hating him was a privilege she had earned. Father Ahearn's words struck him suddenly: *Hating sin . . . belongs to us poor fools who believe in right and wrong.* Was that her pitch? That she was on the side of the angels?

"Don't do that," she said suddenly.

"What's the matter?"

"I don't want you to touch me."

Carmody took his hand away from her slowly. "I'm not good enough, is that it?"

"Don't make a big thing out of it," she said wearily. "I just don't want you to touch me, that's all. Not because I think you aren't good enough and not because I don't like it." She looked at him, her face a small white blur in the dim room. "Can't you understand that?"

"Wait until you're asked before you say no," he said, wanting to hurt her as she had hurt him.

"That's a cheap thing to say. It isn't what I meant, Mike, I was just—"

"Cheap?" he said, cutting across her sentence. "That sounds funny coming from you." There had been a delayed reaction to the feel of her body under his hand; now the memory of it crowded sharply and turbulently against his control. "What about Danny Nimo?" he said, his voice rising angrily. "Would you call that just a little cheap around the edges?"

"Oh, damn you, damn you," she said, pounding a fist against her knee. "That's all you've got on your mind. You're infatuated with evil. Goodness bores you. Because the devil is more exciting to you than God. He's your kind of people, a real sharpie. All right, I'll tell you about Danny Nimo."

"I don't want to hear about it."

"Oh, yes you do. It's low and depraved. It's your meat, Mike."

"Stop it," he said sharply.

"I lived with Danny Nimo for a year," she said. "This was six years ago. Then there was the automobile accident. Danny paid the bills and took care of me for two years although I was in a cast most of that time. That was goodness of a sort, although you'd never understand it. During that time I had plenty of time to think about myself and Danny. I tried to understand why I had got mixed up with him. But I couldn't figure it out. Not neatly and simply, anyway. My father was an electrician, my mother was a good-hearted woman and I'd had a fair education. And I had a little talent for music. It didn't add to the way I was living. Maybe it was the fun of being a racketeer's girl. Living high without working for it. Being on the inside. I don't know. But I did know that I'd taken a big step in a direction I didn't want to go. So when I was well enough to walk I told him how I felt and left him. There's the whole story. Did you get a kick out of it?"

The bitterness in her voice confused him. "I'm sorry I spoke out of turn," he said slowly. "Who am I to be judging people?"

"Excuse me," she said and stood quickly. He saw that she was close to tears.

"Wait a minute. Please. Is it that easy to get out? Like you did, I mean?"

"Easy?" She was silent a moment. Then she laughed softly. "Try it, if you think it's easy. Just say, 'Forgive me, I've been wrong.' That's all. But keep a drink close by. The words may choke you a little."

" 'Forgive me,' " he said quietly. "Who do I say that to?"

"To whatever you've got left. Maybe yourself."

Carmody shook his head slowly. He couldn't say he'd been wrong and mean it. And how could anybody forgive himself? It was too simple and pat.

Nancy stirred on the couch, and then sat up suddenly, her eyes bright with fear.

"Relax, everything's all right," Karen said gently. "Lie down and finish your sleep."

Nancy recognized Carmody and drew a long, relieved breath. "Old tough Mike," she said, and put her head down on the pillow. She laughed softly. "I guess I had a bad dream."

Carmody sat beside her and took one of her hands. She looked cool and comfortable under the single white sheet.

"How do you feel?" he asked her. He heard Karen cross behind him and leave the room.

"Pretty good, I guess."

"Ackerman is afraid of you," he said. "What have you got on him, baby?"

She smiled at him but it was a shaky effort. "My mother told me a man could get anything from a woman if he called her baby," she said.

"Don't play around, please," he said. "You told Fanzo's men you were going to send Ackerman to jail. What did you mean by that?"

Her eyes filled with tears. "I'm afraid, Mike. I don't want to get mixed up in it."

"They can't hurt you," he said. "You're safe here."

"You don't know them, Mike."

"I know them," he said. "They're scared and on the run. If you keep them running you'll be safe. But if they beat this trouble you're in a bad spot. Don't you see that?"

Karen returned and sat at the foot of the couch. For a moment Nancy stared at her in silence, her eyes round and frightened in her childish face. "Should I tell him?" she said softly.

"I think so," Karen said. "It would be a big thing to do."

"All right," Nancy said, the words tumbling out rapidly. "Ackerman is afraid of a man named Dobbs. Dobbs lives in New Jersey. That's all I know, Mike, I swear it."

"Dobbs?" The name meant nothing to Carmody. "How did you find this out?"

"Beaumonte told me. When he was drunk one night. You see, something had gone wrong and Ackerman phoned him and raised the devil for fifteen or twenty minutes. When it was all over Dan was in a terrible mood. He drank a full bottle of whiskey, and then started knocking the furniture around and smashing bottles and records all over the place. I never saw him so wild. When I finally got him to bed, he started talking about Dobbs. He didn't know what he was saying, I knew. But he said that Dobbs was the only guy smarter than Ackerman, the only guy Ackerman was afraid of. It meant nothing at all to me. The next day I pretended I'd been drunk too. Beaumonte seemed a little scared. He asked me half-a-dozen times if I remembered what he'd been talking about, but I played dumb. Listening out of turn is just as bad as talking out of turn."

"You must have used Dobbs' name with Fanzo's men," Carmody said.

"I guess I did," Nancy said sadly.

"And it went back to Ackerman." Carmody stood up and turned the name around in his mind. He knew men named Dobbs but none who fitted the role of Ackerman's blackmailer. "Where's the phone?" he asked Karen.

"In the kitchen."

Carmody went into the tiny kitchen, took the phone from the wall and dialed his Headquarters. When the clerk answered, he said, "I'm looking for George Murphy, the reporter. Is he around?"

"Well, he was here half an hour ago. He said he was going up to the press room, I think. Wait, I'll switch you."

The clerk transferred the call and another voice said, "Press room."

"Is George Murphy around?"

"Hold on. He's talking to his desk on another phone."

"Okay."

Murphy came on a moment later. "Hello?"

"Mike Carmody, George. Are you busy right now?"

"Nothing that won't keep. What's up?"

"I want to talk to you. Can you meet me at the South end of City Hall on Market Street in about fifteen minutes?"

"Sure, Mike. I'll be the man with the press card in his hatband."

Carmody walked into the living room and said to Karen, "I'm going now." His whole manner had changed; the lead was in his hands and his hunter's instincts had driven everything else from his mind.

"Be careful, Mike," Nancy said. Karen watched him in silence.

"I will." He left the apartment and went down to his car.

Murphy was waiting for him at the north entrance of the Hall, his hat pushed back on his big round head, a fresh cigar in his mouth. He looked sleepy and comfortable, as if he'd just finished dinner; but behind those drowsing eyes was a mind like an immense and orderly warehouse. "Hi, Mike," he said, taking the cigar from his mouth.

"Let's walk," Carmody said. "What I've got is very private."

"Okay."

They strolled across the avenue that wound around the Hall, and started down Market Street, walking leisurely through the crowds that were pouring out of shops and office buildings.

Without looking at Murphy, Carmody said, "I've got the start of the biggest story you ever saw. But I need help. When I get the whole thing, it's all yours. How about it?"

"Let's hear the start of it," Murphy said, putting the cigar in his mouth and clasping his hands behind him.

"Ackerman is afraid of a man named Dobbs," Carmody said. "Dobbs lives in New Jersey. That's all I know. I want you to help me find him."

"It doesn't sound right," Murphy said, after walking along a few feet in silence. "Ackerman's not afraid of anybody. He's got rid of anybody who could hurt him, and don't bet against that."

"My tip is straight," Carmody said. "If we can find Dobbs, and spade up what he's got on Ackerman, then you've got a story."

Murphy took the cigar from his mouth and looked at it as they waited for a light. "The story I'll get is your obituary, Mike. You can't buck Ackerman now. Six months from now, maybe. But the city isn't ready yet."

"I'm ready," Carmody said. "To hell with the city."

"You couldn't keep them from killing your brother," Murphy said thoughtfully. "What makes you think you can stay healthy?"

"We're different types," Carmody said.

"I guess you are," Murphy said cryptically. Then he shrugged his big soft shoulders. "Let's walk over to the office. Maybe we can find this Dobbs in the library. But I don't see much hope for it."

They spent the next three hours in the *Express* morgue, studying items on those Dobbses whose fame or notoriety had rated interment in this mausoleum of newsprint. There were obits, news and sports stories, announcements of promotions, luncheons, engagements, divorces, weddings. Murphy pawed through the yellowing clips with patient efficiency, occasionally embellishing the stories with scraps from the warehouse of his memory. Finally, he weeded out all but five clippings. "I'll check these," he said. "Each one of these guys knew Ackerman in the old days. And that's where the dirt is, I'll bet. Here we got Micky Dobbs, the fight promoter. And Judge Dobbs who worked for Ackerman before he retired. And Max Dobbs, the bondsman. Tim Dobbs, the fire chief." Murphy grinned crookedly. "He used to condemn joints that didn't cooperate with Ackerman. And last is Murray Payne Dobbs, who was a big trucker before Ackerman ran him out of the state." He made a pile of the clips and then got up from the table and rubbed the top of his head. "You want me to handle this? I can do it through the paper without causing too much talk."

"Okay. Call me when you learn something."

"Where'll you be? At the hotel?"

"No. I'm staying at the old man's."

Murphy glanced at him queerly. "I thought you hated that place."

"It's quieter out there," Carmody said.

At ten-thirty that night a slim, dark-haired man stepped into a telephone booth, fished in the return slot out of habit then dropped a coin and dialed a number. When a voice answered, he said, "Sammy Ingersoll. I got a message for Mr. Ackerman."

"Just a minute."

"What's the word?" Ackerman said, a few seconds later.

"Carmody's bedded down for the night. At his brother's home in the Northeast. He's been huddling most of the evening with a guy from the *Express*. Murphy."

"What about the girl?"

"Only got a guess so far. But it's a good one, I think. She's stashed away in the apartment of that dame who saw the shooting. Karen something-or-other."

"You don't get paid for guessing," Ackerman said angrily.

"I know, Mr. Ackerman. But Carmody took some dame there. I got that from a neighbor who was up early with an earache. This neighbor saw Carmody and the girl go in about four in the morning. I can't check it because they got police guards there. In the lobby and up at her apartment."

"All right," Ackerman said, after a short pause. "We'll handle the police detail. You've earned a vacation. Take a couple of weeks in Miami and send us the bill. And keep what you told me to yourself."

Sammy made a small circle with his lips. His sharp little face was completely blank. "Mr. Beaumonte asked me to let him know if I learned anything."

"I said to keep it to yourself. You'd better not misunderstand me."

"No chance of that. I'm on my way."

When he left the booth, Sammy wiped his damp forehead with a handkerchief. There was no future in getting in the middle between Bill Ackerman and Dan Beaumonte. Miami seemed like a beautiful idea to him, not just for two or three weeks but maybe two or three years.

# 11

CARMODY SLEPT THAT NIGHT IN HIS OLD ROOM. IN THE MORNING HE discovered that someone had taken care of the things he had left here years ago. His suits hung in plastic bags, and his bureau drawers were full of clean linen. Carmody looked at them for a moment, remembering his father's finicky concern over his and Eddie's things. Neatness wasn't his strong point, but he had worked hard at being father and mother to them, repainting their wagons, trimming their hair, getting after them about muddy shoes and dirty fingernails. "Cleanliness is next to godliness," he had usually intoned while herding them to the bathroom. I suppose he always expected me to come back, Carmody thought.

He had finished a breakfast of orange juice and coffee when the phone rang. It was Murphy.

"Can I pick you up in about twenty minutes?" he said. "We got some work to do."

"What did you find out?"

"Something damned interesting. I'll be out as soon as I can."

Carmody lit a cigarette and walked into the living room. The early sun slanted through the windows, brightening the somber tones of the furniture and pictures. For some reason the room didn't depress him this morning. He thought about it as he smoked and looked at his father's piano. Ever since he had started trying to save Eddie his thoughts had been returning restlessly to the old man. He should have no time for anyone but Ackerman. His thoughts should be on what Murphy had dug up, but instead they swerved irrelevantly into the past. Back to unimportant details. Like his clothes hanging neatly and cleanly in the closet upstairs. And an image of the old man at the piano booming out something for the Offertory. *Redemptor Mundi Deus.* Even now the somehow frightening Latin words could send a shiver down his spine. But why? They were just words, weren't they?

A footstep sounded on the porch and Carmody went quickly to the door. Father Ahearn smiled at him through the screen. "I just thought I'd see if you were home," he said.

Carmody let him in and the old man sat down gratefully.

"It will be hot today." He sighed and looked up at Carmody. "You asked for understanding from me yesterday but I left you. That wasn't the way for a priest to behave. I'm sorry."

"That's okay."

"I wish I could help you. You know, Eddie gave me his will the last time I spoke with him. He wanted you to have this house. Did he tell you that?"

"No, he didn't," Carmody said slowly.

"You don't want it, do you?"

"I haven't thought about it. But I guess not. Why should I?"

"You're a stubborn man," Father Ahearn said. "Just like your father. If you understood him, you might understand yourself, Mike. He was a proud man, and very set in his ways. But they were pretty good ways." The old priest smiled slowly. "Remember how touchy he was about his singing. And the truth was he didn't have a very good voice."

"But big," Carmody said.

"Oh, it was that, I grant you." Father Ahearn got to his feet with an effort and went to the piano. "Eddie kept all the music, I see." He picked up one of the sheets and smiled at it. *"O, Blame Not the Bard."* His eyes went across the music. "'Twas treason to love her, twas death to defend," he murmured, shaking his head. Then he looked sharply at Carmody. "That's something to remember about your father, Mike. He wasn't allowed to love his own country. Like thousands of other Irishmen, that love was a kind of treason. Can't you understand their bitterness when their sons went wrong over here? Instead of being grateful for a country to love and live in, some of the sons seemed bent only on spoiling the place. That hurt men like your father. It makes them angry and unreasonable, which isn't the best tone to use on hot-headed young men. Can't you see that, Mike?"

"Well, it's all over, anyway," Carmody said. "He's dead and I'm still the rotten apple. Talking won't change it."

"How did you get so far away from us?" Father Ahearn said, shaking his head slowly.

"I don't know. It wasn't one decision." Carmody shrugged. "Little by little, I guess."

"Couldn't you try coming back the same way? Little by little, I mean."

"Admit I've been wrong? Ask for forgiveness." Carmody turned away from him and pounded a fist into his palm. "It's no good. If I did that I'd come to a dead-center stop. And I can't stop while my brother lies dead and his murderers are living like kings." Turning back, he stared angrily and hopelessly at the priest. "All I've got is a certain kind of power and drive. I can do things. The way I am, that is. But I'd be nothing if I turned into a confused sinner, begging for forgiveness."

"You'll be nothing until you see that Eddie's murder was wrong," Father Ahearn said sharply. "Not because he was your brother, or a police officer, but because he was a human being whose life belonged to God."

A car door slammed at the curb. Through the windows Carmody saw George Murphy coming up the walk. "I've got to be going, Father," he said, relieved to end this painful and pointless argument.

"Remember this," the old priest said, and put a hand quickly on his arm. "Don't get thinking you're hopeless. St. Francis de Sales said, 'Be patient with everyone, but above all with yourself.' Keep that in mind. All sinners flatter themselves that they are hopeless. But no one is, son."

"Okay, okay," Carmody said shortly; he wanted to be gone, he wanted no more talk about sin and forgiveness. Turning, he left the house and met Murphy on the front porch.

"We've got to take a ride," Murphy said. "You set to go?"

"Yes."

When Father Ahearn came down the steps, Murphy's sedan was moving away from the curb. He watched until it had disappeared at the corner, and then shook his head and started back to the rectory. His expression was weary and troubled.

"Well, what is it?" Carmody asked, as Murphy headed through the bright streets toward the River Drive.

"The Dobbses we found in the clips didn't add up to anything," Murphy said. He looked tired and hot; his day-old beard was a black smudge along his jaws, and his eyes were narrowed against the sunlight. "I worked all night on them and didn't get a lead. But I found another Dobbs, and he could be our man."

"Who's that?"

"This fell into my lap, from an old guy named Sweeney who's been a rewrite man on our paper since the year One. I got talking to him this morning, and he told me about a Billy Dobbs who worked on the *Intelligencer* years back. Not a reporter, but a photographer. The only memorable thing about Dobbs, Sweeney told me, was that he once stumbled accidentally into a bank stick-up. This was in '38. Dobbs was coming in from a routine assignment, driving south on Market Street, when three guys ran out of the old Farmer's Bank with satchels of dough and guns in their hands. They killed two cops right in the street, and a bullet hit the windshield of Dobbs' car. He stopped and scrambled into a gutter to get out of the fire. All he thought about was taking cover instead of taking pictures. He could have been a hero by photographing the gunmen, but he'd probably have been a dead one. That's what he said, at any rate. Two years later Dobbs quit the paper and that's all Sweeney could tell me about him." Murphy glanced at Carmody. "You see where this might be leading?"

"I've got an idea."

"Right now we're going to where Dobbs used to live. A guy in the *Intelligencer's* personnel section gave me his old address. It's in Avondale, in a pretty average neighborhood. Dobbs lived there with his mother and father. But they've all been gone for a long time."

"We'll have to ring a lot of doorbells to find someone who knew them," Carmody said.

"I can't think of any short cut," Murphy said, and rubbed a hand wearily over his face. "I wish there was. I could use some sleep."

They parked in front of the two-story wooden house in which the Dobbs family had lived, and got out of the car. The street was shady and quiet, in a neighborhood that was deteriorating steadily but gradually.

"You want the odd or even addresses?" Murphy said dryly.

"I'll take the other side. Let's go."

It was in the middle of the afternoon and two blocks from the Dobbs home that Carmody got his hands on a lead. She was a pleasant little woman, starched and clean in a blue house dress, and she had known the Dobbses very well. "Funny you should ask," she said, tilting her gray head at Carmody. "I was just thinking of Ed and Martha the other day. Something brought them back to mind, what I just can't remember. But come in, won't you? No sense baking there in the sun."

In the dim old-fashioned parlor, Carmody said, "Do you remember when they moved away?"

"Yes, it was just before the war. The Second World War, I mean. About '40 or '41. Ed quit his job on the cars, and off they went. To California."

"Did you know their son? Billy Dobbs?"

"Indeed I did. He was a quiet, steady youngster, and got himself a fine job on the paper. Took pictures for them. We used to see his name on them sometimes. Fires, accidents, all sorts of things you'd never expect little Billy Dobbs to be mixed up in."

"But he quit his job, didn't he?"

"That's right. Moved off to another paper. It worried his mother, I can tell you, but it turned out pretty well, I guess."

"Do you know what paper he went to?"

"His mother told me but I forgot," the woman said, with a little sigh.

"Anybody around here ever hear from the Dobbses?"

"No, not for years anyway. Old Mr. Johnson, he's dead now, looked them up when he was in California. He was out seeing his son who was in camp there, you see. And the Dobbses had come into good luck. Some relative of theirs in Australia had died, they told Mr. Johnson, and left them a nice little bit of money. They were living in style, he said. Flower garden, nice home, a maid even." She smiled and shook her head. "A far cry from the days when they were on the cars."

"Was their son around?"

She frowned. "Mr. Johnson never said anything about Billy . . ."

Carmody went quickly down the stairs to the sidewalk and looked along the street for Murphy. He saw him in the next block and yelled at him to get his attention. When Murphy turned, Carmody shouted, "Let's go. I've got it . . ."

"Everything fits," Carmody said, as they headed back toward his home. "Dobbs did take pictures of the stick-up. He waited two years, probably protected himself from every angle and then parlayed them into a pension plan."

"Nice guy, Dobbs," Murphy said, nodding. "Didn't forget the old folks either. The thing is, I guess, to find Dobbs."

"We won't find him," Carmody said. "Ackerman has sent him on the road by now. Dobbs is on his way to South America or Newfoundland, I'd bet."

"Then we got to find the pictures," Murphy said.

"I want to think about that angle a little," Carmody said.

"We got something good here, Mike. This is what Delaney had on Ackerman. He must know about Dobbs. And that pressure was strong enough to make Ackerman take the big risk of killing your brother. So if we get Dobbs' pictures we get Bill Ackerman. On a rap he can't beat."

"That's it." Carmody glanced at Murphy's tired profile. "You'd have made a good cop, George."

"So would you, Mike," Murphy said. Then he rubbed his lips with the back of his hand. "Forget that; okay? It's no time for cracks."

"Nobody's mad," Carmody said bitterly.

They said good-by in front of the house and Carmody went inside and tossed his hat on the piano. He was on his way to the kitchen for a beer when the phone began to ring. Picking it up, he said, "Yes?"

"Mike, this is Karen. The police took me downtown this morning to look at more pictures. There was no guard here while I was away." Her voice began to tremble. "Nancy's gone, Mike."

"Who picked you up?" he said sharply.

"A Captain Green. From the records station."

Green was on Ackerman's leash, Carmody knew. Technically, he had the right to bring a witness downtown . . . And someone else could have pulled off the police guard . . . Carmody swore furiously.

"Stay right there," he said. "I'm coming over."

Nancy might have walked out by herself, he thought, as he ran down to his car. But in his heart he knew he was kidding himself. This was Ackerman's work. He wanted her and he had taken her.

# *12*

IT WAS TWENTY MINUTES LATER WHEN HE REACHED KAREN'S APARTMENT. She let him in and sat down on the edge of the sofa, locking her hands together in her lap.

"I've got to know just when this happened," he said. "Right to the minute."

"I'll try to remember."

Carmody saw that she was holding herself under control with an effort. Her small face was pale and strained, and her lower lip was trembling slightly. "If you can hang on you'll be helping her," he said. Sitting beside her, he took her clenched hands between his and rubbed them gently. "Start from the time the police picked you up here."

"That was ten o'clock. Captain Green got here then and said he wanted me to come downtown. I told him I'd get ready. Nancy was frightened. She didn't want to stay alone, but I said it would be all right." Karen drew a long breath and a little tremor went through her body. "I didn't get back until two-thirty. Captain Green showed me dozens of pictures and took his time about it. When we got back he made me wait downstairs until he radioed the local district and told them to put the police details back at the apartment. That was the first I knew that they'd been taken off. I was scared then. And when I came in I saw that she was gone."

Carmody looked around the room. "Was there any sign of a struggle?"

"No. But she left a diamond ring on the basin in the bathroom." Her hands tightened in his. "Wouldn't she have taken that if she decided to walk out?"

"I don't know. She might have forgotten it." Carmody didn't believe this and he saw that Karen didn't either. "We'll find her," he said, squeezing her hand tightly. Then he went quickly to the phone in the kitchen and dialed Police. It took him a minute to get through to Wilson. "Jim, Mike Carmody," he said. "I want to report a missing person. It could be a kidnap job."

"I've been trying to get you, Mike. You've got to come in. Myerdahl didn't buy my brief on you. He insists—"

"Jim, hold that, will you?" Carmody said. "This is the lead to Ackerman. Let's get it rolling. We can talk about Myerdahl later."

Wilson hesitated. Then he said, "Let's have it," in his crisp official voice.

"The missing person is a girl, Nancy Drake. She's blonde with blue eyes and a good figure. About five-three, a hundred and ten, I'd say."

"Nancy Drake? Isn't that Dan Beaumonte's mistress?"

"That's right. She left, or was kidnaped from, the Empire Hotel this morning, sometime between ten o'clock and two-thirty."

"The Empire? That's Karen Stephanson's hotel, right?"

"Yes. I stuck Nancy in her apartment. I thought she'd be safe here with guards at both doors."

"Damn it, what are you trying to do?" Wilson demanded angrily. "Did it occur to you that Beaumonte's girl might have blown the head off our only witness? You said you'd work straight with me, Mike. But you can't drop the prima donna act, even for your brother's murder."

"I guessed wrong," Carmody said. "I didn't figure Ackerman would pull the guard detail off."

"That was a mighty bad guess. Look, now; I'll get an alarm out for this Nancy girl. But you get in here, understand? And bring your badge and gun. Myerdahl wants 'em both."

"Okay," Carmody said bitterly, and replaced the phone with a bang. When he returned to the living room Karen was pacing the floor nervously. "I can't forget that I talked her into helping you," she said.

"This isn't your fault. It's mine."

"She'd just written a letter to her agent," Karen said, putting the palms of her hands against her forehead. "She was sure she'd started back uphill."

"The police of three states will be looking for her," Carmody said. "Remember that." He put his hands gently on her slim square shoulders. "I'll call you as soon as I hear anything," he said.

Carmody walked through the swinging wooden gates of the Homicide Bureau twenty minutes later, and nodded to Dirksen and Abrams who were working at their desks with a suspicious show of industry. Dirksen pointed to Wilson's closed door and said softly, "Very high-priced help at work, Mike. Myerdahl and the D.A."

Carmody smiled faintly at him and rapped on the door. Wilson opened it and said, "Come on in, Mike."

"Anything on the girl yet?"

"No, but the alarm is out."

Carmody walked into the office and took off his hat. Captain Myerdahl, acting superintendent of the department, sat in a straight chair beside

Wilson's desk, puffing on a short black pipe. Standing at the windows was Lansing Powell, the city's District Attorney. Myerdahl was a short stocky man with a coarse dark complexion, and small blue eyes that glittered like splinters of ice behind his rimless glasses. He was a tough and shrewd cop, who took his responsibilities with fanatic intensity. As a rookie he had supported his wife and family on two-thirds of his meager salary and spent the remainder on Berlitz lessons to modify his heavy German accent. He had moved up slowly through the ranks, never compromising his standards, and giving every job the full measure of his dogged strength and intelligence. Detectives and patrolmen hated the discipline he enforced but they relished working for him; in Myerdahl's district a cop could do his job twenty-four hours a day without worrying about stepping on sensitive toes.

Myerdahl stood solidly behind his men when they were doing honest work, and he couldn't be intimidated by threats or pressure. Now he looked up at Carmody and took the pipe from his mouth. "I asked the lieutenant for an unfitness report on you this morning," he said bluntly. "But I didn't get it. Instead I got some excuses. Well, I don't take excuses. I've got no use for wealthy cops. They're in the wrong business. So you better find another one."

Carmody's expression remained impassive. "They should have tied a can to me years ago," he said. "Was that all you had to say?"

"That's all I got to say."

"How about listening to me then?" Carmody said quietly. "I've got a case against Bill Ackerman. I want to give it to you."

"Hah! You think I'd believe you?"

"Forget about me. Listen to the facts. Ackerman's your target, isn't he?"

"I'll get him with men who aren't carrying his money."

"Now just a minute," Powell said, cutting calmly through the tension. "I'm interested in Carmody's information, Superintendent." He came around Wilson's desk, a tall, slender man who wore horn-rimmed glasses and conservative clothes. There was a scholarly, good-humored air about him, the intangible endowment of a good family, excellent schools and a background of noteworthy achievement in the law and politics. But his graceful manners camouflaged a shrewd and vigorous intelligence, as dozens of defense attorneys had learned to their clients' dismay. Perching on the corner of Wilson's desk, he smiled impersonally at Carmody. "In my job I'm forced to use instruments of dubious moral value," he said. "I understand the superintendent's position, but I can't afford the philosophic luxury of observing absolute standards. Call it fighting fire with fire, or whatever you like. I don't justify it or condemn it. It is a condition I accept. However, let me say this much, without any personal rancor, I don't like using crooked cops. To me they're a lost and frightening breed

of men, and I would prefer to keep as far away from them as possible."
He studied Carmody's hard impassive face, a curious frown gathering
about his eyes. "You're what some people call a smart operator, I suppose.
I've known others like you, and I think I understand your reasoning
processes. When you join the force it occurs to you in time that there is
a way to make the job pay off more handsomely than the taxpayers
intended. In short, to cheat, to trade on your position of public trust.
What doesn't occur to you is that the same course is open to every man
in the department. They can cheat, or play it straight. Thank God, most
of them play it straight. But you don't give them credit for that. You see
their honesty as stupidity, their integrity as a lack of nerve. This is why I
find you rather frightening." Powell shrugged and crossed his long legs.
But he was still frowning thoughtfully at Carmody. "You rationalize your
dishonesty with more of the same deadly cynicism," he said slowly. "You
say, 'If I don't take the graft then someone else will.' This isn't logic, of
course, it's merely an expression of your lack of faith. If you were logical
you would test the proposition by being honest. Instead, you simply assume
that everyone else is dishonest. You prejudge the world by yourself and
steal with the comforting defense that you're only beating the other crooks
to it. The thing you—"

"That's an excellent speech, sir," Carmody said abruptly. "I'd like to
hear the rest of it sometime. I mean that. But *I* want to talk now."

Powell nodded. "Okay, Carmody. What have you to tell us?"

"A story about a man named Dobbs. A man Ackerman is afraid of."
He gave it to them in rapid detail, his trained mind presenting each fact
in its damaging order. When he finished the attitude of the men facing
him had changed; Wilson was grinning with excitement, Myerdahl had
hunched forward to the edge of his chair and Powell was walking back
and forth before the desk with a grim little look on his face. And the
atmosphere of the room had changed, too; it was charged now with
excitement and tension.

"Well," Carmody said, "is it a case?"

"It may very well be," Powell said. "It's a logical inference that Dobbs
took photographs of Ackerman participating in a robbery and murder.
The robbery isn't important, but the murder can still send him to the
chair. And I'm quite sure that Dobbs has taken every precaution to make
his case against Ackerman airtight. The pictures are probably in a vault,
and his attorney probably has a letter instructing him to present them to
the police in the event anything sudden and fatal happens to Dobbs.
Ackerman must be efficiently trapped, or he wouldn't have paid off all
these years. He would simply have shot him. So our job is to find the
pictures."

"We can get them," Myerdahl said, thumping the desk with his fist.

"A court order can open vaults. And we'll smoke out his lawyer. Or if the letter is with his family, we'll drag them back and make them talk."

"It will finish Ackerman," Powell said, turning to Carmody. "But it doesn't touch Beaumonte or the organization."

"I can wrap them up for you," Carmody said.

"How's that?"

"I've got a witness they won't like," Carmody said. "A man who knows every name, every date and every pay-off connected with the city's rackets. He's been on Beaumonte's payroll for six years and he's willing to talk. Can you use him?"

"I most certainly can," Powell said. "Who is he?"

"Me," Carmody said quietly.

A silence grew and stretched in the smoky room. Wilson let out his breath slowly and Myerdahl rubbed his jaw and studied Carmody suspiciously. "Well," Powell said at last. "You'll be an almighty big help. But since there's a good chance you'll go to jail, why are you doing this?"

"I'm tired of that question," Carmody said, shrugging his wide shoulders. "And what difference does it make? If we get a case, what else matters?"

"Several things," Powell said, smiling slightly. "The most important thing, however, is to make men like you recognize the difference between right and wrong, to make you realize that you're responsible for understanding the distinction. We can get Ackerman and Beaumonte a good deal easier than the border-line cases who support them by a cynical indifference to their moral obligations. That's why I'm interested in your motive. Is it just a grudge? Or is it something a little different, a little better perhaps?"

Carmody was about to speak when the phone rang. Wilson picked it up and said, "Yes, go ahead." He listened a moment, a slow frown spreading over his face, and then he nodded and said shortly, "Let me know the minute anything else comes in." Replacing the phone he looked at Carmody. "That might be Nancy Drake, Mike. Radio has picked up a report from a New Jersey traffic car. They've got an accident a mile south of Exit 21 on the Turnpike. The victim fits the description of Nancy Drake. But the identification isn't positive."

"It's positive," Carmody said slowly. "They took her out and killed her. Because she gave me the lead that may hang them." There was no anger in him, only a cold and terrible determination. He looked from Powell to Myerdahl, breathing slowly and deeply. "You two did all the talking so far," he said. "Now listen: while you were talking they killed her like they'd swat a fly. Dobbs will be next, then me, then any other fool who gets in their way. They know they can get away with it because while their guns are banging you sit talking and drowning out the noise. There's no case against them here, there's nothing but talk. And I'm sick of it.

You treated me like a leper because I wanted to help and I'm sick of that, too. Now I'm going to settle this without any more conversation."

Carmody backed toward the door and Wilson said, "Don't go off half-cocked, Mike."

"More talk," Carmody said, smiling unpleasantly. "Keep it up! Mr. Powell, tell them about right and wrong and the evil in the city's scout packs. Myerdahl, come up with some stories of your early days as a cop. Talk your heads off, but for God's sake don't do anything."

"I'd suggest you relax if I thought it would do any good," Powell said pleasantly.

"You're suspended!" Myerdahl shouted, leaping to his feet.

"You're suspended, too," Carmody said. "In a big tub of virtuous incompetence. Maybe that's why I went crooked. Because I got tired of you good little people who can't get anything done."

He walked out and pulled the door shut behind him with an explosive bang.

State troopers had channeled all northbound traffic into one lane to by-pass the scene of the accident. The darkness was split by the red lights of squad cars parked on the grass off the highway. Carmody pulled up behind them and walked down to the gully where a fire-blackened convertible lay upside down, its wheels pointing grotesquely and helplessly at the sky. Men were working around it, measuring skid tracks, beginning the tests on brakes, wheel alignment, ignition system. A uniformed patrolman stood beside a small, blanket-covered figure on the ground. Carmody walked over to him and said, "Has the doctor gone?"

"Yes. He couldn't do anything. What's your business?" he added.

"Metropolitan police," Carmody said opening his wallet. "I want to check an identification."

"Sure, Sarge. Go ahead."

Carmody knelt down and drew the blanket gently away from the small figure on the ground. He stared at her a moment, his face grim and hard in the flaring shadows thrown by the police lights. The fire, rather miraculously, hadn't touched her face or hair. She must have crawled halfway out the window before the smoke and flame got her, he thought. For half a moment he stared at the frozen, inanimate pain on her face, at the leaves and twigs caught in her tangled blonde hair. He kept his eyes away from the rest of her body. You didn't get back to show business, he thought. You just got murdered. He put the blanket over her face and got to his feet.

"Do you know what happened?" he asked the uniformed cop.

"I heard the talk," the cop said respectfully; the look in Carmody's face made him anxious to help. "She was alone in the car when the first motorist got to her and pulled her out. But nobody saw the crash. She lost control about fifty yards from the bridge, judging from the skid tracks. Then she barreled down here and tipped over."

It was phony all the way, Carmody knew. Nancy had never been behind the wheel of a car in her life.

"She didn't have much of a chance," the cop said, and shook his head. "Not a ghost."

Carmody walked up the grade to his car. The single line of traffic passed him on his left, moving slowly despite the shouted orders from the troopers. Everyone wants a glimpse of tragedy, he thought, while faces peered out of the slowly moving cars, eager for the sounds and smells of disaster. Carmody looked down the hill at the blanket-draped figure on the ground, and then he slipped his car into gear and headed back to the city.

Half an hour later he rapped on the door of Beaumonte's apartment. Footsteps sounded and Beaumonte, in his shirt-sleeves, opened the door, the big padded roll of his body swelling tightly against the waistband of his trousers. Without a jacket he didn't look formidable; he was just another fat man in a silk shirt and loud suspenders.

"I'm in kind of a hurry, Mike," he said, not moving aside. "What's on your mind?"

The long room behind was empty and Carmody saw three pigskin bags in the middle of the floor. "You're taking a trip?" he said.

"That's right." Beaumonte's smile was a grudging concession which didn't relieve the annoyance in his face. "I'm catching a plane in half an hour."

"You asked me to find Nancy," Carmody said. He walked into the room, forcing Beaumonte to step aside, and tossed his hat in a chair.

"Well, where is she?" Beaumonte asked him anxiously.

Carmody faced him with his hands on his hips. "She's under a blanket, Dan. They pulled her out of a wreck on the Turnpike about an hour ago. She's dead."

"Dead?" Beaumonte stared at him incredulously. "No, you're kidding," he whispered. His face had turned white and his lips were beginning to tremble. "She can't be dead," he said, shaking his head quickly.

"I saw her. She burned to death."

Beaumonte put both hands over his face and lurched blindly toward the sofa. He sat down, his body sprawling slackly on the cushions, and began to cry in a soft, anguished voice.

Carmody lit a cigarette and flipped the match toward the ashtray. He watched Beaumonte's efforts to get himself under control with no expression at all on his face.

"I loved that girl," Beaumonte said, in a choking voice. His eyes were closed but tears welled under the lids and coursed slowly down his white cheeks. "I loved her and she never looked at another guy. She was all mine. Where did it happen? Who was with her?"

"She was alone," Carmody said.

It took several seconds for this to register. When it did, Beaumonte opened his eyes and struggled up to a sitting position. "She never drove, she couldn't," he said hoarsely. "What are you saying, Mike?"

"She was murdered," Carmody said.

Beaumonte shook his head so quickly that tears were shaken from his fat cheeks. "Ackerman said he wouldn't hurt her," he cried in a rising voice. "He said he wouldn't touch her."

"And you believed him. Like I believed you when you said you'd give Eddie forty-eight hours."

"Why did he kill her?" Beaumonte said, mumbling the words through his trembling lips. "He didn't have to do that. I could have kept her quiet."

"She was killed because she told me about Dobbs," Carmody said coldly. "That's going to hang Ackerman. And it may hang you, too, Dan."

Beaumonte began to weep. "Mike, please. I been through enough."

"You've put hundreds of people on the same rack," Carmody said bitterly. "I could laugh at you if you were lying in hell with your back broken. Now get this: you and Ackerman are going down the drain and I helped pull the plug. I'm going with you, but that seems a fair price. You can sweat out the next six months in jail, or you can die right now. The choice is yours."

"What do you mean?"

Carmody took out his revolver and shoved the barrel deep into Beaumonte's wide stomach. "I want the name of the guy who killed my brother," he said gently. "And his address."

"Ackerman made the plans," Beaumonte said, his voice going up in a squeal. "He got a guy named Joie Langley from Chicago."

"Is he still in town?"

Beaumonte wet his lips as he stared into Carmody's cold gray eyes. "Don't shoot, Mike," he whispered. "I'm talking. Langley's staying in a rooming house on Broome Street. The address is 4842. Ackerman didn't want him to leave while there was a witness who could finger him. If he couldn't get rid of the witness, then he planned to get rid of Langley. Langley's got no money at all, and he can't move. He's a bad kid, Mike."

"I'll make an angel out of him," Carmody said, putting away his gun. "Now don't move until I'm gone."

When the door closed Beaumonte struggled to his feet, breathing heavily, his eyes glistening with tears. Sweat was streaming down his body, plastering his silk shirt to the slabs of flesh that armored his ribs. He walked around the room, wandering in a circle, occasionally moaning like a man goaded by an intense, recurring pain. Finally, he went to the telephone, lifted the receiver and dialed a number. Staring at the wall, he wet his lips and attempted desperately to get himself under control.

A voice said, "Yes?"

"Ackerman? This is Dan."

"I thought you'd gone. I told you the ceiling was ready to fall in," Ackerman told him shortly.

"Carmody's picking up Joie Langley, Bill. He's spread the story about Dobbs. Now he's after his brother's killer. I thought you'd like to know."

"Is he alone?"

"Yes." Beaumonte put the phone down abruptly and walked to the bar. While he was making himself a strong drink the phone began to ring. Beaumonte stared at it and sipped his drink. He wasn't crying any more; his pale face was set in a haggard expression of hate. "Go after him, Bill," he whispered to the ringing phone. "He'll pay you off for me, he'll send you to hell."

# 13

BROOME STREET STRETCHED FROM THE RIVER TO THE HEART OF THE city and terminated in a dead end a half-block below the Municipal Building. Its upper section was smart and prosperous, with excellent shops and department stores facing each other across a broad asphalt surface. But the street changed character as it wound through warehouses and slums to the river. Overhead lights gave way to street lamps set far apart, and the gutters were clotted with newspapers, garbage and refuse. The tall, red brick buildings had been converted into rooming houses for dock laborers, and the neon signs of cheap bars glittered at every corner.

Carmody parked in the 4800 block and when he switched off the motor a dark thick silence settled around him. The warehouses and garages were locked up at this hour, and the dawn-rising longshoremen were in bed for the night. Moving quietly, he walked down the empty sidewalk to number 4842, a narrow, four-storied brick building, identical with a dozen others in the block. He ascended the short stoop of stone stairs, hollowed by decades of use, and tried the door. It was locked, as he'd expected it would be. He rang the night bell.

A few minutes later a stockily built Irishman wearing only a pair of trousers peered out at him with sleepy, belligerent eyes.

"Now what's your pleasure?" he said.

Carmody held out his badge and let the slanting light from the hallway fall on it. "Talk as natural as you can," he said quietly. "Answer my questions. Have you got a spare room?"

The man cleared his throat and stared at the badge. "We're all full up," he said.

"Think I'd have better luck somewhere else in the block?"

"Couldn't say for sure. You can try across the street, at 4839. They might have an extra."

"A big blond man with a wide face," Carmody said quietly. "If he's here nod your head."

The man's eyes became round and solemn. He nodded slowly and jerked his thumb in a furtive gesture to his right. "Just beside me," he said, breathing out the words. "Front room."

"Thanks, anyway," Carmody said, and moved silently past him into the small airless hallway. He closed the front door and pointed to the stairs. The man needed no urging; he took the steps two at a time, his bare feet noiseless on the faded carpet.

Carmody waited until he had turned out of sight at the second-floor landing. Then he rapped sharply on the door of the front room. His breathing was even and slow, and his hands hung straight down at his sides.

Bedsprings creaked beyond the door and footsteps moved across the floor.

"Who's that?" a voice said quietly.

"Message from Bill Ackerman," Carmody said.

The door opened an inch and stopped. Carmody saw one eye shining softly from the light in the hallway, and below that the cold blue glint of a gun barrel.

"Walk straight in when I open the door," the voice said. "Stop in the middle of the room and don't turn around. Get that straight."

"Okay, I've got it."

"Start walking."

The door swung open. Carmody entered the dark room with the hall light shining on his back. He was a perfect target if the killer wanted to shoot. But he wasn't worried about that. Not yet.

A switch clicked and a bare bulb above his head flooded the room with white harsh light. He heard the door swing shut, a lock click and then a gun barrel pressed hard against his spine. The man's free hand went over him with expert speed, found his revolver and flipped it free of the holster.

"Take off your hat now," he said. "Real slow. Raise it with both hands."

He knows his racket, Carmody thought, lifting his hat. Occasionally even a cop might forget that a small gun could be carried on the top of a man's head under a fedora.

"Lemme look at you now," the man said.

Turning slowly, Carmody faced the man who had killed his brother. Look down here, Eddie, he prayed. This is for you.

"You're Joie Langley, right?" he said quietly.

"Don't make conversation. What's with Ackerman?"

Langley's youth surprised Carmody. He was twenty-four, or twenty-five at most, a big muscular kid with tousled blond hair and sullen eyes set close together in a wide brutal face. The gun he held looked like a finger of his huge hand. He was wearing loafers, slacks and an unbuttoned yellow sports shirt that exposed his solid hairy chest. About Eddie's age, Carmody thought, but a different breed. He was a hard and savage killer; Eddie wouldn't have had a chance with him, even from the front.

"Ackerman wants you to clear out," Carmody said. "I'm a cop, and I work for him. I'll set it up for you."

"A cop?" Langley said softly, and took a step back from Carmody. He went down in a springy crouch, his sullen eyes narrowing with suspicion. "I don't like this, buddy. The whole deal stinks. I'm the hottest guy in the country but he won't pay off, won't let me clear out. Where's your badge, buddy?"

"I'll take my wallet from my hip pocket," Carmody said quietly. "I'll do it nice and slow. You're getting all excited, sonny. What's the matter? This your first job?"

Langley swore at him impersonally. Then he said, "I'm making sure it ain't my last, that's all. Take out your frontpiece."

Carmody opened his wallet and flashed the badge. "Look at the name on the identification card," he said. "That's important, too."

Langley stared at him, the gun steady in his big fist. "I like this less all the time, buddy," he said.

"You'd be spending your dough in Las Vegas right now if you hadn't fumbled the job," Carmody said. "Look at the name in that wallet. Then we'll get moving."

Langley took the wallet in his free hand and held it at eye-level. He was still watching Carmody. "You sound like you think you're tough," he said casually.

"Look at the name."

Langley grinned and glanced at the identification card, keeping the gun fixed steadily on Carmody's stomach.

"Michael T. Carmody," he said, reading the name slowly. A puzzled line deepened above his eyes. "That's the name of the guy I—"

Carmody had raised his hand casually—as if he were going to scratch his chin—and now he struck down at Langley's wrist, gambling on the hoodlum's momentary confusion and the speed and power of his own body.

He almost lost his bet.

Langley jerked back from the blow, his lips flattening in a snarl, and the rock-hard edge of Carmody's hand missed his wrist—but it struck the top of his thumb and knocked his finger away from the trigger. For a split second the gun dangled impotently in his hand, and Carmody made another desperate bet on himself and whipped a left hook into Langley's face. It would have been safer to try for the gun; if the hook missed he'd be dead before he could throw another punch. But it didn't miss; Langley's head snapped back as Carmody's fist exploded under his jaw and the gun spun from his hand to the floor. Carmody kicked it under the bed and began to laugh. Then he hit Langley in the stomach with a right that raised him two inches off the floor. When Langley bent over, gasping for breath, Carmody brought his knee up into his face and knocked him halfway across the room.

"It was your last job, sonny," he said, grabbing the slack of the sports shirt and pulling him to his feet. "You shot a good kid, my brother. But you shoot nobody else."

Langley stared at him, breathing raggedly, hate shining from his bleeding ruined face. "I'd cut off my hands and feet for one chance at you, copper," he cried softly. "I'd fix you good."

"You had your chance, sonny," Carmody said. "A thousand more wouldn't help." Turning Langley around, he twisted his wrist up between his shoulder blades and locked it there in the vise of his own big hand. "Eddie could have taken you front to front," he said. "You're not big-time, you're all mouth. We're going downtown now and I'll turn you over to my brother's friends. If you want your troubles to start sooner just get balky. I'll break this arm of yours off and make you carry it."

"I don't scare, copper," Langley said angrily.

Carmody hesitated in the bleak room and stared with bitter eyes into his own past. "No, we don't scare, sonny," he said. "God Himself can't scare us. So we wind up like this. Little men begging for a break."

"Who's little?"

"You're little enough to fit in the chair," Carmody said. "That's what counts. How old are you?"

"Twenty-six my next birthday."

"A ripe old age," Carmody said, and sighed. "Let's go."

He retrieved his revolver, opened the door and shoved Langley out into the dimly lighted hallway. The house was still and quiet. It was just about all over, Carmody knew, and he was restless and impatient for the final end of it. The power and drive that had always been a pressure within him seemed to be gone; even his anger had watered down to a heavy pervading bitterness. He was reaching for the knob when the doorbell broke clamorously through the silence.

Carmody froze, tightening his grip on Langley's wrist.

"Easy now," he whispered.

"Maybe you got trouble, copper."

"You'll get it first."

Carmody was in an awkward position. With one hand he couldn't open the door and still keep an effective grip on the gun. And Langley might break if he put away the gun to open the door.

"Maybe we got action," Langley said, laughing soundlessly.

"You won't see it," Carmody said; raising his gun he slugged him at the base of the skull, not hard enough to injure him but hard enough to silence him for a few moments. Langley sagged against him and Carmody caught his arms and lowered him to the floor.

Then he turned the knob, releasing the catch, and stepped quickly back to the shadow of the stairs. The door swung open and Myers, the little detective from his shift, walked into the hallway.

"Good Lord," he said closing the door quickly, and glancing from Carmody down to Langley's sprawled body.

"How did you find me?" Carmody said.

Myers was breathing rapidly, his small cautious face tense with excitement. "That can wait, Mike. Ackerman's sitting across the street in his car. With Hymie Schmidt. Did you know that?"

Carmody felt a quiver of excitement go down his spine. It wasn't over yet; not by a long sight. Ackerman was the man he had come closer to fearing than anyone else he had known in his life. And now Ackerman was waiting for him.

"There's an alarm out for him," Myers said. "He's wanted for questioning. And he's on the run."

"How did you know I was here?"

"I spotted your car down the block. That old mobster at my wife's sanitarium gave me the tip on this guy." He glanced down at Langley. "Someone in Chicago told him a guy named Joie Langley had come East to do a job on a cop. A pet stoolie of mine tipped me off he was staying here. I came out just to look around and then I saw your car. That scared me. So I decided to come in. That's when I saw Ackerman and Schmidt pull up and stop across the street."

"They've seen my car, too, then," Carmody said. "We don't have much time. They'll either clear out or come in here shooting."

"I got it all thought out," Myers said, gripping his arm. "They don't know me from Adam. To them I'm just a little guy who lives here or is hunting for a room. Well, look: I'll walk out again and go down to the sidewalk. I take out cigarettes, pretend I need a match and cross the street to their car. When I get there I put my gun in their face. And that's the end of it. You can cover me from here. Okay?"

Carmody hesitated. It was a good bold move but Myers wasn't the man for it. "No," he said.

"It will work."

"What the devil are you trying to prove?"

Myers shook his head slowly. "They killed a cop, remember? I'm going to prove they can't get away with it. That's what's important to me. Don't you ever know what makes people tick, Mike?"

"No, I'm too dumb," Carmody said wearily. Then he put his hand awkwardly on Myers' shoulder. "Forgive me, will you? You're a better cop than I could be in a thousand years. Go out and arrest those bastards."

"You watch me." Myers opened the door and went down the stone steps to the sidewalk. From the crack of the partially open door Carmody saw Ackerman's long black car parked across the street, and the faces of the two men in the front seat, pale triangular blurs in the darkness. He watched Myers fumble through his pockets, bring out cigarettes and stick one in his mouth. Weaving slightly, Myers dug around again in his pockets for matches. Carmody felt perspiration starting on his forehead; the little detective was overdoing it, playing it like a drunk on a stage. But it was too late to drag him back. Myers had started across the street to Ackerman's car, weaving on rubbery legs.

"You guys got a match?" Carmody heard him call.

"I think so." It was Ackerman's voice, carrying clearly across the silent street.

"Good guy," Myers said, laughing cheerfully.

That was when Ackerman shot him, as he approached the car, doing his imitation of a drunk's lurching walk. The report blasted the silence and sent shattering echoes racing along the dark blocks.

Carmody charged down to the sidewalk as he saw Myers fall, and heard his shrill incredulous cry of pain. His gun banged twice and the glass in Ackerman's windshield shattered with a noisy crash. He saw Ackerman clearly then but before he could fire again something struck his shoulder and spun his body around in a full circle. There was no pain at first, only the incredible, sledge-hammer impact of the bullet. He was on his knees, feeling for his gun when the pain hit, driving into him like a white-hot needle. The breath left his body in a squeezing rush and he put a hand quickly on the pavement to keep himself from falling on his face. When he raised his head, Ackerman was standing above him, looking as tall as the buildings. "You rotten filthy dog," he said, staring at Carmody with furious eyes. "You fixed me good. But you're where you belong now, on your knees and ready to die."

Carmody fought against a dizzying pain and nausea. "You're through," he grinned, and the effort stretched the skin whitely across his cheekbones. "It wasn't a bad night's work."

"I'll be alive when you're dead," Ackerman said, his voice trembling with passion.

Windows had gone up along the block and from a distance came the faint baying of a police siren.

"Boss, let's go," Hymie Schmidt shouted from inside the car.

"Just one more second," Ackerman said, putting the cold muzzle of his gun against Carmody's forehead. "Don't worry about me," he said, leaning forward and speaking slowly and clearly. "I've got judges and lawyers in every pocket. And shooting a crooked cop is an easy rap to beat."

"Damn you!" Hymie Schmidt yelled, and let out the clutch with a snap. The car shot forward with a deep roar of power. Ackerman spun around, his face twisting with alarm. "Stop!" he shouted, and ran a few yards down the street, waving both arms in the air. Finally, he halted, cursing furiously at the fading tail-light.

When he turned around, Carmody was kneeling as he had left him, but Myers was sitting up in the street with a gun in his lap, his little face frozen and white with pain.

"You won't kill any more cops," he said weakly, and shot Ackerman through the head.

# 14

A POLICE CAR TOOK CARMODY TO ST. DAVID'S HOSPITAL WHERE A DOC-tor cut away his shirt, removed the bullet and dressed the wound in his shoulder. Afterward, Carmody sat on a bench in the starkly clean accident ward and smoked a cigarette. He felt empty and drained but in a little while strength began flowing sluggishly back into his body.

"Hell, man, you're indestructible," an intern said, as Carmody got slowly to his feet.

"Don't bet on that," Carmody said. The uniformed cop who was wait-ing to drive him to Headquarters put a coat gently over his bare shoulders. "Ready, Sarge?" he asked.

"We'll wait until we hear about Myers," Carmody said.

A nurse came down from the operating room a few minutes later. "How's he making it?" he asked her.

The nurse was a pretty girl with soft warm eyes and something about Carmody made her feel like taking him in her arms. For all his size and toughness he seemed so bewildered and lost.

"He has a chance," she said.

"How good?"

"Pretty good, I think."

"Thank you."

"You're welcome," the nurse said, and touched his arm timidly.

Carmody smiled at her, then glanced at the cop. "Let's roll," he said.

The record room at Homicide was jammed with police and reporters, and the noise of their excited, splintered conversations rumbled through the smoky air. There was an uproar when Carmody came in. Reporters on deadline tried to get to him for any kind of statement, but Abrams begged them to shut up and clear the hell out of the way. "You'll get your stories," he shouted, circling Carmody like an indignant hen. "But give us a break first, for the Lord's sake."

Over the heads of the crowd Carmody saw Karen and George Murphy standing against the wall. She stood on tiptoes, watching him anxiously, and Murphy was patting her shoulder with a big clumsy hand. Abrams took Carmody's good arm and said, "They want you in Wilson's office, Mike."

"Just a second." Carmody pushed through the ring of reporters and cops and walked over to Karen. "Can you stick around?" he asked her. "I'm going to be busy for a while."

"Yes, I'll wait. Are you all right?"

"What? Oh, sure." He glanced down at the splint and sling on his arm. "It's not bad." He felt suddenly as if he were walking through a dream. "Did you identify Langley?"

She nodded and wet her lips. He saw that she was very pale. "The police took me to see him a few minutes ago."

"You'll stick around?" he said, frowning slightly.

"Yes, Mike."

Murphy smiled at him and patted his shoulder gently. "It's a great story. 'Cop Nabs Brother's Slayer.' The copy desks can ring some beautiful changes on that one."

"Wouldn't it be nice if that's the way it was," Carmody said.

"Yes, that would be pretty," Murphy said with a little sigh. "Well, I'll see you later, Mike."

"You'll get the whole story, George. That was the deal."

"Sure, I'm not worried. Take it easy, pal."

"I'll see you as soon as I can," Carmody said to Karen. "You'll be here?" Even in his confusion he realized he was pressing the point with absurd insistence.

"Yes, Mike."

Wilson's office, in comparison to the record room, seemed like a haven of peace. Myerdahl and Powell were talking together at the window, and Wilson was seated at his desk. When Carmody came in Wilson jumped to his feet, grinning with pleasure and excitement, and led him to a chair. "It was a fine night's work, Mike," he said. "The best we've had since I've been in the department. How're you feeling?"

"Pretty good, I guess."

Powell sauntered over and patted Carmody's shoulder. "I'll say amen to Jimmy's comment," he said. "It was a great night's work. We've got your brother's killer and Ackerman is dead. The organization is in for a terrific thump."

"How about Beaumonte?"

"He caught a plane for Miami a few hours ago. But Langley has already confessed that Beaumonte hired him to do the job on your brother. So we'll bring Mr. Beaumonte back on a murder charge. We still haven't found the pictures Dobbs was using to blackmail Ackerman, but they've already served their purpose. They made him stampede."

Carmody fumbled for a cigarette and discovered he had none. Powell brought out his case quickly. "Have one of these?"

"Thanks." Carmody blew a stream of smoke at the floor and rubbed his forehead. He could feel fatigue settling on him with a ponderous pressure. "I wonder how Ackerman knew I was going to get Langley?"

Wilson said, "Hymie Schmidt answered that for us. Beaumonte tipped off Ackerman you were going out there."

Carmody sighed wearily. "He used me as his executioner. I was still on the payroll."

The mood in the room changed slightly. Powell looked at his watch and said, "I've got to get up to my office. We'll be working all night, as it is."

Myerdahl took the short black pipe from his mouth and said bluntly, "I don't take back my words this afternoon, Carmody. But I say this now. You were all cop tonight."

Carmody smiled faintly. "Thanks, Superintendent."

When they had gone Wilson sat on the edge of his desk and drew a long breath. He studied Carmody for a few seconds in silence. Then he said lightly, "The peace and quiet is kind of a relief, isn't it?"

"Peace?" Carmody said, smiling crookedly. "Where is it, Jim?" He sat slumped in the chair, head bowed, staring at the cracks in the floor. The overhead light gleamed on his thick blond hair, on the hard flat planes of his face, on the white sling stretching diagonally across his bare chest. Sighing, he shook his head slowly. "I was wrong, Jim," he said. Karen had told him to say that, he remembered. And had warned him that the words might choke. But nothing like that happened. It was a relief to say the words. It was like putting down an intolerable burden. "Yes, I was wrong," he murmured. What came next? You asked for forgiveness, that was it. He'd done that, he recalled, he'd asked Myers to forgive him. But it didn't seem enough. He hadn't changed; no bells of hope pealed in his soul, no promise of salvation blazed before his eyes. Maybe what Father Ahearn had suggested fitted in here. Come back little by little. The way he'd gone away.

"What will happen to me, Jim?" he said quietly. He was curious about that in an impersonal manner; it didn't really matter because the big thing had already happened. He knew he was ruined. The mainspring that was the core of his strength had been smashed. Goodness had destroyed him. And that was almost comical. Mike Carmody had been hunted down, surrounded and destroyed. Cops like Myers and Wilson, women like Nancy and Karen, even big fat George Murphy had been in on the kill. He had thought they were fools, pushovers, weaklings—looking at them but seeing himself—and they had calmly smashed him to bits with their decency and goodness. Everything he believed had been proven invalid. So what was left of Mike Carmody?

Wilson came over beside him and put a hand on his shoulder. "Damn it, we all make mistakes," he said, hunting awkwardly for words. "Don't let this thing beat you all the way down, Mike. What will happen to you is anybody's guess. The papers will play you up as the fearless cop who avenged his brother's murder. When the rest of it comes out, that you were on Ackerman's team, well they may switch around and make you out the biggest bum in the city. Powell is on your side though, and so is Myerdahl, if he'll ever admit it." Wilson frowned and then rubbed a hand over his face. "The best thing you can hope for is that they'll let you resign without pressing charges."

So I'm through as a cop, Carmody thought, still staring at the floor. That had been important once, but now it didn't matter. Nothing mattered really. He felt as if his body and soul were vacuums, drained and empty, without even a promise of hope to sustain them.

"What's the worst I can expect?" he asked.

Wilson shrugged. Reluctantly he said, "Three, four years, maybe."

"Am I under arrest?"

"No, but you'll have to stick around. Powell wants me to take a statement from you tonight on your connection with Beaumonte and Ackerman."

"That fast?"

"We've got to do it fast. Before the organization can grow another head."

"Okay. Can I go outside and say good-by to a friend?"

"Sure, of course."

The record room had returned to its normal state of quiet efficiency; the reporters had gone up with Powell to work on the story of Ackerman's death and the patrolmen had been detailed back to their squads and wagons. Abrams was at his desk, studying a file, and the clerk was typing out a report, occasionally pausing to stare through the dirty windows at the dark city. The bright overhead light was merciless on the battered furniture, the cigarette-littered floor, the curling flyers tacked on the bulletin board. It was a room that had been part of Carmody's life for years, but after tonight that would be all over.

Karen sat alone on the wooden bench at the wall, striking an incongruously elegant note against the drab and dusty office. She was wearing a black suit, high-heeled pumps, and her hair was brushed back from her small serious face. Good people, he thought. That had occurred to him before, but grudgingly and suspiciously. Now it was a simple unqualified tribute.

She rose lightly to her feet as he crossed the room.

"Let's sit down," he said. He felt clumsy and constrained with her, hopelessly at a loss for words. "I've just got a few minutes," he said at last. "There's a lot of routine to get out of the way, you know."

"Yes, of course. Don't worry about me, Mike. I'll get a cab."

"Where will you go?"

"Well, I haven't thought about it. Some hotel, probably."

The room was silent except for the occasional rattle of the clerk's typewriter.

"You told me to say I was wrong," he said, dragging the words out with an effort. "I did that. I wanted you to know."

She looked at him gravely. "Did it hurt?"

"It wasn't too bad." He frowned at the floor, feeling weary and helpless. It wouldn't work. There was no way to get to her, no way to bridge the barrier of bitterness he had built between them.

But miraculously, she came to him. "Don't try to do too much all at once," she said, putting a hand on his wrist. "Take it in easy stages. That works, you'll find."

"Look, I was wrong about you," he said. "That was as wrong as I ever got. Can you believe that? Can you forgive me?"

"That won't be hard, Mike. But let's do it the way I suggested. In easy stages. Okay?"

"All right, whatever you say," he said. Then he sighed and looked at the big clock above the police speaker. "The lieutenant's waiting for me."

They walked around the counter together and stopped at the swinging doors that opened on the corridor. "Eddie's funeral is tomorrow morning," he said. "Would you want to go with me?"

"I'd like that, Mike."

"Look, I may be going to jail," he said abruptly. "They can let me resign, or send me up. Either way, can I find you afterwards?"

"You'll be able to find me," she said slowly.

Carmody smiled into her small brave face, and put a hand on her shoulder. For just that instant there was a suggestion of the old hard confidence in his eyes. "I'll see you, Karen," he said.

"Good-by, Mike," she said in a soft voice, and pushed through the swinging doors and walked quickly down the corridor.

Carmody watched her until she turned out of sight. Standing alone, he stared into the dim empty corridor, still seeing in his mind the graceful swing of her legs and the high proud look of her head and shoulders. After a few moments he shook his head and rubbed his forehead and eyes with the back of his good hand. Then he turned and walked slowly into the record room. The door to the lieutenant's office stood open, and Carmody saw that Wilson was waiting for him, an empty chair pulled up beside his desk.

Carmody wet his lips, suddenly swept by an emotion that he couldn't define. Part of it was fear, but there was something else, too. For a moment he stood indecisively, staring at the empty chair that waited for him at Wilson's elbow. Finally, it came to him; this was what he felt as a child when he waited in the line at the confessional. Fear, yes, but something else. And the other thing was the sweeping relief that came from the anticipation of forgiveness.

Smiling slowly, Carmody walked into the lieutenant's office. "Let's go," he said, and eased himself gratefully into the empty chair.

*The Seven File*

# 1

AT TEN-THIRTY IN THE MORNING A BIG MAN IN A BLACK LEATHER JACKET
turned off Second Avenue into Thirty-first Street. He stopped for a moment to check the number on a building, then continued down the block,
limping slightly, favoring his left leg.

The day was bright with early spring sunlight. Children played along
the sidewalks, piercing the iron sound of traffic with laughter, and here
and there old men sat out on fire escapes, soaking up the soft, thin sun.

The man in the leather jacket kept his eyes on the numbers as he
limped past a tailor shop, a cigar store and several old tenements which
had recently been converted into smart and functional town houses. The
area was in a state of inevitable transition; drab old shops were giving way
to florists and interior decorators; and families that had lived here for
half a century were being displaced by people who had the taste and
means to turn these stately relics into chic, in-town homes. There were
children in the block who had grown up like a fungus on the city's sidewalks; there were others who went to school in taxis, who spent their
week ends in the country, and who never went outside unless accompanied
by maids or nurses.

The limping man stopped halfway down the block and looked up at a
tall building which had been lavishly restored to respectability. He smiled
then, admiring the freshly painted trim, the tuck pointers' handsome effects and the elegantly massive door, with its antique knocker and heavy
brass numerals.

The man's name was Duke Farrel. Smiling now, with the sun brightening his dark bold features, he seemed strikingly handsome. Good humor
dissolved the suggestion of coarseness in his face; the wariness in his eyes,
and the sullen heaviness about his mouth were less evident when he was
smiling. And he smiled much of the time. He was in his late thirties but
looked ten years younger than that; his shoulders were wide and powerful,
his waist was trim as an athlete's and his smile was charged with youthful
humor and confidence. Except for the limp, which he could accentuate
or minimize as he chose, he might have been taken for a lifeguard or a
professional football player, a man used to exercise and sun, who lived
simply and cleanly, enjoying good plain food and plenty of rest.

Now he started up the stone stairs, one hand on the black, wrought-iron
railing, and moving in spite of his limp with an air of businesslike efficiency. He lifted the heavy brass knocker and chimes sounded faintly

within the house. Smiling, he listened to their echoes trembling away into silence. He was still smiling when the door was opened by a slender, dark-haired girl in a nurse's uniform.

"Telephone company," he said, touching the peak of his cap in a casual salute. His jacket was open and the nurse saw the leather tool pouch that was attached to his belt. The head of a small hammer glinted sharply in the sunlight. "Any trouble on your line this morning?" he said.

"There've been no incoming calls," she said. "And I've had no occasion to use the phone myself." Her accent was Irish, faint but unmistakable.

"Lucky you didn't." He smiled easily at her, making her a participant in the little joke. "There's some trouble with the wiring along the block. It might be here. I'd better take a look."

She hesitated an instant, and he understood why. *Be very careful about letting strangers in. Make sure they have proper identification. This is New York, my dear, and you must remember.* . . . She'd undoubtedly received some such injunction from her mistress. Frowning, he looked at his watch. "There's more than one phone here, I guess," he said.

His manner disarmed her; he seemed completely businesslike, anxious to get on with his work. "Yes, there are phones on the first and second floor," she said. "Come in, please. But be as quiet as possible, won't you? The baby is asleep."

"I've got kids of my own," he said, with a reassuring smile. "I'm an expert at tiptoeing around the house. What is it, boy or girl?"

"A girl, just a year old."

Duke Farrel shook his head, still smiling. "They're really terrific at that age."

"Yes, aren't they?" She was smiling back at him now, completely won over.

It was always so easy, Duke Farrel thought, as he stepped into the foyer and waited for her to close the door. People simply didn't believe in evil. It was a staggering fact. They read the papers presumably, they had a front-row view of the world's meanness and viciousness, but they still reached for their wallets when someone whined, "Look, I ain't had a bite since—," or they took strangers in, picked up hitchhikers, went to the aid of vagrants and derelicts, behaving in short as if human beings were worthy of love and trust.

"The phone is in the study," she said, walking ahead of him into the living room.

It was all very choice, Duke thought, glancing around with alert, appraising eyes. The original flooring had been restored and the old wood glowed softly and warmly. Fresh flowers and vivid paintings stood out in bold contrast against the charcoal-gray drapes and wallpaper. A group of three low chairs was arranged before the fireplace, and lavishly ornate candelabra stood at either end of the marble mantelpiece. It was a charming room, done with loving, experienced care.

This would be Mrs. Bradley's triumph, Duke knew. Fashion was her business. He could imagine her planning these effects, chic and slender, laughing as an idea struck her. "Let's try a pickup of honest-to-goodness *red* right here!" And her husband, crewcut and healthy, the product of Boston's best studs. "It's fine with me, honey. You do what pleases you."

The telephone was in a small study which had been decorated solidly and conventionally—a concession, Duke guessed, to Boston and background. Green leather chairs, book-lined walls, hunting prints—a man's room, yes indeed. That would be the lair of Bradley the broker. "A man needs a place to relax in, dear." And she'd humor him, of course. Because he was handsome, gentlemanly and very, very wealthy. And they were in love, too. Mustn't forget that. Duke didn't know the Bradleys personally, and he didn't want to. But he had become something of an authority on their tastes and habits.

For several minutes he went through the motions of checking the telephone, paying no attention to the nurse who watched him from the doorway.

"Well, this looks okay," he said, replacing the plate on a black metal box that was attached to the floorboard. "I'll check the wiring down here, and then the upstairs phone. I can find my way around, I think."

"As long as Jill is asleep I don't have anything very urgent to do."

"Jill? That's cute." He glanced at her, his smile casual and friendly. "You're Irish, eh?"

"Yes."

A bit cool, he wondered? Not mixing with the maintenance staff? Or was it just shyness? "My father was Irish," he said. "He always called me Duke because he used to work for one in Belfast." Duke shook his head. "He was a great old boy, but he never got used to America. Always said it was too big for one little Irishman."

Most of this was impromptu invention; but it happened to be true that his father had nicknamed him Duke. And the tag had stuck ever since. Through school, in jail . . .

Duke talked casually while he made a pretense of checking the wiring in the dining room and kitchen. He was an instinctively good actor because he enjoyed deception for its own sake. Now he played a sincere, obvious, salt-of-the-earth type—and played it well. She relaxed after a bit, and began to smile at his good-natured chatter. Duke also knew how to listen, and she found his impersonal but attentive manner very flattering. Without realizing, she did most of the talking. Her name was Kathleen Reilly, he learned, and she had been with the Bradleys since Jill was born. Kathleen had left Limerick when she was fifteen, emigrating to America with her father. She was twenty-three now, and had decided to go back to school at the end of the summer and complete her training as an X-ray technician. But it would be very hard to leave. Jill was such a funny, dear child. . . .

Duke listened with a convincing show of interest, but all the while he was noting the position of doors and windows and light switches. He drew a plan of the room in his mind so that he could walk through them in the dark if necessary. Or run . . .

In the kitchen he opened a door that led onto a small porch. Steps went down to a garden, in which there was a playpen and sandbox.

"That's wonderful for the kid," he said, estimating the height of the brick wall at the back of the small yard.

"Yes, she loves it," Kathleen said.

Duke stopped and raised his hand. "Hey, I think I hear her."

She turned, listening, and then walked lightly and quickly down the hall to the foot of the front stairs. Duke took a key from his pocket and eased it into the lock of the kitchen door. The tumblers turned under the pressure of his fingers . . .

"Maybe I imagined it," he said, when she came back to the kitchen. Smiling at her, he shook his head. "When we had our first I never got a full night's sleep. I used to keep popping in to see that he was still breathing."

She laughed and said, "I know how that is."

She was quite a dish, he thought, looking at her with more interest. A very nice bundle, but not for him. She had long, silky black hair, dark blue eyes and a complexion that was white and soft as doeskin. In the immaculate white uniform her body was excitingly virginal, lovely and trim and vulnerable. She was obviously one of the world's innocents, he thought. But worth cultivating in spite of that. Or because of it, rather. It would be fun to take off her rose-colored glasses and let her take a good look at what the world was like. But that wasn't going to happen. Not with him anyway. He felt a little stab of envy for the man who would be in charge of that stage of her education.

"The nursery is at the head of the stairs," she said, leading him along the hallway. "The phone is just beside it, in Mr. and Mrs. Bradley's room."

Duke let her move ahead of him on the stairs so that he could enjoy the view of her ankles. And it was quite a view, he thought. Even in low-heeled shoes and white nylons her legs were slim and beautiful. There were few girls who could do as well in sheer stockings and high heels. This was talent. She stopped at the landing and looked back at him. "I'm sorry," she said, with a quick compassion in her voice. "I didn't mean to rush you."

It was difficult not to laugh; he could have taken these stairs in three strides. "I can get around as well as the next guy," he said sharply. This went right through them, he knew. Proud, hating pity—it melted them down like butter.

"I'm sorry," she said again, helplessly.

He put her at ease with a smile. "The guy who nicked me is even sorrier."

"Was it the war?"

"Germany, a long time ago." Still smiling, he said, "And now I'm more interested in what's wrong with your boss's phone. What's over is over. That's the nursery, eh?" he said, nodding at a door that stood a few inches ajar.

"Yes."

Duke stared at the creamy white paneling, the shiny brass knob and hinges. Little Jill was sleeping in there—little Jill, the granddaughter of Oliphant Bradley, whose name was synonymous with directorates, banking firms, brokerage office and money—mustn't forget plain, vulgar old money. Jill was a million-dollar baby without a doubt. Duke felt excitement stirring in him. The next time he stood here the house would be dark and silent. . . .

"The phone is in the bedroom," she said quietly.

"Sure," he said, wondering if she had attached anything to his interest in the nursery.

The Bradleys were living it up, Duke thought, as he entered their bedroom. Housekeeper (off today, as he well knew), nurse, cute little baby, cute big house, money in the bank—living it up, yes indeed. There was a fireplace opposite the bed, and wall-to-wall carpeting that felt a foot thick under his heavy shoes.

The décor of the room was pink and black—humorously erotic, sex with a broad smile, modern and uninhibited. Real cute kids, he thought. This was information he could do without.

While he checked the phone and wiring Kathleen contributed a few more bits about the Bradleys. None of it struck him as essential or significant. They were delightful people, wonderful to every one.

"Democratic, eh?" he said.

She felt the edge to his voice. "It's not something they put on," she said.

"Sure," Duke said. He studied her with a crooked little smile. "You know something? You were smart to come to America."

"Why do you say that?"

"Because people in America like beautiful things."

"And people in other countries don't?"

"We put a higher price on them," he said. "You'll find that out."

"Well, thanks for the warning," she said lightly; but his words had brought a flush of color to her cheeks. She was aware of the hard and speculative interest in his eyes.

Duke knew he was behaving stupidly. Worse than that, dangerously.

But the stillness of the house, the faint perfume of the bedroom, her innocent vulnerable beauty—they were working in him like whiskey on a cold day. A sensuous warmth was blunting the edge of his caution. "A girl like you could have the world for a cupcake," he said. "You know that, I guess."

"I haven't thought about it," she said evenly. She wasn't smiling anymore. "Are you through in here?"

"Not quite," he said, studying her with a hard, intent smile. His instincts warned him to clear out, but the call was muted and distant. He wasn't thinking about playing it smart now. He was thinking that she had the whitest skin he had ever seen. And that his two hands would almost circle her waist.

Turning slowly, he moved between her and the door. And it was then the baby woke and began to cry. The girl stepped around him and hurried across the room. "I'm coming, honey," she said in a cheerful, reassuring voice.

Duke let out his breath slowly and walked into the hall. His heart was pounding hard. "I'll be leaving now," he said, watching the half-open nursery door. He could hear the sleepy gurglings of the child.

"Did you find the trouble?" Her voice was friendly and impersonal. An act? He didn't think so. She wasn't that clever.

"No, it's probably across the street on another circuit."

"Will you let yourself out, please? I've got my hands full with Jill."

"Sure thing. So long."

Outside in the bright spring sunshine Duke took a handkerchief from his pocket and patted his damp forehead. Fool, he thought, but without anger or rancor. Risking a deal that had been in the works for three months. And for what? A pair of good-looking legs and a healthy body. A real prize, he thought. There were probably only a million girls in the city with the same qualifications for immortality. But he wasn't really annoyed with himself. He had always taken what he wanted—ignoring circumstances and consequences—and he wasn't likely to change now. It was the exact moment of the present that he knew and savored.

Crossing the city to his hotel, he enjoyed the warm sun on his face and the sense of excitement generated by the hurrying crowds and noisy traffic. He felt absorbed in the millions of lives that were flowing around him, pleasurably sustained by the limitless promise of the city. Luxury, women, sensation—all of it crammed for convenience into a few square blocks. And all of it for sale; the city kept its promise to the rich. He knew that much. Only to the rich . . .

His hotel was in the west forties, a narrow, soot-colored building that looked as if it had been squeezed into place in the block. The street itself was gaudy and illicit, with its cheap bars and strip joints, suggesting the cleverly camouflaged entrances to a huge trap. At the lobby desk Duke picked up his keys and asked the clerk if there were any messages for him.

The clerk was a plump, pink-cheeked young man with a contempt for the hotel's trade which he didn't bother to disguise. He knew that most of the men who stopped there were only a notch above vagrants, and he saw no earthly reason to treat them as anything else. Without looking up he shook his head in answer to Duke's question.

"I'm expecting a wire from my brother," Duke said gently. "From up in Maine. It's important."

"I'll watch for it. Don't worry."

Duke hesitated a second or so, smiling at the clerk. Then he said dryly, "It's nice of you to put yourself out. Thanks very much."

The clerk stared after him as he limped toward the elevators. Then his lips tightened with exasperation. He knew the type. Sarcastic and boorish. If they weren't kept in place they became impossible. . . .

Upstairs Duke removed his work clothes and put on a gray flannel suit and a white shirt with a neat dark blue tie. Smiling at his reflection in the mirror, he poured a drink of whiskey into a plastic toothbrush glass. He liked the look of his dark, arrogant features and the hard expression in his deep-set eyes.

Then the smile left his face and he swore softly. Why hadn't Hank answered his wire? It wasn't like his kid brother to ignore him; Hank had been trained like a dog, painstakingly and thoroughly. Even after all these years he wouldn't have forgotten his lessons. But still—he hadn't sent word that they could use his cottage. Grant wouldn't understand the delay. And he wouldn't like it.

Sipping the whiskey, Duke smiled slightly. Well, to hell with Grant, he thought. He couldn't keep his thoughts from straying back to the nurse. In fact, he didn't try; he gave himself over to them with relish. She didn't know much about men. Start with that. She'd be thinking about marriage and babies and a house with a little garden in back of it. But not about men. Not until she grew up some more. He began to place her in different frames; at a bar, walking among trees, fighting her way through the crowds in a subway, with men of all kinds. And he imagined her in evening gowns, in sports clothes, in filmy lingerie in a warm, scented bedroom, lying almost naked on a beach. Would she tan? He wondered, looking at his own dark hands. Probably not. But that would be okay. A pink tone would go great with her black hair and blue eyes.

Duke finished his drink, suddenly irritable and restless. It was time to call Grant. Tell him there was no word on the cottage yet. . . .

When Duke dropped his key at the desk the clerk looked up at him, and said, "A wire came in for you about five minutes ago." Turning, he took a telegram from the key rack and slid it across the counter toward Duke.

Duke stared at him, ignoring the yellow envelope. He had been drinking for the last hour, and his eyes were ugly and dangerous. "Why didn't you send it up?"

"Well—I'm here alone at the moment. The bellboy is out for coffee."

"Didn't I tell you it was important?"

"I'm sorry, but you can't expect . . ."

"I expect service," Duke said, his voice cutting harshly across the clerk's. "You're here to say 'yes, sir' and 'no, sir' and do exactly what you're told. That's why you're paid a small salary. Trained monkeys come cheap."

The clerk's cheeks trembled with indignation. "There's no cause to be abusive," he said. "I know your type—" He paused and wet his lips, finding it suddenly very difficult to meet Duke's eyes.

"What's my type?" Duke said gently. "Tell me about it."

"I merely meant—" The clerk's voice became high and uncertain; all of his dignity dissolved in fear. "We try to be of service, sir. This won't happen again, I assure you."

Ignoring the apology, Duke ripped open the telegram with an abrupt angry gesture. The wire was from his brother, Hank. As he read it, a slow, secretive smile relieved the sullenness in his face. The kid hadn't forgotten his lessons. . . . Turning, Duke limped across the lobby toward the public phones, and the clerk stared after his broad back with wide frightened eyes.

# 2

REPLACING THE PHONE IN ITS CRADLE, EDDIE GRANT GLANCED AT THE slender graying man who sat facing him in an overstuffed chair on the opposite side of the living room. "The cottage is all set," Grant said, without expression. "That was Duke. His brother will be away fishing during the week we need it. Nice timing, eh?"

The man in the chair smiled faintly. "Simply perfect," he said, in a mannered British accent; its inflection and tone were meant to suggest a good school and good regiment, but they smacked unmistakably of pretense and phoniness, of small shady deals rushed through in an atmosphere of anxious haste and pressure. It was a voice trained to say such things as "Your coat? Why, so it is! I say, what a stupid mistake. . . ."

The man's name was Howard Sydney Creasy. He was small and frail, a gnome of a creature in a shiny black suit that was relieved by a gray silk tie and a tiny pearl stickpin. There was nothing unusual about his appearance; his features were small and commonplace and over the years he had cultivated a simpering smile that was, to his thinking, both civil and superior at once. He seldom allowed his confused hatreds to break through the barriers he had set up against them—and then only when he was alone. To the world he presented a bland, good-humored mien, and a whimsical courtesy that was his only defense against ridicule or anger.

Now he said to Grant, "Are you quite sure of Duke's brother? I mean, are you sure he'll go off fishing on schedule?"

"Duke is sure of him," Grant said.

"Then the question is—are we sure of Duke?"

Grant stared at him for a second or two, then shrugged his wide shoulders. Lighting a cigarette, he sat down on a window seat that ran beneath the front windows of the room. From here he could look down the length of the apartment—living room, dining room, short hallway, kitchen. The furniture was cheap and the colors had been chosen without imagination; it was a depressing prospect, relieved only slightly by the knowledge that he would never see it again after a week or so. He had sublet it for two months, and the original tenant had replaced the furniture with bargain-basement specials before turning over the key. Only two more weeks, Grant thought. And then the big-time again.

Stocky and powerfully built, he was a big man, clumsy with muscle and heavy bone; he worried constantly about his weight. The morning sun touched his lifeless blond hair, and revealed the network of tiny cracks that gave his face the surface look of yellowing parchment. He was only forty-five, but the stamp of worry and tension was on him; most of those forty-five years had been spent solving the simple but violent problem of keeping alive.

"Duke's okay," he said at last. "Don't worry about him."

"Do you know anything about his brother?" Creasy said.

"I've never met him, if that's what you mean. But Duke's filled me in on him. They're different types." Grant smiled faintly. "There's an understatement for you. The kid brother, Hank, went off to Korea and piled up a big record. After that he didn't come home. His parents were dead. Maybe it was that. Or maybe he wanted to get away from Duke. Anyway he went to Maine, and got into the real estate business with an old-timer up there. He's a very respectable type, which is just what we want."

"They don't sound like chips from exactly the same block," Creasy said.

"Splinters is the word maybe. They're half-brothers. Same father, different mothers."

"Do they see each other regularly?"

"No, they had trouble in the past. I don't know just what, but Duke's got the kid over his hip. When he needs dough he just shoots off a wire, and back comes the cash. The kid's afraid of him, I guess. But that doesn't matter to us."

"But Duke matters to us."

Grant stared at him. "I told you he's okay. I've known him for years. I met him in stir, back in '43."

"Forgive me, but I don't consider that last any recommendation," Creasy said, with a mannered little smile.

"Shut up!" Grant said, spacing the words slowly and deliberately.

"I say, it was only a joke." Creasy's smile became strained. "No offense meant."

"I said shut up!" Grant stood and pounded a fist into his palm. "I don't like being kidded." He stared at Creasy, his big chest rising and falling slowly. "Understand that? Fifteen years ago I ran two wards in Chicago. The numbers, horse rooms, everything. I was just thirty then, and I had it made. Dough, cars, broads, a job that was getting bigger every year. I was on the inside of the city. I saw the wheels that ran it, and I watched them turn, fast or slow, the way the big boys wanted. You know where I'd be today if I hadn't been sent up?" He shook his head disgustedly, as some of the anger drained from him. "I'd be running the city, that's about all. But I shot a bookie, a thieving little creep, and there was a lot of reform talk in the air, so I got tossed to the do-gooders. Yeah." He jerked a thumb at his broad chest. "Me, Eddie Grant, the bogey man behind all the dirt in the city. They talked like I was Capone. And I got twenty years. So don't kid me about making mistakes. Understand that?"

"Yes, of course—"

"And do you think the big boys got a place for me now?" Grant said, staring down at Creasy. "Like hell they have. So I'm on my own. But they'll hear from me again." He made an abrupt, dismissing gesture with his hand. "That's my baby, not yours. Now: you got everything clear?"

"Certainly. We've been over it a hundred times, at least."

Grant was obviously pleased by Creasy's answer. "That's right. I planned this job good. We've got nothing to worry about."

A key turned in the front door and a blonde woman with a bag of groceries in her arms entered the room. "Hello, Eddie," she said, closing the door with her foot. She was in her early forties, with a good but matronly figure and a plump pretty face. Her eyes were large and blue, and hopelessly nearsighted. She narrowed them down to slits as she noticed Creasy. "Oh, it's you, Howard," she said at last.

Creasy was standing like a guardsman. "How are you, Belle? Silly question. I can see you're blooming as usual."

"Why, thank you!" Belle put a finger under her chin and made a playful curtsy. "Eddie, can I bring you two a drink?"

"No," Grant said shortly. "Creasy is just leaving."

Creasy cleared his throat. "I must be popping off, actually." Picking up his Homburg and umbrella, he glanced at his watch. "I'm late now, as a matter of fact." He smiled winningly at Belle. "Do you think she'll forgive me?"

"Oh, I'm sure of it," Belle said.

And Creasy made his exit, bowing gracefully to her and bobbing his head at Grant, hurrying off to his customary rendezvous with himself and loneliness.

Grant was methodically performing his setting-up exercises when Belle returned from the kitchen with a glass of sherry. Smiling at him, she sat down in a deep chair and adjusted her skirt to reveal a smooth round knee. She had pretty legs and enjoyed displaying them; flirtation was a habit with her, a reflexive response to men of all kinds. "You're cheating," she said. "You're bending your knees."

"Like hell I am."

"I was just teasing. You take this physical culture stuff pretty grimly. Are you aiming at the Mr. America finals?"

Grant didn't bother answering her. He completed his waist exercises and went into the bedroom. Belle sipped her sherry and picked up a magazine. She was used to his indifference, and rather liked it. In the bedroom Grant was staring at himself in the mirror above the dresser, critically examining the wrinkles that covered his face like fine lace. It was natural enough at forty-five, he thought. He pulled a lock of his gray-blond hair down on his forehead, and then cautiously touched the thinning area at his crown. Plenty of it left . . . He thought: I don't look any older than when I went to jail. Harder maybe, but not older. They'd know him when he came back. They wouldn't frown and say, "Wasn't that Eddie Grant?" No, they'd know him. He wasn't one of the slobs who went old and weak in stir. Whining for a handout, broke, old . . .

"Belle, did you get that face cream I told you about?" he called to her.

"Yes, it's in the medicine cabinet."

Grant studied his reflection for a few more seconds, drawing in his breath to accentuate the size of his chest, the hard line of his waist. All right, all right, he thought, and walked back into the living room. "That place in Maine sounds great," he said. "Duke's brother's place. Good fresh air, clean living."

"Judas! You talk like we're going on a camping trip."

"I know where we're going," he said, staring at her, suddenly irritable and nervous. "Don't make cracks like that."

"What's the matter with you?"

"Nothing. Nothing's the matter."

"Which one of them worries you?" she asked in the mild, little girl's voice she affected occasionally. "Duke or Creasy?"

Grant frowned at her, his eyes sharp and cold. "Don't talk trouble. They're both okay. As good as I could hope for."

"Well, what is it then?" she said plaintively.

Without answering her he turned back to the windows and stared at the sunlight that glinted in the leaves of the little maple trees along the block. Finally he said heavily and quietly, "I'm worried, sure. We're trying something the biggest mob in the country wouldn't touch for ten million bucks. That's something to worry about."

"But you're going ahead with it," she said, turning the sherry glass slowly against her lower lip.

"A kidnaping is different from any other job," he said, still staring down into the street. "Contacts, cash, they're no good. You don't have a friend in a deal like this. We'll be hot the way no killer or bank robber is ever hot. They can go to the mobs and pay for a hideout, transportation. But no mob would help us. They'd finger us straight to the cops." Turning, he looked at her then, his eyes curiously flat and pale. "That's going to work on us, you and me, on Duke and Creasy. That's what we got to fight. The feeling that we're all alone, that if we slip we'll be in the chair thirty days later."

"But you're going ahead with it?" she asked him again, moving her foot about in a slow circle.

He nodded at her, his eyes bright and hard and dangerous. "You're damned right I am. And nothing is going to stop me. . . ."

At five o'clock on the afternoon of the 17th, a black Jaguar pulled up and stopped before the Bradleys' brownstone on Thirty-first Street. A young man in a leather windbreaker hopped out, closed the door neatly and reverently, then trotted up the stone steps and rang the bell. When the Bradley's housekeeper, Mrs. Jarrod, opened the door, he tossed her a mock salute. "One Jaguar, all set to growl," he said. "You keep an eye on him, I've got to get back to the garage."

"They'll be leaving directly," Mrs. Jarrod said.

The young man smiled up at the rectangular section of blue sky and white cloud that was visible from the street. "They got a nice week end coming up," he said. "They going sailing?"

"I presume so," Mrs. Jarrod said.

"That's the life." He sighed. "When I make my pile, that's for me. The blue sea, the bounding main, a bottle of beer—living, eh?"

Mrs. Jarrod stiffened. Gray-haired, stout and conventional, she brooked no nonsense from the world; and this struck her as nonsense. "You won't make your pile, as you put it, wasting time chattering with me," she said.

The young man laughed and trotted down the steps to the sidewalk. He headed toward Third Avenue, swinging his arms briskly, obviously savoring the clean feeling of the spring air.

From his room across the street Howard Creasy watched the scene. He stood in darkness, peering through the heavy curtains that covered his windows. The room behind him was close and warm, smelling faintly of the liver-sausage sandwich and coffee he had brought in for his supper. Creasy's body was motionless, almost inert, and his face was impassive. Only his eyes seemed alive; behind rimless glasses they burned now with a curious intensity.

When the door opened and the Bradleys appeared, Creasy felt the sudden nervous stroke of his heart. He moved closer to the window and a shaft of sunlight touched the beads of perspiration on his forehead.

Dick Bradley, a dark-haired young man in his middle thirties, took the luggage down to the car. Two pigskin bags, a leather cosmetics case, luxuriously thick car robe—Creasy made a bitter and envious inventory. No stickers on the suitcases, he noticed with a stab of anger; they'd been around the world more than likely but they wouldn't use labels for fear people would take them for common tourists. They were the Bradleys, so naturally they stopped at all the fine places—no need to paste up the itinerary for fools to stare at.

Creasy was enjoying his anger; it quickened his pulse and respiration, and suffused his body with a sense of power and urgency that was almost unendurably exhilarating.

Mrs. Bradley (who was called Ellie, he knew) was having a last word with the housekeeper while her husband stowed their things away in the back of the car. Final orders, Creasy thought sullenly. "Do this, do that," he said aloud, and his voice was a mincing little snarl. "Use up the meat loaf and left-overs. And don't be hanging on the telephone."

Creasy knew all about people with money, people like Ellie Bradley. And he hated them with all the power and strength of his small body and soul. She had the stamp of money on her, he saw. It was something they couldn't camouflage. She was beautiful and correct, of course, in a great gray tweed topcoat that went perfectly with her ash-blonde hair and cool, stylish manners. Anointed and perfumed and pampered, he thought, with alligator pumps and matching handbag, and the bright yellow cashmere scarf blazing at her slim throat. But it wasn't only the clothes that marked her in his eyes; he saw the arrogance in the turn of her narrow elegant head, the contempt in every studied line of her tall graceful body. That's what they couldn't hide, he thought, watching them with cold, cunning eyes. Their merciless disdain for the poor and the weak. . . .

He felt his heart lurch with fury as he stared at them; they were so fabulously equipped, so sure of themselves, so casual and secure in their acceptance of privilege. They wouldn't notice him if he were lying in the gutter at their feet with a broken back. Oh, but if he didn't leap to open a door, or bow and smile to her—yes, that would be different. They only noticed you if you inconvenienced them, intruded on their serene pleasure. There was only one way to gain their attention—by hurting them.

"Enjoy yourselves, my chickies," he murmured into the silence of his room. He thought with bitter relish of their week end—of tennis and golf and sailing, of the salty wind whipping ruddiness and health into their clean-limbed handsome bodies. And then the long nights, reveling in pleasure, creating more of their own to enjoy the blessings of the rich. "Enjoy yourselves," he said, and his voice was suddenly harsh and ugly in the dark room.

Dick Bradley called to his wife, smiling up at her, and she said a last good-by to Mrs. Jarrod and came quickly down the stairs, her slim legs flashing in the sunlight. They climbed into the car, waved to Mrs. Jarrod and drove off. She watched them for a second or two, then went inside, closing the door against Creasy.

He walked across the room and picked up the telephone. Enjoy yourself, he thought, smiling faintly. When you come home life will be very different.

Grant answered and Creasy said, "They've just gone."

"Good. Call me when the housekeeper leaves."

"Of course," Creasy said.

The receiver clicked in his ear.

# 3

AT MIDNIGHT A BLACK SEDAN PULLED UP AND PARKED ON THE EAST side of Second Avenue, a few doors below Thirty-first. Grant was at the wheel, hat brim low across his forehead, a cigarette gleaming in the dark triangle of his face. Belle huddled close to him, the collar of her bulky opossum coat turned up about her throat; the night was cold and a sharp wind churned through the empty, silent streets.

Duke sat behind them, leaning forward, and only the sharp glint of his eyes was visible in the darkness.

"I got a minute after twelve," he said quietly. "How about you?"

Grant raised an arm and looked at his watch. "That's it. We'll be around front in just ten minutes."

They had timed this operation as carefully as possible, estimating to the half-minute how long it would take Duke to reach the nursery in the Bradleys' home, to bring the child down to the sidewalk on Thirty-first Street. It was necessary to rendezvous on Thirty-first Street; the lane that ran behind the Bradleys' brownstone was not wide enough to admit a car.

Grant shifted and stared at Duke. "You all set?"

"I'll see you in ten minutes," Duke said. His smile was a vivid slash in the darkness. "There's nothing to worry about."

"Sure, sure," Grant said in a light sharp voice. "Get started."

Duke left the car and walked rapidly toward the narrow lane that passed behind the Bradleys' home. He wore a black leather windbreaker and a black scarf wrapped tightly about his throat. In spite of his limp he moved swiftly and silently, and only the white flash of his face was visible in the dark stretches between the yellow street lamps. . . .

In the car Belle lit a cigarette and Grant looked at her and swore under his breath. "You have to smoke now?" he said. "You can't wait till we're on our way?"

"What's the matter, Eddie?"

"I asked you a question. Can't you wait till we—" Grant wet his lips and stared through the windshield at the wide dark emptiness of Second Avenue. Only an occasional truck rumbled past them, and the sidewalks were deserted. "You'll have your hands full with that baby pretty soon," he said.

"I'll be through with this cigarette by then," she said.

"Okay, okay." He wished she wouldn't quibble about things; he wished she would do as he told her and shut up; and he wished his nerves were in steadier shape. It had come as a surprise, this sudden jittery conviction that something was going to slip. There was no reason for fear; the plan was sound, its details had been checked painstakingly and he had no serious doubts about Duke or Creasy. So why was he worried?

She laughed softly. "Eddie, you're a funny guy. Until tonight I'd of sworn you didn't have a nerve in your body."

"What are you talking about?"

"It happened right after supper, didn't it? I saw you get a funny look on your face. It came real suddenly, as if you'd just woke up in a strange place and didn't know where you were. And were afraid to turn your head to see what was behind you."

"You got some imagination," Grant said, trying to make his voice flat and bored. "Stop thinking so much about me. You packed everything for the baby? And did you put my cable exerciser in the grip?"

"Yes, of course. Everything is perfect."

*It happened right after supper, didn't it?* She was right, of course.

That's when it had hit him, the weakening fear that he was risking his life in this deal—literally his naked vulnerable body. That wasn't true in other jobs; you risked your freedom for ten years, say six with good behavior thrown in, but in a kidnaping there was nothing but the chair. Grant looked at his watch and saw that seven minutes had passed. Duke must be in the nursery now! He cleared the dryness from his throat and started the motor. "We'll go around the block," he said, keeping his voice soft and quiet. "If everything's okay he should be waiting for us."

There was no parking space near the Bradleys' home, Grant saw. Cars were lined bumper to bumper on both sides of the street. And there was no sign of Duke. But they were a good two minutes ahead of schedule. He double parked three doors from the Bradleys' house, and cut the motor and the lights. Silence and darkness closed about them; along the block only a few windows showed yellow squares against the night.

Grant watched the double doors of the Bradleys' home, prepared to turn the ignition the instant they swung open. In his mind he could see the sequence vividly—the opening doors, then Duke's dark figure, bulky with the child in his arms. And he could almost feel his own arms and legs moving as he drove slowly to meet them. And in his imagination he could hear the smooth roar of the motor as they picked up speed and disappeared into the dark. . . .

But the door remained closed.

"He's late," Grant said, willing the door to open.

Three minutes passed away—three minutes in which each second died separately and slowly.

"Duke said a minute after, didn't he?" Grant turned to Belle, his voice strangely high and sharp. "Not a minute before, was it?"

"You both had your watches set at a minute after," Belle said.

In the rear vision mirror Grant saw a car turn into the block off Third Avenue. A red rectangular light gleamed on the roof of the car above the windshield.

"Christ!" he said softly.

"What is it?" Belle looked at Grant and saw the blisters of sweat that had suddenly broken out on his forehead. "What is it?" she said again, reaching for his hand.

"A squad car." He put his arm around her shoulder and drew her close as the light from the police prowl car swept up to them. "If they stop we're just saying good night, see?"

But the police car didn't stop. It went by slowly, the driver glancing at them without expression, his face hard and young under the shiny visor of his cap.

Grant took his arm from Belle's shoulders and watched the squad's red taillight until it disappeared at the intersection of Second Avenue. Then he said softly, "Next time around those jokers will stop and ask questions."

He wet his lips and looked at the closed door of the Bradley home. "I had a feeling something would slip."

"He's only six or seven minutes late," Belle said.

"We'll go around the block, once more," Grant said. "Just once."

"What do you think happened?"

"How the hell would I know?" Grant said, as he let out the clutch.

The circuit took two minutes. As they came down Thirty-first Street for the second time, the car rolling slowly and quietly, Grant saw no sign of Duke; the steps and sidewalk in front of the Bradley home were empty. And then, as he gunned the motor, a shadow moved between two parked cars and Duke stepped suddenly into the glare of the headlights.

He was alone—Grant saw that as he pressed his foot powerfully against the brake. The car stopped short, swaying on its springs, and Duke limped toward them, his eyes bright and reckless with excitement.

"Get in!" Grant said. "Get in, damn you."

"No, I've got to go back inside."

"Are you crazy?" Grant's voice rose suddenly. "Get in, I tell you."

Duke caught his shoulder with a huge hand. "Now listen," he said sharply. "Shut up and listen. The nurse woke up. She was sleeping in the room beside the nursery. I—"

"Stay here if you want," Grant said, staring into Duke's hard, dangerous eyes. "I'm clearing out."

Duke tightened his grip on Grant's shoulder. "We got time, Eddie. The nurse is out cold. She'll be out for ten minutes. Relax, for God's sake." He glanced up and down the dark sidewalks then, still holding Grant by the shoulder, and finally he swung his eyes over the dark windows in the building across the street. "We got time," he said, in a low, insistent voice. "We look all right. I'm just a guy saying good night to some friends. Listen to me, will you?"

"Did the nurse get a look at you?" Grant asked.

"No, I took her from behind," Duke said. "She didn't see anything." He looked past Grant at Belle. "You've got to come back with me. We've got to take the nurse and the kid. I can't handle it alone."

"Have you flipped?" Grant said, jerking free from Duke's hand. "What the hell are you talking about?"

"We're taking them both, Eddie," Duke said. He was grinning but his eyes were cold and ugly. "If we leave the nurse she'll blow a whistle on us when she comes around. And that will louse up the whole deal. But if we take her with us and the cops get into it, they'll blame the job on her. Don't you see that?" His voice suddenly hardened. "Damn it, what's the matter with you? We ran into trouble. Does that mean we chicken out? Are you kids or grownups?"

Grant wet his lips and glanced at Belle. She looked lonely and frightened, her eyes large and shiny in the darkness. This was what he'd feared and expected; some freakish development that would make all their planning worthless. The conviction of disaster had become a superstition with him; a certainty based on emotions impervious to logic or reason. "Okay, get moving," he said to Belle. "It's okay."

"But, Eddie—"

"It's okay," he said, but he knew that was a lie. They were acting impulsively, improvising to circumvent trouble, and he knew this was no good. "You go with Duke," he said.

When Belle hesitated he said sharply, "Get moving," and at that she opened the door and walked around the car. In the glare of the headlights he saw the fear in her pale face. Duke took her arm and said to Grant, "Ride around for ten minutes. We'll be ready by then."

Grant let out the clutch and when the car moved away Duke said to Belle, "Come on. We got to work fast. . . ."

Everything was as he had left it, Duke saw, as he entered the nursery. The baby was in her crib, the nurse lay on the studio couch against the wall and the air was heavy with the nauseating smell of ether. A blue night-light cast a soft glow over the room, touching the smiles of big-eyed dolls, gleaming on brightly colored picture books and pull-toys. It was a charming room, warm and scented, luxurious with satin-smooth blankets and big cuddly pillows.

Duke said quietly, "The nurse's room is upstairs. Pack a grip with her things, enough to last her a week or so. Don't forget jewelry, perfumes, letters. Personal stuff."

"Will she need all that?" Belle stood close to him, speaking in a nervous whisper. She was staring at the nurse's slender figure, at her black hair spread in disorder against the pillow.

"Make it look like she planned to leave," Duke said, still very quietly. "Go on now, Belle. And hurry."

When Belle tiptoed from the room, Duke sat on the couch and studied the girl's pale face. She was breathing slowly and heavily, moving her head from side to side in confusion and pain. In the glow of the night-light he could see the fine softness of her skin. She was smaller than he remembered her. Actually she was more girl than woman, with a tiny waist and small but promising hips and breasts; it was the way she held herself and walked that gave an illusion of height. She wasn't just pretty, he thought, smiling at her shadowed eyes. She was beautiful, hard and fine at the same time, full of breeding and spirit. The kind that needed training and curbing—lots of it. But breaking them in was fun. And then they worked just that much harder to please you. Like his brother, Hank . . .

He realized that he was wasting precious time. "Okay, wake up," he said, slapping her cheeks sharply and deliberately. When her eyes opened, when the cords in her throat suddenly went tight with terror, Duke put a heavy hand across her mouth and said, "No noise now. You understand?"

She struggled helplessly against him, arching her slim body against his weight, twisting her head away from the suffocating pressure of his hand.

Duke said quietly, "Cut it out now. You want the kid to be hurt?"

At that she ceased the unequal and pointless fight; her body became taut and rigid under his hand. Only her eyes continued to move; they went back and forth across his face, intent with a sudden new fear and understanding.

"That's better," Duke said. "You remember me, I guess. Now listen: we're taking the baby. And we're taking you. If you do what you're told the kid won't be hurt. You understand? It's up to you whether the kid lives or dies. You got that straight?"

He moved his hand to let her speak. She said, "Yes, don't hurt her. Please—"

Duke put his hand down, cutting off the sentence. "Okay, that's smart. We've got a long drive ahead of us tonight. You get dressed, get in the car and enjoy the ride. If you make a fuss, we'll tie you up like a Christmas turkey and put you in the trunk. You won't like that. You won't get any circulation in your hands and feet, and there's not much air back there. After eight or ten hours you'll be glad to be a good little girl. You understand me?"

Belle came into the room carrying an overnight bag, a sweater, gray tweed skirt and a pair of black sling pumps. "I've got everything," she said.

"Okay," Duke said. He took his hands from the nurse's mouth and stared into her dark eyes. "You going to be good?"

Her eyes went to Belle, and then back to Duke. Only the sound of her rapid shallow breathing disturbed the silence of the room.

"Well?" Duke said.

Staring up at him, she wet her lips and nodded slowly.

The cold blue of the Medomak River was on their right as they turned into the narrow gravel-topped road that wound past Hank Farrel's cottage. They had made two stops since leaving New York; one, on Third Avenue, to post the ransom demand, the second for coffee and fried egg sandwiches several hours later. Now they were eight hours out of New York, ninety miles north of Portland and the sun had already burned away the last of the mists that had hung in thick layers over the land at dawn.

It was clean hard country they had been driving through the past two hours, a winter country softening now with spring; thick scrub bushes were touched with bright green and the frozen earth had turned dark in patches, as snow melted and freshets trickled toward the river from the high ground. It was a land of silences and small brilliant ponds, of rocky coastline and forests of squat, salt-bleached fir trees.

When they stopped in the lane beside Hank Farrel's house no one spoke for a moment; they were held by the silence around them, and the curious sense of distance that pervades coastal lands. Finally Duke stirred and that served as a cue for the others; they climbed from the car then and stared at the house.

It was a snug and tidy salt box, the original structure two stories high and the addition extending out sharply from the level of the first floor windows. Everything about it was spick-and-span; the clapboard was bright with fresh white paint and the windowpanes sparkled cleanly in the sun. From its elevation, the views were dramatic; on one side a vividly green stretch of fir trees sloped down to the tidal river. On the other side there was the winding road, a pond semicircled by forests and finally the peak of another house outlined sharply against the blue sky. The house was a half-mile down the road and the nearest village, Williamsboro, was five miles away.

Grant narrowed his eyes against the brilliance of sun, sky and water. He didn't like the look of this country; it was hard and cold and unyielding. But then, staring around at the silent forest and feeling the desolateness of the area, he began to smile faintly. This wasn't a pleasure trip, this was business. And for their business this place was perfect. Grant had recovered his confidence and was thinking clearly and sharply again. Their schedule would have to be altered, he knew, but not seriously. Originally he hadn't planned to make the trip up to Maine; he was to stay in New York and pick up the ransom money. But with the nurse on their hands he had been forced to come along. Belle didn't drive and Duke couldn't watch the nurse and the road at the same time. But they could handle her all right now and he would take the train back to New York in the morning. "Let's get inside," he said.

Twenty minutes later he stood with Duke in front of the fireplace, soaking up warmth from the blazing pine logs. Duke was pouring rum into two thick mugs on the mantelpiece. They had found the fire laid for them and the bottle of rum on the kitchen table—with a note from Duke's brother telling them to make themselves at home.

Grant was in high spirits; the lines of tension had disappeared from around his mouth and eyes. The fire was loosening his cold, stiff muscles, and the smell of the strong rum had quickened all of his senses. He glanced around the long, comfortable room, noticing the shelves of books, the small piano, the well-worn rugs and furniture—and suddenly he began to laugh.

Duke handed him a glass of rum. "What's so funny?"

"It was so damned easy, when you think about it. We walk in and pick up the granddaughter of one of the biggest guys in the country—with no more trouble than you'd have stealing a newspaper."

Duke glanced at him, smiling faintly. "Sitting out in the car was easy enough, I guess."

"Let's don't argue about who was the hero." Duke's sarcasm didn't affect Grant's good humor. "The thing is we licked this deal. I'll go back to New York in the morning and arrange to pick up the cash. All you have to do is keep the nurse quiet. That shouldn't be hard."

"Just the opposite," Duke said, grinning.

Grant looked at him, and then turned his eyes toward the low beamed ceiling. Belle had taken the nurse and baby upstairs, and they could hear the click of high-heeled shoes above their heads.

"Be smart," Grant said. "She'll play along. She'll do anything to save the kid."

"I was thinking about that," Duke said, and took a sip from his drink.

"I told you to be smart," Grant said, staring at him. "Leave her alone."

"Supposing she throws herself at me?" Duke said. He sighed comically. "It might take all my strength, Eddie."

"Get this straight," Grant said. "Don't touch her."

And then, as Duke grinned at him with easy challenge, a knock sounded on the front door.

For an instant neither man moved; standing perfectly still they stared at each other, their breathing a slow, laboring sound in the silence. Then Grant swore softly and dropped his hand into the pocket of his suit coat.

"Relax," Duke said, grabbing his arm.

"You said nobody ever came by here."

"Take your hand off that gun." Duke's voice was an angry, insistent whisper. "It's probably a friend of my brother's. I'll handle this."

Grant swallowed the dry constriction in his throat. The yellow, old-parchment color had faded from his face; in the morning light his skin was a dirty gray. "See who it is," he said hoarsely.

There was a second knock on the door as Duke limped across the room. "Coming," he called.

He pulled open the door and the smile stiffened on his face as he stared at the slender sandy-haired young man who stood on the porch. For a few seconds the two men stared at each other in a tense, unnatural silence; they were both smiling, but there was no humor in their watchful, appraising eyes. Then Duke laughed suddenly and boisterously and slapped the younger man on the shoulder. "Well, I'll be damned," he said. "Talk about surprises. Come on in, kid."

Turning his head he looked at Grant, who was moving slowly across the floor, one hand deep in the pocket of his suit coat. "Eddie, how about this!" he said. Duke's voice was big and hearty, but his eyes were alive with dark and unmistakable warning. Laughing, he said, "Eddie, meet my kid brother!"

# 4

HANK FARREL GLANCED PAST HIS BROTHER, AND NODDED TO THE POWER-fully built man who was moving slowly toward them with a hand buried deep in his pocket, and no expression at all on his broad, pale face. This would be Eddie Grant, he thought. Duke had written that he wanted to bring Grant and his family up for a week or so. Grant and Duke were going into business together, and they needed to thrash out all the details in peace and quiet. Fine, Hank thought. Grant looked as if he could stand a little peace and quiet.

And then, as his brother closed the door behind him, Hank became aware of the tension in the room. It hit him so abruptly that he felt the smile tighten awkwardly on his lips. Grant and his brother were staring at each other like fighters waiting for the gong to sound.

"You told me he was going fishing," Grant said in a hard, bitter voice.

Duke smiled carelessly. "Maybe I got it mixed up," he said. "No harm done, eh, Eddie?"

Hank felt the edge of warning in his brother's voice. And then he saw that Grant was holding a gun in his pocket; the muzzle made a round, unmistakable bulge against the cloth of the jacket.

Hank's arms moved out from his body, an instinctive preparation for trouble. Grant glanced at him, and Hank realized he was behaving fool-ishly; this trouble didn't concern him. It was between Duke and Grant. Maybe he'd walked in on an argument.

Hank took out his cigarettes and moved between the two men, trying to ignore the tension in the room. But this wasn't easy; the gun in Grant's hand was now pointed squarely at his own stomach. "The plane we chartered developed engine trouble," he said. "We had to postpone our trip, so I thought I'd drive over and say hello."

"Postponed your trip?" Grant's eyes were hard and cold. "For how long?"

"Just a few hours," Hank said. He offered his cigarettes to Grant, making an effort to reduce the curious strain with this commonplace gesture. But Grant shook his head, and continued to study him suspiciously. What are they afraid of? Hank thought. And with that came a fear he hadn't felt for a long, long time: what was his brother mixed up in now? "You found the rum, I hope," he said, glancing at Duke.

"Sure, we found it," Duke said heartily; his manner was suddenly effusive and cordial. "Eddie and I started working on it, too, don't worry." Laughing he put his hands on Hank's shoulders, and looked him up and down, grinning in what seemed to be pleased and genuine astonishment. "Kid, this is great. It calls for a drink all around. How the hell long has it been? Five years, eh?"

"Almost eight," Hank said.

"Ye gods! That long! Eddie, I haven't seen this kid brother of mine for eight years."

The tension in the room had eased, Hank saw; Grant's hand had come out of his pocket, and Duke had switched over to a favorite role, the boisterous, high-spirited, life-of-the-party.

Grant put out his big square hand, and said, "It's nice to meet you, Hank." He was smiling, but the effort did nothing but tighten the network of wrinkles around his curiously pale eyes. "It was nice of you to let us use your place for our confab."

Duke put an arm around Hank's shoulder and hugged him roughly. "Did you think he'd tell me to get lost when I needed a favor?" He grinned at Grant. "We Farrels stick together. Right, kid?"

"Sure," Hank said shortly. He didn't like the feel of his brother's arm on his shoulders. And he didn't like the unctuous good humor they were exuding now; in its way this was more ominous than the fear and tension of a moment ago. What were they covering up?

Duke let his hands drop to his sides, and Hank saw the change in his smile, the hardening around his eyes and mouth. Duke had sensed his coldness, he knew. This was a gift of his brother's, a shrewd, intuitive awareness of what people were feeling and thinking. Particularly if they were trying to hide anything; he had an instinctive flair for fear and guilt. Smiling at Grant, Duke said, "Hank and I had our troubles, but we kept them in the family. Sometimes I had to teach him a little respect for his big brother." He rapped his knuckles lightly against Hank's stomach. "You remember those little lessons, eh, kid?"

"I learned a lot from you," Hank said slowly.

"And now you're all grown up," Duke said. Studying his brother, Duke's smile was tentative, faintly challenging. "Let's see, you're twenty-eight, eh? And you've been off to the wars. I read that you got some kind of a decoration. It was in the home-town paper, right on the front page with a picture of you and everything. That was something, having you turn out to be a hero."

He sighed and slapped his bad leg. "The doctors just told me to go home and buy war bonds."

Hank realized with relief that Duke's self-pity didn't touch him at all; in fact it struck him as slightly comical. "How many did you buy?" he said casually.

For an instant Duke looked startled. Then he recovered and punched Hank on the arm. "Hey, they turned you into a humorist."

Hank smiled at him, savoring the awareness of his own freedom. The old slavery was over and done with. He knew that now. He could face Duke without fear or shame, without the guilty sense of responsibility that had oppressed him all his life. The eight years on his own had cut the bonds that held him to his brother. He had been sure it would be this way: he had felt free of Duke. But he'd been compelled to put it to the test. That was why he had driven back here tonight. . . .

Duke was a stranger to him now, he thought, studying the bold, heavy features, the cold eyes recessed under a jutting ridge of forehead. A guy who'd thrown away his chances, who had drank or fought his way out of every job he'd had, and who blamed the world for all his troubles. He doesn't mean a thing to me any more. Even the bad leg meant nothing. I ruined that leg, and it doesn't bother me at all, he thought. Hank realized that he had never seen Duke clearly until this instant. The image of his brother had always been distorted by fear and guilt. But now the picture was sharply and vividly in focus. A bully, a liar . . . Was this what I feared? he thought, with a touch of bitterness.

He was surprised at his lack of feeling. There was no pity left in him, no mercy, nothing. It was all gone, paid out in blackmail to Duke over the years. In hourly installments. . . .

"Well, let's have that drink," Grant said, directing the impatience in his voice at Duke. "Your brother's got to be on his way, I guess."

Hank glanced at his watch as Duke limped into the kitchen. "Yes, I don't have much time," he said, moving toward the fireplace. Why were they so anxious to get rid of him? "This feels pretty good," he said, stripping off his jacket and holding out his hands to the welcome heat. And why was Grant carrying a gun?

"It's getting colder, I think," Grant said. There wasn't much resemblance between the brothers, he thought. Hank was light-colored and quick, with short sandy hair, and a slim, rangy body. A deceptive kind of build. So smooth and easy that you didn't figure it for anything else. But he saw the power in Hank's big bony wrists, and the suggestion of speed in the way he moved and handled himself. He was taller than his brother, but Duke had forty pounds on him, all of it in his massive shoulders and arms. The kid, that's what Duke called him. But Grant wondered. This didn't look like a kid to him. Not with that jaw, and the hard, serious face. There was a thin white scar across his forehead, and this added to his grave, businesslike appearance; the scar drew a permanent frown above his eyes. He didn't have Duke's wildness or violence, but he'd be harder to handle than he looked, Grant knew. But he wasn't worried about a physical showdown.

What worried him was that the kid seemed sharp and alert, nobody's fool. He'd seen the gun. Grant was sure of that. So what would he do? Have a drink with them, wave a big good-by—and then head for the cops? Could they let him go?

Grant drifted across the room toward the fireplace. "You got a fine spot here," he said, his eyes going toward the ceiling. Everything was quiet up there. Maybe this would work out. Maybe they could send him off thinking nothing was wrong. "You know, you gave me a real jolt when you knocked," he said. His laugh was a good effort, solid and cheerful, but just a bit embarrassed. "I'm a city boy, and too much peace and quiet gets on my nerves. Duke said nobody ever came by here, and when you banged on the door—" He laughed and shook his head. "I damn near went out of my skin. Look!" He took the revolver from his pocket and showed it to Hank. "That's how nervous I was. I don't know what I expected. A gang of drunken Indians maybe."

"I'm sorry I startled you," Hank said, smiling easily. "But this is pretty peaceful country. We haven't had an Indian raid up here for weeks."

Grant laughed and dropped the gun into his pocket. "But I didn't know that," he said.

"You might get in some target practice on the river," Hank said. He was still smiling, playing out the farce. "But don't waste time looking for Indians."

A footstep sounded above them, and Hank glanced at the ceiling. Grant cleared his throat and said, "My wife will be sorry she missed you. She was pretty tired after the drive."

"Maybe another time," Hank said.

"Sure."

Duke came into the room carrying a tray of hot rum drinks, his manner charged with a jovial bustle. "Here we are," he said, "the old painkiller." The pungent smell of the liquor was sharp in the warm room. Firelight blazed on the satin-smooth pine floor, and sun glinted brightly on the clean windowpanes. A cute picture, Hank thought, taking a glass from Duke. Add a gun though, and it didn't look so cute.

"Well, I hit the jackpot this time, kid," Duke said, grinning at him. "Eddie and I can't miss."

"Let's drink to that," Hank said. Duke had written vaguely about his connection with Grant: a mail-order business, no overhead, vast profits and so forth. Hank had heard this sort of thing before. Duke was always just one step away from the pot of gold. Then something went wrong. Never through his fault, of course.

"You'll have to get used to me being a big shot," Duke said. He winked at Grant. "The kid was always after me to make something out of myself. Be a credit to the family. Like he was." Duke's voice was good-humored, but there was a needle in his manner.

Hank found the old mockery faintly tiresome. And this pleased him. Another bond broken. . . .

Grant put his empty glass on the mantel and glanced at his watch. "That was a rough drive," he said, covering a yawn with his hand. "I hate to be a killjoy, but I'm going to turn in."

As Hank put his glass down, footsteps sounded above them, moving with a sense of determination and urgency. Looking up, he caught the sharp, warning glance that flicked between Grant and his brother. Then a woman's voice, high with anger and desperation, cut through the silence. "You can't keep a baby in this icebox. She'll die up here!"

"Now, now, don't shout so!" It was another voice, soothing but stern, speaking as an adult might speak to a difficult child.

"Stay here, Duke," Grant said. He stared at Hank, then turned and started up the stairs, his thick legs driving like pistons beneath his heavy, powerful body.

Duke closed the door behind him and looked at his brother with a lazy little smile. "You can always trust dames to provide some fireworks," he said. "Don't worry though, it doesn't sound serious."

"It doesn't sound exactly cheerful," Hank said. He heard Grant's voice then, sharp and angry, and above it the note of desperation in the girl's protest.

"Family squabbles usually sound like four-alarm fires," Duke said. Leaning against the door he seemed completely at ease; he was like a fighter facing an opponent he had no reason to take seriously. "Just forget it, kid," he said.

"Who's the girl?" Hank said. "And who's the baby she's worried about?"

Duke glanced toward the sound of the argument upstairs, and then sighed and shrugged—gestures that suggested good-natured capitulation. "I guess you got a right to know," he said. "It's your house. The girl is Grant's daughter. And the baby belongs to her. It's a real cute little baby. But Grant's daughter just doesn't happen to have any real cute little husband." Duke smiled whimsically. "You know how it is. People make mistakes."

An ominous little chill went through Hank as he realized that Duke was lying to him. "That's a shame," he said casually. The instinct for survival had made him an authority on his brother's poses; Duke's shifting and deceptive masks had been an anxious preoccupation of his for years. And now he knew that Duke was lying. The lazy smile, the air of worldly compassion—they were both false. Underneath that indolent façade Duke's muscles were tightening for trouble.

"It's a shame, all right," Duke said, sighing heavily. "And it's a load on Grant. That's why he acts so damn jumpy. Maybe you noticed it. His daughter is a hot-tempered kid, and they aren't hitting it off so well. He was hoping they could patch things up if they had a little peace and quiet."

"This is the place for it," Hank said. Would they let him go? he wondered. Would they risk it?

The argument above them reached a climax. Grant shouted something, a door slammed with a crash and the echo of the two sounds trembled through the house, fading slowly into silence.

Duke sighed and took out his cigarettes. "Old Eddie's got his troubles," he said. "We were in our share of scrapes, but we never handed the old man that particular kind of headache. Eh, kid?" He smiled and offered the cigarettes to Hank. "Want one of these?"

"Thanks." Hank accepted a cigarette and tapped it against the back of his hand, playing along with Duke's mood of casual indifference. But he knew that Duke was watching him closely; over the flame of the match his brother's eyes were sharp with speculation.

Would they let him go now? Hank wondered, as he heard Grant coming down the stairs. A little earlier they had been eager to get rid of him. But there was something wrong here. And they might wonder what he thought, what he suspected. . . .

"Well, I've got to be on my way," he said, as Grant stepped into the room. Turning, he strolled over to the chair where he had left his jacket. He didn't want to look at either of them just now. Something in his face might give him away. While his back was turned they would make their decision about him. . . .

"It was fine seeing you again, Duke," he said, picking up his jacket. "And you, too, Eddie. I'm just sorry I couldn't stay longer."

"Sure, kid," Duke said. "Let's don't put off the next reunion quite so long, eh?"

"Of course not," Hank said. He laughed. "Eight more years and we'll be old men."

They were settling the issue now, with a glance, a gesture. . . .

Hank turned slowly, frowning at his wrist watch. This was the appropriate gesture for the charade he was acting out—concern over time. "I'll have to hurry," he said, glancing up at Grant.

And then he saw they didn't intend to let him go.

Grant was standing six feet from him, big hands hanging limply at his sides. There was no expression at all in his broad, strangely old face; even his eyes were blank and unrevealing. Duke stood with his elbow resting on the mantel, his teeth flashing in a smile against his healthy brown skin.

It was the smile that gave them away. Hank knew that smile; as a boy he had learned to watch for it with dread. It was a special smile, mettlesome and reckless, and it meant that trouble was on the way. Trouble for someone else . . .

Grant cleared his throat, and the sound was hard and significant in the waiting silence. "How long out to the airport?"

"About half an hour," Hank said, as casually as he could manage it. He moved closer to Grant. They weren't expecting trouble, he realized; they didn't rate him that high. "Well, it was pleasant meeting you, Eddie," he said. "I hope you and Duke make a mint."

"We kind of expect to," Grant said, without smiling. There was an edge of sarcasm to his voice. "Next time maybe you can stay longer, kid."

"Sure thing," Hank said, still smiling. Grant's hand was moving slowly toward his coat pocket and Hank thought, *now*— Deliberately, almost casually, he flipped his bulky woolen jacket into Duke's face and then he slugged Grant in the stomach with his right hand, putting every bit of strength and weight behind the blow. The move was so fast and unexpected that both men were caught completely off guard; Duke stumbled toward the mantel, and Grant went for his gun in a desperate reflex, just as Hank's fist sank into his stomach and smashed the air from his body.

Grant shouted hoarsely as the pain doubled him up, and the sounds came out of his straining throat in convulsive gasps. The gun was almost clear of his pocket but his fingers were too weak to hold it; Hank tore it away from him, and swung the butt down heavily against the back of his head. As Grant went to the floor, his body sprawling in a slack, clumsy heap, Hank stepped back quickly and twisted the gun up to cover his brother.

Duke had recovered his balance, and was staring at him in what seemed to be complete bewilderment. "What's got into you, kid?" he said, in a high, shocked voice.

"Don't move," Hank said.

"Have you gone crazy? Is that what they taught you in the army? To slug people for no reason at all?" Duke took a limping step toward his brother. "Eddie's a friend of mine," he said angrily. "He may be dying, you crazy fool."

"I told you to stay put," Hank said.

Duke stopped, his eyes flicking to the gun. "You're acting damn strange," he said slowly. "You're in bad trouble, kid. There are laws about breaking people's skulls open." Shrugging, he moved toward Hank. "But maybe we can square this. I'm your brother, remember."

"Don't take any bets on brotherly love," Hank said. The gun in his hand was steady on Duke's stomach. "I want to know what's going on here."

"You sure grew up," Duke said thoughtfully. His manner had changed; he seemed relaxed and at ease, and there was an approving little smile on his lips. "I couldn't have handled Grant any better myself. They taught

you that in the army, eh?" He stood indolently, lazily, a sleepy glaze alter-
ing the look in his eyes.

But Hank wasn't fooled; he knew how fast Duke could move from any
position.

"You're real tough," Duke said, grinning. "But that gun is on safe."

"You heard that one in the movies," Hank said. "Just stand nice and
quiet." Stepping over Grant's body he put a hand on the knob of the
upstairs door.

"Wait!" Duke said.

"There's nothing to wait for."

"Wait, for God's sake," Duke cried, and Hank stopped short, arrested
by the desperation and fear in his brother's voice and eyes. Watch yourself now, he thought, as Duke rubbed a hand over his forehead with a
despairing gesture.

"You've got to help me, kid," Duke said. "I got nobody else. You've
got to help me."

"What kind of trouble are you in?"

"I tried to keep you out of this," Duke said, rubbing his hands on the
sides of his trousers. "I wanted you to go, to get out of here. You know
that, don't you?"

"What are you mixed up in?" Hank said coldly; he knew Duke too well
to pity him.

"Grant lied to me," Duke said, his voice rising sharply. "You've got
to believe that. Grant said it was a stick-up. I was broke, kid. I went along
with it, because I was broke. I was supposed to drive, that's all. I didn't
know about the baby. I'll swear that on my knees."

A chill went through Hank. "What in God's name are you talking
about?"

"It's a kidnaping, a snatch," Duke said in a rough, trembling voice. He
turned away from his brother and rubbed his hand across his lips. "Grant
suckered me into it. But I tried to get you away from here, kid. You know
I did."

Hank stared at his brother, feeling the straining silence beating at his
ears. He was conscious of his pounding heart, the sound of his breathing,
the cold butt of the gun in the palm of his hand. "You crazy fool," he
said, barely whispering the words.

"It wasn't my fault," Duke stared down at Grant, his big chest rising
and falling rapidly. "He lied to me, the bastard. You think I'd touch a
kidnaping with my eyes open?"

"Who's the girl upstairs?"

"The baby's nurse. We had to take her along." Duke wet his lips.
"What are you going to do, kid?"

"I'm calling the police. Now."

"It'll be the end of me. Think of that, for God's sake."

"If the cops believe your story you may get a break."

"They won't believe me," Duke said harshly. "I've done time. That's all a cop cares about. I'm wrong to start with. It's a form bet. That's the way their minds work. No, they'll burn me." He raised his hands desperately, imploringly. "You got to help me, kid."

"No," Hank said.

"Listen to me for a second. That's all I'm asking."

"No." Stepping around Grant he moved carefully toward the phone, holding the gun on his brother. He was aware of his danger now. There was a woman upstairs with the nurse. She might be armed.

Duke moved sideways with him, edging slowly toward the telephone. "Give me a break, kid," he said hoarsely. "Just till tomorrow morning. The baby goes home then. Grant's taking her back. It will be all done, finished. In just ten or twelve hours. Give me that much of a break."

"Not a chance."

"Listen, kid! If the cops bust in here that baby's going to get hurt. Grant will use her to cover himself. Let's get her out of here before the fireworks start. Isn't that smarter? Or don't you give a damn?" Duke's voice rose angrily. "You want to be the big hero, is that it? Call the cops, get your name in the paper. But supposing the baby is killed. Will that make you happy?"

Hank said gently, "The baby isn't going to be killed. I'll shoot you and Grant first. You'd better believe that."

"Don't talk that way," Duke said, shaking his head quickly. "This is Duke, remember. Your brother, kid." His lips were trembling, and his limp was very pronounced as he dragged himself across the floor. "We can make a deal, kid. Let Grant take the baby home. Then I'll go with you to the cops. They'd believe me then. We'd turn Grant in." He wet his lips. "Just a few hours. That's all I'm asking. I don't want to die, kid."

Unconsciously, Hank hesitated. He wanted to believe him; that had always been his trouble. Even now, listening to his wheedling lies, he wanted to believe him. The story about Grant—it could have happened that way, he thought.

And Duke, six feet from the phone now, watched him with narrowing eyes. "What do you say, kid? Just a few hours?" With what seemed an immense effort, he shifted himself closer to the phone. "You can't blame me for wanting to stay alive. It's not much fun with one leg, but it's better than nothing, I guess. How about it?"

"No," Hank said sharply. Duke's words were beginning to work on him. "No deals, no stalls."

"Go ahead and shoot then!" Duke leaped sideways for the phone, his big body moving with the speed and precision of a pouncing cat. "Shoot me, hero," he said, bringing his hand down with a crash on the receiver. "Kill me. That's what you want." The slackness was gone from his body;

he was like an animal ready to charge; his muscles were drawn up tight, his weight was balanced on the springs of his legs. Crouching low, an arm swinging wide, he laughed bitterly, and said, "Go ahead, pull the trigger. They taught you about guns, didn't they? What are you afraid of?"

"Get away from that phone," Hank said softly. "I don't want to shoot you, Duke."

"You don't want to shoot!" Duke said, in a hard, mocking voice. "Have you sold yourself that lie? You always hated me. You want to blow me to hell. So here's your chance. Haven't you got the guts?"

"You're raving," Hank said. "Get away from that phone."

"Raving?" Duke brought his hand down against the thigh of his bad leg, and the sound was like a pistol shot in the silence. "You did that, remember? You tried to kill me when you were a kid. Now you want the cops to finish the job for you."

"You've got a lot of mileage out of that accident," Hank said, and his voice was as bitter as his brother's. "You've been whining about it for twenty years. Don't you think that's enough?"

"Sure it's boring," Duke said. "You try limping through life and see if it's boring or not. We called it an accident, didn't we? Everybody covered up for little Hank, the boy with the matches and the yen for homicide."

"Shut up," Hank said.

"Don't want to talk about it, eh?" Duke laughed as he saw the tense frown tightening on his brother's forehead. "Of course you don't, kid. It's no fun to talk about your mistakes. And you made a big one. Because you didn't kill me. But you tried, by God. Doesn't that make you feel better? You set the fire, and walked away from it. You knew I was sleeping upstairs. And you didn't think I'd wake up. But I did. And I jumped. I stayed alive."

"Get away from that phone." Hank rubbed the scar on his forehead, and then dropped his hand guiltily to his side; it was a gesture of confusion and anxiety that he hadn't used for years. And he realized with a sudden sickening fear that Duke could still hurt him.

"Am I boring you now?" Duke said, in a low, passionate voice. He took a step toward Hank, staring at him with sullen, furious eyes. "That jump put an end to football and track for me. You can't run with a stiff knee, kid. Paste that away with your collection of interesting, but little-known facts. I was All-State in my sophomore year, the first time that ever happened in Wisconsin. Lots of things ended with that jump, kid." Watching the frown deepen on his brother's face, he laughed bitterly. "And lots of things started. Limping around like a crab. Taking side streets to school because I didn't like dragging myself down Charles Avenue for everybody to stare at. Watching other guys play football, and running on the beach. That all started for me. And ducking away from girls who wanted to tell me they didn't mind that I walked like a crane with a broken leg." Duke laughed again, but his eyes were alive with scorn and anger. "You never knew about this, I guess. You got all the sympathy. 'Mustn't let little Hank know he tried to burn his brother up like a pig on a spit. That might give him nightmares!' Sure, that's what they said. Poor Hank!"

"A spark from the fireplace set the rug on fire," Hank said in a low, savage voice. "When I woke the room was full of smoke. I couldn't get up the stairs to wake you."

Staring at the fury in his brother's face, he knew he was fighting for his freedom, for his very life. Duke's words had stormed against him, scattering his resolution into splintered fragments. He'd been a fool to underestimate him, to think he had earned his freedom without striking a blow.

"An accident," he said again, gathering all his strength for what he must say next; this had been in his mind for years, evolving from his tortuous examination and reassessment of his relationship with Duke. Now he said coldly. "You loved being a martyr. It gave you an excuse to be any kind of a heel you wanted. You always had an out. A cripple could get away with a murder—if he was a phony to start with. You used that stiff knee to blackmail people for pity and sympathy and forgiveness—and anything else you could squeeze out of them."

"I told you you were full of hate," Duke said softly. "Can't you hear it in your voice?"

"No," Hank said. He was breathing hard, his chest rising and falling quickly. "Get away from that phone."

"Why did you hate me?" Duke went on. "You had a good life, didn't you? You went off to the wars while I limped around with the women and children. You loved that, didn't you? Being the hero at last, picture in the paper for shooting some Korean slobs in the back. You pushed me aside all right—it's easy to do with a guy who has only one leg. But you're still not satisfied," Duke said, taking a half-step toward him. "You want to hand me over to the cops. You want them to burn me. But they won't do your dirty work. You'll have to shoot me yourself. Go ahead, you crawling little bastard. Go ahead and shoot."

Hank tried to squeeze the trigger, but his fingers were numb and helpless. "I don't want to kill you," he said, wetting his lips. Without realizing it his free hand had moved to touch the thin, white scar on his forehead.

Duke grinned suddenly. "You aren't going to kill anybody at all, kid." His eyes shifted past Hank's shoulder. "Is he, Eddie?"

Hank spun around, a cold shock of fear streaking through his body. He saw Grant lying on the floor, limp and motionless, and he knew that he'd been tricked, that he'd lost everything. . . .

His reactions were anticlimactic; spinning around, he tried to bring the gun back on Duke, but it was far too late for that. The edge of Duke's hand struck his wrist and sent the gun spinning halfway across the room. And before he could raise his hands, Duke's first blow snapped his head back and the second caught him alongside the jaw and knocked him reeling against the wall.

Duke came after him quickly, his eyes measuring him for destruction. He was grinning now, and his teeth flashed against his dark skin. "You poor fool," he said, beginning to laugh.

Hank couldn't get his hands up; they felt as if weights were riveted to his wrists. He had forgotten the power in Duke's fists. He had forgotten so much. . . .

Duke hit him with clinical precision, once in the stomach, once along the jaw, his arms swinging with the finality of an executioner's stroke. He was laughing as he hit, and that was what Hank heard as he fell toward the spreading blackness at his feet. . . .

# 5

THERE WAS PAIN FIRST, A HEAVY THROBBING ACHE BELOW HIS HEART, and then the confusing memory of an old dream that had haunted his childhood; he had angered and disappointed Duke in some way. That was always the essence that filtered into his consciousness, an oppressive despair at having forfeited his brother's approval.

There was no reference point for his slowly turning thoughts, only the isolated memory of the dream, and the odd sense of confusion. But why confusion? The dream was a familiar weight, a familiar fear. . . .

"Get up!" Duke said. "Come on, move!"

"All right."

"Move, I said."

"All right." He was lying on his left side, his knees drawn up toward his chin. As he rolled onto his stomach the pain below his heart spread toward the small of his back. He gasped softly, trying to lift himself on his elbows.

"You're not hurt," Duke said.

Hank opened his eyes and brought them into focus with a painful effort. Duke and Grant were looking down at him, and behind them stood two women; a dark-haired girl and an older woman, a blonde. The blonde held the girl's arms behind her with soft but competent-looking hands. They were watching him, too—everyone was watching him.

"Get on your feet!" It was Grant speaking, his voice thick and ugly with anger.

"He's not faking," Duke said. "I tagged him pretty good." His tone was judicious, faintly amused. "He forgot his manners in the army. Can you imagine that? What the hell are they doing to these kids of ours?"

"I'll give him a refresher course," Grant said.

Duke began to laugh. "I'll have to hold him for you then. He suckered you real good. He's got a nice right, hasn't he?"

"Sure, he's got a nice right," Grant said. Duke's laughter had brought a rush of angry color into his cheeks. "So we'd better fix it."

Hank twisted convulsively as Grant's steel-capped heel came down on the back of his outstretched hand. He couldn't pull himself free; Grant ground his weight down slowly, viciously, driving the steel cleat like a knife against tendons and bone.

"A nice right," Grant said, "but he won't use it on me again."

Hank put the other fist against his mouth. Tears started in his eyes, and he began to tremble as a cold, sickening sweat squeezed out of his body. But he didn't cry out; the only thing that gave him away was his rapid, tortured breathing.

Duke said, "Well, you asked for it, kid," in an indifferent voice.

And then the girl cried furiously, "Stop it, stop it! Leave him alone!"

The older woman said, "Now, dearie, just keep nice and quiet. It's nothing for you to get excited about."

"What kind of men are you?"

"I may have to show you, baby," Duke said gently.

Hank raised himself up on one elbow; his right hand was numb now, but a fiery little pulse was starting to hammer beneath the smashed bone. It was going to get worse fast. . . .

"Now let's everybody relax," Duke said, putting his hands under his brother's arms and lifting him easily into a chair.

"His friends are waiting for him," Grant said. "They'll start wondering about him pretty soon." He was controlling himself with an effort; an undercurrent of tension trembled in his voice.

"That's why we should all relax," Duke said. "We've got to do some thinking. Snap to, kid. That's better," he said and Hank looked up at him with dark, staring eyes. "Well, it's the old story," Duke said. "You get in my way and you get hurt. You thought that was all changed. Big army hero, and everything." There was no anger in his voice; he sounded faintly amused. "You're a real square. Slugging Eddie, trying to call the cops. Who do you think you are? A boy crime-fighter or something, for God's sake?"

"Let's get on with that thinking," Grant said. "What are we going to do with him?"

"Sure, sure," Duke said. He looked at Hank's hand, studying the broken skin, the blood, the deep, thickening bruise above the knuckles. Finally he turned and limped slowly to the middle of the room. He stood there with his hands on his hips, frowning as he stared from his brother to the girl. "You two listen good, now," he said. His mood had changed again, and his big, dark face was hard and cold. "You got the same stake in this deal that we have. Your lives. If we make a slip, we die. You make a slip, you die. Get that straight. Hank, I'll drive you to the airport. You tell your friends you hurt your hand changing a tire. You can't go fishing with one hand. You got that?" His voice sharpened. "Speak when I talk to you."

"I've—I've got it."

"Look at this girl. Look, I tell you."

Hank moved his eyes slowly to the girl. She had been crying, he saw; her eyes were dark and swollen, and her face streaked with tears. She was slender and small, with long black hair that fell like a shadow across one pale cheek. The woman behind her was softly, unimportantly pretty, with an expression of patient worry on her face. She held the girl's arms in a grip that was expert and efficient; if the girl struggled she would only hurt herself.

"Take a good look," Duke said. "She's the baby's nurse. The baby is upstairs, a real cute little girl. Think of them at the airport, kid. You make a mistake out there and they die. Get it? You try to pull something funny and they're through, finished."

Hank stared at the girl, conscious of the laboring stroke of his heart in the stillness of the room. A wind from the river banged the sides of the house with heavy blows, and the sudden crack of a burning log was sharp and loud against the silence. She was very frightened, he saw; the threat to the baby had done it. And he saw the appeal in her eyes. "Don't hurt her," she said, smiling shakily at Duke, like a child trying to buy the favor of a bad-tempered adult.

"It's up to him," Duke said, nodding casually at his brother. "If he convinces his friends—well and good. If not—" He shrugged his big shoulders, not bothering to finish the sentence.

It was the old trick, Hank thought with weary despair. Duke never accepted responsibility; if anything got in his way that wasn't *his* fault. Hell, *he* couldn't stop. People should know that.

"You both got a job to do," Duke said, staring at the girl. "Remember that. Either of you make a mistake and that kid dies."

"I can get rid of my friends," Hank said. He saw the swift hope kindling in the girl's eyes, and he wondered: what kind of a fool is this? Doesn't she know there's no hope?

"Fine, kid," Duke said. "I knew we could count on you."

"You won't make it," Hank said, staring at him. "You can kill us all but you won't make it."

Duke smiled slowly. "You'd better pray that we do. You're in this, right up to your neck. You had a gun on me, remember? And you knew this was a kidnaping. You could have shot me and called the police. So you're as guilty as we are."

"I couldn't shoot you," Hank said. The eight years of freedom were over, he knew. He was caught again in the hopeless web of fear and guilt, love and hate. Duke was always with him; he could never put down the burden of that dark presence.

"Why not?" Duke was grinning but his eyes were sharp with bitter mockery. "Because we're brothers? That's a cute one. Supposing you try to cross me up. You think I won't shoot?"

"Sure, you'll shoot," Hank said, swallowing the dry pain in his throat. The girl was staring at him with another expression now, and he felt the guilty color rising in his cheeks.

"Let's get rolling," Duke said. "Come on, kid. Move."

Grant came with them to the door. "You want me to go along?"

"Hell, no." Duke's tone was amiable, but there was a challenge in his eyes. "You need some rest, I think."

"Rest, that's good. I can't go back to New York now. You know that, I guess?"

"Why not?"

"You and Belle can't handle your brother and the nurse. We'll have to let Creasy pick up the money."

Duke smiled gently. "Don't you want to go back, Eddie?"

"That's not it. You two can't stay awake every minute."

"We'll talk about it when I get back."

"Creasy knows the pickup plan perfectly. There's nothing to it."

"You trust him, eh?"

"Yeah. Sure I do."

"All right." Duke's smile was gone; he was studying Grant with a sceptical frown; "While we're away take a look around for guns, knives, pokers, that kind of stuff. I want 'em all locked up. And nail the upstairs windows shut. Every room. Understand? This joint is going to be a jail, so make it a maximum security job. You should know how to go about that."

"Sure, I'll get at it. Don't be gone any longer than you have to."

"I thought the kid and I might stop for a few beers."

"Cut the clowning," Grant said, in a voice tightening with strain. "This isn't a comedy hour."

"Relax, relax," Duke said, patting his shoulder. "Do some push-ups. It's only Saturday morning. Nobody knows the kid is gone yet. We don't have to start worrying until Sunday afternoon. That's when the Bradleys get home. . . ."

# 6

At five o'clock on Sunday afternoon the traffic approaching the Triborough bridge was fairly light. Three hours later every lane would be clogged with streams of cars, winding their way in from Long Island to Manhattan. It would take a full hour then to cross the bridge, and the pleasant memories of the week end would dissolve into the city-hard realities of blasting horns, exhaust fumes and irritable traffic cops.

Dick Bradley was thinking along these lines as he slowed down to pay his fare at the toll house. Ellie was probably right, after all: check out early, avoid the tedious drive back to the city. He glanced at her as they started up again under a smooth rush of power. They hadn't spoken since leaving the Kimbles', and she showed no evidence of recovering her normal good humor. His own irritation quickened again; her peremptory insistence on leaving had embarrassed everyone at the party. They had all known something was wrong. Frank Kimble had been fine about it, of course, tactful and casual, taking Ellie's side against him with comic belligerence, and shooing them off with cheerful good-bys. Trust old Frank, he thought, smiling slightly.

Well, it was over and done with. And it wasn't as if she'd made a scene —that idea deepened his smile—she had simply insisted they leave. And no one could talk her out of it.

As they swept into the wide concrete curve that led them down to the river drive, he found himself admiring the warm sun on the surface of the water, and the clean, precise tracery of the bridge against the blue sky. Sunday was the best day of the week in New York. Everything was so blessedly quiet and peaceful. In spite of Ellie's withdrawn silence, his mood was benign and cheerful; the sun and exercise had been a magnificent tonic. He enjoyed feeling in shape, and he always got out of sorts if he were cooped up in the city too long.

He glanced at his wife. They were only a few minutes from home; it was time for a truce.

"You look nice and rested, honey," he said.

"Have I been so noticeably haggard lately?"

"No, of course not," he said, grinning at her set profile. She was coming around, he knew; her sarcasm was usually a token shot fired just before the white flag was run up. All he'd have to do now was jolly her up a bit.

"You've got to learn how to sail though," he said. "That's the main reason for a week end at Frank's and Polly's." He remembered with pleasure how excellent she had looked in white shorts and one of his shirts—very slim and chic and elegant. "We'll put you in training this summer," he said. "Polly is a great sailor, you know."

"I'm sure she does everything magnificently," Ellie said. "Sailing, hunting, wrestling—all the feminine virtues."

"That's a hell of a thing to say." His voice was formal and stiff, and she realized that she had hurt him deeply; loyalty was an intense business with him. "Polly happens to be an excellent sailor," he said. "It's odd that should annoy you."

"Well, why shouldn't she sail well? It's about like playing an oboe, I imagine. If you keep at it you'll get the hang of it. And she's kept at it for about thirty years."

"Some people never learn to sail," Dick said, in a stubborn, deliberate voice. "There's a thing to it, a spirit, that you either have or—" He frowned and took out his cigarettes. "Perhaps you don't understand this at all."

"You either have it or you don't," Ellie said dryly. "We used to say that back home about playing a game called duck-on-the-rock. You either had it or you didn't."

"I hate it when you start being cute and advertising gameish," he said. "Things matter. Period. You can't pretend they don't by making wise-cracks about them."

"All right, I'm sorry," she said, smiling at the frown that had settled above his clear, direct eyes. "Polly's an angel. You know I adore her."

"Maybe I'm being stuffy," he said. His voice was still odd and stiff. "But I think it's bad form to carp at someone who's tried her best to make you feel at home with our crowd."

"Bad form? Yes, that's a little stuffy, Dick."

"All right then, I *am* stuffy." He knew he was being cranky and censorious—but that couldn't be helped; he *was* prudish, and he couldn't pretend a Bohemianism that he didn't believe in. He felt (as his father had taught him to feel) that narrow-mindedness was preferable to a wishy-washy, indiscriminate tolerance. To *not* have convictions, and strong ones, about behavior, dress and language—that was surrendering to anarchy out of sheer timidity or laziness.

"My father always said a house guest should leave two things behind him: one, a tip for the servants, and second, anything he might have seen or heard that would reflect discredit on his host."

"Your father has mentioned that to me," Ellie said. "Several times, in fact."

"It's a good point, don't you think?"

"Oh, damn it. I don't care *what* your father says."

Ellie felt close to tears; normally she admired Dick's tribal loyalty to his father and friends. It was a sweet, old-fashioned virtue, and she respected him for not covering his feelings with layers of brittle irreverence. But occasionally she was hurt by the lack of an equal loyalty to her. And there were so *many* old friends, a great free-masonry of them, initiated at birth into the cabalistic rituals of the Unionville Hunt, the horse shows in Raleigh, the skiing at Stowe, the sailing and swimming and fishing here, there and everywhere—so *many* of them, she thought, bound together by nostalgic memories of dancing schools and prom dates, or foolish old camp songs, of football games and tennis matches, of poor old Jerry who got the Navy Cross posthumously, and old Tim who dove into an empty swimming pool one night without so much as spraining a finger—memories that drew a magical circle around and kept out the new friends, the new wives, the squares in general. The old days were best. And what of the new days?

Dick made the light at Forty-second Street with a burst of speed, and there was anger in the smooth, reckless way he handled the car. "I hope I haven't bored you talking about my father," he said.

"Dick, I'm frightened. I can't help it."

He stared at her and saw that she was very close to tears. "Damn it, what's the matter, baby? I didn't mean to—" He reached over and patted her hand. "Come on, cheer up. We'll be home soon."

"I told you I was worried about Jill," she said. "I told you that last night, and again this morning. The phone didn't answer. I called twice last night, and twice again this morning. But it didn't bother you at all. 'Stop being a howling Jane.' That's what you said. 'Let's go sailing, or play tennis or lift some dumbbells.' That's all that mattered."

"Now, honey, don't be unreasonable. Cheer up, that's it. They're probably out walking. Kate may have taken her to the park for the day." In spite of his cheerful manner he was beginning to feel guilty—Ellie had been worried about the baby and he had behaved like a sulking boor. Of course, there was nothing the matter. But Ellie was worried, which was only natural. And it *was* a little odd that Kate had been out so long. . . .

"Look, if anything was seriously wrong, Kate would have called you. This isn't the Congo, honey."

"I suppose I'm being a complete fool," she said. "Me, the modern mother, calm and casual. Dr. Spock would send me back to chapter one if he heard about this."

They were at Thirty-fourth Street now, traveling south on Second Avenue. Only three more blocks, then a right turn. . . . The neighborhood was familiar and comforting, lazy and peaceful in the late afternoon sun. They passed the shops that Mrs. Jarrod ordered from: Bailey's Meats, Ragoni's delicatessen, Mercury drugs, and the names were reassuring symbols of the commonplace and ordinary. Nothing could be wrong . . . this is where we live, Ellie thought, as Dick swung into Thirty-first Street.

Kate and Jill walk by these stores and homes every day on their way to the river or the park.

But she couldn't completely silence the little voice of fear. Jill was too final and precious a goal. They had been married five years when she was born, and the wait had made her seem much more important. All her own life had been made of goals, Ellie thought. She had been poor for much of it, gracious and shabbily poor, the daughter of a general practitioner who had died before wartime demands might have made him worth his weight in gold.

She had worked her way through school—the first big goal. Then she had made the long jump from a job in fashion in Milwaukee to a better job in New York. Always there were small, immediate goals in sight; a new dress, a tightly budgeted vacation, slip covers for one of the half-dozen chic little apartments she had lived in before meeting Dick. Money was important to her and it had been fun earning it; she was happy making lists and accounts, budgeting herself carefully, keeping her balances as neat as her figure.

But the Bradley money was something else again. It was simply *there* —a solid, unexciting substance surrounding her on all sides. No one earned it on a week-to-week basis, or worried about how long it would last. It was as permanent as the ground beneath their feet. When they wanted something they discussed buying it in terms of quality and convenience, not in dollars and cents. Dick was careful with money, but in a way she didn't understand; he regarded it in the abstract, as counters put *here* to accomplish *this* or that—he didn't think of dollars in terms of food and clothing and rent.

Dick slowed down as they passed a group of youngsters who were playing ball against the side of a building. "Well, here we are," he said. "You'll see, everything will be fine. Jill, sticky with pablum, Kate in her usual sunny mood. Want to bet?"

"I don't think so," she said, smiling at him. She was suddenly sure that he was right. The Bradleys had a long-term lease on good luck. The house would be shining and peaceful. Kate and Jill would be romping around in the nursery. The evening would follow a safe, pleasant pattern. Dick would mix martinis, and very probably would mention the time he had drunk four in a row at the Goldstones' hunt party. They would have Jill to themselves downstairs for an hour or so, and then Mrs. Jarrod would announce dinner. . . .

As Dick stopped in front of their house, she said, "I'll leave you to cope. Okay?"

"Sure thing. You dash on in."

Dick stretched gratefully. The hour's drive after a week end of tennis and sailing had stiffened him up a bit. But it was a pleasant feeling. Coming around the car he glanced up and down the street, savoring its

Sunday emptiness. Ellie loved this place, he knew. And he didn't mind making this concession to her happiness; she wanted to go on working for a while, and living in town made that possible. It wouldn't do when Jill was ready for school, of course. Then they'd move out to the country. And Ellie couldn't commute to a job. He couldn't see that at all; it wasn't that he objected to women having careers if they wanted them, but in the country he knew that her time would be taken up completely with running their home, and participating in the activities of the community.

As he went up the stairs he was thinking of her with an especial tenderness and warmth. He was lucky to have her—she had been easily the most attractive woman at the Kimbles'. Frank had shepherded her around like a happy mastiff, and the women had seemed honestly delighted with her. . . . She was a new experience for them, with her funny, humorous slant on things. And, of course, her figure and clothes had set them right back on their heels.

She had turned the key in the lock and was pushing open the door, and his eyes were on a level with her shining black sling-pumps. He smiled appreciatively at the sharp turn of her ankles, the sleek elegance of her legs—he loved the way she walked, each step precise and sure and graceful.

As he went up another step he saw the letter that was lying on the polished floor of the foyer. Something was wrong about that, he thought. Why hadn't Kate put it in the study?

Ellie hadn't noticed it; she was looking up toward the nursery, smiling with anticipation and pleasure. "Jill, baby," she sang out. "We're home, darling." She stepped on the letter as she crossed the foyer, and the sharp heel of her pump left its square outline just below the special delivery stamp. "Jill, it's Mummy," she called, as she ran quickly up the stairs. "Where's my big girl?"

Dick bent and picked up the letter, aware of Ellie's voice echoing flatly throughout the big house. He noted automatically that there was no return address on the envelope, and that the stamp had been cancelled in Manhattan early Saturday morning. It had been lying here all day then. And all day yesterday. . . .

As he ripped open the envelope and removed the single sheet of note-paper, he heard Ellie calling Jill's name again and again, her voice high and frantic against the echoing silence.

He read the note quickly, and it made no sense to him. Standing in the open doorway with a square of yellow sunshine falling across his legs, he frowned and rubbed the tips of his fingers across his forehead. What the devil is this? he thought. What kind of nonsense?

Then—scanning the note again—the meaning struck him with sickening, physical impact; the paper shook in his hands, and he realized that he was trembling from head to foot. Ellie's voice sounded louder and louder around him—she was coming down the stairs now, her heels clattering with frantic speed, and she was calling his name desperately and helplessly.

"Dick, Dick, they're not here!"

"I know—I know."

She stopped and stared at him, her body tense and rigid in the straining silence. "Dick, what is it?" Her voice trembled and broke as she saw the fear in his face. "Tell me what's wrong."

He couldn't speak. He tried, but couldn't; his throat was dry and tight with pain.

"Tell me, Dick," she whispered.

He caught her to him, pulling her tightly against his chest. The note was before her eyes, and she read it then, crushed against her husband, standing in the yellow sunlight that poured into the foyer from the street.

"We've got to do exactly as they tell us," he said, whispering the words against her cheek in a high, straining voice. The week end color had drained from his face, and his eyes were bright with desperation and fear. "You understand? Exactly as we're told."

She was sobbing words against his chest. "No, God, no, no, no—"

"Stop it, stop it!" he said harshly. He stared into the street, sliding his eyes over the familiar sights with pointless, terrible fear. They were exposed, helpless and vulnerable. The sun-splashed sidewalks, the calm façade of the church that faced their house, a shouting boy on a bicycle— all of this was hostile and evil to his eyes. "We must do what they want us to do," he said, tightening his grip around her shoulders. "I'll call my father. Please stop, please, please stop," he said, in a breaking voice. And then he swung the door shut against the bright, menacing world.

From his room across the street Creasy watched the door close with a sense of infinite and majestic satisfaction. He nodded slowly, deliberately, as a judge might nod while reading an inevitable and irrevocable sentence. "Yes," he said, softly and quietly. "Yes, they will understand now." His mood was judicial and calm, and this surprised him slightly. There was none of the frenzied anger that gave him such exquisite pleasure—instead he felt rather solemn, almost disinterested. . . .

They had never known pain or humiliation, of course. But now they would learn. This was just and proper. Pain belonged to the rich and poor alike. But the rich refused to accept this fundamental law. They bought immunity at the expense of the poor.

He glanced at his watch. Fifteen minutes had passed. And the door remained closed—no sirens were wailing, no police cars were rushing to comfort the privileged beautiful couple in the silent house.

Creasy chuckled softly, and the smile brightened his tiny ugly face, puckered the corners of his eyes. They wouldn't call the police, he thought. They would wait for *his* bidding. . . .

And what were they doing now? Bradley, the handsome sportsman, the young man with big bank accounts and a beautiful wife to batten his vanity. What would *he* be doing? At the phone now, talking to his father in hysterical whispers, begging for help, for speed . . . or perhaps they hadn't reached his father yet. "We'll try his club, sir, and call you back—" And he would hang onto the receiver like death itself . . .

And what of her? The disdainful, elegant beauty, too choice for any but a millionaire's taste. Not so beautiful now with her make-up streaked, and her eyes red from weeping. Screaming at her playboy husband to *do* something, kicking her feet like a child in a tantrum.

Creasy watched the Bradleys' home for a full hour, standing motionless behind the thick curtains. At six o'clock the Bradleys' housekeeper appeared, a model of stout, complacent efficiency. Creasy knew her sort. Loyal to those who hired her, grateful for the dog-to-master relationship. Standing up for them against her own kind.

There were no other callers. It was apparent that the Bradleys were following instructions. By now they would have been in touch with the old man in Boston. The wheels were turning. . . .

At seven o'clock Creasy put on his topcoat and left his dark, ill-smelling room. He stood on his stoop for a moment, smoothing his gloves over his small, neat hands. The sun was down now, and there was a chill edge to the wind. Finally he started down the steps, holding the iron railing with a gloved hand, setting his feet down with mincing care. A passing couple smiled at him; he was so obviously a bachelor or widower, a tidy little man setting off on a Sunday evening stroll. With a casual glance at the Bradleys' home, Creasy turned and walked briskly toward Third Avenue. It was time to phone Grant now, to tell him that everything was all right. . . .

Oliphant Bradley let himself into his Beacon Street apartment shortly after six-thirty on Sunday afternoon. He dropped his hat and stick in the foyer, and strode into the long, comfortable living room, a tall spare man with white hair and snapping blue eyes. At the moment he was in excellent spirits, and this was evident in the way he walked, and the expression on his face. He seldom bothered to hide his feelings or reactions; if he was pleased he laughed, if angry he shouted, if bored he turned off his hearing aid. There was enough egotism in his make-up and enough money in his banks to let him display his moods externally—and now he was grinning with pleasure because he had spent the afternoon with Joe Piersall and had won thirty dollars from him at pinochle.

"Anderson," he called, switching on a lamp beside his reading chair. In the twilight he found the shadows in the big room depressing; he liked things bright and vivid and lively. Earthy, his wife had called it. He straightened, smiling at this chance recollection. *In spite of your cold*

*showers and proper Boston background, my dear, very earthy. . . .*
Well, maybe I am, he thought, savoring the memory of Joe Piersall's
choleric bad temper.

The dining room door opened and his valet, Anderson, came in. He
was younger than Mr. Bradley by several years, but not so well preserved;
his hair was gray and thin on top, and he walked as if he were carrying a
fragile and carelessly wrapped package. "I was just about to ring up the
Piersalls, sir," he said. "Your son has been calling from New York since
five o'clock. He said it was quite urgent."

"Oh. Anybody sick?"

"No, sir, he said that everyone was fine. He and Mrs. Bradley had been
out to the Frank Kimbles' for the week end."

"Get a nice sunstroke with that crowd and not much else. How about
Jill?"

"Well—I don't believe he mentioned her, sir."

Oliphant Bradley pulled out his watch, studied it for a second and then
let the slim golden disc slide back into his vest pocket. The habit was a
compulsive one, and his addiction to it annoyed him; why in the devil
was he always fiddling around with clocks and watches? Timing his
breakfast, timing his walks, even timing hands of bridge—a silly habit, the
reflexive twitch of an idle old fool. He resolved to stop it—for the fiftieth
time. Let the time go by. Stop staring at it. That won't help. . . .

"I'll call him from the study," he said. At the doorway he stopped
and grinned at Anderson. "I clipped Joe Piersall for thirty bucks this
afternoon. How about that?"

Anderson smiled back at him. "I'm sure that put him in a good humor."

"Sure, sure. He didn't quite claim I cheated, but that was only because
I was a guest. If we'd been playing here it would have been different.
Do you remember the time he insisted on staying until he got even? 
Slept on the sofa finally."

"Yes, I do, sir. He was here two days, I believe."

Oliphant Bradley was still chuckling as he picked up the phone in his
study and gave the operator his son's number in New York. . . .

Anderson was setting the tea tray when he heard Mr. Bradley call
for him in a high, unfamiliar voice. The urgency of the tone made him
start; the cup and saucer he held rattled alarmingly as he put them down
on the sideboard. "Yes, sir," he said, as Mr. Bradley called his name again.
He hurried through the apartment to the study, a small alcove off the
library.

"Would you bring me a brandy, please." Mr. Bradley stood beside his
desk with one hand resting on the cradled telephone. There was a smile
on his lips, but Anderson thought his eyes looked odd—bright and hard and
intense.

"Is anything wrong, sir?"

"No, no. They just called to say hello. Everything is fine."

"You look upset, sir. If there's something—"

"No, it's just that damn twinge again." Still making an effort to smile, he touched the area above his heart. It would be hard to deceive Anderson; they had been together thirty years and knew each other very well. But he must deceive him. No one must guess. . . .

"The brandy will do the trick," he said.

"Shouldn't I call Dr. Playton?"

"He'd be delighted if you did. The only pleasure he gets out of life lately is hospitalizing his friends. No, just bring me the brandy, please. And another thing. I'm going down to New York for a few days. I'll need a grip. No evening things, thank God."

"Yes, of course." Anderson lingered in the doorway, obviously worried and uncertain. Mr. Bradley cursed himself silently; he was handling this like an hysterical child. Stupidly . . . giving everything away. "Dick wants me to go over a list of stocks with him," he said, forcing an easier note into his voice. "He seems to think I've developed clairvoyance in my old age."

"Well, it will be pleasant for you, sir. Seeing Mrs. Bradley and Jill again."

"Yes, yes, of course."

While Anderson was packing his grip Mr. Bradley put in a call to Joe Piersall. A baby girl watched him from a silver frame on his desk. Round and rosy as an apple, with doll-like curls and dimples, she beamed out at the world with a sense of breathless wonder and excitement. He had made her smile for that picture, he remembered; the photographer, a stupid, clucking fool, had only frightened her, and Ellie and Dick hadn't done much better. But he had got her laughing . . . the old trick of staring solemnly at her and widening his eyes very slowly had done it. Suddenly he slammed his fist down on the desk. Don't get excited, Playton had said. Damn Playton! He had never known such a cold, deliberate fury in all his life. They would pay for this. Every dollar he owned would be used to hunt them down. . . .

The Piersalls' butler told him that Mr. Piersall had gone for a walk in the woods but was expected back for tea. Mr. Bradley left a message asking Piersall to call him back the minute he came in.

Replacing the phone he stood and walked around the room, rubbing his hands together anxiously. Gone since Saturday night at least. But where was the nurse? The Irish girl, Kate. Dick hadn't even mentioned her. Was she involved in this?

He drank the brandy Anderson had brought him, but it didn't dissolve the nervous pain in his stomach. A sudden terrible fear had gripped him; Jill was already dead. Why should they let her live? The money would be paid anyway. A finger's pressure on her throat, a few spadesful of earth on her body, and she wouldn't cause them any more trouble.

Yes, she was dead. He was sure of that. And all of his own foolish dreams were dead. Of being around when she started to talk, of watching her learn to ride, of summers with her at the big old place at James Harbor. They never went there any more. It was made for children. . . . Ellie wouldn't have minded, he thought, rubbing a hand over his eyes. These were the dreams that had kept him alive. Bait, nothing more. The carrot in front of a tired donkey. Fooling himself with Playton's blessing. "Just to see her, that's all I want." The only grandchild he would ever see. "That will satisfy me completely. I'm not asking for the moon, am I?" That was the start of it. And then: "I'd like to hear her talking." And: "If I could see her in a party dress—they start early, you know." An old dreaming fool. Encouraged by Playton.

He stared at the baby's picture, fighting back his tears. He couldn't help her, he couldn't spare her an instant of fear and pain. With all his money, all his influence. . . .

The phone rang and he lifted the receiver quickly. "Joe? This is terribly important. Can you talk? Are you alone?"

"I'm in my study, and the door is closed. Why?"

"All right, listen closely, Joe. I can't repeat this."

"Yes, yes. Shoot."

"Get this then." Oliphant Bradley's voice was low and harsh. "I need two hundred thousand dollars tonight. Within the next two hours. I need—"

"Ollie, for God's sake—"

"Listen to me. The bills must be in denominations of five, ten and twenty. They must be old."

"Good God! When did this happen?"

"I can't tell you on the phone. I'll be at your bank in an hour. And I want a plane standing by for me when we've got the money counted."

"Certainly." Piersall's voice sharpened. "I'll call two of my managers to help us. And I'll have my son arrange for the plane. I'll see you in an hour, Ollie."

Bradley put the phone down and rubbed the tips of his fingers over his forehead. Yes, they would pay the money. That was the least of it. There were fifty men he might have called, but Joe Piersall happened to be the handiest. The money meant nothing. It would go into the hands of human scum who had already murdered his son's baby. And would they ever be caught? Ever punished? Not by tired old men and frightened parents. Dick and Ellie didn't want the police brought in. It might be weeks before they faced the brutal fact that their baby was dead. And then it would be too late. The trail would have vanished; already it was cold. What did Dick and Ellie know about such things? he thought. They were hysterical children, unable to think or plan.

A knock sounded and Anderson looked in on him. "Your bag is ready, sir. And will you have tea?"

"No—no, thanks. I'll have something downtown."

When the door closed Mr. Bradley reached slowly for the phone. His old face was suddenly set in hard, bitter lines. This wasn't his decision to make—but by God he would make it. He knew best. That's what mattered. He picked up the phone and cleared his throat. When the operator answered, he said, "Get me the FBI, please. Right away."

# 7

AT SEVEN-THIRTY ON SUNDAY NIGHT THE PHONE RANG AT THE LODGE. Duke was sitting before the fireplace, sprawled comfortably in his chair, a cold cigar in the fingers of his trailing hand. He was nodding drowsily and his dark, strong face was flushed with the heat from the log fire. The room was warm and snug, the old furniture and flooring gleaming softly under lamplight, the windows and doors closed against the storm that had sprung up in the gathering darkness. Wind and rain drove against the sides of the house in swerving erratic bursts, buffeting them with great banging blows.

Grant was pacing the floor, drawing nervously on his cigarette, and occasionally glancing at his wrist watch. He looked tense and preoccupied; his heavily muscled body was clumsy with strain and his eyes were on the move constantly, switching from side to side, pointlessly checking the corners of the room, the shadows thrown by the spurting flames.

When the phone rang he turned and stared at Duke. "It's the phone," he said.

"You were expecting maybe something by Mozart?" Duke said, grinning at him.

"Cut it out," Grant said sharply.

"Cut what out? Pick up the phone."

"Sure, sure," Grant said. Crossing the room quickly, he lifted the receiver and said, "Yes," in a cautious voice. He listened for a few seconds, frowning faintly, and then, little by little, his expression cleared and a smile began to turn the corners of his lips. "Good," he said. He drew a deep breath. "That's fine."

Duke looked at Grant. "Tell him not to start spending the dough yet."

Grant made an impatient gesture with his hand. "So far, so good then," he said, speaking into the phone. "But we've had a mix-up. I can't get back to New York. You know what that means?" He listened, shaking his head slowly. "No, I can't tell you on the phone. You understand what it means?" Finally, after another pause, he said, "That's right. There's nothing to it. It's all worked out. We'll be in touch right along, of course. If there's any question at all, let me know. Yes, yes. Of course. . . ."

When Grant put the phone back in place, he came over and sat down beside Duke. He lit a cigarette and patted his damp forehead with a handkerchief. Some of the tension had eased in his big body. "So far, so good," he said, glancing sideways at Duke. "The Bradleys got home at five. Creasy saw them pick up the note. They went inside, and that was that. The housekeeper got in at six. Nobody else showed."

"They'll do what they're told," Duke said, stretching his arm over his head. "They want the kid back. How's Creasy? All charged up?"

"He sounds fine. He's going to handle the payoff. We worked out the plan between us, you know. He's studied every step." Grant smiled then, but he was watching Duke's profile from the corner of his eyes. "He can handle it just as well as I could. He's a damn shrewd little guy."

"I don't like him," Duke said yawning. "I can always spot oddballs. You watch. He'll be picked up for undressing in the park one of these days."

"That will be his first pinch then," Grant said. "Lots of guys can't say that much. You and me, for instance. But he's never been picked up, never mugged or printed. And he's lived in that room across from the Bradleys' for two years. Even if the cops got into this they couldn't get a line on Creasy."

Duke yawned again and got to his feet. "And if they do get a line on him, squealing won't do him any good. That's the nice thing in a deal like this." He put his hands on his hips and grinned down at Grant. "You can trust your partners. The cops don't provide incentive for weasels. They just burn everybody."

"Stop talking about burning," Grant said, and threw his cigarette into the fire.

The door that led upstairs opened and the nurse stepped into the room. "Well, well," Duke said, turning to look at her. "Everything okay in your department?"

"Yes, thank you."

"That kid must be pretty good company."

"She needs a lot of attention," Kate said. Then she added quickly, "All babies that age do." She weighed each word carefully; contempt was too dear a luxury. *If I don't anger them they won't hurt her . . . this wasn't hope, it was prayer.*

It had come as a shock to her that she could accept the conditions of evil so readily. At first she had known fury, and a kind of terrible surprise—they *dare* not do this. That had been her first outraged thought. Until then she hadn't known that men like Duke and Grant existed; God wouldn't create creatures without pity or mercy, as callous as animals to the suffering of others. But now that feeling of surprise, of incredulity was gone. Duke and Grant existed. Evil existed. And it must be appeased. . . .

Duke drifted over and lounged in the kitchen doorway, filling it with his big body. He smiled down at her, sensing something of her thoughts. "If you got any complaints, think of me as the manager of the joint," he said.

"No, everything is all right," she said, making herself meet his eyes steadily. This was the one she feared; not only because he was brutal and pitiless, but because she knew he could see right through her. . . .

"Your room okay?" he said. "And that big bed? Is that okay?"

"Yes, it's fine." She made a move to pass him, but he didn't step aside. Lounging in the doorway, he watched her growing confusion with a little smile. "I worry about you in that big bed. It seems so big and cold. I keep thinking you'll be lonesome."

"Please don't worry," she said, as he began to laugh softly. She knew her cheeks were blazing. He was doing this deliberately but pointlessly, and this was what infuriated her—the casual quality of his sadism. This was a game for a rainy evening, a substitute for darts or checkers. . . .

"I must bring Jill a bottle," she said.

"Sure, sure. I never kept people from their work." Straightening slowly, he gave her room to pass. "But all work and no play does you know what."

She had to squeeze past him to go into the kitchen, and she knew this was deliberate on his part, too; he wanted to watch her shrink away from him, watch her involuntary reflex of distaste. This told him precisely what she was thinking; all her politeness and tact couldn't conceal that physical revulsion.

"See you later," he said, watching her with his knowing little grin. "We've got to figure out some way to kill time up here." Turning from her he strolled back into the living room. Grant looked up at him, frowning faintly. "I told you to lay off," he said.

Duke shrugged and smiled; his mood was cheerful and he decided to ignore the rebuke. "What a housemother you'd make," he said, shaking his head.

Hank was sitting at the kitchen table, his injured hand resting in his lap. A pulse under the broken bone was beating sluggishly, and each heavy stroke sent splinters of pain streaking along his forearm. This had been going for thirty-six hours now, and his face was drawn and pale beneath a two-day smudge of beard. Belle sat opposite him, staring blankly at the glass of rum she held in her small, plump hand. They hadn't been talking; they were hardly conscious of one another's presence.

Hank glanced up when the nurse came into the kitchen. He had heard the exchange between her and Duke, and now he saw the angry color in her cheeks. Duke's work, he thought; he always regarded innocence as something of a personal challenge. Nothing delighted him like proving that virtue was a result of fear or apathy. Or lack of opportunity. . . .

He watched her as she moved from the sink to the stove, putting the nursing bottles on to boil. There was no way he could help her, nothing he could do. The completeness of his loss had numbed him; he hardly noticed the pain beating rhythmically as a metronome through his hand and arm. Everything he had fought for in those eight years away from Duke had blown away like dust in a high wind. Freedom, self-respect, the secret, almost sheepish pleasure he had taken in the discovery of courage —that was all gone. But had it ever been his? No; he had only kidded himself. Away from Duke he could deny the fear and guilt. But it was there all the time.

Belle looked up and stared at the heavy rain rolling down the black windowpanes. "How long does this go on?" she said.

"It could last a week," he said.

Belle sighed and took a sip of rum. "Great, just great." She was in a miserable mood, blue and dispirited. Unless she was clean and looking her best, she took no pleasure in anything. The house was damp, with drafty currents swirling around her feet; she had put on a coarse woolen shirt over her dress, but that had made her feel sloppy and shapeless. A big fat blonde, she thought unhappily. The rum kindled a warm self-pity in her breast. And not so blonde at that . . .

"You want some help?" she said to the nurse.

"No, thank you."

"I know all about babies, if that's what you're worrying about."

"No, I can manage."

"Why, sure you can, dearie." Belle's tone was querulous; she wanted to move around, get her mind off herself. "But it won't hurt you to take a break. Have a cup of coffee and I'll give the baby her bottle."

"She's used to me," Kate said. "But thanks anyway." She spoke casually, almost pleasantly, but Hank could see the anger in the line of her jaw.

"All right, all right," Belle said. "I just thought I'd ask. Proves my heart's in the right place." Standing, she hugged her arms to her body and strolled out of the kitchen.

Hank stood slowly when he heard Grant talking to Belle in the living room. The girl turned from the stove and watched him steadily as he moved around the table. This was the first moment they had been left alone together and the tension between them tightened in the straining silence. Fear and danger had heightened their perceptions; each word, each flickering expression was charged with significance.

"I couldn't shoot him," he said. Unconsciously his hands rose in a gesture of appeal. "Do you understand?"

She stared at him, her eyes dark and watchful in her pale face. "No," she said.

"He's my brother. Don't you understand?"

"I tried to."

"And you can't."

"No." She looked down at his injured hand then, and said quietly, "It should be in a sling." There was no feeling at all in her voice.

She took a folded dishtowel from the rack above the sink, and with a swift, precise gesture, ripped it down the middle. Knotting the ends together, she said, "If you can, soak your hand in hot water every few hours. That won't help the pain, but it will keep it clean. Raise your arm now. Higher. That's about right." She looped the dishtowel around his wrist, then put the ends over his shoulders and tied them behind his neck.

"Thanks," he said.

She looked closely at his hands then, and he heard her draw a sharp little breath. "A doctor should see to it."

"You don't understand why I couldn't shoot him?" he asked her again.

"It doesn't matter." She looked up at him, her eyes dark and empty. "Understanding, I mean. You didn't. That's what matters."

Hank heard Belle's footsteps coming back toward the kitchen. He moved away from the girl and sat down at the table. There was nothing more to say to her now; she didn't trust him, and that was what he needed to know. He couldn't trust her then. For he understood what she probably hadn't realized yet; that Duke and Grant couldn't possibly let them live.

Belle came in, still hugging her arms to her body, and when she saw the nurse take the bottle from the stove, she said, "You're going to feed her now?"

"Yes."

"Let me do it. For heaven's sake, dearie, I won't drop her. I was taking care of kids while you were in your cradle."

"No." Kate started past her but Belle put a hand on her arm. "Wait a minute. You act like I've got something catching. Don't you think I'm good enough to touch that precious little brat?"

"Good enough?" Kate turned and stared at her for an instant in silence. She looked puzzled and fascinated—as if she were seeing some strange but repellent animal for the first time. "Good enough?" she said, shaking her head slowly.

"That's what I said, good enough!" Belle's voice had become shrill and strident. The contempt in the girl's eyes cut her painfully; she felt her eyes beginning to sting. "You don't have to act so high and mighty," she said. "You don't even know me."

The revulsion she felt was nakedly apparent in the girl's eyes and face. "I wouldn't let you feed a dog of mine," she said in a low, trembling voice.

"Well, that's a fine thing to say!" Belle tried to laugh, but there was no conviction in her effort; she couldn't face the contempt in the girl's eyes. Turning, she smiled shakily at Hank, appealing to him for understanding. "You hear her?" she said. "Real temper, eh?" She wanted sympathy now, a friend to say, "Forget it. She's bats—"

But Hank's eyes gave her no such comfort.

Kate walked out of the kitchen and Belle sat down slowly at the table and poured herself a short shot of rum. The girl's footsteps passed over their heads, clicking softly down the hall to the baby's room, and Belle said, "She's got her nerve, eh?" Glancing at the ceiling, she shook her head. "To hear her talk you'd think I built concentration camps as a hobby. You'd think she was the only woman in the world who could take care of that baby. And it's not even hers, get that. She don't have any kids at all. And giving me all that holier-than-thou talk. Me, a better mother than she'll ever make. I've got a kid, did you know that?" She smiled at Hank. "A boy, what's more. He's sixteen. And you talk about being a good mother. I gave him everything, but he wasn't spoiled. I could be strict when I had to." She sipped her drink and nodded, involved with her recollections. "I've seen what happens in these spare-the-rod homes. Of course, I never had to be real strict with Tommy. He was always a good boy."

"Where is he now?" Hank asked her.

"With my mother." She smiled at him again, pleased at his interest. "He needs a home, you know. And I've been on the move pretty much. He's on the track team. Runs the mile. He's good about writing me, and my mother sends me all kinds of pictures."

"Supposing you didn't know where he was?"

She looked puzzled for an instant. "But he's with my mother. I just told you." Then her expression changed and she smiled slowly. "Oh, oh, digging traps for me, eh?" She didn't seem annoyed; she was studying him with friendly interest. "You mean supposing he was kidnaped. Well, if I had the Bradleys' money I'd just pay up and get him back. What else? That's what will happen to the baby upstairs. Nobody's going to hurt her. I told Eddie that from the start. 'You take that baby home safe and sound or count me out.' That's what I told him. And the Bradleys won't miss the money, you can bet. The worry may even do 'em good. They never had a worry in their lives, I'll bet."

She believes all this; Hank thought, watching her without expression. What kind of woman is she? There was no clue in her physical appearance; dyed blonde hair, plump, still-pretty features, surprisingly good legs

—the cataloging meant nothing. A moral spastic, he thought. A spiritual idiot, physically incapable of defining behavior in terms of right or wrong. She saw nothing wrong in a kidnaping—she could even discuss the therapeutic effect the worry might have on the parents. But her feelings were hurt because the nurse despised her. Like a child, he thought, a stupid, evil child.

Grant walked into the kitchen, his expression sullen and irritable, and looked at Belle. "Well, what about dinner? You started anything?"

"There's nothing to start except those cans of beans and frankfurters."

Grant made an effort to control his exasperation; it wasn't her fault they were eating out of cans.

"Well, fix something then," he said. "And why the devil don't you clean yourself up?"

"In this icebox? Are you crazy?" She stared at him defiantly, but the distaste in his expression made her feel shaky and vulnerable. Why was he yapping at her? He was the one whose nerves were going to pieces.

It was because of him that she had forgotten to bring nail-polish remover and peroxide. Everything else had been neatly packed away; the baby supplies, powder, cream, food, diapers; and her own clothes had been ready for days. She had planned carefully for the trip, making up little lists each morning and crossing off the items as she bought them—the only thing she had skipped was a last stop at the corner drug store for peroxide and nail-polish remover. Grant had been so jumpy that she had stayed in the apartment, bringing him coffee, listening to his stories about the old days in Chicago. Belle's mood became righteous and angry. In a day or so the roots of her hair would be turning dark, and that would give him something else to gripe about. "You shouldn't be worrying about food all the time," she said. "It would do you good to skip a few meals. You're getting a nervous stomach. I eat anything that's put in front of me."

"Yeah, or drink it," he said, staring at the bottle of rum. "You think frankfurters are T-bone steaks because you're loaded most of the time."

"Look, you got a nerve. I—"

"Belle, shut up!" he said, and she saw that his irritation had grown swiftly and dangerously; his eyes were blank and shiny, and there was a small white circle around his tight lips. "Get the supper started," he said.

She knew he was ready to hit her. "Sure, Eddie. I'll get right at it. I'll fix up something. Something you'll like."

"Okay, *okay,* stop chattering. Get with it." He looked at Hank for an instant, then turned and walked back into the living room.

Belle rubbed her fists into her eyes, like a child fighting back tears. "He doesn't mean half of that," she said. "It's just that he's got a lot on his mind."

"I'll help you with supper," Hank said. He could hear Grant moving about in the living room, his heels making a steady rhythmic sound on the pine flooring. Pacing back and forth, lighting one cigarette after the other. "I know a way to dress up those beans," he said, watching Belle. She would crack first, he thought. "How about it?" he said. "Can I give you a hand?"

"Why, sure." She looked at him, blinking away her tears. "It's always easier when you've got someone to talk with. That's the only reason I wanted to help with the baby." She stood and smoothed down her skirt. "Let's go, friend. I'm a lousy cook, but willing, so help me."

Later, while the coffee was heating they sat down at the table for a cigarette. "What's your son's name?" he said.

"Tom, so he's a Tommy, naturally." Belle was in more cheerful spirits; the bustle and talk had restored her normal good humor. "I shouldn't have told you about him, maybe," she said, grinning into his eyes. "You'll be thinking of me as an old lady in a bonnet."

He smiled at that. "He's on the track team, you said?"

"That's right. Let me get you a cup of coffee, okay?"

"Fine." When she stood up Hank glanced toward the living room, listening again to Grant's slow, heavy footsteps. . . .

INSPECTOR WEST WAS PLAYING BRIDGE WHEN THE PHONE SOUNDED IN the foyer of his apartment. It was nine-thirty, a cool, lovely spring night; a breeze off the Potomac had blessed Washington with two days of surpassingly pleasant weather. The ringing phone was a reprieve for the Inspector; he was facing the formidable job of making four spades with the king and queen of trump out against him. He didn't know where they were, he only knew they weren't in the dummy. His wife and Tom Wilkins, a next door neighbor, sat on his left and right and he hadn't learned anything from their expressions or first round of play. If Wilkins held the honors there was no chance of a finesse. And Wilkins would set him with relish. Tom Wilkins was a frank and pleasant chap, but bridge turned him into an irritating sort of person. The high, shrieking laugh was the worst of it, the Inspector thought.

"Excuse me," he said, standing.

"Take your time," Wilkins said, beginning to laugh. "And take a peek at your Blackwood while you're away. It might help."

The Inspector smiled as he felt a good sport would smile, and walked into the foyer to answer the phone. He was curious about the call, of course; as an FBI agent he was never off duty.

When he recognized the voice of the caller he knew immediately that this was top priority. The very top. "Yes, sir," he said, and listened. . . .

A few minutes later he returned to the bridge table, smiling ruefully. "Just my luck," he said. "The indispensable man, that's me."

"Oh, Dave, no!" his wife said.

"What's the matter?" Tom Wilkins asked.

"It's work, that's what's the matter," Mrs. West said, sighing with humorous resignation. She had caught her husband's eye as he entered the room, and knew he had to leave immediately—but that he wanted to leave without any suspicious flurries or fanfare.

"We're bringing a lot of files up to date," the Inspector said, picking up his cards. "It's a round-the-clock job, and when they reached my section—they planned it for Sunday night, I'm sure—they just yell for me to come in. Okay, where were we now?"

Tom Wilkins was laughing again. "Just so you don't run out before we set you, Dave."

"We'll see about that," the Inspector said.

He played carefully and deliberately, seemingly engrossed in the game. There was nothing in his manner to indicate that his thoughts were turning around a brownstone on Thirty-first Street in New York, and a baby named Jill Bradley. The nurse was gone, too. There was hope in that. A neurotic perhaps, fancying slights, unhealthily involved with the child—women like that usually turned up in a day or so, frightened silly, hysterically repentant. With the baby in perfect shape. He played a card and took the trick, controlling his impatience. Oliphant Bradley was on his way to New York with two hundred thousand dollars. The New York office would cover him from La Guardia. So far there had been no news break. That was luck—if anything about a kidnaping could be called lucky. If the story broke the chances of bargaining for the baby went down ominously.

He took another trick and grinned at Tom Wilkins' discomfiture—but seeing him only as a red face and spectacles, an unavoidable source of delay. A hundred agents were on their way to New York now. From New Jersey, Pennsylvania, Ohio, from as far west as Chicago—specialists at this kind of work. They would be spread around the city in hotels, boardinghouses, the homes of local agents. There would be no observable increase of activity in New York headquarters, no sudden concentration of out-of-town agents. This was fundamental security. Elevator men, waitresses, cab drivers, janitors—they might talk, innocently but disastrously. "You watch, something's breaking. I'll bet I saw fifty new FBI guys in the building today—" and who might be listening to this? A bartender, a wife, a girl friend—or someone involved in the kidnaping?

"Darn it, you squeaked through," his wife said, as he took the last trick. She had held the missing honors, after all. He hoped with all his heart that this was an omen. . . .

When Wilkins left the Inspector strode into the bedroom and began packing. It was a quick and simple task; he was an orderly, systematic man, with a physical discipline like that of a professional soldier. Everything he wanted was in its proper place; there wasn't a second wasted searching for clothing or toilet articles. The Inspector was in his late forties, but his hair was still thick and black, and his reflexes were those of a man half his age. He was designed for function; his memory was precise, his eyes were shrewd and intelligent, and his voice, when he was angry, could cut through evasions or excuses like a whip. He was as hard to please as he was sparing of praise. But men considered it a privilege to work for him.

When he came out of the bedroom his wife was waiting for him with his hat and coat. "When will you call?" she asked him.

"Tomorrow night," he said.

"Take care of yourself, Dave." She had no idea of where he was going, or what his job might be, and it didn't occur to her to ask; over the years she had succeeded in suspending her curiosity if not her fears.

He hesitated an instant, smiling quickly at her. "I'll take care of myself," he said. Then he kissed her and turned to the door. She watched him as he hurried down the corridor toward the self-service elevator. He was looking at his watch.

On Sundays the FBI in New York normally operated on a reduced work schedule; the heavy flow of routine correspondence was cut down to a trickle and hundreds of typewriters and teletypes were silent. Many clerical employees were off duty and several floors of the huge old building on lower Broadway were empty and dark. Only a skeleton force manned the research labs in the basement. Even the neighborhood was calm and quiet. A few cabs cruised the area, and an occasional truck rumbled through the comparative silence of Sunday night. Couples strolled the sidewalks, enjoying the first spring weather, and down the block a newsie was shouting a garbled version of Monday morning's lead story. It was a typical end-of-the-week scene, quiet, lazy, almost drowsy.

At nine o'clock Jerry Roth, an assistant-in-charge of the New York office, came in and took an elevator up to his sixth floor office. Several agents had come in before him, and two more entered the lobby as his elevator was on the way up. The uniformed guard in the lobby gave them a soft smiling salute as they passed by his desk. It was normal traffic; agents were in and out around the clock, dictating reports, checking files, running down leads. There was nothing to indicate to him, or to anyone else who might have been watching the building, that all the resources of an intricate and powerful organization were being readied for action.

Jerry Roth stood behind the desk in his brightly lighted office, a bear of a man with features that looked as if they had been cut from dark, well-seasoned wood. In spite of gray hair and the deep lines at the corners of his mouth and eyes, he was a belligerently formidable man; anyone with sense would have kept clear of him in a barroom brawl.

Now, staring at the four agents before him, he rapped on his desk, not for attention but for emphasis. "I'll go through this just once," he said quietly. "A girl named Jill Bradley was kidnaped from her home at 715 East Thirty-first. An extortion note has been received, so we're in on it now. We don't have to wait five days for a presumption of an interstate violation. The parents don't know for certain when the baby was taken. Possibly Friday night or sometime Saturday. They've made arrangements to meet the ransom demand." Roth let his eyes touch each face deliberately. "So far nobody else is in on it. That's the way it's going to stay. Washington is sending an Inspector over to handle the job at this end. It's Dave West. You've heard of him. I've worked with him. When this is all over you'll know why I think he's the best we've got. Now let's go. We've got things to do before he gets here." Roth picked up a paper from his desk and glanced at it briefly. "Okay then: Burns, I want you to get out to Thirty-first Street. Photograph the block from your car. We'll need a blow-up of that neighborhood to work with here.

"Doorways, alleys, newsstands, shops, houses, warehouses, everything. Check for spots from where we can keep the Bradleys' home under surveillance. Make sketches, so we can get the scale right. When you're finished report to the photo lab. They'll be ready for you. Get moving now. Nelson, you go down to our library and dig up everything you can find on Oliphant Bradley. Check Dun & Bradstreet, Poor's Directory of Executives, Who's Who. I want every line you can find on the family's business associates, in-laws, clubs they belong to, where their summer homes are, everything. There'll be yards on the old man. The son is Richard Townsend Bradley. He's married to a girl whose maiden name was Eleanor Sims. There may be something on her; I don't know. Put it all on tape, and get two girls to type it up. I want it on my desk when West arrives."

Nelson, a tall redhead, said, "Do you want me to check the morgues on the local papers?"

Roth hesitated, then shook his head. The newspaper morgues were more complete sources of information, but no matter how they camouflaged their interest in the Bradleys, an alert editor or reporter might guess at the truth. . . . Their prime consideration was returning the child safely to its parents. Nothing else mattered. Catching the kidnapers, trying them, executing them—these were secondary considerations. "Never mind the papers," he said. "Work with what we've got in our own files."

"Right, sir."

Two agents remained. To the one on his left, Roth said, "Bell, I want you to set up a headquarters for the Inspector on this floor. Get a dozen of our best clerks in here tonight, and line up communications men. Have extra cars and trucks standing by, and fingerprint kits, assault equipment, tear gas rifles—anything we might need. Set up a file on this case, and keep it clear of the regular records."

Control and speed were essentials; if West wanted an agent, a file, a lead card, anything at all, he would want it right away—not thirty seconds from now. A ton of paper might bulge in this file before they were through, and each separate piece had to be instantly available. The clerks would set up indexes to channel the flow of tips and action reports, and a register would be provided to account for the minute-by-minute location and activity of each of the hundred-odd men under West's command. This was routine, standard operating procedure; when West walked in an hour or so from now his headquarters staff would be standing by, ready for action.

"Open our file with this," Roth said, and handed Bell the telephone memorandum from Washington.

"A seven file," Bell said.

"That's right." Roth's voice was suddenly hard and angry. "Seven." This was the general file number for kidnapings, and its implications touched bitter memories in these men. "Get with it," Roth said, and then turned to the last man who stood before his desk. "If it had been any other job, I wouldn't have called you in, Crowley."

"That's okay, sir."

Roth rubbed his wide hands together, and a frown deepened the lines at the corners of his eyes. "How is she?" he said. "Any word at all?"

"No, they're still making tests."

Roth cleared his throat. "I called you because I remembered you've got an uncle living on Thirty-first Street. In the same block as the Bradleys."

Crowley nodded, and said, "That's right." He frowned faintly, a pleasant-looking young man with curly black hair and intelligent eyes. "He's lived there ever since he took his pension from the city police."

"And you visit him, don't you?"

"Yes, every couple of weeks. He's all alone now, except for a son in New Mexico."

"Well, you can probably see what I'm getting at," Roth said. "West will want a man inside the Bradleys'. You could go to your uncle's and cross the roofs to the Bradley house."

"That would work," Crowley said.

"I know," Roth said. "And you've got an excuse to be in the block.

You've been going there to visit your uncle. If the street is being watched, you won't give anything away. If anyone asks questions about you, they'll get safe answers."

"Sure," Crowley said. "It makes sense."

Roth looked down at his desk. "Once you go inside the Bradleys' house, you stay inside. No matter what happens to your daughter. We can't pull you out after you go in. You understand that, don't you?"

"I understand," Crowley said.

"You want me to leave it up to the Inspector?"

Crowley hesitated, then smiled slightly and shook his head. "He's got his problems. Don't worry him with mine. Look, I don't want to make a speech. If I can help find that Bradley baby, I'll go in. Tell the Inspector I'm his boy."

Roth nodded slowly. "All right, Tom."

Oliphant Bradley walked into La Guardia's terminal building at ten-thirty that night, only four hours after receiving his son's message in Boston. He carried a grip in each hand, but shook his head at a porter who offered to assist him; in one bag was a change of clothes, in the other was two hundred thousand dollars in used bills of small denominations. The old man was frowning as he strode through the crowded terminal toward the cab rank; during the flight he had begun to worry about having called the FBI. It was the wisest thing to do, of course. That wasn't what worried him. It was the question of propriety. It was his son's decision to make. . . .

The agent he had talked with in Boston had held him up for several interminable minutes with questions: *What was the exact wording of the note? Had there been any threatening letters in the past? When was he leaving for New York? When would he arrive? Would he bring a picture of his granddaughter?*

Bradley had finally hung up on him and driven off to the bank. He had his work to do, let them get busy with theirs! But it wasn't this interrogation that had started him worrying—it was the task that faced him now; the business of explaining his decision to Dick and Ellie. Dick had stressed the need for secrecy; no one must know the baby was missing. Jill's life depended on their swift, silent obedience, he had said. But Dick was wrong there. The baby was already dead. All they could do now was make certain that retribution was swift and final. But to exact payment you needed the machinery of investigation and enforcement. Oliphant Bradley was convinced he had done his duty. But he wondered uneasily if Dick and Ellie would understand. . . .

A cab door opened for him. He was too preoccupied with his thoughts to notice that several inconspicuous young men had blocked off that taxi from the rest of the crowd. He climbed in, gave the driver his son's address and settled back, holding the satchel of money in his lap. As they turned into the fast bright stream of Parkway traffic, the driver looked up and caught his eye in the rear-vision mirror.

"Do you have the child's picture, Mr. Bradley?"

Bradley started. The abrupt question demoralized him. He felt confused and nervous, menaced by the onrushing headlights, the roar of speeding traffic. "What did you say?" He leaned forward, hugging the bag of money close to his body.

The driver reached back without taking his eyes from the road and handed him a flat, black leather case. "Identification, sir."

The case opened like a little book. Inside there was an oblong card under a protective sheet of clear plastic. Mr. Bradley studied the photograph on the card, then leaned still further forward to peer at the driver's profile. "Your name is Shattuck?" he said.

"Yes. Do you have the child's picture with you?"

"Yes. Of course."

"Just drop it over the front seat, please. Then sit back and relax."

As they turned off Second Avenue half an hour later, Shattuck said quietly, "When we stop don't forget to pay the fare, Mr. Bradley. We don't want anyone to think I'm anything but a cab driver."

"Are they watching the house?"

"There's no point in assuming they aren't."

Thirty-first Street was peaceful and quiet at this hour of Sunday night. Yellow shafts of light shone from home and street lamps, and groups of men and women sat on the stoops of the old brownstones. Everything seemed secure and safe; this was one of a thousand city streets in which life was going its casual, ordinary way. A burst of studio laughter sounded from a television set, and a woman on the sidewalk said to her husband, "Do you want to go in and watch the last of the show?"

Mr. Bradley climbed from the cab and paid the fare that had registered on the meter. He added an appropriate tip, and said good night to Shattuck, playing his part with scrupulous care. Turning, he squared his old shoulders and started up the steps of his son's home, his eyes raised to the shining brass numerals on the door. When the door began to open he felt his heart lurch heavily. They were watching for him. They would understand, he thought. But the weight of his decision had suddenly become a terrible burden. . . .

Shattuck drove three blocks down Lexington Avenue before pulling up at an all-night restaurant. He walked inside with a folded newspaper under his arm and took a seat at the counter. The man beside him was finishing his dessert, and he and Shattuck began to talk casually about the weather, and then the Saturday night fight at the garden. The man pulled a newspaper from his pocket to refresh his memory on the scoring. "You see, they gave him seven out of ten," he said.

Putting his newspaper down beside Shattuck, he finished his coffee and lit a cigarette. "Take it easy now, Mac," he said.

"Sure thing," Shattuck said.

The man picked up Shattuck's paper, which was folded over Jill Bradley's picture, and strolled out of the restaurant.

Shattuck pushed his cap back on his forehead and sipped his coffee. . . .

# 9

GRANT DID NOT EXPECT A SECOND CALL FROM CREASY ON SUNDAY NIGHT. When the phone rang he was sitting close to the fireplace, chain-smoking cigarettes. For some reason he wasn't able to relax; everything was moving on schedule, but he couldn't make himself settle down for the tedious but inevitable wait. There were too many irritants rubbing his raw nerves; Belle's drinking, the sloppy, tasteless food, Duke's casual assumption of authority—as if he'd been elected to a partnership in this deal. I'll run things, Grant thought, flipping his cigarette into the dying fire. I'll straighten Duke out. And Belle. His thoughts were sullen and vindictive. What the hell were they taking him for?

When the phone rang the sound of it went through him with an excruciating shock. He sprang to his feet, tipping his chair over with a crash, and stared at the telephone as if it were some strange and dangerous enemy. Above him he heard Duke's limping steps going down the hallway toward the stairs. Grant hurried across the room and picked up the receiver. . . .

It was Creasy, excited and triumphant. The grandfather had arrived at his son's home an hour or so ago. Carrying two grips. The money, undoubtedly. . . .

"Okay, fine," Grant said. "Everything else look quiet?"

"Oh, delightfully quiet." Creasy's voice squirmed with pleasure. "They're behaving like lambs. . . ."

Grant put the phone down as Duke came into the room, looking rested and fresh; he had been napping since dinner. "Don't tell me," he said. "Let me guess. Creasy's been arrested."

"I'm getting tired of your comedy routine."

"Okay, okay," Duke said, limping toward the fire. "I thought you'd appreciate a laugh or two."

"The old man checked in from Boston an hour ago. He's probably got the cash."

"On Sunday yet. How about that? That's the advantage of owning your own bank. We couldn't cash a check on Sunday to buy penicillin for our dying mothers."

"You got a nice humorous slant on life."

"Stop worrying," Duke said. "We're home free, I tell you." He glanced about the softly lit room, frowning slightly. The shadows cast by the fire leaped and flickered on the wide, pine floorboards, against the gilt bindings of a set of classics. Outside the wind and rain still banged against the sides of the house. "My brother's really an oddball," he said. "I'd rather be in jail."

"Don't talk like a fool. Look." Grant moved closer to him. "You notice anything going on between your brother and that nurse?"

Duke grinned at him. "I said it before, you'd have made a great housemother. The kids wouldn't fool old lady Grant."

"Stop thinking of me as your straight man, Duke," Grant said softly, and his eyes were odd and cold.

Duke shrugged. "You know me, Eddie. I like a little gag every now and then."

"Now is the wrong time," Grant said. His dominant passion was for survival; he had killed more than once to stay alive and something of that showed in his face when he felt threatened or insecure.

"Sure," Duke said, putting on a thoughtful expression. He had thought of Grant as shrewd and competent—but not dangerous. That could have been a serious error, he realized. "My brother and the little Mick?" He shook his head. "I think you're imagining things, Eddie."

"Maybe, maybe not. They don't talk to each other. They don't often look at each other. But when they do I get a feeling it means something." Grant put a cigarette in his mouth, and stared at Duke with his flat pale eyes. "She came down awhile ago with a bandage for his hand. I let her take care of him."

"That's a normal kind of impulse," Duke said.

"Sure, sure. But if they get interested in each other they might try something foolish. They might work up the guts to give us trouble."

"You think ahead, don't you?"

Grant lit his cigarette. "That's why I'm running this deal, Duke. . . ."

Hank was sitting at the kitchen table. Belle had gone up to bed after helping him with the dishes. She had been in a mood of sodden sentimentality, telling him story after story about her son's childhood, and insisting endlessly that she would never leave him again under any circumstances. He wasn't sure that he had impressed her as anything but a tolerant ear, but that was enough for a start. She was a simple woman, but not stupid; she would suspect any obvious overtures. After she had gone the nurse had come down and dressed his injured hand, washing it with warm water and bandaging it with strips torn from a pillow case. This was done with Grant's approval; he had stood in the doorway, a cigarette in his mouth, watching them with careful, thoughtful eyes. They hadn't spoken to each other; Hank had stood close to her, seeing the light gleaming on her dark hair, the deep shadows under her eyes and the fine pale texture of her skin. But there was no communication between them, nothing but the gentle touch of her fingers on his hand. And that was an impersonal kindness, an instinctive reaction to suffering of any kind.

Now Grant and Duke were in the living room together, and Hank could hear the murmur of their voices. They took no chance in leaving him alone; the back door was locked, the key was in Grant's possession and the windows had been nailed shut. The only way in or out was through the front door and one of them was on guard in the living room all the time. Even with two good hands he wouldn't have had a prayer.

Hank rubbed the tips of his fingers against his forehead. The phone had rung a few moments ago, and when he heard Grant talking, he had succumbed to an old, wistful hope; perhaps Duke would have a change of heart and turn against Grant. Maybe it would happen. He was a victim of hope for he had never stopped trying to understand Duke.

Even now he was trying to understand how his brother had gotten involved with Grant. The habit of apology was too strong to break; there must be powerful reasons for what Duke had done, he thought. If he could understand him, he could forgive him. That had always been his hope.

He couldn't judge Duke coldly, dispassionately. Never . . . because he was responsible for what Duke had become. He couldn't forget that. He could only try to understand him. . . .

They had been raised in a small town in Wisconsin, a land of brilliant lakes and fresh-smelling pine trees, a land with a nostalgic frontier feeling to it; the Chippewa reservation was only a few miles away, and most of the boys in the area had learned their trapping and hunting and fishing directly from the Indian guides. And Duke had learned more than anyone else. Even the old Indians admitted there was little they could show him. At fifteen he could disappear into the woods and live there for weeks at a time, without matches or blankets or camping equipment. He took nothing but fishhooks, line and a coil of rope for trapping. And his knife, of course. Duke was never without that. He ignored fish and game laws —a doe was meat to him, nothing else. He peddled venison to the tourists, and sold whiskey to the Indians, a federal offense. But no one was particularly exercised by his wildness. He was tall and dark, beautifully built, and was well aware of the value of his smile. If he couldn't bully people, he charmed them. If neither tactic worked he ignored them—or struck back when they weren't expecting it. A few people in town were on to him, of course. Horchmyer, the druggist for one. Duke had tried to buy certain items from him, and since then the old man had watched him with a cold eye. And the Rawlings family. There had been quite a bit of talk about how Jimmy Rawlings' shoulder was broken in football practice—the whistle had blown several seconds before Duke came down hard on little Jimmy. But nothing came of the talk. There were men who took Duke's side. Nobody blames him when he bangs over for a touchdown, do they?

That was true enough. Lamson High won twenty-two straight games with Duke as fullback, and the University scouts were all down to watch him play.

But he wasn't popular at school. Some girls liked him, but he had little interest in that type. He preferred conflict; his favorite targets were the innocents who had been raised in families with gentleness and dignity. They weren't prepared for his kind of attacks; they were his choice victims.

What was *wrong?* Hank thought, rubbing his forehead. It seemed that he had spent a lifetime trying to understand Duke.

Maybe it was his mother. He and Duke were half-brothers. Duke's father had married a second time when Duke was eight years old. Hank had been born a year later. Duke had been a difficult youngster and Hank had grown up in an atmosphere tense and uneasy with propitiation; his mother feared she was failing with Duke and went to distracted lengths to earn his affection. Duke played on her fears; he demanded bribes, not for good conduct but as a hostage against worse; if he got *this*, he would not do *that*. These were his terms to his stepmother.

The whole house had revolved around his moods and tempers. Even his own father was involved in this blackmail; he too wanted peace in the family at any price. He was an easy-going sort, a small-town store keeper, a man who would rather lose an issue than win it, if the winning was going to cause hard feelings. He was modest and retiring: "If anyone wants my opinion, which I know isn't likely—" That was his father's smiling preface to any argument or discussion. Tactful, obliging—*weak*. The way I'm weak, Hank thought.

His father simply couldn't handle Duke. He smiled and talked of "boys' hi-jinks" when complaints were brought to him. And he promised that he'd have a talk with his son. But he said and did nothing. He was afraid Duke might walk out if he attempted to discipline him, but at the same time he was proud of the boy's looks, his arrogance, his superb physical talents. The big men in town had got in the habit of dropping by the store to chat before and after games, and this was a very pleasant thing; cigars were passed, backs were slapped and there was an illusion of warm, easy equality. It would be very hard to give all this up. They were things he had never known before. It was asking a lot of him (as one teacher had asked) to take Duke off the team until his marks improved. It made lying for him almost an instinctive reflex—as he lied twice, once to the police and again to Jo Reynold's father: "The boy was in bed at ten-thirty. Yes, I looked in on him." It was an easy thing to say.

It went this way until the accident. And that was the end of many things, the start of many things . . .

The living room fire was a soft red eye, watching Hank as he fell asleep on the sofa. He was nine then, the night of the accident, but he had remembered the look of the fire all his life—that soft red eye in the darkness was a part of his nightmares. Duke was asleep upstairs and his father was in town for the monthly dinner of one of his service clubs. Perhaps if his mother had been alive it would have been different. But she had died six months before.

A falling spark must have landed on the carpet. A newspaper had caught, and then the curtains . . .

Hank had awakened a few minutes later, screaming through the smoke for his brother. There was no way to get up to him; the flames were six feet high in front of the stairs. And Duke couldn't get down. So he had jumped.

Hank was under his windows by then, shouting his name over and over, and he saw Duke kick through the pane, balance himself for an instant on the ledge and then leap out into the darkness. He was grinning as he landed, his teeth flashing in his face; the danger exhilarated him, the physical challenge fired his blood. He was supremely confident, contemptuous of the risk—but the drop was long and the earth was hard as iron. Duke's right leg was broken at the knee. After three months in the hospital he was sent home on crutches. The improvement the doctor had cautiously predicted never materialized. Duke's limp became as much a part of him as the color of his eyes. . . .

Hank lifted his head. Grant and Duke had stopped talking, and in the silence he heard the nurse's soft footsteps coming down the stairs. She opened the door and crossed the living room to the kitchen, walking with quick, precise strides. She was very tired, he saw; her face was pale and drawn, and there was a tiny pulse beating rapidly in her throat. And he saw something else in her expression . . .

He stood up and said, "What's the matter?"

"I think Jill is sick. She's running a fever."

"Well—" He wet his lips, hating to put his helplessness into his words. What could he say? That it was too bad, and he was sorry as hell? "Should she have a doctor?" he said.

"I'm not sure. Sometimes these flare-ups go down overnight."

They stared at each other, and again (as it had happened the first time they were alone) the tension between them was charged with significance; it was an instant of silence, probing appraisal, an attempt at a communion that might be truer than any they could establish through words. There was no time for a leisurely comparison of attitudes and values. Trust between them could only be intuitive. Hank had known this sort of thing in the army. Sometimes you looked at a man and wondered if he would still be alongside you in the next few seconds. What you knew of his poker habits, his taste in liquor and women or the fact that he loved or was bored with his wife and kids—none of that told you what you needed to know. You made a snap judgment based on criteria you could never define or articulate. And sometimes you were wrong. He understood her fear.

"Let's hope she gets over it," he said.

"That's all we can do," she said, watching him steadily. She used the plural deliberately, with an unmistakable emphasis; and she told him with that word, and with her eyes, that she believed they were on the same side.

He had no time to answer her, for Duke sauntered into the kitchen then, a speculative little smile on his lips.

"You two look pretty solemn," he said. "Well, that's the younger generation for you."

Neither of them answered him and he said dryly, "Secrets, eh? You'd rather I left? And Grant, too, I suppose."

"The baby's running a temperature," Hank said.

"Well, that's a shame." He seemed to accept this as an explanation of their curious silence. "What's the matter with her?" he said to the nurse.

"I don't know. It could be the ride, the change."

"She'll get used to that in a day or so," Duke said. "Fevers don't mean much in kids. Keep her nice and warm. If she's no better tomorrow we might try a little terramycin."

"I wouldn't unless a doctor prescribed it," she said.

"Sure, a doctor would be the best bet," Duke said. He rubbed his jaw. "But that's a pretty tough order."

"You won't call a doctor? Even if she gets worse?"

"We'll do what we can," he said. "You think we'd stand around and let the kid get real sick?" Duke put his big hands on her shoulders. "Don't you worry, it's going to be all right."

Hank saw her stiffen at his touch, and he felt the heat of anger in his own cheeks.

"You're what the doctor would order anyway," Duke said, smiling down at her pale face. "The kid's lucky to have you. I'll bet you're great with babies."

"She may be awake now." She attempted to turn but he held her easily with his big hands.

"You'll hear her if she wakes up," he said.

"Please let me go."

"Why sure," Duke said, grinning into the revealing anger in his brother's eyes. "You got to go, you got to go." He tightened his grip slightly, not to hurt her, but to let her feel the power in his hands. When he released her she stood quietly for a moment, rubbing her shoulders with the tips of her fingers, and then she turned and walked quickly from the kitchen. The two brothers watched each other in silence as she crossed the living room and started upstairs. When they heard the click of her heels above their heads, Duke shook his head and began to laugh. "Kid, forgive me, but it's pretty funny. You've fallen for her! Boom! Like that!" He struck the table with the flat of his hand. "You're ready to bump your forehead on the floor when she walks by—and for what? A couple of soulful looks. Is that all?"

Hank shrugged lightly. "She's nice-looking, or hadn't you noticed?"

"You're pretty casual about it. You got used to dames in the army, eh?"

"As a matter of fact she reminds me of an old friend of yours."

"Yeah? Who's that?"

"Jo Reynolds."

"Must be a couple of other people."

"You don't remember Jo?" Hank watched his brother with a little smile. "She had dark hair and a fair complexion. Just like this girl. You must remember her, Duke. Someone slapped her around pretty badly one night behind the football stadium. You can't forget the row that caused. Her old man had the police on it for months."

"Oh, that girl," Duke said slowly.

"Sure, you know her. You used to try to date her, I think."

Duke's face had gone dark and hard. "Let's forget about old times, and the kids from Big Springs," he said. "This is now. And I got advice for you. Lay off this girl. A long way off. This is your big brother, Duke, talking, so you better listen."

Hank shrugged again and put a cigarette in his mouth. Staring at his brother's strangely troubled eyes, he thought: *Will I be able to kill him if I get another chance?*

# 10

THE MILKMAN SOUNDED THE KNOCKER ON THE BRADLEYS' DOOR AT EIGHT o'clock Monday morning. It was a cool and lovely day; long golden shafts of sunlight were striking through the soft white mists that had blown in from the sea. The air was fresh and the sky was a brilliant blue. Later traffic would increase, the air would be thick and gray with exhaust fumes and the people would be irritable and preoccupied as they bought papers and lined up for buses or disappeared into damp echoing subway tunnels. But now the streets were quiet and cheerful in the bright sunlight.

The milkman was whistling serenely when Mrs. Jarrod opened the door. He smiled at her and tugged the peak of his cap. These were excellent customers; they bought everything from him, cottage cheese, yogurt, ice cream, the items most people shopped for in the supermarkets. As he took the weekly order, he said, "And how's the little girl? Getting fat and saucy on our milk?"

"Yes—yes, of course."

The milkman glanced up at her, surprised by the edge in her voice. She didn't look cross, he thought. Nerves probably. Getting to that age. Everything either fine or hopeless. No middle ground. When he went down to his truck he turned to give her a big wave and a smile, but she had already closed the door. Tomorrow she'll probably be perky as ever, he thought.

The FBI agent and Mr. Bradley were still at the table when she entered the dining room. They had been up all night, the FBI agent asking questions, prowling through the house, talking on the radio that he had installed in the study.

Dick Bradley glanced up at her, and said, "Could we have more coffee, please?"

"Yes, Mr. Bradley." Mrs. Jarrod's manner was crisp and impersonal; they needed service from her, she knew, not sniffles and tears.

Crowley ran a hand through his thick black hair, and lit a cigarette. "Let's see, where were we? Princeton, I think. No trouble there?"

"No." Bradley tried to smile, then sighed and shook his head. "Just with math."

Crowley had been going over his past with him for the last hour or so, on the chance that he might recall someone who disliked him, someone he had wronged or embarrassed—intentionally or otherwise. But so far they had uncovered nothing more significant than a scuffle in the cloakroom of his dancing school. Bradley's past stretched quietly behind him, pleasant, well-cared-for terrain; all the bumps had apparently been smoothed over by his father. School, camps, trips to Italy and France—it had all been arranged thoughtfully and pleasantly. Then the Navy—flying a desk in Washington—and finally the partnership in the old man's brokerage firm.

There had been no trouble about his marriage. Crowley got the impression that Bradley, Senior, had been unenthusiastic about it, but hadn't stood in his son's way.

"How about your business friends?"

Bradley shook his head and fumbled for a cigarette. He was exhausted and on edge; his face was white and there was a desperate expression in his eyes. "We're getting nowhere," he said in an uneven voice. "I—I don't have enemies. I don't have enough guts. I never got into fights, I never played around with other men's wives. I—I never did anything. I'm Dickey Bradley, model young man. The good loser, the guy who comes in second, wearing a smile and carrying the winner's coat. Nobody hates me." He rubbed his forehead wearily, seemingly spent by the bitterness of his outburst. "Not this much anyway."

"Let's take a break," Crowley said. He wished there was some way he could ease Bradley's fears. But he had no hope to offer yet, and he couldn't lie to him. "I've got to report to the Inspector," he said, rising. "Just relax for a while."

In the study between the living room and dining room Crowley had installed an ultra-high frequency receiver and transmitter which put him in round-the-clock communication with FBI headquarters on lower Broadway. He had arrived at the Bradleys' the night before, entering through the trapdoor in the roof of their building and since then had been in hourly contact with Inspector West. He had dictated the original ransom demand to West, and West had relayed it to Washington where its peculiarities of construction and spelling would be checked for similarities with every note in the vast extortion files. Crowley had learned nothing significant about the baby's nurse, Kate Reilly; Dick Bradley and his father, Oliphant Bradley, both were convinced that she wasn't involved in the kidnaping. She was loyal, intelligent, devoted to the child—they repeated all this several times, but they couldn't offer any explanation of why she had packed up and left. He hadn't met Mrs. Bradley yet; she had taken a sedative and was asleep when he arrived. Now, at eight-thirty in the morning, she was still in bed.

So far Crowley had followed routine. The ransom money was under lock and key in the guest-room closet, and he had checked every door and window to make certain that no one had forced his way into the house. None of the locks had been tampered with . . . There was a faint smell of ether in the nursery, but no signs of a struggle.

He had fingerprinted the nursery, but had found only prints of the nurse and child—establishing the identity of the nurse's by checking them against prints taken from her room. He had questioned Mrs. Jarrod about the people who had access to the house: the delivery boys, garbage collectors, peddlers, milkmen, door-to-door salesmen, the tradespeople who came and went in the ordinary business of the day. She knew them all, and was careful about whom she let in; and she was certain there had been no strange face about in the past few months. Crowley had asked Bradley and his father about servants they had discharged in the past, of employees they had let go for one reason or another, of individuals or firms they might have hurt in business competition. Then he had begun the long interview with young Bradley about his friends, his clubs and associations, his wife and her friends and family, searching his past for enemies—which was just as fruitless as searching a penthouse garden for big game.

Crowley had done the routine things, he had followed the book—and had made no progress. That was all he could tell West. He had covered the logical areas thoroughly, but without results. Crowley was beginning to feel the tension building up in him; in ten hours he hadn't picked up a lead. He knew there were a hundred men standing by on the outside; he knew that West had the vast resources of Washington at his finger tips; he knew that anything needed could be produced in minutes—but none of that was any good unless he could find a lead here. . . .

When he finished his report, West said, "Have you talked to Mrs. Bradley yet?"

"No, she's still asleep."

"Try to talk to her as soon as possible. We want more on that nurse. Either she's in it or not. Get a line on her boy friends, her family, where she worked before she came with the Bradleys. Find out if she went to church, and where; if she belonged to any clubs or groups."

"Yes, sir."

"Crowley—Roth had a call from your wife. Your daughter—well, there's no change."

"I see." Crowley looked at the mike he was holding, and let out his breath slowly. "Thanks, sir. I'll call you as soon as I've talked to Mrs. Bradley."

"I'll be here."

When Crowley walked back into the dining room Oliphant Bradley was sitting at the breakfast table. He nodded at him and said, "You were talking to headquarters, I gather. Any news there?"

"Nothing definite," Crowley said.

"These crimes fall into patterns, don't they? The same types go in for the same kind of activities, I mean."

"That's generally true, sir."

Oliphant Bradley put his coffee cup down, and said, "Well, it seems to me you might have some information by now. If you picked up everyone ever connected with an extortion case and sweated them properly—you might have something." In spite of his worry over the child the old man's mood was executive and aggressive; his son had agreed that he had done right in calling the FBI; and that had taken a load off his mind. All of his vigorous confidence in himself had returned, and the tensions of the past night had charged him with an artificial energy. "Another thing, I understand that the ransom note is still here in the house. Shouldn't that be in your laboratory in Washington? Fingerprints, chemical analysis—isn't that your specialty?"

"Dad, they know their business," his son said.

"Yes, of course they do. I'm not implying they don't," the old man said impatiently. "But they're open to suggestions, I hope. I always was, and still am—from any clerk in our organization."

"Sir, we're after the baby, not the kidnapers," Crowley said quietly. "If we made wholesale arrests we might get a lead—but your granddaughter would become a death sentence to the men who kidnaped her, to anyone connected with the crime in any way at all. We'd put her on the spot, but good. About the kidnap note: supposing we sent it to Washington for analysis. And supposing the kidnapers sent a messenger here and asked for the note? That's happened in cases like this. What would you say? That you'd lost it? That you threw it out with the garbage?" Crowley shook his head. "It wouldn't wash. The kidnapers, if they weren't fools, would know you'd called in the police. They'd know they couldn't dare bargain with you any longer for the baby."

"I see, I didn't think—" The old man rubbed his jaw.

Crowley said, "The hardest thing in the world is to wait, to do nothing. That's our job right now."

Young Bradley stood up from the table abruptly and walked into the living room. His father said, "You'll excuse me?" to Crowley, and joined his son who was standing at the window, staring into the street. Crowley picked up the three cups and saucers from the table and carried them into the kitchen. "Where do you want these?" he said to Mrs. Jarrod.

She didn't answer him immediately; she was frowning faintly, counting on her fingers. Finally she looked at him and said, "What?"

He nodded at the cups he was holding. "Where do you want these?"

"Oh, anywhere at all. Right on the sink is fine." Her voice was edged with impatience. "You asked me if there had been any strangers around in the last few weeks."

"Yes?" Crowley felt the sudden stroke of his heart. "You remember something?"

"I'll tell you what it was. Three weeks ago Thursday there was a man here to look at the telephones. I wasn't here, it was my day off. But Kitty told me about it the next day, just talking casually. She didn't think it was anything unusual, mind you." Mrs. Jarrod seemed determined to be an exact and unemotional witness. "She just mentioned it over a cup of tea, as you would say."

"You're sure of the date?"

"I just counted it back. It was three weeks last Thursday. I know because I'd been at my sister's in Roslyn for the day."

"Please try to tell me exactly what Kitty said. Don't leave out anything, no matter how trivial it might sound."

"I'll try my best." Mrs. Jarrod drew a deep breath. "Well, for one thing she thought he must have kissed the Blarney Stone. He was full of smooth talk, about how beautiful she was and all like that. A chatterbox

—but an amusing one, she said. He was big and good-looking, with dark hair and dark skin. He was Irish, she mentioned that for sure. Talked about his father over there, she said. And what else now?"

Mrs. Jarrod frowned at the floor, and Crowley said nothing. "I can't remember anything else," she said at last.

"What was wrong with the phones?"

"Ah, that's it. Nothing at all. They were all right. He went through the house, checking the wires and all, downstairs and upstairs, and then went off. Said it was probably somewhere else in the block."

"This could be important. Keep thinking about your talk with Kitty. Something else might occur to you."

"Ah, there was another thing. He was hurt in the war, he told her. He had a limp in his leg."

This last bit dampened Crowley's enthusiasm slightly. It didn't seem likely that a man with such memorable characteristics would be used on the inside part of the job. The breezy line of chatter also seemed out of place. He wouldn't be calling attention to himself that way; he would slide in and out as inconspicuously as possible. . . .

As Crowley pushed through the swinging doors of the kitchen he saw a slim young woman in mules and a blue robe standing with Dick Bradley at the living-room fireplace. He hesitated, suddenly conscious of his shirtsleeves, his day-old beard, the gun in the holster at his hip. This would be the mother, he thought. Ellie Bradley. He hoped they had told her why he was here. Although they were not facing each other, he wasn't sure that she had seen him; her eyes were unrevealing shadows in the whiteness of her face. Even without make-up though, he saw that she was chic and elegant, with thin classic features in the fashion magazine style, and a cap of sleek yellow hair.

She put a hand suddenly on her husband's arm. "Dick," she said, and Crowley knew that she had seen him; instinctively she had crowded close against her husband.

"It's all right, dear, don't be upset."

"Who is he?" Ellie said, and there was a tremor of hysteria in her voice.

Oliphant Bradley was standing a few feet from them, tall and straight and handsome, his appearance a tribute to healthy living, a number of active interests, and a very good tailor. He had been born to a tradition of duty, trained to make the unpopular decision and stick by it. But yesterday he had done what he felt was right, and now he was nervous and uncertain as he stared at the growing fear in Ellie's eyes.

"My dear," he said, making placating little gestures with his hands. "Ellie, my dear, it's quite all right."

The fools, Crowley thought. They might have spared her this. . . .

"Who is he?" she cried, clinging to her husband's arm.

"My name is Crowley, Mrs. Bradley. I'm an agent of the Federal Bureau of Investigation. We're working to bring your baby back home safe and sound."

She shook her head slowly, as if he had just told her a preposterous lie. "That can't be," she said, in a soft puzzled voice. "They told us not to call the police. They said they'd kill our baby if we called the police."

Dick Bradley held her close to him. "Honey, honey, everything is all right. We stand a better chance with the FBI."

"But they told us not to call them."

"We need help to find the men who kidnaped her."

"I don't care about them!" she cried. "I want my baby back!"

"Please, honey. Hang on to yourself. Father thought it was smarter to call in the police. It seems—"

She twisted herself from his arms with convulsive strength. "Your father," she said, shaking her head slowly. "No, no," she said. "No, Dick."

The old man cleared his throat. "Ellie, I acted hastily, I admit that. I should have consulted with Dick. But time was precious, and I thought—"

"Stop it, stop it!" she cried, pressing her fingers to her temples.

"I acted with your interests at heart. You know that, Ellie."

"How could you do it?" She shook her head desperately. "It's Jill who'll suffer. How could you do this to us?"

"My dear—"

"Oh, but it was easy for you, I'm sure," she cried, turning on him with cold, deliberate fury. The change in her expression was sudden and shocking; she looked dangerous then, savage and pitiless, her eyes shining oddly in the marble-whiteness of her face. "You thought it was all for the best," she said, in a low, trembling voice. "So that settled it. It's *my* baby who is gone. She may be dead now, or crying for comfort and attention. It was our right to decide what to do. But you took over as you've always tried to do, with your college funds, and plans for schools and summer vacations and trips abroad. Only this time it's her life—"

"Ellie!" her husband said hoarsely.

She ignored him; her dark, shining eyes were fixed on the old man. "If she's killed will you still think you acted for the best?"

Crowley knew that nothing he could say would help the situation. She wouldn't trust him or believe him; he was the law, the symbol of the new threat to her child. But changing the direction of her anger might help to dissipate it.

"Mrs. Bradley, the chances of getting your baby are better with our help," he said. "A hundred trained men are working for you now. And a thousand more will be used if they're needed. They know their jobs. They don't often fail."

She turned slowly to face him, and there was a touch of wonder in her eyes. "Yes, that's how you would think of it," she said. Then tension was gone from her body, her arms hung straight at her sides and she seemed hopelessly weary and despondent. "Winning and losing," she said, in a soft, empty voice. "Keeping score. Put the losses in one column, the wins in another. And then add them up at the end of the year."

Her husband touched her arm tentatively but she turned away from him and leaned against the mantel. From there she could see the dining room, cheerful and bright with the morning sun. The breakfast things were still on the table; silver creamer and sugar bowl, the jam pot, crumpled-up napkins. The Bradleys had breakfasted as usual, she thought, stifling a giddy impulse to laugh. That's what breeding did for you, taught you to be orderly, taught you to keep busy. . . .

Crowley saw that she was ready to break. He caught young Bradley's eye. "Take her upstairs," he said.

Bradley started at his tone. "Yes, yes, of course. Come on, honey, you need to rest."

"Is that what I need?" she looked at him thoughtfully, as if she were memorizing his features.

"I'll take you up to your room."

"I can manage, thanks." She crossed the room and went slowly up the stairs. The men stood in an uncomfortable silence, avoiding each other's eyes.

"She's very tired," Oliphant Bradley said. He looked suddenly old and vulnerable. "I think—I believe she'll feel differently when she's rested—when this is over, that is."

"I wonder," Dick Bradley said.

It's hardest on him, Crowley thought. He doesn't have what she needs. It's a tough thing to find out. If this hadn't happened he probably wouldn't have known. . . .

"She was right," Bradley said, staring at his father. "It was our decision. I didn't have the guts to tell you that."

"You'd have done the same thing, son. In my place you would have acted as I did."

"I hope to God I wouldn't. I hope I can let my children think for themselves. You can't obviously. We didn't want the FBI. Jill's chances are better without police interference."

"You're wrong, son."

"That's my privilege then. Freedom includes the right to be wrong." Dick Bradley turned suddenly on Crowley. "You heard me? We don't want you here, we don't need you."

It would be nice if he could win this time, Crowley thought. But this wasn't a game of bean-bag. This time he couldn't win. "I'm sorry," he said.

"I'm telling you to clear out," Bradley said, his voice rising shrilly.

"We're not a catering service," Crowley said. "You don't get the FBI through an employment agency. We're law officers, and a federal law has been violated. That's why we're here. That's why a hundred men and a million dollars' worth of equipment is standing by—to get your baby back home."

Bradley tried to find an answer to this, but finally turned away with a dispirited shake of his head. There was nothing to say, nothing to do; his father's decision would stand. This had been the pattern of his life.

In the silence that followed the chimes from the front door knocker sounded clamorously through the house. Crowley glanced at his watch: it was eight-thirty. "Mail?" he asked Bradley.

"Yes, yes," Bradley said, already moving toward the foyer. His father started after him but Crowley caught his arm. "No point meeting the mailman in a group. It might give him something to wonder about."

"I see . . . yes, of course," the old man said, and there was a strange humility in his voice.

Dick Bradley returned with a bundle of bills, letters and magazines, but he was obviously too nervous to sort through them; his hands were trembling so badly that several pieces of mail slipped through his fingers. Crowley took the stack from him and retrieved those that had dropped to the floor.

He discarded bills and magazines quickly, and finally came to it, a cheap plain envelope with the name Bradley printed on it in block capitals. As he opened it he noted automatically that it had been posted in the city the night before. The message was also in block capitals, on a sheet of ruled, copybook paper. Crowley read the message aloud: "When you have the money in the house, close the venetian blinds on the middle window in the front room upstairs from twelve to two p.m. The little girl is still fine."

That was all.

Bradley was watching him with an expression of strained, haggard hope. "We've got the money," he said. "There's no need for any delay."

"That's right. We'll follow these instructions to the letter." Crowley turned and walked quickly into the study. He had two items to report to the Inspector: this note, and the fact that a telephone repairman had gone through the Bradleys' house three weeks ago last Thursday. . . .

But West didn't get Crowley's message until nine o'clock. He had spent the early hours of the morning driving through the Bradleys' neighborhood, marking points of surveillance, checking the directions of traffic and familiarizing himself with the look and feel of the streets. When he returned Roth was standing at his desk, and the Inspector knew from his expression that something was up.

"Crowley called a half hour ago," Roth said. "The second note arrived with the regular mail." He handed West the memo sheet on which he had written the kidnap message.

West read it through, frowning faintly. "From twelve to two the streets will be crowded," he said finally. "Anything else?"

Roth told him of the telephone repairman who had been at the Bradleys'.

"You've checked with the telephone company?" West asked him—but it was more a statement than question.

Roth nodded. "They're looking up their records."

West pushed his hat back on his forehead, a gesture that seemed curiously out of place with his usual precision and exactness. He hadn't been to bed yet but there was no evidence of fatigue in his face; his color was fresh and his eyes were alert and clear. Around him work went on swiftly and efficiently; a half dozen agents sat at desks that fanned out from his command post. They were running cautious checks on individuals and families living in the Bradleys' block on Thirty-first Street, using tax records and credit services as sources of information. From other desks the clatter of clerks' typewriters almost drowned out the traffic noises drifting up from Broadway.

West stood facing a long table set in the middle of the headquarter's area and bounded by irregular ranks of desks and filing cabinets. On the table, gleaming under the bright overhead lights, was a small-scale sketch of the Bradleys' block done in black ink on a huge square of white cardboard. Spread around it were glossy prints of the adjoining area— doorways, shops and stores, parking lots, the church opposite the Bradleys', the warehouse at Second Avenue.

West seemed unaware of the disciplined tension around him; he was studying his watch, a faint frown darkening his lean features. Finally he said to Roth, "Okay, we've got a little under three hours to work in. Starting at noon I want motion pictures taken of the street and sidewalk in front of the Bradleys'. Every car, every cab or truck that goes through there, every man, woman, child or dog that walks by—we're going to have them on film. It's a long shot. The kidnapers don't have to check personally to see if the blinds are closed. They could hire a boy to do it for a quarter. They could drive by in a cab. Or they might be watching from a window across the street. It's a long shot, but we'll take it. Now let's see where we can put cameras."

The two men bent to study the small-scale sketch of Thirty-first Street that covered almost half of West's desk. Finally Roth put his big forefinger on the church that faced the Bradleys'. "How about that?" he said, glancing sideways at West. "From the tower we'd have good coverage."

West nodded slowly. "That's okay. And Crowley's uncle lives on the opposite side of the street. We can put another camera there." Turning, he waved for a clerk. "Get Brunner in the photo lab. Tell him to come up right away."

"Yes, sir."

"There's a job I want you to start on," West said to Roth. "The wife, Eleanor Sims. She's from Chicago, and she's worked here and in Milwaukee. Now she's with an ad agency, Masterson and Thomas. I want a thorough check on her. Associates, family, men she's dated, girls she's shared apartments with, everything. Find out what agencies used to have the accounts she's working on now. See about business feuds, ad people who might have her job if she were out of the picture. And keep working on the Bradleys. Who inherits that baby's share of the old man's money. That's way out in left field, but check it anyway. And I want a rundown on every grocery boy, every deliveryman, every salesman who makes regular stops at the Bradleys'. Crowley gave me the list. Run it down."

Roth had been making quick notes on a memo pad. "Right. I'll get at it." As he turned away an agent stood quickly and walked to the Inspector's table. "The telephone company says they had no calls for service on the Bradleys' phone. It wasn't their man who was in the house."

The Inspector nodded and sat down on the edge of his desk. He stared out across the long, busy room, at the men fishing patiently for information, at the rows of girls hammering away at typewriters. The corners of his eyes began to narrow slightly; it was an unconscious reaction, a reflex as old as man himself; it was the hunter's reaction to the first sign of his quarry.

# 11

"Is the baby feeling better?"

"You heard the nurse, didn't you?" Grant's tone was abrupt and irritable. "The baby's fever went up, she thinks. So how could the kid be better?"

"Well, don't bite my head off," Belle said.

It was nine o'clock Monday morning. Grant was fully dressed, but Belle wore only a slip and a pair of pink mules. The windows of their room faced the water, and Grant stood in front of them doing his deep-breathing exercises. The day would be clear and mild, he thought. And quiet. . . . He was developing a compulsive anger at the look and feel of this countryside. The vivid colors hurt his eyes, and after last night's storm the stillness seemed to be drumming against his nerves. He was becoming grateful for any noise that shattered the serene spreading silence. In the silences he found himself listening for things . . .

"What can we do for the baby?" Belle asked him.

She sat on the edge of the bed painting her nails. The smoke from her cigarette stung her eyes, and she tipped her head sideways to avoid it; the pose was rather birdlike and attentive, as if she were listening for sounds in another part of the house. She had decided that morning to make an effort at more careful grooming. If she let herself go to pieces she'd be miserable. She knew that from experience. No more liquor, she had decided. Just one or two highballs after dinner. Sometimes that helped her sleep. She had got up early this morning and forced herself under a cold shower, and now she felt not only clean but virtuous. With her foundation on, and plenty of make-up, she'd look fine. But she was almost too cold to care; her lips were stiff, and she could see the goose pimples on her bare arms and legs.

She realized that Grant hadn't answered her question about the baby. He stood with his hands clasped behind his back, head thrust forward, staring out the windows. Like an ox, she thought. And just as communicative. But her reflections were good-humored; she admired his bulk, his silent indifference to her feelings.

"This is really no place for a kid," she said.

"We could have stayed at the Waldorf, of course."

"Well, you might have found a place with central heating," she said.

"Jails have central heating," he said with heavy irony. "Would that make you happy?"

"What are you going to do about the baby?"

"Don't worry, a fever won't kill her." Grant turned from the window and began pacing up and down the small room. Nothing could slip, he thought. They'd know this afternoon if the Bradleys had the money in their house. Undoubtedly they had; the old man wouldn't have come all the way down from Boston without it. So it was just a question of the payoff. There was no problem there, either. The arrangements were sure fire. All Creasy had to do was pick up the money. Then they could split up.

"I don't like the way Duke is acting," Belle said, inspecting one hand critically. "He behaves like a high school kid when he's trying to impress somebody."

"Who's he trying to impress?"

"Our road-company Florence Nightingale, who do you think?"

"So he likes girls. It's not a Federal rap."

"But he's reckless, Eddie. Nothing matters to him. Not even his own neck."

"Stop worrying about him. He'll do what I tell him."

Belle smiled and resumed work on her nails. She liked a certain amount of rough handling; it was a man's world and that suited her perfectly. Considerate and gentle men made her uncomfortable. "I'm glad you're running this deal," she said.

Grant was smiling faintly as he sat down by the window and lit a cigarette. He wouldn't have admitted it, but he was grateful for her complacent confidence in him. "You should have known me in the old days," he said. "I had a dozen characters like Duke hanging around me just to light my cigarettes."

"Oh, come on now."

"Well, half a dozen anyway. I had it made all right," he said, settling himself more comfortably in the chair. "There was a place called Donovan's in my ward, Belle, a big steak house right near North Clark Street and McCormick. All during the Twenties it ran as a speak. It never closed." Staring at the tip of his cigarette the smile faded slowly from his broad, pale face. "I went to lunch there every day. So did all the big shots in the city. The mobsters, the bookies and politicians, the big union wheels, even the mayor. They all turned up at Donovan's two or three times a week. It was like a big club. A tourist couldn't get a stool at the bar." Grant frowned faintly, caught up in memories. The smell of the place hit you first, he was thinking; liquor and food and thick expensive cigar smoke, a smell as exciting as the idea of power. Next there was the bustle and noise, the waiters in starched shirts and black ties hurrying around with shots of whiskey and big steak platters, smiling and bobbing their heads to old customers, hardly seeing the people who didn't count. It was a kick just to walk into the place. Being on the inside of all the deals, that was the big thing though. Getting the straight dope on horses, fights, the shiftings in the police department and the Hall, knowing why things happened when they did, who pulled the strings. . . .

"I never had to order," he said. "I had the same table for years. I drank twenty-year-old Scotch and ate nothing but steaks that cost six bucks a throw. Every waiter in the joint knew my order." He glanced up and saw that she had stopped working on her nails and was smiling at him. "It sounds wonderful, Eddie," she said.

"What's wonderful?" he said, shrugging; he knew he had been talking foolishly and revealingly. "It's just a steak house." He dropped his cigarette on the polished pinewood floor and ground it out with the tip of his shoe. "I'll go back there one of these days," he said, and unconsciously his voice became bitter and hard. "They'll be glad to see me." The idea of Donovan's had become a symbol of everything he had lost; in jail he had longed for the feeling of importance that came when the brass-bound door swung open for him, when he strolled into the big noisy room, at ease and at home with the big men who ran the city. And all those years in jail he had dreamed of returning to Donovan's, planning his entrances to the smallest detail; he would wear a gabardine suit, a two-hundred-dollar job the color of well-creamed coffee, with brown-and-white shoes, a dark blue shirt and red tie, and he'd stop just inside the door for a few seconds, nodding to Joe and Max behind the bar, looking around slowly and easily, and then he'd light a cigarette and walk straight down the room to his regular table. Just like those years in jail had never happened . . .

Duke's voice fell across his thoughts. "Hey, Eddie, come down here a second."

"He couldn't come up, of course," Belle said.

Grant looked at her irritably, and then went downstairs to the living room. Duke and the nurse stood at the front door, obviously ready to leave; they wore topcoats, and Duke was tossing the car keys up and down in his hand. His brother was standing at the fireplace.

"Keep an eye on him, Eddie," Duke said. "See that he doesn't get into the jam."

"Where do you think you're going?"

"Into town." Duke smiled and took the girl's arm. "Errand of mercy. The kid's fever seems better, but she needs nose drops, a salve for her chest, that sort of stuff."

Grant fought to control his swelling anger. "And you're the hero that's going to get it?"

"No, not me, the nurse," Duke said easily. "The people in town know I'm Hank's brother. If I was shopping for a sick kid the word would get around. Neighbors and friends might drop in to see if they could help. But nobody knows the girl. She can buy what she likes without causing any talk. See what I mean?"

He was right, Grant realized, but that wasn't important—what mattered was that Duke hadn't bothered to consult him first.

"We're ready to go," Duke said quietly. "Anything you want us to bring you?"

Grant hesitated, reluctant to force the issue. "Did you check the radio this morning?" he said. "The news show, I mean?"

"Sure. There's nothing on us. Nothing at all."

"Okay, get back here as fast as you can," Grant said shortly. He tried to sound as if he were granting Duke permission to leave, but it didn't come off that way; they all realized he was avoiding a challenge.

Belle came downstairs as Duke was starting the car. The noise of the motor was a series of shattering sounds against the silence. She smiled a good morning at Hank and then glanced at Grant who was still staring at the front door.

"Duke going somewhere?" she asked him.

"We need groceries. And the baby needs some things."

"Oh." Belle glanced at Hank, sensing that Grant's mood was ugly. "Where's the girl? The nurse, I mean."

"She went with Duke," Hank said.

"Was that smart?"

Hank shrugged. "I wouldn't know."

"Judas Priest, Eddie, what did you let them go for?"

"Don't worry about it," Grant said, without looking at her. "It's all right."

Hank knew that Grant's temper was dangerously short; he had lost to Duke by default and that was eating at him.

"Eddie, it wasn't smart," Belle said. "Duke's after that girl. You don't know what kind of a dumb thing he might do while he's alone with her."

"Don't worry about it, I told you," Grant said.

"How do you know Duke didn't wake the girl up the night he took the baby?"

"What do you mean?" Grant said, turning and staring at her.

"Maybe he woke her up deliberately, that's what I mean. He says she caught him in the nursery, but how can you be sure? It's his story, that's all. I wouldn't be surprised if he woke her up just so he could bring her with us."

"Shut up!" Grant said, making an abrupt, silencing gesture with his hand. "Stop talking up trouble."

"I may be saving us trouble, Eddie."

"And I told you to shut up. Duke isn't crazy. He's thinking of his hide just like the rest of us."

"That's right," Hank said.

They both looked at him and Grant said dryly, "Thanks a lot, Junior."

"He's his brother after all," Belle said. "He should know."

"All right, he *knows*. And he knows his brother is no crackpot. That's why I'm telling you."

Hank put a cigarette in his mouth and struck a match with his good hand. "It's not quite that simple," he said. "Duke makes sense to himself. But sometimes other people can't see that so they're liable to think he's a little cracked."

Belle smiled at him as she sat down and crossed her legs. "That's an interesting way to look at it," she said, moving her foot about in a small circle. "I'm not sure I understand it, but it's interesting anyway."

"It's pretty deep," Grant said dryly. "It means Duke is smart. It means he gets what he wants."

"That's it exactly," Hank said. "Regardless."

Grant turned away from them and strolled to the windows. He stood there for a few seconds and the silence in the room stretched into a curious tension; the conversation wasn't over yet, and everyone realized that. Duke was a subject of desperate importance to Grant and Belle; they didn't trust him but their lives were in his hands. They wanted clues to his character, indices to his patterns of behavior. They had to know what made him tick. Hank had guessed this earlier, but now he was sure of it; he could feel their uneasiness in the silence.

Grant turned slowly and looked at him. "What do you mean 'regardless?' " he said.

"Regardless?"

"You said that he got what he wanted 'regardless.' " Grant gestured irritably with one hand. "What do you mean?"

"Oh. Well, I simply meant that he'd scare you with the chances he'd take. If he wanted something, that is." Hank smiled and shook his head as if he were savoring an old, bitter-sweet memory. "One summer, for instance, Duke looked like a cinch to win the first prize for the biggest muskie caught in Lake Sandstone. The prize was twenty-five dollars, quite a bit of money in those days, and it was put up by one of the big lodges on the lake. Duke caught a beauty in July, a forty-six-pounder, and the contest ended on Labor Day. By the first of September he looked like a shoo-in. No one else had caught anything close to his big one." Hank took a drag on his cigarette, all of his movements casual and deliberate. Then he smiled at Grant who was watching him with a hard little frown.

"You wouldn't think twenty-five dollars would mean such a lot to a man," he said. "I mean, a fish is a fish. But Duke wanted that prize."

"Okay, okay, so what happened?" Grant said.

"He won the contest, all right," Hank said, "but it was no shoo-in. A day before the contest ended the word came into the lodge that one of Duke's friends had caught a whopper. He was still out on the lake with it, but he'd showed it to a man coming in. And this fellow said the fish might go sixty pounds. This was around dusk, and there was only a little bit of light still showing on the horizon."

"Never mind the nature touches," Grant said. "Let's have the results. You said Duke won. How come—when somebody else caught a bigger fish?"

"Well, that's what I meant by 'regardless,' " Hank said. "Duke took out a motorboat and cut his friend's boat in half. Ran him down. He said he didn't see him in the dark."

Belle drew a sharp breath. "I've never heard of anything so terrible."

"But Duke got what he wanted. His friend lost all of his tackle, plus his record fish. And he almost lost his life. But Duke got the twenty-five bucks. So it made sense to Duke. Other people might not see it that way, of course."

"Kids are always pulling damn-fool stunts like that," Grant said. "How old was he then?"

"About twenty-three," Hank said quietly.

Grant let out his breath slowly and turned back to the windows. He stared at the gravel road that wound past the house. The sun was stronger now, sparkling on the dew in the fields.

"Eddie?"

He turned and looked at her. She was very pale and her fingers moved nervously along the sides of her dress. "Well, what?"

"Oh, nothing."

He swore softly and turned back to the window. Belle smiled tentatively at Hank, as if entreating him to ignore Grant's bad manners. "This is going to be a nice day, isn't it?" she said.

Hank glanced at the sun-bright windowpanes. "They picked a good morning for their shopping," he said. "Half the county probably has the same idea."

"That's right," Belle said slowly. She glanced at Grant's tense shoulders, a worried little frown on her face. "The stores will be crowded, I suppose."

Hank nodded. "Mobbed."

# 12

CROWLEY TAPPED LIGHTLY ON MRS. BRADLEY'S DOOR AND WHEN SHE said, "Yes?" he hesitated for a second, wishing to God there was some way of avoiding this session. It would be difficult for him, and painful for her—but it had to be faced. "This is Crowley," he said. "I need to talk to you for a minute."

"Please come in," she said.

Crowley opened the door and stepped into her darkened room. He didn't see her at first; the shades were drawn, and only a night lamp gleamed above the tufted crimson bedspread; its reflection shone on the face of an illuminated clock and struck splinters of brilliance from a bracelet on the dressing table. Then she said, "I'm over here," and he turned and saw that she was sitting in a lounge chair near the windows, her arms folded tightly over her breasts. A bar of light from the blinds touched her sleek blonde head, but her face and eyes were in darkness.

"We've got what may be a lead," Crowley said quietly. "Three weeks ago last Thursday a man came here to check your telephones. That's what he told the nurse. But he wasn't sent by the telephone company. We want to find that man, and we need your help."

"I haven't been much help so far, have I?"

"There's been nothing you could do."

"I might have kept quiet." She looked up at him and he saw the misery in her eyes. "I don't know why I took it out on Dick and his father. But I can't think straight—I know the men who took Jill won't bring her back. I've been through her room. They didn't take the things she'll need. Clothes, blankets, powder and oil—they didn't touch them. They just took her."

"They would have the things she'd need ready in advance, Mrs. Bradley. They wouldn't bumble around the nursery, collecting them."

"But I can't hope, I can't even pray. That's the terrible thing."

"I can understand that. I have a daughter, too. I can guess how you feel, believe me."

"She's home with her mother. There's—a difference."

Crowley wet his lips. "No, she's in the hospital. She—she's been having headaches, and the doctor thought a few tests might show up the trouble."

"But what's wrong with her?"

"They don't know."

"But that's impossible." Her voice was puzzled. "They'd know right away unless—" She stopped and made a futile little gesture with her hands. They looked at each other in silence.

"Sure," he said finally. "They'd know right away unless it's cancer or a tumor maybe."

"I'm sorry." A reflection of light touched her face and when she looked up at him he saw that she was crying. "Why aren't you with her? Why aren't you home with your wife?"

"Oh, Christ!" Crowley said, "I didn't want to get started on my troubles. All I want you to understand is that I'm not just an adding machine sent out here to keep score. Look, how about a cigarette?"

"No—no thanks."

Crowley lit his own and then stared at the lighter, turning it around slowly in his big hand. "I spent last night talking to your husband. About his schools, friends, business associates, your marriage. But I got a better picture of you than I did of him. You're tougher than he is. Maybe stronger is a better word. You've worked for things all your life. That's something I understand. Maybe there's no particular credit due people like us. It just happened. But it didn't happen to them. This is the first jolt they've ever taken that their money can't fix. They've got to get their help somewhere else."

"From me?"

"You're all they've got. It's your job."

"What can I do?"

"Help me," Crowley said. "I need a line on that fake repairman. Did Kate talk to you about him? Think hard."

She raised her head slowly and he knew from the expression in her eyes that she was coming over to his side. "I—I'll try," she said.

"Good," Crowley said, sitting down beside her.

Ellie's mental processes had been trained and molded by years in the business world. Her thinking habits were organized and precise. Within a minute or so she had pinpointed the day the repairman had been in the house.

"Yes, it was Thursday," she said, and then, frowning slightly, she recreated the day in terms that had little or no meaning for Crowley. "There was a staff meeting on the Milburn account that morning, then a layout conference, lunch with the fashion group. I talked to a space salesman from *New*—let's see, Dick called and we had cocktails at the Algonquin. We went on to dinner at a place in the Fifties. We were home around ten at the latest."

"Did you talk to the nurse when you came in?"

"I—let's see. I know I went up to the nursery. Yes, Kate was giving Jill a bottle. I took the baby and Kate stayed to talk for a while." Ellie rubbed her fingers over her forehead. "It—it was about the baby. I can't remember anything specific."

Crowley didn't press her. He waited, hoping, but finally she shook her head helplessly. "I'm no help, I'm afraid."

"Did Kate have any particular men friends?"

"No, I don't believe so. There was a young man last winter—his name was Delancey, Bill Delancey—she saw him quite regularly. But it wasn't anything serious. He was a lieutenant in the army and on his way to Germany, I think it was."

"Has she any relatives in the city?"

"No. Her family is in Ireland."

"I see. Did she have any close girl friends?"

"Several, I think. I can find you their names if you think it's important."

"I wish you would, please. Was Kate attached to Jill? I mean, did you ever think she was too fond of her perhaps?"

"She loved Jill, of course." Ellie turned away from him and shook her head quickly. "No, Kate wouldn't do this."

"There was no sign of a struggle," Crowley said. "No locks forced. But she's packed and gone."

"No—" Ellie shook her head again. "She's loyal and kind and good. We—knew her perfectly. She was like a younger sister to me. I knew all about her family, her younger brothers and sisters. They made little presents for Jill—colored post cards, wooden animals on wheels—you know. She *isn't* involved in this. You can't tell me she is."

Crowley was silent for a few seconds. Then he said, "Would you come up to her room with me, please?"

"Yes, of course," Ellie said.

The nurse's bedroom was at the head of the stairs on the third floor, a bright and cheerful place that had been decorated with the same care as the rest of the house; the walls were a shade of blue-green, the furniture was smartly simple, and the blue-and-white coarse linen draperies matched the spread that was folded at the foot of the wide studio couch.

Crowley stood in the doorway and watched Ellie as she looked through the closet. "She took her new spring suit, the tweed skirt, blouses." Her voice was troubled and low. "Everything she'd need . . . street shoes, loafers. Raincoat. . . ." She turned and crossed swiftly to the bureau and began to pull out the drawers.

"They're empty," Crowley said.

"Yes—I see." Ellie moved to the small combination desk-table and touched the top of it with her fingers. "She—she always kept her diary right here."

"That's gone," Crowley said. "Her overnight bag is gone. And her toilet articles. Comb and brush, cologne, perfume, toothbrush, toothpaste, soap—the works." Without realizing it, Crowley had put a sharp, demanding edge to his voice. "Personal letters, pocketbook, cash, keys. All cleaned out. How do you explain that?"

"I—I can't."

"No locks were forced. There was no sign of a struggle. The baby and nurse are gone. Those facts may be interpreted a dozen different ways. But right now I see only one."

"If Kate took her away then Jill won't be frightened," Ellie said in an empty, lifeless voice. "Jill knows her. They've been together since Jill was born."

Ellie sat down on the edge of the studio couch and looked at the faint indentation in the smooth white surface of the pillow. The bed had been slept in; the spread had been turned back, but the blanket and sheets were only slightly disarranged. "She went to bed that night," Ellie said softly. She was frowning. "That's strange—"

"Why?"

Then Ellie said, "Wait!" in a high, breathless voice, and put her hand quickly under the pillow. "I knew there was something. Yes, yes!"

"What is it?" Crowley stepped around the foot of the bed as Ellie stood up quickly. "Look," she said. She held a rosary in her hands, an old-fashioned one with heavy wooden beads and a large cross. "She wouldn't have left this," Ellie said.

"She might have forgotten it."

"No, you don't understand. In the daytime she kept it on the bureau. At night she put it under her pillow. She said a rosary before she fell asleep."

"Yes but—" Crowley hesitated, then shrugged. "It's a nice habit, Ellie. That's all."

"Don't you see? She was in bed ready to go to sleep. Otherwise the rosary wouldn't have been under the pillow. Something must have waked her. She got up to see what it was—and she never came back." Ellie shook her head impatiently. "Don't you understand? Why should she have gone to bed if she intended to take Jill away?"

Crowley looked down at the rosary she held in her hands. Yes, it made sense. Whoever had taken the baby had also taken the nurse. Very probably. . . . Professionals then, organized and competent, able to improvise. . . . And that was bad. Professionals would have no compunctions about getting rid of the baby.

"I told you Kate wasn't involved," Ellie said. She was looking up at Crowley, her eyes suddenly bright with hope. "We know that now. Won't that help?"

"Yes, of course," he said. She didn't understand, he realized. "Now I think you'd better go back to your room and rest. I'll call the Inspector."

Ellie looked down at the rosary in her hands. She hesitated a second, then put it in her pocket and walked quickly from the room.

# 13

When they heard the car turning into the drive Grant glanced at Hank and then walked to the windows, his hand instinctively moving toward the gun in his pocket. As he pulled the curtains back, Belle said, "Is it them, honey?" Her voice was like an anxious child's, uneasy and guarded, appealing to grownups for reassurance.

"Sure, it's them," Grant said bitterly. "With their arms full of junk. They must have hit every goddam store in town."

"Williamsboro is quite a shopping center," Hank said, and Grant looked at him, his eyes narrowing irritably. "The psychology bit, eh? Don't strain yourself, Junior."

Hank glanced at his watch: eleven o'clock. Duke had been gone about two hours and the tension had been building steadily; Grant was worried and his fears had infected Belle. She had attempted a few chattery gambits to break the long silences, but Grant was in no mood for small talk. For the past hour there had been little conversation. Once Grant had said to Hank, "You don't like Duke, eh?" but Hank had shrugged off the question. Later Grant had come back to the subject from a different direction. "What did he do to you? You must have crossed him. He's a loyal guy. I know him. He sticks to his friends."

"You'd have to ask his friends about that," Hank said.

"Yeah? I don't have to ask anybody."

There was a step on the porch and then the door was pushed open and Duke and the nurse came into the room. In the movement and noise of their entrance Hank caught her eye, trying to read something in her expression; but she seemed distracted and nervous, and there was no communion between them, no warmth or awareness or recognition. He wondered if he had imagined her reaction to him last night.

"The baby's fine, I think," Belle said to her. "I haven't heard a peep out of her."

"I'll go up," Kate said, turning to the stairs.

"If she's awake, tell her we've got the stuff to fix her up," Duke said. He was in a jubilant mood; a cigar jutted at a comical angle from his mouth, and his cheeks were flushed with sun and air and excitement. Hank knew the reason for his high spirits; the danger of being in town with the girl had exhilarated him. He always needed such stimulants; without them he became bored and sullen and troublesome.

"Take some of this loot," he said, handing a big shopping bag to Belle. "We're going to eat for a change. I've got steaks here two inches thick, and a dozen big Idahos." He whacked Belle lightly on the hip with the flat of his hand. "Come on, shake it. I'll make the sauce for the potatoes—a Duke Farrel special with cheese and butter. We'll hate ourselves in the morning, eh, Belle?"

Belle responded gratefully to his enthusiasm. "Well, we'll be a long time dead," she said, laughing, "so let's live it up a little."

Belle loved a good time. Food and drink in generous amounts, jokes, horseplay, kidding around—this was her notion of a party. She knew from long experience that nothing mattered unless the men were in a cheerful mood; if they just ate and drank and got mad when you tried to cheer them up—that was murder. Now Duke seemed to be coming to life, and she was hoping some of it would rub off on Eddie.

"Steaks for lunch," she said, smiling at him. "Black on the outside, pink on the inside. Like that place in Chicago you were talking about. Donovan's."

"Donovan's?" Duke said, still grinning. "Everybody in jail thought about women. Except Eddie. He was torching for a steak house."

"It was good enough for the biggest people in town," Grant said shortly.

"Sure, sure," Duke said. "Look, we need something to drink. We got nothing here but rum."

"Rum is all right," Belle said. She noticed unhappily that Eddie wasn't responding to Duke's good humor. Just when they had a chance for a little fun. . . .

"Rum is for old men," Duke said. "I want some whiskey." He glanced at Hank. "Why didn't you tell me this jerk town of yours was dry?"

"You didn't ask me."

"Sure, sure, and naturally you wouldn't guess that I'd want to buy a bottle. Where's the nearest place I can get one?"

"Jameston. That's about twelve miles from here."

"What a crazy mixed-up state," Duke said. "One town is dry, the next sells booze. Just the kind of place you'd pick to settle in. Well, I can make a liquor run in half an hour."

"The rum won't kill you," Grant said.

"That's for sure. I'm not drinking it."

"Then stick to water," Grant said sharply.

Duke looked at him for a second or so, and then he smiled easily. "Water won't do, Eddie."

"You're not going back into town, get that straight." Grant stood facing Duke, his hands swinging free and clear from his body. "We may be the hottest guys in the country right now. We aren't taking any extra chances."

"Sure, but we don't have to go out of our way to be miserable," Duke said. "Wearing hair shirts and eating bread and water isn't going to help."

"We aren't going to argue about it," Grant said.

Duke smiled slowly, and an uneasy little silence settled on the room. "Maybe we are, Eddie. Maybe we'll have to."

Hank stood perfectly still, not looking directly at either man. He had seen what was coming; Duke wanted to run things, not because he thought he was better qualified than Grant but simply because he was bored. And if Duke took over, Hank knew that they had a chance. . . .

"You're not being smart, Duke," Grant said. "If you were, you'd see I'm right."

"Brains are your department, eh?"

"Yeah, they're my department," Grant said, his voice rising suddenly. "You don't think. You've got nothing to think *with*. Steaks, Idaho potatoes, cigars, booze. You must have been about as inconspicuous as a drunk elephant on Main Street. We're *hot*. Do you know what that means?" He took a step toward Duke, trembling with rage. "If we're picked up we'll be dead three weeks later. That's what it means. But you act like you're the advance party for a convention of picnickers. You got to have this, got to have that. Can't drink rum. Can't eat canned food. You think a few days off steak will stunt your growth?"

"I told you wearing hair shirts isn't going to help." Duke was smiling, seemingly amused at Grant's anger. "You got to relax, Eddie. No sense in making it hard for ourselves."

"We'll relax when this is over. I planned this job for six months and you're not going to louse it up."

"We wouldn't have the kid if it weren't for me," Duke said. "Remember that."

"Sure, and we wouldn't have the nurse if it weren't for you," Grant yelled. "You woke her up and brought her along. You put all our necks on the block. Isn't that the way it was?"

Duke was still smiling, but his eyes had become wary. "It's your story, finish it."

Grant knew he had made a dangerous mistake, but he was too furious to care; unless Duke were kept in line they might pay for his foolishness with their lives. "You're going to do what I tell you," he said, in a low, trembling voice. "I'm not going to the chair because you want a certain kind of booze to drink." Grant's anger was almost choking him; Duke seemed determined to behave recklessly stupid. Crazy. . . . Belle had seen it. And his own brother knew it. "Get this," Grant said, staring at him. "We're staking our lives against two hundred thousand bucks. We're not after a prize for catching a goddam fish. This is the biggest job you've ever been cut into. And I'm running it. Don't ever get any different idea."

"Sure, you're the boss," Duke said. "The big wheel. So let's don't argue about that any more." He was smiling faintly, but Hank could see the pressure building in him; his eyes were sharp, and his big body was ominously passive and slack. "But what's all this about catching fish?" he said gently.

"What do you mean?"

"You said we weren't after a prize for catching fish. Why did you bring that up?"

It had slipped out, Grant realized; he didn't remember saying it. He made an irritable gesture with his hand. "I forget. It's not important."

"We were talking about that muskie Duke caught," Hank said casually. "It was probably on your mind."

"Don't worry about what's on my mind."

Duke looked sharply from Grant to his brother. "How come you told them about the muskie?"

"I forget," Hank said, smiling faintly. "We were talking about you, and something must have reminded me of it."

"Talking about me?" Duke turned back to Grant, his eyes puzzled and irritable. "That's great. I'm out getting us something decent to eat and you haven't anything better to do than sit around bum-rapping me. Yeah, great."

"Don't get excited," Grant said. "It was just passing the time."

"I was explaining to Grant that you're really pretty smart," Hank said.

"He's a cute one," Grant said to Duke.

"You need him to tell you I'm smart, eh?"

"I tell you it wasn't anything."

"Okay, okay," Duke said, looking at his brother. "You want trouble, eh? Making up stories about your big, bad brother."

"Making up stories? Ed Daley would like that."

"I ran him down by accident. Everybody knows that."

"Everybody knows that's your story," Hank said.

"You've taken your lumps," Duke said, frowning slightly. "I'd think you'd be tired of it. But keep yapping and you'll get hurt again."

"Don't waste time scaring me," Hank said. "You can't worry a man in a death cell by telling him he can't have cream in his coffee. Do what the hell you want, Duke."

Duke stared at him, still frowning; for an instant he seemed honestly interested in his brother. "We don't have to kill you," he said slowly. "Don't you realize that? When this job is over we'll turn you loose. You can't go to the cops. You're in this deal, kid. Get used to that idea. Relax and take it easy."

"Let's everybody relax," Belle said in an uneasy little voice. "We've got a nice lunch today. Isn't that something to be grateful for?"

Duke looked at her and shook his head slowly. "Don't ever change. Promise me that."

"You're still worrying about your whiskey. *I* could go to town, if that's all you want. Would that be okay, Eddie?"

Grant rubbed his forehead, and then he said, "Judas Priest!" in a harsh, explosive voice.

"What's that supposed to mean?"

"It means nobody's going to town," Grant said, staring at her. "What in hell do you think we're talking about? Don't you ever listen, for Christ's sake?"

"Sure, I listen. You didn't want Duke to go—" She stopped and wet her lips. "But he—he's conspicuous."

"And you think you're the type who's just lost in a crowd?" Grant's eyes were mean and ugly as they moved slowly down to her high-heeled sandals, then back up to her shining blonde hair. "Well, think again. This is a nice quiet little town. Full of nice quiet little people. They'd think you were in town trying to bring back burlesque."

A painful flush of color had come up in Belle's cheeks. "I look respectable," she said. "I've been in towns like this before. Lots of times. And I never attracted a crowd. People didn't stop on the sidewalks and stare at me." Her voice was trembling slightly. "I've got a son who'd like to hear you talking this way. It would be nice for him, wouldn't it?"

"All right, all *right*," Grant said. "Let's knock it off. Get with lunch, okay?"

Belle hurried into the kitchen, fighting back her tears. She felt as if her whole body had been assaulted and bruised—he could hurt her without even trying to, she thought bitterly. The fact that he didn't try to made it worse. All men know that trick. They were born knowing it.

She took the bottle of rum from the pantry and poured herself a long drink. Why shouldn't I? she thought. He doesn't care what I do. I'm like a dumb animal as far as he's concerned. A pat on the head, a kick in the ribs—neither gesture had any feeling in it.

Duke limped into the kitchen a little later and she raised her glass to him. "First today."

He didn't bother to answer her. Filling a tumbler with rum, he turned back into the living room. "Laughing boy," Belle muttered, and raised her glass.

As Duke settled himself into a chair the stairway door opened and the nurse stepped into the room. "How's the kid?" he said.

"She's asleep, but she feels quite cool. I'm just going to heat her bottle."

"I told you there was nothing to worry about."

"Yes, she seems better." She waited for him to continue, but he was obviously bored with the subject; picking up a magazine, he began to leaf through it, occasionally reading a title aloud in a flat, listless voice. The nurse turned, met Hank's eyes briefly and walked into the kitchen.

"This'll send you," Duke said. "How To Keep Your Wife's Love After Forty. You need a little help in that department, Eddie?"

Hank stood up and Grant said, "Where are you going?"

"I thought I'd shave. Okay?"

"Yeah—go ahead."

As Hank started up the stairs Duke said, "There's the old man's training for you. Clean minds in clean bodies."

"He sounds real interesting," Grant said.

Duke dropped the magazine on the floor and took another long swallow from his drink. He felt the rum burning in his stomach, and then the sensuous heat moving slowly and pleasurably downward, warming his belly and his loins.

"We'll get the news from Creasy in a few hours," Grant said. He sat forward on the edge of the chair, his elbows resting on his knees. "We'll know if the Bradleys have the dough. After that there's nothing but the pickup."

"They'll have it," Duke said. "They want the kid back." He lit a cigarette, then settled himself comfortably in his chair and flipped the burnt match in a high and accurate arc toward the fireplace. From where he sat he could watch the nurse working at the kitchen sink. It was a pleasant sight; a square of sunlight struck the wall beside her and its reflections gleamed like tiny jewels in her silky black hair. She wore a white silk blouse with short sleeves, and a skirt that fitted her neat waist and hips without a wrinkle—sprayed on, he thought smiling faintly.

"I wish to hell we didn't have to let Creasy handle the pickup," Grant said.

Duke noticed that she had changed her pumps for slippers—high heels were probably too noisy in the baby's room. That must be it. His thoughts drifted around her pleasantly and languorously. She wasn't sexy. You couldn't call a blouse and skirt a sexy outfit. But something about her got to him.

"Creasy's a sharp little character," Grant said.

"Sure he is," Duke said.

"And the pickup plan is perfect. Even if the cops were in on this they couldn't cover it."

Duke was staring at the girl, his lips curving in a smile, his eyes soft and sleepy.

"But I'd rather be there myself," Grant said. "I'm going stale here." He flexed his arms and shoulders and drew in his stomach. "Too many starches, too much sitting around. I'd like to spend some time on a beach. Get a tan. You ever notice how a few days in the sun makes you look younger?" Grant fumbled for his cigarettes. "Look, Duke, you think Creasy can handle the pickup?"

"What?" Duke was paying very little attention to Grant; his worried voice was nothing but a droning accompaniment to Duke's lazy thoughts.

"You think Creasy can handle it? Hey! Are you asleep?"

"No, just dozing. Yeah, Creasy's all right." The nurse was measuring something into a spoon and with her arms raised he could follow the soft curve of her breast against the silken blouse. He remembered the time they had been together in the Bradleys' bedroom. Everything came back to him with a curious vividness; he could close his eyes and see the cool, spacious room, the uncompromisingly suggestive pinks and blacks of the color scheme; he could almost feel the thick nap of the carpeting under his shoes, and smell the faint but compelling scent of the perfume that permeated the air. And she had been clean and sweet in her white uniform, chatting away innocently with him, unaware of his sudden, reckless need for her . . .

"Duke? You think Creasy will get ideas about an extra slice of the money?"

"Why not?" Duke said irritably. Grant's voice was becoming a nuisance, a nagging interruption. "People always get ideas. That's why they're always in trouble."

"That's all he'll get then—ideas," Grant said.

When she had come into the nursery (almost taking him by surprise) he had caught her from behind—an arm around her body and a hand on her mouth to cut off her screams. She had fought and squirmed like a wildcat. Duke took a slow sip from his drink. The slim light body straining against him had been very exciting; he remembered that he had almost been sorry when the fight went out of her.

Duke put his glass down and sat up straight in his chair.

"You bring any cards?" he asked Grant.

"No, I wasn't planning to stay, you know."

"You picked the nice end of the deal. Waiting in New York wouldn't be so bad. You could at least get a drink and the papers."

"We won't be here much longer."

"Great," Duke said. He could feel a restless ferment in his breast.

The need for whiskey, the conflict with Grant, the wait that stretched ahead of him—it all seemed to be churning inside his head.

The girl left the kitchen and started up the stairs. She wasn't wearing stockings, he noticed; the fine down on her legs gleamed brightly as she stepped through a splash of sunlight. Her skin was very white. He watched her as she went up the stairs, studying the fluid swing of her hips and the delicate muscles drawing together in the backs of her slim legs. Innocent, hell. She knew what she was doing, he thought as his turbulent, illogical anger suddenly found a channel deep enough for its pounding violence.

"I'm going up to keep an eye on my brother," he said to Grant. His voice was casual and Grant didn't look up from the magazine he had been leafing through. "Good idea," he said, turning a page.

Hank heard his brother's heavy limping footsteps as he was drying his face awkwardly with his one good hand. He put the towel over the rack and then stood completely still, following Duke's progress along the hallway. A door opened, creaking faintly through the silent house, and he knew from the sound which room Duke had entered—the one the nurse and child were using.

Hank stepped into the hall and stared at the closed door of the nurse's room, caught in a paralyzing inertia. It was the fear of Duke that held him, the fear that had been part of him all his life; like the color of his eyes and skin, it was something that would never change. And with the fear there was guilt. Together they formed a ruthless twisted syllogism: Duke deserved the breaks, so keep out of his way and let him have everything he wanted—if you had this beaten into you a sufficient number of times it began to make a crazy kind of sense . . .

And then he heard a cry from the nurse's room. The sound was smothered abruptly, but by then he was moving down the hallway, his paralysis snapped by the desperation in her voice. He wasn't aware of his decision until the door opened under his hand and he saw them struggling together in the middle of the darkened room. Duke held her against him with one arm, his free hand forcing her head back at a sharp angle. She was helpless against his effortless strength; her arms were locked against her sides and her slippered feet churned futilely in the air.

"Let her go!" Hank said.

"You goddam fool." Duke stared over his shoulder at him, his eyes gleaming and furious in the darkness. "Beat it, get moving!"

"Let her go!"

Duke swore savagely and released the girl. She stumbled away from him, and he turned on Hank, still swearing, and struck him viciously across the face with the back of his hand. Hank staggered under the power of the blow, and Duke moved after him, and said, "Get your fists up, kid."

Hank looked away from him, his injured hand hanging limply at his side. He felt a stinging pain in his mouth, and then the sticky warmth of blood on his lips.

"No?" Duke said. "Take a beating and then turn around to be kicked in the tail. I had a hound like that once and I shot him." Turning slightly, he glanced at the girl. He was breathing heavily but there was a little smile on his lips; the instant of violence had purged most of his anger and frustration. "No point in being upset," he said. She was looking at the floor, her pale face in shadows, but he saw that her lips were trembling. "My brother always butts in where he isn't wanted. Next time there won't be any interruptions. That's a promise, baby." He moved toward the door, staring at Hank. "There hadn't better be any interruptions, kid." He stood for a second or so, watching both of them, and then he shrugged his big shoulders and walked out of the room.

"Are you all right?" Hank said.

"Why didn't you kill him when you had the chance?" Her voice shook with anger and contempt.

"Stop thinking about that. It won't help."

"Nothing will help. They can't let us live. It's just a matter of time before they kill us."

"That's right, a matter of time," Hank said. "But time is working for us, not them." He took a step toward her. "Listen to me: they're kidnapers. You know what that means? They'll be dead within a month if the police get hold of them. And they know it. Every second we stay alive puts more pressure on them." Hank glanced toward the closed door; he heard a footstep on the stairs. "They can't afford one slip, one bad break. This isn't Siberia. There are hikers, picnickers in these woods. I've got friends in town who might drop by. If the police are in on it, there are hundreds of men looking for you and the baby. A knock on that front door could put them straight into the death cell. And they're sweating that out." He gripped her shoulder with his good hand. "Hang on," he said, in a low, urgent voice. "You've taken what they've handed you so far. You've got to keep taking it. Can you do it?"

She stared at him, and he saw the fear and doubt in her eyes. "Don't you want to fight?" he said harshly. "Don't you think I've got enough guts to help you?"

"No, it isn't—" She turned swiftly from him and opened the door of the closet. A thin edge of light touched the clothes that hung there, his jackets, suits, odd slacks. "I saw this," she said, putting her fingers on his army blouse. The gaudy rows of campaign ribbons and decorations gleamed in the ray of sunlight. "Don't they mean something?"

"Maybe," he said, staring at the three rows of ribbons. "Maybe they did."

"I think they did," she said.

A step sounded in the hall and the door swung inward. Grant stood there, staring at them with ominously alert eyes. In his right fist he held a gun. "Downstairs, you," he said to Hank. "And keep away from her. This isn't a college house party. You get out of line again and I'll bust your other hand wide open. Remember that, Junior. Now move!"

# 14

CROWLEY CAME ON HIS SECOND LEAD SHORTLY AFTER HIS TALK WITH Ellie Bradley. Since then he had been working in the study, fingerprinting every surface the telephone repairman might conceivably have touched; the phone itself yielded nothing, but he was hoping for prints in a less obvious place—around the window or desk perhaps, areas that weren't dusted and handled every day.

He found a single print on a small black metal box attached to the floorboard behind the desk. The box contained the bell and telephone coil, he knew, an arrangement which was peculiar to older buildings. Crowley opened his fingerprint kit and removed a silver powder, white lifting tape, a brush and scissors. Then he went to work.

When he finally straightened up and turned he saw that Mrs. Jarrod was watching him from the doorway. "I didn't want to disturb you," she said, with her stiff, old-fashioned dignity. She was a woman, Crowley guessed, who had little tolerance for scatterbrains and idlers; she was direct and relevant, and she knew the difference between fact and guesswork. She wasn't here out of curiosity, he was sure of that.

"I've been trying all morning to remember something else Kitty told me," she said.

"Yes? What is it?"

"I—I can't remember," she said, and her plump cheeks became pink with annoyance. "I can't quite get hold of it."

"Well, that happens to all of us," Crowley said easily. He lit a cigarette and sat down on the edge of the desk. "And the harder you try, the blanker your mind gets."

"That's it exactly."

Crowley began replacing the fingerprint equipment, making each movement deliberate and casual. If he could get her mind on to something else the information she wanted might pop into her head. "Have you got a scissors?" he asked her.

"Why, yes, of course."

"I don't need it now. Later perhaps. Mine seems kind of dull."

"You use a scissors in taking fingerprints?"

"Yes, to cut the lifting tape. First we powder the prints, then photograph them, then lift them with this tape which, as you can see, is about like the kind you use to repair an automobile tire. Then we put a cellophane cap over the tape to prevent smudging. And that's it."

"It's complicated, isn't it?"

"Just routine, that's all."

Mrs. Jarrod was frowning. "It was something about a nickname. There, I've got that much. The man told Kitty something about this nickname."

"Good. That's a start."

"But I can't remember what it was."

"Let's see now. Nicknames usually fall into categories, don't they? How about physical characteristics? Fatty or Fatso, Slim, Tiny, Baldy, Blackie—" Crowley was speaking quietly and slowly. "Or Lefty perhaps. Then there's Pudge, Specs, Four-eyes—"

"No, it's nothing like that."

Crowley took a pull on his cigarette. "We'll hit it, don't worry. Was it unflattering? You know, like Gimpy or Creep or Humpy?"

But Mrs. Jarrod was shaking her head. "It's just the opposite."

"You mean flattering? Like Handsome or Big Boy or—let's see— Romeo?"

"It's not flattering. It's—special. I thought when Kitty told me about it that it was pretty high-and-mighty for a repairman."

"High and mighty, eh?" Crowley frowned and took another deliberate pull on his cigarette. They were close; he could feel it. But he didn't want to stampede her thoughts. "How about Champ then? Or Ace?"

"That's it, that's it. Ace!" Mrs. Jarrod suddenly shook her head irritably. "No, that's not it. But it's closer than anything else you've said."

"Ace? How about cards? Ace, King, Queen, Jack—any of those fit?"

"No, no, no."

"Just relax, we'll get it." Crowley was smiling easily, but he felt like shaking her. "Let's work on the cards a little more. Joker or Thirty Days —that's poker slang for three tens. How about Full House, Royal Flush, Deuce—"

"Deuce, deuce! That's it," she cried in a high, excited voice. "That's it exactly."

"Deuce? You're sure."

"No—" She gave a little moan. "It's not Deuce. But that's close, so close—Duke! It was Duke! I'm certain of it. His father nicknamed him Duke. He told Kitty that."

Crowley glanced down at the black metal box from which he had lifted the single fingerprint. "Duke," he said softly.

"It was silly of me to forget it," Mrs. Jarrod said.

"You did fine," Crowley said, reaching for the mike to flash Inspector West. . . .

Shortly after eleven o'clock that same morning a florist's station wagon pulled up and stopped in front of St. John's Church on Thirty-first Street. A man wearing a visored cap and a smart green twill uniform climbed out, checked through a sheaf of bills, then took two long boxes from the rear of the car and walked briskly into the vestibule of the church. He returned in less than thirty seconds, hopped into the car and drove off. It was a commonplace occurrence, a millionth part of the city's daily logistical problem; flowers for a baptism or wedding, a floral piece for the altar—the most alert observer could hardly suspect anything else.

The flower boxes had been placed on a table in the baptistery, and standing beside them now (and trying not to stare at them) was the church's pastor, a tall, middle-aged man with strong features and deep, thoughtful eyes. He checked his wrist watch every few seconds, and occasionally cleared his throat and patted his forehead with a handkerchief. The baptistery door opened a few minutes later, and a young man in a business suit came in and smiled at the priest.

"My name is Nelson, Father."

"Yes—I was expecting you. Your office called."

The young man showed him an identification card with his picture on it, and the priest studied the photograph carefully. "Yes, yes, of course," he said at last. "Is there anything else I can do? Any way I can be of help?"

"No, everything is all set." The agent was a generation younger than the priest, and possibly many generations less wise, but he had a veteran's confidence about him that put the older man at ease.

"The stairs are just there," the priest said, nodding at a closed door. "I'll see that no one else goes up."

"Perfect." The young man raised the lid of one of the flower boxes and checked the equipment inside; his alert eyes moved over the reels of film, the camera, the foot-long telescopic lenses. . . . "I'll get busy then," he said. "Thanks again, Father."

Shortly after this an old but rakish convertible pulled up before the brownstone building where Crowley's uncle lived. The driver, a tanned, crewcut young man in slacks, grinned at two small boys who were staring at his car. "She'll do sixty-five in second," he said.

"Yeah?" The boys sounded skeptical.

"Yeah. It's got a special carburetor and a high compression head."

Still grinning at them, he lifted a bag of golf clubs from the back seat, and then went around to the trunk and removed two tennis rackets and a sagging leather suitcase. His manner was brisk and cheerful; he was whistling as he locked the car, apparently a healthy young animal with nothing on his mind but the latest popular songs and the price of tennis balls.

"You fix up your car yourself?" one of the boys asked him.

"Sure. That's the only way to be sure of what's under the hood. Take it easy."

As he trotted up the steps the two boys stared after him, not speaking, hardly breathing, caught in the sudden intense thrall of hero-worship.

Inside the house the young man showed Crowley's uncle his identification card, and then said, "I'll go up and get things ready now."

"Can I help you with your grip?"

"No. I can manage. Thanks anyway. . . ."

Crowley was frowning at his watch, following the steady inevitable sweep of the second hand with his eyes. He stood facing the windows in the Bradleys' living room, and he held the venetian blind cords in his right hand.

"How much longer?" Dick Bradley said.

"Two more minutes."

Bradley lit a cigarette quickly, his movements a little flurry of nerves and tension. "They'll be outside, that's what I can't take," he said. "They'll come right to the house and look to see if the blinds are closed. And we sit here and can't do one damn thing about it."

"We've just got to sit tight," Crowley said. He knew the cameras were turning by now, covering the Bradleys' house, and the sidewalks and doorways and windows on both sides of the street. There were dozens of agents scattered through the neighborhood, in trucks and cabs, strolling through the block on carefully arranged time schedules. It was highly unlikely that any known criminal could walk through the area without being spotted. They wouldn't be picked up, of course, but they'd be put under close, thorough surveillance.

"How much longer must we wait?" Ellie Bradley said. She sat on the edge of the sofa with her arms crossed over her breasts.

"One minute more," Crowley said, looking at her. She had come down only a few minutes before, and so far had said very little to her husband. They were a million miles apart, Crowley thought. This crisis had marked the enormous gulf between their temperaments and backgrounds. They had drifted along without realizing this, lulled into a facsimile of unity by the variety of casual interests they shared; under ordinary circumstances the fact that they hardly knew each other might never have disturbed their placid and privileged existence. But now they were strangers; the pressure of the past day and night had driven them apart.

He felt sorry for them. It would help if they could help one another, but they had nothing to give, nothing to receive.

Ellie was looking at her husband, who was pacing up and down before the fireplace. She was very pale, and the strain and fear in her face was pitifully evident. "You took your father to a hotel?" she asked him.

"Yes, yes—it seemed better."

"How is he feeling?"

Dick Bradley said a very smart thing then, probably the smartest thing he had ever said in his life. "I don't know," he said. "I didn't ask him." In a guileful man it would have been a guileful remark. But he had no guile. She knew that much about him.

"Sit here beside me," she said. "Please."

"Yes—certainly."

They sat close to each other and he put an arm tentatively and awkwardly about her shoulders. "It's going to be all right, honey," he said. "I feel sure of it."

"You—may be right." She was looking down at her hands. "You've always had lucky hunches, haven't you?"

"Yes, I have at that. But this is more than a hunch."

Crowley glanced at his watch. "Twelve o'clock," he said quietly, and pulled the cord that closed the blinds on the middle window. Take a good look at it, he thought with cold anger. Look hard. And maybe we'll be looking at you. . . .

Standing behind his heavily curtained windows, Creasy had been watching for the sign from the Bradleys since ten o'clock that morning. He had enjoyed the vigil; it was strangely exciting to watch the house, and speculate on the anguish growing behind those handsome walls. There was the street to study also; he didn't let pleasure distract him from duty. His small, glinting eyes were alert for strange faces, suspicious behavior, out-of-the-ordinary circumstances. He watched each car and truck that stopped within his range of vision, scanned all passengers stepping out of taxis, every person strolling along the sidewalks. He had a flair for the police; they couldn't hide from him.

But in two hours he saw nothing to arouse his suspicions. The life of the block rolled casually past him, reassuringly routine and familiar to his searching eyes.

The signal came exactly at twelve o'clock, and when Creasy saw this evidence of capitulation a strange excitement shook his frail body; this was a climax too exquisite to squander in a greedy burst—this must be prolonged and savored.

For several minutes he stared at the closed blind, a soft smile brightening his small, gray face. Their knees were hinged, oh yes, he thought. Quick to bend. All they needed was practice. He laughed quietly. It was all a matter of leverage and purchase. Once you turned the screws they went down as nicely as you please, whining like any poor mortal.

How were they taking it? he wondered. The lady with her haughty beauty? And him? What good were his clubs and schools and money now?

Creasy's smile faded slowly. The money would buy back the baby, of course, and with that realization came a sharp flick of disappointment. Yes, their money would help—they always had that advantage. They could buy what they wanted; a car, a yacht, the safe return of their child—it was always so easy for them. A curious premonition of defeat grew in him; they would have an anxious day or two at the most, and then it would be over. The baby would be safely home again, and they would go on as before, pampered and protected, snapping their fingers for service, knowing their whims to be laws. . . .

Perhaps they hadn't even been worried about the child's safety. Why should they be? They knew the power of their money; this conviction would temper their anxiety and allay their fears.

It was infuriating. Creasy turned petulantly from the window and pulled the short cigarette stub from his lips. Then he grimaced with pain; the paper had become stuck and a sliver of his dry skin came off with the stub. He looked about his dark, close-smelling little room, feeling restless and irritable. His lunch was on his bedside table, an egg salad sandwich and a container of coffee. He sat down to eat, taking what pleasure he could in the greasy food, the cold coffee that tasted nauseatingly of the cardboard carton. The cut on his lip stung painfully and his mood became despondent.

He glanced around his room, a frown gathering over his eyes. Normally he was happy enough here; he liked this gloomy little box, it was quiet and warm and safe. But now it depressed him. Even his photographs and genealogical charts—the latter was more an obsession than a hobby—even looking at them failed to restore his good humor.

The pictures adorned the wall at the foot of his bed, dozens of faded and cracked photographs of once-famous movie stars. Most of them were now dead or forgotten. They watched Creasy with the expressions and smiles fashionable in their generation: the women were stark and pale for the most part, with low bangs and dramatically widened eyes; the masculine accent was on the suave and mysterious, the cynically raised eyebrows and patent-leather hair. Creasy hated them all. They had been young when he was young, but they had been famous and beautiful and happy. This was his revenge, to pin them helplessly to his walls and speculate on what they must look like today—if they were still alive. In a sense he won a victory over them every night. He lay in bed, reconstructing their faces, mentally drawing in the marks of age, the white or thinning hair, the sagging jowls, the squints, the lines of worry and fear, the toothless gums and sunken cheeks.

This was his hobby—but genealogy was his passion. He had been collecting family trees for years; against the wall three steel filing cases held the results of this mania.

Creasy read the society pages from the Boston, New York and Philadelphia papers avidly, making careful notes of births and marriages, of who went where and who was doing what in the world of fashionable people. Then, like an excited ferret, he scrambled after those names in his files, tracking them through labyrinthine breedings and connections, to their original source, sniffing out frauds and phonies, the *nouveau riche*, the pretenders and climbers. Most of them were common as dirt, he had found out; it didn't matter to him whether the blot was one generation removed or thirty—bad blood was bad blood and time wouldn't purify it. He had made a careful study of the Bradleys, of course, and had discovered (as he had expected) that the tree was full of bad fruit.

He was thinking of this as he stood up from his lunch. Blackguards and rogues . . . and the latest issue from that rotten trunk put on such airs. He and his lady! They might have paid some of their debt. In cleansing fear and pain. But no, not even that. They simply paid the ransom—as they would pay a light bill—and back came the baby.

Creasy moved to the window. Yes, their blind was still down. It didn't seem to matter. Rain was falling, he saw, and this increased his annoyance. He hated wetness of any kind. But he must go out to phone Grant.

Creasy put on rubbers, then wound a scarf around his neck and got into his raincoat. Taking his umbrella and gloves, he left his room. When he stepped outside he shivered involuntarily at the impact of the cold wet wind. He put up his umbrella and picked his way down the steps like a cat, avoiding the shallow puddles and flinching at the feel of the damp iron railing against his hand. There would be no point in trying to find a cab; he had resigned himself to walking.

But as he reached the foot of the stairs a small city miracle occurred; a cab stopped directly in front of him to let out a fare. Creasy called to the driver in a high, excited voice, and bobbed his umbrella up and down to catch his eye. The cabby glanced at him and nodded, as his passenger, a big man in a tweed topcoat, climbed out of the taxi. The big man grinned as he walked by Creasy. "She's all yours. Luck, eh?"

"Yes," Creasy said.

The rear door of the cab was open, the interior was a warm, dry haven awaiting him—but he hesitated, glancing uneasily after the man in the tweed coat.

The driver said patiently, "Let's go, mister."

"Yes," Creasy said, stepping carefully down from the curb. The passenger had gone into an interior decorator's shop next door. Quite normal . . .

But suddenly Creasy felt a small warning chill go through him. This cab—so opportune, so unexpected—was that coincidence? He hesitated again, staring at the casual, everyday look of the street. His eyes strayed across the brown bulk of the church, moved up to its steeple and then switched to the second-story windows on the opposite side of the block.

"All right, all *right*," the driver said. "I got a living to make, Mac."

"Never mind," Creasy said curtly.

The driver reached back and closed the door of his cab with a crash. "Just so I know," he muttered, and drove off with a roar of power.

Why take a chance? Creasy thought, as he walked with mincing haste toward the corner. You never lost if you never gambled . . . perhaps he was being overly cautious, but he didn't think so. The arrival of the cab might have been simple good fortune, but he knew it paid to look carefully at the unusual, the unexpected, the seemingly lucky break. That was how they caught you. Enough rope . . .

Creasy walked to the intersection of Third Avenue where, after a reassuring wait of several minutes he succeeded in hailing another cab. The driver had turned into Thirty-first Street before catching his signal, so they had to go around the block—but Creasy knew the extra twenty cents was a small price to pay for being careful.

As they passed the Bradleys' he glanced out at the closed blind, and then settled himself comfortably and lit a cigarette.

# 15

IT WAS SHORTLY AFTER TWO ON MONDAY AFTERNOON THAT THE PHONE sounded through the oppressive silence of the lodge. Grant lifted the receiver, frowning nervously, but after a few seconds his expression cleared, and he said, "That's fine, everything's going right on schedule." He winked at Duke who was sitting at the fireplace, and made a circle with his thumb and forefinger. "Okay now, there's nothing to worry about. Nothing at all. You just remember what I've told you . . . that's right. Fine . . . fine."

Grant put the receiver back in place and slapped the table with the flat of his hand. He began to laugh then, his voice high and giddy with relief. "Like clockwork, Duke," he said. "The blind closed right on the dot of twelve."

"They've got the money then," Duke said.

"Sure they've got it; they're playing ball. We're going to pull this off, Duke."

"Great," Duke said. Since his run-in with Hank in the girl's room, he had been drinking steadily, sitting and staring into the red eye of the fire. A frown hardened his dark features, and the leaping flames gleamed on the backs of his hands and cast a faint sheen on his thick black hair. "We're coming to the payoff," he said.

"That's right. Tonight Creasy sends the note telling them about the money. The Bradleys get it in the morning. The cash register rings tomorrow night. Creasy picks up the dough, and it's all over."

"Except for the loose ends," Duke said.

"Yeah." Grant rubbed a hand over his face. "The loose ends." He glanced at the door to the kitchen; Hank and Belle were in there finishing up the lunch dishes. The nurse was upstairs with the baby. "You got any ideas?" he said.

"It's pretty obvious, isn't it?"

They sat close together, speaking so softly that their voices were covered by the crackle of the fire. Duke took a sip of his drink. They were silent, avoiding each other's eyes. Finally Grant let out his breath slowly. "What are we going to do?"

Duke smiled faintly. "You're running things. It's up to you."

"Don't clown around."

"We'll do what we've got to do, Eddie. There's no choice. Not the way I see it. Maybe you got another idea."

"No—but how's it going to look?"

"We'll make it look all right."

"Duke—" Grant hesitated, swallowing something in his throat. "You mean both of them?"

"Hold it," Duke said.

Belle came into the room, carrying a white porcelain dish filled with clean, damp diapers. "I just rinsed these out," she said. "Takes a little load off the girl." Belle's manner was righteous and complacent, but her eyes were slightly glazed over; she was proving something but she wasn't quite sure what. "Can you move back a bit, Eddie? I want to hang 'em before the fire."

"For Christ's sake, we're talking."

"All right, you're talking. It won't hurt to move your chair, will it?"

"Hang the diapers in the kitchen."

"They won't dry, Eddie. I know."

Duke said quietly, "Take the diapers and yourself back where you came from, Belle. This isn't a nursery."

"Well, that's a fine—"

"Beat it!" Grant said. "Will you do what I tell you? We're busy!"

"And that's more important than the baby being clean and comfortable. Sure." Belle shook her head and wandered back into the kitchen. They heard her say to Hank: "The brain trust is in session in there."

Grant stared at the doorway for an instant, and then turned back to Duke. "Both of them? The nurse *and* the kid?"

"That's my idea. You got another one?"

"Will it look all right?"

"The cops will have their answer in one package. The nurse and the kid. They won't look any farther."

"A note would help," Grant said. "From the nurse to the family. Saying she's sorry, maybe. Wouldn't that help?"

"That's pretty good. In fact, it's damn good." They sat without speaking for another minute and then Duke looked at Grant and said irritably, "Well, what are you waiting for?"

"Okay, okay. I'll get the note. Don't worry about it."

"And I'll get some wood. We'd freeze if I waited for anybody else to stir his tail."

As Duke limped toward the front door Grant walked into the kitchen and said to Hank, "I need some paper and a pencil. You got any?"

"I think so."

"Fine, get 'em." Then he looked down at Belle who was sitting at the kitchen table. "Go upstairs and tell the nurse I want her. Come on, move."

"All right," Belle said, trying to strike a note of disinterested dignity, but she had been drinking steadily that morning and the words slurred together in a liquid murmur. Grant ran himself a glass of water at the sink and said, "You might try some of this stuff for a change. It's a little-known beverage called water."

"Dear, dear," Belle said, patting the back of her head. "Some people around here are just getting lousy with virtue."

"Beat it," Grant said sharply. "You aren't funny, you're pathetic."

"All right, I said I was going." Her defiance wilted under the coldness in his eyes. She knew he was disgusted with her, that he thought her a slatternly nuisance; he made no effort to hide his feelings. It wasn't fair, she thought, getting unsteadily to her feet. It was cruel . . . If he was tired of her, well okay. They'd had good times together, they'd meant something to each other. She wouldn't spoil all that now. She'd bow out. She had some pride after all. It wasn't fair of Eddie to make her feel so cheap and small. She hadn't done anything to be ashamed of. . . .

As she left the room, Hank returned with a pencil and a notebook. "These okay?" he said to Grant.

"Yeah, they're fine. Just put 'em on the table."

"Everything going all right?" Hank said casually.

"What do you mean?"

"I was just wondering if you're going to make it. What's your guess?"

Grant stared at him for a few seconds in silence. Then he said slowly, "I don't have to guess, Junior."

"You'd better be nicer to Belle. That's a friendly tip. If you don't brush her off gently, she might blow the whistle on you some day. Women are like that."

"You'd better write an advice to the lovelorn column," Grant said. "Better than that, you better just shut up. Understand?"

"Sure."

Grant sipped his water, still staring at him. Then he said, "Why do you care? Don't tell me you're pulling for us."

"Just because you're underdogs? No, it's not that," Hank said.

"We're not underdogs. We're on top. That's how I planned it."

"You didn't plan on the nurse," Hank said. "You didn't plan on me."

"That's right. So we'll improvise. You watch." Grant turned as the nurse came into the kitchen, with Belle holding her elbow lightly.

"Sit down," he said, nodding to a chair in front of the pencil and pad. "You're going to write a note to the Bradleys. In your own words, you tell 'em the kid is okay, and you're sorry if they've been scared or worried. You got that?"

She sat down slowly at the table, and one of her slim hands moved across the table and touched the pencil. "Is that all?" she said, watching Grant without expression.

"That's the start. The rest goes this way: tell them you're sorry you took the baby, but that you needed money. You didn't know what a terrible thing it was until it was too late to turn back. Ask them—" Grant gestured irritably. "To forgive you, I guess is all right. Put it in your own words without trying for anything fancy. You want me to run through it once more for you?"

"No—I've got it." She sat perfectly still, one hand touching the pencil. The room was quiet, and in that instant of oppressive silence her other hand moved reluctantly to the writing tablet.

"Get with it," Grant said.

She moved her hand back from the pencil. "No—I can't."

"You're going to write that note just like I told you," Grant said quietly. "You'll write it now, or a little bit later maybe. But you're going to write it."

"No," she said, and Grant's frown deepened at the sudden conviction in her voice. "You've hurt them enough. I won't do this to them."

"You won't be worrying about them if you don't do what I tell you," Grant said. "You'll have enough to do worrying about yourself." He leaned toward her, putting his hands flat on the table, and the overhead light gleamed brightly against the dangerous anger in his face. "We've got a full day to work on you, baby. We've got time to bring you around slow. But I like to work fast. And I know quite a few tricks. You learn things in jail. You learn things from crazy bastards who spend all their time figuring out ways to hurt people they don't like. You want to find out what I learned? It's up to you, baby. What's it going to be?"

She was gripping the sides of the chair with her hands, and all the color had drained from her face.

"Well, how about it?" he said gently.

"No—no," she said, in a high, straining voice. "I won't do it."

"We'll see about that," Grant said, walking slowly around the table. He brushed past Belle, paying no attention to her; his eyes were fixed on the girl. "You're going to wish you'd never been born."

"Don't touch her, Eddie," Hank said.

Grant turned on him, and his gun came out so quickly that Hank hardly saw the motion of his hand. "Sit down!" he said, his voice swelling angrily.

"I don't think you can afford fireworks," Hank said. He didn't believe this; there was little chance that anyone was within half a mile of the cottage. But he was aware of a profound change within himself. Earlier he had come to a state of fatalistic acceptance; they planned to kill him anyway, so what happened before that didn't matter very much. That had been his armor. But it wasn't enough now. She and the baby were alone and helpless. He had to protect them until he died. That was more important than the dying. Staring at Grant he said, "You'll wake up the area, Eddie. Is that what you want? Company? Are you getting bored?"

"Nobody's going to hear the shot," Grant said.

"There might be a hunter fifty yards from the house," Hank said. "Or a fisherman over on John Adam's pond. You're taking a chance you don't need to, Eddie. You're starting to act like Duke."

"Yeah?" Grant's face was hard and impassive; he had got his first compulsive rage under control. "Maybe you're right at that. Gambling's a luxury at this stage of the game. But there's a way without any risk at all." He turned slightly toward Belle. "Go upstairs and get the kid."

"What's the idea, Eddie?"

"Just bring her down, that's all."

"You wouldn't hurt her," the nurse said, in a soft, incredulous voice. "You wouldn't do that."

"Put it this way," Grant said, smiling slightly. "I'd hate to. Belle, do what I tell you."

"Eddie, I—" She wet her lips, avoiding the sudden anger in his eyes. "It wouldn't be right. A baby—"

"Get her, I said," Grant yelled. "You think this is a goddam debating club? Do what I tell you!"

Belle stumbled toward the door as if his words had struck her with a physical impact. "It's wrong, you know it's wrong," she said.

"Please don't," the nurse said, in a breaking voice.

Belle stopped in the doorway and looked at her. "Nobody has said 'please' to me for years," she said slowly.

"Please," the nurse said again, but she was crying now and the word was an indistinct sound in the silence.

"Sure, sure," Belle said, staring at Grant. "Nobody is going to hurt that baby. You promised she wouldn't be hurt. A fine word of honor you've got. I couldn't ever look at myself again if anything happened to that kid. I'm a mother. I've got feelings, Eddie."

"Belle, get moving," Grant said in a thick, choking voice. "I can't take any more of this." The gun had swung around to her and Hank saw that he was ready to shoot; he was breathing with a kind of desperate urgency, as if he couldn't get enough air, and his eyes were blazing with fury.

This wasn't what Hank wanted; the explosion had to be between Duke and Grant.

"I think you'd better write the note," he said to the nurse. He spoke as quietly and calmly as he could, trying to reduce the dangerous tension in the room.

"Yes," she said quickly, desperately. "I will."

"Okay, *okay*," Grant said. The gun came down to his side and he wet his dry lips. "That's what I wanted in the first place. . . ."

They watched in awkward silence as she wrote the note. The light shone on her dark head and touched the tears on her cheeks with flickering brilliance. There was no sound but the soft pull of the pencil, and the uneven catch in her breathing.

When she stopped writing Grant picked up the note and read it through several times, nodding his head slowly. "You could have done this right away and saved all the commotion." Then he stared at Belle until she flushed under his intent, impersonal scrutiny.

"There's no reason to look like that," she said uneasily. "It wouldn't have been right, Eddie. You know that."

He walked into the living room without answering her. "You know it, Eddie," she said, staring after him anxiously.

Hank walked around the table and put his hand on the girl's shoulder. She had lowered her head on her arms and was weeping helplessly.

There was nothing he could say; words of comfort or hope would be grotesque. He patted her arm gently, and at last she raised her head and pressed her cheek against the back of his hand. It was an impersonal response, he knew; she was like a frightened child turning impulsively and instinctively toward the kindness in a stranger's voice.

# 16

By six o'clock Monday night the film which had been shot in Thirty-first Street was delivered to the Bradleys' by two agents wearing the uniforms of a rug-cleaning service. The film, along with screen and projector, was inside a neatly wrapped carpet.

Crowley set up the screen in the long dining room, after closing the doors and drawing the blinds on the windows. He seated Ellie and Dick Bradley to the right of the projector, Oliphant Bradley and Mrs. Jarrod to the left, and now they stared up at him, their faces pale anxious blurs in the semidarkness.

They were watching him with a mixture of fear and hope, he realized; they hoped for miracles, but feared he was going to play a conjurer's trick on them. And he felt the same way himself. . . .

Crowley snapped a switch and a beam of blue-white light illuminated the square screen at the end of the room. "Before we start I want to point out a few things," he said. "This will be a long session. Don't be discouraged if we seem to be getting nowhere. Keep watching. Now, about what to watch for: first of all, faces you've seen before, people who may have worked for you, or with you at some time in the past. Secretaries, chauffeurs, maids, gardeners, butlers, handymen. Anyone you might have had contact with at clubs, parking lots, garages, shops, restaurants." Crowley ticked off categories on his fingers. "Caddies, locker room attendants, bartenders, waiters, elevator operators, maintenance men, shoeshine boys—speak up if you see anyone you've known before. Mrs. Jarrod, I want you to watch particularly for anyone you've ever seen around this house—delivery boys, window washers, plumbers, painters, part-time maids, part-time catering help, that sort of thing. Do you all understand?"

"Yes, yes, of course," Oliphant Bradley said sharply.

"The next point is a little more difficult," Crowley said. "I want you to be alert for anything that strikes you as odd or unusual . . . no matter how trivial or inconsequential it may seem. For years you've been soaking up unconscious impressions of this street. You know how it looks normally, you know the *feel* of it. If anything strikes you as off key—I want to know about it. I can't give you an example. I wouldn't if I could. I don't want you *looking* for peculiarities. And I don't want to suggest what you should look for. It won't work that way. Something may jar your unconscious picture of this street. That's what I want to know about. I'm putting this badly, I think. But do you have an idea of what I mean?" He glanced from face to face and they all nodded solemnly—like children in a classroom, he thought.

"All right, let's go," he said, flicking a switch.

The film began to run. . . .

For the first half-hour there was hardly a stir in the room; their mood was expectant and tense as the life of the street moved before their eyes. Cars, trucks and cabs rolled by and people of every kind and type filled the screen: delivery boys, postmen, pedestrians of all ages, smartly dressed girls, an occasional soldier, a few drunks, a construction worker in a metal helmet biting into a long Italian sandwich—the group could have been duplicated on a thousand of the city's streets. Crowley stopped the camera several times to study specific faces, freezing the flowing scene into a grotesque and unnatural immobility. Oliphant Bradley stood up once and said, "Wait! Look there!" in a high, excited voice, but when Crowley stopped the scene the old man sat down shaking his head slowly. "No, it's not the same chap. It was someone who'd worked for my father, I thought. But that could hardly be, eh?" He asked the question in a confused voice.

When the rain began the people thinned out, and there followed seemingly interminable stretches of building fronts and wet sidewalks.

"This doesn't seem to be getting us anywhere," Dick Bradley said, taking out his cigarettes. "Smoke, Ellie?"

"No, please keep watching."

The atmosphere in the room had changed; hope was dying. There would be no miracles; only a conjurer's trick. . . . Crowley sensed this in the flurries of talk, the restless shiftings of position.

Finally it was over and the screen gleamed white and blank at the end of the room. Crowley turned off the projector and snapped on the overhead lights. "The footage we've just seen was shot from a house on this side of the street. The film from the church steeple is next. But first: did you notice anything unusual?"

"Two more hours of film," Oliphant Bradley said wearily, "I—it seems a waste of time."

"Did you see anything odd or curious?" Crowley said, watching them alertly. He had seen something near the end of the film. "Anything at all?" he said, and his voice was sharper now, prodding their memories.

Ellie was sitting forward on the edge of the chair, a faint frown shadowing her smooth forehead. "I'm not sure," she said slowly. "It's probably silly. I know it can't mean—"

"What was it?" Crowley said quickly. "Come on."

"The little man," Ellie said, watching him with a frown. "That seemed strange, didn't it? I mean, about the cab."

"Exactly," Crowley said, slapping the table.

"What's all this?" Dick Bradley said, staring at his wife.

"We'll take another look," Crowley said. He ran the film back for a few minutes, then snapped off the overhead lights. "Now watch . . ."

They saw the front of a brownstone, the rain slanting against its brick façade and darkening the old-fashioned wooden doorway. A few seconds later the door opened and a small neatly dressed man started cautiously down the stone steps, one hand clinging to the iron railing. He was obviously repelled by the weather; his distaste was evident as he picked his way down to the sidewalk.

"Who's that chap?" Oliphant Bradley said.

No one answered him. The little man waved his umbrella to catch the eye of a cab driver who had stopped before him to let out a fare. Later, when the passenger had hurried past him, the little man stepped carefully down from the curb and approached the open door of the cab. Then he hesitated, staring up and down the street. Finally he raised his eyes and looked full into the camera; they could see his small, commonplace face, the mirrorlike flash of his glasses, the mark of caution in his hunched shoulders and slowly turning body.

The driver spoke to him apparently, and he took another step toward the cab. But again he hesitated, and finally he shook his head quickly and walked toward Third Avenue.

"What's that supposed to mean?" Oliphant Bradley said.

"Keep watching!" Crowley said.

A few minutes later a cab came down the street and they were able to see the passenger clearly; he was sitting forward and peering out the window. "It's the same man," Dick Bradley said, in a surprised voice.

Crowley turned on the lights and switched off the machine. "It struck you as odd, eh?"

"Well, yes—but there's probably a simple explanation for it."

"Of course," his father said. "The man hailed a cab and decided not to take it after all. I daresay every one of us has done the same thing on occasion. You remember another appointment, you've forgotten something—it's a commonplace sort of thing."

"This is a bit different," Crowley said. "Our friend turned down a cab in the rain, and then walked a block and got another cab going in the same direction—that doesn't strike me as normal. There may be an explanation for it. Frankly, I'd be surprised if there weren't. But it's odd enough to interest me." He glanced at Ellie. "Have you ever seen this chap before?"

"No—I don't think so."

Crowley rubbed a hand along his jaw. A man had turned down a cab under curious circumstances—that's what it amounted to. Ostensibly at least. A freakish bit of behavior, nothing more. But the man had come out of a building directly opposite the Bradleys'. That put another twist to it.

"Just wait here," he said. "I'm going to back this hunch of mine a little bit further."

Crowley stepped into the study and opened the suitcase he had brought in with him Sunday night. He picked up his binoculars and then walked through the darkened living room to the windows. Stooping a bit, he sighted through the slats of the venetian blinds, focusing his glasses on the tall brownstone that faced the Bradleys'. In spite of the evening's dusky gloom, the powerful lenses pulled the building right up to his eyes.

He saw nothing significant until he lowered the glasses to the first floor windows—and then a sudden shock of excitement ran through him. Someone was standing behind those curtained windows, looking out toward the Bradleys' house. He couldn't tell whether the shadowy outline was that of a man or woman, but he knew which way the person was facing; he could see the tiny orange glow of a cigarette, flaring and fading rhythmically through the curtains.

Crowley backed slowly away from the windows, keeping his glasses trained on the watching figure across the street. He knew he couldn't be seen, but he was taking no chances; this was fitting together too neatly for coincidence.

Halfway across the room he realized that Ellie and Dick Bradley had joined him. "What is it?" Ellie whispered. "What do you see?"

Crowley brought the binoculars down and let out his breath slowly. She was staring at him, and in the faint light he saw the fear in her eyes, and the deep weary lines in her face. "Someone is watching this house from across the street," he said. "It may mean nothing. But we'll find out, don't worry. I'll call the Inspector. Then we'll look at the rest of the film."

As he turned toward the study she put a hand on his arm. "Has he— has he told you anything about your child?"

"No, not yet. Say a prayer, okay?"

"Yes—okay."

At FBI headquarters in downtown New York, Roth and Inspector West were watching a copy of the film that had been shot in Thirty-first Street that afternoon. Alerted by Crowley's call, they were studying a certain section of it with new and sharper interest.

Roth was in shirt-sleeves, perspiring in the small, close projection room. Without his jacket he looked even more formidable; the damp fabric of his shirt was molded to the heavy muscles of his arms and shoulders. "Crowley's got a good pair of eyes," he said, frowning at the screen. "Or maybe I'm getting old."

"We both missed it," the Inspector said. "Thank God Crowley didn't."

"What do you make of it?" Roth said, when the operator switched off the machine.

"A man being cautious, that's all. But why should he be cautious? That's what interests me. Let's go upstairs."

They left the projection room and took an elevator to West's office on the seventh floor. Roth lit a cigarette as they sat down in front of the big cardboard map of Thirty-first Street. Around them typewriters and teletypes clattered, and half a dozen agents were studying reports or talking on telephones. The FBI's nets were being cast in ever-widening circles. Business associates of Ellie and Dick Bradley, Mrs. Jarrod's friends and relatives, the service record of Bill Delancey, the army lieutenant who had dated Kate Reilly, clerks and delivery men in the shops and stores patronized by the Bradleys—all of these people were being brought under a close, discreet surveillance.

But so far the nets had come up empty. . . .

The Inspector was studying the map of Thirty-first Street. He put his finger on the building that faced the Bradleys'. "Who lives in that front room, Jerry?"

Roth picked up a file card in his seemingly clumsy fingers. "Howard Creasy, age fifty-five. He worked last as a locker room attendant at the Manhattan Athletic Club. No police record. We got this information from a personal loan company."

"How long has he lived there?"

"We don't know exactly. But he was living there when he got the loan and that was six months ago."

"The loan was paid off?"

"Yes. He settled in cash. Three hundred dollars. That was four months ago. He left the club then, and hasn't worked since."

"What I want to know is this: are Howard Creasy and the little chap who turned down the cab—are they the same person?"

Roth looked at him and nodded. "I'll find out."

West turned to the agent who was covering the line to Washington. "Anything come in while I was downstairs?" It was an unnecessary question, he knew; if there was anything the agent wouldn't have to be asked for it. But West's patience was short; the waiting had worn his nerves down to a fine edge.

"Nothing, sir," the agent said.

Nothing, West thought. And this was Monday night. The baby had been gone since Friday night. Seventy-two hours. And they had nothing yet. Washington had been working all day on the print Crowley had found in the Bradleys' study. So far, no luck. And no leads had developed from the Bradleys' friends and business associates, nothing from the tradespeople in the neighborhood. Blanks everywhere, he thought. But in spite of this, he was developing a feeling about the case—a bad one. They couldn't hope that the kidnapers would bring the baby back home. Because that wasn't the kidnapers' plan. . . .

In Washington, fifteen fingerprint examiners had been working ten hours on the print Crowley had lifted from the Bradleys' study. They had a frame of reference in which to work—their hypothesis being that the print belonged to a man whose nickname was Duke. Photographic enlargements had been made of the latent print, and from the criminal file jackets had been pulled on every individual nicknamed "Duke"; there were 1603 such individuals, and each of their cards had to be checked against the print found in Bradley's study. There was some elimination; the latent print was a loop category, and so it wasn't necessary to examine minutely all the whorls and arches. The job was, nevertheless, immense, and there were no short cuts. Fingerprints are counted and coded in sets of ten fingers—and such a set can be traced in a matter of minutes. But tracing a single print to its mate would mean examining each of the one hundred and twenty million prints in the bureau's files—a job as difficult as tracing a leaf back to the twig it had blown from during a storm.

There was the chance that an identification could be made on the first card—but it might as easily be the last. Examiners worked steadily through the afternoon and evening, turning down card after card after failing to match them with the photographic enlargements which were propped up before their desks. Occasionally they stopped to rest their eyes, or take a quick drag on a cigarette, and then they resumed the patient, dogged search.

Finally a slender man with graying hair stood quickly and walked down the aisle to the supervisor who was in charge of the detail. "Here it is," he said quietly. "Age thirty-one at time of last arrest. Served four years in Joliet for armed robbery and assault. Edward John Farrel, nicknamed 'Duke.' "

The supervisor looked at the dark, bold front face and profile shots of Duke Farrel. Then he nodded and said, "I'll call Inspector West. Get this card over to him by wire photo. I hope this does it. . . ."

# 17

ON SPRING EVENINGS DARKNESS SETTLED WITH DISQUIETING SUDDENNESS about the lodge. There was no softly shadowed dusk to foretell the end of day; reflections from the tidal river preserved the illusion of daylight for a time, but when they disappeared, winking out abruptly, the night rushed in to fill up the vacuum.

Duke stood at the window with his hands in his pockets, and Grant was at the fire, looking through a newspaper. A single lamp and the leaping flames provided the only illumination in the room. The corners were dark, and giant shadows moved on the white ceiling as Grant flipped over the pages of his paper.

Hank sat at the piano, occasionally brushing the keys with his left hand. The pain had started again in his right, and a heavy pulse beat like a hammer against the shattered bone.

There had been very little conversation since dinner. The mood in the house was tense and wary; as the climax approached, nerves were tightening painfully. And there was still a day to go, a full twenty-four hours, Hank thought.

He touched a key and Grant looked over his paper at him. "You play that thing?"

Hank shook his head. "Just pick out the tunes."

"Then what's it here for?"

"The owner threw it in with the deal when I bought the place."

Without turning Duke said dryly, "He'd have to throw in a band and a chorus line to get me interested."

Hank began picking out *Swanee River* with one finger and Grant shook his head and blew a stream of smoke at the ceiling.

"Too jazzy?" Hank said.

"No, it's just great," Grant said with heavy sarcasm.

"How's the wood situation?" Duke said.

"It looks all right."

"Looks all right? I see three logs."

"That should get us by."

"And if it doesn't I can always lug in some more, I guess."

"Don't be a martyr," Grant said. "I'll get the wood. But you were the guy brought up by Indians. I thought you'd love playing Boy Scout up here."

Duke didn't answer him. His head was tilted slightly toward the piano. "What are you playing that for?"

Hank had drifted to another melody without realizing it. And it took him a second or two to identify it. *The Kerry Dancers,* he thought. That wasn't quite right, but it was close. "It's a nice old song," he said.

"Yeah, nice and dismal," Duke said. He frowned slightly, then shook his head and walked to the mantel to pour himself a drink. "You take your kicks real square."

Hank was trying to remember the words as he picked out the tune with one finger. A phrase or two came back to him, poignant and bittersweet with the mystery of loss: *Gone, alas . . . all those hours of gladness, Gone, alas! like our youth too soon.*

This song had had a curious significance in their home, he remembered. But why? No one in the family was musical. Where would they hear it? On the radio occasionally. . . . And when that happened his father had become pensive. Not sad, but thoughtful. And his mother would ask him who had been in the store that day (or something equally chattery), and prod him into a different mood.

Hank started the song again, trying to puzzle out its significance. He was quite sure he hadn't been aware of his parents' reaction to it when he was young; he had absorbed his impression unconsciously. And now he was dredging it up . . . but why? Then, glancing at Duke's back, he thought he knew the answer to that question.

The room was very still. Hank played softly, and the notes of the sad old song fell with a haunting clarity into the silence. "She liked this, I guess," he said.

"Who?" Duke didn't turn but Hank heard the surprise in his voice.

"Your mother."

"Yeah? Who told you that?"

"I forget." Hank picked out the tune with slow insistence. "She was young when she died, wasn't she?"

Duke turned slowly. He stared at his brother for a few seconds, and then made an awkward little gesture with his hand. "I don't know, twenty-eight, twenty-nine, something like that."

"You were only about seven, I guess. Do you remember her?"

"Sure, I remember her. At seven you remember things. You think seven-year-old kids are still in the cradle?"

"I never saw a picture of her," Hank said. "There weren't any in the house. Funny."

"What's funny? We moved around a lot. I mean before the old man married again." Duke made another awkward gesture with his hand; he seemed suddenly defensive and vulnerable. "Things kept getting lost. You know how it is."

"Sure, that's the way it goes," Hank said. And then he thought of the scar on his forehead. The picture had reminded him of it. That had happened when he was very young, four or five at the most. He had been poking around in Duke's drawer, and had come across a small photograph wrapped in tissue paper. He hadn't removed the picture—only looked at the faint image he could discern through the filmy wrappings. And then Duke had come in, noiselessly as always, and caught him. What had he hit him with? A tennis racket, that was it. The first thing he had picked up. . . .

"It's a stupid song," Duke said. "A whining old dirge." His voice was harder now, arrogant and challenging. Hank looked at him and shrugged lightly. "You don't want me to play it?"

"Why should I give a damn? Play whatever the hell you want." He limped back to the mantel to refill his glass.

Hank began picking out the song again and Duke wandered back to the window and stared out at the night. Belle came out of the kitchen a moment or so later and drifted over to the piano. "That's nice," she said.

"Sing it," Hank said.

"You asked for it, mister." She began to hum the song softly in a low and surprisingly pleasant voice. "It's so dreamy and sad," she said at last. "I just love it. Let's see if I can remember the words."

"Knock it off," Grant said irritably. "That's all we need, campfire songs."

"Let her sing if she wants to," Duke said. He didn't turn around but they could hear the anger in his voice. "She can sing if she wants to."

"Okay, *okay*," Grant said. "But does she have to stick to that cornball Mick song?"

"What do you know about music?" Duke said, turning and staring at him. "You never heard anything but an organ grinder in that Polack neighborhood you grew up in."

"A lot of big men came out of that neighborhood, and don't forget it," Grant said.

"But not including you," Duke said.

"What's the matter? You want Belle to sing Irish songs? Fine! Great! She can sing *Mother Machree* and *Paddy McGinty's Goat* until dawn for all I care." He returned pointedly to his newspaper. "Just let me know when it's over so I can clap."

Hank smiled at Belle, and she began singing again, slowly and shyly; her eyes switched to Grant for some sign of interest or approval, but he was buried in the paper.

"You're doing fine," Hank said. He glanced at Duke and saw that he put his drink on the windowsill and was rubbing his forehead with both hands. The music was a thin lament in the silence and Belle's voice as soft and sad as a weeping child's. "You're doing fine," Hank said again, and she gave him a grateful and nervous little smile.

Hank looked at Duke again, seeing the crack in him now. But where was the wedge to fit into it? And the hammer to drive it home?

# 18

MAIL WAS DELIVERED AROUND EIGHT-FIFTEEN ON THIRTY-FIRST STREET, but at seven o'clock Crowley and the Bradleys were waiting in the living room for the postman. If things were as they hoped, the morning's mail would bring the instructions for paying the ransom money—the last step before the return of the baby.

Crowley stood at the front window with his binoculars trained on the building across the street. The watcher was there, he saw, a dark outline behind the heavy curtains. Creasy, Howard Creasy. A neatly dressed little man who hadn't had a job for four months. And who spent a great deal of his time watching the Bradleys' home. Crowley had got another name from West: Duke Farrel, the man who had posed as a telephone repairman. So far they had only the names—but now a hundred agents were on the trail.

Ellie Bradley was pacing the floor slowly. She wore a dressing gown and slippers. Mrs. Jarrod had brought in a tray of coffee, but after one sip Ellie had put her cup down on the mantel. Dick Bradley was watching the front door and his father sat on the sofa, nervously sucking on a dry pipe.

No one made any attempt at conversation; small talk or banalities would have fallen grotesquely into the silence.

When the chimes sounded they were all caught by surprise; they weren't expecting the mail for another hour. Oliphant Bradley stood quickly, his breathing loud and heavy in the stillness. Dick Bradley looked helplessly from his wife to Crowley.

"See who it is," Crowley said.

"Yes—yes, of course." Dick hurried down the short hallway and opened the door. A postman stood on the doorstep. "Special, sir," he said.

"Thank you."

"Going to be a nice day, eh? So long."

Bradley returned to the living room and said, "We didn't think about special deliveries." His voice was high and breathless. He fumbled at the envelope for a few seconds, and then shook his head and handed the letter to Crowley. "You open it. I—I can't seem to manage."

Crowley opened the letter and removed the single sheet of lined, copy-book paper. It had been folded twice, and as he opened it he saw that it had been torn from a pad or tablet; the left side of the paper was ragged and uneven.

Ellie walked toward him slowly, her hands pressed tightly against her breasts. "What do they want us to do?"

Crowley was staring at the note and she saw the frown gathering above his eyes.

"What is it?" she said. "What is it?" Her voice was beginning to shake.

Each word in the note struck Crowley with a sickening impact; where did we slip? he thought despairingly. For the note, in neatly penciled capitals, read: *You didn't follow instructions, chickies! So you don't want her back, after all.*

Dick Bradley took the note from his hands. "What's the matter? What do they—" He stopped then, as abruptly as if his words had struck a physical barrier. "God!" he said. "They know the police are in it." His face was suddenly white and old as he stared at his wife. "It's all over," he said in a high, terrible voice. "It's over."

"This kind of letter is standard," Crowley said. "At this stage they want to keep you scared. If you've been thinking of going to the police, this will stop you." No one was listening to him, and he hadn't expected them to; he hoped only that the sound of his voice might distract them for a second or so—give them an instant to adjust to this new terror. He hadn't lied to them; a bluffing note might come in about this time. But they wouldn't believe that. And, in this case, neither did he. . . .

Ellie sat down very slowly. "They've killed her, I know. She's dead." The lack of emotion in her voice was more shocking than any outburst; she sounded as if she were discussing the weather. And her eyes were empty and dry.

Dick Bradley was staring straight at his father. "They didn't kill her," he said quietly, almost thoughtfully.

"Son—"

"We didn't want the police. We wanted to pay the money and get Jill back safely. But you knew better. You called the police."

"Son, listen to me. I swear I thought—"

"It doesn't matter what you thought. It doesn't matter what any of us thought. What matters is that our daughter is dead. That's what you've done."

"No, no," Ellie said, shaking her head. "Don't say that, Dick. Please."

"Ellie—" The old man sat down beside her and his lips were trembling helplessly. "I did—what I thought was best for our baby. You must believe me. I don't want forgiveness. I don't deserve it." His voice was shaking. "But you must believe me, Ellie."

"I do, I do, of course I do," she said in a soothing voice.

Crowley felt a dry pain in his throat. She was making it easy for him, for all of them.

"Dick, bring us a drink, please," she said. "I think your father might have a brandy." She looked at his white face, the little circle of pain around his lips. "Then you'd better lie down for a while. There's nothing —more to do now."

And it was then, as Dick Bradley left the room, that the chimes sounded for the second time. Ellie stood up quickly, a hand moving to her throat, and Crowley said, "Could you go to the door?"

"Yes, I'm all right, I can manage."

He looked at her steadily for a second or so, and then said, "You could manage anything, for my money."

Ellie sighed wearily and walked through the foyer to the doorway. She opened the door, narrowing her eyes slightly against the morning sun. "Yes?" she said.

The man on the stoop was small and neatly dressed, and his glasses winked like mirrors in the sunlight. There was a simpering little smile on his lips. "Ah, good morning, ma'am," he said, removing his hat with an awkward little flourish. "I hope I'm not disturbing you."

"No—no," Ellie said. She recognized him then, and her heart began to pound with sudden violence.

"My name is Creasy and I live opposite you on the block," he said. "I just stopped by to ask about your little daughter."

"Yes—" Ellie's lips were dry, and she could feel a pulse fluttering with terror at the hollow of her throat. "Yes?"

Inside the house Crowley waved a warning hand to Dick Bradley who had just entered the living room with a tray. Then Crowley dropped a hand on his gun and moved as close as he could to the front door. . . .

Creasy's smile was secretive, and there was a curious blend of humility and arrogance in his manner. This was his moment of triumphant climax; he had been driven to do this, compelled against all common sense and caution to see her, to see the ravages of pain and fear in her face—for he had reached the point beyond which his imagination had become stale and unrewarding. That was why he had sent the special delivery letter to the Bradleys. Turn the screw once more. . . . The instructions for paying the ransom were in the regular mail, and should arrive within an hour or so. Then the bonds of the rack could be loosened again. They could hope. . . . Grant's schedule wouldn't be affected at all. This moment was pure luxury, an exquisite dividend.

"We haven't met, of course," he said, bobbing his head rhythmically. Yes, she had suffered—he saw that now. The shadows under her eyes were like deep purple bruises. "In the country I daresay it would be different." He smiled to let her know he understood these protocols. "One still leaves cards, doesn't one?"

"Yes—" Her voice was high and strained. "There's—more time."

"Precisely. Here it's all rush, rush, rush." He studied her drawn features carefully, memorizing each mark of anguish with clinical care. "But we who value such things find time for—what shall I say?—the older graces?"

"That's true, I'm sure." Ellie had known this feeling in nightmares: the rending need to scream and be silent at one and the same time.

No make-up, Creasy observed, and unconsciously his smile became a trifle superior. Where was the elegant coiffeur, the luxurious attention to skin and eyes and nails? Without the expensive props what was she? A drab. . . .

"I must tell you why I've taken this liberty," he said. "Lately, I've enjoyed a smile or two from your charming little daughter. We pass in the street, and I bow quite formally to the little princess, and she rewards my fealty with a clap of her dimpled hands—the beginning and end of life saluting each other, one might say." He pretended not to notice her trembling lips and dark, staring eyes. "Nothing much by the standards of the busy world perhaps, but quite a lot to one facing—why not confess it?—his autumn years. But I've missed my princess the last few days. I was afraid she might be ill. That's why I stopped by." Creasy chuckled softly. "I rather like to think I am her first gentleman caller."

"It's sweet of you to be worried. Jill has been under the weather, and we thought it best to keep her in for a few days."

"What a pity! She'll miss her outings."

"Yes, she is restless." Ellie was fighting as only she could; her smile was warm, and her voice was almost casual. *He knew Jill was gone—* that thought pounded in her mind.

"I'm sure she'll be bright and chipper very soon," Creasy said. "These indispositions don't bother children at all. Please tell her I stopped by, and that I'm looking forward to seeing her in the near future."

"Thank you. I will."

"How fortunate you're right here to take care of her," Creasy said, smiling a little. He allowed himself a final savoring look at her white face, and then he nodded briskly, and said, "Well, I must be toddling along. Good day!"

"Good-by."

Creasy crossed the street, beaming with a smug sense of accomplishment. Inside his room he lit a cigarette with a debonair gesture and took up his post at the windows. It had been risky, of course, he thought, still smiling brightly. But so well worth it. . . .

When he saw the mailman go up their steps an hour later, Creasy experienced an odd moment of deflation and loss. Now it was over. Finally. . . . The reprieve was in the postman's leather pouch. The ransom instructions, detailed and explicit. Now they would hope again. He sighed and dropped his cigarette into the dregs of a coffee cup where it sputtered out with an angry and final little hiss. Over, he thought sadly. So soon, so terribly soon. . . .

On Inspector West's desk at FBI headquarters there were two enlarged glossy prints of Duke Farrel, one full face, the other in profile. The pictures had been wired from Washington, only a few minutes after the dossier on Farrel had come in by telephone. Since that time—ten o'clock the previous night—Roth had been in communication with Joliet Penitentiary in Illinois, and police authorities in Chicago, and Madison, Wisconsin. Now it was nine o'clock, Tuesday morning. Long beams of cheerful sun slanted in the windows and from the streets below could be heard muted sounds of traffic and occasionally the shrill piping of a traffic cop's whistle.

The Inspector stood at his desk with Roth. He had talked with Crowley twice this morning; he knew about the special delivery letter, Creasy's subsequent visit and of the ransom instructions which had arrived an hour later in the regular mail.

The Inspector was studying Duke Farrel's dark bold features.

"According to Joliet, he's dangerous," Roth said. "He took solitary like it was a suite in a luxury hotel."

They were assembling, bit by bit, a portrait of Duke Farrel. They knew that he was unmarried, seemed to have no close friends, that both his father and mother were dead. His only relative was a half-brother, Henry Todd Farrel, who had left Big Springs, Wisconsin, at the start of the Korean War. There was no indication that the brothers had been in contact since that time. The younger brother had enlisted in the army and served in Korea. They were waiting now for his service record. They had no idea of his present whereabouts. . . .

West drummed his fingers on the desk. "We've got to get a line on him, Jerry."

"We'll have something when we get his service record. Right now all we know is that his mail was forwarded from Big Springs to Boston for a few months four years ago. Care of general delivery."

West glanced at the big clock on the wall; the gesture was compulsive, almost desperate. Time had assumed a heightened and precious value now; the minutes seemed to be flowing away on a prodigal tide.

"Let's check the pickup plans," he said. On his left a small-scale map of Pennsylvania had been tacked to a bulletin board. The kidnapers' plan was nearly perfect, West had seen instantly; it was simple, ingenious, safe. He could no longer hope that he was dealing with amateurs or neurotics.

West looked at a copy of the payoff instructions and then turned to the map of Pennsylvania. "Step one," he said to Roth. "Dick Bradley takes the money to Philadelphia at three this afternoon. There he rents a convertible. He stays in Philly until ten o'clock. Then drives to—" West glanced at his memo. "Kennett Square."

"That's about here," Roth said, putting his finger on the map. "Fifteen miles from Wilmington, Delaware, thirty miles southwest of Philadelphia."

"He leaves Kennett Square at midnight on Highway One and drives south at thirty miles an hour," West said. "He keeps going until dawn if necessary—he keeps going until a car pulls up behind him and signals him to stop with three blasts of the horn. Then Bradley drops off the money and continues south for another fifty miles."

"That will be tough to cover," Roth said.

"If we cover," West said slowly.

"The baby may be down that way. South, I mean."

"Sure. Virginia, Florida, Panama, Peru. There's a lot of territory south of us."

"But if they take the money and disappear, where does that leave us?"

West glanced at him. "And suppose they spot us? Where does that leave the baby?"

Roth shrugged his big shoulders and said nothing. . . .

Afterwards, West knew, the correct decision would seem the inevitable one—a wrong decision would be attributed to the judgment of a fool or an incompetent. The only thing that mattered was the baby's safety. But either path he chose might cost the baby its life. And a million jurors would sit in judgment on the bureau's decision over their morning coffee and papers. "What the hell was he trying? A grandstand play? Why didn't he let them have the money? The baby's the important thing, right?" And if it went the other way: "Chicken-hearted, that's what they are. They had the bastards right in their hands and didn't have the guts to close their fists. Why didn't they have a hundred men waiting when they tried to grab that money? Where were they?"

West didn't give a damn about those million jurors. He was thinking only of the baby—but the jurors' arguments were the same ones that sounded in his own mind.

"Let's set up to cover," he said quietly. "Let's be ready."

"Right," Roth said.

"Call Philadelphia first. The instructions don't specify where Bradley is to rent the car. That's one break. Have Philly plant a convertible for him, equipped with a camera and transmitter that works off a foot pedal. Now let's see: at thirty miles an hour Bradley will travel about one hundred and eighty miles on Highway One by dawn. Okay, get enough men to cover that stretch thoroughly this afternoon. Spot every garage, diner, restaurant and all the side roads. Prepare small-scale maps of the area on both sides of the highway, secondary roads, rivers, bridges, overpasses—everything. And mark out deserted stretches on Highway One —places where the contact is likely.

"If we decide to cover, everything's got to be ready. Enough cars on an intercom hookup, enough men to follow any length of tail job."

"They'll be ready."

West turned back to his desk, still studying the ransom instructions. Regardless of their preparations, this would be risky; the kidnapers had every advantage. They could be miles ahead of Bradley, or miles behind him, choosing their moment of contact from a wide latitude of times and places. They could wait until the road was dark and empty—then make their move.

Roth came to his side later and said, "It's rolling. What next?"

Nothing more had come in on Duke Farrel, nothing at all on his brother.

"I want more on Creasy," West said.

"You aren't sure of him?"

"There's no proof. He could be the neighborhood crank or a Peeping

Tom. He turned down a cab in the rain. Maybe he likes getting wet. He's watching the Bradleys' house. Maybe he likes old brownstones. I want more."

"We've been covering him since last night," Roth said. "We've made a duplicate key to his room. Maybe if I took a look around there—"

West glanced at him, a little frown on his face. "We've got to know," he said. "Right now all we've got is a handful of smoke."

Roth said nothing. He wanted to go, he wanted to be doing something positive, but he controlled his impatience; he didn't want to influence West's decision.

"Okay," West said at last. "But for God's sake be careful, Jerry. . . ."

Roth and an agent named Carstairs parked on Third Avenue just below Thirty-first Street. They waited there almost an hour before the radio in the car crackled, and a voice said, "Subject just leaving building, walking toward Second Avenue."

Roth picked up his telephone. "All right, I'm going in. Keep your eyes open."

The agent who had given him this information was stationed in a room at the intersection of Third Avenue and Thirty-first Street. From there he had a clear east-west view of Thirty-first Street.

A few moments later Roth walked briskly into Creasy's building with a zippered brief case under his arm. In the case were insurance literature, application forms, a rate book—and beneath these a receiver and a transmitter by which he could keep in touch with Carstairs and the agent stationed in the room at the intersection. The hallway was empty and dark, and the house smelled faintly of old wood and German cooking. Roth listened for an instant, and then let himself into Creasy's room and closed the door quickly.

He was alert for anything and everything. There were phone numbers on a desk pad, and he made a note of these, and then went rapidly through Creasy's bureau drawers. The files of genealogical data had no significance for him, but he stared for a few seconds at the faded pictures of silent film stars that covered the wall at the foot of his bed. A movie fan? A hero worshiper? Speculation was pointless, but something in that collection of handsome, forgotten faces alerted his highly developed sense of the incongruous—which in Roth was an intuitive faculty, an almost *a priori* awareness of significant peculiarities. Scientists have similar antennae, as do doctors and priests, and occasional politicians.

But Roth ignored these ephemeral promptings; there was no time for anything but facts. He turned to the top of the bureau where Creasy's toilet articles were spread in a disorderly heap, a sorry little monument to a man's lack of respect for his own body. The bristles of his hairbrush, dark with scurf and oil, were worn down to the wooden backs, and the tubes of shaving cream and toothpaste had been squeezed and twisted into little accordions of ugly economy. His bar of soap, partially wrapped in a damp wash cloth, was festooned with sworls of drying suds, and flecked with little curls of hair. All of this added to Roth's picture of Creasy—from these data he could have drawn a hundred accurate inferences about the man. But they didn't need inferences now; they needed facts.

Finally he picked up a notebook from a table in the middle of the room—the sort school children use, with ruled paper and cardboard covers in black and white check. Roth leafed through it, aware of a little stir of excitement. Crowley had said the special delivery letter had been written on ruled, copybook paper—and the front page had been torn from this book, and there were pen or pencil indentations on the second page. The message to the Bradley's had been brief—two short sentences—and the marks on the second page were also brief—two short sentences.

Roth made himself think clearly, trying not to give way to a precipitate impatience. The special delivery note was just across the street and it would take only a split second to match its torn edges against the backbone of this book. He glanced at his watch; he'd been inside five minutes. But time was no yardstick of safety; Creasy might be gone all day, or he might be heading back home this minute.

Roth was suddenly aware that perspiration had broken out on his forehead. To bring the note here might crowd the limits of safety to dangerous lengths. If something slipped it could mean the baby's life. Arresting Creasy would do no good; they couldn't know what codes or signals had been arranged between him and the other kidnapers.

Roth stared at the notebook for half a minute in silence. Then he said, "God help me," in a low voice, and reached for his brief case.

Having made the decision, he worked quickly: he zippered open the brief case and flashed Carstairs with movements that were maximums of precision and economy. He said quietly, "I'm going to phone Crowley. Get every word. You'll know what to do then . . ."

"Right," Carstairs said. "I'm standing by."

Roth placed the radio beside the phone and dialed the Bradleys' number, and when the buzzing started he heard the sudden heavy stroke of his heart. He talked first to Dick Bradley and then to Crowley. "This is Roth," he said. "I'm across the street in Creasy's room." Crowley didn't answer him and Roth said, "your middle name is Francis, your card number is one, two, four, eight, you've got a bullet scar on your left forearm. The guy who shot you was named Miller. Okay?"

"Right," Crowley said.

"Okay, listen carefully now . . ."

Roth crossed the room after putting the phone down and looked out at the windows of the Bradley home, at the sun gleaming on the massive brass knocker and antique numerals. A moment later Mrs. Jarrod came out and walked briskly toward Third Avenue, a mesh market bag in her hand. Roth patted his forehead with a handkerchief. Mrs. Jarrod had the note in her purse, and Carstairs was waiting for her in the supermarket. She would leave the note in a freezer and he would be standing beside her to retrieve it . . .

Five minutes passed. Then two more. "It's got to work," he said softly, using the words as a wall against his fears. He stood perfectly still, breathing as deeply as a man who had been running hard for blocks. Then he heard footsteps in the hallway, a man's footsteps brisk and sharp in the silence. The man was whistling *Dark Eyes*. Roth let out his breath slowly. The tune was a favorite of Carstairs' . . .

He crossed the room, turned the knob and took the sheet of paper from Carstairs. No words were needed. Roth opened the notebook and placed the sheet of paper on top of the second page, moving the torn edges toward each other, lining them up with his eyes until they fitted together, meshing exactly. . . .

Roth's thoughts leaped ahead. They had Creasy. Now they must get Duke Farrel.

But as he turned toward the door the radio clicked softly, and the agent in the room on Third Avenue said, "Clear out!" in a sharp, imperative voice. "Creasy just pulled up in a cab. Move! Fast!"

Creasy fumbled in his pockets for change. He wasn't sure why he had returned home. Something had frightened him and he always felt safer in his room—that was all he knew. All his life he had been spied upon; he had caught people staring at him from windows and doorways since he had been a child. And today the awareness of these hostile watchers had been very strong. . . .

He discovered he had no change. He gave the driver a five-dollar bill and said, "Please, I'm in a hurry."

"In a hurry? This all you've got?"

"Yes. You should have change for a five." Creasy's voice almost shot out of control. "You can't expect your passengers to carry the fare in silver. *You're* supposed to carry change. Isn't that correct?"

The driver looked at him in silence, his head tilted slightly. Finally he said, "Mac, I asked you a simple question. I said, 'This all you got?' All you got to do is say no. Lecturing me ain't going to help. There's nothing to yak about. No hard feelings, nothing." He counted out Creasy's change carefully, smiled philosophically at the size of his tip, and drove off, shaking his head.

Creasy's room was dark and empty. He leaned against the door, drawing confidence from the silence, the familiar shadows, the musty smells. Finally he snapped on the nightlamp beside his bed, fearful as always that the shadows might begin to move. He looked in the closet and under the bed for his enemy. Some day he would find him. When the shadows moved. . . . But today he was safe. His fears subsided slowly into the depths of his unconscious. He lit a cigarette and walked to the windows, smiling at the Bradleys' house. He felt secure again, dominant. . . .

Roth stood on the stairs leading to the second floor of Creasy's building. He had barely made it. When he heard Creasy go into his room, he glanced at his watch. He waited five minutes, then came briskly down the stairs and walked into the bright sunlight. Now to call West.

# 19

GRANT WAS DOZING BEFORE THE FIREPLACE WHEN A CAR TURNED INTO the driveway in front of the lodge. As he came to his feet, shaking his head in confusion, headlights swept brilliantly across the windows and a train of grotesque shadows leaped through the fire-lit room.

"Duke!" he cried, in a hoarse, sleep-thickened voice. "Duke, for God's sake!" He drew the gun from his pocket and faced the front door, shaking his big head groggily as the lights passed the windows and darkness plunged back into the room. Outside the sound of a motor faded and trembled away into silence.

Duke turned on the lamp beside his chair and glanced at his watch. Hank had been stretched out on the sofa but now he sat up, his eyes switching from his brother to Grant.

"It's only nine-thirty," Duke said, as a step sounded on the porch. "Sociable hour for callers."

"Get up!" Grant said, as the steps came solidly toward the front door. "Get up, damn you."

"Put that gun away," Duke said. His face was blurred by the shadows, but his eyes were hard splinters of light in the darkness. "We got a caller, a friend of my brother's maybe." Without raising his voice he said harshly, "Put it away, you fool!" Duke stood and hitched up his trousers. He looked at Hank and said, "Play along, kid. If anything slips you get it first. Then the nurse and kid."

A knock sounded and Duke said, "You're the host, kid. Act like it."

Hank nodded and got slowly to his feet. As he crossed the room a second knock shook the panel, and a third sounded just as he pulled open the door. Light from behind him slanted through the doorway and touched the smiling face of the big man who stood on the porch: it was Adam Wilson, Hank saw, an amiable giant who ran a sporting goods store in Williamsboro.

"Not too late for a visit, I hope," Adam said, smiling first at Hank, and then at Grant and Duke who stood together at the fireplace.

"No, come on in," Hank said. "We were just sitting around talking. You haven't met my brother, I know, or his friend, Eddie Grant."

"Glad to meet you both," Adam said. He smiled at them, turning his hat slowly in his big hands. "I drove out this way to see Pop Macky and I thought I'd drop in on Hank here. I heard he missed his fishing trip because he hurt his hand. A fellow out at the airport told me about it. How's it coming along, boy?"

"It's coming along okay," Hank said.

Adam was staring at the dirty bandage and the deep purple color of his wrist. "You sure?" he said doubtfully.

Duke came across the room smiling. "Nice to meet you, Adam. Maybe you can make him be sensible about that hand of his. I tried to get him in to the doctor twice, but he's got a superman complex."

"I'd listen to your brother," Adam said, glancing at Hank. "That paw don't look a bit good."

"Tomorrow he goes to the doctor if I have to carry him," Duke said. "Sit down now and I'll find you a drink. Rum okay?"

"Rum's my drink," Adam said, smiling again. He took off his heavy jacket, a big man, tall and broad, with a padded, comfortable-looking body. There was a quality of gentleness in his manner; his eyes were clear and innocent behind rimless glasses, and his humor was of an old-fashioned, friendly sort, completely without sting or malice.

Duke turned into the kitchen and Hank and Adam settled themselves before the fire. Grant remained standing at the mantelpiece, watching Wilson with narrow, cautious eyes.

Silence settled in the room. "You in business in town?" Grant said suddenly.

"Yes, that's right, Mr. Grant. I run a little sports store. Guns and fishing tackle mostly."

"That's a pretty good deal, eh?"

Adam looked at him, polite and attentive. "Well, yes and no, I'd say. Not much money, but quite a bit of fun. There's a good bunch in town, and it's not too hard sitting around swapping lies with them."

Grant ran a hand over his forehead and Hank saw him glance at his watch. Adam saw it too. . . .

The silence closed around them once more. Hank knew Adam was no fool; in spite of his bland good humor he was a successful trader in a country of historically good traders. Nothing much escaped his big clear eyes. He knew what went on behind people's faces; when he lost at poker it was news in town. Now he was curious about Grant's strained manner, turning it over slowly in his uncomplicated mind.

"Small towns have their points, eh?" Grant said. He made a nervous gesture with his hand. "Everybody knows everybody. A man feels at home, I guess."

"Yes, that's true. You live in the city, Mr. Grant?"

"Always have, always will, I suppose," Grant said, smiling quickly. He put his elbow on the mantel and the cloth of his jacket tightened over the gun he carried in his pocket. Adam saw that; Hank was sure of it. His eyes passed over that significant bulge casually; he paid no more attention to it than he did the buttons on Grant's coat. But he had recognized it; he knew the shape of guns.

Duke came back into the room with a bottle of rum and a tray of glasses, his manner cheerful and ebullient. "Good thing rum's your drink, Adam. It's all we've got."

"Rum's the next best thing to a good wife," Adam said. "Some old fellows around here been drinking it since they were kids. Nobody knows how old they are now. They go on about hearing Dan Webster talk though." Adam raised his glass smiling. "Take it or leave it, that's their story."

"I'll take it," Duke said. "Well, long life, eh?"

Everyone drank and shifted into more comfortable positions. Duke's mood was genial and expansive. "The good life, eh? A fire, something to drink—pretty good, eh?"

"You said it."

"That's what we city slickers miss," Grant said. He was taking his cue from Duke now, Hank saw—striking a note of jovial normality. "We don't relax enough. We think life is just something that gets in the way of work—instead of the other way around."

"That's well put," Adam said, nodding. "We're just the opposite, eh, Hank? Too much fishing, not enough work."

"You mean Hank's turned into a playboy up here?" Duke said.

Adam laughed. "Telling tales out of school. There I go again."

"Well, watch it," Hank said easily; but all his senses were suddenly alert. *Too much fishing*—Adam's sport was gunning. He was no fisherman.

Adam sipped his drink and smiled into the fire. "Speaking of work, which I hate about as much as working itself, I got those new reels you wanted. Two of 'em, real beauties. It'll take a lot of fish to make that investment pay off."

"It's fun trying," Hank said. Now he could feel the slow heavy pounding of his heart; he hadn't ordered any reels from Adam.

"They're out in the car, as a matter of fact," Adam said. "In the back under a lot of junk. You want to help me dig 'em out? Or let it ride till you're in town?"

"Oh, let it ride," Hank said. Duke wasn't smiling any more, he saw; he was watching Adam with a puzzled little frown. "I can't do much fishing with this hand." They were taking a dangerous chance with Duke; he was always alert for betrayal and deception. When he double-crossed a friend he felt he was simply beating him to the punch.

The conversation drifted into casual channels. Adam told some of his favorite hunting stories, and Duke poured another round of drinks. Grant said he had always wanted to go on a hunting trip in Africa—that had been his ambition as a kid. Adam seemed interested in this, and Duke added a bit of rum to everyone's glass. The time passed uneventfully. Finally Duke yawned and said, "Look, I hate to be the wet blanket, but I'm bushed."

"I didn't mean to keep you up," Adam said. "I've got to be going along."

"Finish your drink," Duke said. "Don't let me spoil things." He shook hands with Adam and said, "We'll stop by one of these days. I'd like to see the shop."

"You do that," Adam said. "I want you to meet some of the boys."

After Duke went upstairs the silence that followed was normal, almost comfortable: Grant had his nerves under control and was waiting for Adam to leave without visible impatience. They sipped their last drinks and watched the fire, seemingly suffused with lazy contentment. Finally Adam said, "There's something I forgot, Hank. I ran into Harry Davis yesterday and he asked me if you still wanted that job done on the roof. Said he'd drop out and give you an estimate if you were interested. I told him I'd ask you."

"I don't know," Hank said, shrugging lightly. The wrong word here might finish them; Harry Davis was no contractor, he was the sheriff of Williamsboro. "It's a job for him, all right," he said finally. "But I'm worried about the price. It may be pretty steep. He can't handle it alone, I know."

"The longer you let it go, the worse it gets," Adam said. "Like me, for instance. I let a leaky roof go one year, next thing I knew I had a plastering job on my hands." Puffing on his pipe, he seemed completely relaxed and at ease. "So I'll tell him to come out, eh?"

"Okay, do that," Hank said.

"Now I've got to be going. Eddie, I hope you can stop by the store before you leave. I'd like to have you all up to my place for a bite to eat. And who knows? Even a drop to drink."

"That sounds good."

"Come when you can. I don't need advance warning."

They all went to the door, and Hank said, "Watch the road, Adam, you've been belting that rum tonight."

Adam laughed as he put on his hat. "Don't worry about me," he said.

Smiling at Hank, his expression changed slightly. "Don't worry about a thing, boy. Get back to the fire now, both of you."

"So long," Grant said. "Take it easy."

"That's my middle name. Good-by now."

Grant closed the door and listened for a few seconds to Adam's heavy footsteps crossing the porch. Then he shook his head. "The local wit, eh? The Jackie Gleason of the crackerbarrel crowd."

"He's a pretty nice guy," Hank said casually. He was estimating the time it would take Adam to reach Williamsboro, find Harry Davis—an hour at least. Then Davis would be back out here in another half hour . . .

"Those village clowns are all nice guys," Grant said, strolling toward the fireplace. "They haven't got brains to be anything else. I'd hate to be stuck with him in a stalled elevator, that's all I can say."

But supposing Adam couldn't find Harry Davis? Would he call the State Police? Yes, of course. They could make it in two hours or less. Hank glanced at his watch. Ten-thirty. By twelve-thirty then. . . .

A heavy footstep sounded on the front porch. Grant straightened spasmodically, the tendons in his throat drawing tight with fear. "You expecting anybody else?"

"Don't do anything in a hurry, Eddie. Adam might have forgot something."

"Shut up! Just sit there."

The door was pushed inward with force; it swung around, crashing against the wall, and a blast of cold air swept into the room, shaking the windowpanes and stirring the smouldering logs into a guttering panic.

Hank came to his feet as he saw Adam standing in the doorway, his face white against the night, a dark, liquid mass gleaming on his forehead. "Adam!" he cried.

And then Adam staggered forward and went down to his knees, his breath coming in deep, laboring gasps, and behind him Hank saw Duke standing, with a piece of firewood in his hand, an expression of sullen fury on his dark features.

"You crazy maniac!" Grant yelled at him. "What the hell have you done now?"

"Saved your goddamned necks, that's all," Duke said.

Hank knelt beside Adam, hardly hearing the argument crashing above his head.

"You're acting like a madman," Grant said in a high, wild voice. "The cops will be out looking for him. Didn't that enter that crazy thick head of yours?"

"He was on his way to the cops," Duke said harshly. "So relax, Eddie. I'm getting tired of your temperament. If you can't keep calm, maybe you'd better go upstairs with the women."

"What do you mean, on his way to the cops?"

"He didn't have any reels for Junior here in his car. I checked that."

"He might have forgot 'em. I tell you, Duke—"

"Don't bother telling me things," Duke said. "They threw signals past you as if you weren't here. Harry Davis! Roofing job! Lucky for us I waited on the stairs. Harry Davis! He is the sheriff of Williamsboro. His posters for re-election are plastered on every telephone pole in town. And Adam was on his way to get him. I got a window open and slid down a drainpipe—and just in time, Eddie."

"But what do we do now, Duke? I—I can't think."

"We keep him quiet. That's all. He'll phone his store in the morning, tell them he won't be in. He'll—"

"He won't do anything," Hank said. "He's dead. You killed him."

"Don't talk a lot of foolishness," Duke said. "I just tapped him." Kneeling, he slipped a hand under Adam's coat. "Just enough to put him out for a few minutes. I can time that swing to the second, kid. If I'd wanted to—" He stopped there, frowning faintly, staring at Adam's face. For a moment or so no one spoke; Grant's heavy breathing was loud in the silence.

"Duke?" he said.

"Yeah, the kid was right," Duke said thoughtfully. He rocked back on his heels and shook his head. "I can't understand it, Eddie. I just tapped him." He stared across the still body at his brother. "You see, kid, he asked for it. It wasn't my fault. He was trying to be a smart guy."

Hank got to his feet. "You don't believe that. Nobody else does either."

"He wanted to cut himself into the deal," Duke said. "He just wanted to be smart, that's all."

Hank looked at his brother, seeing him clearly for the first time, the image unsoftened by the filters of guilt and fear and sentiment; he saw the grossness, the twisted mixture of cunning and boldness, the defiance and fear—yes, over all of it, the mark of fear.

"He asked for it," Duke said, dismissing responsibility with a little shrug.

"And the baby upstairs asked for it," Hank said. "And the nurse. Every time you club somebody from behind you limp away, whining that they asked for it. Aren't you getting sick of that routine?"

"Now you just better shut up," Duke said slowly, but the contempt in his brother's face stung him into a defensive anger. "Go on, stare all you like. Make gags about my crooked leg. It's a sure-fire laugh. Anybody with two good legs loves it. I—"

Duke stopped abruptly as the upstairs door opened and Belle stepped into the room. "Eddie, I thought—" Then she saw Adam's sprawled body and a little cry of terror broke through her lips. "What's the matter with him? Who is he, Eddie?"

"He's dead," Grant said.

"Oh, God!" she whispered, and her eyes became wide and dark in her pale face. She turned slowly to Duke who had stretched out in a chair and clasped his hands behind his head.

"Did you do it? Did you do it, Duke?"

"That's right, look right at me," he said with an ironical little smile. "There's a dead body around, so good old Duke must have done it. Sure, I killed him, Belle. I busted his head open with that hunk of wood you're almost standing on."

She stepped back quickly, her breath coming in uneven little gasps. "Don't joke about it. For God's sake, don't joke about it. He's dead. Why did you do it?"

"Because I'm crazy," Duke said. "I'm a screwball. That's what Grant says, and he's the boss so he must be right."

"Please, *please!*" she whispered.

"All right, calm down," Grant said. "He had to do it, Belle. This guy was going for the cops. Now we've got to decide what to do next." He looked at Hank. "Did anyone know he was coming out here?"

"You heard everything I did."

"Was he married? Has he got a family expecting him?"

"He wasn't married," Hank said. "He took care of his mother and his brother's wife and two kids. They all live over in Eaton about thirty miles from here. Adam's brother was an infantry sergeant who was killed on Iwo Jima."

"I don't want a family history," Grant said.

"You and Duke were in jail then. You might have missed the news-papers."

"Don't get wise," Grant said, but it was an automatic injunction, with-out any strength or conviction behind it; caught between fear and anger, he couldn't find an attitude, a course of action. "Come on, Duke," he said anxiously. "We've got to decide what to do."

"Count me out, Eddie. I've tried my best so far and you don't like it. All I get is a lot of yap." He shrugged his big shoulders. "You're the boss. Do what the hell you want."

"That's great. You kill him and then you act like it's some parlor game you don't want to play any more."

"Yeah, I quit," Duke said. "I'm bored. I'm tired of saving your ass. Save it yourself, Eddie."

Grant stared at him. "Do you know what you're saying? There's a body on the floor. Cops will be here looking for him. We got the baby upstairs and the nurse." Grant's voice rose angrily. "Am I boring you with details? Will you be bored when they strap you into the chair?"

"You got us into this," Belle said. "It's not fair just to sit there and do nothing."

"We got different ideas about what to do," Duke said. "So I'll just step out of the picture."

Hank knew this tactic of Duke's—he wanted submission, nothing else. If he couldn't get it, he walked out, brutally disengaging himself from all promises, responsibilities or commitments. He wouldn't argue. He just turned his back and quit. Hank had seen this pressure work on football coaches ("Okay, I'll turn in my suit after practice then."); and with girls ("Find somebody else to take the rap, baby, I'm shoving off.") and with their father, again and again. ("Okay, I'll clear out. Yeah, I'll write —but don't hold your breath.")

And now, watching Grant's shifting, worried eyes, Hank knew it would work again. They needed Duke and they would meet his terms.

"Look," Grant said, "we don't have to argue about who's running things. You want to take over—fine. The thing is, we're in trouble. Let's don't sit here debating about who's in charge."

"That's sensible, I guess," Belle said, looking uneasily at Grant.

They had disintegrated more than they realized, Hank thought, as he watched the complacent little smile growing on Duke's face. They weren't thinking, they were hoping—trusting Duke blindly and foolishly. They didn't see that Duke's confidence was based only on this moment of personal triumph—that it had nothing to do with their final safety. They wouldn't have made that mistake yesterday—or even a few hours ago.

"Well, first we've got to get rid of this guy," Duke said, getting to his feet. "I'll drive him out into the woods. That's all. When he's found the cops will probably think a hitchhiker did it."

"And they may not," Grant said.

"That's right," Duke said, glancing from Grant to Belle. "Understand this. We're in trouble. The job went sour. Eddie, you aren't going to make your entrance at Donovan's on schedule. That's all you wanted out of this deal. Ten minutes of glory, ten minutes of pretending that jail never happened and you're not an old man with a fat stomach and a bald spot. Listen!" he said harshly as Grant took a step toward him. "You don't get your entrance. We're running now, dodging and hiding, using the alleys and corners until we're clear. And you're doing what I tell you. Or I run alone. Belle, you get upstairs and stick with the nurse. Get moving."

Belle hurried out of the room, and Hank said, "You had a chance with Grant running things. Now you're through."

Duke smiled at him, balancing his weight on the balls of his feet. "I've watched you building up your nerve, kid, bit by bit, like a guy making a house of matches. It's a long hard job for you, isn't it? Everything's got to be just so, right in balance. Otherwise you fall apart. Now you're ready to start acting like a man. Well, I can't let you play hero—funny as you look trying. There's no time for laughs." He glanced at Grant. "Eddie, there's a springhouse built right into the basement. Stone walls, a heavy door with a lock on it. That's our solitary wing. Hank's going in there until we need him again. If he makes a racket, beat him senseless. You're handling this end. Check the car, have some coffee and food ready and sit tight. Got that?"

Hank knew they had lost. The waiting, the hoping, the pressure on Grant and Duke—none of it was any good. And he wouldn't have another chance after the door of the springhouse swung shut on him. None of them would. . . .

"All right, Junior," Grant said.

"Sure," Hank said. He turned toward the door, then spun around, dropping into a crouch. Grant said, "Why, you bastard," charging at him—and Hank came up fast, swinging a left hook from the floor. The blow caught Grant on the forehead, staggering him, and Hank clawed at the pocket in which he kept his gun.

Duke bent down and picked up the piece of firewood. "Hero," he said. His voice was disgusted. He raised his arm and brought the club down in a vicious arc. As Hank fell to the floor, Duke shook his head and looked at Grant. "He almost took you," he said. "Start being a little sharp, okay?"

Grant stared down at Hank's limp body. "I'll fix him before we leave," he said. "That's a promise."

"Just stay sharp, okay?"

# 20

CREASY COLLECTED THE RANSOM MONEY EARLY WEDNESDAY MORNING on a deserted stretch of Highway One, just south of Oxford, Pennsylvania. There was no difficulty, no confusion, no possibility of surveillance, Creasy was certain; the highway was dark and empty for miles in either direction when he came up behind Bradley's slowly moving convertible, and sounded his horn three times. Bradley stopped obediently, and within sixty seconds Creasy was on his way back to New York with the suitcase full of money in the rear of the car.

Grant's plan had been brilliantly ingenious, he thought, as he drove through the darkness; maximum simplicity, minimum risk. Creasy had been free to choose the time and place for the contact; Bradley's car, traveling at a constant thirty miles per hour, had been absurdly easy to keep under safe observation. Creasy had passed it several times, then pulled up at a gas station or diner to let Bradley resume the lead. If anything had seemed suspicious he would simply have turned off the highway and gone back to New York. But everything was exactly as Grant said it would be; there was little traffic, chiefly interstate buses and trucks traveling slightly over the legal speed limit. And there were dozens of deserted stretches along the road where contact would have been safe and easy—and all those areas had been carefully checked by Grant weeks before. Yes, it had been simple. . . . Even the business about the transmitter had gone smoothly. Grant had been afraid that Bradley—or the police—might have installed a radio transmitter in the convertible to flash a signal when Creasy made the contact. To circumvent this, Creasy (on Grant's instructions) had turned his car radio on as he drew up behind the convertible. Grant had warned him to listen closely for signs of static or interruptions then—evidence that a transmitter was operating in Bradley's car. But there had been no suspicious interference or noises, only one or two normal little cracklings. Not two, one, Creasy remembered. The reception had been quite perfect.

Then he had honked three times. And a minute later was in possession of two hundred thousand dollars. He had opened the suitcase to make sure—that had taken fifteen seconds at the most—and then he had turned around and started for the New Jersey Turnpike, heading for New York.

When Creasy reached the outskirts of Wilmington, Delaware, he turned off the highway into a dark residential area, and parked in a block of arching trees and handsomely landscaped homes. Only a few cars and buses had passed him since he had picked up the money, but he decided to wait here in the darkness and make absolutely certain he wasn't being followed. . . . No precaution was ever pointless.

Creasy took a road map from the glove compartment. If a police car happened to stop, he would have his story. . . . "I seem to have gotten turned around, officer. Could you tell me the best route to the Memorial Bridge? Ah, yes. Silly of me. Thanks so much. . . ."

Creasy lit a cigarette, and then settled back and smiled at the dim reflection of his glasses in his windshield. Grant had been so worried—giving him instructions as if he were lecturing a backward child. So meticulous, so exasperatingly repetitious. Grant seemed unable to believe that Creasy could actually drive a car. But Creasy was an excellent driver, having been in service as a chauffeur for a number of years. In Old Westbury, he thought, remembering the quiet, winding roads and gardens, its air of spaciousness so incongruous with the proximity of New York. There was regal privilege, he thought—to have nine-hole golf courses on land that was worth ten or twenty dollars a square yard. An elegant life, oh yes, with indoor tennis courts for the winter months, heated pools and polo fields and endless chatter about horses and games and schools, and how well old Mrs. So-and-So would cut up for the lucky survivors. He had worked for the Winthrops. Not the good branch, not the direct line—but second cousins. Nobodies, actually. He had traced them thoroughly. And how superior and disagreeable they had been! The daughter . . . He remembered her so well. Haughty little bitch. Lying on her back in white shorts, toasting her slim brown body in the sun. Cool drink at her side. . . . Now she had a son, he remembered. Michael Desmond. The christening party had taken up quite a bit of space in the society pages. Little Michael was about a year old now. . . .

Creasy was puzzled by the direction of his thoughts, and by the splintered, irrelevant anger that was growing in his breast, spreading pleasurably through his body. The Winthrops, yes, indeed. They needed a comeuppance. Doting on their first grandchild. So many people needed a lesson. And it was so easy.

With a start he glanced at his watch. He must be on his way. There would be time for all this later. But time for what? His thoughts were strangely confused. Only the sustaining sense of anger churned clearly and satisfyingly in his mind. With a vicious thrust of his small foot he tramped down on the starter. . . .

The radio on Inspector West's desk cracked through a tense silence, and Roth sat up quickly and leaned toward the speaker, his face hard with strain and fatigue.

A voice said, "Davis, Philadelphia office. Subject crossed the Memorial Bridge a few minutes ago, on the approach to the New Jersey Turnpike."

"Okay," Roth said.

"I'm turning off now."

"Good work, Davis."

Roth glanced up at West who was sitting on the edge of the desk with an unlighted cigarette in his mouth. The days of strain had drawn lines of exhaustion in his lean, youthful face, but his eyes were hard and bright as marbles.

"Looks like he's coming back to New York," Roth said.

West nodded slowly, and glanced at the clock.

The radio sounded again, and a voice said, "This is Brandell, Philadelphia. Subject is on the Turnpike. I'm going to pull ahead of him. He's doing forty-five. I'll check off in ten or twelve miles."

"Right, Brandell," Roth said.

West stood up, glancing at the clock again; it drew his eyes like a magnet. It was three o'clock Wednesday morning. Time was working against them now; each minute that passed lengthened the odds against the baby. The ransom had been paid, the kidnapers had their money. Now the baby became dangerous and incriminating excess baggage. A nuisance. . . . Why risk taking her home? That would be the question they'd put to themselves. And West knew how they would answer it. . . .

The FBI had covered the payoff for that reason—hoping that the pickup car would lead them to the baby. More than a hundred cars, trucks, cabs and station wagons had participated in the coverage—even a few motorcycles. Creasy had been followed leaving Kennett Square, Pennsylvania by a relay of cars, working on a split-second schedule. Bradley's convertible had been equipped with a radio transmitter and camera by agents from the Philadelphia office. When Creasy had pulled up behind him Bradley had touched a foot pedal—and the camera had recorded Creasy's license plates, and the transmitter had thrown one signal to the cordon of agents who were patrolling the secondary roads that ran parallel to Highway One.

It was an intricate maneuver, demanding perfect timing and synchronization from the dozens of agents participating in the surveillance. And it had been brought off flawlessly. Now Creasy was apparently returning to New York with the money. And time was running out. . . .

West threw his unlit cigarette aside with an abrupt, angry gesture. He stared at the two blown-up photographs on his desk: Duke Farrel and Howard Creasy. Where in the name of God was Farrel?

A half-dozen agents sat at the desks surrounding West's long table. They were waiting for phones to ring, teletype keys or radio signals to break the silence; the nets had been cast wide—to Chicago, Madison and Detroit, south to Mobile, as far west as Colorado, to any place where there might be a lead on the Farrel brothers.

An agent had talked to the younger brother's commanding officer, a retired colonel living in Red Bank, New Jersey. Another had spent three hours at Joliet penitentiary, talking with the warden and trustees who had known Duke Farrel.

They had the two brothers in sharp relief now; army service, prison record, credit ratings, hobbies, tastes in food, clothing, women—that had all gone into the file. They didn't have much on Creasy, but a file was growing on one Edwin David Grant, a seasoned Chicago hoodlum who had been an intimate of Duke Farrel's in prison. They had been around Chicago for a while after being released from jail, and had gone on together to Detroit, and later to Denver. There the trail ended, there was nothing to indicate that Grant was with Farrel now. . . .

Roth said, "I'll be surprised if the younger brother is in on it."

"You can't tell," West said.

Roth picked up a card from the desk. "He doesn't fit. Two decorations, damn fine record, and you know what his CO thinks of him—it just doesn't fit."

"We'll see."

They knew that Henry Farrel lived and worked in Portland, Maine, as a junior partner in a real estate office. Agents had checked his apartment, but found it empty; he was away on a fishing trip in Canada, but his secretary didn't know just where.

"It could fit," West said. "Maybe the Farrel brothers met in Canada."

"Sure," Roth said, dropping the card back on the table. "I'll be surprised though."

There was nothing to do but wait. Everyone in the room looked up when the radio broke the silence with a periodic report on Creasy's approach to New York. And occasionally, with almost furtive glances, they watched the relentless sweep of the second hand around the face of the clock.

At three-thirty the phone on West's desk rang. He picked up the receiver and said, "Yes?" in his sharp official voice. Then: "Yes—certainly I've got time. What is it?" His voice was almost gentle then; the crisp official note was gone. Roth glanced up as he said, "Well, that's fine news, absolutely great. I'll get word to him . . . yes, of course. He'll be—well, he'll be just as happy as you are."

West put the phone down and said to Roth, "There's one break. That's Crowley's wife."

"The baby's okay?"

"Not okay. It's polio, but a mild case, she says. The doctors feel sure the child is in no real danger."

"How about the aftereffects?"

"She just said the baby's going to live. She's taking the bridges one at a time." He put another cigarette in his mouth. "Give Crowley a flash. He's standing by. . . ."

It was four o'clock when the direct phone to Chicago began to ring. An agent lifted the receiver, then glanced at West. "For you, sir. Agent-in-charge, Chicago office."

West took the receiver and said, "Yes?"

"Jim Keely, Tom. We've got another line on Duke Farrel. I can't vouch for it. It's third-hand. But you can run it down. One of our sources here just phoned me. He came across a bookmaker who had a letter from Duke Farrel. He was in New York then, staying at either the Wells Hotel or the Bell Hotel—the bookie wasn't sure."

"When was this?"

"About a month ago. Farrel was in to the book for a couple of hundred bucks, and they were after their money. He wrote that he'd be in Chicago in six weeks and straighten it out then. That's all we've got."

"It may help," West said. "Thanks, Jim."

When he put down the phone Roth stood and said, "What is it?" The other agents had come to their feet, too, and were watching him with alert eyes.

"The Wells Hotel, or the Bell Hotel," West said. "Farrel was at one of those places a month ago. Do you know them?"

"I know the Wells," Roth said. "On Forty-seventh Street between Fifth and Sixth. It's a trap. Vags, hustlers, horse players, that sort of thing."

"The Bell is up in Harlem," another agent said. "It's run by some kind of a mission. You've got to be a member of the church to stay there."

"The Wells sounds right," West said. "We'll try it first."

"What do we do?" Roth said. He had already put on his coat; he was tense, ready to go, his big face hard and mad. "Take it apart brick by brick? Give the clients a memory lesson?"

"Farrel might have friends there," West said.

"I'll bet he does. And I'll bet they know where he is."

"We can't go in with sirens," West said.

"Someone in that hotel may have a lead for us," Roth said, and unconsciously his eyes shifted to the clock. "I'd like to bust it loose. While there's time."

"Yes, and someone there might be on the phone to Farrel ten minutes later," West said. "The bellhop, the night desk clerk, elevator man—any one of them might be in on this deal."

"What the hell *can* we do?" Roth said, pounding a fist into the palm of his hand.

"Relax—and start doing it right now," West said, and there was a sudden snap of command in his voice. "We're handcuffed till that baby is safe. We're not taking any chances yet. So let's go to work. Check the post office to see if any registers were delivered to Farrel while he was at the Wells. And the telephone company for long distance calls. And Western Union for wires."

West swung around to the agents standing in front of his desk. "All right, move! Don't waste time explaining what you want to clerks. Go right to the top. We want this information now."

Turning, he beckoned to the agent on the Chicago phone. "Let that go now, Bill. I want you to check the police precinct covering the Wells Hotel. Find out what paroled convicts they've got in the area. Get their names and addresses. Find out if they're watching anyone at the Wells— for any reason at all. Say you're on a security job. Phone me here when you've got that dope."

Roth came back to West's desk after assigning three agents to phones. "I'm sorry I blew my top," he said.

"Forget it," West said. "We may hit something now." He was thinking of the million jurors with just a touch of bitterness. They'd quarter-back this decision, too, from the stands, not knowing or not caring that a kidnaping put law officers in a strait jacket; the police didn't have the breaks in this case. Not as long as the baby was missing. . . .

A few minutes later they had a final radio report on Creasy; he had left his car and the ransom money at a garage on Second Avenue. From there he had walked to his room on Thirty-first Street. He was now inside.

Phoning, West thought, saying, *"This end is all wrapped up. Sure, I've got it. You can fade now. Don't take anything you don't need. . . ."*

They'd get Creasy, of course. And Farrel and the others. That was no problem. They'd try them and execute them as quickly as the law would allow. . . .

But would that compensate the Bradleys for a dead baby?

The minutes seemed to be rushing by now. West tried not to watch the clock but his eyes shifted there compulsively—and on each occasion another precious amount of time was lost forever.

And then, at four-fifteen, an agent scrambled to his feet and knocked his chair over backwards. "Here it is," he yelled in a sharp, breathless voice. He spun around, kicked his chair from his path, and reached West in two long strides. "Here it is, sir. From Farrel's brother."

West jerked the paper and scanned the message. Yes, he thought, feeling the pounding beat of his heart. Yes. . . . The message read: "My cottage available two weeks. More if you need it. Won't see you. Sorry. Am leaving for fishing trip Canada. Regards. Hank."

"Where was it sent from?"

"Williamsboro, Maine."

West stood perfectly still for an instant, staring at the message. "Now listen carefully, Jerry," he said—and as quiet and deliberate as his voice was, it brought silence over the room. "I'm going up there. I'll call you from the Boston airport. You phone Washington, tell them what we've got, and have them on a conference line for my report. After that, call Boston. I want a dozen agents to meet me at the airport. Men who know the country around Williamsboro. You've got that?"

"Right."

"Tell Boston I want to know where Hank Farrel's cottage is. I want to know who lives in every house near it. Tell them to be set to block the roads leading away from Farrel's place. I want to use local trucks—power company trucks, moving vans, delivery trucks. Equipped with two-way radio apparatus. They can fly men up now to get that detail ready. I'll phone Washington again from Williamsboro. You've got all this?"

"Yes, I've got it. You want me to call the Bradleys?"

West hesitated, then shook his head slowly. "They'll want to know one way or the other. And we don't know—not yet."

He pulled up his tie and without looking, reached out for his coat and hat; an agent held them ready. With a last quick glance at the clock, West started for the elevators at a run. . . .

# 21

DUKE STOOD AT THE KITCHEN WINDOW, A CUP OF RUM-LACED COFFEE IN his hand, and watched the new day spreading along the horizon. The sky was gray and pink above the green waters of the tidal estuary, and the tips of the fir trees were gleaming in the first thin sunlight. Duke felt pleasantly sleepy as he sipped the hot coffee and stared out at the fresh countryside. He'd had very little rest the past three days, and he had been drinking steadily most of that time; the combination had worn him down to a state of comfortable, almost luxurious drowsiness.

When he did sleep it would be a sensuous pleasure, as rewarding as food or drink or a woman. But he couldn't sleep yet. There were still a few loose ends. Creasy had called at four-thirty: he had the money. So that was set. And Adam Wilson's body had been taken care of; Duke had driven deep into the woods and left it there sprawled behind the wheel of the car, alone and staring in the empty stillness of the forest. Duke had come back to the lodge on foot, leaving no more sign of his passage than a canoe would leave on water. He had enjoyed the silent, stealthy return; it reminded him of his boyhood in Wisconsin, the old Indians, the hunting and fishing and the powerful excitement that had always gripped him when he was alone in the secret darkness of the woods. When you knew how to handle yourself you could come within ten feet of a camping party and listen and watch for hours without being seen or heard. . . .

He glanced at his watch: six-thirty. The girl would be ready with the baby. The last loose ends. He had told her he was taking her home, but she hadn't believed that; she had stared at him, knowing he lied, watching him with eyes that were like a trapped animal's.

Duke stretched his arms above his head, then put his hands on the small of his back and twisted sideways and forwards, limbering up his big body. A cramping pain tightened his chest. He still felt stiff as he limped upstairs. Stale, he thought. He needed exercise.

Grant hadn't been sleeping. He opened the door at Duke's knock, wearing slacks and a sports shirt. A cigarette burned at the corner of his mouth and the perspiration on his forehead glistened in the light of the flaring ash.

"You set to go?" he said.

"All set." In the big double bed behind Grant, Belle's body was a soft mound under the blankets. She was breathing softly, evenly. "Nothing wrong with her conscience," Duke said.

"She's good for hours. It's that booze. Don't worry, I'll get her up when you've gone."

"That's right. We're moving when I get back."

"With your brother?"

"We're taking him, sure," Duke said. "We'll stop in town, let folks see him. That will keep anybody from coming out here and nosing around."

"Okay. You'd better get going."

"I found a nice spot for it," Duke said. "A hundred-foot drop, straight into water."

"There's no point talking about it."

Duke smiled faintly. "I get the nice jobs, don't I?"

"Why talk about it?"

"The water is deep there," Duke said. He knew Grant was ready to fly apart; his eyes were bright with tension. "They won't find the car for days."

Grant wet his lips. "The engine number is a phoney, the plates are registered to a John Doe in Seattle, Washington. They can't ever trace it."

"Sure, there's nothing to worry about," Duke said, smiling at the sickly sheen on Grant's face. "But maybe you'd like to handle this last job yourself. Just to make sure. Just to make sure you'll get back to Donovan's."

"No—no, you go ahead."

"You're sure you trust me?"

Grant's smile tightened the lines of fear in his face. "Don't clown around," he said. "You go ahead."

"Okay, be ready to go when I get back. We'll use Hank's car. Understand?"

Grant nodded quickly, then closed the door and leaned against it, his breath coming in deep laboring gasps. He heard Duke moving toward the girl's room, then the rap of his knuckles and the protesting creak of a door hinge.

She must have been waiting for him, he thought. Standing there with the kid in her arms. They were coming down the hall now, the tap of her high heels sounding a light accompaniment to Duke's dragging footsteps. As they started down the stairs Duke said something to her, his voice good-humored and cheerful. Grant knew from the cautious sound of her steps that she was carrying the baby. . . .

When Grant heard the door close behind them he shook Belle's shoulder. "Come on, time to be going," he said. "Come on, let's go." He was surprised at the casual note he was able to put into his voice. It would be all over in twenty or thirty minutes, he thought, as he heard the car turning over protestingly in the cold morning silence.

"Come on," he said again.

"All right, Eddie. You want some breakfast?"

"Just coffee. We'll eat on the road. Come on."

"I'm awake, honest." Her voice was thick with sleep. "I'll be down in a few minutes."

"All right, don't go back to sleep, hear?"

When the door closed Belle sat up quickly and swung her legs over the side of the bed. For an instant she felt as if she might be sick; her flesh was cold, and a nauseating knot of fear had gathered her stomach. "God!" she whispered, staring at the closed door. "Why did I hear it? Why did I have to know?"

But she did know. She hadn't been sleeping; she had heard the conversation between Duke and Grant and she knew the baby was going to die. After all Eddie had promised . . . They mustn't do it, they couldn't, she thought, as she pulled on a robe and stepped into her slippers. But from the driveway she heard the powerful, accelerating roar of the car as it swung toward the road. Turning to the right. . . .

And from downstairs Grant shouted, "Damn it, are you up, Belle?"

"Yes, I'm coming." The roar of the motor was fading away, but the echoes seemed to be growing louder in her mind. And Grant's voice was a deafening, menacing sound in the silent house; the combination beat with a confusing clamor against her ears. Belle stepped into the hallway, drawing the belt of her robe tightly around her body. To her right she saw the open door of the room the nurse and baby had been using. She saw a baby's empty bottle on the bureau, a small square can of powder on the night table. Tears started in her eyes.

"Belle!"

"I'm coming, Eddie. Stop yelling."

She went quickly down the stairs, holding one hand tightly against her body. "Look what you made me do with your yelling," she said. "I burned myself trying to light a cigarette. Oh, *damn* it," she moaned, turning away from him and pressing the hand deeply into her side. She had gone this far, done this much without thinking or planning; her actions had been automatic, a reflexive response to the sight of the baby bottle and powder can in the nurse's room. They couldn't kill a little baby. . . .

"Well, let's see it," Grant said. "Hell, a match burn couldn't be that bad."

"Let's see, let's see! A lot of good looking will do. It's not bad! No, *you* can't feel a thing, naturally. It's my hand."

"Don't blow a fuse. We got things to do."

"Yeah, I'm supposed to cook and pack and everything else now."

"Is there anything around here good for a burn? How about baking soda?"

"Baking soda is for hangovers. I saw a tube of Unguentine in the bathroom. Get it for me, honey. Oh, *damn!* What are you always yelling for?"

"All right, all *right*," Grant said. "Let's get it fixed up, and then let's get to work."

"Sure, sure," Belle waited until his footsteps sounded above her, and then she turned and ran into the kitchen, her breath coming in whimpering little gasps. The door leading to the basement was stuck, and she began to weep, pulling at it, trying to control her mounting terror. Finally she saw the key. Locked, she thought, and her relief was giddy, hysterical. Only locked. . . . Turning the key, she opened the door and clattered down the steps, swaying precipitously and crazily on her high-heeled mules. From a tiny window at ground level a shaft of light fell onto the cement floor and spread ineffectually toward the dark corners of the basement. There was only one door in sight, solid and old, secured with an iron bar, a hasp and padlock. The key was in the lock. . . .

She slipped the lock from the hasp and let the iron bar drop to the floor. The door was pushed open violently, almost upsetting her, and Hank came out in a crouch, his left hand ready to strike.

"No, no," she said, backing away from him. "Duke's gone with the baby. He's going to kill her. Eddie said they wouldn't. He kept saying that all the time."

"Where's Grant?"

"I sent him upstairs for a minute. But hurry! You've got to hurry. Before he comes down. The car turned right. I heard it turn right. Your car is still here. Go after him. Tell him he can't do it."

Hank picked up the iron bar in his left hand and started up the steps to the kitchen. He would have to go out the front door; Duke had the keys to the back door and the kitchen windows had been nailed shut. He was conscious strangely of a sense of no-consciousness; he wasn't thinking, planning, hoping, fearing. A stiff strand of blood-matted hair fell down over his forehead, and the pain in his right hand was like smouldering fire. But he was hardly aware of these things.

In the kitchen he stopped for an instant, staring into the living room. Belle was coming up the stairs behind him, panting heavily, and this was the only sound in the house. Should he tiptoe toward the front door? Or make a run for it? Better to take it naturally; Grant would assume the footsteps were Belle's.

He moved into the living room, staring at the front door, estimating the time it would take to start the car rolling—and then a voice beside him said, "Drop it, Junior. Drop it fast!" Hank turned, feeling the heavy, sickening stroke of his heart as Grant came toward him, his big pale face tense with fear and anger. "Drop it, goddam you," he yelled suddenly. "What do you think I'm talking to you for?"

Belle stopped in the doorway, a little scream of terror breaking past her dry lips. "Eddie, Eddie, don't! There's been enough—don't."

Grant stared at her, his big chest rising and falling slowly. "You let him out! You gave him the chance to put me in the chair. That's what you did. That's how you pay me back."

"You said you wouldn't hurt the baby!" Tears trembled in her swollen eyes. "You said that, Eddie, over and over. Didn't you, Eddie?"

"Go ahead, shoot both of us," Hank said, his voice low and savage. The iron bar swung at his side. "You killed Adam Wilson. Duke's going to kill the nurse and baby. So you kill us. You're in the wholesale business now."

"Shut up, I'm warning you."

"Go to hell! You're nothing now. You'll be dead in three weeks. You think you can beat this? You think you can kill five people and drive away like a summer tourist? What kind of a fool are you?"

"Eddie, he's right. Help him to stop Duke. That's your only chance."

"Shut up!" Grant shouted, his body trembling with impotent fury. "We had this deal made. Creasy's got the money, you hear that?" Grant sounded as if he were strangling on the words; they came out thick and swollen from his straining throat. "He called us, he's got the money. No hitches, nothing. We were ready to leave when Duke got back. And you threw it all away. You crazy, sniveling bitch, you threw it all away. The only thing I ever wanted, the only thing. . . ."

"You're the crazy one!" Belle was sobbing now. "All you wanted to do was go back to the steak house like a big shot. Nothing else counted. You're the crazy one!"

"Belle, don't—"

"It's the truth! It's all you wanted. Just walking into Donovan's, or whatever it's called, and pretending you were a big shot again. Pretending you were never in jail, and that you were fifteen years younger. Duke knew it. You didn't want the money from this job, you didn't want to make a life for you and me—you just wanted to make an entrance and order drinks like some down-homer in town with a bankroll." Belle brushed a tear from her cheek. "Why didn't you just go to an easy-loan outfit and borrow a couple of hundred bucks? That would pay for ten minutes at Donovan's, wouldn't it? Instead you kidnap a baby and kill people you never saw before in your life. Crazy! You're the crazy one. You probably couldn't get a table at Donovan's. Those years in jail happened, Eddie. You're old. You can't change that by dreaming and doing exercises. You're like old chorus girls who're always torching for guys who gave them flowers thirty years back, old bags nobody wanted to—" Belle's voice faltered. She took a step backward shaking her head slowly. "No, I didn't mean that, Eddie. No, Eddie, you can't—"

Grant was swearing at her then, softly and mechanically, and when the gun jumped twice in his hand, he was still swearing, spitting the words into the sudden terrible pain in her eyes.

And when she staggered and fell, whimpering his name into the floor, he was still cursing her in a weary, hopeless voice.

Hank stepped toward him, raising the iron bar. Grant tried to bring the gun around, but his face blurred with surprise and fear as he saw that he was going to be too late. "No!" he shouted, but Hank was on top of him then, the bar swinging viciously at his head. The blow landed just below Grant's temple, and it drove him down to his knees. Hank didn't wait for him to fall; he knew from the impact that he wouldn't get up for a long time.

He picked up Grant's gun and knelt beside Belle. She was lying in a widening pool of blood. "Baby," he heard her say. She was staring at Grant's closed eyes; their faces were only inches apart. "Eddie, baby, I shouldn't have—about Donovan's. I shouldn't have said that. They'd know you—" She tried to finish the sentence but the words died in her throat, died with her; tears stood out brightly on her chalk-white face.

Hank touched her shoulder, and then he stood and ran for his car. Duke had turned right, she'd said. He thought he knew where Duke was going. . . .

# 22

DUKE DROVE SLOWLY ALONG THE GRAVEL-TOPPED ROAD THAT FOLLOWED the curving coast line. It was seven o'clock, and the flat, blue water was sparkling in the hot, brilliant sunlight. The early morning mists were lifting from the green fields, and the breeze off the sea was fresh and clean and cool.

Duke lit a cigarette and inhaled deeply, savoring the satisfying bite of the smoke in his lungs. Another few miles, he thought. He held out the pack to the girl. "You want one of these?"

She sat beside him in the front seat, holding the sleeping baby in her arms. "No," she said. He glanced at her and saw that she was staring straight ahead, her eyes dark and wide in her pale face. "Where are you taking us?" she said.

"Just up the road aways."

"You don't have to kill the baby," she said. "She could never cause you any trouble."

So she knows, he thought, taking a long pull on his cigarette. Duke didn't like the job ahead of him. But it would be over fast, at least; a blow at the back of her neck, that was all. Then let the car go over and down—

way down—taking both of them with it. Fast . . . thirty seconds at the
most. His concern puzzled him. He wasn't used to reflection. How was he
going to feel afterward? Well—he'd know soon enough.

"You don't have to kill her," she said, watching him.

"Who said anything about killing her?"

"You think if we're found together—the police won't look for anyone
else. Isn't that it?"

"That idea crossed my mind," Duke said dryly. He glanced at her,
then back to the road. It was such a damned waste. He could see her
legs reflected in the windshield, slim and beautiful, the color of honey in
the sunlight.

"Please listen to me," she said.

"Why sure." He frowned slightly, knowing from the tone of her voice
that she was going to beg. She had come alive suddenly; all the weary
resignation was gone. Every cell in her body was fighting . . .

"You could trust me," she said.

"I don't see how."

"You wanted me the other day, didn't you?"

That brought a small smile to his lips. "You're pretty observant, eh?"

"I'll go anywhere with you—be anything you want me to be."

"Now don't start fussing. It's too late, don't you see?"

"No—listen to me. Let me take the baby home. I'll say you dropped us
off somewhere—anywhere."

"I'd come through as quite a gent, wouldn't I?" Duke said. "They'd
probably even dust off the seat of the chair before strapping me into it."

"No, no! I'd say I never saw you, never saw anyone. Then—later—I'd
come to you, anywhere you wanted me to. I swear that, I swear that to
God."

Duke smiled slightly. Like all the women he'd ever known—when they
wanted something badly they put the body on the block. What a funny
kind of conceit! Their sacred goddam bodies. . . .

"You'd like to live with me, eh?" He smiled at the reflection of her
legs in the windshield. It was a crazy idea, but not impossible. Nothing
was. . . .

"I'll stay with you as long as you want me. Just let me take the baby
home. Just let her live."

"You don't have to take her home. We could leave her right here on
the road, or near a village." It could work out, he thought. She was a
Catholic. They kept their words. . . . A laugh bubbled up suddenly in
him. Supposing they pulled it off—and the two of them dropped in casually
on Grant some day. In Mexico maybe. Duke struck the steering wheel
with the flat of his hand. He'd have a hemorrhage!

Duke realized that he was quite drunk. He blinked his eyes, focusing
them on the sunny road that stretched ahead of him through the green

fir trees. This was a surprise; liquor had never affected him this way
before. He sat up straighter, hunching over the wheel. They weren't
home free yet. Caution was instinctive with him; he had an uncanny flair
for danger.

"I would be good to you," she said.

"Don't oversell it."

"I know I would."

Duke was pained by her innocence; she sounded like a teen-ager
ordering a double shot—covering fear with boldness. But this was what
had attracted him to her in the first place.

"What would you do for me?" he said. "Let's hear your sales talk. I
like details."

"You know," she said, so softly that he barely heard the words. But
he heard the shame in her voice, and saw the rising color in her cheeks.

In the rear vision mirror the road stretched straight as a string behind
him. He slowed down, watching the mirror, seeing nothing but the fine
dust spun into the air by his tires. The motor idled gently in the silence.
A crow flew over them, crying an insistent warning. They were good sport,
Duke thought, watching the bird's arrowlike flight. Great wing-shooting.
If you could hunt crows, you could hunt anything. If men came back as
birds, an old Indian had told him, damn few of them would be smart
enough to be crows.

Duke smiled at the girl. "We might have fun, you know," he said.

"I—I'd please you."

"Sure you would." He squeezed her knee lightly, and saw the darkness
of his hand against her white flesh. She wasn't wearing stockings and her
skin was soft and smooth as a flower petal under his fingers. "You mind
this?" he said.

"No—no, I don't mind."

"You'll strain yourself with all that enthusiasm." Was it worth it? he
wondered.

From down the road he heard the sound of a car or truck, throbbing
faintly against the silence. Duke stepped on the starter, frowning into the
sunlight.

"Will you let her live?" the girl said.

"Just a minute. I'll think it over." He patted her knee again, without
taking his eyes from the road. "We could have fun, eh?"

Duke went into a curve and when he came out of it there was a truck
ahead of him attempting a turn in the narrow road, blocking his way
completely. He touched the brake with his foot and said, "Take it nice
and easy now. I'm thinking about your idea."

Duke stopped about twenty yards from the truck and looked out the
window. The driver was pulling the steering wheel around, working

swiftly and efficiently. He waved to Duke and called, "Be out of your way in a second."

"No hurry, take your time."

"Thanks. I should have turned at the crossroads." He was young, his cheerful handsome face shadowed by a visored cap.

Duke lit another cigarette and glanced up at the rear vision mirror. Everything looked quiet and peaceful. Somewhere in the brilliant sky above him he heard the faint drone of an airplane, a purring sound under the churning roar of the truck's engine.

Duke sat up straighter behind the wheel, his eyes narrowing under his thick, black brows. "Honeybun Bakery," he murmured, reading the sign on the red and white sides of the truck. "Deliveries every day. Life in the country is getting real cushy."

Duke's voice was casual, almost bored, but all of his senses were sharp and alert. When he had driven away from the lodge a half hour ago a man had been fishing the little lake near John Adam's house. There was nothing especially significant in this; it might have been old John, or one of his neighbors. At two hundred yards he couldn't pick out details. All he'd seen was the silhouette of a man in waders against the pink and gray sky. But it was the first time anyone had been around that early in the morning. He leaned out the window and peered up at the sky, searching for the airplane. What had the crow seen? he wondered. Crying a warning to the nests . . . a man in the fields carrying a gun maybe. Not a farmer then . . . not this early.

Duke stared at the truck. "Honeybun Bakery. Cute name, eh?"

"Yes—yes, of course."

"Kind of square though. Come on, let's talk. If we're going to see a lot of each other we've got to talk. We can't go around like zombies. And how about trying a smile on for size."

"Yes—"

"That's better."

The truck's motor sputtered and died, and in the silence that followed Duke listened to a bird singing in a nearby tree and to the far-off beating sound of the airplane. The truck driver was shaking his head. He pressed the starter and the motor began to grind, turning over and over, monotonously, futilely.

"I think I flooded it," he called to Duke.

"Give it a few minutes. It'll be okay."

"I'm sorry as the devil."

"Don't worry about it."

The driver climbed down from the cab and strolled toward them, pushing his cap up on his forehead. A college boy, Duke thought, noting the blond crew-cut, the bland, good-looking, evenly tanned face. An athlete probably; he was nicely put together and moved with a natural, swinging

grace. Tennis or track maybe. Not football. He didn't look solid enough.
Duke sighed, depressed for some reason by the boy's youth. I had more
to start with than he's got, he thought. I was bigger and faster, and a hell
of a lot tougher. All-State as a sophomore. Nobody had ever done that
before me. If I'd gone on to Minnesota or Purdue my name would be
right alongside those great ones from the Big Ten. The Purvis brothers,
Jim and Duane, Pug Lund, Beattie Feathers, Nagurski, Berwanger from
Chicago . . . fans still talked about them. But if he'd gone on playing
they'd mention him first. Duke Farrel! Why did it all go wrong?

The youngster stopped beside the car and looked at them with an
embarrassed little smile. When he saw the girl he took off his cap. "I'm
sorry to delay you like this."

"Don't worry about it," Duke said. He saw that the young man's forehead was smoothly tanned—all the way up to the roots of his short,
healthy hair. There was no line marking the rim of his cap. Normally,
if you wore a cap in the sun, half of your forehead stayed white. . . .
Normally.

"I'll take a break and stretch my legs," Duke said. His body had
responded instantly to challenge; every muscle was ready for trouble.
"We've got a great day," he said, stepping into the road.

"Sure thing. Can't beat it. How about a smoke?"

"Well, no thanks. Just finished one."

They were standing about three feet apart, their eyes narrowed as
they smiled into the brilliant sunshine. "I'll bet you played tennis in
school," Duke said, as the young man's hand moved casually toward his
back pocket.

"No, track was my sport. The eight-eighty."

"Some difference," Duke grinned.

The young man's hand came up from his pocket and the gun he held
was not much bigger than a pack of playing cards. "Don't move!" he
said, and his voice was suddenly hard and sharp with authority.

But the command came a fraction of a second too late; Duke was
already moving. He struck downward with vicious force, and the edge of
his hand chopped across the young man's rising wrist—snapping a bone
and sending the gun flying into the dirt at their feet. "Tennis player!"
Duke yelled, caught in a furious, senseless anger.

The young man lunged at him, swinging for his jaw with his good
hand, but Duke slipped the punch and struck him twice, once in the body
and once in the face, and the blows drove him to his knees. "Lot of
spirit, eh?" Duke said, as the man tried to grab him about the waist.
"Dead game college kid!" He slapped his arms away and hit him again
in the face, putting all his strength and anger behind the blow. The
young man went over backwards and rolled to the side of the road, his
body flopping like a rag doll's in the dust. Duke picked up the little toy

of a gun and dropped it into his pocket. He was breathing hard, and his heart pounded insistently against his ribs. It felt as big and solid as a bowling ball inside him, crowding everything else out of place. Booze, he thought, looking at the limp body lying in the road. Too much of it . . . But I still do all right. I still haven't met the guy I can't take.

He turned around and said, "Wise young punk—" and there he stopped, the grin fading from his face, staring at the empty car. She was gone. Duke stood listening, an ear turning to the wind. There was no place she could go. . . . Finally he heard her, in the woods to his left, running, heading toward the sea. He hesitated a moment, staring into the sky, listening to the plane. The cops were in it—which meant they'd been in it all along. It was everybody for himself now. Duke glanced up and down the empty road and then hopped the ditch that ran beside it, and melted into the green darkness of the woods. He could hear her ahead of him, running.

# 23

HANK HIT THE BRAKE AS HE CAME OUT OF THE CURVE AND SAW DUKE'S car and the bakery truck parked sideways across the road. The skidding tires shot gravel through the air; he was almost hidden by the dust as he climbed out and crouched beside the car.

The countryside hummed with drowsy, commonplace sounds; a bird called plaintively from the low branches of a fir tree, and off to his right came the steady, sighing wash of the sea. When the dust settled he moved slowly toward Duke's car, holding Grant's gun in his hand, checking both sides of the road with his eyes. Then, from the direction of the sea, he heard a faint, indistinct cry. The bird flew from the branch chattering with angry excitement. Hank turned to the sound, listening for a second or so, and then he crossed the ditch beside the road and entered the woods at a scrambling run. Someone was moving ahead of him—not more than thirty or forty yards away—and he took his bearing on the dry noise of crackling leaves and branches.

He traveled a straight course, ignoring the branches and underbrush that cut and tore at his legs. Once he fell, his foot sinking six inches into bog mud, and he went down again when a ropy vine whipped around his ankle.

At the edge of the trees a shelf of rock jutted out high above the water and formed a small clearing. He was close to it now; already he could see tiny patches of blue sky glinting like decorations in the branches of the trees. He knew it was the girl running ahead of him; if it were Duke he wouldn't have heard him—Duke made no more noise in the woods than a snake.

A sudden fear went through Hank, and he stopped short, staring about at the green shadows. Where was Duke? The fear grew in him as he lowered himself carefully to his knees, trying to control the sound of his heavy breathing. Where was his brother? He could hear the girl plainly; she was fifteen or twenty yards away, hidden by a screen of trees. She had stopped running; beyond the clearing that faced the sea, there was nowhere else to run. But he could hear the sound of her weeping, and the sound of the whimpering baby.

Where was Duke? Never where you expected him to be. Always ready to strike when your back was turned. He needed the girl and baby as hostages; that would occur to him inevitably. They were his only chance of getting clear. But he wouldn't go directly to them. No . . . he'd wait to see who might be following.

Hank crawled back toward the road on his hands and knees, moving with infinite caution. After a dozen yards or so, he swung out on a wide circle to his left, traveling faster now, moving through the shadows in a half crouch; his body was hidden by the thick underbrush, and he picked patches of soft, moist earth to cushion his footsteps.

A moment later he approached the clearing once more—from the side now—following the rocky, curving shore line. Scrub firs grew thickly along the coast, and the sunlight was caught and held in the fine network of thick green branches. Turning a bend in the trail, Hank stopped suddenly, all of his muscles tightening spasmodically; Duke was standing with his back to him just a dozen feet away, motionless in the shadow of a tree. He was staring into the clearing, and in the silence Hank heard his deep, labored breathing. That sound had covered his approach. Duke held a gun in his hand, a tiny weapon not much bigger than a pack of cigarettes.

"Drop it, Duke!" Hank said. "Drop it fast!"

"Kid?" Duke's voice was low and amused; he didn't turn around. "Is that you, kid?"

"Drop it, Duke. Drop it, or I'll shoot."

"I was waiting for you, kid." The gun slipped from his fingers and he turned slowly and looked at Hank. In the clearing beyond them they could hear the girl's sobs.

"Go back to the road," Hank called to her. "Go back to the road and wait there. It's all right."

"Sure, it's all right," Duke said, watching him with an ironical little smile. "I let her go. She's okay. So is the baby. I told you they wouldn't be hurt." He jerked his head toward the clearing. "She thinks a big scene is expected now, that's all. You know how dames are, kid." In spite of the smile Duke's face looked weary and old; a two-day beard smudged and coarsened his jawline, and his eyes were narrowed against the light filtering through the trees. He leaned against a tree trunk and hooked his thumbs carelessly on his belt. His red flannel shirt was open at the throat, and the sunlight glinted on the black hair springing up from his deep chest. "How did you get out?" he said. "Belle let you go, eh?"

He was guessing, Hank knew; shrewdly and accurately. But guessing. . . . He said nothing and Duke shrugged lightly. "I figured it would be that way. That's why I waited for you. I let her go, kid, and waited for you."

"Fine," Hank said. "We'll both wait now. For the cops."

"They were in it all along, I guess," Duke said dryly. "Grant and his big brain." He lifted a hand suddenly; in the distance they could hear cars approaching at high speed, the motors wailing through the soft green silence of the woods. "The boys in buttons," Duke said. "The heroes."

Hank heard the girl moving away from them, pushing her way through the underbrush on the opposite side of the clearing—taking the baby toward the road.

"Kid, we've got to do some thinking," Duke said quietly. "What happened at the lodge?"

"You guessed it. Belle let me out. She's dead now. The police probably have Grant. You're next."

"Kid, it doesn't have to be that way," Duke said gently. "Don't you see? With Belle dead we can pin the whole job on Grant." He took a limping step toward Hank, his face and voice hardening with excitement. "Listen: everybody's going to talk. Talk a mile a minute. The girl, Grant, Creasy—he handled the New York end for us and picked up the dough. But there're two of us. If we stick together we can laugh at them. You and me, the Farrel brothers. That's the way the old man would want it to be."

"Is that what he'd want?" Hank said coldly. "A couple of sons lying to the cops?"

"It's our necks, kid. We can pile this whole thing on Grant." Duke turned toward the approaching cars, and Hank saw the tendons straining in the powerful column of his throat. "We can say he forced us into it, and that we waited for a chance to jump him." He stared at his brother again, his big hands opening and closing slowly. "You got to help me, kid. We need a simple story. Nothing fancy. And then we've got to stick to it. You understand? No matter what happens, we stick to that story."

"Tell any story you like," Hank said. "I'll be there to say you're lying."

Duke let out his breath slowly. "Sure, there's no sense in jamming yourself up for me," he said bitterly. "You're in the clear. But do you want to see me killed?" He took another step toward Hank, and wet his dry lips.

"Listen: give me a start on them. That's not asking much. If I can get down to the water and find a boat I'll have a chance. I can live all summer in the woods. I'm begging now, kid. I don't want to stand trial." Duke was breathing heavily. "You know what that means? People looking at me like I'm an animal, a judge ripping me up and down for the benefit of the newspapers and the slobs on the jury getting their kicks by sending me to the chair. Knock-kneed little punks and sour women that no guy ever wanted—having a ball thinking about me being strapped down and split wide open with five thousand volts of electricity. That's what it's like, kid. Can you blame me for wanting to make a break for it? To go out clean and fast?" He shook his head quickly. "Kid, this isn't some stranger talking to you," he said in a desperate, pleading voice. The wind had blown a tangle of hair over his forehead, and his eyes were hard and bright in his shining face. "This is Duke, your brother. I taught you to swim, remember. I lent you dough for dates. There wasn't a guy in town would lay a finger on you because you were my kid brother. You got to remember that, kid. I'm not some character you met at a bar. I'm your brother. And I'm crawling now, begging for a break."

"Ask somebody else for a break," Hank said. "Ask the jury."

Duke took a dragging step toward him, his hands swinging out from his sides. "You little bastard," he said savagely. The change in him was abrupt and violent; he moved forward slowly, his eyes bright with fury. "You're a rabbit trying to act like a man. That's all you ever were." He slapped his bad leg with the palm of his hand, and the sound was like a pistol shot in the stillness. "That's your work, remember. Now you want the cops to finish me. But think again. A gun won't help you. I'm going to shove it down your throat. You'll do your squealing without teeth."

"Don't try," Hank said quietly.

Duke lunged at him, his right arm swinging in a long arc, but the speed and power were gone from his body; as close as he was, Hank was able to slip the punch, and Duke lost his footing and sprawled awkwardly onto the slick mossy earth. Swearing hoarsely, he struggled to his feet and started for Hank again, purposefully and slowly now, his big fists swinging low at his sides.

"Rabbit," he said, breathing harshly. "Put yourself back together again, eh? Piece by piece, like a building made out of matches. Well, I'm going to knock you apart for good."

Hank shook his head slowly. With no particular feeling, he pulled the trigger and shot Duke just above his right kneecap. The report of the gun crashed through the woods, chasing eerie echoes before it; the noise almost smothered Duke's surprised shout of pain. He leaped toward Hank, swearing wildly, but when he landed the leg buckled under him and he sprawled forward on his face. Lashing out spasmodically with his good leg, he began to curse in a high, raging voice.

Hank stepped away from him and checked the gun to make sure there was another round in the chamber. The cars had stopped on the road not more than fifty or sixty yards from them. He heard commands snapped in a clear, sharp voice and then the sound of men moving into the woods.

Duke had worked himself up to a sitting position. He stared at the blood staining his trouser leg and shook his head slowly as if he couldn't quite understand what had happened to him; the conviction of his own invulnerability had always been his strongest faith. "It hurts like hell," he said finally, looking up at Hank. A frown shadowed his dark eyes, and he seemed to be having difficulty getting enough air into his lungs. "You hit the bad leg, at least," he said, with a bitter, pain-tight smile. "Should I say thanks for that?"

There was nothing Hank wanted to say; it was over and done, and that's all there was to it.

Duke picked up a few loose pebbles from the ground and began to toss them up and down in the palm of his hand. He watched them as they bounced aimlessly in the air, oblivious to Hank now, oblivious to everything. "I never thought it would be like this," he said. "It's funny. I could have been anything. Anything at all." He stared away into the green shadows of the woods and his voice was low and wistful. Sighing, he tossed the pebbles aside and looked up again at his brother. "You're going to have a lot to live with, kid."

"I'll live with it," Hank said. "Don't worry." He felt infinitely weary. This was maturity for him, growing up; to realize that he owed himself and the world just as much as he owed his brother.

"Don't count me out yet," Duke said. A grin touched his lips. "I can beat this thing. They won't send a cripple to the chair. I know how to handle people. There won't be a dry eye in that courtroom. You watch."

Yes, he's probably right, Hank thought, staring at the secretive little smile growing on his brother's face. Strangers might weep for him. But I can't. Not any more. I have no tears left for him. He believed this, staring at his brother's face. But when the men with shotguns broke into the clearing he knew it wasn't true. . . .

# 24

AT EIGHT O'CLOCK THAT MORNING CREASY PICKED HIS WAY DOWN THE steps of his rooming house, one hand maintaining a cautious grip on the brim of his old-fashioned bowler. It was the start of a cheerful spring day, sunny and clear, but a lusty wind was blowing down the block, scattering refuse in the gutters and sending little eddies of dust spiraling into the air.

Creasy's mood was benign and mellow. Everything was over now; before him stretched a calm interval for reassessment and recapitulation. Grant had told him to follow his usual routine and wait for further instructions. He hadn't mentioned the baby and the nurse, but undoubtedly plans had been made for them; Grant had sounded confident and cheerful. Everybody was safe then; Grant and Duke and Belle were probably a couple of hundred miles from the lodge by now.

Creasy glanced casually at the Bradleys' as he stopped to smooth worn gray suède gloves over the backs of his thin hands. A black car had parked in front of their house and a young man in a gabardine topcoat and a snap-brim hat had gone inside. The driver had remained behind the wheel. Creasy had seen this from the windows of his room. But he wasn't curious about the waiting car, or the man who had gone into the Bradleys'; the Bradleys no longer interested him particularly. They were like shipboard acquaintances, he thought; drawn together interestingly for a time, but now going their separate ways, busy with other pursuits and activities. Other activities . . . Yes, indeed. He had already made a complete check of the Winthrops in his files.

This was *au revoir*, he thought, smiling at the clean, handsome façade of the Bradleys' home. Savoring the moment, enjoying its ceremonial flavor, Creasy didn't notice the car that was parked a dozen yards from him on the same side of the block. Four men stepped out while Creasy stood on the sidewalk, smiling and smoothing on his gloves. They sauntered toward him casually, fanning out to approach him from three angles.

Roth reached him first. Creasy felt a hand close on the lapel of his overcoat, and at the same instant he became aware of a man on either side of him, and the powerful hands gripping his arms. Creasy stared up into a face that might have been carved from iron.

"You're under arrest," Roth said.

"I say—this is some mistake." Creasy felt himself trembling helplessly. "I'm hardly the sort—" He began to titter; his thoughts were suddenly spinning in a dizzy fashion. "Well, I should think that's obvious. Gentlemen aren't accustomed to—well, we'll say no more about it, eh? I shan't file a complaint. Rather a good joke, actually. Mistake . . ."

"Let's go," Roth said, nodding at the men who held Creasy's arms.

"Now see here!" Creasy suddenly started and blinked his eyes; the street was full of leaping shadows. Moving—yes, moving like quicksilver, twisting with bewildering speed into intricate and strangely ominous designs. He laughed triumphantly; this was what he had always expected, the shadows and the enemies. He had been right. Yes, indeed.

The Bradleys were leaving their house, he saw, hurrying to the car parked at the curb. They moved through the shadows as if they weren't there, protected and shielded by their magic circles of youth, beauty and money. She was truly beautiful now, pale and drawn, refined by pain, all the dross consumed by the cleansing fire. Creasy tried to wave to her, but he found that he couldn't raise his arms. "They're friends of mine," he said petulantly. "A fine old family. We're quite good friends." He struggled helplessly against the hands that carried him toward the car. "She's a nobody, of course. But we're friends. I've called on them. You don't believe that, do you?"

"We'll talk about it later," Roth said. His face was still hard, but his voice had changed slightly; he saw the sickness in Creasy's face and eyes. "Let's go now."

"Yes, of course." Creasy was smiling slyly now; they didn't realize that he was wealthy—that was *his* little joke. The suitcase full of money belonged to him, and it represented a permanent barrier against rudeness and insult. He would put these vulgar fools in their place, oh, yes indeed. But not yet. Give them a bit more rope . . . Creasy was beginning to laugh as they put him into the car. It was so funny he didn't know how he would ever stop.

On the sidewalk across the street Ellie Bradley was looking up at Crowley. She hadn't seen Creasy's arrest; Crowley had spotted Roth, and had stepped in front of her just as he had closed in on Creasy. Ellie had been crying; her face was streaked with tears, but her eyes were radiant —clear and incredibly happy.

"I can't say good-by properly now," she said, holding his arms with both hands. "Will you come over tonight? With your wife? I want you to see Jill. Will you?"

"Yes, I'll call you," he said, smiling at her. "Now hop in. Your baby's waiting for you."

"And so is yours," she said. "We can't ever be grateful enough, can we?"

"I don't see how."

"Okay, honey," Dick Bradley said, touching her arm. He was waiting for her at the side of the car. The driver had already started the motor.

"Yes, yes," she said, in a voice that was trembling with eager excitement.

She turned and climbed into the rear of the car. Bradley grinned and shook hands with Crowley. "You'll call us? For sure?"

"For sure," Crowley said.

The car moved away from the curb, gathering speed as it headed toward Third Avenue. Ellie looked out the rear window and blew him a kiss, as the driver swung into the intersection.

Crowley waved a good-by to them. He stood there for a few seconds, smiling faintly at the early morning serenity of the street; trucks and cabs went by on their way to the new day and there were children playing in front of the old brownstones down the block. Women walked toward the avenues with shopping bags folded over their arms, and on the landings of fire escapes a few old men were soaking up the thin spring sunlight.

Crowley lit a cigarette and flipped the match toward the curb. He buttoned the top button on his shirt and pulled up the knot of his tie. Still smiling faintly, he glanced up at the massive black door of the Bradleys' home. Inside another agent was on duty, tidying up loose ends. Crowley's job was over. The tension of the last three days was flowing out of him and a bone-deep tiredness was settling in; he felt very weary, very eager to be home. Taking a deep drag from his cigarette, he walked to the curb and waved down a cruising cab.

# 25

INSPECTOR WEST HAD USED THE OFFICE OF SHERIFF DAVIS AS HIS HEAD-quarters during the tense, exhausting day. Now it was almost dark and he was relaxing for a few moments at the sheriff's desk. In the square below him groups of people stood talking in the gathering dusk; he could hear the faint murmur of their voices, see the flare of their cigarettes in the deep gloom. They were discussing the kidnaping, he knew; no one in Williamsboro had talked about anything else that day. The village had been swamped by newspapermen, photographers, television crews; the wire services and big dailies had flown in reporters, and mobile TV units had been cruising through the streets all day long, covering every detail they could get a camera on. Anyone who had been in contact with the kidnapers had become exciting and newsworthy; the druggist, the grocery clerk, friends and relatives of the dead Adam Wilson—they had been interviewed, quoted, photographed, their likenesses and comments preserved forever on tapes and film.

West had held two press conferences, and had faced TV cameras every time he stepped from his office into the corridors of the courthouse. These were chores, irksome but necessary; the public had first rights to the story now. But there was also a vast amount of work to be done—fingerprints, photographs, personal inventories—the routine but exhaustive processing of the prisoners. And their stories had to be checked and rechecked, the contradictions examined from every possible perspective. Leads had to be run down, fast; this morning West hadn't been able to assume that he had caught all the kidnap mob in one bag. There might be a lookout, a courier, a pickup man, still free, and he didn't intend to give anyone a chance to run for cover.

This work had gone on at a furious, orderly pace, but now, at last, things were blessedly quiet for a few minutes. The clerks had gone home, his agents were out for dinner, and even the reporters and TV crews had drifted away from their posts in the corridor. The sheriff's second floor suite was calm and peaceful, and West sighed as he lit a cigarette and shifted into a comfortable position in the swivel chair. But the door to the inner office opened a moment or so later, and Hank Farrel walked into the room.

West smiled at him. "Pretty short nap."

"There's not much point trying to sleep," Hank said.

"You've been churning along at about three times normal speed for quite a while. It takes time to slow down. How about a cigarette?"

"Thanks." Hank sat down slowly and rubbed a hand over his forehead. He was completely spent, but he wasn't able to sleep. The doctor had given him a sedative half an hour ago, and West had told him to stretch out on the sofa in the sheriff's inner office. But sleep hadn't come; he had lain staring at the dark ceiling, keeping a vigil with his thoughts. This day had been the longest of his life. They had dressed his injured hand, and then listened to his story—not once or twice, but twenty times. Fifty. . . . They had checked his statement point by point, cross-examining him on each detail. Not merely to trip him up, he knew; they wanted to be sure he hadn't been involved in the kidnaping. Eventually they had accepted his story; the girl's testimony had supported his statement fully and exactly. And Grant had talked. . . .

"Is there any reason I can't go home?" he said.

"I don't see why not."

"Are the reporters still out there?"

"No, you won't be bothered. Your car is parked in back of the courthouse. I think you can get away without posing for any more pictures."

"Fine. Were there any calls for me?"

"There was a message from Mr. Bradley," West said. "He's grateful, which is putting it about as mildly as possible. He wants to talk to you, up here or in New York, at your convenience. And on the same subject, let me say I'm grateful, too, Hank. You had a very tough job and you handled it perfectly."

"Thanks," Hank said, getting to his feet. He felt awkward and stiff. "And there were no other calls?"

"No."

She had said she would call him—here or out at the lodge. When she had a minute . . . They hadn't spoken more than a dozen words this morning. West had listened to their stories and then she and the baby had been driven out to the airport to meet the Bradleys. But before that she had crossed to him and put a hand on his arm. She had said she would call him, as soon as she could. . . .

"There's one favor I'd like to ask," Hank said.

West sighed and came around his desk. "I can guess," he said. "You want to see your brother."

"Yes—can I?"

"Sure, but why not wait a day or so?"

"I'm ready now."

"It won't be easy."

"I didn't expect it to be."

"Adam Wilson is dead, Hank," the Inspector said, and now there was a hard, angry edge to his voice. "A friend of yours, a good, decent guy. The woman, Belle, is dead. It's only through the grace of God that the baby and nurse are alive. You, too, for that matter. The baby's parents were put through three days of unrefined hell, waiting to know if they'd ever see their child again. This is the dirtiest crime in the book, for my money." West made a sharp, abrupt gesture with his hand. "And how do you think your brother is taking it? Can you guess? He's playing it for laughs. Wisecracking, acting as if he's a celebrity besieged by autograph hounds. He's loving every minute of it, enjoying the attention and excitement. If you think he's touched by repentance, or any kind of regret— think again." West sighed and shook his head. "I sound pretty tough, I know. But I don't want you to walk in on that right now. Don't you think you've taken enough in the last three days?"

"I don't know," Hank said. "But I want to see him. There isn't much time left."

"Time for what?"

Hank shrugged wearily. "I don't know. It's just the way I feel."

"All right then," the Inspector said, turning to his desk. "I'll arrange it." He was reaching for the phone when it began to ring. "Excuse me," he said, lifting the receiver. "Hello, this is West." The Inspector listened a moment, nodding slowly. Then he said, "When was this? All right . . . thanks very much. Yes, yes, of course. Good-by."

Frowning faintly, West put the receiver back into its cradle. He stared at the top of the desk for a few seconds, then sighed and looked up at Hank. "I don't know whether this will be good or bad news for you, son."

"What happened?"

"Your brother died a few minutes ago," West said quietly. "He complained of a pain in his chest after dinner. He suffered two heart attacks within half an hour. He didn't recover from the last one."

"He's dead?"

"Yes. The doctor said his heart must have been in bad shape for some time. I don't suppose he'd had a check-up lately."

"Check-up? No, I'm sure he hadn't. He—he didn't have much use for doctors." Hank stood perfectly still, staring out the window behind the sheriff's desk. He saw the branches of a maple tree stirring slowly in the darkness, and beyond that the lights of the village, shining in the night. "And he's dead now," he said softly. The fact was almost impossible to credit; it was as if half of himself had died. Even when he was away from Duke he had never been free from the dark, insistent presence; he had carried his brother with him all his life. Now the burden had been lifted and he knew he would miss it—ache for it at times.

Hank turned toward the door and Inspector West came after him and put a hand on his arm. "Why don't you stay here and have supper with me?"

"Thanks—I think I'd rather go home."

"We won't make a production out of it," West said. "Just a steak and a bottle of beer. How about it?"

"Can't I take a rain check on it?"

"Of course you can. But I thought you might want to talk a while."

Hank shook his head slowly. "There's nothing to talk about. It just doesn't make any sense to me. My brother was—" He shrugged tiredly, realizing the futility of explanations. "He was trouble," he said bitterly. "For himself, for everybody. He could have been anything. He said that after I shot him. It was true. Instead he was trouble. Two hundred pounds of trouble, swinging crazily at anything in its way. Does that make any sense to you?"

"I don't have any snap answers," West said. "In my job I've seen all kinds of people, all kinds of evil. When I was younger I kept watching for a pattern in human behavior, an equation that would make it all clear and significant to me. I thought I could find a few words that might explain all the mysteries and contradictions I kept running up against. But I never found those words. Now I know I never will."

"So it makes no sense to you either?"

"I didn't say that. I've found out this much, Hank. Sometimes evil is clear and understandable. Sometimes it makes no sense at all. But it's still our responsibility to face it—as you've done. Someone else may understand it. Someone with perfect understanding. Do you know what I mean? With that kind of understanding there may be sympathy, even forgiveness."

Hank was silent for a moment or so, and then he smiled faintly at the Inspector. "I'll be at the lodge if you need me. Good night."

"There's one other thing." West stepped across the room and took a wallet from the middle drawer of the sheriff's desk. "This belonged to your brother," he said. "It was all he had on him. I thought you might like to take it along."

Hank hesitated a moment, staring at the worn, black leather wallet.

"Yes, I'll take it along," he said, and when he spoke he felt the sudden tightness in his throat. "So long, Inspector."

"You've got a rain check on that steak, remember."

"I won't forget." Hank smiled quickly at him and left the office.

Half an hour later Hank crossed the porch of the lodge and fitted his key into the lock. He hesitated then, glancing over his shoulder at the dark shadows that crowded the house. The parking light on his car was a futile yellow gleam against the night; he could just see the white curve of the gravel road, and the uneven silhouettes of fir trees against the black skyline. The woods were quiet and unmoving; the faint wash of the water and the far-off cry of a hunting owl were harsh sounds against the unstirring silence.

Hank stared around, listening; it would be like this for a long time, he realized. When he came up here he would be watching for movement in the shadows beside the porch, cocking his head toward a snapping twig or the sudden rustle of a bird in the trees. Finally he opened the door and went inside. The silence in the house struck him as unnatural; he became aware that he was holding his breath, listening for a soft footstep on the stairs, the sound of whispering, conspiring voices in the kitchen.

Someone had put everything in order. Probably Sheriff Davis had sent a woman out, he thought. The floor was scrubbed clean, the lamps and chairs had been straightened, embers glowed faintly in the fireplace. But you couldn't get rid of ghosts with soap and water, he thought; the house was like a big empty stage, ready and waiting for actors to make their entrances.

Hank rubbed both hands over his face. There would be no entrances; he was letting his nerves run riot. Duke wouldn't saunter in from the kitchen, a grin on his dark face, his eyes alert for trouble. Duke was dead. And Belle and Grant were gone. He might write Belle's son some day, he thought. Soften it a little. She had helped at the end.

Hank walked slowly across the room and put another log on the hot ashes. With a hand resting on the mantel he watched smoke curl around the log, and the little spears of fire attacking the dry bark. Finally the wood crackled and burst into flames, and the draft shot up the chimney with a breathless roar. He stood watching the fire, not knowing what to do next; he was hungry but he didn't want to eat, he was exhausted but he couldn't sleep. After a while he sighed and took Duke's wallet from his pocket. He turned it around in his hands, examining the dry cracks along the fold, the broken stitches in the seams. Inside there was a five-dollar bill, and a collection of business cards under a celluloid shield. Five dollars . . . a bottle and a package of cigarettes. The cards were without significance; a liquor store that promised night and day deliveries, a garage, a men's clothing shop with a salesman's name printed in the right-hand corner.

One compartment of the wallet was zippered shut. Hank opened it and removed a carefully wrapped packet that was about the size of a playing card. A faint memory tugged at him. Turning toward the light, he saw that the packet contained a snapshot protected by layers of fine tissue paper. He had seen this before . . . he remembered the look of the blurred features through the paper. He had found this picture in Duke's drawer, rummaging about with a child's pointless curiosity. And Duke had caught him. Unconsciously Hank's fingers moved up to trace the scar on his forehead. What had Duke hit him with? A tennis racket. . . .

Hank removed the layers of silk-smooth paper, and studied the snapshot of Duke's mother. She had been in her middle twenties when this picture was taken, more girl than woman, awkward and shy, pretty, with long, dark hair and a thin, animated face. The print was hazy and blurred, but he could see her clear, direct eyes and the little smile pulling at her full lips. She wore a print housedress with a soft, round collar. She looked friendly but somewhat tentative, as if she might be uncomfortable with people until she got used to them. She had only completed one year of high school. His mother had told him that, he remembered.

Duke had been eight when she died, and he had carried her picture for more than thirty years, hiding it from everyone else, guarding this relic of her with sullen, passionate jealousy. What did that tell you about him? Nothing. . . .

There was no way to know—no way to guess at what this shyly smiling woman had meant to him, or what her death had destroyed in him. Had he tried to revenge himself on the world for taking her from him?

Guessing was futile. What had the Inspector said? Someone might understand him. Someone with perfect understanding. Staring at the picture, he remembered what an army chaplain had once said to him: "I believe in hell, certainly. But if you were to ask me if anyone is *in* hell—well, I might give you an argument. Who am I to put a limit on God's mercy?"

The phone began to ring then, and the sound was clear and welcome in the silent house. He turned toward it, a smile touching his lips. She had said she would call. . . .

He stared around the room, seeing the firelight on the smooth pine flooring, hearing the wind pressing against the windowpanes. The phone called to him again, and he let the faded snapshot slip from his hand into the fire. He didn't wait to see the flames take it. This was the closing of a door, the final good-by. He went quickly to the phone and lifted the receiver. His movements were sure and confident, and a smile came on his face as he heard her voice.

# The Darkest Hour

# 1

STEVE RETNICK'S RELEASE FROM SING SING CAUSED A BRIEF AND SEEM-
ingly casual stir of interest in the file room of the Thirty-First Detective
Squad. There were three men present when Sergeant Miles Kleyburg,
after a glance at his desk calendar, said: "Today's the day. You think
he'll come back here?" There was no particular emphasis in the tone of
his voice.

Lieutenant Neville stood in the doorway of his private office packing
a short black pipe, and it was difficult to tell from his expression whether
or not he had heard Kleyburg's question. He was frowning slightly, and
there was an impersonally irritable set to his lean, intelligent features.
"You mean Steve," he said at last, and walked past Kleyburg's desk to
the wide, dirt-streaked windows that overlooked the river. Lighting his
pipe, he stared without enthusiasm at the view. Snow had fallen that
morning and a high steady wind had packed it slickly and tightly on the
streets and sidewalks. Gulls stood out brightly against the swollen, soot-
dark river.

"I don't know about Retnick," Lieutenant Neville said, shaking his head
slowly. "He'll want to know about Ragoni. I hope—" Shrugging he left
the sentence incomplete. "He'll do what he wants, I suppose."

"I'll be glad to see him," Kleyburg said, and the lack of inflection in
his voice gave the words a curious weight.

Neville glanced at him. "I will too," he said, and went about the business
of lighting his pipe.

The third man in the room, a detective named Connors, studied a report
on his desk and took no part in the conversation. When the lieutenant
returned to his office a moment or so later, Connors stretched and got to
his feet. He was a tall young man with even features and wavy blond
hair. Except for excellent clothes and a certain aloofness in his manner,
there was nothing distinctive about his appearance; his face was handsome
but blankly so, unrelieved by humor or intelligence.

"I'm going out for a few minutes," he said casually.

Kleyburg, a heavily built man with thin white hair and horn-rimmed
glasses, nodded briefly at him but said nothing. He watched Connors
saunter through the double doors of the squadroom, with no expression at
all on his tired, solid face.

Connors went quickly down the dusty stairs, nodded to the uniformed
lieutenant at the desk, and crossed the mean slum street to a small candy

store. Edging through a crowd of youngsters at the comics book rack, he walked to the telephone booth at the rear of the shop. He dialed a number and when a voice answered, he said, "Mr. Amato, please. This is Connors." After a short wait another voice spoke to him, and he said, "Connors, Mr. Amato. I just thought I'd remind you. Retnick is out today." Listening then, he smiled faintly at the back of his well-groomed hand. "Sure," he said at last. "I'll find him. I'll take care of it."

Connors replaced the phone and went outside. A cold wind swept down the crosstown block, stirring up flurries of snow. Connors turned his collar up and hurried toward the station.

But Steve Retnick didn't return that day or the next. And along the waterfront and in certain police stations there were men who waited uneasily for him. . . .

It was eight-fifteen the following night when Retnick walked into Tim Moran's saloon on Twelfth Avenue. He stopped just inside the door, a tall, wide-shouldered man who wore cheap clothes and a felt hat pulled down low on his forehead. His face was expressionless as he glanced around, but his eyes were cold and sharp under the brim of his hat.

The place wasn't crowded at that hour; two dockworkers sat at the end of the bar, red-faced men in caps and bulky jackets. Standing between them was a huge, deceptively fat man whose round, childish face was slightly flushed with liquor. He wore an expensive camel's hair coat that accentuated his size, and his voice rumbled over that of the tenor who was singing shrilly of Killarney from the juke box. Retnick knew the big man; he was called Hammy, and before showing up on the waterfront he had made his living as a sparring partner, a punching bag for fighters who had some brains as well as bulk. He was a simple-minded bully, dangerously strong and arrogant. Retnick wasn't interested in him so he turned and walked slowly to the bar.

Tim Moran looked up from a glass he was polishing and his mouth sagged open in surprise. "Steve!" he said, as a smile spread slowly over his small red face. "Steve, boy! Welcome back, boy."

"Thanks, Tim," Retnick said, taking a seat.

"You've not changed at all," Moran said.

This was almost true; the five years in jail hadn't marked him physically. The planes of his dark face were sharp and hard. There was no gray in his close-cut black hair, and his body was like something made of seasoned wood and leather, tough and flexible, designed to endure. But there were changes.

"Five years older," Retnick said, pushing his hat a bit higher on his forehead. Moran looked into his eyes then and saw the change in the man. He said, "Well, let's celebrate, Steve. What'll it be?" He looked away from Retnick as he spoke, troubled by what he had seen in those flat gray eyes. "What'll it be, boy?"

"I'll skip the drink," Retnick said. "I'm looking for Frank Ragoni. Has he been in here?"

"No, Steve, I haven't seen him for a week."

"You know he's missing, I guess."

"Yes, I know that," Moran said. "But it just don't make sense."

"Have you heard any talk about where he might be?"

"Not a word. I'd like to help. I know you were good friends, but—" He shrugged again, watching Retnick's dark, hard face.

"Ragoni finished his shift at midnight," Retnick said. "He was working at Pier Five, in the hold of a North Star Lines ship that night. He never got home. I've talked to his wife. She says he was in a good mood when he left for work. That's all I've found out."

"Why should he up and disappear?" Moran said. "He's got a nice wife and family, and he's the steady type. It don't make sense, does it, Steve?"

"Not yet it doesn't," Retnick said.

The big man in the camel's hair coat rapped on the bar and stared peevishly at Moran. "What do I do for a drink?" he said, his eyes switching to Retnick. "Send you a gold-plated invitation or something?"

Moran smiled quickly. "I was just talking to a friend I haven't seen for a while. What'll it be?"

"Whisky all round," Hammy said, staring at Retnick. "Give your long-lost friend one, too. He looks like he could use it."

"Right away, Hammy."

When the drink was set before him Retnick studied it for a moment or so in silence, realizing that Hammy was still watching him from the end of the bar. The room was silent as Retnick finally lifted the glass, took a sip from it and nodded to Hammy. "Thanks," he said, and the curious little interval of tension dissolved. Hammy began talking to the dock-workers again, and Moran put his elbows on the bar in front of Retnick.

"Watch yourself with him, Steve," he said, rubbing a hand over his mouth to blur the words. "He's mean."

"Who's he working for?"

"Nick Amato."

"I picked up that drink too fast," Retnick said. "Is Amato still riding high?"

"The men in his local stick behind him."

"Do they have any choice?"

Moran found a rag and began to work on the shining surface of the bar. "I sell beer, Steve. To anybody who wants it. I don't take sides in union politics. You know how it is."

"Sure," Retnick said. "I know how it is."

"Steve, this is none of my business, but—" The little Irishman shrugged and smiled uncertainly. "Have you been to see your wife yet?"

Retnick stared at him for a moment or so without any expression on his face. Then he said, "No," in a cold tight voice and got to his feet. "Take it easy," he said, and started for the door.

Hammy called after him, "Hey, you didn't finish your drink, buddy!" Retnick turned around slowly. "I don't want it," he said.

"That's no way to treat a free drink," Hammy said, studying Retnick expectantly. "Go on, toss it down."

Retnick kept a tight grip on his temper; he couldn't afford trouble with this fool. "You've got a point," he said, and walked to the bar and finished off the drink.

Hammy sauntered toward him then, a little smile touching his big simple face. He was a ponderous bulk of a man, with a chest and stomach that were barrel-like in their proportions. His eyes were small and confident, reflecting the simple trust he held in his own size and strength. He enjoyed the power his huge body gave him over others, and he looked for occasions to exercise it; fighting made him feel brave because he hadn't the wit to distinguish between strength and courage.

"I guess I'm a little slow," he said, still grinning amiably. "You're Steve Retnick, aren't you?"

"That's right," Retnick said turning again toward the door.

"The big tough copper," Hammy said, with a different edge to his voice; he was whetting his temper now, waiting pleasurably for it to take charge of his judgment and senses. "The big tough cop who got sent to jail for murder. How was it in jail, copper?"

Retnick said, "It wasn't good, Hammy."

Hammy cocked his big head and smiled slightly. "You don't sound tough any more," he said. "I guess they softened you up some." There wouldn't be any fight, he knew then. This was a big slob whose guts had turned to water in a cell. "You better get going," he said, leaning against the bar. "I don't like ex-cops any better than I like cops."

Retnick hesitated briefly, memorizing the look of Hammy's big stupid face, the arrogant pose of his body at the bar. "Okay," he said and walked out. The opening and closing of the door let a rush of cold air into the warm bar; a swarm of snowflakes whirled dizzily across the floor before melting into little black spots of water. Hammy put his head back and began to laugh . . .

Outside, Retnick turned his collar up against the bitter wind that came off the river. The graceful bulk of a liner loomed directly ahead of him, blacker than the night. He lit a cigarette, cupping his powerful hands about the match, and the small flame glinted on the sharp planes of his face and drew a vivid outline of his head and shoulders against the darkness. Inhaling deeply he waited for his anger to subside; this was a new anger, hot and impulsive, completely alien to the frozen lifeless anger that had been locked inside him for five years. He could control this new anger, subjugate it to a proper place in his plans. The old anger was something else again; that existed of itself, independent of his will or desire. Flipping the match aside he walked uptown and turned into a slum block, where only a few yellow lights winked from the tall old brownstones.

This was an area he had learned by heart; the river first with its slow booming traffic, and then the piers, the switching yards, and the mean tough waterfront streets of the West Side. This was a jungle on the edge of the city and Retnick knew most of its secrets.

Retnick walked east for three blocks, occasionally stopping in the shadow of a car to study the street behind him; but nothing moved in the darkness. In the fourth block he passed the heavy incongruous bulk of St. Viator's and went up the stone steps of the rectory that adjoined the church. For an instant he hesitated before the stained glass cross that was inset in the frosted pane of the door. Then he rang the bell.

Mrs. Simmons, the white-haired housekeeper, opened the door, and when she recognized him she let out a little cry of surprise and pleasure. "Steve, it's really you," she said, as he stepped into the lighted foyer. It was obvious she didn't know quite what to say after that; she made several false starts, stammering with the excitement of it all, and then said, "Wait, I'll tell Father Bristow. Just wait, he's in his study."

Retnick removed his hat and turned down the collar of his overcoat. Brushing flakes of snow from his shoulders, he glanced about the little room, studying the familiar furniture and pictures. Nothing had been changed here. The Madonna, the Crucifix, the faded carpet and old-fashioned hall-tree mirror, they were all the same, just five years older. Everything was five years older.

A door opened and Father Bristow came down the hall, a warm grin spreading on his round brown face. "Well, well, this is wonderful," he said, putting both hands on Retnick's shoulders. "Come on into the study and we'll celebrate properly."

The study was a small room at the back of the rectory, cluttered with books and magazines, smelling of wood smoke and pipe tobacco. Retnick shook his head as Father Bristow took a bottle of wine from a tiny closet beside the fireplace.

"Never mind the drink," he said. "I've got nothing to celebrate."

Glancing at him curiously, Father Bristow saw the cold, dispassionate expression in Retnick's face. He hesitated a second, and then put the bottle away. "All right, Steve," he said quietly.

"I'm looking for Frank Ragoni," Retnick said.

Father Bristow sighed. "I wish I could help you."

"When did you see him last?"

"About two weeks ago."

"Did he have any message for me?"

"No, he and his wife stopped by after Mass, but he didn't have anything specific to say about you, Steve. Their oldest boy is being confirmed pretty soon, and that's what he wanted to see me about."

Retnick was silent a moment, staring at the priest with cold eyes. "Well, it was a long shot," he said. "Thanks, anyway."

"What's all this about?"

"Six weeks ago I had a letter from Ragoni," he said. Staring into the fire, Retnick's eyes narrowed against the small, spurting flames. "He said he knew who killed Joe Ventra."

The silence stretched out between the two men, straining and tight in the cozy little room. Father Bristow was quite pale. "Joe Ventra," he said slowly.

"That's right," Retnick said. "Well, take it easy, Father."

"Now wait a minute, Steve," the priest said, putting a hand quickly on Retnick's arm. "What are you going to do?"

"I'm going to find Ragoni. He'll tell me who killed Ventra. After that, everything will be simple."

"Please, Steve. I'm not going to make a sermon, but I want you to listen to me. Everyone knows you didn't kill Joe Ventra. That's common knowledge from one end of the waterfront to the other. You were framed. Everyone knows that."

"That's right," Retnick said, with deceptive gentleness. "I was framed. Everybody knew it. The cops knew it, and so did the unions. But that didn't keep me out of jail. I got thrown off the force as a murderer." Retnick's voice thickened as he jerked his arm away from the priest's hand. "I lived in a cage like an animal for five years," he said, drawing a deep breath. "Sleeping alone, eating what they put in front of me, never moving without rifles pointing at my back. I paid five years of my life for Joe Ventra's death. Now somebody else is going to pay."

"Steve, you're heading for trouble."

"I want trouble," Retnick said, staring at him bitterly. "I need it." And then, because he owed the priest this much, he said, "Forget the guy you remember, Father. The guy who taught boxing to your boys clubs and took the kids on fishing trips up to Montauk. I'm somebody else."

"I doubt that," the priest said. "But what about Marcia?"

"She'll get along. She's good at that."

"Aren't you going to see her?"

"Sure," Retnick said. "She knew Ragoni."

"Is that the only reason you're seeing her?"

"Tell me a better one," Retnick said coldly.

A touch of color appeared in the priest's face. "I don't know all your problems," he said, "but I know your duties. And one of them is to treat her with compassion and sympathy, no matter what mistakes she's made."

"And what about her duties?" Retnick said, staring at the priest. Then he turned away sharply. "Talking's no good. I've got to be going, Father."

The priest went with him to the door. From the steps he watched Retnick walking toward the avenue, walking like a man advancing on an enemy. Father Bristow shivered involuntarily, not from the cold but from the memory of the coldness in Retnick's eyes.

# 2

THE GRAMERCY WAS A SUPPER CLUB IN THE EAST FIFTIES, AN INTIMATE spot that featured excellent food and unobtrusive music. There was a small bar and several banquettes at one end of the room to accommodate patrons waiting for tables; it wasn't a place for stags to get drunk in. The bartender looked dubiously at Retnick's cheap suit, and said, "Do you have a reservation, sir?"

"No. Give me a whisky with water."

"Very well, sir." The bartender didn't argue the point; as a judge of men he bet himself that this one wouldn't start trouble. Finish it, more than likely—

Retnick glanced into the crowded, dimly lighted dining room and saw the tiny white piano placed against the far wall.

"When does the music start?" he asked the bartender.

"Nine-thirty, or thereabouts."

"Is she here now?"

"You mean the pianist?"

"That's right, Marcia Kelly."

"I believe she's changing, sir."

Retnick took the paper coaster from under his drink and wrote his name on it. "Would you send this back to her, please?" he said, pushing the coaster across the bar.

"Well, sir, we have a rule about that, you know."

"It's all right. I'm an old friend of hers."

"In this case—" The bartender hesitated, smiling uncertainly. Then he signaled a waiter, hoping that his estimate of this man had been accurate.

The waiter returned in a moment or so and said to Retnick, "She'd like to see you, sir. Will you come with me?"

Walking through the little flurries of laughter and conversation in the dining room, Retnick noticed the piano again and remembered that a piano had figured in their first meeting. This was no feat of memory; there were few details of their days and nights together that he couldn't recall effortlessly and vividly. When he met her he had been bird-dogging for Father Bristow, looking for someone to give piano lessons to three kids in the boys club. The priest had suggested Marcia Kelly, a girl from the parish who had studied music in college.

She had been willing to help out . . .

They were married in the summer, six months or so after they had met. And a short while after that, a month to the day before Christmas, he was in jail on a murder rap.

They turned into a short corridor and the waiter pointed to a door at the end of it. "Right there," he said.

"Thanks." When the waiter had gone Retnick hesitated, feeling nothing but the pressure of the lifeless anger in his breast. It was all right then, he knew. Nothing could touch him.

He walked down the corridor and rapped on the door. She said, "Come in, please," in a light, expectant voice. Retnick smiled and twisted the knob.

She stood in the middle of the softly lighted dressing room, a small girl with close-cut, curly black hair. There was humor and intelligence in her delicate features, and her body looked slimly mature and elegant in a simple black evening gown.

Retnick closed the door and stood with his back to it, watching her with a cold little smile. For an instant neither of them spoke and the silence became oppressive in the perfume-scented room.

She's twenty-eight now, he thought irrelevantly. The years had touched her; the planes of her face were more sharply defined and the look of gay and careless happiness was gone from her eyes. He noticed that her bare shoulders were lightly tanned but that her face was very pale.

"Steve," she said, and took a tentative step toward him, smiling uncertainly into the coldness of his eyes.

Retnick leaned against the door. "This isn't a social call," he said.

"I waited at home for you yesterday," she said.

"Home?"

A touch of color came into her face. "The apartment then. I—I hoped you'd come back. I had a steak, a bottle of wine—" She made a helpless little gesture with her hands, smiling too brightly now. "It was quite a production, Steve. Too bad you had to miss it."

"A big welcome for the hero, eh?" he said. "The kind GI's get, with all the neighbors in to add to the festivities."

"I thought—"

"I didn't get out of the army, I got out of jail," Retnick said.

She brought her hands up slowly to her breast. "Why didn't you come home?"

"What for?"

"I'm still your wife."

"That's your decision, not mine," Retnick said. "I told you to get a divorce."

"I didn't want a divorce. I wanted to wait for you."

"And did you wait?" Retnick said evenly. "Like a pure and faithful wife in some medieval romance? Is that how you waited?"

"Please, Steve," she said. She turned away from him, hugging her arms tightly against her body. "Let's don't talk about it. Not now. Can't we go somewhere and have a cup of coffee?"

"I don't have time."

"Can't you give me the tiniest break?" she said, turning and looking steadily into his eyes. "I want to tell you what happened. It's not a long and fancy story. There aren't any twists or surprises in it. And I don't come out as the brave and lonely little heroine." She took a step toward him, smiling with trembling lips into his hard face. "I'm not trying to make it sound cute, Steve. You know me better than that."

"I thought I knew you," he said.

"You left me with nothing," she said, shaking her head helplessly. "Why did you do it to me? You told me not to visit you in jail. You wouldn't even see me when I went there. You told me to get a divorce the day the trial ended. And you acted as if you hated me. I couldn't understand it. I tried to wait for you, Steve, I tried. I—"

"There was a man, right?"

"Please, Steve." She turned away from him and put a hand to her forehead. "I wrote you everything. I needed your help. I still need it."

"You needed something," Retnick said, "but it wasn't me. So let's forget it. When did you see Frank Ragoni last?"

She stared at him with something like wonder in her eyes. "What did they do to you, Steve? You used to understand people, you used—"

"When did you see Ragoni last?" Retnick's voice fell across her words like a cold dead weight.

She sat down at the dressing table and shrugged her slim bare shoulders. "Okay, okay," she said wearily. "You think I'm a leper and that's that. I'll stop trying to change your mind. So on to something important. Frank was in here about a month ago, I think. With his wife. They were celebrating an anniversary."

"A month ago. Did he give you any message for me?"

"Nothing in particular."

"Are you sure?"

"I don't know," she said, shaking her head. "What am I supposed to remember?"

"This would have to do with Joe Ventra's murderer."

She looked at him and her hand moved slowly to her throat. "I'm sure he said nothing about that."

Retnick hesitated an instant. "Did he ever mention Ventra to you?"

"Only to say you'd been framed for his murder. He said that over and over."

"Did you see Ragoni often?"

"He asked me to come out for dinner every few months. And I had his family up to the apartment occasionally for breakfast after Mass." She smiled bitterly. "We got along fine. He used to tell what a great fullback you were at Fordham. His wife liked me, too."

Retnick turned abruptly to the door.

"Steve, wait!" she said, coming swiftly to her feet.

Without looking at her, he said, "I've waited five years. I'm through waiting. So long."

It was ten o'clock when Retnick stepped into a telephone booth a block from the Gramercy. He dialed a number and a woman's voice answered the phone. "I'd like to speak to Mr. Glencannon," Retnick said.

"Who's this?"

"My name is Retnick, Steve Retnick."

"Is there any other message? This is his sister speaking."

"I want to see him tonight, if that's possible."

"Just a moment, please."

Retnick lit a cigarette and waited, staring out at the shining counters of the drugstore, at the couples sitting at the fountain.

"Hello? My brother would be glad to see you tonight. Do you have our address?"

"Yes. I'll be there in about ten minutes."

Retnick left the drugstore and picked up a cruising cab on Lexington Avenue. He gave the driver Glencannon's address and settled back to think. Jack Glencannon was the president of Ragoni's local, 202. And that local was heading for trouble. It adjoined Nick Amato's area of operations, and Amato was preparing to expand in an obvious direction. Retnick had learned this the day before from Frank Ragoni's wife. Amato and Glencannon were as dissimilar as two men could be; one was honest, the other was a thief. But Retnick wondered if Amato were big enough to take on Glencannon; if so it was a tribute of sorts to his nerve and cunning. Glencannon was a tough and powerful old man, a legend on the docks for more than thirty years. He was Union Jack to his boys, and they had always stuck to him with fierce loyalty. Glencannon's hold on his men was simple; he ran an honest local. He didn't believe in short-gangs, loan sharks, kickbacks or organized theft. It was a formidable set-up to oppose, Retnick knew; but he also knew that Amato never started a fight if there was a chance of losing it.

Glencannon lived on the fifth floor of an apartment building in the West Seventies. Retnick knocked and the door was opened by a gray-haired woman who smiled and said, "Come in, please. I'm Jack's sister."

"I'm sorry to be calling so late," he said.

"Goodness, don't let that bother you," she said, with a little laugh. "People keep coming in at all hours. Friends, judges, politicians, the mayor himself sometimes, they just drop in when it suits them." She took off her rimless glasses and smiled philosophically. "I've looked after Jack since my husband died eighteen years ago, and I tell you frankly I marvel to this day at his patience. Well, now, was it something in particular you wanted to talk to him about?"

"It's about Frank Ragoni."

"I'll tell him you're here. Please sit down and make yourself comfortable." Then she hesitated. "Jack hasn't been well lately. I know you'll understand."

Retnick sensed something behind the literal meaning of her words. "I'll make my visit brief," he said.

Retnick lit another cigarette and glanced about the large, comfortably furnished room. He had known Glencannon pretty well in the past. The old man had followed his football career with interest, and had been one of his references for the police department. Which certainly hadn't hurt.

The door opened and Glencannon's sister came in. Retnick knew from her expression that something was wrong.

"I'm sorry," she said, making an awkward little gesture with her hands. "My brother just doesn't think he's up to seeing anyone tonight."

"That's too bad," Retnick said slowly. "Is it anything serious?"

"No, thank heaven, it's just one of those heavy colds that is working down to his chest."

"He was all right when I called," Retnick said. "That was ten minutes ago."

"Ups and downs are fairly common at his age," she said, in a cooler voice. "Some other night would be better, I think."

"He didn't go down until he heard Ragoni's name," Retnick said. "Was that what bothered him?"

"It isn't my place to interpret his messages," she said. "He doesn't want to see anyone tonight. That's all I can tell you."

"Maybe the name Ragoni bothers you," Retnick said.

"It means nothing to me."

"You'll be an impartial audience then," Retnick said quietly. "Frank Ragoni was a member of your brother's local. He's been missing for more than a week. Could you guess why?"

"I don't know anything about these matters."

"No, I suppose you don't," Retnick said. "That's why I wanted to talk to your brother. Ragoni is missing, and he may be dead. Maybe he got killed for standing up to Nick Amato. That's not his job, of course, that's your brother's."

"You know all about killing, don't you?" she said, in a rising voice.

"What do you mean?"

"You're Steve Retnick, aren't you?"

Retnick stared at her. "That's right."

She took a step backward, flushing at the look in his eyes. "I didn't mean that," she said. "But you have no right to be badgering me this way. My brother is a sick, overworked man."

"Tell him I'm sorry for him," Retnick said. "Nick Amato won't be. Good night."

Retnick's room was on the first floor of a brownstone that had somehow preserved a remnant of dignity over the years. The wide, high-ceilinged hallway was clean and freshly painted and the beautiful old woodwork had been treated with care; it shone like satin in the light from the ornate brass chandelier. Kleyburg had rented this place in his name a month ago, after checking the landlady's reputation, and making sure that none of the other tenants had police records; this was a parole board requirement and Kleyburg had satisfied it with scrupulous care.

Retnick was searching for his key when a faint scratching noise sounded behind him. He turned quickly, his instincts alerting him to danger, but it was a thin, gray-and-white cat that stared up at him from the shadowed corner of the hallway. Its eyes gleamed like blue-green marbles in the darkness. Retnick let out his breath slowly, and rubbed the back of his hand over his forehead. Relief eased the tension in his arms and shoulders. He knew he was in a dangerous mood, ready to explode at the slightest pressure. But there was nothing he could do about it. He picked up the cat and felt its claws tighten nervously against the rough cloth of his overcoat.

As bad as I am, he thought, rubbing the little animal gently under the chin. But you'll get over it. A cup of milk and a sweater to curl up on will fix you up fine. Shifting the cat to his left hand he opened the door of his room and snapped on the lights. He had nothing to feed her, he realized, and the delicatessens in the neighborhood were closed by now. Annoyed with himself, he turned back to the hallway. He didn't want to be responsible for anything, even a kitten. But he couldn't leave her now. After this promise of attention and company she'd keep the whole house awake scratching and crying at his door. Finally he walked down the hall and rapped gently on his landlady's door. This was a fine way of getting thrown out of here, he thought, waking Mrs. Cara in the middle of the night over a stray cat. But he was wrong. Mrs. Cara opened the door, tightening the belt of her blue robe, and her fat brown face broke into a smile as she saw the cat in Retnick's arm.

"Well, you found Silvy," she said, in a fond, pleased voice.

"She was in the hallway. I thought she was probably hungry."

"No, she's been fed. The trouble is she just likes to wander around." She looked up at him then, an appraising little smile on her lips. "Look, you like cats?"

"Well enough," Retnick said. "Why?"

"You could help me out maybe," Mrs. Cara said. "Silvy slips out of here whenever the door is open, and that's practically all the time with the mail, the laundry, and people asking for messages or paying their rent. Then she roams all over the house keeping people awake."

"Well, how can I help out?" Retnick said, as Mrs. Cara paused expectantly.

"Let me keep her in your room. Okay? She won't be no bother, no mess or nothing. I'll take care of her but she lives with you." Smiling, she patted his arm. "How about it?"

Retnick shrugged and smiled faintly. "You made a deal, Mrs. Cara."

"You're a good man," Mrs. Cara said. "Lots of people don't care about cats. They think cats got some trick so they live without food or any attention at all. 'Drive out in the country and throw 'em anywhere. They'll get by.' That's what some people say. I'd like to throw *them* out in the woods and see how they like it. 'Eat some bark,' I'd tell 'em. 'You'll get along fine.' "

Retnick patted the cat. "We'll see that she gets along okay. Don't worry."

When he returned to his room the cat leaped from his arms and made a tense trip along the walls, peering around as if she expected to find mastiffs in every corner.

Retnick watched her for a few seconds, and then took off his overcoat and dropped it on the bed. By the time he had stripped to the waist the cat was curled up on the coat, blinking drowsily. Smiling faintly he moved her aside and hung his overcoat in the closet. He stretched tiredly then, and the action brought a web of heavy muscles into play; he was built like a weight-lifter, with tremendous arms and shoulders, but there was nothing freakish or narcissistic about the development of his body. He was designed for function, not display.

He was tired but sleep was impossible, he knew; he would only lie staring into the darkness, thinking. And he had done enough of that in the last five years.

He was lighting a cigarette when a knock sounded on the door. Retnick hesitated, frowning. No one had this address but the Parole Board. The knock sounded again, imperatively this time. Retnick stepped to the door and opened it an inch.

"Retnick?" a voice said.

"That's right."

"I'm Connors, Thirty-First Detectives." An open wallet appeared at the crack in the door and Retnick saw the gleaming face of a police shield. "I want to talk to you."

"Sure, come in," he said, opening the door.

Connors studied Retnick, taking his time about it, and then he smiled slightly and sauntered into the room. "Cozy little spot," he said, glancing around casually. "Mind if I take off my coat?"

"Go ahead."

Connors removed his handsomely cut tweed overcoat and folded it neatly over the foot of the bed. When he saw the cat he looked at Retnick with a quizzical little smile. "I didn't figure you as a benefactor of stray kittens," he said.

"How did you figure me?" Retnick said.

Connors shrugged lightly. "You had quite a reputation at the Thirty-First," he said. "Very rugged, very tough." There was just a trace of malice in his smile. "I believe I've heard Sergeant Kleyburg refer to you as quote, a cop's cop, unquote."

"How is Kleyburg?" Retnick said, ignoring Connors' sarcasm.

"Fine, just fine," Connors said. He sat down and crossed his legs carefully, shifting his trousers to protect their sharp crease. Then he ran a hand over his wavy blond hair and smiled at Retnick. "Is there a drink in the house?"

"Sorry." Retnick found Connors' manner annoying, but he didn't let that show in his expression. He knew nothing about him, but the quality of his clothes was suspicious; the handsome gray flannel suit, the white-on-white shirt, the expensive neatly figured tie—you didn't buy items like that on a detective's salary.

"What are your plans?" Connors said, after lighting a cigarette with a mannered little flourish.

"Nothing definite yet," Retnick said. "Why?"

"I thought I might help you get your bearings," Connors said.

"That would be nice."

Connors was looking about for an ashtray. Retnick picked up one from the bureau and Connors accepted it with a nod of thanks. Balancing it on one knee, he looked at Retnick, a small smile touching his smooth handsome face. "Think of this as a briefing," he said. "Things have changed since you went to jail. Specifically, things have changed on the waterfront. It will save you time and possibly trouble to keep that in mind. Things are peaceful now. The unions and shippers are getting along, and the locals aren't squabbling among themselves any more. There's a rumble every now and then, but strictly on an intramural basis."

"Intramural?"

"That means all in the family."

"It didn't when I went to college," Retnick said. "But go on."

Connors inclined his head and smiled slightly. "I forgot you weren't an ordinary cop. You were a cop's cop. But as I was saying: the docks are quiet. The man who starts trouble won't have any friends. Do you understand?"

"I think so," Retnick said.

"Good. Another point. Do you have any plans for a job?"

"No."

"Maybe I can help out there." Connors took a deep drag on his cigarette and blew a thin stream of smoke toward Retnick. "When you killed Joe Ventra you inadvertently did Nick Amato a favor. That probably hasn't occurred to you, but Amato is grateful, even though your efforts in his behalf were completely accidental."

"You're sure I killed Ventra," Retnick said.

"I couldn't care less one way or the other," Connors said, with an easy smile. "If you say you took a bum rap, I'll buy that. But the fact is you hit Ventra in a bar, and he went outside and died."

"I pushed him away from me," Retnick said. "He went outside and got slugged to death with a blackjack."

"I'll buy all that," Connors said, still smiling. "As I say, if that's your story it's okay with me. But the jury heard witnesses say you knocked him around brutally, and that he was half-dead when you kicked him into the street. And they found you guilty of murder in the second degree. But to come back to the point: Ventra and Amato were fighting for control of Local 200 at the time. With Ventra dead, Amato naturally took over. *Whoever* killed Ventra accidentally did Amato a favor."

"Maybe Amato did himself a favor," Retnick said.

Connors looked thoughtfully at him. "You're forgetting what I told you already. No one wants trouble. But cracks like that can lead to trouble. For you, my friend."

"Let's get to the point," Retnick said. "What's your deal?"

"Amato's got a job for you. Chauffeur, bodyguard, something like that. The dough is good."

"You like it, I guess," Retnick said.

A slow tide of color moved up in Connors' cheeks. "Brother, you are stupid," he said gently. "You're an ex-cop, an ex-convict. You're all washed up. If you start any trouble you'll get your head knocked right off your shoulders."

Retnick turned away slowly, grinding a big fist into the palm of his hand. "You punks all sound alike," he said, in a low, savage voice. "Messenger boys, carrier pigeons, doing dirty little jobs for hoodlums so you can dress like dudes and sneak a few week ends off in Miami or Atlantic City. Who's going—"

"Listen—"

"Shut up!" Retnick said, turning swiftly and dangerously. The anger was a tight cruel pain inside him, a pressure screaming for release. "Who's going to knock my head off? You?"

Connors got to his feet, wetting his lips. Instinct warned him his gun and badge wouldn't prevail here. "Don't fly off the handle," he said, smiling with an effort into the murder in Retnick's face. "I've told you what Amato is thinking. What you do about it is up to you."

"You can tell Amato I've got a job," Retnick said. "I'm going to find Frank Ragoni, and I'm going to find out who killed Ventra. And the guy who killed Ventra is going to wish to God he'd shot himself the same night."

Connors shrugged and picked up his overcoat. "I gave you good advice," he said. "You'll appreciate it eventually." Then, in the doorway, he smiled at Retnick. There was a new confidence in his manner. "Part of that job you mentioned won't be too difficult. Finding Ragoni, I mean."

"What's that?"

"You'll see it in the papers. Ragoni's body was pulled out of the river tonight. I saw the report on it before I came over here. Someone stuck a knife into him." Connors sighed. "Those things happen, Retnick. Good night." He closed the door.

Retnick sat down slowly on the edge of the bed and rubbed his forehead with the back of his hand. Ragoni was dead. Connors wouldn't lie about it. For an instant he felt a curious surprise at his own lack of reaction. Ragoni had been a good friend of his, but he felt no sense of pain or loss at all, nothing but a certain selfish disappointment; this would make his job far more difficult. He swore bitterly and pounded a fist into his palm. It would have been so easy. Find Ragoni, listen to a name. That was all. Now he was on his own. There would be no help for him on the waterfront, no friends. The cat had curled up beside him but he was unaware of its warm presence. He sat perfectly still, staring at his big hands, and the single bare bulb drew deep shadows under his bitter, lonely eyes.

# 3

AT MIDNIGHT NICK AMATO SAT BEHIND HIS DESK, SLUMPED DEEP IN the chair, with one foot propped up against a pulled-out drawer. The strong overhead light filled the small office with harsh brilliance, revealing cracks in the uncarpeted floor, the worn spots on the furniture, and the chipped gilt lettering on the windows that read: Headquarters, Local 200.

Joe Lye stood with his back to the wall, his hands deep in the pockets of his black overcoat, and watched the single door.

Amato was studying a Christmas card, a small frown on his broad, swarthy face. Smiling at him from the card was a photograph of his own face, looking absurd under a Santa Claus hat. The inscription read: Happy Holiday Greetings From Uncle Nick.

"This stinks," Amato said, glancing at Joe Lye. "It's cheap. Why did you use my picture? I'm not running for office."

"Okay, I'll tell Dave to take it back to the printer," Joe Lye said.

"The picture would be in every ash can in the neighborhood after Christmas. Great, eh? Figure out something else."

"Okay," Joe Lye said.

Amato tossed the Christmas card on his desk and glanced at his watch. Then he yawned comfortably, a stockily built man of fifty, slightly below middle height, with a face as dark and hard as mahogany. Except for his eyes, which were cynical and pitiless, he could have passed for any sort of small businessman. He usually wore cheap brown or gray suits, and his only curious mannerism was an occasional air of abstraction; he gave the impression then that he was listening with amusement to some invisible story-teller.

"How old is Glencannon?" he said, glancing again at Joe Lye.

"I don't know. Seventy-five maybe."

Amato shook his fingers gently in front of his face. "That's too old to be up this time of night," he said.

"Did it have to be tonight?"

"Yeah, tonight, tonight, right away," Amato said, and yawned again. Then he began to laugh.

"What's funny?" Joe Lye asked him, not sure of what to expect. You never knew with Amato when he was in these dreamy moods. Sometimes he wanted to talk, sometimes he wanted you to shut up. You never knew.

"Glencannon is worried," Amato said, smiling gently. "He can't wait till morning. Maybe he wants to give us 202."

"*I* wish he'd waited till morning," Lye said. He crossed the room, a thin figure in black, and leaned against the wall. His eyes were irritable in the unhealthy pallor of his small, lean face. There was the suggestion of a smile about his lips but this was a matter he couldn't control; a tic pulled his mouth into a tight grimace when he was nervous or worried. It looked like a grin at first glance, but the illusion of humor was shattered by the dangerous tension in his face.

"*You* wish he'd waited till morning?" Amato said. "What was you doing that was so important?"

"Well, I don't go to Kay's to watch television," Lye said. He wished he'd kept his mouth shut; Amato loved this little game.

"What was you doing?" Amato said.

"Getting ready to eat, if you want details."

"This late?"

"Sure." Lye gestured nervously with a slim pale hand. "I didn't get there till nine. We had a few drinks, Martinis, if you're interested, and she was just ready to put in the steak when you called."

"Martinis and steaks," Amato said, smiling and shaking his head slowly. "Just like the movies. You got the life, Joe. Not like it was in jail, eh?"

Lye felt his mouth twisting painfully. Lighting a cigarette, he changed his position against the wall, turning the unmarked side of his face to Amato; it filled him with a sick rage to be stared at. "Why talk about jail?" he said, flipping the burned match across the room.

"Because it's interesting," Amato said, watching Lye with a little grin. "Those guards up there used to tell me how you were doing."

"I know, I know," Lye said. "They should keep their big fat mouths shut."

"They said you prayed every night," Amato said. "Down on your knees like you was in a church. That's funny, eh?"

"You got a funny idea of what's funny."

"What were you praying for?"

"The place gets you," Lye said. He looked quickly around the room, his eyes switching like those of an animal in a trap. Since those two weeks in the death cell a dream the color of blood had plagued his sleep, turning every night into an occasion of potential terror. It was always in red, a dull crimson shot with flecks of black, and there were laughing guards who rushed him down a corridor to the chair. Only it wasn't a chair when they reached it, but a high rude altar, and they stretched him on it and tightened the straps about his body until he couldn't breathe.

"It must be pretty bad," Amato said, shaking his head. "But I don't get the praying business. What's that going to help?"

"I don't know," Lye said, dropping his cigarette on the floor. "The place softens you up, that's all. You act buggy."

Amato said casually, "You ought to get your face fixed up, Joe. It looks like hell, you know."

"Sure I know," Lye said, rubbing his mouth nervously. "You think I like it? But the doc says it's in my head."

"He thinks you're nuts?"

"He's the nutty one if you ask me," Lye said. Relax, the doctor said. But how could he relax when he couldn't even sleep?

"You shouldn't have worried in jail," Amato said. "Didn't you know I'd get you out?"

"Time was getting short," Lye said.

"Trust me," Amato said. "Don't waste time praying to anybody else. Well, what about Retnick?"

"Connors talked to him," Lye said. He felt the tension easing in his straining lips. "Retnick's in no mood to play ball. Connors couldn't get anything definite from him."

"That Connors never has anything definite," Amato said. "It's getting bad when you can't buy anything better than a dummy like Connors."

"Retnick's got a one-track mind. He's still thinking about who killed Ventra."

Amato frowned slightly at the top of his desk. "That's a Polack for you," he said. "Stubborn."

A step sounded on the stairs and Amato raised a hand quickly for silence. But it was Hammy who opened the door and sauntered into the room, a drunken grin on his big red face. "Sorry I'm late," he said to Amato, and slumped into a chair that creaked under his great weight.

"Where've you been?" Amato said, in a deceptively pleasant voice.

"Around. Here and there." Hammy laughed and massaged his bumpy forehead with the back of his hand. "Celebrating."

"I didn't say twelve o'clock just to be talking."

The look in Amato's eyes sobered Hammy. "Sure thing, boss, it won't happen again. I—"

"Okay, *okay*," Amato said, cutting him off irritably. "Joe, you figure something for Retnick."

"All right," Lye said.

Hammy was smiling. "Retnick? That guy couldn't lick his upper lip. I can take him, boss."

"Where? To a movie, maybe?"

"I deliver, you know that." Amato's sarcasm didn't diminish Hammy's childish confidence in his own ability. There were many things his small brain didn't understand; but he understood perfectly well that he could kill most men in a matter of seconds with his hands. Not in a ring maybe, but an alley or barroom was different.

A bell jangled from below, and Amato said, "Well, here's the old man. Go bring him up, Hammy."

"Sure, Boss."

Amato smiled faintly at Lye as they heard the slow, heavy footsteps ascending the stairs. "We should have had an oxygen tent handy," he muttered.

The door opened and Jack Glencannon came into the room, blinking at the harsh overhead light.

"Take a seat," Amato said, staring at the old man's flushed face. "You don't look so chipper."

"The stairs get my wind these days," Glencannon said, taking a deep breath. He sat down slowly and patted his damp forehead with a hand-kerchief.

"Relax a second," Amato said, smiling coldly. "You're no spring chicken any more. You should be soaking up the sun in Florida on a nice pension. Maybe it's time to let somebody else run your local."

The old man straightened his shoulders then and tried to put a suggestion of defiance into the thrust of his big jaw. But it was a futile effort. Everything about Glencannon was old and weary and beaten; the clothes hung loosely on his once-powerful frame, and there was a good inch of space between his collar and the withered skin of his throat. Networks of tiny blue veins had ruptured in his cheeks; he had been drinking heavily that night, and for many nights in the past, but he hadn't numbed himself sufficiently for this showdown. There was a core of fear in him that the liquor hadn't been able to dissolve.

"We need a frank talk, Amato," he said, trying for a hearty tone. "We've needed it for a long time." He hesitated then, conscious of Lye's bright stare, and Amato's supercilious smile. "I guess you know what I mean," he said.

"You're talking," Amato said. "Keep going."

"We don't have to fight each other," Glencannon said, smiling with obvious effort. "Some of your boys are pressuring the men in my local— I guess we both know that, Nick. And it's got to stop."

Amato didn't answer him for a moment. Then he said gently, *"You* say it's got to stop. Okay. *You* stop it, then."

"It's your men that need the stopping," Glencannon said, standing and putting his hands on Amato's desk for support. "I don't hire the likes of your bums and hoodlums. You tell 'em to keep away from my local. It's a clean place. The men are satisfied. They don't want killers with guns telling 'em how to vote."

"Killers?" Amato said, raising his eyebrows. "That's a pretty strong word, old man."

Glencannon stared at Amato, his breathing loud and harsh in the silence. "Frank Ragoni didn't stab himself in the back and jump into the river," he said.

"You're talking real stupid," Joe Lye said.

"Shut up," Amato said casually. "You think we killed Ragoni?"

"He was told to get off the docks by your men," Glencannon said, struggling to keep his voice steady. "He was told to stop talking about the elections. He got a last warning. Shut up or get killed. He didn't shut up, and he got a knife in his back."

Amato leaned forward, and his face settled into cold ugly lines. "Now listen to me, you washed-up old slob," he said, softly and quietly. "You want your local, you fight for it. Elections are next month. The boys will make their choice. That's all there is to it. I got nothing else to say to you."

"Wait a minute, Nick. I didn't come here to start a fight. This thing can be worked out peacefully." Glencannon's smile was a travesty; his lips were pulled back against his teeth but his eyes were bright with fear.

"We're on the same side, after all. We're union men, Nick. How will it look for us to be squabbling? I—"

"I told you I had nothing more to say." Amato stood up and stared with distaste at the old man's trembling lips. "You're a drunk and a slob and I'm tired of looking at you. Now beat it."

Glencannon fought to say something, anything, but there were no words in his sick, tired old mind. Thirty years ago, he thought, remembering what he had once been, seeing again the man who could shout down a hall full of workers, and if necessary enforce his orders with rock-hard fists. He put a hand to his forehead and took an involuntary step backward, wanting nothing now but to get away from the contempt and anger in Amato's eyes. "You didn't understand me, Nick," he said weakly.

"Take him home, Hammy," Amato said.

"No. I'll look after myself."

"You need a nurse. Take him home, Hammy."

When they had gone Amato shook his head and sat down at his desk. "He'd do himself a favor if he laid down and died," he said.

"You handled him right," Joe Lye said.

"Hell, a two-year-old baby could handle him," Amato said. "But he used to be quite a boy. Years ago, that was. Well, turn out the lights. You can drive me home."

"Look, Kay is waiting for me," Lye said, and wet his lips. "I mean, she's right downstairs."

Amato was getting into his heavy black overcoat. He stopped, one arm in a sleeve, and looked blankly at Lye. "How come she's here?" he said at last.

"She drove me down and I told her to wait," Lye said. Anger ate at him like a corrosive acid. Amato was playing the puzzled peasant now, one of his most maddening roles. Everything would have to be spelled out for him in capitals. "You said to hurry," he explained. "I thought I'd make better time if she drove me."

"And she waited for you?"

"Well, I didn't think we'd be long."

"I see." Amato nodded and finished putting on his coat. "You don't want to drive me, is that it?"

"No. I'll tell her to go on home."

"It's no trouble?" Amato was smiling slightly.

"Of course not."

"Where does she live?"

"On the East Side. Near Park." He knew damn well where she lived, Lye thought bitterly.

"Pretty fancy neighborhood," Amato said shaking his head. "You're flying high, Joe."

"Well, it's her place, not mine."

Amato smiled cynically. "What does she pay the bills with? She ain't been in a show in ten years. How old is she anyway?"

Lye felt his mouth tightening. Turning away from Amato he said, "She's thirty-five."

Amato laughed and strolled to the door. "Yeah," he said. "Well, let's go."

Lye went downstairs ahead of him, his footsteps clattering noisily through the silent building, and Amato smiled as he snapped off the lights. The smile lingered on his lips as he went slowly down to the first floor.

Moving with short jerky strides, Lye crossed the street to the gray convertible that was parked in the darkness opposite union headquarters. He rapped his knuckles against the window and the girl at the wheel rolled the glass down quickly.

"What is it, Joe?" she said. "What's the matter?"

"Nothing the matter," he said in a low tense voice. "Does there have to be something the matter? You always act like the world's about to blow up in your face."

"Joe," she said pleadingly.

"I got to drive him home," he said. "I'll be up later."

"Sure, Joe." She was a pretty blonde woman, expensively cared for, but her eyes were miserable with fear. "Don't get excited," she said, and touched his hand gently. "Is he riding you again?"

"I got to take him home, that's all," he said, spacing the words deliberately and coldly. "Why do you make a Federal case out of everything?"

"I know what he does to you," she said.

"Will you stop it?"

"All right, Joe. But hurry."

"I'll make it as soon as I can."

Amato stood in the darkness across the street, listening to the murmur of their conversation. He saw the small pale blur of her face, and the pearls gleaming at her throat. Kay Johnson, he thought, turning the name slowly in his mind. He had seen her in a movie once, back in the late thirties.

She wasn't a very good actress, but she was damn good-looking, one of those long-legged, pink-and-white college-kid types, full of healthy sex and bounce. Amato had met her a couple of times with Joe, but always briefly. She was thin and elegant now, with a shining blonde hair-do, and very classy clothes. Nice for Joe, he thought. Too nice for Joe.

The engine turned over, filling the dark silence with the sound of power, and Joe Lye crossed the street and joined Amato on the sidewalk. When the car was halfway down the block, Amato said abruptly, "I'll take myself home."

Lye turned and stared after the red tail lights of her car.

"You can't catch her," Amato said irritably. "Get a cab."

"Sure," Lye said. He was breathing hard, but his anger was dissolving in relief and anticipation. "You sure you're okay?"

"For Christ's sake, yes."

"I'll see you in the morning."

Amato put his hands in his pockets and watched Lye hurrying off into the darkness, his thin black figure moving in a jerky, puppet's rhythm. In a sour and bitter mood, Amato finally turned and walked down the block to his sedan. With a conscious effort he tried not to think of the home he was going to, the cluttered, close-smelling apartment with its profusion of holy pictures and expensive, tasteless furniture. He shook his head quickly, as if trying to dislodge a disagreeable memory. Money meant nothing to his wife. If he gave her a hundred dollars she'd buy something for their nephew, or drop it in the poor box. Nothing for herself but a black dress that looked just like every other black dress she'd bought in the last twenty years. Amato slid behind the wheel of his car and made an attempt to change the direction of his thoughts. He didn't want to be envious of Joe Lye. That could mean trouble.

AT SEVEN O'CLOCK RETNICK LEFT HIS ROOM AND WALKED TO A RESTAURANT on the avenue for breakfast. The day was cold and beautiful; clean winter sunlight sparkled on the snow in the gutters and brightened the faces of the old brownstones. When he returned Mrs. Cara was waiting for him in the hall.

"There's a telephone call for you," she said. "The woman says she's your wife."

Retnick hesitated and Mrs. Cara watched his dark hard face with frank curiosity. "Okay," he said at last.

"And how was the cat?" Mrs. Cara said, catching his arm. "No trouble, eh?"

"No, not a bit."

"See? I told you," she smiled.

Retnick said, "That's right," and walked down the hall to the telephone. "Hello," he said.

"Steve—I saw the story on Frank," she said quietly. "I'm terribly sorry. I know what you meant to each other."

"Sure," he said. Then: "Where did you get this number?"

"From Lieutenant Neville. Steve, I want to go out to see Mrs. Ragoni this afternoon." She hesitated, then said tentatively, "Would you come with me?"

"I'm going to be busy," he said.

"Please, Steve, I want to talk to you. Last night was so terribly wrong."

"What do you want to talk about?" he said.

"Steve, Steve," she cried softly, and he knew that she was weeping. "Don't throw everything away. Won't you let me see you this morning?"

He hesitated, frowning at the phone. "Okay," he said at last. "I'll stop by Tim Moran's saloon around ten. Can you make that?"

"Yes, yes, of course."

Retnick put the phone down, irritated with himself. He didn't want to see her, not for any reason.

Twenty minutes later Retnick walked into a sturdy, red-brick station house on the West Side of the city. Nothing important had been changed, he noticed, as he stopped at the high wooden information desk. A new painting of the flag hung above the switchboard where a sergeant worked in contact with the district's squads and patrolmen. But everything else looked the same.

"Is Lieutenant Neville in?" he asked the lieutenant behind the desk.

"He's upstairs in the Detective division. Take the stairs at the end of the hall."

Sergeant Kleyburg was sitting alone in the long file room, frowning at a bulky report on his desk. When Retnick stopped at the counter that divided the office, Kleyburg glanced up and removed the horn-rimmed glasses from his broad, impassive face. Then he said, "I'll be damned," in a hoarse, surprised voice. He crossed the room, grinning, and pushed open the gate at the end of the counter. "Come in, boy," he said.

They shook hands and Retnick glanced around at the familiar dusty furniture, the height chart, the bank of gray steel filing cabinets, the bulletin board with its cluster of yellowing flyers.

"It hasn't changed much," he said, looking at Kleyburg.

"You haven't either," Kleyburg said, punching him lightly on the arm. "You look great."

"I feel great," Retnick said.

Kleyburg nodded slowly, his eyes grave and hard. "I can imagine, Steve. You took a lousy rap."

"You should have been on the jury," Retnick said. "Is the lieutenant busy?"

"Hell, no. You want to see him alone?"

"It doesn't matter. But one thing first. Do you have a detective here named Connors?"

"He's on my shift."

"Does he work for anyone else?"

Kleyburg shrugged. "I couldn't prove it. That answer your question?"

"Yeah," Retnick said. "He's real smart, eh?"

Kleyburg shrugged again. "We get smart ones occasionally. You know that. They don't last long. Let's go see the boss."

Lieutenant Neville, a slim man with an air of competence about him, looked up from his desk when they opened the door of the office. "Well, well," he said, standing and grinning at Retnick. "You should have given us a little warning. We could have had drinks and dancing girls. How the devil are you, Steve?"

"Fair enough," Retnick said.

"I suppose you don't have any plans yet," Neville said.

"Oh, yes," Retnick said, staring at him. "I'm going to find out about Ragoni."

A small silence settled in the room. Kleyburg shifted his weight from one foot to the other, and Neville ran a hand slowly over his thinning brown hair. "That was rough," he said. "I know you were friends." He picked up a report from his desk, frowned at it for a second, and then offered it to Retnick. "That's all we have so far," he said.

Retnick skimmed through the detective's report, picking out the important information quickly. Body of deceased had been observed by a barge captain, floating just under the surface of the river at Eighty-seventh Street. Identification had been made by wife of the deceased. Cause of death was listed as knife wounds.

"That's all you've got, eh?" Retnick said, dropping the report on Neville's desk.

"We just found his body last night."

"You haven't questioned Nick Amato, of course," Retnick said gently.

"Why the 'of course'? We'll pick him up if there's a reason to, Steve."

"He's moving in on Glencannon's local," Retnick said. "Ragoni was warned to stop lobbying against Amato and his hoodlums. Now Ragoni's dead. I'd say this is a good time to pick up Nick Amato."

"You don't pick up Nick Amato with a case like that," Neville said. "Now listen to me, Steve. I'm a cop, not a tea-leaf reader. And I've got to talk to you like a cop. You get in trouble with Amato and I won't be able to help you out of it. Do you understand?"

"I'm not asking for help," Retnick said.

Neville's face was troubled. He came around the desk and put a hand on Retnick's arm. "Don't be so touchy," he said. "Off the record, I'll do what I can. And I think that goes for Kleyburg here and lots of other cops. But officially you're an ex-cop and an ex-con. Those are two strikes against you, Steve. Keep that in mind."

Retnick smiled coldly. "There's not much chance of forgetting it. Take it easy, Lieutenant."

"Now don't barge off this way," Neville said, tightening his grip on Retnick's arm. "Calm down and listen to me. Will you do that?"

"I'll listen," Retnick said.

Neville sat on the edge of his desk and took out his pipe. "You're thirty-three now, right?"

"That's right."

"You've got a long life ahead of you. Don't throw it away, Steve."

"A long life," Retnick said. "And what do I do with that nice long life?"

"You can start over, Steve."

"The big bright dream," Retnick said, staring at him with a bitter smile on his lips. "Work hard, make good. I did that once, remember? I worked my way through school, and earned eight major letters while I was doing it. I took the police exams when I was twenty-two, and was a third-grade detective eighteen months later. Working hard, making good. I've had enough of it. Let somebody else work hard and make good. I've got other plans."

Neville was silent a moment, staring at his unlighted pipe. Then he said: "Do those plans include your wife?"

"No," Retnick said. "They concern the guy who killed Joe Ventra."

"Steve, you're heading for trouble."

Retnick started to say something, but changed his mind. He made a short, chopping gesture with his hand, and said, "Why waste each other's time? Take it easy, Lieutenant."

Kleyburg followed him down the stairs and caught up with him on the sidewalk. He blinked into the bright sunlight and said, "Steve, if you need anything, just yell. Remember that. Anything."

Retnick said, "Is Ben McCabe still the super over at the North Star Lines?"

"Yes. Why?"

"That's where Ragoni worked," Retnick said. "It's the last place he was seen alive. It's a good place to ask a question or two."

Kleyburg's eyes were worried. "Watch yourself, boy."

The North Star Lines terminal boomed with noise and commotion; two ships were loading that morning, and winches, trucks and men were straining against the inflexible pressure of time and tides. Retnick stopped before the checker's office and here, at the mouth of the cavernous warehouse, the noise beat against him in waves.

A guard in a leather jacket stepped out of the office and looked at Retnick with close, sharp eyes.

"Is Ben McCabe around?" Retnick said.

"Yeah, but they got two ships working. He's pretty busy. What'd you want to see him about?"

"Tell him Steve Retnick is looking for him."

"Will that be enough?"

"Let's try it," Retnick said.

The guard shrugged and said, "You wait here." He walked onto the pier and turned out of sight around a wall of cargo. In a minute or so he reappeared and said, "It's okay, Retnick. You know the way?"

"I can find him," Retnick said. The terminal was cold and drafty; above the whine of winches and rumble of trucks the wind sang through the superstructure of the ships, and swept refuse in frantic eddies along the thick planking of the floor. The air smelled of coffee and oil and the river. Retnick turned into an aisle formed by crates of cargo and went up a flight of steps to McCabe's office, which overlooked the length of the pier. McCabe's chief clerk, a thin, balding man with a shy smile said, "Well, Steve, it's nice to see you again."

His name was Sam Enright, Retnick remembered. They shook hands and Enright said, "Go right on in. The boss is expecting you."

"Thanks, Sam."

McCabe stood up when Retnick entered his office, a short, stockily built man in his fifties, with thick, gray hair and a bold, good-humored face. "I didn't expect to see you for a couple of months," he said, as they shook hands. "I thought you'd go off on a long fishing trip or something. You look fine though, like you'd been fishing instead—" He smiled apologetically and didn't finish the sentence.

"Well, I was up the river anyway," Retnick said.

McCabe smiled. "Sit down. What's on your mind?"

"I want to find out about Ragoni."

McCabe said slowly, "You know he's dead, I guess."

"I heard about it last night. That's why I'm here."

McCabe wasn't smiling now; his manner was cautious. "You probably know as much as I do, Steve. Ragoni was last seen in the hold of the *Santa Domingo,* nine days ago around midnight. He went on deck and didn't come back. The crew thought he'd gone home." He hesitated and shrugged. "The next day we learned that he hadn't gone home. Last night we learned that he'd been murdered. It's a police matter from now on."

"How about the accident a couple of weeks ago?" Retnick said, casually. "Was someone trying to get Ragoni then?"

McCabe's eyes narrowed slightly. "Who told about an accident?"

"I spent my first afternoon out of jail at Ragoni's home," Retnick said. "His wife told me about the accident."

"Well, there was an accident, as you obviously know," McCabe said. "We investigated it thoroughly. It was a mix-up in orders. The winchman lowered a draft while Ragoni was on the loading platform. Fortunately, he saw it coming and got clear."

"Did you notify the police?"

"That isn't customary, as you know." McCabe's manner was cold and sharp. There were spots of color in his cheeks.

"You know Amato's moving onto your pier, don't you?" Retnick said. McCabe stood up abruptly and said, "That's a matter I won't discuss."

"Which means the answer is yes," Retnick said.

"Neither yes or no," McCabe said, coming around his desk. "We're shippers. We're not philosophers of labor, and we aren't police officers. We work with what the unions give us. I wish the public understood that. Union squabbles aren't our concern."

"Sure," Retnick said coldly. "And because of that Ragoni is dead."

"I don't like the implication," McCabe said angrily.

"I don't like it either," Retnick said. "It stinks, if you ask me. Ragoni was fighting as an individual to keep Amato's killers from taking over the place he worked. They warned him to keep quiet, but he wouldn't. So they tried for him with a few tons of cargo, and then they stuck a knife in his back. And the same thing will happen to any man who doesn't want to take orders from Amato's stooges."

McCabe turned away and ran a hand through his hair. "All right, all right," he said bitterly. "If Amato wins the election he's in. He supplies our terminal. And what in hell can we do about it?"

"You could close down the pier and ship out of Boston or Philly," Retnick said. "You could post a notice that you wouldn't come back to the city until Amato's killers were out of the union. How would that sit with your stockholders?"

"You guess," McCabe said.

"Well, I didn't come here to tell you your business," Retnick said. "I need a favor."

"What's that?"

"I want to talk to Ragoni's crew."

"Why?"

Retnick shrugged. "I was a good friend of his."

McCabe hesitated, staring with worried eyes at the river that flowed sluggishly past his windows. "Put it that way, and it's all right. But this can't be official, Steve. You understand my position, I think."

"Sure. Can I see them now?"

"Come with me. Ragoni's gang is on the *Executive*."

Retnick followed McCabe downstairs to the pier. Ahead of them the terminal jutted out a hundred yards into the river, a peninsula of noise and light and movement. The *Executive* was loading to their right, its long graceful hull curving high above the docks.

Retnick and McCabe walked down an aisle flanked by small mountains of cargo, and boarded her amidships. The wind hit them with buffeting force as they stepped from a companionway to the ship's unsheltered aft deck. At the moment cargo was being stacked in the hold, and the winchman and deck gang were idle; they stood about the open hatch with their hands in their pockets and shoulders hunched against the weather. A big man in a leather windbreaker walked over to them and tugged the brim of his cap.

"Everything's on schedule, Mr. McCabe," he said.

"Fine. Brophy, this is Steve Retnick."

Brophy tilted his big square head to one side and studied Retnick with narrow eyes. "I think we met," he said. "Didn't you used to be at the Thirty-First?"

"That's right."

"What can I do for you?" Brophy said. Several men drifted over and fanned out in a semicircle behind him, their eyes flicking curiously from Brophy to Retnick.

"I was a good friend of Frank Ragoni and his family," Retnick said. "His wife is in pretty bad shape right now, as you can imagine."

"Sure." Brophy nodded, and several of the men behind him murmured appropriately.

"I talked to her this morning," Retnick said. "The only thing on her mind was an accident Frank had had on the job a few weeks ago. The doctor told me that this kind of thing is common in shock cases. She was trying to think about anything except the fact that Frank was dead. To calm her down, I told her I'd come over and talk to Mr. McCabe about it. He was good enough to let me see you boys."

His words made an impression on the men. They all looked solemn and thoughtful. Brophy said, "I can tell you about the accident, Retnick. But it wasn't an accident, I guess you know. It was a near-miss. I was in the hold next to Ragoni when it happened. There was some dunnage on the loading platform and Ragoni said something about it. I guess he asked if he should pick it up. Well, I'd already given the signal to lower away, so I said never mind." Brophy took a deep breath that filled his body out like a circus fat man's. "But he didn't hear me, I guess. Or he misunderstood. He scrambled onto the platform just as the winch let the draft go. It missed Ragoni by an inch or two. That's the story, Retnick, all of it."

Retnick nodded. "I know how those things happen. By the way, who was on the winch?"

"An extra man, fellow name of Evans. Grady here had been out sick for a week or so."

"I had the flu," a red-faced little man in the group said importantly. "Couldn't get out of bed for two weeks."

Retnick looked at him. "Did you know this fellow Evans?"

The question seemed to put Grady on the defensive. He looked from side to side as if expecting an attack from either direction. "No, I didn't know him. He was a new man."

"Did you know him, Brophy?"

"Me?" Brophy looked surprised. "No, Steinkamp, our hiring boss, picked him out of the shape when Grady called in sick. Evans knew his stuff, that's all I cared about."

Retnick didn't ask any more questions. He sensed that the mention of Evans had changed the mood of the men.

"Thanks a lot," he said to Brophy. "I won't take up any more of your time."

They walked back to the terminal office through the noise that crashed between the iron hulls of the two big liners. McCabe sat on the edge of his desk and looked at Retnick.

"That's as much as I can do for you," he said. "You heard the story. It's straight."

"Yes, I think it is," Retnick said. He shrugged and smiled. "Thanks a lot, Mac."

"Anytime, Steve."

Retnick nodded good-by to him and left his office. Sam Enright glanced up from his desk in the outer room and said, "Well, the boss looks pretty good, wouldn't you say?"

"Yes, he does," Retnick said.

"I suppose it's too early to ask about your plans."

"I'm going to loaf a while." Retnick sat on the edge of Enright's desk and lit a cigarette. "By the way, what kind of fellow was Evans?"

Enright ran both hands over his bald head, and then frowned as if he were both surprised and a little hurt to find that his hair was gone. "Well, Evans wasn't here more than eight or ten days. He was a big guy, a redhead. They called him Red. Quite a hot-tempered character, I heard. Why?"

"I think I knew a friend of his in jail. Do you have an address for Evans?"

"Just a minute." Enright went to a filing cabinet and took out a card. "We have the dope on him because of that accident. Normally these extra men just float in and out. Got a pencil? He had a room on Tenth Avenue. 201, Tenth. Got it?"

"Yes, thanks. When did he leave here?"

"About a week ago, I think."

Right after Ragoni disappeared, Retnick thought. "Well, it may not be the same guy," he said casually.

"From what I heard of Red Evans you're lucky if it isn't," Enright said.

Retnick smiled, but his eyes were cold and deadly. "We'll see," he said.

Outside Retnick crossed the avenue and waited for a cab. Traffic was heavy now; trucks rattled by him in steady streams, rushing the city's supplies to terminals, docks, freight yards. The sun had gone under a bank of low black clouds, and the day was stark and cold. Retnick's hunter's senses told him he had struck a hot trail; it was hardly coincidence that Evans and Ragoni had disappeared at the same time. This was a lead the police might not come across. There was no report of the near accident and the longshoremen, even Ragoni's friends, wouldn't be likely to mention it. The penalties for talking were too high.

Evans' attempt to kill Ragoni a week before would be smothered in silence. And the facts would change mysteriously; the file on him might disappear from Enright's office, and men would remember him as dark-haired and small, if they remembered him at all.

Retnick flagged a cab and gave the driver Evans' Tenth Avenue address. It was a run-down rooming house crowded in between a small factory and a dead storage garage for automobiles. He talked with Evans' erstwhile landlady, a plump middle-aged woman with an orderly enthusiasm for detail. Evans had been with her for a month to the day, and had checked out a week ago. He was a man who kept mostly to himself; she saw him only when he stopped by to pay his weekly rent. But he kept his room neat, which wasn't surprising since he seldom slept there. She didn't know where he slept.

"Is he in some kind of trouble?" she asked him at last.

Retnick smiled. "Just the opposite. We've got some money for him on a damage claim he filed last year."

"Oh. Well, I wish I could help you."

"Did he send his laundry out in the neighborhood?"

"Yes, I believe he took it around to the Chinaman's. That's in the middle of the next block."

"Thanks a lot," Retnick said. "If I catch up with him I'll tell him to send you a box of candy."

She smiled cynically. "That'll be the day."

Retnick walked down to the Chinese laundry, playing a hunch; Evans hadn't used his room at night, which suggested a girl friend. And in that case he might have had his laundry sent to her place. The laundry man was small and young, with smooth blank eyes. Two children played behind the counter, and a woman in a shapeless dress and slippers was ironing shirts on a table against the wall. The room was warm and smelled cleanly of soap and fresh linen.

The young man remembered Evans. Yes. He had work shirts and dress shirts, lots of them. He dropped them off himself, usually in the morning, and his oldest boy delivered them. No, not down the block, but over on the East Side.

Retnick's fingers were trembling slightly as he wrote down the address and apartment number.

"You a cop?" the young man asked him then.

Retnick smiled at him, letting him believe what he wanted, and the young man sighed and nodded. "Good job," he said.

Retnick thanked him and left. It was almost ten o'clock, the time he'd agreed to meet his wife at Tim Moran's. He hesitated on the cold, slushy sidewalk, staring at the address he had got from the laundryman. That would keep for a bit. The session with his wife wouldn't take long.

# 5

RETNICK WALKED INTO TIM MORAN'S SALOON A FEW MINUTES AFTER ten. The bar was crowded then with longshoremen who had been skipped over at the morning's shape-up. They were smoking and chatting over their beers, killing time until they could shape again in the afternoon. Several of them glanced curiously at Retnick as he moved to a vacant spot at the bar, his hands deep in the pockets of his overcoat. Tim Moran waved a greeting and came to meet him, a tentative smile touching his small red face.

"Has my wife been in here this morning?" Retnick said.

"I haven't seen her, Steve."

"I'll take a booth. Send her back, will you?"

"Sure. Can I bring you something to drink?"

"No, never mind."

Retnick walked to the rear of the big noisy room, moving down a narrow corridor formed by the crowded bar on his left and the line of brown wooden booths on his right. He hung up his hat and sat down in the last booth without bothering to take off his overcoat. From here he could see the length of the bar, the front doors and the big plate glass windows that faced the avenue. It was snowing again and the wind was higher. The big soft flakes rushed past in fast formations, straight lines of white against the windows.

Retnick lit a cigarette and stared at two longshoremen who were regarding him with simple curiosity. They turned away, confused by the cold anger in his eyes, and went back to their beer and talk. He settled down in the booth then and watched the smoke curling in slow spirals from his cigarette, isolated from the cheerful noises of the bar, by the dark and bitter cast of his thoughts. He glanced up when his wife came in. She closed the door quickly against the rush of cold air that swirled into the room, and stood indecisively for an instant, a small uncertain smile touching her lips. Her cheeks were flushed from the wind. She wore a gray tweed topcoat with a flaring skirt, and flakes of melting snow glistened in her close-cut, curly black hair. Moran saw her and waved, and she went to the bar and shook hands with him, moving with a quick light grace that seemed appropriate to any place or occasion. The men at the bar made room for her, grinning sympathetically as she stamped the snow from her small black pumps. There was a quality of direct, unself-conscious friendliness about her that put them completely at ease. A pretty picture, Retnick thought, staring impassively at her clean warm beauty. Charming the simple souls with a quick smile, the turn of a slim ankle. No wonder she looks good, he thought, putting out his cigarette. She's had five good years. Big good years. Anger twisted in his breast like the turn of a cold blade. She hadn't missed anything, anything at all.

She smiled at something Moran said in parting, and then walked quickly toward the rear of the room. But the smile left her face when Retnick stood up and she saw the look in his eyes; she faltered for an instant, as if a heavy weight had suddenly been placed on her shoulders.

"I'm sorry I'm late," she said, sliding into the booth. "There weren't any cabs. Have you been waiting long?"

The words meant nothing; they were defensive little flurries against the barrier in his face and eyes.

"It doesn't matter," he said. "What's on your mind?"

She was silent a moment, frowning at the backs of her hands. Then she sighed and looked at him. "Last night was all wrong, Steve."

"What did you expect?"

"I thought we could talk to each other, at least."

"We talked," he said.

"We just made noises," she said. "There was no more communication than you'd find between a Martian and a—a Zulu."

"Did that surprise you?"

She stared at him for a few seconds, studying the lines in his hard face. Then she said slowly, "Do you hate me so much you won't even listen to me? I want to explain what happened. Don't I deserve that much of a break?"

Retnick laughed shortly. "A break," he said. "That's very funny."

"It isn't funny," she said, with a sharp note of anger in her voice. "Who says I'm dirt on the floor? Who treats me like God's greatest slut? You, the final judge! But you won't listen to my side of it. You've made up your mind and the case is closed. I can go whistle."

Retnick lit a cigarette and flipped the match aside. "Is that all you've got to say?"

She put her hands over his suddenly. "I want a break and I don't deserve one. Is that so terrible? You've got to have some compassion left. They couldn't change you that much."

"I'm not interested in forgiving people," Retnick said.

She withdrew her hands from his slowly. "Forgiving your enemies isn't optional," she said. "It's something you've got to do. There's a direct order, isn't there? 'Father forgive them'. Or maybe that's not it. You could check with Father Bristow."

"I've got nothing to talk to him about," Retnick said.

"This is just a waste of time then," she said slowly.

Retnick's hands burned from the touch of her cool fingers. He swallowed a tightness in his throat and said, "Sure, it's a waste of time."

She looked down at the surface of the table and moistened her lips. For a moment she was silent. Then she said dryly, "That's that, I guess. If you want to play it like the great stone face, all right. What I wanted to talk to you about was this: I saved some money while you were gone. About six thousand dollars. I'd like you to take it and go away and do what you want with it. Go fishing or hunting, or go to Florida and lie in the sun, or get drunk for a year if you like. Then come back. Maybe we could talk by then. Would you do that, Steve?"

He smiled bitterly. "You think I'm mixed up, eh? Like a GI with battle fatigue. Give him a few helpings of apple pie and let him loaf in the sun and he'll be okay."

"Then what *is* wrong with you?"

"Nothing's wrong with me," he said sharply. "I'm going to find the men who killed Ventra and there'll be a big, loud pay-off. That makes sense to me. If you don't think I'm right, then I suggest you take the dough and go on a therapeutic binge. You need it."

As he was talking Retnick heard the front door open and felt the sudden draft of cold air about his ankles. But he paid no attention to it until he became conscious of the strange, expectant silence that had settled over the room. He looked up then and saw Joe Lye and Hammy standing at the far end of the bar.

"Steve," she said. "Listen to me. I want—"

"I'll get you a cab," he said.

"Please. If you leave this way we can never fix it up."

"Let's go," he said, standing. "I don't want to talk any more."

She slipped from the booth, buttoning the collar of her coat, and Retnick picked up his hat. The longshoremen along the bar sipped beer in silence, minding their own business with scrupulous care. Tim Moran stood at the spigots, his face grave and impassive, but Retnick caught the little flash of warning in his eyes.

Marcia walked quickly toward the front door, her high heels sounding sharply in the unnatural stillness. Retnick followed her, ignoring the cautious glances shot at him by men at the bar. Then, when he was at the door, Joe Lye said, "Hello, Steve," and his voice fell softly into the silence.

Retnick hesitated. Marcia stopped with her hand on the knob and looked up at him, suddenly aware of the tension in the room.

Lye said, "Don't hurry off because of us, Steve."

Retnick turned around slowly, hands deep in the pockets of his overcoat. Under the brim of his hat his face was expressionless. He knew it would be wise to clear out before there was trouble; but his control was slipping.

"What do you want, Joe?" he said quietly.

Lye and Hammy stood together at the turn of the bar, with space on either side of them; the men nearest them had drifted casually toward the juke box and lunch table at the rear of the room. Lye, tall and thin in black clothes, looked relaxed and easy, but the straining little smile was flashing like a danger signal at the side of his pallid face. Hammy was grinning expectantly. His hands were hooked onto the lapels of his tan overcoat, pulling it back from his huge chest. He looked slightly drunk; there was a hot gleam in his little eyes, and his round, flat face was flushed and beaded with perspiration.

The smile tightened on Lye's face. "There's some talk that you got dumb in jail," he said. "I wanted to check on that."

"How do you plan to find out?" Retnick said.

Lye laughed gently. "Well, maybe I'll give you one of those I.Q. tests. Hammy here can ask the questions."

Marcia caught Retnick's arm. "Steve, let's go."

"There's no hurry," he said, staring at Lye.

"They want trouble. Don't be a fool."

Hammy laughed happily. "Your wife says you're a fool and I guess she should know. How come you're living with a little kitty cat when you got a dish like that waiting for you, Retnick? That's the first question in the big I.Q. test."

The little grin on Retnick's lips did something ugly to his face. "I've got questions too," he said. "Who killed Frank Ragoni? Who killed Joe Ventra? Those are mine, Joe. Tell Amato I'll be around to try them on him one of these days."

Lye's unnatural smile strained his mouth in a tight, twisted line. "You still talk real big, Steve. I bet Hammy can fix that."

"He can try," Retnick said gently.

"Steve, don't!" Marcia cried.

Hammy laughed again. "You big clown," he said, and surged toward Retnick, a long powerful arm swinging in an arc at his neck. He loved this work; all he needed was a grip and then he could maul and batter any man to pieces.

But he never got his grip; Retnick slapped his arm away with a blow that spun him around in a half-circle. Then he hit him twice in the body, deliberately and cruelly, bringing the punches up with effortless, terrible power, and Hammy's breath left his body in an agonized gasp. His hands dropped quickly, as if invisible weights had suddenly been shackled to his wrists, and he fought for breath through a wide, straining mouth. He stared at Retnick, his eyes bulging piteously, and Retnick hit him again, slugging the wide exposed jaw with all the strength in his body. Hammy's knees quit under him then, and he went down to the floor in a lugubrious sprawl, falling like an old man, limply and helplessly. Lying on his side, he panted for breath, a bloody froth bubbling on his lips.

Retnick stared at Joe Lye, who stood perfectly still, his face twisted into a fixed weird smile. "Do you want to go on with your little question game?" he said softly. Already, the short, hot anger was gone, purged by the simple moment of action. But the old anger was with him still, cold and lasting, running powerfully under all his emotions.

Lye shook his head slowly. When he spoke his voice was barely audible. "It's your round."

"You're smart, Joe," Retnick said. The room was silent and still as he looked down at Hammy's helpless bulk. "Next time I'll kill you," he said. "Remember that."

Then he walked past his wife, opened the door and started uptown, moving with long strides into the driving snow. He heard her call his name and he heard her footsteps behind him, but he kept walking. She caught up with him finally and took his arm in both of her hands. "Steve, stop," she said. "Don't run away from me like this."

He looked down at her. She was very pale; her lipstick stood out as a vivid slash, and her eyes were dark with fear. "Why did you do it?" she said. "What's wrong with you?"

"They asked for it, they got it," he said.

"You wanted to kill him," she said. "Steve, you've got to stop. You're —you're like an animal."

"I'm not stopping. I haven't started yet."

She stared at him and then shook her head quickly. "It's not just me you hate. You hate everybody. You'll go on hating until you're killed."

"That shouldn't bother you," he said, and pulled his arm away from her and walked toward the avenue. She stared after him, one hand touching her throat, until his big body disappeared into the clouds of swirling snow.

# 6

THE BUILDING WAS A HANDSOME BROWNSTONE IN A QUIET BLOCK EAST OF Park, a street of neat iron grill-work and well-kept window boxes. The apartment number was 4 B, and the name on the tiny white card was

Dixie Davis. This was where Red Evans had told the laundryman to deliver his shirts.

Retnick paused in the small lobby, smoothed down his thick black hair and brushed the snow from his shoulders. He pressed the buzzer then, knowing there was nothing to do but move ahead and hope for luck. Everything else was gone from his mind; his wife, Lye and Hammy, these were phantoms he could dissolve with an exercise of will. A tiny, scratching noise sounded from the speaker and a girl's voice said, "Hello?"

"This is a friend of Red Evans," he said. "I'd like to talk to you."

"Talk away, friend," she said indifferently; her voice sounded as if it hadn't registered surprise in a long, long time.

"I'd rather make it private. Can I come up for a minute?"

There was an interval of silence. Then she said, "Where'd you know Red?"

"At the docks. At the North Star Lines."

Again she hesitated. Then: "Okay, friend."

She stood in the doorway of her apartment, a small redhead with very cold blue eyes. There was no interest or friendliness in her pale face; she studied him with instinctive caution as he walked down the short hallway from the landing. She was in her late twenties, he guessed, and nobody's innocent little doll. The sharp blue eyes, points of light under the red bangs, had seen more than their share of fakes and deadbeats and frauds.

He said, "I hope I'm not breaking up your schedule." She wore a blue silk robe and slippers, but her eyes and face were made up for the street.

She shrugged her thin shoulders, dismissing the apology as irrelevant. "When did you see Red last?" she said.

"Not for quite a while." Retnick glanced at the closed doors along the hall. "I'd rather not talk about it out here. It's pretty important."

"Okay, come on in."

The room was small, but attractively furnished with conventional modern pieces. Everything was primly neat and clean; magazines formed orderly designs on the coffee tables, and the tiny felt pillows on the sofa were lined up as neatly as marshmallows in a box. The only personal note was a floppy Raggedy Ann doll which was propped up on an ottoman before the small television set.

"Mind if I smoke?" he said as she closed the door.

"Go ahead. What's so important about finding Red?"

"How about you?" He offered her the pack, but she shook her head and sat down in a deep chair beside a liquor cabinet. A door stood open behind her, and Retnick noticed an overnight bag on the bed and, beside it, a slip and nylon stockings. A pair of anklestrap sandals were placed neatly together on the floor. He lit his cigarette and glanced around for an ashtray.

"On the coffee table," she said.

"Thanks."

"Let's get on with it," she said. "Why'd you come here looking for Red?"

"I'll level with you," Retnick said. "I don't know Red. I never met the guy. But I want to find him."

She stared at him, one foot swinging slowly, her eyes shining and cold in her pale face. Then she said, "I don't go for jokers like you. What's your angle?"

"I want to find Evans. It's simple as that."

"Are you a private cop or something?"

Retnick shook his head. "I just got out of jail. My name's Retnick. Does that mean anything to you?"

She shook her head slowly. "Should it?"

"Not particularly. Before I went up I gave some cash to a man I thought I could trust. A man by the name of Ragoni. Ever hear of him?"

"We must move in different crowds, friend," she said.

"You'll never meet Ragoni. He's dead," Retnick said. "He got killed about the time Red Evans disappeared from the docks. I learned that from some buddies of mine at the pier. I guess you see why I'm looking for Evans."

"You think maybe he's got your dough?"

Retnick smiled slightly. "It's worth checking, don't you think?"

"How'd you find out I knew him?"

"From his landlady. He gave her this address for forwarding mail."

"That's my redhead," she said, with a bitter little smile. "Give me one of those cigarettes, will you?"

"Sure." Retnick held a light for her and she murmured a thank you and let her head rest against the upholstered back of the chair. The bitter little smile was still on her lips. "So Red uses me as a forwarding address, eh? That's like him. He's a guy who takes over. And then he takes off. I can't help you, mister. I haven't heard from him since he walked out on me."

"That's too bad," Retnick said.

She laughed shortly. "It's the kindest thing he ever did. He took me for plenty, including what was left of my girlish dreams. I met him at the place I work, which is a saloon that calls itself a rendezvous. Okay, he's good-looking, and he's got a nice line. I buy it. Pretty soon he's moved in on me, which wasn't bad. We were a permanent deal, he said." She smiled cynically and shook her head. "I'm believing all this, remember. We were going to Canada where everything was new and fresh. He wanted to raise cattle or something. You should hear him on the evils of cities. Corny, eh? Well, girls like corn, mister. It makes them fat and sleepy. One day he didn't show up, and I found the three hundred bucks gone from my piggy bank." She spread her hands. "End of story. No

Canada, no good life on the plains. If you find him, mister, you got my permission to use his head for a golf ball."

Retnick frowned slightly. "You think he might have gone to Canada alone?"

"I wouldn't know. He talked like he'd discovered the damn place, but he could have got all that from a book."

"Would you get in touch with me if he shows up again?"

She smiled at him, swinging one foot in a little circle. The silken robe slipped apart at her knees, revealing slender, chalk-white legs. "Was it a lot of money, mister?" she said slowly.

"It's enough for two people to have some fun with," Retnick said. "How about it?"

"You don't want to raise cattle and live the good life, by any chance?"

Retnick smiled and shook his head. "I'm a city type. I like my cattle with french-fries on the side. Do we do business?"

"So what can I lose?" she said. "If the bum shows up I'll let you know."

"Fine." Retnick took a pencil from his pocket and wrote his number on the back of a packet of matches. "You can get me there," he said, dropping the matches on the table. "And I know where to find you."

She stood and smoothed down the front of her robe. "This is a business deal, I think you said."

"That's right," Retnick said, smiling into her small hard eyes. "If you want to change the rules, let me know."

"Fair enough," she said, moving to the door. "Good luck, big boy."

"Thanks." Retnick walked past her into the short hallway and started down the stairs. When he heard her door close he stopped and listened to the silence for a moment or two. Then he went quietly back to her apartment and put his ear against the door. She was speaking to someone in a low, urgent voice, but he couldn't distinguish the words; her voice was a blur of anxious sound.

Retnick went down to the street then and walked a block before hailing a cab. "This is a tail job," he said to the driver. "Is that okay with you?"

The driver, an intelligent-looking old man, looked around at him. "Are you a cop?"

"I'm a husband," Retnick said. "Okay?"

"All right, get in," the old man said without enthusiasm.

Retnick lit a cigarette and settled back in the seat. From there he could see the entrance to Dixie's building. He felt reasonably certain that she was still in contact with Red Evans; her version of their relationship didn't fit her type. Things happened that way to some girls, but not to hard-shelled little characters like Dixie Davis.

She came out of her building about five minutes later and glanced at her watch as she started toward Park Avenue, picking her way awkwardly through the slush in high-heeled shoes.

"That your wife?" the driver said, shifting into first.

"Yes. Give her a little lead."

Dixie Davis crossed Park and stopped on the corner, obviously looking for a cab. "She's going downtown," Retnick said. "You'd better get ahead of her."

"I got you," the driver said. He swung into Park and stopped at the canopied entrance of an apartment building. The doorman came out from the lobby, but the driver held up a street-guide, and called, "Just checking an address, buddy."

The doorman nodded and went back to the lobby. In the rear-vision mirror Retnick saw Dixie climb into a cab that had pulled up for the red light. "Pick up the first Yellow that passes us," he told his driver.

"All right."

They followed the Yellow across town to the Pennsylvania station, and the driver said, "They're heading into the back tunnel. You want to go down?"

"Let a couple of cabs get ahead of us," Retnick said. When they stopped for a light he gave the driver a bill and waved the change.

"I hope this is where she told you she was going," the old man said, looking back at Retnick.

Retnick smiled slightly. "She's running true to form."

In the brightly lighted tunnel Retnick waited until Dixie had paid off her cab and started for the revolving doors that led to the station. Then he went down the ramp and signaled a Red Cap. "I've got a job for you," he said. "It's worth five bucks. Okay?"

"Sure, if it's legal," the Red Cap said.

"Come on with me." Inside the vast waiting room Retnick saw Dixie heading for the coach ticket windows. He pointed her out to the Red Cap and said, "Find out where she buys a ticket to. I'll wait here."

Retnick was able to follow Dixie's bright red hair through the crowd without difficulty. He saw her stop briefly at the ticket window, and then hurry toward the train shed with short quick steps. The Red Cap came back and said, "She's going to Trenton, sir. At least she bought a ticket there."

"Thanks very much," Retnick said, and gave him his money.

"Thank you, sir."

Trenton, Retnick thought, as he walked toward a rank of telephone booths. Was that where Red Evans had holed up? If so, one small part of the problem was solved. But the greater part remained: to establish who had paid him to do the job. Even then Retnick knew he might be no closer to the man who had killed Ventra. He was suddenly swept with a sense of oppressive futility. And when it was all over, when he had proved that a cop named Retnick had been framed, what the hell would it mean? Where would he be? Still sitting in a cheap bedroom, or standing at a cheap bar, as isolated from humanity as he was right now. For a moment or so he stared at the crowds passing him, experiencing a curious bitter loneliness. Some of the people looked happy. He wondered what they knew. Or what they didn't know. Finally he shrugged and stepped into a telephone booth. He called Kleyburg at the Thirty-First, and got through to him after a short wait. "You said to yell if I needed anything," he said.

"Sure, Steve. What is it?"

"Take this down." Retnick gave him Dixie Davis' name and address. Then he said, "I'd like to know all about her. Where she works, what her days off are, who she sees, and so forth. Is that possible?"

"I can manage it. She lives in the Twentieth, but I've got some friends over there. Between us we'll get a fix on her. Look, I'll have to cut this short. We're busy today." He hesitated, then said, "Maybe you haven't seen a paper."

"No, what's up?"

"They found old Jack Glencannon's body a couple of hours ago. On a siding just off Twelfth Avenue."

"What happened to him?"

"Nobody's sure yet. But it looks like a homicide."

Retnick sat in the booth for a moment or so, staring at the bustle and commotion in the cavernous station. There was a hard little smile on his lips. This would tighten the screws on Nick Amato, whether he was responsible for the old man's death or not. The papers would set fires under the cops and unions now. The pot would boil and the public would want a victim or two tossed into it. That was fine. Let them all burn.

# 7

AT FOUR O'CLOCK THAT AFTERNOON RETNICK STOOD WATCHING THE ENtrance to the North Star Lines terminal. It was almost dark then; the snow had stopped falling but a damp heavy fog swirled in massive clouds off the river. Floodlights, mounted on the piers, picked up shifting gleams on the surface of the water, and the moan of fog horns was a threatening sound above the rumble of traffic. Retnick smoked one cigarette after another, and kept his eyes on the entrance to the North Star Lines. Finally the little Irishman, Grady, appeared, leaving work with a group of longshoremen. This was the man Retnick wanted to talk to, Grady, the winchman whose job Red Evans had taken over. The men crossed the street, their figures black and clumsy in the gray fog, heading for the welcoming yellow gleam of Tim Moran's saloon. When they disappeared inside Retnick lit another cigarette and settled down to wait.

It was six when Grady came out of Moran's. He was alone now, and his step was brisk but slightly unsteady as he started uptown.

Retnick followed him through the darkness for a block or two and came up behind him in an empty stretch of the avenue. He put a hand on Grady's arm and crowded him against the brick wall of a warehouse. "I've been looking for you, Grady," he said.

Grady was slightly drunk and he didn't quite understand what was happening. "What's the matter with you now?" he said, blinking at Retnick. "Let me by. What kind of funny business are you pulling?"

"I was a friend of Frank Ragoni's," Retnick said.

"Sure we were all his friends," Grady said. His mood changed and he sighed. "It was a dirty shame, a dirty shame. Him with a family and everything." He stared up at Retnick, a frown twisting his small, flushed face. "You were at the pier this morning, weren't you?" he said. "You're Retnick."

"That's right. I want some answers. You got sick and Evans took your job. Did somebody tell you to get sick?"

Grady shook his head quickly. "No, it's God's truth I had the flu. I couldn't get out of me bed."

"And while you were sick Red Evans took your winch," Retnick said. "That's right, isn't it?"

"Yes, that's right," Grady said, nodding vigorously.

"And Evans dropped a load on Ragoni. It missed by an inch. That's right, isn't it?"

Grady shrugged and smiled weakly. "I wasn't there, you know. But that's what I heard." He looked up and down the dark street, wetting his lips. "My old lady is waiting supper for me. I'd best be going."

"Don't be in a hurry," Retnick said. "Do you know why I went to jail?"

"Well, they said you killed a man, but I never put any stock in that."

"Put some stock in it," Retnick said staring into Grady's watery blue eyes. "Why did you stay off the job?"

"It was the flu, I told you."

"Will you stick to that when the cops get to you?"

Grady looked up at Retnick and a strange fear claimed him completely. He began to breathe rapidly. "They told me not to shape for a week," he said, catching hold of Retnick's hands. "They said I'd get myself killed."

"Was the hiring boss in on it? And Brophy?"

"I don't know, I swear to God. Nobody talks about it."

"Amato is ready to take over your local, eh?"

"It'd be worth your life to stand up to them now," Grady said, glancing anxiously up and down the dark street. "Old Union Jack, himself, is dead, you know. Happened today. Who knows who'll be next? Hah! Ask Joe Lye. Or Hammy. Or Dave Cardinal. They can tell you maybe." Grady smiled shakily, trying to coax sympathy into Retnick's bitter eyes. "I—I didn't feel good about laying up pretending to be sick. I knew they were after somebody. But what could I do? A man can't stand up alone to them killers, can he? My boy is in the Army, and there'd be no one to look after the old lady if something happened to me. You see how it was, don't you?"

"Sure, it never changes," Retnick said shortly. "Who was it told you to stay home? Which one of them?"

"That was Mario."

"Mario?"

"Nick Amato's nephew. He's a punk, but he's got them others behind him."

"Go on home," Retnick said. "Enjoy your dinner."

"What else could I do?" Grady said, staring guiltily into Retnick's dark hard face. "What else could I do?"

Retnick turned without answering him and walked into the darkness. Now he had two names: Mario Amato and Red Evans. It was a good bet that Mario had engineered the execution. If that were true, if young Mario had hired Red Evans, they would have to be thrown together under pressure. One of them might crack. Not Evans, who was probably a cold and tough professional, but young Mario was another matter; Retnick remembered him as a boy of seventeen, weak and petulant, vain about his looks and clothes, getting by on his uncle's reputation. Now he would be twenty-three, Retnick thought. A tough boy, doing man-sized jobs for Amato, arranging murders like an old hand. Retnick smiled coldly into the darkness. We'll see how tough he is, he was thinking . . .

Retnick ate a lonely dinner that night, savoring his dark thoughts like a miser. They were all he had, these bitter anticipations of vengeance, and he didn't realize how dear they had become to him; he lived in a sense on anger, and he hadn't thought very much about what he would be when his anger was finally satisfied.

When he finished dinner he walked uptown on Broadway, going all the way to Harlem, barely noticing the people and streets he passed. Then he turned around and came back downtown, with no destination in mind, but only hoping to tire himself enough to sleep. At nine-thirty he stopped in front of the Gramercy Club staring at his wife's picture, which was in a glass panel to one side of the entrance. It had been taken a long time ago, shortly after they were married; her hair had been long then, brushed down to her shoulders in a page-boy, and her eyes were bright with careless happiness. Retnick studied the picture for a full minute, tracing the soft curve of her lips with his eyes.

Finally he turned away and walked slowly toward the corner, staring at the bright busy street, and the cheerful-looking people coming in and out of bars and restaurants. Snow was falling again, softly and lightly; the wind had died away and the bright flakes fell in slow straight lines, gleaming prettily in the colored light from neon signs. Retnick stopped, confused by his feelings and walked back to the Gramercy. He went inside and took a seat at the bar, not bothering to check his hat and coat. The bartender remembered him and smiled and said hello.

"It was whisky with water, I believe," he said.

"That's fine," Retnick said, staring across the dining room at his wife. She was playing an old show tune, lightly and stylishly, smiling down at the keyboard. A light behind her threw her face in shadows; he could only see the soft gleam of her lips.

The bartender leaned toward him and said, "Do you want me to send word to her that you're here?"

Retnick rubbed a hand over his forehead. "No, never mind." Standing abruptly he started toward the door. He had to wait an instant to let a group of people come in, and it was then, as he glanced once more at his wife, that he noticed a dark-haired man sitting alone at a table that faced the piano. The light was uncertain, soft and hazy with cigarette smoke, but Retnick was able to pick out the man's features, the heavy lips, the dark full eyebrows. He hesitated a second or two, frowning, and then walked back to the bar. When the bartender came over to him Retnick pointed out the man, and asked if he were a regular customer.

"Not a regular, certainly," the bartender said thoughtfully. "This is the first time I've noticed him."

"Okay, thanks," Retnick said. Outside he crossed the street and stood where he could watch the entrance of the Gramercy Club. The man watching his wife with such interest was Davey Cardinal, one of Amato's enforcers.

It was an hour later that Cardinal strolled out of the club and waved to a cab. He was short and stockily built, with the manners of a show-off; he played to an audience always, delighting in his role of tough guy. But behind this childish, arrogant façade, Retnick knew he was extremely shrewd and ruthless. Watching the tail light of his cab winking into the darkness, Retnick began to frown. His concern was blended of anger and exasperation; it wouldn't do them any good to strike at him through Marcia. But they didn't know that.

When he got to his room that night he found a note from Mrs. Cara under his door. Sergeant Kleyburg had called and asked if Retnick would stop by his home in the morning. Around eight.

# 8

MILES KLEYBURG LIVED ALONE IN A SMALL APARTMENT A FEW BLOCKS below Yorktown. His wife had died in childbirth leaving him two sons to look after. But they, too, were gone now. One had married and moved to California to live, and the other had chosen the Army as a career and was presently stationed in Germany.

Retnick knew all about the boys; he had served as the chief outlet for Kleyburg's parental pride during the years they had worked together as partners. Then he had sympathized with the old man's loneliness. Now he knew that it was an inescapable factor of existence. Everybody's alone, he was thinking, as he rang the bell to Kleyburg's apartment. The sooner people learned that, the better off they were. But it was a bitter truth, and they fought against it. They wanted to belong to someone, anyone at all, and they closed their eyes to the fact that they were nakedly alone. They went through ritualistic rites pretending the opposite was true, making faith a hostage against loneliness and betrayal. Trusting their friends, repeating words like love and honor to their brides before solemn altars, believing out of fear in someone who was all-kind, all-loving, all-powerful. And, to that someone, they made the most pathetic commitments of all, because they thought they could belong to him forever. But none of it was true, none of it signified anything. I know, he thought, and felt a bitter sterile pride in the knowledge.

Kleyburg opened the door and grinned as he put out his hand. "Well, it's good to see you," he said. "Come on in."

"Did you get a line on Dixie Davis?" Retnick said, as he entered the warm, clean living room.

"I think I got what you need," Kleyburg said. "Go on, take off your coat. We're not heading for a fire." Kleyburg was freshly shaved, and wore an old jacket and a pair of slacks. "I'm off duty today and I thought we could sit around a while and chew the rag. After we chew up some breakfast. How about it?"

Retnick took out his cigarettes and said, "I'm in a hurry, Miles. What about the girl?"

"Sure, if that's the way you want it." Kleyburg ran a hand over his gray hair and smiled awkwardly. He looked old and tired, Retnick thought. "Remember, though, how we used to come up here for breakfast sometimes after finishing the twelve-to-eight shift? I thought we could do it like that. Come on, Steve, I've got fresh sausages and fresh eggs on tap. How about it? You look like you could stand a solid meal."

"I'll have coffee if it's ready," Retnick said. "The big breakfast will have to wait."

Kleyburg was obviously disappointed. "Okay, Steve," he said, shrugging and smiling. "Sorry I can't sell you the whole menu though. Sit down, I'll get the coffee."

When he left Retnick lit a cigarette and glanced around the room. The place had a comfortable, cluttered look to it. Sports magazines, pipes, a couple of big reading chairs, and the pictures of the boys on the mantel. Dozens of pictures, ranging from large tinted portraits to informal snapshots. The soldier boy, his silver bars agleam, stared solemnly into the future from one end of the mantel, while opposite him his brother stood tall and erect in a wedding picture with his bride. There were snaps of the married couple in California, lounging in shorts in the sun, and several of the soldier boy preparing for his trade. Sighting over a forty-five, posing on the turret of a tank, lying in the prone position with a rifle tucked expertly under his chin.

Kleyburg came in with the coffee and said, "Here we are!" Then he smiled at the pictures of his sons. "They're doing okay, don't you think?"

"They look good," Retnick said. He took a cup of coffee and sat down on the edge of the couch. There should be something else to say, he thought. Kleyburg obviously expected it; this was like old times for him, relaxing after a night's work, bragging inoffensively about his kids. But these weren't old times for Retnick, and he hadn't the warmth or interest to pretend that they were. "How about the girl?" he said.

"I got a break on her," Kleyburg said, changing his tone to match Retnick's. "Nielsen at the Twentieth had her up on a charge a few months ago. Her name is Dorothy not Dixie, but the last name is honest. She works at an Eighth Avenue clipjoint. Nielsen arrested her and a few others like her on a Navy complaint. Seems the girls were taking the gobs for everything but their gold fillings, and the Navy asked us to look into it. Dixie's twenty-nine and she's been in and out of lots of trouble. Shoplifting, hustling, con games, you name it. Dixie takes off two days a week, Tuesday and Thursday." Kleyburg shrugged. "That's about it, Steve."

"No line on her boy friends?"

Kleyburg shook his head. "She's the Navy's friend."

"Any mention of a guy named Red Evans?"

"I gave you all Nielsen gave me, Steve."

"Does that name mean anything to you?"

"Red Evans? Nothing in particular. Why?"

There was no humor in Retnick's smile. "I'm looking for him," he said, standing.

"Hold it a second," Kleyburg said, frowning at the bitter smile on Retnick's lips. "I want to say something to you. I was awake most of the night thinking about it, and I want to get it off my chest." He paused and took a deep breath. "You're on a downhill slide, boy, and you'll end in a crash. You've got reason to be mad. Sure. But you can choke on hate easier than you can a fishbone. I know. I know because I felt that way when my wife died. I thought I'd got a kick in the teeth from the whole world. And you can't live feeling like that."

Retnick shrugged. "I'm alive, Miles."

"Now wait," Kleyburg said, shaking his head. "I want to finish. If I get sidetracked I'll never get this said. When my wife died I hated everybody. I didn't even want the kids. But I couldn't walk away from my responsibility. It would have been easy to give the kids away; my sister was itching to get her hands on them. But I stuck it out, and it was no fun doing the job alone. And this is what I want to tell you, I guess. Lots of people helped me over those tough times. My mother-in-law took care of the kids until I got a housekeeper, and neighbors came in with all kinds of assistance, and even my house sergeant, the old crab, Bill Rafferty, gave me details close to home so I could duck in and see that everything was going all right. Most people are decent, Steve. They'll help you over this trouble. Don't go on thinking everybody is rotten."

"I'm not interested in people," Retnick said. "I'm interested in the men who framed me. Nobody else matters."

"You'll ruin yourself," Kleyburg said, making a futile gesture with his hand. "You were a fine decent guy, Steve. You had sympathy for everybody. Remember how you listened to me talk about the boys? You probably won't realize what that meant until you have some kids of your own."

Retnick wished the old man would stop talking so that he could leave, but Kleyburg went on, moving his hands about in anxious little flurries. "I've got to make you understand what I'm saying," he said. "Look, I was never the cop you were. I didn't have the brains and the drive. You carried me. I know that. You walked into trouble, you went through doorways first, and into dark alleys, and I held down the radio in the car. You think that didn't mean anything to me? That's why I can't stand by and let you wreck your life."

The words didn't touch Retnick; they were noises that meant nothing. "Don't worry about me," he said. "I'll take care of myself."

"It isn't a matter of just living or dying," Kleyburg said, shaking his head stubbornly. "It's how you live and die, Steve. I'm an old man, and I understand some things better than you can. You've got to live in peace. You've got to forgive people. You've—"

"Stop it," Retnick said abruptly. "You're getting comical." Kleyburg put a hand on his arm, but Retnick pulled away from him and turned to the door. "Save your sermon. I don't need it."

At seven o'clock that night Retnick walked into the West Side funeral home where Union Jack Glencannon would receive his last mortal respects. He had spent most of the day making a cautious effort to get on young Mario Amato's trail; but so far without luck. Now he checked the register of names at the door, knowing that Mario would probably show up at the wake. That was protocol on the docks; everyone went to funerals. But Mario hadn't made his visit yet.

Retnick signed his name on the mourner's page and walked into the thickly carpeted chapel, which was heavy with the scent of flowers. The place wasn't crowded; two men he didn't know stood before the casket and a third was wandering along the ranks of massed floral pieces inspecting the names of the donors.

Glencannon looked sad and stern in death, his big bold face incongruous against the quilted lining of the coffin. Beside him lay the scabbard and sword of the Knights of Columbus, and a worn Rosary was intertwined about his heavy hands. Instinctively Retnick crossed himself and said a prayer. The words came back effortlessly, which surprised him; it had been so long since he had prayed for anyone.

Leaving the chapel, he found a secluded chair in the adjoining room from where he could watch the foyer. There were half-a-dozen men sitting about in this room, talking in low voices and filling the air with smoke from pipes and cigars.

The crowd began to arrive an hour or so later. It was a solemn and important occasion, and it brought out top officials from the city, the unions and industry. The mayor stayed almost an hour and that word was passed with quiet pride to later arrivals. There was a steady stream of cops, firemen and longshoremen, friends of the old man's for nearly half a century. And with these came shipping executives, railroad men, heads of the various firms that sprawled along the waterfront.

Retnick saw Nick Amato and Joe Lye when they came in around ten o'clock. Amato wore a bulky brown overcoat and smiled at people he knew like an eager-to-please fruit peddler. Only his eyes gave him away; they reflected his cynical contempt for this exhibition.

Lye stayed behind Amato, his eyes quick and alert in his tense face; he carried his body as if it were a ticking bomb, a thin black cylinder of potential destruction. It was this strange explosive quality about Lye that made him feared and hated along the waterfront. And it was no act. He didn't play at being a toughie like Dave Cardinal. The dangerous pressures inside him were nakedly apparent in his pale eyes and queer straining lips.

The night wore on. The five Antuni brothers arrived, dignified, rather courtly men who ruled five thousand longshoremen in Jersey with hands of steel, and who feared nothing in the world except their youngest brother, a priest on Staten Island. The crowd kept coming, ex-fighters, cops, newspapermen, dockworkers, saloon keepers, union officials, hoodlums and politicians. But there was no sign of young Mario Amato.

Retnick was putting out a tasteless cigarette when Lieutenant Neville drifted over to him and said, "Who're you waiting for, Steve?"

Retnick hadn't seen him come in. He said, "No one. Why?"

"Don't kid me. You haven't taken your eyes off the front door. Who're you expecting?"

"Mario Amato."

"What's your interest in him?"

Retnick shrugged. "Let's say it's personal."

Lieutenant Neville lit a cigarette and stared thoughtfully at the glowing tip. There was a puzzled expression on his lean intelligent face. "What's the point of being cozy with me, Steve?" he said. "We're after the same thing, but your way is wrong. I told you yesterday to keep out of trouble."

"Am I in trouble?" Retnick said, looking at him evenly.

"That fight with Hammy was a pretty stupid business."

"He wanted it, I didn't."

"It gave Amato a chance to gripe," Neville said. "Not to me, but downtown. I get the repercussions. He doesn't want a labor-hating ex-con roaming around the docks beating up his boys."

"Labor hating," Retnick said. "That's good."

"So I have an official order to keep an eye on you."

"That must make you feel fine," Retnick said. "Getting orders relayed to you from that hoodlum."

"I don't want to argue about it," Neville said.

"Thanks a lot," Retnick said. "Now we can move to important considerations. Such as who killed old man Glencannon. And Frank Ragoni."

Neville ignored the bitterness in Retnick's voice. "The lab isn't sure about Glencannon," he said. "It could be a homicide, or it could be a natural death. He went to Amato's office around midnight, and Amato says he was in good shape when he left. He was found a dozen blocks from there yesterday, behind a string of gondolas on a storage siding."

Retnick grinned coldly. "You want some advice? Arrest Nick Amato for the murder."

"We aren't calling it a murder yet," Neville said. Spots of color had come up in his pale cheeks. "Glencannon was an old man. His heart could have quit on him. The bruise on his head could have resulted from the fall. He could have crawled to where he was found."

"That's very logical," Retnick said dryly. "Or he might have been hit by lightning, or died laughing at old jokes. Investigate those angles, too. But don't bother Nick Amato. He's too busy planning his next murder."

Neville said coldly, "I'm getting fed up with you, Steve. You think you're a lonely tragic figure who's been wronged by everybody in the whole world. That may fatten up your ego but it's lousy logic."

"You don't get logical in jail," Retnick said. He was starting to say something else when he noticed Mario Amato moving through the thinning crowd with two young men about his own age. He was slim and dark, with soft brown eyes, and he walked with a little swagger, as if he were certain that everyone in the room knew who he was, and was staring at him with interest and respect. He wore a beautifully fitted topcoat and carried a white fedora. Smiling broadly, he seemed in high spirits, obviously delighted to be leaving this place of gloom and death.

When he had passed through the doors Retnick said, "I've got to go, Lieutenant."

"Yes, I guess you do," Neville said wearily. He had seen Mario, too, and his eyes were troubled as he watched Retnick crossing the floor, moving with the deliberate stride of a hunter.

# 9

MARIO AMATO STOPPED AT THE AVENUE WITH HIS TWO COMPANIONS AND tried to decide how to spend the rest of the evening. It was cold and windy on the corner and he pulled the collar of his fancy overcoat up tight about his throat. The traffic was light and the sidewalks were empty. Ahead of them the neon signs of bars winked invitingly into the black tunnel of the street. But he didn't feel like drinking; liquor had never had much appeal to him. A girl would be more like it. He wanted to forget the look of Glencannon's face, and the heavy depressing scent of the flowers. A girl would do that.

Retnick came silently from the darkness behind him and put a big hand on his arm. "I've been looking for you," he said.

Mario started nervously. "What the hell's the idea?" he said in a high, angry voice. One of his companions surged forward, but Retnick struck him across the chest with a forearm that was like a bar of iron, and the young man backed off quickly, gasping for breath. "Keep out of this," Retnick said. The two young men stared at him, breathing hard, checked by the look in his face.

Mario tried to pull free but Retnick's hand was like an iron collar about his arm. "What's the idea?" he said again, but plaintively now. "I don't know you, Mac."

"Tell me you don't know my sister."

Mario smiled weakly. What he saw in Retnick's eyes made him very nervous. "I don't think I know your sister," he said. "Maybe I met her somewhere. What's her name?"

"Nancy Riordan. And you aren't running out on her, get that straight."

"Look, mister, I don't know anybody by that name."

"I want to hear you tell her that," Retnick said. "Come on, let's go."

"Now wait a minute," Mario cried.

"That's Nick Amato's nephew," one of his friends said. "You better be sure what you're doing."

Retnick stared at him. "You mean he's too good for my sister?"

The young man shrugged and tried to smile. "No, I just thought I'd tell you."

"Well, don't bother telling me things," Retnick said. "You guys aren't involved in this. But you will be if you keep shooting off your mouths. I'll deal you in for free."

Both young men shook their heads quickly. "It's between you and him," one of them said.

"Fine. Beat it."

"Sure, we were going." They nodded jerkily to Mario. "See you around," one of them said. Mario stared wistfully after them as they hurried off, their heads pulled down into the collars of their coats. There was no one else in sight. Not even a cop. The city was dark and empty.

"Mister, you got me wrong," he said, smiling uncertainly at Retnick. "I never treated any girl wrong, I swear."

"That's what we're going to make sure of," Retnick said. "Maybe you're not the guy. If so, there's no harm done. Let's walk. She's waiting for us a few blocks from here. . . ."

Retnick unlocked his room, ushered Mario in ahead of him and closed the door. When he snapped on the lights the little cat blinked at them from the bed. It yawned and stretched a paw tentatively into the air.

"What's the gag?" Mario said, looking around with a worried smile.

Retnick tossed his coat on the bed and unloosened his tie. "Sit down, Mario," he said. "You know Red Evans, I guess."

"Yeah, I know him," Mario said slowly.

"We're going to talk about him," Retnick said, walking toward young Amato. "Sit down, I told you."

"Yeah, but your sister—"

"There's no sister," he said, and shoved Mario into a straight-backed chair. Standing over him, his eyes bright and hard, Retnick said, "There's just you and me, sweetheart. We're going to talk about how much you paid Evans to murder Frank Ragoni."

Mario wet his lips and tried desperately to keep the fear inside him from showing in his face. He was no stranger to violence, but not at these odds. As Nick Amato's nephew he lived in a cocoon of security and privilege. He had never faced trouble alone; his uncle's men saw to that.

"I don't know what you're talking about," he said, putting what strength he could muster into his voice. "You got me all wrong, I tell you."

"Where did you know Evans?"

"Well, around the docks. Just to say hello to. You know how it is?" He tried to meet Retnick's eyes directly, but it was almost impossible; there was something in them that was like the frightening stillness in old Glencannon's face. "I wasn't a friend of his," he went on anxiously. "We just nodded to each other, that's all."

Retnick stared at him in silence. Then he said quietly, "We won't have any trouble if you tell the truth, Mario. I know you hired Evans to do the job on Ragoni. I got that from the winchman, Grady. Did your uncle tell you to hire Evans? That's what I want to know."

"You got no right to accuse me of being a murderer," Mario said. He was becoming excited now and some of his fear left him. "You're asking for real trouble, buddy. I'm no punk you can push around."

He started to get up but Retnick put a hand against his chest and slammed him back into the chair. "I told you to sit down," he said, smiling unpleasantly. "Why did your uncle want Ragoni killed?"

Mario's breath came unevenly; he was suddenly close to tears. "I don't know anything about it," he said. "Somebody gave you the wrong dope on me."

Retnick knew he was lying; fear and guilt were stamped on him like a brand. For an instant he debated the wisdom of knocking the truth out of him; it wouldn't be hard. This was a punk, a pretty boy with soft nervous eyes and skin like a girl's. He'd be hopping bells or jerking sodas if it weren't for his uncle. But Retnick decided against force. Amato could toss him to the parole board.

Turning away he took out his cigarettes. "You can beat it," he said. "We'll have another talk one of these days."

Mario stood up and edged nervously past Retnick to the door. "You got me wrong, I'm telling you."

"You're in trouble, sonny," Retnick said. "And your uncle can't fix it. Tell him a guy by the name of Retnick told you that."

When Mario had gone Retnick locked the door and sat down on the edge of the bed. The cat curled up beside him and closed its eyes. Retnick stroked her absently and she began to purr. Frowning through the smoke of his cigarette, he tried to guess what was coming. Trouble, of course. Mario would run squealing to his uncle and that would start it. But there was no other way to play it. He had to push until something started to give.

# 10

NICK AMATO LISTENED TO HIS NEPHEW'S STORY AS HE SIPPED BLACK coffee in the kitchen of his West Side cold-water flat. The kitchen was the only room in which he felt comfortable. His wife had filled the rest of the house with holy pictures, dull heavy furniture, and retouched portraits of her relatives in Naples. And everything smelled of furniture polish.

Amato was in shirtsleeves, with his elbows on the table and a cup of coffee cradled in his hands. He was mad, and getting madder every minute, but he kept the musing little smile on his lips. Joe Lye sat at the end of the table watching Mario, and Hammy, a bandage along his right cheek and jaw, stood in the corner, twisting his hat around in his hands and breathing noisily through his damaged nose.

"So that's all," Amato said, staring with cold brown eyes at his coffee cup. "You haven't forgot nothing, eh?"

"I told you just the way it happened," Mario said, rubbing his damp forehead. He was frightened by his uncle's reaction; if Amato had laughed or cursed he would have felt better. Maybe the big guy, Retnick, knew something. *You're in trouble your uncle can't fix!* That's what he'd said.

"So that's all," Amato said. "He asked you about Evans and Ragoni and you told him nothing. Is that it?"

"I swear that's all," Mario said. "I told you about him hitting me and the rest of it."

"Yeah," Amato said. He looked up at his nephew, staring at him as he would stare at a bug crawling on his plate. "Did you hit him back? I forget."

"What could I do?" Perspiration shone on Mario's face, dampened the little curls of hair along his temples. "He might have killed me."

"Retnick?" Amato laughed softly. "Don't worry about him." He turned to Hammy. "He's not tough. Ain't that right, Hammy?"

"I was drunk," Hammy said. He shifted his great weight from one foot to the other, and smiled stupidly at Amato. The beating from Retnick had effected a change in him; the dumb trust in himself was gone, and his eyes were sheepish and puzzled. "I was drunk," he said again. "He caught me when I was fouled up from drinking."

"You'll get him the next time, eh?" Amato said, staring at the shame in his eyes. Like a castrated bull, Amato thought. "Next time, eh."

Hammy smiled as if this were a joke; he wanted no more of Retnick. The memory of those blows to his body was frighteningly vivid; another one would have killed him, he knew. "Sure, Nick," he said, laughing nervously.

"Next time he'll kill you," Amato said, knowing what was going on in Hammy's mind. "Remember that."

A soft knock sounded on the door. Amato looked around irritably and called out, "Yeah?"

His wife entered the room smiling an apology at Amato. She was stout and middle-aged, with a dark complexion and large brown eyes. Her black dress, shapeless and old, fell almost to her ankles, and she wore her gray hair in a large bun at the back of her neck. There was a heavy resignation in her manner, but it didn't stem from peace of mind or calmness of soul; instead she looked as if she had signed an armistice with life before a shot could be fired.

She stood close to Mario, almost touching him, and said to her husband, "He's upset and tired, Nick. Can't he go to bed?"

"Sure, he can go to bed," Amato said, drumming his fingers on the table. Once he had seen a blasphemous picture of a cow saying a rosary and the image nagged at him when he looked at his wife.

"I did all I could," Mario said, making a last attempt to alter the ominously hard expression around his uncle's lips.

"Go to bed," Amato said. "Don't worry about it."

His wife shepherded Mario from the room and before the door closed Amato heard her promising to bring him some warm milk with a little brandy in it. Amato put down his cup and swore softly.

Hammy, guessing at the source of his irritation, nodded solemnly and said, "That kid will turn out spoiled, I bet. Anna's too good to him."

"Joe, give Hammy a thousand dollars," Amato said.

Lye hesitated, smiling uncertainly; the request made no sense but he knew Amato was in one of his dangerous, unpredictable moods.

Amato suddenly pounded his fist on the table. Glaring at Lye, he said, "You want to know what for? You want to vote on things maybe, be democratic?"

"Hell no, Nick," Lye said hastily. He counted out ten one hundred dollar bills from his wallet and handed them to Hammy.

"What's this for?" Hammy said, staring in confusion at the money.

"That's your severance pay," Amato said, getting to his feet.

"Wait a minute, you can't—"

"Shut up!" Amato yelled at him. He crouched slightly, as if the weight of his anger was more than he could bear, and Lye moved slowly to the wall and covered Hammy with the gun in his overcoat pocket.

"You killed old man Glencannon," Amato said, in a low thick voice.

"I didn't mean to," Hammy said, shaking his head desperately. "I just cuffed him and he—well, he fell over."

"You're lucky I'm letting you quit," Amato said, pounding a fist on the kitchen table. "What'll it look like when I take over his local next month? The International can move in and call the election a phony. The papers are going to have a lot to say about hoodlums and killers on the docks. Sure, but that doesn't mean anything to you." Amato paused, breathing heavily, bringing his anger under control. "There's five hundred men in my local who do what I tell 'em to do. I say work, they work; I say strike, they strike. But you got to be different, you got to do things on your own."

"Boss, I was trying to make him wait for a cab," Hammy said, rubbing his big hands together nervously. His little eyes were wide and frightened. "He pulled away from me, and I grabbed him. Maybe I hit him. But not hard. And he just fell over. I—I dumped him then. That was all I could do. You got to give me a break."

"You're getting a break," Amato said coldly. "I could turn you over to the cops. But I'm letting you go. But I want you to go fast, understand? Get out of town and stay out."

Hammy looked desperately puzzled and hurt, like a child whose values had been ridiculed by a trusted adult.

"This ain't a fair shake," he said at last. "It's because of that Polack, Retnick. You think I'm no good because he dropped me. I told you I was drunk."

Lye said softly, "You're crowding your luck, Hammy. You heard Nick. Don't let me see you in New York again."

Hammy looked away from Lye's fixed and deadly smile. He knew what that smile meant. "I'm going," he said wetting his lips. "I ain't mad."

"I'll see you to the door," Lye said. "Then I don't want to see you again anywhere."

When Lye returned to the kitchen, Amato was seated at the kitchen table puffing on a cigar. "Has Retnick got a phone?" he said, looking up at Lye through the ropy layers of smoke.

"Yeah. There's one in his boarding house."

"Call him up and tell him I want to see him. Right away. Here."

"You think he'll come?"

Amato shrugged. "Sure. That's why he roughed up the kid."

"You should let me handle him now," Lye said. "He's trouble, Nick. And he's getting help from the boys at the Thirty-First."

"Go call him up," Amato said. "I don't want any more loud bangs along my stretch of the docks. You call him."

"Okay, Nick."

While Lye was out of the room his wife came in and put a saucepan of milk on the stove to heat. The kitchen was crowded with equipment, all of it gleaming and new. Anna seemed at home among these mechanical marvels. They were a big thing to her, Amato knew. Mario, the church and the kitchen. That was her life. He watched her, frowning slightly, as she took down a large breakfast cup and measured out two table-spoonfuls of brandy into it. Then she stirred the steaming milk slowly, and a little smile touched her full patient lips.

"For the kid?" Amato asked her.

She nodded, without looking at him; her attention was claimed by the simmering milk. "He's upset," she said.

"He'll be okay."

Anna poured the milk into the cup and put the saucepan back on the stove. Then she turned and looked at her husband. There was a curiously cold expression on her dark face. "He told me a man hit him tonight," she said. "Can't you keep him safe?"

"Things like that happen. They don't mean nothing."

"This mustn't happen to him, Nick. He's all I got. You know that."

"Sure, sure," Amato said irritably. Most of the time he was glad he'd arranged to have Mario shipped to America. But there were moments when he wished he'd let him rot in Naples. The boy gave Anna something to think about besides polishing the furniture and hanging around the church. That part was fine; but her simple-minded anxiety about him was a bore. Amato had bought little Mario the way he'd buy an ice box or a suit of clothes; they had no kids and Anna cried about it at night, so he got her sister to ship them her oldest boy, Mario. That was fifteen years ago, and since then Anna had lived for the boy, coddling and smothering him with her frustrated maternal longings.

"I'll take care of him," Amato said, hoping to end the matter.

"He's not strong like other boys," Anna said. "He's not rough and wild. He should make something out of himself. It's no good that he works with your men. He should be a priest or a teacher." Anna spoke with dogged insistence, as if emphasis alone might make her dreams come true.

Amato puffed on his cigar, avoiding her eyes. The cow with the rosary, he was thinking. The idea of Mario as a priest or teacher—or anything at all for that matter—struck him as slightly absurd. "Don't worry about him," he said. "He'll be okay."

"I try not to worry," she said. "You don't know how hard I try." Then she left the room without looking at him and went quickly down the hallway to her son.

Lye returned in a moment or so and sat down at the end of the table. "I talked to him," he said. "He'll come."

Amato grunted and puffed on his cigar. His mood had turned sour and bitter. He wouldn't have admitted it, but Anna's jealous preoccupation with Mario made him feel unimportant. "You seeing that broad of yours tonight?" he asked Lye.

"It's pretty late," Lye said, trying to be casual about it.

"Can't you answer a simple question?" Amato said. "I know it's late. I got a watch, too."

"Yeah, I'll see her, I guess," Lye said.

"You got a nice life," Amato said, staring at Lye. "Martinis and steaks, real high style." The thought of Kay Johnson made him restless and irritable; he had never seen her apartment but he imagined it as a place of soft lights and deep chairs, with music playing, maybe, and lots of good liquor in crystal decanters. And he saw her there, very pale and blonde, with white shoulders that smelled of perfume, and a long robe that showed off her breasts and hips. "How'd you get to know her?" he asked Lye.

"A friend of mine, a bookie, introduced us at the track," Lye said. The conversation made him uneasy; he felt his mouth beginning to tighten. "I drove her home that afternoon, and—" He shrugged. "Well, I started seeing her, that's all."

"You must have hidden talent," Amato said, staring deliberately and cruelly at Lye's twisted mouth. "You ain't the best-looking guy in the world, you know."

"I get along," Lye said, trying to control his growing tension.

"Maybe it's them prayers of yours being answered," Amato said. "You prayed when you were in jail, but God didn't get you out, Joe. I guess the prayers went into another account."

"How the hell would I know?" Lye said, lighting a cigarette and throwing the match aside nervously. "Things just work out, that's all."

"Then why pray?" Amato said.

"Why don't we talk about something else?" Lye said.

"Maybe you pray for the hell of it," Amato said. "For fun, maybe." He didn't know why he was needling Lye; it wasn't improving his own temper. "I can arrange for you to start praying again, if that's what you like. There's that Donaldson rap still hanging over your head. I guess you remember that."

Lye took a deep drag on his cigarette and tried to smile; but it was a ghastly effort. "Why should you send me back to jail?" he said. "I do my work. I'm with you all the way. You know that, Nick."

"Sure, I depend on you, Joe," Amato said, frowning faintly. "Let's forget it. How did Retnick sound?"

"No way in particular. He just said he'd come over."

"He may be your next job."

Lye nodded quickly. "I ain't worried." He felt the tensions easing in him, flowing mercifully from his rigid body. It filled him with shame to be so vulnerable to unreasoning fears; but those nights in the death cell had driven a shaft of terror into the deep and secret core of his manhood. The dream had come again last night, the violent red dream that repeated itself with the monotony of a stuck phonograph record. There were always the profane, laughing guards, the rush along the corridor, and then the rude altar and the straps that tightened across his bare chest until he could no longer breathe. And the guards stared at him, laughing obscenely, and there was nothing he could do about it. The dream sickened him; there were parts of it he had never been able to tell Kay about . . .

# 11

IT WAS A FEW MINUTES PAST ELEVEN WHEN RETNICK RANG THE BELL at Amato's home. A cold wind hammered at the garbage cans set out along the curb, and street lights thrust cones of pale yellow light into the deep shadows along the sidewalk. Joe Lye opened the door, nodded jerkily at him, and said, "Come on along with me."

Retnick stepped past him and walked down a hallway to the kitchen. He wasn't worried about Lye's advantageous position behind him; it wasn't likely that Amato would try to kill him in his own home. Amato was sitting in his shirtsleeves at the kitchen table, smoking a short black cigar. The room was brightly lighted and smelled of peppers and ground coffee.

"What's on your mind?" Retnick said, as Lye drifted to one side of him and stood with his back to the wall.

Amato smiled and shook his fingers gently before his face. "You could turn that around, eh?" he said. "What's on *your* mind?"

"You wanted to see me," Retnick said. "Here I am."

"Come on, don't be so hard," Amato said. "How about some coffee?"

"Don't bother."

Amato shrugged and sighed. "So you're mad at me," he said. "Maybe you think you got reason to be. Maybe you think I put Hammy up to picking a scrap with you. Well, that's wrong, Steve. Hammy was working on his own, and I fired him for it. Now don't that prove I'm trying to get along with people?"

"Everyone knows you're a decent, generous guy," Retnick said, smiling coldly. "Tell me something new."

Amato cocked his head to one side and studied him for a second or two with narrowing eyes. Then he said gently, "There's no point being sarcastic. I'm trying to be fair. You thought I turned Hammy loose on you. All right, that's understandable. So you pick up my kid and rough him up a little. I don't like that, Steve. It was a dumb move. But I figure the two mistakes cross each other out. I'm ready to forget them. How about you?"

Retnick shrugged. "I've already forgot about the fight with Hammy," he said. "But he won't forget it that fast."

"Yeah, you really landed on him," Amato said slowly. "Now I got something else to say. How would you like his job?"

"Let's don't strain to be funny," Retnick said.

A little flush of color moved up in Amato's dark cheeks. "I ain't being funny, Steve. That ain't my way. The job pays two hundred bucks a week. And you can do better than that in a fairly short time. A business agent ain't a bad job, as I guess you know. You could make it in a couple of years if you played everything smart. You listening to me?"

"Sure, I'm listening," Retnick said.

"There's no point worrying about the past," Amato said. "Here's how I feel. You live today. You got a living to make, a family to take care of, things like that. That you got to do *now*, today, not last year or five years ago. Carrying grudges don't pay no bills. So how about it? With a steady job you can get an apartment, get back with your wife, start living a good normal life again. And there's plenty of room with me, I guarantee you. So how about it?"

"I don't need a job," Retnick said slowly. Amato was serious, he knew, and that was the most disgusting part of it. Men compromised themselves in order to work. That was the rule and Amato understood it well. The choice was not between good or bad, but between bad and worse; a man was either an active participant in evil, or a silent accomplice. To stand in a middle ground meant economic suicide. And the necessity to compromise performed a moral alchemy on men; it altered them drastically and made them very easy to manage.

Amato shrugged and smiled. "Everybody needs a job, Steve."

"I'm wasting time. You have anything else to tell me?"

"Sure, sure," Amato said softly. He stood and came around the table, looking up at Retnick with cold sharp eyes. "You want to be a hard guy, eh? Make trouble, bother me. How long you think you'll last, eh?"

"What's your guess?"

"I don't have to guess," Amato said. Tilting his head to one side he flicked the back of his hand across Retnick's lapels in a contemptuous gesture. "Big tough guy, eh? Make trouble for me." Amato's grip on his temper was slipping; his voice was suddenly hoarse and thick. "Well, I tell you this. You're a big mouth, that's all. A big-mouth slob. I tell you now keep out of my way. You put your nose in my business and I'll cut it off for you. You forget about Ventra, forget about Ragoni, forget about my business. Then you'll stay alive. You bother me and you'll get your head blown off. You understand that?"

"Why should I forget about Ventra?" Retnick said, very softly.

"Because I say so," Amato shouted, and with the back of his hand slapped Retnick across the chest. "You do what you're told if you want to stay alive. I tell you—"

Retnick smiled and hit him in the stomach then, almost casually, and Amato bent over with a convulsive flurry of motion, hugging his arms tightly to his body and sputtering feebly through his straining mouth. His face was very red as he sagged helplessly against the kitchen table and put out one hand quickly to prevent himself from sliding to the floor.

Retnick turned with dangerous, menacing speed and struck Lye's forearm with a chopping blow of his hand. The gun Lye was raising clattered onto the floor, and he stiffened against the wall, one arm hanging uselessly at his side, his mouth twisting cruelly in his small pale face.

Retnick picked up the gun and put it in his pocket. He was breathing hard, trying to control his anger; it wasn't time to make a final move. Staring at Amato he said thickly, "You're lucky. Don't crowd it."

Amato's eyes were strange and wild. "You'll die for this, Retnick. I swear to God."

Retnick backed to the door, his hand sliding down onto the gun in his pocket. "Don't say anything else, Nick. I don't want to kill you."

Amato stared at him, breathing raggedly. He shook his head slowly from side to side then, knowing he was close to death.

"Not yet," Retnick said.

Outside he crossed the dark street and stopped in the shadow of a parked car. For a moment or so he watched Amato's door, but it remained closed; Lye wasn't coming after him tonight.

Retnick walked quickly toward the avenue. Turning left at the intersection he went by closed shops and markets, dark theaters that advertised Spanish subtitles. He wanted to find a phone, but everything was closed for the night. Two sailors across the street were arguing with drunken good humor about something or other, but there was no one else in sight. And there were no cabs. Retnick walked four blocks before coming on an all-night drugstore, and from there he put in a call to the Thirty-First. Lieutenant Neville was on another line, a clerk said. Would he hang on?

It was a short wait. Neville said hello, sounding tired and impatient.

"This is Steve," Retnick said. "I want to see you tonight."

Neville hesitated. Then he said, "Where are you?"

Retnick told him and Neville said, "This had better be interesting. I was on my way home. I'll pick you up in ten minutes."

Retnick waited in the darkness a few doors from the drugstore, his back to a brick wall and a cigarette in his lips. When Neville's black sedan slowed down at the intersection, he moved out to the curb and held up his hand. The car pulled up alongside him and stopped. Retnick climbed in, Neville released the clutch, and they headed north on Tenth Avenue, cruising evenly to make the lights.

"Well, what is it?" Neville said.

Retnick glanced at him, and in the faint light from the dashboard he saw the hard lines around his mouth, the cold impersonal cast of his features.

"I've got a link between young Mario Amato and the guy who murdered Frank Ragoni," he said. "You want to hear about it?"

"I'm surprised you thought of me," Neville said dryly. "I got the impression earlier this evening that you figured me for one of Amato's boys."

"I didn't mean that," Retnick said. Neville's tone bothered him. Most of what he had learned about police work had come from Neville; not the routine of it, but the important intangibles, the need for patience and fairness, the objective, sympathetic consideration of human beings, this had come from Neville. There was no man in the department Retnick had respected more, no man whose approval meant more to him. But the significance and warmth of that relationship were gone. And it was he who had changed, not Neville. That was what seemed to hurt. "I need help," he said. He wished he could explain what he felt, but there was no way to unlock the words. "I've gone as far as I can on my own."

Neville slowed down and pulled over to the curb. When he cut off the motor the silence settled abruptly and heavily around them. There was very little traffic; an occasional truck rumbled past, briefly disturbing the silence. Ahead of them the wide avenue stretched into empty darkness. "Let me have a cigarette, Steve," Neville said. His voice was weary. Retnick gave him a cigarette, held a light for it, and then Neville pushed his hat back on his forehead and settled down in the seat. "You're going to tell me about Red Evans, I suppose," he said. "Is that it?"

"You know about him?" Retnick said. He couldn't keep the surprise from his voice.

"We try to earn our money," Neville said. "We know he drifted into Ragoni's gang, and disappeared the night Ragoni turned up missing. What have you got?"

"Quite a bit more," Retnick said. He told Neville what he had learned then; of Ragoni's letter to him in jail, of Ragoni's conviction that he knew who had killed Joe Ventra; of the winchman, Grady, who had been warned to stay off the job by young Mario Amato; of the accident by which Red Evans had almost killed Ragoni, and of Dixie Davis and his certainty that she was still seeing Red Evans in Trenton. "Here's how it looks to me," he said finally. "Ragoni was on the spot. Either because he knew who had killed Ventra, or because he was fighting as best he could to keep Amato and his hoodlums from taking over the local he belonged to. Mario Amato hired Red Evans to kill him and make it look like an accident. That didn't work, so Evans stuck a knife in him and blew. Doesn't that sound like the script to you?"

Neville shrugged lightly. "It could be, Steve."

"I talked to Mario tonight," Retnick went on. "He's a scared little punk. But he denied any connection with Evans. I could have beaten the truth out of him, but that wouldn't have held up in court."

"You're developing an odd common sense," Neville said, glancing at him sharply. "How did you get to talk to Mario?"

"I took him to my room."

Neville shook his head. "Steve, you're begging for trouble."

"Okay, okay," Retnick said. "But I'm getting what I want. I just left Nick Amato's home. Joe Lye called and asked me to come over, this was about an hour after I let Mario go. Amato offered to forget the whole business, and then he offered me a job. When I told him what to do with it, he blew his top and told me to forget about Ventra and Ragoni. He threatened to kill me if I didn't. That caused a row. I belted Amato and slapped a gun out of Joe Lye's hand. Then I left. Don't you see this the way I do? If we throw young Mario and Red Evans together we'll get the whole story."

"And you want me to pick up Mario? Is that it?"

"Yes."

"I might," Neville said slowly. "I might if I caught him stabbing my wife or something like that."

"But not to sweat him?"

"This job isn't much, but it's all I've got," Neville said.

"So it's no, eh?" Retnick said, staring at him. "I give you a case against a murderer and you talk about losing your job. Is that it?"

"Now listen to me: you were trained as a cop and you know the meaning of evidence. But you seem to have forgotten it. You've got suspicions but you won't prove them by slapping people around. We've got two detectives working on the Ragoni murder. They'll stay on it until they get results. Leave the job to them. They're paid for it."

"I'm giving you a short cut," Retnick said. "But you want it the long way." He knew there was no point in further talk; no one cared as much as he did. No one had his reasons. Neville could wait for the slow turn of the wheel of justice, and meanwhile draw his pay and live his quiet pleasant life. But for him the waiting was over.

"Forget Mario Amato," Neville said. "We couldn't hold him for two hours. And what would I say when Amato sprung him? That I'd picked him up on the word of an ex-convict?"

"Supposing I got Red Evans?"

"We'll get Red Evans," Neville said. "You keep out of this. That's all I can give you, Steve, a piece of damn good advice."

"Save it," Retnick said. "Put it away with your pension."

"Okay, if that's the way you want it," Neville said angrily. "Where can I drop you?"

"The boarding house. It's on Fortieth and it's on your way. Otherwise, I wouldn't trouble you."

"You're a stubborn Polack," Neville said, and let out the clutch with an exasperated snap. The car leaped forward, the wheels whining at the pavement.

Retnick's street was dark and empty. The lieutenant coasted to a stop and let the motor idle. "Now hold it a second," he said, as Retnick opened the door. He turned toward him, a troubled frown on his face. "I want to say one more thing."

"More advice?"

Neville sighed. "I'm trying to help, Steve. In my way. I think it's the right way. But let's assume for argument's sake that I'm wrong. Say I'm a pension-happy cop who's afraid to rock the boat, afraid of hoodlums like Amato. Say that if you will. All I want you to do is think hard about what I've said. Get this chip off your shoulder and start thinking sensibly. Will you do me that favor?"

"I've thought about your advice," Retnick said. "Good night." Stepping from the car he slammed the door and went up the short flight of worn concrete steps to the doorway of his building. He took his keys from his pocket and turned halfway around to get some light from the street lamp. Neville started up the block under a rush of power, and Retnick turned back to the door and fitted his key in the lock. A high cold wind was blowing and a tin can tumbled along the gutter with a sudden clatter of sound. Retnick's key stuck and he pulled it out and turned once again to the light. And it was then that he saw the shadow of a crouching man moving along the line of cars at the curb. He hesitated an instant, feeling the sudden heavy strike of his heart, the warning tension in his muscles. The shadow moved again, rising slowly as the man came to a standing position behind a black sedan.

Retnick turned back to the door. Standing perfectly still he counted to three, giving the man time to aim, and then he dropped to his knees and dove down the stairs toward the sidewalk. He landed on his right shoulder and tucked his head into his chest to keep from being brained on the concrete; the momentum of his lunge rolled him over, and he came to his feet in a crouch at the curb. And by then the street was echoing with a report of a gun and the scream of a ricocheting bullet. A second shot bounced from the front of the building, sending fine particles of brick whining into the darkness.

Retnick saw the flash of the gun's muzzle two car lengths ahead of him, on the curb side of the cars.

He held Lye's gun in his hand. The silence was complete now and he knew that Neville's car had stopped somewhere up the block. That meant the lieutenant had heard the shots.

The man who had fired at him was only two car lengths away, and Retnick heard the scuff of his shoes on the sidewalk as he moved closer through the darkness. There was no place for Retnick to hide. The cars were parked bumper-to-bumper along the curb and he couldn't slip between them to the street. He could only wait for Neville.

Somewhere down the block a window went up with a protesting shriek and a woman shouted into the silence. And the wind rattled the can near Retnick's hand.

He knew Neville would probably come back along the line of cars on the opposite side of the street. Crouching low he felt around for the tin can in the gutter. Then he tossed it over the cars into the street, and flattened himself on his stomach.

A big figure loomed in the darkness a dozen feet from him. Swearing hoarsely, the man clambered over the fenders of a car, and leaped into the street. He fired again, still cursing, and then Retnick heard Neville yell sharply, "This is the police. Drop that gun."

Retnick scrambled to his feet. A lamp on the opposite sidewalk threw a pale yellow light into the street, and Retnick saw a big man in a camel's hair coat, and saw the fear and rage working in his face as he wheeled and raised his gun in the direction of Neville's voice. A shot sounded off to the right and he heard the man cry out hoarsely. Turning in a frantic circle the man dropped his gun and hugged his stomach tightly with both hands. Finally he went down to his knees and began to sob. And when he fell forward his voice broke and he cried, "No!" in a high, incredulous voice.

Retnick put his gun away and climbed over the bumpers of a car to the street. Hammy lay sprawled on the pavement staring with wide frightened eyes at the dark sky, his big chest heaving for air. Noises sounded up and down the block as people shouted at each other from open windows. Several men were hurrying to the scene, their running footsteps loud and clear in the night.

Neville stepped from behind a car and crossed the street to Retnick's side. He was pale, and there was a sharp glint of excitement in his eyes. "Are you okay?" he said, watching Retnick closely.

"Yes. He missed twice."

Neville knelt beside Hammy. It was obvious the big man was dying. He looked lonely and scared and his face was very white.

"Did Amato tell you to get Retnick?" Neville said, speaking sharply and distinctly. "Come on, Hammy, get squared away before you die."

Hammy shook his head slowly. "I can't die," he said, wetting his lips. "It's not time. I'm young—" His voice broke and he began to cough.

"Who killed Ragoni?" Retnick said quietly.

Several men had crowded around them and Neville raised his head and glared at them. "Get back home where you belong," he said. "I'm a police officer."

The men backed off to the sidewalk and stared in fascination at Hammy.

"I don't know who killed anybody," Hammy said. He looked as if he were trying to cry. "You didn't have to shoot me, I had a lot ahead of me."

"Help us," Retnick said. Neville folded Hammy's fedora and slipped it under his head. "You don't owe Amato anything," Retnick said. "Who killed Joe Ventra? Do you know, Hammy?"

"Amato threw me out," Hammy said weakly. His eyes closed and he drew a deep breath. "Everybody said he killed Ventra. I don't know. Don't let me die."

"We'll do what we can, Hammy," Neville said. "Who says Amato killed Ventra? Tell us that." A police siren wailed in the distance. Neville shook Hammy's arm gently. "Tell us that," he said.

Hammy opened his eyes and reached for Neville's arm. "Wait," he said in a high clear voice. "It ain't over so soon. I just—" He tried to sit up then, staring in sudden fear and understanding at Retnick. When he began to cough the strength left his body and he slumped back to the pavement. Tears glistened in his staring eyes.

A squad car pulled up and a big patrolman came toward them with a hand resting on the butt of his gun.

Neville got slowly to his feet and looked at Retnick. "You come on to the station with me," Neville said. "We'll need your statement. Then we'll have a talk."

Retnick gave his statement to a young detective named Myers, mentioning his fight with Hammy as a possible reason for the ambush. Neville typed out a report without bothering to take off his hat or coat. Then he tossed it in his basket and came into the file room and nodded at Retnick. "I'll wait for you on the sidewalk," he said.

When Retnick came out of the station Neville turned to him, his face sharp and white in the darkness. "Amato didn't wait long to take a crack at you," he said.

"He believes in direct action," Retnick said. "He doesn't wait for an airtight case. You could learn a lot from him."

"Let's stop yapping at each other," Neville said. "Do you know where Red Evans is now?"

"I think he's in Trenton."

"You said earlier that you could get him to New York. Does that still stand?"

"I don't need Red Evans," Retnick said coldly. "Didn't you hear Hammy say Amato killed Joe Ventra? That's all I've been trying to find out."

"A hoodlum's word isn't enough to convict Amato."

"It's enough for me," Retnick said.

"Now listen," Neville said sharply. "We can get Amato my way. But you'll get nothing by acting like a one-man jury and firing squad. We need Red Evans, but we can't extradite him. If you get him, I'll pick up Mario Amato. Then we'll get the truth. And the truth will point at Amato."

Retnick hesitated a second, staring at Neville. "Do I have your word on that?"

"You have my word," Neville said. "But be careful, Steve. Red Evans is a very tough boy."

"Sure," Retnick said. "So was Hammy."

# 12

FROM THE THIRTY-FIRST RETNICK WALKED TO TENTH AVENUE AND picked up a cruising cab. What he had to do was simple and clear; find Red Evans and drag him to New York. How he would do this was neither simple nor clear, but he wasn't worrying about it. What worried him now was Davey Cardinal, and the thought of that hoodlum's interest in his wife. Retnick's concern was illogical, but he couldn't shake it. Why should he care what happened to her? The logical answer was that he didn't, but the logical answer wasn't accurate. He did care what happened to her and he didn't understand why. The driver looked around at him inquiringly, and Retnick gave him an address in the East Eighties, a half block from where he had lived with Marcia. Lighting a cigarette he tried to analyze his feelings on the ride uptown through the dark city. But he got nowhere. It was tied up with Amato, he decided at last. If Amato thought of hitting at him through Marcia, then that put her on his side, even though the involvement was needless and pointless. That must be it, he thought . . .

He paid off the driver and walked along the dark sidewalk, on the opposite side of the street from her apartment.

This was a neighborhood he knew well, although he had lived there only a few months. But in that time he had memorized the street; it was clearer in his mind than the streets of the lower East Side where he had been born and raised.

Retnick stopped in the shadow of a tree and looked up at his wife's apartment. One light shed a faint golden glow through the curtains. She wouldn't be home yet, he knew. For a moment or so he stood completely motionless, staring at the windows of the apartment. It was difficult to realize that he had once lived there, and more difficult still to imagine what sort of man he had been then. The image of himself at peace, living normally and casually, was too strange and incongruous to believe in.

He knew in an objective way he had once been happy, that he had laughed easily, that there had been friends in his life, and the warmth and sustenance of love, but when he tried to examine these memories they became distorted and blurred, twisting out of shape under the corrosive action of his anger.

But there were moments when he could think of Marcia apart from himself, without bitterness, without any feeling at all, as if she were some beautiful lifeless object he had known in a strange dream. It proved something to him that he could think of her at times without any sense of pain or loss. But what it proved he was never quite sure.

He always thought of her in motion; smiling or talking, looking up quickly to laugh at something in the paper, attacking the housework in brief shorts and sandals, her legs slim and brown and quick, and fussing in the kitchen over dinner, making enough for six people because she was proud of his appetite. Her world was gay. And she had thought him too serious. "Don't *worry* so much," she used to say, laughing at him. But it wasn't worry that made him thoughtful, it was caution. Caution was in his background; it was part of the lower East Side, part of working your way through school, part of being a cop. He wasn't afraid of life, but he had been taught to respect it. She could be careless and casual because she had never been hurt. This was a touching thing about her, the conviction that life was sunny and gay, that anyone you met could be your friend. He never quite understood this unreasoned optimism; it amused and puzzled him at the same time. But his attempt to fit her into any of the categories he knew had always failed; she was too direct in some ways, too subtle in others, and when he tried to hold her fast she went through his fingers like quicksilver.

He could think of her this way, dispassionately and calmly. It was the thought of her with someone else that brought up the cold lifeless anger, made his memories of her unendurable.

To his left the gleaming yellow light of a cab turned into the block. Retnick moved closer to the trunk of the tree as the cab slowed down and stopped a few doors from Marcia's apartment. A man climbed out, paid off the driver, and the cab started up again, picking up speed as it went by Retnick. The silence settled heavily as the noise of the motor faded away in the night. For a few seconds the street was quiet, and then Retnick heard the flat ring of the man's heels on the sidewalk. He came out of the darkness directly across from Retnick, and stopped to look casually at the doorway of Marcia's apartment. Then he strolled on, hands deep in his overcoat pockets, his hat brim pulled down low over his swarthy features. Retnick recognized him as he passed through the cone of light falling from the street lamp. Davey Cardinal, Amato's enforcer. Not a mad dog like Joe Lye, but a dangerous show-off, a man in love with his role as tough guy. Perfect for the job of terrorizing a girl.

Cardinal stopped two doors beyond Marcia's building, and glanced casually up and down the sidewalk. Then he stepped quickly into the shadows near the curb and merged with the darkness.

Retnick checked the gun he had taken from Joe Lye, made sure the safety was off and that there was a round in the chamber. Then he crossed the street and walked down the sidewalk toward Cardinal, alert for any sudden movement in the shadows. When he saw the pale shine of his face, and the blur of his body beside a car, he stopped and said, "Hello, Davey."

Cardinal came out of the shadows slowly, a stocky man with a tight little grin on his dark features. He crossed a stretch of lawn to the sidewalk and looked up into Retnick's face. "You keep funny hours, Steve," he said.

"I thought you'd stopped siphoning gas out of parked cars," Retnick said. "I thought you'd turned into a big shot."

"I was obeying nature, that's all," Cardinal said. Still smiling, he touched Retnick's chest lightly with the back of his hand. "But what I do ain't any of your business. And where and how I do it falls in the same class. Nothing about me concerns you, big boy. Keep that in mind. Keep that in mind while you turn your big tail and clear out of here."

"My wife lives just two doors from here," Retnick said gently. "She'll be coming home in a few minutes. Did you know that?"

Cardinal raised his eyebrows. "Maybe I'll run into her."

"No you won't," Retnick said, still speaking gently. Then he took the lapels of the little man's coat in one hand, and when Cardinal's arm dropped swiftly, Retnick drove the muzzle of his gun into his stomach with cruel force. A cry of pain broke past Cardinal's lips, and his hands came up from his pockets and tugged impotently at Retnick's wrist.

"Steve!" he cried out softly, as Retnick shoved him roughly against a tree. "You hurt me inside."

"Listen to me," Retnick said, staring into the pain and fear in his eyes. Their faces were inches apart and he could see the sweat on Cardinal's lip and forehead, the pinched lines of terror at the corners of his mouth.

"Steve—"

"Listen, I said. You beat it now. If anything happens to her, I'll come after you first. Understand that? I won't ask who did it, remember. I'll get you."

"Steve, I swear you got me wrong."

Retnick stared at him for another second or two in silence.

Cardinal wet his lips. "Don't kill me," he whispered. "God, don't kill me, Steve."

"I want to kill you," Retnick said. "I'd like an excuse. Remember that. Now get out of here."

Cardinal straightened his tie and without meeting Retnick's eyes slipped away from the tree and started up the sidewalk, walking like a man who is controlling a desperate impulse to break into a run.

Retnick watched the short dark figure until it disappeared in the shadows of the next block. He didn't think Cardinal would be back; the little hoodlum knew he wanted to kill him. Retnick drew a deep breath. It was stamped on him like a brand then, this need to hurt and destroy. Cardinal had seen it clearly.

A car door slammed behind him and Retnick turned quickly, irritated at himself for having failed to notice the sound of the motor. His wife said good night to the cab driver and started for the entrance of her building, pulling the collar of her coat up against the cold wind. Retnick stood perfectly still in the shadows, hoping she wouldn't see him. But she hesitated at the sidewalk and then turned uncertainly, seeming to sense his presence in the darkness.

"Steve?" she said softly. "Is that you, Steve?"

Retnick walked toward her, his hands in the pockets of his overcoat, and the cab driver, who had waited, said, "Everything okay, Miss Kelly?"

"Yes, Johnny, it's all right," she said, glancing at him with a quick little smile.

"Just checking," he said. "Good night now."

Retnick looked down at his wife and rubbed the back of his hand across his mouth. They were silent then in the cold darkness until the sound of the cab's motor had droned away in the next block.

Then she said, "The bartender told me you were at the club last night. Why didn't you wait?"

"I wanted a drink," he said. "Nothing else."

She shrugged lightly; her gray eyes were puzzled and hurt, but she managed a little smile. "That's direct enough," she said. "And do you want a drink now? I have one upstairs."

"Never mind." It was hard to look at her, to see the tentative, hesitant appeal in her face. She had changed more than he had realized. Not physically; her skin and eyes, the clean grace of her forehead, these would never change. She would always be beautiful but she would never again be unafraid. The careless, unreasoned belief that everything would turn out for the best—that was gone.

"Why were you waiting here?" she said.

"It's too involved to go into," he said. "Look, could you manage to get out of town for a week or two?"

"It's curious you should mention it. I'm planning to leave. Did you know that?"

He felt suddenly confused and angry. "How the hell would I know it? Where are you going?"

"Chicago. It's a better job, my agent thinks."

"You do what he says, eh? Just like that?" he said, snapping his fingers.

"Not quite. He's wanted me to leave for two years, but I thought there was something to wait for in New York."

"You'll be better off in Chicago."

"Why do you want me to leave?"

"I told you it's an involved business," he said. "I'm not making friends these days, and some of them might think of causing you trouble. It's a long shot, but it's there."

She was frowning slightly, watching him with thoughtful eyes. "And you'd care if something happened to me?"

There was no guile in her question; she seemed honestly puzzled by him now.

"I couldn't care less," he said, and his voice was bitter with anger at himself, at the stupidity of his answer. Why was he here if he didn't care? That's what she'd ask him next, trapping and hounding him with her eyes. "I don't want you dragged into this. I don't want you on my side, even by accident."

"Steve, Steve," she said, breathing the words softly. "Stop doing this thing to yourself." She caught his arm impulsively as he tried to turn away from her. "Look at me, Steve. Please! I want to talk to you, I want to tell you what happened—how it happened while you were away." She shook her head quickly, staring helplessly into his eyes. "It was so unimportant, Steve, so tragically unimportant. That's what I want to make you understand. It had nothing to do with my loving you. Can't you believe that?"

"I might," Retnick said, "if I were a complete fool. I suppose you told him I was unimportant—tragically unimportant in your nice phrase."

She took a step backward and withdrew her hand slowly from his arm. Then she said, "It's a waste of time to go on hurting me, Steve. If you knew me at all you'd realize you've hurt me enough." Her lips were trembling but her eyes were suddenly as cold as his own. "Maybe you think I should be stoned in the public square by the righteous daughters of the community? Or be beaten and branded and hung up by my thumbs? Is there any limit to what you think I deserve? How much should I pay for my mistake? I've been lonely and afraid for years. Isn't that payment of a kind? Isn't that enough? I'm in love with a man who can look at me as if I'm something loathsome. Isn't that some kind of payment? Well, to me it is. As far as I'm concerned the account is in balance. I've got nothing to be ashamed of. From now on I'll judge myself by my rules, yes, and by Father Bristow's. His rules are based on love, and yours are based on hate." She drew a deep, unsteady breath. "That's a long speech, but it's the last you'll hear from me."

"Wait a minute," he said.

"No." She shook her head quickly, speaking the one word with difficulty. Turning, she hurried toward the entrance of her apartment. He saw the gleam of her slim legs as she began to run, and he knew from the way she held her shoulders that she was weeping.

"I never wanted to hurt you," he shouted, but the door was already closing swiftly against his words.

Why had it happened to him? he thought, rubbing both hands over his face. He realized his mind was spinning senselessly, demanding answers to impossible questions. There was no reason to any of it; his life had been smashed casually and carelessly, destroyed in a whimsical collision with another's will. The only way to give it sense was to destroy whoever ordained these fateful collisions. An uncomfortable chill went through his body at the thought, and he shook himself quickly and began walking. He knew then that part of his hatred had shifted from Amato to someone infinitely more powerful. What worried him was that his anger was directed at someone he no longer believed in. It was this that made the shadows of the night, and the shadows in his mind, so strange and menacing.

# 13

RETNICK LAY ON HIS BED SMOKING ONE CIGARETTE AFTER ANOTHER, UNable to find relief from his painful, turbulent thoughts. When a knock sounded on the door he got quickly to his feet, grateful for the distraction. Mrs. Cara stood in the hallway, an anxious and worried frown on her face.

"Mr. Retnick, I shouldn't bother you, but one of my old men is sick." She sighed and shook her head. "Not sick but drunk. He is weeping and drinking and I can't do nothing for him. I thought you could talk to him, maybe."

"What good would that do? If he wants to drink he'll drink."

"But he's not like that. Mr. Nelson is very steady all the time. Something just happened to him, that's all."

"You could call the cops," Retnick said.

"Oh, I wouldn't do that. He's a very nice man."

"Where is he?"

She smiled then, and some of the worry left her eyes. "Good, I show you. Come with me. Maybe another man can help him."

Mr. Nelson had a room on the first floor at the back of the house, a clean, neat cubicle with a window opening on an air shaft. He was lying on the bed staring at the ceiling, a tall thin man with silver-gray hair and gentle brown eyes that were sunk deep beneath bushy eyebrows. A half-empty bottle of whisky was on the floor near his trailing hand. He was fully dressed. His overcoat was folded over the back of a chair but he still wore a gray wool muffler. He had been crying, obviously; his nose was red and tears glittered in his staring eyes.

"You go back to bed," Retnick said to Mrs. Cara. "I'll sit here with him awhile."

"Can I get him anything?"

"I don't think so."

Nelson was apparently unconscious of their presence, but Retnick knew from the altered rhythm of his breathing that he had heard their voices. He pulled up the chair and sat beside the bed. Mrs. Cara looked uncertainly at the two men for a moment, and then sighed and tiptoed from the room.

"You can't help," Nelson said, without looking at Retnick. His voice was unexpectedly clear. "You might as well go, too. I'm not likely to become violent."

"You gave Mrs. Cara a scare."

"I didn't mean to. I—she's a good friend of mine. But I couldn't help it."

"She'll understand. She's just worried about you, that's all. You mind if I smoke a cigarette?"

"No, I don't mind. But you might as well go back and sleep. You can't help me."

"I'll just finish the cigarette then," Retnick said.

Nelson said nothing for three or four minutes. Retnick glanced around the small, tidy room; it was a still life of sterile loneliness. No snapshots, no pictures, no personal notes. The clutter of life was absent; the change and keys to use tomorrow, the stamped letter to mail on the way to work, there were no such things in this wrapped-up little box. A toothbrush stood in a clean glass on a shelf above the sink, and a bar of soap gleamed dully in the bright light. But they looked new and unused, like props in a department store window. Except for a tiny crucifix above the bed the walls were bare.

"My cousin died this morning," Nelson said, in his clear distinct voice. "That's—well, that's why I got drunk. Would you explain that to Mrs. Cara?"

"That's too bad," Retnick said. "She'll be sorry to hear it."

Nelson shook his head. "She didn't know him. I haven't seen him for fifteen years. He lived in Boise. He was a school teacher. Never married. But he was the only relative I had. It—just hit me today. I'm alone. There's nobody to bury me. The police will come when I die and they won't know what to do with my body. I—I just started drinking this morning. I couldn't stop thinking about what would happen to me, and I couldn't stop drinking. I'm not a drinking man. I worked thirty-two years in the post office and I don't suppose I had a dozen glasses of beer in all that time. You might as well go to bed, mister."

"When I finish the cigarette," Retnick said. His eyes moved to the crucifix, and he stared defiantly at the suspended figure. "You believe in God, don't you?" he said.

"I don't know. Not enough, maybe. I don't know."

"What did you do in your spare time when you were working?"

"I used to go out to the track," Nelson said. "I never bet, but I liked to watch horses. Thoroughbreds, I mean. I was born in Virginia and I got the look of them stamped in my head. I just like to watch them run." He smiled nervously and turned to look at Retnick. "You ever do that?"

"No, I was born on the East Side. I thought horses came with milk wagons attached to them until I was about ten, I think."

"Well, you missed something. They're pretty to watch, I tell you."

"Maybe you could show me what to look for some day. They'll be running at Belmont in a few months."

"Sure they will. I'd be glad to show you, too. A kid misses a lot growing up in the city."

He was okay now, Retnick knew. Maybe he could even get to sleep. "How about a nightcap?" he said casually.

"You go ahead. I—I think I had enough."

Retnick rinsed the toothbrush glass, and poured himself a small drink. Then he said good night. But Nelson didn't answer him. His eyes were closed and his breathing had become regular.

When Retnick stepped into the dark hallway, Mrs. Cara put her head out of her door. "He's all right?" she asked him quietly.

"I think so. His cousin died this morning, and it hit him hard. But he'll be okay."

"I'm glad. He's a nice man. He's lived here eighteen years."

"Good night," Retnick said, but Mrs. Cara put her hand on his arm. "You were good to him. Your voice was almost like a woman's. You don't mind my saying this, I hope, but it ain't like the voice you used with your wife on the phone."

Retnick stared at her. "My trouble didn't come from a bottle. And it won't go away with a hangover."

"Things are never as bad as you think they are, Mr. Retnick. You remember that."

"Sometimes they're worse," Retnick said. "Good night."

He slept little that night and was up at six in the morning. He went to the corner restaurant for coffee and returned to his rooming house without bothering to eat breakfast. Today he had to look for Red Evans. This was Thursday, Dixie Davis' day off, and if she followed her customary pattern she would go to Trenton to meet Evans. Retnick decided to pick her up there. That would be less risky than attempting to trail her from New York.

The day was clear and crisp with an occasional flurry of snow in the air. Two men stood talking together in front of his rooming house. They were staring at the place in the street where Hammy had died. Retnick heard one of them say, "The guy who shot him was a cop. It says that in the paper. Some luck, eh? Pull something and find a cop in the same block waiting for you."

Retnick let himself into the room, trying not to think of anything at all, trying particularly not to think of his wife. That was over. She would go to Chicago and he would stay here with his dark heavy thoughts. The little cat, Silvy, blinked at him from an open drawer, stretching comfortably on his small stack of new shirts. He put her down on the floor and then took Joe Lye's gun from his pocket and looked at it for a moment, unable to decide whether or not to take it with him. There were risks either way. But he finally decided against it. He would go right back to jail if he were picked up carrying a gun. He put the gun under his shirts, closed the drawer and left.

It was an hour's ride to Trenton and by eight o'clock he had taken his post in the waiting room, sitting where he could watch the passengers who got off the New York trains. He spent the morning in the dusty, overheated room, using a newspaper to shield his face when people trickled in off the hourly trains. He wasted the morning and most of the afternoon before he became convinced that she wasn't going to show. It would have been more reasonable to trail her from New York and take the risk of being seen, he thought. Evans had probably left Trenton when he heard that Retnick was looking for him.

It was five o'clock when he got back to New York. He ate a sandwich and drank a cup of coffee, and then tried to find a cab. But the evening rush had started by then and the increasingly heavy snow had created traffic snarls throughout the midtown section. Retnick joined an exasperated group of people under a hotel canopy. A red-faced doorman stood in the street whistling for a cab with pointless optimism, while the snow fell softly and silently into the black congested city.

Retnick didn't get to Dixie Davis' apartment until almost seven o'clock. In the foyer he brushed the snow from his hat and shoulders before pressing her buzzer. She answered almost immediately, "Who is it?"

"Retnick," he said. "Remember?"

"Sure. What's on your mind?"

"I want to see you."

"Look, Buster, there's a thing called a telephone," she said. "People use it to make dates with."

"I didn't have time to call," he said. "This is important."

There was a brief silence. Then she said, "Important to who? You or me?"

"It could be for both of us."

"Okay, come on up."

She was waiting for him in the doorway, a bored little smile twisting her freshly painted lips. Except for her eyes, which were cold little points under the red bangs, everything about her was designed as part of an obvious piece. The red silk dress straining tightly at the curves of her small body, the sheer nylons and wedge-soled ankle straps, the huge junk bracelet on her wrist, they all advertised an old, old product.

"Well, what's the good news?" she said. "You strike gold in a back tooth or something?"

"It's better than that," he said, smiling slightly. He strolled past her into the scrupulously neat and impersonal room. "We're all alone, eh?" he said, tossing his hat into a chair.

"Make yourself at home. You want a robe and slippers maybe?"

"It's a tempting idea."

"Okay, stop clowning," she said, staring at him coldly. "What's on your mind?"

"You don't sound very friendly," he said.

"I don't like guys barging up here like it was a saloon with a free lunch," she said. "I told you once, I'll tell you twice, use the damn telephone if you want to see me."

Retnick stared at her, his face and eyes hardening slowly. "I don't want to see you," he said. "Given a choice I'd prefer to play pinochle with somebody's eighty-year-old aunt. But I don't have a choice."

"You know where the door is," she said, putting her hands on her small, bony hips. "If you don't like it here, blow."

Retnick's smile did something ugly to his eyes. "You're pretty tough, aren't you?"

"I get by, Buster. I take care of me and mine."

"But you're sitting in a very rough game," Retnick said. "You could get hurt. Doesn't that worry you?"

"I sleep just fine," she said.

"You're still seeing Red Evans," Retnick said slowly. "And he's a murderer. I didn't buy the cute story about the trusting little doll who lost her heart and bankroll to the con man. Life in Canada, a big fresh start, it was all corn, Dixie. Where is he? That's what I'm going to find out."

She laughed softly. "You're an ex-con who got kicked off the police force for murdering a man. Do you think that makes you something special? You think I'll get down on my knees for a creep like you? Get this straight now, Buster: if I see Red Evans that's my business. He could be a murderer fifty times over and he'd still be a better man than you are."

Something in her manner puzzled him; she was relishing this moment, chin raised, eyes flashing, playing it as if she were facing an audience.

"You could get hurt in this deal," he said, watching her closely. "Hasn't that occurred to you?"

"I'm scared to death," she said.

Retnick caught her suddenly by the shoulders and jerked her close to him. "I'll bet you don't want to get hurt," he said softly.

The speed and power in his hands had wiped the wise little sneer from her face; she stared up at him, breathing unevenly, terrified by the strange look in his eyes.

"Don't," she whispered, and her eyes flicked past him to the closed bedroom door. It was an involuntary betrayal; she looked quickly back at Retnick, a new fear touching her face.

An audience, Retnick thought, and a little shock went through him. They weren't alone.

He heard the metallic whisper as the doorknob turned and he saw the straining effort Dixie was making to keep her eyes on his face. Raising his voice he said, "You said you'd finger him for a thousand bucks. So why stall? You want more dough?"

"Don't move," a voice behind him said quietly. "That's good. Now take your dirty hands off her. And don't turn around."

Retnick released the girl and she backed away from him, grinning with relief. She rubbed her thin shoulders and said, "We'll see what a big man you are now, Buster."

Fast expert hands went over Retnick's clothes and body. Then the voice said, "Okay, big shot, let's look at you."

As Retnick turned, a fist struck the side of his face and the sharp edge of a ring slashed across the cheek bone. The man who struck him stepped back quickly, the gun in his hand centered on Retnick's stomach. "All right, start something," he said, smiling faintly.

Retnick touched his cheek and felt the warm blood under his fingers. "You're Red Evans, eh?" he said.

"Yeah, that's it. How come everybody thinks you're dumb? You sound real sharp to me."

Evans was a tall man with sloping shoulders and a loose, reckless mouth. His hair was bright red, and he needed a shave; the lamplight glinted on the blond whiskers along his heavy jaw. He wore a gaily colored sports shirt with dark slacks, and his brown eyes looked muddy and dangerous.

"The love tap was necessary," he said, balancing himself on the balls of his feet and keeping a safe distance from Retnick. "My story goes like this: you broke in, started beating up my friend and I had to kill you in self-defense. Does it sound all right? You used to be a cop. You should be a good judge."

Retnick shrugged. "It sounds okay. But what's your story for Ragoni? Did you kill him in self-defense too?"

"I don't need any story for Ragoni," Evans said, and he wasn't smiling any more. "I never touched him. But it annoyed me when I heard you were talking pretty loud about me and Ragoni. That kind of talk can cause trouble. I checked with Amato and he told me you got this delusion I killed your pal. So I decided to come over and set you straight."

"You didn't trust Amato to handle it, eh?"

Evans said gently, "They sounded a little scared of you. Tough cop and all that crap. But things like that don't scare me, Retnick."

"Before you shoot you'd better be sure your chum here will back up the story."

Evans smiled at Dixie. "She'll back me up, she's smart."

"Sure, she's smart," Retnick said. "She offered to lead me to you for a thousand bucks."

Dixie laughed softly. "Did I, big shot? Did I lead you to him? Or was it the other way around?"

"She held out for more dough," Retnick said, watching Evans. He had little hope this would work. They weren't fools; they were shrewd and tough and ruthless.

"So she's double-crossing me," Evans said, with a sigh. He looked sadly at Dixie. "You're a naughty one, selling out the old redhead."

"It's funny," Retnick said, hardening his voice. "Real funny. Cops make most of their pinches because clowns like you have such fine senses of humor. How do you suppose I knew you killed Ragoni? You think I heard that on a newscast?"

Evans' expression changed slightly. He still smiled, but a wary glint appeared in his muddy eyes. "Okay, big shot, where'd you hear it?"

"Ask her," Retnick said.

"Sure," Evans said slowly. "I'll ask her. Dixie knows better than to kid around with me."

"He's just trying to steam you up, Red," Dixie said. One thin hand moved uneasily along the seam of her skirt. "I never told him anything."

"But he knows something," Evans said, looking thoughtfully at Retnick. "If he ain't guessing, then somebody's been talking."

"I'm guessing, sure," Retnick said. "I guess Mario Amato paid you to do the job on Ragoni. And I guess it was Mario who got you the job on the winch in Ragoni's crew. And I guess it was just damn carelessness when you almost hit him with a load of freight." He smiled coldly at Evans. "You want me to keep guessing?"

"You know about Mario Amato, eh?" Evans said. He looked genuinely puzzled. "Who's been talking to you?"

"Ask her," Retnick said.

Evans sighed deeply. "You goofed that time, big shot. I never told her about Mario."

"Somebody did," Retnick said. "Before you blast me and hit tomorrow's front pages, ask yourself who's been spreading the news about you."

"Red, wake up!" Dixie cried. "He's just stalling. Can't you see that?"

"Something cute is going on," Evans said. He looked mad and dangerous. "Come here, baby. Don't cross in front of him or you'll get a bullet through you."

"What do you want?"

"Just come here."

When she reached his side he put an arm around her and twisted his fingers into her hair. His eyes and gun stayed on Retnick. "I want to get things straight," he said, very quietly. "We'll take our time and find out what's going on. You first, Dixie," he said, and forced her head back until the tendons in her throat stood out tightly under the white skin.

"Red, don't!"

"I'm not going to hurt you," he said. "I just want you nice and quiet. Now listen: if you talked to anybody I got to know about it. Understand me? Maybe somebody put pressure on you or offered you a big payoff. That's okay. I don't care if you talked. But I got to know if I'm being fitted for a frame."

"Red, I swear to God," she cried.

"Let me finish. If you squealed say so. I won't hurt you. But I got to know."

"I swear I never talked, Red. Stop it, please."

"I think I believe you, baby," Evans said, watching Retnick with his muddy, dangerous eyes. "Now it's your turn, big shot. Where'd you get your information?"

Unconsciously, his hand tightened in Dixie's hair, and she said hoarsely, "For God's sake, Red, stop it!" The words were thick with pain in her straining throat, and tears started in her eyes. She tried to drive a sharply pointed heel into his foot, and then her right knee jerked upward in a spasmodic, convulsive reaction and knocked his gun hand into the air.

Retnick was on him like an animal. He caught Evans' upraised wrist with one hand, his throat with the other, and slammed him backward across the room. The rush of his body knocked the girl spinning to the floor and sent a chair crashing crazily onto its side. Evans' body struck the wall with a crash, and Retnick saw the dazed pain and fear streak into his eyes when his head snapped against the wall.

"Drop the gun," he said, holding him by the arm and throat. "Drop it!"

Evans struggled against him, desperately trying to twist his pinioned hand and bring the gun to bear on Retnick.

"Tough guy," Retnick said, and closed his fingers with all his strength on Evans' wrist.

Evans screamed in pain, the sound of it high and incredulous in his throat, and the gun clattered from his distended fingers to the floor. Retnick hit him in the stomach then, and something brutal and guilty within him savored the impact of the blow and the explosive rush of air from Evans' lungs.

Breathing heavily, he stepped back and let him slide to the floor. He picked up the gun, dropped it in his pocket and stared for a second or so without feeling or compassion at Evans' red, straining face and jackknifed body. Finally he looked at the girl who sat on the floor supporting her weight with one outstretched hand. Her eyes were wide with terror as she stared at him.

"Get up," he said.

"Don't hurt me, please."

"Get up. Keep quiet and you'll be okay."

Retnick walked to the phone and put in a call to the Thirty-First. Watching Evans, he told the clerk who answered to put him through to Lieutenant Neville. When Neville came on, Retnick said, "I got him. Evans. Can you pick him up right away?"

Neville whistled softly. "Is he marked up?"

"Nothing that will show."

"Where are you?"

Retnick told him and Neville said, "Sit tight."

Retnick put the phone down and lit a cigarette. Inhaling deeply, he felt some of the tension dissolving in his body. But he felt no elation or triumph. Only a curious bitterness and distaste.

"You're working with the cops?" Dixie asked him in a small, uneasy voice.

"That's right."

"You made him think I crossed him," she said. Staring at Evans a little shudder went through her body. "What'll happen to me when he gets loose?"

"Maybe he won't get loose."

"But if he does?"

"That's your problem."

"What have you got against me?"

"Nothing," Retnick said shortly.

She was very pale and her lips were trembling. "Why did you put me in this spot?"

"You put yourself in it," Retnick said, staring at her. "This guy is a killer. He killed a man he'd never seen before, slipped a knife between his ribs for a piece of change. And you knew about it. You thought he was a hero." Retnick made an abrupt, angry gesture with his hand. "Behind every one of these vermin is a dummy like you, loving them, protecting them, treating them like glamour boys. Until you get in the middle. Then you get religion. You think that—" Retnick stopped and ground out his cigarette. He felt disgusted with himself. "You'll be okay," he said.

She was weeping now. Fear had stripped the cynical, wise-guy mask from her face. She looked suddenly childish and vulnerable. Even the cheaply sexy clothes seemed incongruous on her small thin body, like props borrowed from an older sister.

"You don't know him," she said. "You don't know what he's like when he's mad."

"He'll have enough problems without worrying about you."

The buzzer sounded and he went to the speaking tube that was hooked to the wall. He made sure it was Neville, then pressed the button that unlocked the inner door of the foyer.

Neville and Kleyburg walked into the room a few seconds later. Kleyburg put a hand on Retnick's arm, his eyes going worriedly to the blood on his face. "You okay, Steve?" he said.

"It's nothing serious."

Neville was staring down at Evans. "They never look worth the trouble they make," he said. Then he nodded at Dixie, his pale face completely without expression. "Who's this?"

"The girl friend," Retnick said.

"You've got to protect me," Dixie said, smiling nervously at Neville.

"Will you testify against him?" he said.

"There—there's nothing I could tell you," she said, as her eyes slipped away from his contempt. He turned to Retnick, dismissing her completely. "Did you get anything from him?"

"He's your boy," Retnick said. He was sure Evans was listening, so he said, "He knows Amato is trying to frame him and keep the kid in the clear."

Neville picked up the cue. "Amato will get away with it too."

Evans straightened himself painfully to a sitting position. "You guys are real comedians," he said. "Comic book cops, that's what you are."

Kleyburg looked at him with a pleased smile. "On your feet, buddy. We're going to take you some place where you can tell us your life story. I'll bet it's good."

Neville touched Retnick's arm and drew him aside. "You fade," he said quietly. "We'll pick up Mario Amato now and toss these two babies together. I'll call you when there's a break."

# 14

RETNICK WAITED IN HIS ROOM FOR NEVILLE'S CALL. HE SAT ON THE edge of the bed smoking one cigarette after another and checking his watch every few minutes. It was after midnight now; five hours had passed since Evans and Mario had been arrested.

The lamp on the bureau cast a pale yellow light over the old furniture, the dusty, rose-patterned furniture, and drew dark lines across Retnick's rock-hard face. Nothing could slip, he was thinking. Evans was in a savage, nervous mood, half-convinced he was being measured for a frame. Young Mario was a weakling and a fool. Slam them together and you'd get an explosion of squeals and denials. But it hadn't happened yet.

He tried to picture what was going on at the Thirty-First, knowing the cat-and-mouse game Neville would play, knowing the mood of casual but ominous tension he would generate for the benefit of Evans and Mario Amato. He had been part of that scene himself dozens of times but tonight it was difficult to bring it into clear and vivid focus. Another idea slipped softly into his mind, threading itself like elusive music into his hard and bitter thoughts. Tonight would dissolve the swollen fury he had lived with for five years, and then he could see his wife again. Maybe he would understand her then.

The phone rang shrilly and before the echoes died away Retnick was through the door and into the wide dark hallway. He lifted the receiver and said, "Yes?"

"Steve?" It was Neville's voice, edged with weariness.

"Yes. Did they crack?"

Neville drew a deep breath. "It's a bust, Steve. They aren't talking."

"They will, they've got to," Retnick said, tightening his grip on the receiver.

"We used all the tricks, Steve. Nothing worked."

"Evans practically admitted to me that he killed Ragoni," Retnick said angrily. "And he practically admitted that young Mario Amato paid him to do it."

"They won't admit anything now," Neville said. "Now listen: we picked up Mario at his uncle's house four or five hours ago. Kleyburg made the pinch. Amato raised hell. He told his nephew he'd have him out by morning. Mario believed him, I guess. He won't talk. And neither will Evans. I've had two calls from downtown. They're getting hotter about this pinch all the time. So far they buy my story. But I can't convince them much longer."

"So you'll turn them loose," Retnick said bitterly.

"I'll have to. I expect Amato here in an hour or so with a writ for Mario. After Mario walks out Evans will know damn well we were bluffing. I could hold him for a while but what's the point? He isn't going to talk."

Retnick stared down the dark hallway. He could see the yellow gleam of a street lamp through the glass doorway. He said quietly, "Look, Lieutenant, is that creep Connors around? You know, the detective on Amato's string."

"Sure he's around. He's trying to find out what's up. But I've kept him away from this deal. Why?"

"Tell him young Mario has spilled everything," Retnick said.

Neville was silent a moment. Then he said wearily, "Steve, you're out of your mind. Connors would pass that to Amato. Do you want to back a hunch against that boy's life?"

"I'm not interested in Mario's life," Retnick said. "I want to hang Amato. If he thinks his nephew has squealed on him he'll play into your hands."

"No!" Neville said, snapping the single word out with explosive force. "I've gone as far as I can with you. I'm not going to set up a murder to prove that your guess is right. Damn it, Steve, think! Do you realize what you're asking?"

"It was just a thought," Retnick said. He'd been foolish to hope for Neville's help on a shady maneuver; Neville played to strict rules. "I guess we struck out," he said.

"Don't worry, we won't stop here," Neville said.

"Sure," Retnick said. Then he said casually, "Is Kleyburg around, by the way?"

"No, I sent him home an hour ago. Why?"

"It wasn't important. It will keep."

"Get some rest, Steve. And don't think we're licked."

"Of course not. Thanks for the try, Lieutenant."

When Retnick replaced the phone he stood for a moment in the darkness, a strange little smile touching his lips. Neville wouldn't help him. But Kleyburg would.

The old man was obviously ready for bed; he wore a dark-blue flannel robe with slippers and the ends of his gray hair were still damp from a shower. He peered up at Retnick, who stood in the shadows of the doorway, and a surprised smile touched his face. "Steve, this is wonderful," he said. "I couldn't imagine who it was at this time of night."

"I know it's late."

"Forget it. Come on in."

"Thanks." Retnick walked into the warm, comfortable room and dropped his hat on a sofa. Kleyburg had been reading; there was a cup of coffee on the table beside his chair, and a sports magazine on the ottoman. The air smelled pleasantly of coffee and pipe smoke.

"How about a drink, Steve? I'm a long way from turning in. We can jaw away all night if you like."

Retnick looked steadily at him. "Evans didn't talk. Neither did young Mario. That's why I'm here. I need help."

"Sure, Steve. What do you want?"

"We've got to make Evans talk," Retnick said.

Kleyburg spread his hands helplessly. "Easier said than done, Steve. We've tried everything. On him and young Mario. But they didn't break. They're more scared of Amato than they are of cops."

"There's one more thing you can try, Miles."

"Yeah? What's that?"

"Tell Amato his nephew squealed."

Kleyburg smiled uncertainly as the silence stretched and grew in the small, comfortable room. "Now, Steve," he said at last, still smiling nervously and uncertainly. "Amato wouldn't believe us. He'd know we were bluffing."

"Not if he got the word from Connors," Retnick said.

Kleyburg's smile faded slowly. He gestured nervously with one hand and then, to gain time it seemed, removed his glasses and began to polish them with a handkerchief he took from the pocket of his robe. "Yes, he'd believe Connors," he said finally. "That's what he pays him for. Information. But what good would that do?"

"The word would get back to Evans," Retnick said. "Right now he's ready to blow sky high. If he thought the kid had talked he'd start singing, too. And he'd tell us who paid him to kill Ragoni."

Kleyburg shook his head quickly and turned away from Retnick. Without glasses he looked weary and vulnerable; his eyes blinked against the light and a tense frown gathered on his forehead. "You—you can't be serious," he said.

"All it will take is one phone call. From you to Connors."

"No!" Kleyburg said, still shaking his head. "Good Lord, Steve, do you realize what you're asking. Spreading the word that Mario squealed would be like handing him a death sentence. And that's a verdict only a judge and jury are qualified to make. You know that, Steve. I'm a police officer, not an executioner."

"Nothing's going to happen to the kid," Retnick said. "Amato won't kill his own nephew. All this will do is put pressure on Evans. One phone call from you to Connors can break Nick Amato. What are you stalling for?"

"Steve, don't ask me to do this," Kleyburg said, rubbing a hand helplessly over his forehead. Turning away from Retnick he looked at the pictures of his sons on the mantel, staring at them as if he could find some strength and resolution in their earnest young faces. "I've never pulled anything shady or crooked in all my years on the force," he said, and it seemed as if he were speaking to his boys now instead of Retnick. "Maybe that's no claim to fame. But I slept nights. I never had any trouble looking at myself in a mirror." Sighing, he turned and looked up into Retnick's eyes. "You see why it's impossible, Steve? You're taking a chance on that boy's life. I can't go that far."

"You've got a fine bleeding heart for hoodlums all of a sudden," Retnick said bitterly. "I'm after the guy who framed me into jail for five years. But you won't lift a finger to help. All you'll do is make pious speeches about how honest you are and what a pity it would be if a pampered little creep like Mario got hurt. Did you forget that I got hurt too? I lost every goddamn thing that made sense in my life, but that doesn't mean anything to you. To hell with Retnick. This is Be-kind-to-the-Amatos week."

"Steve, don't talk that way," Kleyburg said. He rubbed his mouth nervously and glanced around the room, avoiding Retnick's eyes. "If—if you'd calm down you'd see I'm right about this."

Retnick walked to the mantel and picked up a picture of Kleyburg's older son. He stared at the grave young face, and a bitter smile touched his lips. Then he looked at Kleyburg. "How do you think you lived long enough to raise these kids?" he said quietly. "When we worked together who kicked open the doors, and walked into dark alleys? You or me?"

"Steve, I know you carried me, I know—"

"Sure, I carried you," Retnick said harshly. "I took the tough jobs and let you sit on your can in the car. You think I liked that? You think I was tired of living and wanted some hopped-up punk to blow my brains out?"

"Steve," Kleyburg said helplessly, but Retnick cut him off with an angry gesture. "You made your speech, let me make mine. I carried you because you had kids. Because they needed you alive and on a payroll. Otherwise they might have been on the streets. Think about that when you look at these pictures. Think about that when you're sitting around in Florida on your pension."

Retnick put the picture back on the mantel and turned to the door. Kleyburg hurried after him and caught his arm. "Steve, wait a minute," he said, in a soft, pleading voice. "Don't leave this way. We were friends, remember."

With a hand on the door Retnick turned and stared at him. "Sure, I remember," he said. "You're the one who forgot it."

"Wait, please." Kleyburg rubbed his forehead and shook his head. He looked very tired and beaten; his lips were trembling and his eyes were dull and hopeless. "I can't let you go this way," he said, barely whispering the words. "I—I'll get the word to Connors."

Retnick caught his shoulders in his big hands. "He's at the Thirty-First now. If he's gone try his home. And for God's sake don't be obvious about it."

"I'll handle it," Kleyburg said wearily. "We're working on a case. I'll call him about that and let him pump me. He thinks I'm an old fool anyway."

"That should work," Retnick said. "Don't worry about the kid. It's Nick Amato who's going on the hook."

Kleyburg nodded but his eyes slipped away from Retnick's. "I—I'm glad to be able to help, Steve. I know you carried me. Even if it was just because of the kids I appreciate it."

"We'll have a drink the day they hang Amato," Retnick said. "Make that call now."

# 15

IT WAS AN HOUR BEFORE DAWN WHEN NICK AMATO WALKED INTO THE brightly lighted hallway of the Thirty-First precinct. With him was an attorney named Coyne and a stockily built man who wore a tweed overcoat and a checked cap pulled down over his left ear. This man had several names which were familiar to the police, but he was called Kerry along the waterfront, in recognition of his tweeds and brogue and his incessant, lively chatter about stake racing in Ireland. He had been born on Pell Street in lower Manhattan and had seldom been more than fifty miles away from the place of his birth.

Amato stopped at the information counter and smiled apologetically at the gray-haired lieutenant on duty. A casual observer might have guessed that his awkward little smile was a kind of peasant's armor against the awe-inspiring figure of the officer on duty. But the lieutenant was no casual observer; he knew all about Amato's smile. Leaning forward he said earnestly, "To speak plain, Nick, I thought it was a damn shame to arrest your boy."

"Sure," Amato said, rubbing a finger along his nose. "It scared the old woman half to death. Great police work. Let's have him now. The lawyer he's got the papers."

"A damn shame," the lieutenant said again as he accepted the writ from the attorney. Raising his voice he yelled: "Turnkey! Bring Mario Amato out here."

When Mario appeared he was smiling with a new strength and confidence. The eight hours in jail hadn't marked him physically; he didn't even look in need of sleep. What sustained him was the realization that he had handled himself damn well. He knew that. Joe Lye, Kerry, they couldn't have done better. For a while he had been so scared that he was damn near sick right in the lieutenant's office. Neville, that was his name, had all the facts, and seemed to regard Mario's confirmation of them as an irrelevant detail. A shrewd tough man! Mario would remember the contempt in his eyes for a long time. But it was over now, and he hadn't given them a thing.

"How come the delay?" he said to his uncle, very pleased to be able to joke about it. "These places ain't rest homes exactly."

"Things take time," Amato said. "The lieutenant's got your watch and wallet. Sign out and let's go."

Mario took his wallet from the lieutenant and put it in his pocket without counting the money. This struck him as a nice touch, a patronizing way of letting the cops know he thought they were too dumb to be thieves.

Amato smiled at him but the lights in his eyes were like the points of daggers. I was good to him, he thought. Cars, clothes, money, dames. Anna's little man, pink-cheeked, wavy-haired, with hands that had never known a day's work. My nephew, he was thinking, who would be watching goats on a rocky farm in Calabria if it wasn't for me. I made him a big shot. Just because he hangs his hat in my house and can tell people I'm his uncle he's a big shot. And he'd squealed. At the first hint of pressure he'd crumbled like a piece of stale cake.

Amato kept his little smile in place with a conscious physical effort. He had received Connors' call an hour ago, and since then his anger had been growing dangerously. Connors wasn't sure what the kid had spilled, but he said Neville was happy about it. So this wasn't over yet. They'd pick him up again and again, knowing he was soft and frightened, and eventually they'd get the whole story. If they didn't have it already . . .

Amato rubbed his damp forehead. Take it nice and quiet, he thought. But that was like telling a man with a ticking bomb under his bed to close his eyes and go to sleep. Amato's anger was streaked with a lugubrious self-pity; he felt surrounded by fools and ingrates. Hammy, who'd got himself killed in a stupid move against Retnick; and Joe Lye! Where in hell was Joe Lye? Amato had tried to find him after he'd got Connors' call, but with no luck. So he had been forced to use Kerry, who had a bad habit of boozing and talking too much.

"Let's go," he said to his nephew, and walked outside, making no attempt to conceal his disgust. Kerry joined him on the sidewalk. "Should I be on my way?" he asked briskly.

"Yeah, get going," Amato said, without looking at him. "Don't mess this up. Evans says she's the one who fingered him. All he wants is to pay her off." Amato shook his head and frowned into the darkness. "You guys got to have dames. And you got to tell 'em everything. Brag about every job you pull. Then the cops get hold of them and you act surprised because they squeal. It's the way all you dopes get in trouble."

Kerry smiled faintly. "Sure and that will never change, Nick. I'll see you later." As Mario came out of the station Kerry turned and walked up the block, his leather heels ringing in the silence. He was whistling an Irish air and the melody was clear and sad in the cold, windy night.

Amato glanced at his nephew. "Was it rough?" he said.

"Hell, I could do it standing on my head," Mario said, grinning.

"You go home now. I want you to wait for me in your bedroom. You understand?"

"Look, Nick, I'm all right. I ain't even tired."

"Listen to me," Amato said. "As a favor, okay?"

Amato's attitude confused Mario. "Sure," he said.

"Go home. Wait for me in your bedroom. I'll see you in an hour. We'll have a talk about tonight."

"All right, Nick."

The attorney stood beside Amato and the two men watched Mario walk away toward the avenue. In spite of his uncle's disconcerting manner there was a new confidence in the lift of his head.

Coyne, the attorney, said, "What was this all about, Nick?"

Amato shrugged. "Cops killing time, I guess."

"I suppose. Can I drop you somewhere?"

"No, I got my car."

"Well, good night then."

Without answering him Amato turned and walked down the block to his car. He needed Lye now, and he thought he knew where to find him . . .

Kay Johnson lived in a tall and imposingly respectable apartment house on the East Side. The street was quiet and empty and Amato found a parking place without difficulty. He knocked on the door of the building and peered through the wide glass frames for a sign of life in the lobby. This was great, he thought, savoring the sensuous rush of anger that ran through him. Nick Amato standing in the cold, waiting on Joe Lye's pleasure.

At the far end of the lobby elevator doors opened and a uniformed attendant hurried toward him fumbling with a ring of keys. The man peered through the glass at Amato, frowned indecisively, and then opened the door an inch.

"Kay Johnson," Amato said. "What's her apartment?"

"Six A, sir. But you'll have to phone from the lobby. Most of the tenants insist . . ."

"Okay, okay, we'll phone her," Amato said. "We disturb something, we disturb something. Is that character with the funny lip up there?"

"I wouldn't know, sir." The man led him to a carpeted alcove off the lobby, and nodded to a phone on a desk. His manner was cold and reproving.

I'll show them what crude is, Amato thought bitterly. East Side snobs and Joe Lye playing the gent with Martinis and steaks. No place for Nick Amato. He was just good enough to pick up the checks . . .

Lye answered his ring in a sleepy voice. "Yeah?"

"This is Nick," Amato said good-humoredly. "I tried you earlier but you wasn't in."

"We took in a show and then hit a few spots," Lye said. "Was it something important?"

"So-so. I want to see you now. I'm downstairs."

"Downstairs?" Lye's voice shook slightly. "You mean in the lobby?"

"I guess that's the name for it. Can I come up?"

"Why—" There was silence on the line.

Asking permission, Amato thought. Explaining to her, while he covered the receiver with his hand. *I'll get rid of him fast, baby. You keep out of sight. I'll tell him you've got a headache.*

"Sure, Nick, come on up. Six A."

"Thanks."

Lye met him at the door wearing a gaudy silk dressing gown over a white-on-white shirt and black trousers. He looked as if he had thrown his clothes on in a hurry; the robe was unbelted and a few strands of glossy black hair were plastered against his pale forehead.

"Well, come in, Nick," he said, trying to learn something from his face.

"Sorry to bother you this time of night," Amato said gently. "But I got a job for you."

"Yeah? Who is it?"

Amato didn't answer him. He was staring about the room, a pleased little smile on his lips. It wasn't as grand as he'd thought it would be and for some reason this made him feel better. He noted the record player and bar, the brilliant drapes and bright meaningless pictures, and continued to smile and nod with diffident approval.

"Very cute," he said. "Where's the girl friend? Headache?"

"No, she's just getting fixed up. Were you serious about a job?"

Amato stared at him. "Get out of that clown suit and into your clothes," he said. "There's a job. You want me to do all the work while you lay around here and play footsie?"

Lye rubbed his thin hands together and they made a sound like dry paper rustling in the silence. "Stop riding me," he said, the words coming out in painful jerks. "If you ain't satisfied with me maybe you should get somebody else."

"Sure," Amato said slowly. "And then I'll send you back to catch up on your prayers. Back where you get in a full quota of Hail Marys every night."

A door opened behind him and he turned awkwardly and removed his hat. Kay Johnson smiled at him as she came into the room, her manner that of a flustered wife meeting her husband's boss under less than perfect circumstances.

"This is a wonderful surprise, Mr. Amato," she said. Smiling into his little brown eyes she knew with her sense of audience that she wouldn't fool him for an instant. Words and smiles would be useless against Nick Amato. She recognized his seeming diffidence for what it was, a front for a cynical and contemptuous estimate of people. And she realized also that her own act wasn't a very good one. All of her guile couldn't hide the fear in her eyes. The fear had been part of her so long that she had stopped trying to manage or conceal it.

"This is a nice place, Miss Johnson," Amato said. "If I'd known it was this nice I'd have stopped by sooner. If Joe asked me, that is."

"We've planned to have you up a half-dozen times," she said. "Now, wouldn't you both like a drink? Or coffee perhaps?"

"Take care of Nick," Lye said. "I'll get dressed."

"Are you going out?" She was out of character now; there was no pretty surprise in her manner, and her voice was dull with fear.

Lye walked rapidly into the bedroom and Amato said, "I'm sorry to break up the party, Miss Johnson."

"I suppose it's important," she said, staring at the bedroom door.

"In our business we work around the clock." Watching her, he wondered if she really loved Joe Lye. It didn't figure. She probably was after his cash. That was why she put up with his cheapness, his twisted ruined face. And Lye was getting a bargain, Amato thought, as a strangely complex desire for her began to grow in him. Part of it was physical but there was something else, too. She was class. He had never had a woman like this, and he wondered why. Was it a guilty hangover from his stern childhood training, or was there some lack in him he hadn't recognized or admitted?

He saw with sharp irritation that she wasn't paying any attention to him at all. She paced restlessly, a tense expression around her eyes, and when he turned he saw the gleam of her slim white ankles and the soft press of her thighs against the silken robe. Did he want her because she was blonde and elegant? Because his people were peasants who would have bowed and tugged the peaks of their caps at a woman like this?

"I saw you in the movies once," he said. "That was quite a while back."

"I'm sure it was," she said.

"You played a college girl who didn't wear any make-up," he said, enjoying her strained smile.

"Yes, that was 'Ladies of the Chorus,'" she said.

"You should know. The guy you liked couldn't see you for dust, so you got a job in a cabaret. Then when you were all dolled up he fell in love with you without knowing you were the girl he knew in college."

She laughed and picked up a cigarette from the table. "I'm afraid it sounds just as idiotic now as it did then."

"The guy had a good reason to fall for you," Amato said, watching her. "You were clean and damned good-looking. What else does a man want?"

She saw that he wasn't going to light her cigarette so she did it herself and dropped the match into an ashtray. "I think you're drawing me out now," she said. "You want to hear me say something silly and female."

The door opened then and Lye walked into the room pulling up the knot in his tie. He glanced at Kay and said, "I left the radio on. How about going in and turning it off?"

"Of course," she said quickly.

When she had entered the bedroom Lye rubbed his hands along the sides of his trousers. He looked as if his nerves were stretched to the breaking point. "Okay, what is it?" he said.

"The kid," Amato said quietly.

"You're kidding!" Lye said, and his lips began to strain in spasmodic little jerks.

"I didn't come here to make jokes," Amato said. "He talked. He'll talk again." His voice was suddenly as sharp as a knife blade. "He's home now. In his bedroom. Anna goes to six o'clock Mass. You got to make it look a suicide."

"Nick, this is rough. Can't you figure out something else?"

"You don't like it?"

"No," Lye said.

Amato felt his anger swelling like a cancerous growth inside him. Nobody could take orders any more. That's why there was trouble on the docks. "Maybe you want to go back to jail?" he said in a low, trembling voice.

Lye turned away from him abruptly. The dream flooded his mind at Amato's words, everything in red, the guards, the altar, and in the middle of it his own soft, helpless body, waiting for the impersonal horror of the straps. "I—I just said we might figure out something else," he said.

"*We* don't figure things, *I* figure them," Amato said.

"Sure, sure," Lye said, speaking with difficulty against the constricting pressure around his chest. "I'm ready. Let's go."

Kay returned to the room then, and one hand went to her throat as she saw the tight, unnatural smile on Lye's lips. "What's wrong?" she asked anxiously.

"Nothing," he said, turning away from her. "Come on, Nick, let's go."

Amato smiled at him. "You go on, Joe. I'll take up that drink offer if it's still open."

"You're staying here?" Lye said dully.

"If it's all right with Miss Johnson," Amato said.

"Of course it is," she said.

"I'll check with you later," Lye said, looking at Amato. He hesitated, obviously reluctant to leave.

"It's late, Joe," Amato said gently.

Lye picked up his black overcoat from a chair, nodded jerkily at them and walked out the door. Amato was silent, smiling faintly, as he heard the faint whine of the descending elevator.

"What would you like to drink?" she asked him.

"Never mind." He dismissed the offer with a wave of his hand. "It's morning. No time to be drinking."

"I'm glad you stayed," she said. "I've wanted to talk to you for some time now."

He looked at her in surprise. "What do you want to talk to me about?"

She smiled nervously and lit another cigarette. "Joe would be furious with me for this," she said. "I may be wrong—" She drew a deep breath and tried to meet his eyes directly. "Why do you nag him about the time he spent in jail? Don't you realize how it upsets him?"

"It bothers him, eh?" Amato said slowly.

"You must realize that it does," she said. "I know it's a joke, a form of masculine humor that I don't understand perhaps, but it upsets him terribly. I'm sure you don't mean it seriously, but that needling about the death cell and his prayers, it's on his mind day and night."

"It's no joke," Amato said smiling. "I'm looking for information. What was he praying for? That's all I want to know."

"If you won't be serious there's no point discussing it."

"Oh, I'm serious," Amato said. He smiled at her but his eyes were narrowed and cold. "Maybe you can tell me what he's praying to? You know him pretty well. How comes he prays when he's ready to die? To what does he pray? To who?" He swept an arm around the room, flushing with a sudden anger. "You think those are funny questions? Well, I'll tell you. You like dough, eh? You give me some sensible answers to them questions and I'll load you down with more dough than you ever seen in one lump before. If there's a God, then the prayers make sense. Ain't that right? But if there isn't a God, what's the use of praying?" Amato turned away from her and shook his head irritably. For a moment he was silent, staring at the floor. "It's no time to be talking about it," he said.

"We never settle arguments about religion and politics, do we?"

"I wasn't talking about religion. I was talking about God."

She knew he was serious but his fears struck her as irrelevant and slightly comical; there were so many things to fear in life that she hadn't found time to fear God.

"How come you got mixed up with Joe?" he asked her bluntly.

"That isn't a very graceful way to put it, Mr. Amato."

"You need him, I guess. How long would you last without his dough?"

"With excellent managing, about three months."

He grinned at her. "And then what? Back to the movies?"

"Naturally," she said. "Or television or the theater. It would be simply a matter of picking or choosing." Her voice broke and she turned away from him quickly. "My agent still sends me Christmas cards," she said. "Isn't that an encouraging sign?"

"I could do more for you than Joe," he said. "You're no kid. You need things solid and secure. Joe Lye is one of six hundred guys who do what I tell him. He's nothing." As her expression remained unchanged he made an impatient gesture with his hand. "Well, how about it?"

She managed a smile and said, "I think it's dear of you to flatter me this way." This was safe ground. She had been maneuvering with middle-aged men for twenty years, and she could handle them with ease. It was a simple problem, unrelated to her fear of hunger and age, her terror of Joe Lye's nightmares and the small black gun he carried in his pocket. "I'll make you that drink now," she said.

"I want a yes or no," he said stubbornly.

"Very well," she said. "Before anything else I want to be your friend. Do you understand what I mean?" This was a tested armor, she knew, short, ambiguous questions put very earnestly and thoughtfully.

"Forget the drink," Amato said dryly. He knew she was telling him no, tactfully but finally, choosing Lye ahead of him. And she didn't have to strain to make the decision, he thought with bitter humor. His proposition had struck her as foolish. He was a fat little peasant in her eyes, one of the anonymous people who tugged at their caps when she passed them by. When everything was quiet again, he thought, when the trouble with Retnick was over, then he'd think about fixing her and Lye. He said good-by without looking at her and left the room.

# 16

THE RINGING PHONE WOKE RETNICK AND HE SAT UP IN THE DARKNESS and fumbled for his watch on the table beside the bed. The illuminated hands stood at six-thirty. He heard Mrs. Cara's door open, and then the cautious murmur of her voice. She knocked on his door a second or two later. Retnick crossed the floor and turned the knob. He had been dozing only a few minutes—except for a coat and tie he was fully dressed.

"It's a call for you," Mrs. Cara said.

Retnick nodded his thanks and went down the hall and picked up the receiver. "Hello?"

"Steve Retnick?" It was a girl's voice, low and intense.

"That's right."

"This is Dixie Davis." She laughed but the sound of it was all wrong. "I—I'm scared, I guess. That's why I called. You gave me your number, remember? A million years ago, I guess."

"Take it easy," he said.

"I got a call just a few minutes ago. It was a man and he said he had dialed the wrong number. But it scared me. He hung up right away. It's so quiet here. The whole building is like a tomb. It's—nerves, I know. Isn't that right?"

"Did you call the police?"

"What for?" she said nervously. "I—I just wanted to talk to somebody, that's all. I know you think I'm no good, but a few minutes' talk won't corrupt you."

"I'll call the cops," Retnick said. "Now listen: lock your door and sit tight. Don't open up for anyone but a police officer. Watch the street from your windows and you'll see the squad arrive. Understand?"

"You think I'm in trouble?"

"Why take chances? Keep that door locked, remember."

"All right, sure."

Retnick broke the connection and dialed the police board. He asked for the precinct which covered Dixie's neighborhood, and was put through to a Lieutenant Mynandahl. When he explained what the trouble was the lieutenant said, "All right," in an unexcited voice. "We'll send a car over to look into it. You say she heard a prowler?"

"That's right."

"We'll check it."

Retnick returned to his room, picked up his hat and coat, and left the house. It was black outside, and the streets were empty and cold. He headed for the avenue at a run, knowing that his chances for a cab were slim at this hour. He waited five minutes at the intersection, his collar turned up against the wind, until a cruiser turned off a cross-town street and pulled up for him. Retnick gave the driver Dixie's address and told him to hurry . . .

An empty, black-and-white squad car was pulled up before her building with the motor turning over smoothly. As Retnick paid off his driver he heard the metallic sound of the police radio, and the flat, businesslike voice of the announcer listing routine details and instructions. It was a comforting sound in the darkness and silence.

He went into the small foyer breathing more easily; the cops had got here ahead of him which meant there had been a very brief time-lag between her call and their arrival. Hardly time for anything to happen . . . Then he saw that the inner door stood slightly ajar and that the jamb had been worked on with a jimmy; splinters of torn wood gleamed whitely in the overhead light. Retnick hesitated, feeling the quickening beat of his heart. The cops might have forced their way in, which meant she hadn't answered their ring . . .

He took the steps two at a time and when he turned the landing below her floor a hard young voice said, "Hold it right there. And get your hands up."

A uniformed patrolman stood at the top of the stairs and the gun in his hand was pointed at Retnick.

"I put the call in," Retnick said, standing perfectly still. "I talked to a Lieutenant Mynandahl and he said he'd send a car over here."

The cop said, "How'd you know there would be trouble?"

"She called me."

"All right, come on up," the cop said, after hesitating briefly.

Retnick knew then that he was too late. "She's dead, eh?"

"That's right. You go in and wait for the lieutenant. He'll want to talk to you."

Retnick walked down the short hallway to her apartment, noticing that here too the iron teeth of a jimmy had been at work on the wood above and below the door lock. Inside the neat living room a middle-aged cop was talking on the phone. He glanced at Retnick and a surprised little smile of recognition touched his round face. His name was Melburn, Retnick remembered; they had worked together in Harlem ten years ago.

Melburn waved to him and continued speaking into the phone. "We'll stick here until Homicide shows up," he said. "Right." Replacing the receiver he shook hands with Retnick and said, "Well, long time, eh? You know this girl?"

"Yes, I knew her," Retnick said slowly. And because of that she was dead, he thought. For the first time in five years he experienced something like guilt. "Where is she?"

"In the bathroom." Melburn shifted his weight awkwardly. "Steve, if she meant something to you, well I'm sorry."

Retnick shrugged wearily. "She didn't mean anything to me," he said. Turning he went to the bathroom and pushed open the door.

She looked even smaller in death, curled on the floor in a child's sleeping position, her knees drawn up almost to her chin. The bruises on her throat were partially concealed by the angle at which she lay, but he could see the mindless fear in her face, blurred and magnified by her swollen lips and widely staring eyes. One of her slippers had fallen off and her blue silk robe was twisted up around her thighs. The light above the medicine cabinet gleamed along her thin, chalk-white legs.

Retnick turned back to the living room and lit a cigarette. The smoke tasted hot and dry in his mouth. Melburn said, "We were cruising on Park when we got the call. We got here just a few minutes after it happened. Damn shame, eh?"

"It's a damn shame all right," Retnick said.

"You better stick around, I guess," Melburn said. "The detectives will want to talk to you."

Retnick pushed his hat back on his head and sat down on the edge of a chair with his big hands hanging limply between his knees. "I'll wait," he said. She had been sure that Evans would get her, he was thinking. *Why did you put me on this spot?* That had been her question to him, and he hadn't bothered to answer it. He'd made a speech, he remembered. A pious angry speech. Well, why had he put her on the spot? Now it was an academic question. It was all I could do, he thought, drawing deeply on the cigarette. I had to make Evans think he was being framed. That someone was talking. Otherwise he'd never crack. It was Dixie's life against— He frowned, unable to complete the thought. Against what?

A Homicide detective named Caprizzio came in and Retnick stood and shook hands with him, relieved to get away from his pointless, guilty thoughts. He answered Caprizzio's questions, and Caprizzio nodded gloomily when he was through, and said, "These jobs that don't have a nickel's worth of planning in them are always the worst. The guy jimmies two doors, strangles her and walks out. That kind of murder is like a bolt of lightning, and just as hard to trace. Well, I'll see you around."

Retnick was ready to leave when the door opened and Lieutenant Neville came in, looking tired and worried. He frowned at Retnick and said, "Just a minute, I'll go with you," and then crossed the room and talked to Caprizzio for a few minutes.

Neville was very pale, Retnick noticed, and there was a hard look around his eyes. When he finished with Caprizzio he nodded to Retnick and said, "Let's go downstairs, Steve. I want to talk with you."

The darkness was lifting. A thin pearly light sparkled coldly on the frosted branches of the winter-black trees and shed a soft hazy glow along the well-kept little block. The wagon and three squads were double-parked along the curb, and a group of pedestrians, out early with their dogs, had bunched together across the street to watch the excitement. Two reporters and a photographer were waiting outside the foyer for Caprizzio's okay to go up; they all looked tired and irritable.

"What's going on?" one of them asked Neville. "Come on, don't be like Caprizzio the Cautious. Has she got any relatives in town? That's all the desk wants now. Pictures of her family, if any."

"It's not my case," Neville said. "Caprizzio will give you the works pretty soon, I imagine."

A uniformed patrolman put his head out the door. "Okay," he said to the reporters. "The lieutenant says you can come up."

Neville and Retnick walked down the sidewalk toward Park. The lieutenant took out his cigarettes, lit one and inhaled deeply. "I just left another dead one, Steve. Mario Amato. He blew his brains out an hour ago."

Retnick stared at him, and when he saw the expression on Neville's face the sense of guilt moved in him again, crowding insistently against the weight of his cold heavy anger. "When did this happen?" he asked.

They had stopped and were facing each other in the cold gray light of dawn. Neville said, "Anna Amato found him in bed when she got home from six o'clock Mass. She brought him a breakfast tray. Mario was in bed, a gun in his hand. Half his forehead was gone."

Retnick swallowed a dryness in his throat. "You're sure it's a suicide?"

"It's suicide, all right."

I didn't kill him, Retnick thought. Mario had shot himself after being grilled by Neville. A soft, nervous kid, caught in a murder investigation, he'd taken the easy way out . . .

Neville stared at him with cold stern eyes. "I blame myself for this," he said. "Maybe you blame yourself, too. I don't know. We threw away the book and made a mess of things. It was your idea but I carried it out. I thought you deserved any break I could give you. But all we did was cause two deaths. The girl's murder, and Mario's suicide. My only consolation is that I didn't buy your insane notion to spread the word that Mario had squealed. If I had I might be responsible for another murder. But I didn't, and that's my one consolation. I wonder what yours is."

"You'll let Red Evans go now, I suppose?" Retnick said.

"We have nothing to hold him on. He's in the clear."

"You let him go," Retnick said slowly. "I'll be waiting for him."

"As a cop, I'm warning you," Neville said in a cold official voice. "You get in trouble and I'll treat you like a lawbreaker."

"Thanks all to hell," Retnick said.

"Steve, I—" Neville paused, frowning into Retnick's hard face. "There's no way to get through to you," he said at last, and his voice was empty and tired. "But remember this: the price of vengeance can be too high for any man to pay. You'll know that someday."

"I'll pay it, don't worry," Retnick said.

Neville shrugged. The instant of compassion was gone and his face was once again closed and grim. "Good night, Steve," he said shortly, and walked down the quiet street to the police cars.

# 17

BY NOON NICK AMATO'S HOME HAD BECOME A PLACE OF WELL-ORGANIZED grief and mourning. His wife's friends filled the house, moving solemnly about their duties with funereal expressions on their work-worn faces. There was little they could do to comfort Anna; she lay in bed, turning her head slowly from side to side, pressing Mario's first communion picture tightly against her breasts. She had passed from hysteria to shock; her expression was dazed and incredulous and only at infrequent intervals did tears start in her dull brown eyes. Her friends murmured their sympathies to her and left her room with handkerchiefs pressed to their eyes. Time would help her, they knew. Nothing else. Meanwhile there was work to be done; the house to be cleaned from top to bottom, the plans made for marketing and cooking. The men who came to the wake would need to eat and drink. Nothing ever changed that.

Nick Amato sat in the kitchen, a cigar stub in his hand and a cup of hot coffee before him on the table. He was tired and nervous; his face was gray with fatigue and there was a tiny but annoying tremor in his left eyelid. The knowledge that he was safe hadn't put him at ease, for some reason. With Mario and the girl dead he was safe, but he couldn't relax; every sound in the house grated on his quivering nerves, and there was a cold, painful ache in the pit of his stomach.

Joe Lye stood with his back to the window, smoking a cigarette with quick, hungry drags. Occasionally he glanced at the ceiling, in the direction of Anna's room. "She's calmed down," he said, drawing a deep breath.

"Don't talk about it," Amato said.

A stout gray-haired woman opened the door without knocking. "Father Bristow is here," she said to Amato. "He's gone up to see Anna."

"That's good," Amato said, and stared at her until she smiled nervously and closed the door.

Lye rubbed both hands over his face. "You think he can help her?" he said.

"Anna will listen to him," Amato said. "He'll tell her it was God's will. He'll tell her to be brave."

"What would he tell her if he knew the truth?"

"Don't talk about it, I said."

"That's easy for you."

"Shut up!" Amato said, glaring at him. "It had to be done. Connors told me he'd spilled something to the cops. Supposing he squealed that I told him to hire Evans? It had to be this way, Joe. He could hurt me. Like I can hurt you."

Lye rubbed a fist over his tight mouth. He stood indecisively for a moment, and then pulled out a chair and sat down at the table facing Amato. "We're going to talk," he said. "I got something to say to you."

Amato shrugged. "Go ahead."

"Kay told me about the deal you offered her."

"Women are funny, Joe. You pay 'em a compliment that don't mean anything and they think you're serious." There was a purpose in Lye that Amato didn't understand; but his intuition told him it was dangerous. "So why worry about the funny ideas a woman gets, Joe?" He smiled slowly but his eyes were wary and alert.

"That's not the important thing," Lye said. "So she misunderstood you. Okay. What I'm talking about is you and me, Nick. I'm going to work *with* you from now on, not for you. You understand?"

"You got a gripe, I guess. Keep talking, Joe."

"When we take over Glencannon's local, I'm going to run it," Lye said. "You and I will split up this stretch of the docks. We'll be partners."

Amato dropped his cigar into his coffee and it went out with an angry little hiss. "Joe, I don't like partners," he said gently. "You know that by now. Joe Ventra wanted to be a partner, remember?"

"You remember something now," Lye said, in a tight, straining voice. "Kay is ready to swear she heard you tell me to kill your nephew. You better remember that good. We'll go to the cops—Kay and me—and that will put you right in the chair."

Amato smiled faintly. "That would put you in the chair too, Joe."

"It's a standoff," Lye said. "You got the Donaldson rap hanging over me, I got the kid's murder on you. So we're partners, Nick. You ain't going to needle and hound me about going back to jail. If you do you'll pay a high price for your fun."

Amato kept his anger in check. He raised his eyebrows in a little gesture of good-humored resignation. "I'm a sensible fellow," he said. "You can hurt me, I can hurt you. So it figures we should be friends."

"Partners," Lye said.

Amato shrugged and smiled. "Partners."

Lye rubbed a hand over his damp forehead. He could hardly believe that he'd won; it had taken all his courage to do this, and now he was so spent and drained that his hands were shaking. But he had never known such relief. Already the tense and clotted fear of Amato was easing out of him, and he was suddenly sure that the violent crimson nightmares would never haunt his sleep again. There would be an end to the smothering horror, to the taste of shame in his mouth, as he climbed with agonizing slowness to sanity and consciousness. And the tic that afflicted his face, that sinister barometer of his passions, even that might disappear. Without fear, anything was possible. He was almost grateful to Amato now. "I swear, Nick, we'll get along fine," he said. "You're still the boss. But I had to get out from under you. Kay and I want some kind of life together. We want to live like normal people."

"That's what you want, eh?"

"Everybody does, I guess."

"Maybe you're right." Amato looked at the dead stump of his cigar floating in the coffee. "You know, Joe, she was out of the room when I told you to take care of Mario. She didn't hear nothing."

Lye felt his lips tightening. "She'll swear she heard it all," he said.

"Oh sure. I was just thinking. You can't be normal people." He looked at Lye and smiled. "You're too smart."

"That's a good thing to remember, Nick."

"Don't worry. I'll remember it," Amato said. He stood up then and rubbed his stomach. "I better go up with Anna."

"Okay, Nick. I'll be at the local if you need me."

When he had gone Amato stood for a minute or so staring at the door. He heard Anna's friends moving about above him on the second floor, and from the street the faint noise of children playing. At last he sat down and rubbed both hands over his face, drawing a black curtain over reality for a brief welcome moment. His body felt slack and hot and his left eye was quivering with fatigue. He knew he was in trouble; the knowledge was intuitive but certain. There was Retnick and Neville, and now Joe Lye. They were forcing him to move, prodding him into action, not giving him time to think. That was how they got you; by making you jump. Finally you jumped one time too many . . .

Amato went down the hallway and got into his heavy overcoat. He heard Father Bristow's voice at the top of the stairs, and he let himself out quickly; he didn't want to talk to the priest now. It was one thing with the old woman, listening to them say how terrible it was that the boy was dead, but the priest was different. He looked right through you; Amato knew he had never fooled him for a minute.

The day was cold and overcast with heavy dark clouds. In the steel-gray light the bitter colors of the street were more dismal than usual. The street was dirty, and the black iron fire escapes crawled like a rusty growth up the faces of the mud-colored brownstones. Amato walked slowly to the waterfront, not quite sure why he had left the house. He looked through the fog and saw the terminal his local controlled, a long square finger poking into the gray river. Five hundred men, coopers, checkers, truckers, winch operators, laborers—they paid him to work there. The jobs were safe as long as they stayed in line. That used to mean something to him, but today it seemed flat and pointless.

After a few minutes he turned and started slowly back to his house, to the black-shawled old women and the gloom that permeated every room. But it had to be faced.

The priest had gone, one of the women told him as he hung up his overcoat. He would be back tonight.

"That's good," Amato said. He looked at the woman until she bobbed her head at him and retreated toward the kitchen. Then, sighing heavily, he picked up the phone and gave the operator a number.

Connors sounded sleepy and irritable, but his manner changed instantly when he recognized Amato's voice.

"I just turned in," he said. "It was quite a long night."

"I'm going to make a hero out of you," Amato said, staring down the dark hallway to the kitchen. "You're going to solve that old Donaldson killing all by yourself. You'll have the evidence and you'll make the pinch tonight. You'll like being a hero, won't you?"

Connors' laugh was strained. "It's a role I play pretty well. What's the rest of it, Nick?"

"The guy you arrest don't like it," Amato said quietly. "He puts up a fight, breaks for it maybe. And you got to shoot him."

"Nick, there's been too much of it lately," Connors said, his voice rising nervously. "A month from now would be—"

"Shut up! You're going to be a hero or you're going to be in jail." Amato rubbed his forehead. He was jumping now, without time to think. It happened to the smartest guys. They jumped for safety and landed in trouble. But there wasn't time to think.

"Sure, Nick," Connors said hastily. "I'll handle it, you know that. I only thought the timing was awkward."

"The timing is right," Amato said.

"Okay. Who is it?"

"Joe Lye," Amato said, and put the receiver carefully back in place.

# 18

IT WAS EIGHT O'CLOCK THAT NIGHT WHEN RETNICK RANG THE BELL OF his wife's apartment. He had spent the day in his room trying fruitlessly to find a solution to his problem. It was a moral problem, he had decided irritably, one his Jesuit teachers would have had a field day examining. Take what you want and pay the price! That had made sense to him. But he was beginning to realize that it wasn't as simple as that. If you couldn't pay the price, then what? It wasn't a clean exchange; you didn't make the payment and put an end to it . . .

He heard her light footsteps. Then she opened the door and looked up at him uncertainly. She wore a white silk blouse with black slacks, and her hair was brushed smoothly back from her face. He noticed that she carried two freshly ironed blouses over her arm.

"You didn't say when you were leaving," he said. "I—I wanted to say good-by."

"I'm taking a flight at ten," she said. "I was just packing. I'm glad you could stop by."

"You're busy, I guess."

"No, I'm practically through."

Retnick entered the room and turned his hat around awkwardly in his hands. There were no easy words. Everything seemed to come out with an effort. "You go ahead and finish packing," he said. "Take your time."

"All right, I won't be long."

When the door closed behind her Retnick looked around at the familiar furniture and pictures. She hadn't changed things. His big chair was in the same place, and his pipe rack was still on the table. She'd added a new picture or two, and a bookcase had been built in beside the fireplace. That was about all.

He sat down on a large ottoman without removing his overcoat and rubbed a hand across his forehead. Something was wrong with him, he knew.

When she opened the door he stood quickly.

"Please sit down," she said. "Would you like a cup of coffee?"

"No, I'm fine."

"How about a drink?"

"Never mind."

She sat down on the sofa, tucking her feet beneath her, and lit a cigarette. For a moment or two they were silent, and then Retnick said heavily, "Do you have to go tonight? I mean is there any need to rush?"

"No, not particularly. But I'd like to get settled down a bit before I start work."

"Sure," he said pointlessly. She was a million miles from him, he realized, cool and distant, unmoved by his presence. There was no fear or anxiety in her eyes, no tentative appeal in her manner. She wasn't unhappy in a positive way, she was simply impassive; he knew he didn't touch her any more.

"I want to talk to you," he said, turning and looking into the fireplace. "Will you listen a minute?"

"Of course, Steve."

"Put off your trip," he said. "Stay here until I finish the job I've got to do."

"What would be the point of that?"

"I don't know," he said wearily. "Maybe there's no point to it. But it might make things different. With me anyway. Maybe I could see things in a different light. That's all I'm asking you to take a chance on."

"It's a pretty slim chance, I'm afraid."

"Maybe it is. But it's the only one I can offer you."

"I'm sorry, Steve," she said.

He looked at her then, jarred by the almost casual tone of her voice. "You won't do it?" he said.

"There wouldn't be any point to it," she said, glancing up at him. "I might as well be honest, Steve. You—you've turned into something—well, it doesn't matter. Maybe you were that kind of a man all the time. I don't know." She shrugged lightly. "You think I had a fine roistering time of it while you were away. But for the record they were five miserable years. I was scared most of the time. Scared because I couldn't understand the cruel and stupid pride that made you refuse to let me help you. Did you stop to wonder what that did to me?" She shook her head as he started to speak. "It's not worth arguing about. But I'd like to finish this, please. You told me to get a divorce, you refused to see me, and then you behaved like a madman because there was someone else while you were gone." She smiled sadly. "And my big affair, my great sin! He sang at the club for a while. He was a gentle young man who drank too much and could have written a big book about loneliness. It lasted a month. And that was enough to convince me you were worth waiting for, even if it took fifty years instead of five. I regretted it, I made what amends I could, and I settled down to wait. That's how I put in my five-year stretch, with an occasional dinner with the Ragonis, or a drink with Lieutenant Neville. I might as well have been in jail, too."

If she was angry or bitter, Retnick thought, it would be different. But she seemed disinterested and slightly weary.

"You didn't care about my pride or peace of mind," she went on, studying him thoughtfully with her wide gray eyes. "That's what I couldn't understand. But now I believe you don't care about anybody. You want to kill the men who framed you. And some day you will. You'll be the final judge on that score. Just as you're the final judge on my morals. You're the final arbiter on all behavior, all questions of right and wrong. What you say goes! Well, it doesn't go with me, Steve. I can think of nothing less pleasing than living with you and wondering what suspicions were cropping up in your mind and what action you were planning to take. You—"

"All right," he said, rubbing a hand over his forehead. "I get the general idea."

The phone in the bedroom began to ring and she turned away from him quickly.

"Just a minute," he said. "This man, the singer." He hesitated, frowning. "Did he love you?"

"Why do you ask that?"

"I don't know. Never mind."

She looked at him and he saw that her lips were trembling; his question had pierced her cool indifference. The phone rang again and she said, "Excuse me," in a small, unsteady voice.

When she returned to the room he was staring into the fireplace, a dark frown on his face. "It's for you," she said.

He turned to her, still frowning. "Are you sure?"

"Yes. She asked for you."

He shrugged and walked into the cool, softly lighted bedroom. A gray tweed suit and a lace-edged slip were laid out on the bed, and a pair of brown leather pumps were on the floor beside two pieces of luggage. The room smelled faintly of the lavender sachets she kept with her gloves and lingerie. Retnick sighed and picked up the phone, "This is Steve Retnick."

"My name is Kay Johnson. You don't know me, but I'm Joe—I'm a friend of Joe Lye's." The woman's voice was low and controlled, but he could hear a tremor of fear running under it.

"I'm not very much interested in Joe Lye's friends," he said.

"Please listen to me. Please! I know you don't care anything about him—" She stopped and drew a deep, quivering breath. "No one cares about him! He's just a cheap little hoodlum with a twisted face. I know that!"

"What did you want?" Retnick said. She was almost hysterical, he knew; the tight control of her voice was slipping.

"He's going to be killed," she said. "Nick Amato is going to kill him!"

"You'd better call the police if you're worried about him," Retnick said.

"I can't! The police are going to kill him. Don't you understand?"

"Calm down a bit. You said it was Amato."

"Amato sent a police officer to do it. That's how he works."

"Was it a man named Connors?" Retnick asked her sharply.

"Yes, that's his name. He's going to kill Joe."

"Why did you call me?"

"I don't know. Joe told me you hated Amato. So I looked you up in the book. They're afraid of you."

"And you want me to save your boy friend?"

"No, it wasn't that," she said, laughing softly. "No one can save Joe. The poor guy is all through. But nothing can save Amato."

Retnick's hand tightened on the receiver. "What's that?"

"I can hang him," she said. "I can give you his head on a platter. Are you interested?"

"Where are you now?"

She gave him the address of her apartment, still laughing softly, and Retnick said, "You sit tight. I'll be along in ten or fifteen minutes."

Then he broke the connection and dialed the Thirty-First. Waiting for Neville he turned her story around in his mind. If she were telling the truth there must have been a major row between Amato and Lye. But over what?

When Neville answered, Retnick said, "Lieutenant, this is Retnick. Wait until I finish before you tell me to go to hell. I just had a call from a woman named Kay Johnson, Joe Lye's girl friend. She tells me Amato has put the finger on Lye, and she says she can hang Amato. Whether she's got anything on him or not, I don't know. But I thought I'd let you know. I'm going to her apartment now."

Neville took a deep breath and swore irritably. "Where does she live?" he said at last.

Retnick told him and Neville said, "All right. Meet me in front of her place. I'll leave here now."

Retnick put the phone down and walked slowly into the living room. Marcia looked at him and said, "You sounded excited. I hope it's good news."

"Yes, it's good news," Retnick said. He picked up his hat and she came with him to the door. With his hand on the knob he looked down at her and said, "This could be the end of it. Tonight could end it."

"I hope you'll have what you want then."

He stared into her small familiar face, silently turning the painful thoughts in his mind. Then he said awkwardly, "I thought you'd be better off with a divorce. I thought you would get started over without me. I couldn't let you visit me in jail." He shrugged his big shoulders. "I wasn't built to be a monkey in a cage. And I couldn't come back to you as a jail-bird. It was the way I felt about you. You were like some prize I'd won by a fluke, and I couldn't crawl back to you—" He gestured helplessly. "I had to prove I was framed."

"You never had to prove anything to me, Steve," she said. "You still don't." She touched his arm gently. "Stay here and talk to me until I have to go. Let Lieutenant Neville finish this job tonight. You've done enough."

"But it's not over yet," he said. "I've got to finish it."

"You want to finish it," she said, sighing and taking her hand from his arm. "It isn't clearing your name, coming back to me like a white and shining knight. Be honest, Steve. You want to be in at the kill."

"Maybe that's it," he said. Nothing made sense any more, he thought, watching her with a faint and bitter smile. "You're still planning to leave, of course?"

"There's nothing here for me," she said. "I'll be on the ten o'clock flight."

"Well, good luck," he said.

"Thanks. And take care of yourself, Steve."

"Sure," he said heavily, and opened the door.

She watched him from the doorway as he walked down the hall. He rang for the elevator and stood with his back to her looking down at the floor. The building was still and silent. When the elevator arrived he stepped into it without looking back. She waved tentatively but he was already out of sight. The doors closed on him with a dry and final ring.

# 19

LIEUTENANT NEVILLE WAS WAITING FOR RETNICK IN FRONT OF KAY Johnson's apartment building. There was an obvious constraint in his manner as he greeted him and said, "What do you think this woman has on Amato?"

"I told you she wasn't specific."

"It's probably dynamite," Neville said, throwing his cigarette aside. "She probably knows he played hooky in third grade."

"Then why did you bother coming over?"

Neville glanced up and down the dark street, a humorless grin touching his hard lips. "I'll be damned if I know," he said. "Let's go up."

Kay Johnson opened the door and smiled nervously from Neville to Retnick. She wore a simple black dress with pearls, and she had obviously prepared herself carefully for this role; her make-up was fresh, and her shining blonde hair was meticulously in place. But all the careful grooming wasn't enough to conceal the fear in her eyes and the lines of tension about her mouth.

Neville sensed her anxiety and said quietly, "Miss Johnson, I'm a police officer. My name is Lieutenant Neville. This is Steve Retnick whom you talked with on the phone a short while ago. May we come in?"

"Yes, yes of course," she said quickly. She was looking at Retnick. "I —I didn't know you'd call the police."

"It's better this way, believe me," he said.

Neville glanced around the gracefully furnished room with professional interest. Then he looked at Kay Johnson and said, "What have you got to tell us?"

She sat down on the sofa, so slowly that it seemed the strength was draining from her legs. "Nick Amato is going to kill Joe Lye," she said.

"How do you know that?" Neville said casually.

"Amato sent a detective here, a man named Connors. He rang the bell, I don't know, around eight, I think. Joe was in the kitchen then, but Connors didn't ask to see him. He told me to stay in the living room and he went through the apartment with his gun out. He opened the closet here in the foyer and then started for the bedroom. Maybe Joe saw him coming—I don't know. Maybe he heard him talking to me. Anyway, when this man, Connors, reached the kitchen the back door was open and Joe was gone. I—knew from the way Connors looked and acted that he was going to kill Joe the minute he saw him."

"What did Connors do then?" Neville said.

"He swore at me, he seemed very nervous. Then he went down the back stairs after Joe."

"Did he say he was going to kill Lye?"

She shook her head slowly. "I could tell from the way he acted."

Neville glanced at Retnick and the lack of expression on his face was eloquent. "From the way he acted, eh? Well, do you know *why* Amato wants Lye murdered?"

She seemed puzzled by the question. "Of course," she said. "I—I thought you'd know that, too."

Neville sighed. "We know very little, Miss Johnson."

"Why is Amato going to have Lye killed?" Retnick said, wetting his lips. He could guess the answer, and the knowledge was a guilty terrible weight in his breast.

"Mario Amato didn't commit suicide," she said, taking a deep unsteady breath. "He was killed. Joe killed him." Turning away from them she put a hand to her forehead and began to weep silently. "Amato made Joe kill him. Because Mario talked to the police."

Neville looked sharply at Retnick. Then he sat down beside her and took her shoulders in his hands. "Did you hear Amato tell Joe Lye to kill Mario?"

She hesitated a second or two, and in the silence Retnick could hear the labored, despairing beat of his heart. She was going to lie, he knew, but that didn't matter; she knew the truth. "Yes, I heard him tell Joe," she said, raising her eyes and staring into Neville's eyes. "It was right in this room."

"Will you put that in a statement?" Neville said. "Will you repeat it in court?"

"I'll shout it at the top of my lungs," she said, leaning against him and shaking her head as if she were in pain. "He made Joe do it. And now he's going to kill Joe. He's got to pay for that."

"He'll pay," Neville said. He looked up at Retnick. "Get her coat," he said quietly. "We can hang Amato for murder with a little luck."

"Sure," Retnick said, rubbing his forehead. Turning quickly he went to the closet near the front door. A half-a-dozen coats hung there and he pulled one down without even looking at it. We'll hang Amato, he thought, as the cruel guilty pressure grew within him. But who'll hang me?

They drove in silence across town to the Thirty-First. Neville took Kay Johnson inside to give a preliminary statement, and Retnick waited alone in the car, trying fruitlessly to evade his dark, accusing thoughts. But there was no escape; no matter how he twisted and dodged they clung to him.

He didn't hear the doors of the precinct open and he started when Kleyburg cried, "Steve! You said it wouldn't happen."

Retnick turned and saw the old detective standing on the sidewalk beside the car, staring down at him with wide, frightened eyes. He had come out without a coat and the cold wind had blown his thin gray hair into a tangle over his forehead. "You said it wouldn't happen," he cried again.

Retnick got out of the car quickly and took Kleyburg's shoulders in his hands. "Go back inside," he said. "You'll catch pneumonia out here."

"I heard Neville talking to that woman," Kleyburg said, pulling free from Retnick's hands. "Mario was murdered. We killed him, Steve."

A patrolman coming on duty looked at them curiously, then shrugged and went into the station.

"Not so loud," Retnick said, wetting his lips. He couldn't meet the pain and confusion in the old man's eyes. "Mario was in on it. He deserved killing."

"There was no evidence. Just your say-so. And we killed him on the strength of that."

"Miles, you're wrong. Tomorrow it will look different to you."

Kleyburg shook his head slowly. The confusion and anxiety seemed to fall away from him; he looked at Retnick as if he could suddenly see him very, very clearly. "It won't be different in the morning," he said. "I told you I never had any trouble looking at myself in a mirror. Well, that's over. After forty-two years as a cop I wind up a murderer. That won't change in the morning. For you or for me, Steve."

"Miles—"

Another voice cut coldly and sharply through the silence. "So you used Kleyburg, eh, Steve?"

Retnick looked up quickly and saw Lieutenant Neville standing on the steps of the precinct, his pale face an angry vivid slash against the darkness. "I wouldn't help, so you made an old man do it," he said, walking slowly down to the sidewalk.

"It paid off," Retnick said, in a tight, unnatural voice. "We've got Amato."

"And that's all that matters, eh? Pay off your scores! To hell with everything else." Neville stared at Kleyburg and a touch of compassion gradually softened the lines of his face. "I heard it all, Miles," he said. "You'd better leave your gun and badge on my desk and go on home. We'll talk this over in the morning. If it turns out the kid was guilty we can square it."

"You can't square it," Kleyburg said, looking into the darkness and shaking his head wearily. "It's not a thing you can fix by juggling a report or two around." Then he turned to the lieutenant, and his eyes were helpless and pleading. "I didn't want to pull this deal."

"I understand," Neville said, staring at Retnick. He drew a deep breath. "Okay, Steve. We can pick up Amato now. You got what you wanted."

"That's right," Retnick said, not feeling much of anything at all. "I got what I wanted. . . ."

It was nine-fifteen when they arrived at Nick Amato's home. A line of cars were double-parked before the house, and a group of men stood on the sidewalk smoking cigars and talking in low voices. A crepe hung on the door, gleaming dully in the light that streamed from the inner hallway through the transom window. Neville nodded to the men and went up the stairs. They murmured indistinct greetings and watched him cautiously as he entered the house with Retnick. Then they came together and talked softly among themselves.

Retnick removed his hat and followed Neville into the softly lighted parlor. Floral pieces were banked on three sides of the room; a space along the windows had been left clear for the casket, which hadn't as yet arrived from the funeral home. A half-dozen men and women were present, their faces grave and sad, and Father Bristow was standing in the archway that led to the dining room. Anna Amato sat in a straight chair facing the space the casket would occupy. She wore a heavy black silk dress and her hands lay limply in her lap, palms turned upward in an unconscious gesture of entreaty. There was no expression on her dark, tear-swollen face, but her head was turned slightly to one side, defensively and helplessly, as if she were expecting a blow.

"Excuse me, Mrs. Amato," Neville said.

Father Bristow came forward casually, but his eyes were sharp and interested. Standing behind Anna, he put his hands on her soft round shoulders and watched the lieutenant.

"It was good of you to come," Anna said, without looking up.

"I'm Lieutenant Neville. I'm sorry your son is dead. But I came to see your husband on an important matter. Is he here?"

Anna made a weary little gesture with one hand. "He has gone out."

"Do you know where he went?"

"No."

"Or when he'll be back?"

"I know nothing," Anna said, shaking her head slowly. She seemed hardly conscious of Neville's questions. Two of the men present came and stood beside the priest and looked at the lieutenant with unfriendly eyes. "My son is dead," Anna said, rising to her feet wearily and awkwardly. Tears started in her eyes as she stared hopelessly at Neville. "They bring his body home soon. Can't you let me wait for him in peace?"

"I'm sorry to disturb you, Mrs. Amato," Neville said.

Father Bristow said, "Couldn't this wait, Lieutenant?"

"I think so," Neville said.

Anna Amato suddenly shook her fists in the air, sensing that in some way the sanctity of her grief had been violated. "This is a house of death," she cried, staring at Neville and Retnick with burning eyes. "I wait for my son. I know nothing of my husband. I know nothing except that my son is dead."

"I'm sorry," Neville said gently. "Let's go, Steve."

"Wait a minute," Retnick said, staring at Amato's wife with bitter eyes. "You don't know anything, eh? Nobody knows anything about Nick Amato. They don't see anything, hear anything, or say anything."

"Steve!" Father Bristow said sharply.

"It's time you learned something then," Retnick said, still staring at Amato's wife. "Your son didn't commit suicide. Joe Lye killed him. And Nick Amato gave the orders. That's why the cops are here now."

A stocky man in a black suit swore softly and surged against Retnick, but he might as well have tried to knock down a brick wall with his fists. Retnick shoved him halfway across the room with a blow of his arm. He was breathing slowly and heavily; a bursting pain filled his breast as he stared into the horror in Anna Amato's eyes. "Now you know something," he said thickly.

The room was still as death as Anna turned slowly and awkwardly to Neville. She strained for breath as her eyes searched his face. "Is that true?" she said in a dry whisper. "You say this, too?"

Neville looked away from her and wet his lips. Anna wheeled with a cry of pain and caught Father Bristow's arm in her hands. "They lie, they lie," she said in a sharp loud voice. "Tell me they lie."

"Sit down, Anna," Father Bristow said. "There will be time for this later." He stared coldly at Retnick. "This isn't the time for it. Not now. Not in this house."

Anna turned slowly from him, her lips trembling with silent words. Then she sat down heavily and began to shake her head from side to side. "No one says he lies," she muttered. "No one says he lies."

"I'm not lying," Retnick said, forcing the words out with an effort.

"I said I know nothing," Anna said, smiling softly and emptily. "But it isn't true. For thirty years I watch and see, I listen and hear. I know everything."

Retnick turned sharply and walked to the front door. Outside, in the cold darkness, he lit a cigarette with trembling fingers and then ran the back of his hand over his forehead. The men who had been standing in front of the house were gone; the street was empty and silent. Retnick breathed deeply but he couldn't seem to get enough air. His anger was gone, everything seemed to be gone, and he felt nothing but a cold, draining impotence . . .

It was a few minutes later when Father Bristow came out of the house and walked slowly down the stairs. He looked at Retnick and said, "Did you have to do it that way, Steve?"

"It had to be done," Retnick said. "So I did it."

"She'll never get over it," Father Bristow said.

Retnick glanced at him and it was then the priest saw the change in his eyes. "Neither will I," Retnick said. "Doesn't that make us even?"

Father Bristow sighed and said quietly, "I just don't know, Steve."

Neville came out a little later. He said, "She wasn't kidding when she said she knew something. Amato's on the run. He left here half an hour ago. And she knows where he's running to. I'll call the district from the car and get some help. Good night, Father."

As Neville stepped on the starter of his car a police squad turned into the block and roared toward them under full power.

"I'll see what's up," Neville said. He stepped from the car and walked toward the young patrolman who had climbed from the squad. Retnick watched as the two men talked for perhaps half a minute, and then the patrolman saluted and Neville walked quickly back to the car. His face was pale and drawn in the yellow glare of the headlights. Climbing in beside Retnick, he turned the ignition key and stepped on the starter. Then he let out his breath slowly and settled back in the seat. He looked at Retnick with an odd expression on his face; there was anger in the set of his mouth, but his eyes were sad and bewildered. "I warned you, Steve," he said heavily. "I warned you the best way I knew. I told you sometimes there's a price to vengeance that no man can pay. Now you've run up a big bill."

"What's the matter?" Retnick said sharply, as a strange chill went through his body.

"After we left the Thirty-First Kleyburg went down in the basement and tried to kill himself," Neville said. "He's still alive but it doesn't look good."

Retnick rubbed the back of his fist cruelly over his mouth. "Where did they take him?" he muttered. "I want to see him. I've got to see him before he dies."

"You wanted to get Amato," Neville said. "Let's finish that job." He looked at Retnick and sighed. Then he said gently, "You can't help Miles now, Steve."

"Sure," Retnick said heavily. "I can't help him, I can't help anybody."

# 20

AMATO SAT STIFFLY BESIDE THE DRIVER AND WATCHED THE HEAVY CONcrete supports of the elevated highway flash past them into the darkness. Twelfth Avenue stretched ahead of him, a black, wind-swept tunnel into which the car's headlights bored like thick yellow lances. A small leather suitcase rested on his lap, and his arms were wrapped around it, hugging it tightly against his body. Under the black brim of his hat his cold brown eyes were tense and worried. This was the last big jump. If he slipped now it was all over.

"Everything is set, eh?" he said to the driver for perhaps the fifth time.

"Sure, there's nothing to worry about," the driver said casually. He was a short, slender man with graying hair and features that were pinched together into an expression of foxy good humor.

"I better not have to worry," Amato said. "I don't pay money to have things go wrong."

"It was short notice, Mr. Amato," the driver said. "We done our best. The launch is waiting at Pier 17. The guard there left a door open and took a walk for himself. You'll go down the Hudson, through the Narrows and over to Sheepshead Bay. I didn't get a final check yet, but the fishing boat is supposed to be there with two men to run it. The trip to Cuba takes a week. After that we're out of it."

"I got things set in Cuba," Amato said. "I had that set a long time."

"Well, we done our best on this end," the driver said philosophically. "You got to be lucky, though."

"You better hope I'm lucky," Amato said, glancing at him with his awkward little smile.

"We done our best," the driver said. Some of the good humor left his face as he felt Amato's eyes on him. Most men on the run were at the mercy of those who helped them; they could only pay and pray. But Nick

Amato wasn't like most men. If this thing went wrong the driver knew that the waterfront would be a very unhealthy place for him.

Amato stared straight ahead again and hugged the grip to his chest. Instinct had made him run. There were men who would have stood fast and fought, betting on themselves, betting on money, influence, lawyers. But Amato had a peasant's instinct for survival. He fled without regret, as he would have fled from a volcano that threatened his village. Maybe he would come back some day. But he didn't think about this. Now it was important to get to Cuba and from there to Naples. He carried the harvest of thirty violent but profitable years in his suitcase, and in Naples he could live comfortably, and perhaps think about coming back. Amato needed time to think, and he was buying that as much as safety.

The car slowed to a stop in the darkness before Pier 17's vast silent warehouse. "Well, here you are," the driver said, letting the motor idle. "The door is unlocked, the guard is a couple of blocks away having a cup of coffee. The motor launch is tied up at the end of the terminal waiting for you. Okay?"

"It better be okay," Amato said. "If nothing goes wrong I'll send you a bottle of *Lacryma Christi* from Naples."

"We'll appreciate that, Mr. Amato."

Amato grunted and got out of the car. The driver nodded at him, his face a thin pale blur in the darkness, and then started up toward Ninth Street. Amato stood in the darkness watching the red tail light until it disappeared at the intersection. He was suddenly aware of the silence; it stretched out on all sides of him, spreading hungrily to those distant places where there was noise and laughter and life. He was alone on the little island of sound that was bounded by the rapid beat of his heart. Turning abruptly he walked to the warehouse. The small door used by the guard was open; a light from inside drew a thin bright line along the edge of the jamb. Amato pushed the door in cautiously. A single bulb gleamed in the checker's office, spreading a circle of brightness around the entrance to the warehouse.

But beyond this small yellow pool the terminal was lost in a vast echoing darkness. The launch waited for him at the end of this black cavern, the first link in the chain that would pull him to safety.

Amato closed the little door behind him, breathing more easily. A hundred-yard walk and he was on his way. He shifted the heavy suitcase to his right hand, tugged unnecessarily at his hat brim and started into the shadows.

And one of them began to move.

A little cry of terror broke through Amato's lips. He backed toward the door, feeling the sickening speed of his heartbeat, and tasting the strong bitter fear in his mouth. Something darker than the shadows was coming toward him silently.

He saw the gleam of black shoes as they stepped into the yellow light, and then a voice he knew said, "The trip is off, Nick. It ends here." Joe Lye came out of the darkness, his face pale and tense above the narrow black cylinder of his body. One side of his mouth was pulled up in an unnatural, ghastly smile, and a gun glinted in his hand. "You should have taken me for a partner," he said. "That way you wouldn't have to die."

"Joe, you gave me a scare," Amato said, trying desperately to smile. "I—I been looking for you. We got to clear out, you and me. I waited as long as I could—but it's all right now." He heard the hysterical note in his voice, but he couldn't help himself. "I got plenty of dough here. And the boat's waiting. For you and me. We got to go, Joe."

"You weren't looking for me," Lye said. "Connors was looking for me. You shouldn't have used a punk like him on a tough job, Nick. That's the biggest mistake you made."

"Joe, we got no time for talking," Amato said, trying to swallow the dry constriction in his throat. He dropped the grip and locked his hands together in a desperate appeal. "We're making Cuba the first stop, Joe. I got everything set. Passports, dough, berths on a freighter. It's all set for you and me. You'll like it there. It's hot but the breezes are cool. And they make drinks with rum and lots of lime. It's great, Joe." There was a high giddy tremble in Amato's voice now, and his smile stretched the skin whitely across his cheek bones. "What d'ye say, Joe? I look after things good, eh? And when we get to Italy I show you a fine time. Up in Milan they got night clubs and restaurants just like here. But we got to get moving. You carry the dough." He laughed shrilly. "That's right, you carry the dough. Nick trusts you."

"You're not going to Cuba," Lye said in a cold, empty voice. "You gave Connors that Donaldson rap. That finished me. Now I'm going to finish you. You forgot I knew about this pier, eh?"

"Joe, you're crazy," Amato shouted. "I always did the thinking, didn't I? You do what I say and we'll make it to Naples."

"Just a few seconds, that's all you got," Lye said in the same empty voice. "You used to wonder why I prayed in the death cell. Now you can find out."

"Joe, be smart! We got a whole life ahead of us. With dough and—"

A dry metallic click sounded as Lye cocked the gun. "You're wasting time," he said. "Here you go, Nick."

"Joe!" Amato screamed. He fell on his knees and clasped his hands over his breast. "Don't shoot me. Give me a break."

"So long, Nick."

"God—" Amato's voice was an incredulous whisper. He knew then that he was going to die—here in this cold warehouse, with a satchel of money at his feet and the launch that could take him to safety moored only a hundred yards away. He stared at Lye, while a desolate, hopeless fear spread sluggishly through his body. "God I'm sorry—" His voice broke there; the words of the Act of Contrition spun in his head, eluding his desperate search. "I'm sorry," he said, beginning to weep. "I didn't do wrong. There was no other way—because I dread the loss of Heaven." He groped frantically for the familiar words. "And the pain of Hell. With your help, I amend my life." That was all. He stared through his tears at Lye and shook his head slowly.

"Who were you praying to?" Lye said bitterly, and shot him twice just below the heart.

The echoes of the report rang through the immense warehouse, racing each other in noisy confusion toward the river. And above this clamoring racket Lye heard the keening wail of police sirens.

For an instant he stood perfectly still, the gun hanging limply at his side. A small, perplexed frown touched his forehead as he looked down at Amato. "Nick," he whispered, "can you hear it? It's cops."

But Amato didn't answer him; he lay on his back staring in fear and wonder at the shadows closing slowly over his eyes. His breathing was shallow and rapid, a laboring painful sound in the silence.

Lye looked around uncertainly. Then, moving with jerky strides, he picked up the grip that lay beside Amato, and ran into the darkness of the terminal. Ahead of him was the river and the launch. This wasn't part of his plan; he had no plan beyond killing Amato. But as the desperate illogical hope grew in him, he heard the launch's motors turn over and kick throbbingly to life. "Wait!" he shouted, but the crescendoing roar of the motors smothered his shrill, pleading voice.

When he reached the end of the terminal the small launch was speeding out of the slip toward the river.

Neville braked his car to a skidding stop before Pier 17. Another police squad was approaching on Ninth Street, its siren whining ominously in the darkness. "Watch yourself!" Neville yelled to Retnick, as he ran toward the pier with a gun in his hand.

Retnick was at his side when Neville kicked the door inward and stepped into the warehouse. A single light from the checker's office drew a bright circle on the thick heavy planking and here, in the middle of this brilliant pool, Nick Amato lay dying. Neville knelt beside him and pulled open his tie and collar. "Who did it, Nick?" he said.

"It was Joe. I could've saved him—" Amato's voice dropped away into a dry whisper.

"You're hurt badly," Neville said. "Help us now, Nick."

Retnick was staring down the length of the dark terminal. That's where Lye was. He glanced at Neville, and saw that he had put his gun on the floor while he worked on Amato's tie and collar.

"Is it like telling a priest?" Amato said, staring into Neville's eyes with terrible intensity.

"Who killed Glencannon?" Neville asked him quietly.

Retnick picked up the lieutenant's gun and walked into the terminal. In two strides he had merged with the darkness, and his big body became a shadow moving silently and deliberately toward the faint shifting lights on the river. The clouds had drifted in the high wind; the winter moon glinted on the water and coated the end of the wharf with a pale yellow glow.

Retnick couldn't think clearly; his thoughts circled hopelessly in a despairing maze. But he knew precisely what he was going to do. It was a simple, inevitable choice. There was only one more thing for him to lose.

When he reached the wide doors that led to the open wharf he hesitated and stopped in the last few feet of darkness. Ahead of him was the bright arena; he could see the oil-soaked plankings, the stubby iron mooring posts, and a length of frayed rope that trailed down into the river. He glanced at his watch. Ten:five. She was airborne now, settling comfortably in the deep reclining seat, leafing through a magazine or smoking a cigarette and watching the pinpoints of light on the ground.

The one who had brought him kindness and warmth and love was gone forever. Retnick was suddenly aware of a terrible knowledge; he was a stranger to himself, a stranger to this man who stood in the darkness waiting to die. This was a stalking animal who had reveled in the wrong done to him, putting that wrong above every other right. And Retnick saw him clearly now, studied him with eyes he had closed five years ago.

He hesitated no longer. With the gun hanging at his side he stepped onto the open wharf. The cold wind struck his body, chilling the tears on his face and then above the noise of it, he heard Joe Lye shout: "Don't move, Retnick!"

Retnick turned toward the shrill voice. Lye stood against the wall of the warehouse on his left, his body thin and black in the pale light. The sight on the barrel of his gun gleamed like a splinter of ice.

"You can try shooting if you want," he cried.

"I'm through shooting," Retnick said in a weary, hopeless voice. "Somebody else will have to kill you, Joe. A dozen cops are on the way. Any of them will enjoy the job." The gun fell from his limp fingers.

From the darkness behind him a voice shouted his name and he heard the sound of running footsteps.

"Pick up that gun!" Lye screamed.

For a turbulent instant, Retnick regretted his decision; perhaps he could have paid the price if he lived. But it was too late to think of it.

"You get it in the stomach," Lye shouted at him. "Pick up your gun."

And Retnick knew then that Lye wanted to be killed, too. They were both looking for the easy way out. "You're wasting your time, Joe," he said. "You might as well toss your gun into the river."

"They won't take me back," Lye yelled, and put the gun to his temple. For an instant that seemed frozen in time he swayed back and forth, while his lips twisted into a helpless frenzied smile. And then he began to sob terribly; the gun dropped from his fingers and he went slowly down to his knees. The strength seemed to have been squeezed from his body. He fell over onto his side, and the sound of his weeping was like that of a lost and frightened child.

There were three uniformed patrolmen behind Lieutenant Neville when he came out of the terminal onto the wharf. He gave a short order, and two of them hauled Lye to his feet while a third picked up the gun that had fallen from his hand. Then he glanced at Retnick, who was staring at the river. "You okay?" he said, still breathing hard.

"Sure."

Neville looked at Lye and said, "You're going back to the death house, clever boy."

Lye's face was blank as an idiot's. "I never left there," he said in a soft wondering voice, as if this were something Neville should realize.

Neville nodded at the cops who held his arms. "Get him out of here." When they had gone he looked at Retnick and then at his own gun which was lying on the thick planking of the wharf. Picking it up, he studied it with a little frown. "You didn't mean to use it, I guess," he said.

"That's right," Retnick said. "It seemed like a good idea at the time." He shrugged heavily, staring at the dancing lights on the water. "Like most good ideas it didn't work."

"We got an earful from Amato," Neville said, watching Retnick's face with a frown. "Glencannon, Dixie Davis, the works. Aren't you interested?"

"Sure, it's great," Retnick said heavily.

"And Joe Ventra. Amato killed him, Steve. That will be part of the newspaper story. You're in the clear. Isn't that what you wanted?"

"I was in the clear when I went to jail," Retnick said. "Now that I'm clear I'm guilty. That's a cute twist, isn't it?" The moment of dual perception was gone; there were no longer two men in his mind, there was only one. Retnick, who had taken what he wanted and couldn't pay the price. The moral bankrupt. That was the man he had to live with; the man who could hold him in judgment had died five years ago.

"Steve, part of what you accomplished was good," Neville said, seeing the pain in Retnick's eyes.

"Part of it," Retnick said bitterly. "How's Kleyburg?"

"One of the boys in the squad heard a report. He's got a better than even chance. The old man lived a healthy life and that's working for him now."

Retnick looked at him. "They think he'll live?"

"It looks good," Neville said. "I said you couldn't help him a while ago. But I could be wrong. Will you go to see him tomorrow?"

This would be the start of it, Retnick knew. The payment. "Yes, I'll see him," he said slowly.

Neville glanced at his watch and said awkwardly, "Well, I've got work to do, Steve. We can talk about this later."

"Sure, let's go."

Neville caught his arm. In the moonlight Retnick saw the little smile on his lips. "I meant that. You know where I am. I'll expect to see you."

"Sure," Retnick said, in a different voice. The lieutenant's words reminded him of what Kleyburg had said: *Most people are decent. They want to help.* "I'll see you around, Lieutenant."

It was almost eleven o'clock when Retnick let himself into the hallway of his rooming house. He had walked here from Pier 17, simply because he had had nowhere else to go; even the thought of stopping for a drink had left him without enthusiasm. What was there to celebrate? And getting drunk wouldn't help. There were no easy outs. He had learned that much.

Mrs. Cara looked out of her room at him and said, "You got a phone call to make." She came down the hallway, holding her blue flannel robe tightly about her throat. In the soft overhead light her olive-dark eyes were bright with excitement. "It's important. It's from your wife."

"My wife?" Retnick said, and a little chill went through him. "You're sure?"

"That's what she said."

"Did she call from the airport?"

"No, she was home." Mrs. Cara watched him with frank curiosity. "You going to call her?"

Retnick couldn't answer her; his throat was suddenly tight. Turning he went quickly down the hall to the telephone. Marcia answered the first ring and said, "Yes? Hello?"

She'd been waiting at the phone, he thought, and a hope that was sharper than pain went through him. "This is Steve," he said. "You called me."

"I switched over to an early morning flight," she said. "You told me your job might be over and—I wanted to be sure you were all right."

"Everything is over," he said thickly. She'd switched flights, that was all. Hearing her voice now was almost more than he could bear.

"You don't sound too cheerful about it."

"It's—" His fist suddenly tightened on the receiver. "I need you, baby," he said, in a harsh and desperate voice. "I need you," he said again feeling a tremor shake his body. "You don't owe me anything. It's the other way around. And I can't pay you back. Ever. But let me see you before you go."

She didn't answer him for a moment. Then she said unsteadily, "I thought we'd been over everything important, but—I could be wrong. Do you remember that bar on Seventieth? Tony's?"

"Yes, sure." He stood, breathing as if he had run a race. "I can be there in ten minutes."

"I'll be waiting for you," she said, in a voice so low that he barely heard the words. Then she hung up.

Retnick went down the hall to the doorway, and Mrs. Cara smiled at him and said, "You going out?"

"Yes, I've got to," he said, hardly conscious of her presence. But with a hand on the door, he turned to her. "You'd better look after the cat," he said.

"You're not coming back?"

"I don't know. I hope not." Then he became aware of her smile. "I guess you understand," he said.

"I'll take care of Silvy," she said. "You go home."

Retnick opened the door and went quickly down to the street. In the pale moonlight a soft snow was falling gently over the city. Turning up his collar he started for the avenue where he knew he could find a cab. And then he began to run.